Interior Darkness

Also by Peter Straub

Interior Darkness

Selected Stories

Peter Straub

DOUBLEDAY
New York · London · Toronto · Sydney · Auckland

Copyright © 2016 by Seafront Corporation

All rights reserved. Published in the United States by Doubleday, a division of Penguin Random House LLC, New York, and distributed in Canada by Random House of Canada Limited, a division of Penguin Random House Canada Ltd., Toronto.

www.doubleday.com

DOUBLEDAY and the portrayal of an anchor with a dolphin are registered trademarks of Penguin Random House LLC.

Most of the stories included here were previously published in the following works: "Bar Talk," "Blue Rose," "The Buffalo Hunger," "Going Home," "In the Realm of Dreams," "The Juniper Tree," and "A Short Guide to the City," in *Houses Without Doors* by Peter Straub (Dutton, 1990); "Lapland, or Film Noir," "Little Red's Tango," and "Mr. Aickman's Air Rifle" in *5 Stories* by Peter Straub (Borderlands Press, 2007); "Mallon the Guru" in *Stories: All New Tales* edited by Neil Gaiman (William Morrow, 2010); and "The Collected Short Stories of Freddie Prothero" in *Turn Down the Lights* edited by Richard Chizmar (Cemetery Dance Publications, 2013). "The Ballad of Ballard and Sandrine" by Peter Straub was originally published as a novella by Subterranean Press, Burton, Michigan, in 2011.

Grateful acknowledgment is made to Random House for permission to reprint "Ashputtle," "Mr. Clubb and Mr. Cuff," and "Porkpie Hat" from *Magic Terror: 7 Tales* by Peter Straub, copyright © 2000 by Peter Straub. Reprinted by permission of Random House, an imprint and division of Penguin Random House LLC. All rights reserved.

Book design by Michael Collica
Jacket design by Michael J. Windsor
Jacket image © Silver 30/Shutterstock

Library of Congress Cataloging-in-Publication Data
Straub, Peter, 1943–
[Short stories. Selections]
Interior darkness : selected stories / Peter Straub.—First edition.
pages ; cm
ISBN 978-0-385-54105-3 (hardcover)—ISBN 978-0-385-54106-0 (eBook)
I. Title.
PS3569.T6914A6 2016
813'.54—dc23
2015017962

MANUFACTURED IN THE UNITED STATES OF AMERICA

1 3 5 7 9 10 8 6 4 2

First Edition

For River Royal Fusco-Straub
and
Sebastian Milo Straub

I don't
I don't deny (I wasn't there) but
I'd had the dearest little dream

—Laura Sims, *My God Is This a Man*

Contents

Interior Darkness

From

Houses Without Doors

Blue Rose

For Rosemary Clooney

1

On a stifling summer day the two youngest of the five Beevers children, Harry and Little Eddie, were sitting on cane-backed chairs in the
attic of their house on South Sixth Street in Palmyra, New York. Their
father called it "the upstairs junk room," as this large irregular space
was reserved for the boxes of tablecloths, stacks of diminishingly sized
girls' winter coats, and musty old dresses Maryrose Beevers had mum-
mified as testimony to the superiority of her past to her present.

A tall mirror that could be tilted in its frame, an artifact of their
mother's onetime glory, now revealed to Harry the rear of Little Eddie's
head. This object, looking more malleable than a head should be, was
just peeking above the back of the chair. Even the back of Little Eddie's
head looked tense to Harry.

"Listen to me," Harry said. Little Eddie squirmed in his chair, and
the wobbly chair squirmed with him. "You think I'm kidding you? I
had her last year."

"Well, she didn't kill *you*," Little Eddie said.

"'Course not, she liked me, you little dummy. She only hit me a
couple of times. She hit some of those kids every single day."

"But teachers can't *kill* people," Little Eddie said.

At nine, Little Eddie was only a year younger than he, but Harry
knew that his undersized fretful brother saw him as much a part of the
world of big people as their older brothers.

"Most teachers can't," Harry said. "But what if they live right in the
same building as the principal? What if they won *teaching awards*, hey,

and what if every other teacher in the place is scared stiff of them? Don't you think they can get away with murder? Do you think anybody really misses a snot-faced little brat—a little brat like you? Mrs. Franken took this kid, this runty little Tommy Golz, into the cloakroom, and she killed him right there. I heard him scream. At the end, it sounded just like bubbles. He was trying to yell, but there was too much blood in his throat. He never came back, and nobody ever said boo about it. She killed him, and next year she's going to be your teacher. I hope you're afraid, Little Eddie, because you ought to be." Harry leaned forward. "Tommy Golz even looked sort of like you, Little Eddie."

Little Eddie's entire face twitched as if a lightning bolt had crossed it.

In fact, the young Golz boy had suffered an epileptic fit and been removed from school, as Harry knew.

"Mrs. Franken especially hates selfish little brats that don't share their toys."

"I do share my toys," Little Eddie wailed, tears beginning to run down through the delicate smears of dust on his cheeks. "Everybody *takes* my toys, that's why."

"So give me your Ultraglide Roadster," Harry said. This had been Little Eddie's birthday present, given three days previous by a beaming father and a scowling mother. "Or I'll tell Mrs. Franken as soon as I get inside that school, this fall."

Under its layer of grime, Little Eddie's face went nearly the same white-gray shade as his hair.

An ominous slamming sound came up the stairs.

"Children? Are you messing around up there in the attic? Get down here!"

"We're just sitting in the chairs, Mom," Harry called out.

"Don't you bust those chairs! Get down here this minute!"

Little Eddie slid out of his chair and prepared to bolt.

"I want that car," Harry whispered. "And if you don't give it to me, I'll tell Mom you were foolin' around with her old clothes."

"I didn't do nothin'!" Little Eddie wailed, and broke for the stairs.

"Hey, Mom, we didn't break any stuff, honest!" Harry yelled. He bought a few minutes more by adding "I'm coming right now," and stood up and went toward a cardboard box filled with interesting books he had noticed the day before his brother's birthday, and which had been his goal before he had remembered the Roadster and coaxed Little Eddie upstairs.

When, a short time later, Harry came through the door to the attic steps, he was carrying a tattered paperback book. Little Eddie stood quivering with misery and rage just outside the bedroom the two boys shared with their older brother Albert. He held out a small blue metal car, which Harry instantly took and eased into the front pocket of his jeans.

"When do I get it back?" Little Eddie asked.

"Never," Harry said. "Only selfish people want to get presents back. Don't you know anything at all?" When Eddie pursed his face up to wail, Harry tapped the book in his hands and said, "I got something here that's going to help you with Mrs. Franken, so don't complain."

His mother intercepted him as he came down the stairs to the main floor of the little house—here were the kitchen and living room, both floored with faded linoleum, the actual "junk room" separated by a stiff brown woolen curtain from the little makeshift room where Edgar Beevers slept, and the larger bedroom reserved for Maryrose. Children were never permitted more than a few steps within this awful chamber, for they might disarrange Maryrose's mysterious "papers" or interfere with the rows of antique dolls on the window seat, which was the sole, much-revered architectural distinction of the Beevers house.

Maryrose Beevers stood at the bottom of the stairs, glaring suspiciously up at her fourth son. She did not ever look like a woman who played with dolls, and she did not look that way now. Her hair was twisted into a knot at the back of her head. Smoke from her cigarette curled up past the big glasses like bird's wings, which magnified her eyes.

Harry thrust his hand into his pocket and curled his fingers protectively around the Ultraglide Roadster.

"Those things up there are the possessions of my family," she said. "Show me what you took."

Harry shrugged and held out the paperback as he came down within striking range.

His mother snatched it from him, and tilted her head to see its cover through the cigarette smoke. "Oh. This is from that little box of books up there. Your father used to pretend to read books." She squinted at the print on the cover. "*Hypnosis Made Easy*. Some drugstore trash. You want to read this?"

Harry nodded.

"I don't suppose it can hurt you much." She negligently passed the book back to him. "People in society read books, you know—I used to read a lot, back before I got stuck here with a bunch of dummies. *My* father had a lot of books."

Maryrose nearly touched the top of Harry's head, then snatched back her hand. "You're my scholar, Harry. You're the one who's going places."

"I'm gonna do good in school next year," he said.

"*Well.* You're going to do well. As long as you don't ruin every chance you have by speaking like your father."

Harry felt that particular pain composed of scorn, shame, and terror that filled him when Maryrose spoke of his father in this way. He mumbled something that sounded like acquiescence, and moved a few steps sideways and around her.

2

The porch of the Beevers house extended six feet on either side of the front door, and was the repository for furniture either too large to be crammed into the junk room or too humble to be enshrined in the attic. A sagging porch swing sat beneath the living room window, to the left of an ancient couch whose imitation green leather had been repaired with black duct tape; on the other side of the front door through which Harry Beevers now emerged stood a useless icebox dating from the earliest days of the Beeverses' marriage and two unsteady camp chairs Edgar Beevers had won in a card game. These had never been allowed into the house. Unofficially, this side of the porch was Harry's father's, and thereby had an entirely different atmosphere—defeated, lawless, and shameful—from the side with the swing and the couch.

Harry knelt down in the neutral territory directly before the front door and fished the Ultraglide Roadster from his pocket. He placed the hypnotism book on the porch and rolled the little metal car across its top. Then he gave the car a hard shove and watched it clunk nose-down onto the wood. He repeated this several times before moving the book aside, flattening himself out on his stomach, and giving the little car a decisive push toward the swing and the couch.

The Roadster rolled a few feet before an irregular board tilted it over on its side and stopped it.

"You dumb car," Harry said, and retrieved it. He gave it another push deeper into his mother's realm. A stiff, brittle sprig of paint which had separated from its board cracked in half and rested atop the stalled Roadster like a miniature mattress.

Harry knocked off the chip of paint and sent the car backward down the porch, where it flipped over again and skidded into the side of the icebox. The boy ran down the porch and this time simply hurled the little car back in the direction of the swing. It bounced off the padding and fell heavily to the wood. Harry knelt before the icebox, panting.

His whole head felt funny, as if wet hot towels had been stuffed inside it. Harry picked himself up and walked to where the car lay before the swing. He hated the way it looked, small and helpless. He experimentally stepped on the car and felt it pressing into the undersole of his moccasin. Harry raised his other foot and stood on the car, but nothing happened. He jumped on the car, but the moccasin was no better than his bare foot. Harry bent down to pick up the Roadster.

"You dumb little car," he said. "You're no good anyhow, you low-class little jerky thing." He turned it over in his hands. Then he inserted his thumbs between the frame and one of the little tires. When he pushed, the tire moved. His face heated. He mashed his thumbs against the tire, and the little black doughnut popped into the tall thick weeds in front of the porch. Breathing hard more from emotion than exertion, he popped the other front tire into the weeds. Harry whirled around, and ground the car into the wall beside his father's bedroom window. Long deep scratches appeared in the paint. When Harry peered at the top of the car, it too was scratched. He found a nail head which protruded a quarter of an inch out from the front of the house, and scraped a long paring of blue paint off the driver's side of the Roadster. Gray metal shone through. Harry slammed the car several times against the edge of the nail head, chipping off small quantities of paint. Panting, he popped off the two small rear tires and put them in his pocket because he liked the way they looked.

Without tires, well-scratched and dented, the Ultraglide Roadster had lost most of its power. Harry looked it over with a bitter, deep satisfaction and walked across the porch and shoved it far into the nest of weeds. Gray metal and blue paint shone at him from within the stalks and leaves. Harry thrust his hands into their midst and swept his arms back and forth. The car tumbled away and fell into invisibility.

When Maryrose appeared scowling on the porch, Harry was seated serenely on the squeaking swing, looking at the first few pages of the paperback book.

"What are you doing? What was all that banging?"

"I'm just reading, I didn't hear anything," Harry said.

3

"Well, if it isn't the shitbird," Albert said, jumping up the porch steps thirty minutes later. His face and T-shirt bore broad black stripes of grease. A short, muscular thirteen-year-old, Albert spent every possible minute hanging around the gas station two blocks from their house. Harry knew that Albert despised him. Albert raised a fist and made a jerky, threatening motion toward Harry, who flinched. Albert had often beaten him bloody, as had their two older brothers, Sonny and George, now at army bases in Oklahoma and Germany. Like Albert, his two oldest brothers had seriously disappointed their mother.

Albert laughed, and this time swung his fist within a couple of inches of Harry's face. On the backswing he knocked the book from Harry's hands.

"Thanks," Harry said.

Albert smirked and disappeared around the front door. Almost immediately Harry could hear his mother beginning to shout about the grease on Albert's face and clothes. Albert thumped up the stairs.

Harry opened his clenched fingers and spread them wide, closed his hands into fists, then spread them wide again. When he heard the bedroom door slam shut upstairs, he was able to get off the swing and pick up the book. Being around Albert made him feel like a spring coiled up in a box. From the upper rear of the house, Little Eddie emitted a ghostly wail. Maryrose screamed that she was going to start smacking him if he didn't shut up, and that was that. The three unhappy lives within the house fell back into silence. Harry sat down, found his page, and began reading again.

A man named Dr. Roland Mentaine had written *Hypnosis Made Easy*, and his vocabulary was much larger than Harry's. Dr. Mentaine used words like "orchestrate" and "ineffable" and "enhance," and some of his sentences wound their way through so many subordinate clauses that Harry lost his way. Yet Harry, who had begun the book only half-expecting that he would comprehend anything in it at all, found it a wonderful book. He had made it most of the way through the chapter called "Mind Power."

Harry thought it was neat that hypnosis could cure smoking, stuttering, and bed-wetting. (He himself had wet the bed almost nightly until months before his ninth birthday. The bed-wetting stopped the night a certain lovely dream came to Harry. In the dream he had to urinate terribly, and was hurrying down the stony castle corridor past suits of armor and torches guttering on the walls. At last Harry reached an open door through which he saw the most splendid bathroom of his life. The floors were of polished marble, the walls white-tiled. As soon as he entered the gleaming bathroom, a uniformed butler waved him toward the rank of urinals. Harry began pulling down his zipper, fumbled with himself, and got his penis out of his underpants just in time. As the dream-urine gushed out of him, Harry had blessedly awakened.) Hypnotism could get you right inside someone's mind and let you do things there. You could make a person speak in any foreign language they'd ever heard, even if they'd only heard it once, and you could make them act like a baby. Harry considered how pleasurable it would be to make his brother Albert lie squalling and red-faced on the floor, unable to walk or speak as he pissed all over himself.

Also, and this was a new thought to Harry, you could take a person back to a whole row of lives they had led before they were born as the person they were now. This process of rebirth was called reincarnation. Some of Dr. Mentaine's patients had been kings in Egypt and pirates in the Caribbean, some had been murderers, novelists, and artists. They remembered the houses they'd lived in, the names of their mothers and servants and children, the locations of shops where they'd bought cake and wine. Neat stuff, Harry thought. He wondered if someone who had been a famous murderer a long time ago could remember pushing in the knife or bringing down the hammer. A lot of the books that remained in the little cardboard box upstairs, Harry had noticed, seemed to be about murderers. It would not be any use to take Albert back to a previous life, however. If Albert had any previous lives, he had spent them as inanimate objects on the order of boulders and anvils.

Maybe in another life Albert was a murder weapon, Harry thought.

"Hey, college boy! Joe College!"

Harry looked toward the sidewalk and saw the baseball cap and T-shirted gut of Mr. Petrosian, who lived in a tiny house next to the tavern on the corner of South Six and Livermore Street. Mr. Petrosian was always shouting genial things at kids, but Maryrose wouldn't let Harry or Little Eddie talk to him. She said Mr. Petrosian was as common as dirt. He worked as a janitor in the telephone building and drank a case of beer every night while he sat on his porch.

"Me?" Harry said.

"Yeah! Keep reading books, and you could go to college, right?"

Harry smiled noncommittally. Mr. Petrosian lifted a wide arm and continued to toil down the street toward his house next to the Idle Hour.

In seconds Maryrose burst through the door, folding an old white dish towel in her hands. "Who was that? I heard a man's voice."

"Him," Harry said, pointing at the substantial back of Mr. Petrosian, now half of the way home.

"What did he say? As if it could possibly be interesting, coming from an Armenian janitor."

"He called me Joe College."

Maryrose startled him by smiling.

"Albert says he wants to go back to the station tonight, and I have to go to work soon." Maryrose worked the night shift as a secretary at St. Joseph's Hospital. "God knows when your father'll show up. Get something to eat for Little Eddie and yourself, will you, Harry? I've just got too many things to take care of, as usual."

"I'll get something at Big John's." This was a hamburger stand, a magical place to Harry, erected the summer before in a vacant lot on Livermore Street two blocks down from the Idle Hour.

His mother handed him two carefully folded dollar bills, and he pushed them into his pocket. "Don't let Little Eddie stay in the house alone," his mother said before getting back inside. "Take him with you. You know how scared he gets."

"Sure," Harry said, and went back to his book. He finished the chapter on "Mind Power" while first Maryrose left to stand up at the bus stop on the corner, and then while Albert noisily departed. Little Eddie sat frozen before his soap operas in the living room. Harry turned a page and started reading "Techniques of Hypnosis."

4

At eight-thirty that night the two boys sat alone in the kitchen, on opposite sides of the table covered in yellow bamboo Formica. From the living room came the sound of Sid Caesar babbling in fake German to Imogene Coca on *Your Show of Shows*. Little Eddie claimed to be scared of Sid Caesar, but when Harry had returned from the hamburger stand with a Big Johnburger (with "the works") for himself and a Mama Marydog for Eddie, double fries, and two chocolate shakes, he had been sitting in front of the television, his face moist with tears of moral outrage. Eddie usually liked Mama Marydogs, but he had taken only a couple of meager bites from the one before him now, and was disconsolately pushing a french fry through a blob of ketchup. Every now and then he wiped at his eyes, leaving nearly symmetrical smears of ketchup to dry on his cheeks.

"Mom *said* not to leave me alone in the house," said Little Eddie. "I heard. It was during *The Edge of Night* and you were on the porch. I think I'm gonna tell on you." He peeped across at Harry, then quickly looked back at the french fry and drew it out of the puddle of ketchup. "I'm ascared to be alone in the house." Sometimes Eddie's voice was like a queer speeded-up mechanical version of Maryrose's.

"Don't be so dumb," Harry said, almost kindly. "How can you be scared in your own house? You live here, don't you?"

"I'm ascared of the attic," Eddie said. He held the dripping french fry before his mouth and pushed it in. "The attic makes noise." A little squirm of red appeared at the corner of his mouth. "You were supposed to take me with you."

"Oh, jeez, Eddie, you slow everything down. I wanted to just get the food and come back. I got you your dinner, didn't I? Didn't I get you what you like?"

In truth, Harry liked hanging around in Big John's by himself because then he could talk to Big John and listen to his theories. Big John called himself a "renegade Papist" and considered Hitler the greatest man of the twentieth century, followed closely by Paul XI, Padre Pio who bled from the palms of his hands, and Elvis Presley.

All of these events occurred in what is usually wrongly called a simpler time, before Kennedy and feminism and ecology, before the Nixon presidency and Watergate, before American soldiers, among them a twenty-one-year-old Harry Beevers, journeyed to Vietnam.

"I'm still going to tell," said Little Eddie. He pushed another french fry into the puddle of ketchup. "And that car was my birthday present." He began to snuffle. "Albert hit me, and you stole my car, and you left me alone, and I was scared. And I don't wanna have Mrs. Franken next year, cuz I think she's gonna hurt me."

Harry had nearly forgotten telling his brother about Mrs. Franken and Tommy Golz, and this reminder brought back very sharply the memory of destroying Eddie's birthday present.

Eddie twisted his head sideways and dared another quick look at his brother. "Can I have my Ultraglide Roadster back, Harry? You're going to give it back to me aren'cha? I won't tell Mom you left me alone if you give it back."

"Your car is okay," Harry said. "It's in a sort of a secret place I know."

"You hurt my car!" Eddie squalled. "You did!"

"Shut up!" Harry shouted, and Little Eddie flinched. "You're driving me crazy!" Harry yelled. He realized that he was leaning over the table, and that Little Eddie was getting ready to cry again. He sat down. "Just don't scream at me like that, Eddie."

"You did something to my car," Eddie said with a stunned certainty. "I knew it."

"Look, I'll prove your car is okay," Harry said, and took the two rear tires from his pocket and displayed them on his palm.

Little Eddie stared. He blinked, then reached out tentatively for the tires.

Harry closed his fist around them. "Do they look like I did anything to them?"

"You took them *off*!"

"But don't they look okay, don't they look fine?" Harry opened his fist, closed it again, and returned the tires to his pocket. "I didn't want to show you the whole car, Eddie, because you'd get all worked up, and you gave it to me. Remember? I wanted to show you the tires so you'd see everything was all right. Okay? Got it?"

Eddie miserably shook his head.

"Anyway, I'm going to help you, just like I said."

"With Mrs. Franken?" A fraction of misery left Little Eddie's smeary face.

"Sure. You ever hear of something called hypnotism?"

"I heard a hypmotism." Little Eddie was sulking. "Everybody in the whole world heard a that."

"Hypnotism, stupid, not hypmotism."

"Sure, hypmotism. I saw it on the TV. They did it on *As the World Turns*. A man made a lady go to sleep and think she was going to have a baby."

Harry smiled. "That's just TV, Little Eddie. Real hypnotism is a lot better than that. I read all about it in one of the books from the attic."

Little Eddie was still sulky because of the car. "So what makes it better?"

"Because it lets you do amazing things," Harry said. He called on Dr. Mentaine. "Hypnosis unlocks your mind and lets you use all the power you really have. If you start now, you'll really knock those books when school starts up again. You'll pass every test Mrs. Franken gives you, just like the way I did." He reached across the table and grasped Little Eddie's wrist, stalling a fat brown french fry on its way to the puddle. "But it won't just make sure you're good in school. If you let me try it on you, I'm pretty sure I can show you that you're a lot stronger than you think you are."

Eddie blinked.

"And I bet I can make you so you're not scared of anything anymore. Hypnotism is real good for that. I read in this book, there was this guy who was afraid of bridges. Whenever he even *thought* about crossing a bridge he got all dizzy and sweaty. Terrible stuff happened to him, like he lost his job and once he just had to ride in a car across a bridge and he dumped a load in his pants. He went to see Dr. Mentaine, and Dr. Mentaine hypnotized him and said he would never be afraid of bridges again, and he wasn't."

Harry pulled the paperback from his hip pocket. He opened it flat on the table and bent over the pages. "Here. Listen to this. 'Benefits of the course of treatment were found in all areas of the patient's life, and results were obtained for which he would have paid any price.'" Harry read these words haltingly, but with complete understanding.

"Hypmotism can make me strong?" Little Eddie asked, evidently having saved this point in his head.

"Strong as a bull."

"Strong as Albert?"

"A lot stronger than Albert. A lot stronger than me, too."

"And I can beat up on big guys that hurt me?"

"You just have to learn how."

Eddie sprang up from the chair, yelling nonsense. He flexed his stringlike biceps and for some time twisted his body into a series of muscleman poses.

"You want to do it?" Harry finally asked.

Little Eddie popped into his chair and stared at Harry. His T-shirt's neck band sagged all the way to his breastbone without ever actually touching his chest. "I wanna start."

"Okay, Eddie, good man." Harry stood up and put his hand on the book. "Up to the attic."

"Only, I don't want to go in the attic," Eddie said. He was still staring at Harry, but his head was tilted over like a weird little echo of Mary-rose, and his eyes had filled with suspicion.

"I'm not gonna *take* anything from you, Little Eddie," Harry said. "It's just, we should be out of everybody's way. The attic's real quiet."

Little Eddie stuck his hand inside his T-shirt and let his arm dangle from his wrist.

"You turned your shirt into an armrest," Harry said.

Eddie jerked his hand out of its sling.

"Albert might come waltzing in and wreck everything if we do it in the bedroom."

"If you go up first and turn on the lights," Eddie said.

5

Harry held the book open on his lap, and glanced from it to Little Eddie's tense smeary face. He had read these pages over many times while he sat on the porch. Hypnotism boiled down to a few simple steps, each of which led to the next. The first thing he had to do was to get his brother started right, "relaxed and receptive," according to Dr. Mentaine.

Little Eddie stirred in his cane-backed chair and kneaded his hands together. His shadow, cast by the bulb dangling overhead, imitated him like a black little chairbound monkey. "I wanna get started, I wanna get to be strong," he said.

"Right here in this book it says you have to be relaxed," Harry said. "Just put your hands on top of your legs, nice and easy, with your fingers pointing forward. Then close your eyes and breathe in and out a couple of times. Thinking about being nice and tired and ready to go to sleep."

"I don't wanna go to sleep!"

"It's not really sleep, Little Eddie, it's just sort of like it. You'll still really be awake, but nice and relaxed. Or else it won't work. You have to do everything I tell you. Otherwise everybody'll still be able to beat up on you, like they do now. I want you to pay attention to everything I say."

"Okay." Little Eddie made a visible effort to relax. He placed his hands on his thighs and twice inhaled and exhaled.

"Now close your eyes."

Eddie closed his eyes.

Harry suddenly knew that it was going to work—if he did everything the book said, he would really be able to hypnotize his brother.

"Little Eddie, I want you just to listen to the sound of my voice," he said, forcing himself to be calm. "You are already getting nice and relaxed, as easy and peaceful as if you were lying in bed, and the more you listen to my voice the more relaxed and tired you are going to get. Nothing can bother you. Everything bad is far away, and you're just sitting here, breathing in and out, getting nice and sleepy."

He checked his page to make sure he was doing it right, and then went on.

"It's like lying in bed, Eddie, and the more you hear my voice the more tired and sleepy you're getting, a little more sleepy the more you hear me. Everything else is sort of fading away, and all you can hear is my voice. You feel tired but good, just like the way you do right before you fall asleep. Everything is fine, and you're drifting a little bit, drifting and drifting, and you're getting ready to raise your right hand."

He leaned over and very lightly stroked the back of Little Eddie's grimy right hand. Eddie sat slumped in the chair with his eyes closed, breathing shallowly. Harry spoke very slowly.

"I'm going to count backward from ten, and every time I get to another number, your hand is going to get lighter and lighter. When I count, your right hand is going to get so light it floats up and finally touches your nose when you hear me say 'One.' And then you'll be in a deep sleep. Now I'm starting. Ten. Your hand is already feeling light. Nine. It wants to float up. Eight. Your hand really feels light now. It's going to start to go up now. Seven."

Little Eddie's hand obediently floated an inch up from his thigh.

"Six." The grimy little hand rose another few inches. "It's getting lighter and lighter now, and every time I say another number it gets closer and closer to your nose, and you get sleepier and sleepier. Five."

The hand ascended several inches nearer Eddie's face.

"Four."

The hand now dangled like a sleeping bird half of the way between Eddie's knee and his nose.

"Three."

It rose nearly to Eddie's chin.

"Two."

Eddie's hand hung a few inches from his mouth.

"One. You are going to fall asleep now."

The gently curved, ketchup-streaked forefinger delicately brushed the tip of Little Eddie's nose, and stayed there while Eddie sagged against the back of the chair.

Harry's heart beat so loudly that he feared the sound would bring Eddie out of his trance. Eddie remained motionless. Harry breathed quietly by himself for a moment. "Now you can lower your hand to your lap, Eddie. You are going deeper and deeper into sleep. Deeper and deeper and deeper."

Eddie's hand sank gracefully downward.

The attic seemed hot as the inside of a furnace to Harry. His fingers left blotches on the open pages of the book. He wiped his face on his sleeve and looked at his little brother. Little Eddie had slumped so far down in the chair that his head was no longer visible in the tilting mirror. Perfectly still and quiet, the attic stretched out on all sides of them, waiting (or so it seemed to Harry) for what would happen next. Maryrose's trunks sat in rows under the eaves far behind the mirror, her old dresses hung silently within the dusty wardrobe. Harry rubbed his hands on his jeans to dry them, and flicked a page over with the neatness of an old scholar who had spent half his life in libraries.

"You're going to sit up straight in your chair," he said.

Eddie pulled himself upright.

"Now I want to show you that you're really hypnotized, Little Eddie. It's like a test. I want you to hold your right arm straight out before you. Make it as rigid as you can. This is going to show you how strong you can be."

Eddie's pale arm rose and straightened to the wrist, leaving his fingers dangling.

Harry stood up and said, "That's pretty good." He walked the two steps to Eddie's side and grasped his brother's arm and ran his fingers down the length of it, gently straightening Eddie's hand. "Now I want you to imagine that your arm is getting harder and harder. It's getting as hard and rigid as an iron bar. Your whole arm is an iron bar, and nobody on earth could bend it. Eddie, it's stronger than Superman's arm." He removed his hands and stepped back.

"Now. This arm is so strong and rigid that you can't bend it no matter how hard you try. It's an iron bar, and nobody on earth could bend it. Try. Try to bend it."

Eddie's face tightened up, and his arm rose perhaps two degrees. Eddie grunted with invisible effort, unable to bend his arm.

"Okay, Eddie, you did real good. Now your arm is loosening up, and when I count backward from ten, it's going to get looser and looser. When I get to *one*, your arm'll be normal again." He began counting, and Eddie's fingers loosened and drooped, and finally the arm came to rest again on his leg.

Harry went back to his chair, sat down, and looked at Eddie with great satisfaction. Now he was certain that he would be able to do the next demonstration, which Dr. Mentaine called "The Chair Exercise."

"Now you know that this stuff really works, Eddie, so we're going to do something a little harder. I want you to stand up in front of your chair."

Eddie obeyed. Harry stood up too, and moved his chair forward and to the side so that its cane seat faced Eddie, about four feet away.

"I want you to stretch out between these chairs, with your head on your chair and your feet on mine. And I want you to keep your hands at your sides."

Eddie hunkered down uncomplainingly and settled his head back on the seat of his chair. Supporting himself with his arms, he raised one leg and placed his foot on Harry's chair. Then he lifted the other foot. Difficulty immediately appeared in his face. He raised his arms and clamped them in so that he looked trussed.

"Now your whole body is slowly becoming as hard as iron, Eddie. Your entire body is one of the strongest things on earth. Nothing can make it bend. You could hold yourself there forever and never feel the slightest pain or discomfort. It's like you're lying on a mattress, you're so strong."

The expression of strain left Eddie's face. Slowly his arms extended and relaxed. He lay propped string-straight between the two chairs, so at ease that he did not even appear to be breathing.

"While I talk to you, you're getting stronger and stronger. You could hold up anything. You could hold up an elephant. I'm going to sit down on your stomach to prove it."

Cautiously, Harry seated himself down on his brother's midriff. He raised his legs. Nothing happened. After he had counted slowly to fifteen, Harry lowered his legs and stood. "I'm going to take my shoes off now, Eddie, and stand on you."

He hurried over to a piano stool embroidered with fulsome roses and carried it back; then he slipped off his moccasins and stepped on top of the stool. As Harry stepped on top of Eddie's exposed thin belly, the chair supporting his brother's head wobbled. Harry stood stock-still for a moment, but the chair held. He lifted his other foot from the stool. No movement from the chair. He set the other foot on his brother. Little Eddie effortlessly held him up.

Harry lifted himself experimentally up on his toes and came back down on his heels. Eddie seemed entirely unaffected. Then Harry jumped perhaps half an inch into the air, and since Eddie did not even grunt when he landed, he kept jumping five, six, seven, eight times, until he was breathing hard. "You're amazing, Little Eddie," he said, and stepped off onto the stool. "Now you can begin to relax. You can put your feet on the floor. Then I want you to sit back up in your chair. Your body doesn't feel stiff anymore."

Little Eddie had been rather tentatively lowering one foot, but as soon as Harry finished speaking he buckled in the middle and thumped his bottom on the floor. Harry's chair (Maryrose's chair) sickeningly tipped over, but landed soundlessly on a neat woolen stack of layered winter coats.

Moving like a robot, Little Eddie slowly sat upright on the floor. His eyes were open but unfocused.

"You can stand up now and get back in your chair," Harry said. He did not remember leaving the stool, but he had left it. Sweat ran into his eyes. He pressed his face into his shirtsleeve. For a second, panic had brightly beckoned. Little Eddie was sleepwalking back to his chair. When he sat down, Harry said, "Close your eyes. You're going deeper and deeper into sleep. Deeper and deeper, Little Eddie."

Eddie settled into his chair as if nothing had happened, and Harry reverently set his own chair upright again. Then he picked up the book and opened it. The print swam before his eyes. Harry shook his head and looked again, but still the lines of print snaked across the page. He pressed the palms of his hands against his eyes, and red patterns exploded across his vision.

He removed his hands from his eyes, blinked, and found that although the lines of print were now behaving themselves, he no longer wanted to go on. The attic was too hot, he was too tired, and the toppling of the chair had been too close a brush with actual disaster. But for a time he leafed purposefully through the book while Eddie tranced on, and then found the subheading "Posthypnotic Suggestion."

"Little Eddie, we're just going to do one more thing. If we ever do this again, it'll help us go faster." Harry shut the book. He knew exactly how this went; he would even use the same phrase Dr. Mentaine used with his patients. *Blue rose*—Harry did not quite know why, but he liked the sound of that.

"I'm going to tell you a phrase, Eddie, and from now on whenever you hear me say this phrase, you will instantly go back to sleep and be hypnotized again. The phrase is 'blue rose.' Blue rose. When you hear me say 'blue rose,' you will go right to sleep just the way you are now, and we can make you stronger again. 'Blue rose' is our secret, Eddie, because nobody else knows it. What is it?"

"Blue rose," Eddie said in a muffled voice.

"Okay. I'm going to count backward from ten, and when I get to 'one' you will be wide awake again. You will not remember anything we did, but you will feel happy and strong. Ten."

As Harry counted backward, Little Eddie twitched and stirred, let his arms fall to his sides, thumped one foot carelessly on the floor, and at "one" opened his eyes.

"Did it work? What'd I do? Am I strong?"

"You're a bull," Harry said. "It's getting late, Eddie—time to go downstairs."

Harry's timing was accurate enough to be uncomfortable. As soon as the two boys closed the attic door behind them, they heard the front door slide open in a cacophony of harsh coughs and subdued mutterings followed by the sound of unsteady footsteps proceeding to the bathroom. Edgar Beevers was home.

6

Late that night the three homebound Beevers sons lay in their separate beds in the good-sized second-floor room next to the attic stairs.
Directly above Maryrose's bedroom, its dimensions were nearly identical to it except that the boys' room, the "dorm," had no window seat
and the attic stairs shaved a couple of feet from Harry's end. When the
other two boys had lived at home, Harry and Little Eddie had slept
together, Albert had slept in a bed with Sonny, and only George, who
at the time of his induction into the army had been six feet tall and
weighed two hundred and one pounds, had slept alone. In those days,
Sonny often managed to make Albert cry out in the middle of the
night. The very idea of George could still make Harry's stomach freeze.

Though it was now very late, enough light from the street came in
through the thin white net curtains to give complex shadows to the
bunched muscles of Albert's upper arms as he lay stretched out atop his
sheets. The voices of Maryrose and Edgar Beevers, one approximately
sober and the other unmistakably drunk, came clearly up the stairs and
through the open door.

"*Who* says I waste my time? I don't say that. I don't waste my time."

"I suppose you think you've done a good day's work when you spell
a bartender for a couple of hours—and then drink up your wages!
That's the story of your life, Edgar Beevers, and it's a sad, sad story
of W-A-S-T-E. If my father could have seen what would become of
you . . ."

"I ain't so damn bad."

"You ain't so damn good, either."

"Albert," Eddie said softly from his bed between his two brothers.

As if galvanized by Little Eddie's voice, Albert suddenly sat up in
bed, leaned forward, and reached out to try to smack Eddie with his
fist.

"I didn't do nothin'!" Harry said, and moved to the edge of his mattress. The blow had been for him, he knew, not Eddie, except that
Albert was too lazy to get up.

"I hate your lousy guts," Albert said. "If I wasn't too tired to get out
of this here bed, I'd pound your face in."

"Harry stole my birthday car, Albert," Eddie said. "Makum gimme
it back."

"One day," Maryrose said from downstairs, "at the end of the summer when I was seventeen, late in the afternoon, my father said to my mother, 'Honey, I believe I'm going to take out our pretty little Maryrose and get her something special,' and he called up to me from the drawing room to make myself pretty and get set to go, and because my father was a gentleman and a Man of His Word, I got ready in two shakes. My father was wearing a very handsome brown suit and a red bow tie and his boater. I remember just like I can see it now. He stood at the bottom of the staircase, waiting for me, and when I came down he took my arm and we just went out that front door like a courting couple. Down the stone walk, which my father put in all by himself even though he was a white-collar worker, down Majeski Street, arm in arm down to South Palmyra Avenue. In those days all the best people, all the people who counted, did their shopping on South Palmyra Avenue."

"I'd like to knock your teeth down your throat," Albert said to Harry.

"Albert, he took my birthday car, he really did, and I want it back. I'm ascared he busted it. I want it so much I'm gonna die."

Albert propped himself up on an elbow and for the first time really looked at Little Eddie. Eddie whimpered. "You're such a twerp," Albert said. "I wish you *would* die, Eddie, I wish you'd just drop dead so we could stick you in the ground and forget about you. I wouldn't even cry at your funeral. Prob'ly I wouldn't even be able to remember your name. I'd just say, 'Oh, yeah, he was that little creepy kid used to hang around cryin' all the time, glad he's dead, whatever his name was.'"

Eddie had turned his back on Albert and was weeping softly, his unwashed face distorted by the shadows into an uncanny image of the mask of Tragedy.

"You know, I really wouldn't mind if you dropped dead," Albert mused. "You neither, shitbird."

". . . realized he was taking me to Allouette's. I'm sure you used to look in their windows when you were a little boy. You remember Allouette's, don't you? There's never been anything so beautiful as that store. When I was a little girl and lived in the big house, all the best people used to go there. My father marched me right inside, with his arm around me, and took me up in the elevator and we went straight to the lady who managed the dress department. 'Give my little girl the best,' he said. Price was no object. Quality was all he cared about. 'Give my little girl the best.' *Are you listening to me, Edgar?*"

—

Albert snored facedown into his pillow; Little Eddie twitched and snuffled. Harry lay awake for so long he thought he would never get to sleep. Before him he kept seeing Little Eddie's face all slack and dopey under hypnosis—Little Eddie's face made him feel hot and uncomfortable. Now that Harry was lying down in bed, it seemed to him that everything he had done since returning from Big John's seemed really to have been done by someone else, or to have been done in a dream. He realized that he had to use the bathroom.

Harry slid out of bed, quietly crossed the room, went out onto the dark landing, and felt his way downstairs to the bathroom.

When he emerged, the bathroom light showed him the squat black shape of the telephone atop the Palmyra directory. Harry moved to the low telephone table beside the stairs. He lifted the phone from the directory and opened the book, the width of a Big 5 tablet, with his other hand. As he had done on many other nights when his bladder forced him downstairs, Harry leaned over the page and selected a number. He kept the number in his head as he closed the directory and replaced the telephone. He dialed. The number rang so often that Harry lost count. At last a hoarse voice answered. Harry said, "I'm watching you, and you're a dead man." He softly replaced the receiver in the cradle.

7

Harry caught up with his father the next afternoon just as Edgar Beevers had begun to move up South Sixth Street toward the corner of Livermore. His father wore his usual costume of baggy gray trousers cinched far above his waist by a belt with a double buckle, a red-and-white plaid shirt, and a brown felt hat stationed low over his eyes. His long fleshy nose swam before him, cut in half by the shadow of the hat brim.

"Dad!"

His father glanced incuriously at him, then put his hands back in his pockets. He turned sideways and kept walking down the street, though perhaps a shade more slowly. "What's up, kid? No school?"

"It's summer, there isn't any school. I just thought I'd come with you for a little."

"Well, I ain't doing much. Your ma asked me to pick up some hamburg on Livermore, and I thought I'd slip into the Idle Hour for a quick belt. You won't turn me in, will you?"

"No."

"You ain't a bad kid, Harry. Your ma's just got a lot of worries. I worry about Little Eddie too, sometimes."

"Sure."

"What's with the books? You read when you work?"

"I was just sort of looking at them," Harry said.

His father insinuated his hand beneath Harry's left elbow and extracted two luridly jacketed paperback books. They were titled *Murder, Incorporated* and *Hitler's Death Camps*. Harry already loved both of those books. His father grunted and handed *Murder, Incorporated* back to him. He raised the other book nearly to the top of his nose and peered at the cover, which depicted a naked woman pressing herself against a wall of barbed wire while a uniformed Nazi aimed a rifle at her back.

Looking up at his father, Harry saw that beneath the harsh line of shadow caused by the hat brim, his father's whiskers grew in different colors and patterns. Black and brown, red and orange, the glistening spikes swirled across his father's cheek.

"I bought this book, but it don't look nothing like that," his father said, and returned the book.

"What didn't?"

"That place. Dachau. That death camp."

"How do you know?"

"I was there, wasn't I? You weren't even born then. It didn't look anything like that picture on that book. It just looked like a piece of shit to me, like most of the places I saw when I was in the army."

This was the first time Harry had heard that his father had been in the service.

"You mean, you were in World War II?"

"Yeah, I was in the Big One. They made me corporal over there. Had a nickname, too. 'Beans.' 'Beans' Beevers. And I got a Purple Heart from the time I got a infection."

"You saw Dachau with your own eyes?"

"Damn straight I did." He bent down suddenly. "Hey—don't let your ma catch you readin' that book."

Secretly pleased, Harry shook his head. Now the book and the death camp were a bond between himself and his father.

"Did you ever kill anybody?"

His father wiped his mouth and both cheeks with one long hand. Harry saw a considering eye far back in the shadow of the brim.

"I killed a guy once."

A long pause.

"I shot him in the back."

His father wiped his mouth again, and then motioned forward with his head. He had to get to the bar, the butcher, and back again in a very carefully defined period of time. "You really want to hear this?"

Harry nodded. He swallowed.

"I guess you do, at that. Okay—we was sent into this camp, Dachau, at the end of the war to process the prisoners and arrest the guards and the commandant. Everything was all arranged. A bunch of brass hats from Division were going to come on an inspection, so we had to wait there a couple days. We had these guards lined up, see, and these skinny old wrecks would come up and give 'em hell. We wasn't supposed to let 'em get too near."

They were passing Mr. Petrosian's little tar-paper house, and Harry felt a spasm of relief that Mr. Petrosian was not out on his tiny porch, working on his case of beer. The Idle Hour was only a few paces ahead.

"Anyhow, one of these guards, one of the worst ones, suddenly decided he's going to run for it. He takes off, runnin' like crazy toward the woods. What do I do? I ask. Nobody knows what the hell to do. Shoot him, somebody says. So I shot him in the back. That was all she wrote."

Now they had reached the screen door that led into the Idle Hour, and the smells of malt and hops filled the air. "See you back at the house," his father said, and disappeared through the screen door like a magician.

8

After Harry had read a hundred pages of *Murder, Incorporated*, his favorite murderers were Louis "Lepke" Buchalter and Abe "Kid Twist" Reles. They were dependable professionals. A kind of black light surrounded them and made them glitter. Lepke Buchalter and Abe Reles looked out at the world from the shadows of their hat brims. They lived in shadowy rooms and peered out through the curtains. They appeared on a dark corner before their terrified victim, did their work, and walked away, turning up their coat collars.

Suppose you had some kind of job that took you around the country, like a salesman's job, Harry thought as he read away the afternoon on the porch swing; suppose you had a job that took you from one town to another. Suppose you killed someone in each one of those towns, carefully and quietly, and hid the bodies so it would take a long time to find them. Your work would never be done.

9

"Blue rose," Harry said.

Little Eddie sagged openmouthed against the cane of his chair, his hands loose in his lap.

It had worked. Harry looked around as if he expected applause, and did feel that all the things in the attic looked back at him with warm approval. It was nine-thirty at night; he and Eddie, alone in the house, occupied the attic in perfect safety. Harry wanted to see if he could put other people under and make them do things, but for now, for tonight, he was content to experiment with Eddie.

"You're going deeper and deeper asleep, Eddie, deeper and deeper, and you're listening to every word I say. You're just sinking down and down, hearing my voice come to you, going deeper and deeper with every word, and now you are real deep asleep and ready to begin."

Little Eddie sat sprawled over Maryrose's cane-backed chair, his chin touching his chest and his little pink mouth drooping open. He looked like a slightly undersized seven-year-old, like a second-grader instead of the fourth-grader he would be when he joined Mrs. Franken's class in the fall. Suddenly he reminded Harry of the Ultraglide Roadster, scratched and dented and stripped of its tires.

"Tonight we're going to see how strong you really are. Sit up, Eddie."

Eddie pulled himself upright and closed his mouth, almost comically obedient.

Harry thought it would be fun to make Little Eddie believe he was a dog and trot around the attic on all fours, barking and lifting his leg. Then he saw Little Eddie staggering across the attic, his tongue bugling out of his mouth, his own hands squeezing and squeezing his throat. Maybe he would try that too, after he had done several other exercises he had discovered in Dr. Mentaine's book. He checked the underside of his collar for maybe the fifth time that evening, and felt the long thin shaft of the pearl-handled hat pin he had stopped reading *Murder, Incorporated* long enough to smuggle out of Maryrose's bedroom after she had left for work.

"Eddie," he said, "now you are very deeply asleep, and will be able to do everything I say. I want you to hold your right arm straight out in front of you."

Eddie stuck his arm out like a poker.

"That's good, Eddie. Now I want you to notice that all the feeling is leaving that arm. It's getting number and number. It doesn't even feel like flesh and blood anymore. It feels like it's made out of steel or something. It's so numb that you can't even feel anything there anymore. You can't even feel pain in it."

Harry stood up, and went to Eddie, and brushed his fingers along his arm. "You didn't feel anything, did you?"

"No," Eddie said in a slow, gravel-filled voice.

"Do you feel anything now?" Harry pinched the underside of Eddie's forearm.

"No."

"Now?" Harry used his nails to pinch the side of Eddie's bicep, hard, and left purple dents in his skin.

"No," Eddie repeated.

"How about this?" He slapped his hand against Eddie's forearm as hard as he could. There was a sharp loud smacking sound, and his fingers tingled. If Little Eddie had not been hypnotized, he would have tried to screech down the walls.

"No," Eddie said.

Harry pulled the hat pin out of his collar and inspected his brother's arm. "You're doing great, Little Eddie. You're stronger than anybody in your whole class—you're probably stronger than the whole rest of the school." He turned Eddie's arm so that the palm was up and the white forearm, lightly traced by small blue veins, faced him.

Harry delicately ran the point of the hat pin down Eddie's pale, veined forearm. The pinpoint left a narrow chalk-white scratch in its wake. For a moment Harry felt the floor of the attic sway beneath his feet, then he closed his eyes and jabbed the hat pin into Little Eddie's skin as hard as he could.

He opened his eyes. The floor was still swaying beneath him. From Little Eddie's lower arm protruded six inches of the eight-inch hat pin, the mother-of-pearl glistening softly in the light from the overhead bulb. A drop of blood the size of a watermelon seed stood on Eddie's skin. Harry moved back to his chair and sat down heavily. "Do you feel anything?"

"No," Eddie said again in that surprisingly deep voice.

Harry stared at the hat pin embedded in Eddie's arm. The oval drop of blood lengthened itself out against the white skin and began slowly to ooze toward Eddie's wrist. Harry watched it advance across the pale underside of Eddie's forearm. Finally he stood up and returned to Eddie's side. The elongated drop of blood had ceased moving. Harry bent over and twanged the hat pin. Eddie could feel nothing. Harry put his thumb and forefinger on the glistening head of the pin. His face was so hot he might have been standing before an open fire. He pushed the pin a further half-inch into Eddie's arm, and another small quantity of blood welled up from the base. The pin seemed to be moving in Harry's grasp, pulsing back and forth as if it were breathing.

"Okay," Harry said. "Okay."

He tightened his hold on the pin and pulled. It slipped easily from the wound. Harry held the hat pin before his face just as a doctor holds up a thermometer to read a temperature. He had imagined that the entire bottom section of the shaft would be painted with red, but saw that only a single winding glutinous streak of blood adhered to the pin. For a dizzy second he thought of slipping the end of the pin in his mouth and sucking it clean.

He thought: Maybe in another life I was Lepke Buchalter.

He pulled his handkerchief, a filthy square of red paisley, from his front pocket and wiped the streak of blood from the shaft of the pin. Then he leaned over and gently wiped the red smear from Little Eddie's underarm. Harry refolded the handkerchief so the blood would not show, wiped sweat from his face, and shoved the grubby cloth back into his pocket.

"That was good, Eddie. Now we're going to do something a little bit different."

He knelt down beside his brother and lifted Eddie's nearly weightless, delicately veined arm. "You still can't feel a thing in this arm, Eddie, it's completely numb. It's sound asleep and won't wake up until I tell it to." Harry repositioned himself in order to hold himself steady while he knelt, and put the point of the hat pin nearly flat against Eddie's arm. He pushed it forward far enough to raise a wrinkle of flesh. The point of the hat pin dug into Eddie's skin but did not break it. Harry pushed harder, and the hat pin raised the little bulge of skin by a small but appreciable amount.

Skin was a lot tougher to break than anyone imagined.

The pin was beginning to hurt his fingers, so Harry opened his hand and positioned the head against the base of his middle finger. Grimacing, he pushed his hand against the pin. The point of the pin popped through the raised wrinkle.

"Eddie, you're made out of beer cans," Harry said, and tugged the head of the pin backward. The wrinkle flattened out. Now Harry could shove the pin forward again, sliding the shaft deeper and deeper under the surface of Little Eddie's skin. He could see the raised line of the hat pin marching down his brother's arm, looking as prominent as the damage done to a cartoon lawn by a cartoon rabbit. When the mother-of-pearl head was perhaps three inches from the entry hole, Harry pushed it down into Little Eddie's flesh, thus raising the point of the pin. He gave the head a sharp jab, and the point appeared at the end of the ridge in Eddie's skin, poking through a tiny smear of blood. Harry shoved the pin further. Now it showed about an inch and a half of gray metal at either end.

"Feel anything?"

"Nothing."

Harry jiggled the head of the pin, and a bubble of blood walked out of the entry wound and began to slide down Eddie's arm. Harry sat down on the attic floor beside Eddie and regarded his work. His mind seemed pleasantly empty of thought, filled only with a variety of sensations. He *felt* but could not hear a buzzing in his head, and a blurry film seemed to cover his eyes. He breathed through his mouth. The long pin stuck through Little Eddie's arm looked monstrous seen one way; seen another, it was sheerly beautiful. Skin, blood, and metal. Harry had never seen anything like it before. He reached out and twisted the pin, causing another little blood-snail to crawl from the exit wound. Harry saw all this as if through smudgy glasses, but he did not mind.

He knew the blurriness was only mental. He touched the head of the pin again and moved it from side to side. A little more blood leaked from both punctures. Then Harry shoved the pin in, partially withdrew it so that the point nearly disappeared back into Eddie's arm, moved it forward again; and went on like this, back and forth, back and forth as if he were sewing his brother up, for some time.

Finally he withdrew the pin from Eddie's arm. Two long streaks of blood had nearly reached his brother's wrist. Harry ground the heels of his hands into his eyes, blinked, and discovered that his vision had cleared.

He wondered how long he and Eddie had been in the attic. It could have been hours. He could not quite remember what had happened before he had slid the hat pin into Eddie's skin. Now his blurriness really was mental, not visual. A loud uncomfortable pulse beat in his temples. Again he wiped the blood from Eddie's arm. Then he stood on wobbling knees and returned to his chair.

"How's your arm feel, Eddie?"

"Numb," Eddie said in his gravelly sleepy voice.

"The numbness is going away now. Very, very slowly. You are beginning to feel your arm again, and it feels very good. There is no pain. It feels like the sun was shining on it all afternoon. It's strong and healthy. Feeling is coming back into your arm, and you can move your fingers and everything."

When he had finished speaking, Harry leaned back against the chair and closed his eyes. He rubbed his forehead with his hand and wiped the moisture off his shirt.

"How does your arm feel?" he said without opening his eyes.

"Good."

"That's great, Little Eddie." Harry flattened his palms against his flushed face, wiped his cheeks, and opened his eyes.

I can do this every night, he thought. I can bring Little Eddie up here every single night, at least until school starts.

"Eddie, you're getting stronger and stronger every day. This is really helping you. And the more we do it the stronger you'll get. Do you understand me?"

"I understand you," Eddie said.

"We're almost done for tonight. There's just one more thing I want to try. But you have to be really deep asleep for this to work. So I want you to go deeper and deeper, as deep as you can go. Relax, and now you are really deep asleep, deep deep, and relaxed and ready and feeling good."

Little Eddie sat sprawled in his chair with his head tilted back and his eyes closed. Two tiny dark spots of blood stood out like mosquito bites on his lower right forearm.

"When I talk to you, Eddie, you're slowly getting younger and younger, you're going backward in time, so now you're not nine years old anymore, you're eight, it's last year and you're in the third grade, and now you're seven, and now you're six years old . . . and now you're five, Eddie, and it's the day of your fifth birthday. You're five years old today, Little Eddie. How old are you?"

"I'm five." To Harry's surprised pleasure, Little Eddie's voice actually seemed younger, as did his hunched posture in the chair.

"How do you feel?"

"Not good. I hate my present. It's terrible. Dad got it, and Mom says it should never be allowed in the house because it's just junk. I wish I wouldn't ever have to have birthdays, they're so terrible. I'm gonna cry."

His face contracted. Harry tried to remember what Eddie had gotten for his fifth birthday, but could not—he caught only a dim memory of shame and disappointment. "What's your present, Eddie?"

In a teary voice, Eddie said, "A radio. But it's busted and Mom says it looks like it came from the junkyard. I don't want it anymore. I don't even wanna *see* it."

Yes, Harry thought, yes, yes, yes. He could remember. On Little Eddie's fifth birthday, Edgar Beevers had produced a yellow plastic radio which even Harry had seen was astoundingly ugly. The dial was cracked, and it was marked here and there with brown circular scablike marks where someone had mashed out cigarettes on it.

The radio had long since been buried in the junk room, where it now lay beneath several geological layers of trash.

"Okay, Eddie, you can forget the radio now, because you're going backward again, you're getting younger, you're going backward through being four years old, and now you're three."

He looked with interest at Little Eddie, whose entire demeanor had changed. From being tearfully unhappy, Eddie now demonstrated a self-sufficient good cheer Harry could not ever remember seeing in him. His arms were folded over his chest. He was smiling, and his eyes were bright and clear and childish.

"What do you see?" Harry asked.

"Mommy-ommy-om."

"What's she doing?"

"Mommy's at her desk. She's smoking and looking through her papers." Eddie giggled. "Mommy looks funny. It looks like smoke is coming out of the top of her head." Eddie ducked his chin and hid his smile behind a hand. "Mommy doesn't see me. I can see her, but she doesn't see me. Oh! Mommy works hard! She works hard at her desk!"

Eddie's smile abruptly left his face. His face froze for a second in a comic rubbery absence of expression; then his eyes widened in terror and his mouth went loose and wobbly.

"What happened?" Harry's mouth had gone dry.

"No, Mommy!" Eddie wailed. "Don't, Mommy! I wasn't spying, I wasn't, I promise—" His words broke off into a screech. "NO, MOMMY! DON'T! DON'T, MOMMY!" Eddie jumped upward, sending his chair flying back, and ran blindly toward the rear of the attic. Harry's head rang with Eddie's screeches. He heard a sharp *crack!* of wood breaking, but only as a small part of all the noise Eddie was making as he charged around the attic. Eddie had run into a tangle of hanging dresses, spun around, enmeshing himself deeper in the dresses, and was now tearing himself away from the web of dresses, pulling some of them off the rack. A long-sleeved purple dress with an enormous lace collar had draped itself around Eddie like a ghostly dance partner, and another dress, of dull red velvet, snaked around his right leg. Eddie screamed again and yanked himself away from the tangle. The entire rack of clothes wobbled and then went over in a mad jangle of sound.

"NO!" he screeched. "HELP!" Eddie ran straight into a wooden beam marking off one of the eaves, bounced off, and came windmilling toward Harry. Harry knew his brother could not see him.

"Eddie, stop," he said, but Eddie was past hearing him. Harry tried to make Eddie stop by wrapping his arms around him, but Eddie slammed right into him, hitting Harry's chest with a shoulder and knocking his head painfully against Harry's chin; Harry's arms closed on nothing and his eyes lost focus, and Eddie went crashing into the tilting mirror. The mirror yawned over sideways. Harry saw it tilt with dreamlike slowness toward the floor, and then in an eyeblink drop and crash. Broken glass sprayed across the attic floor.

"STOP!" Harry yelled. "STAND STILL, EDDIE!"

Eddie came to rest. A ripped and dirty dress of dull red velvet still clung to his right leg. Blood oozed down his temple from an ugly cut above his eye. He was breathing hard, releasing air in little whimpering exhalations.

"Holy shit," Harry said, looking around the attic. In only a few seconds Eddie had managed to create what looked at first like absolute devastation. Maryrose's ancient dresses lay tangled in a heap of dusty fabrics from which wire hangers skeletally protruded; gray Eddie-sized footprints lay like a pattern over the muted explosion of colors the dresses now created. When the rack had gone over, it had knocked a section the size of a dinner plate out of a round wooden coffee table Maryrose had particularly prized for its being made from a single section of teak—"a single piece of *teak*, the rarest wood in all the world, all the way from Ceylon!" The much-prized mirror lay in hundreds of glittering pieces across the attic floor. With growing horror, Harry saw that the wooden frame had cracked like a bone, showing a bone-pale, shockingly white fracture in the expanse of dark stain.

Harry's blood tipped within his body, nearly tipping him with it, like the mirror. "Oh God oh God oh God."

He turned slowly around. Eddie stood blinking two feet to his side, wiping ineffectually at the blood running from his forehead and now covering most of his left cheek. He looked like an Indian in war paint—a defeated, lost Indian, for his eyes were dim and his head turned aimlessly from side to side.

A few feet from Eddie lay the chair in which he had been sitting. One of its thin curved wooden arms lay beside it, crudely severed. It looked like an insect's leg, Harry thought, like a toy gun.

For a moment Harry thought that his own face too was red with blood. He wiped his hand over his forehead and looked at his glistening palm. It was only sweat. His heart beat like a bell. Beside him Eddie said, "Aaah . . . what . . . ?" The injury to his head had brought him out of the trance.

The dresses were ruined, stepped-on, tangled, torn. The mirror was broken. The table had been mutilated. Maryrose's chair lay on its side like a murder victim, its severed arm ending in a bristle of snapped ligaments.

"My head *hurts*," Eddie said in a weak, trembling voice. "What happened? Aaah! I'm all blood! I'm all blood, Harry!"

"You're all blood, you're all blood?" Harry shouted at him. "Everything's *all blood*, you dummy! Look around!" He did not recognize his own voice, which sounded high and tinny and seemed to be coming from somewhere else. Little Eddie took an aimless step away from him, and Harry wanted to fly at him, to pound his bloody head into a pancake, to destroy him, smash him . . .

Eddie held up his bloodstained palm and stared at it. He wiped it vaguely across the front of his T-shirt and took another wandering step. "I'm ascared, Harry," his tiny voice uttered.

"Look what you did!" Harry screamed. "You wrecked everything! Damn it! What do you think is going to happen to us?"

"What's Mom going to do?" Eddie asked in a voice only slightly above a whisper.

"You don't know?" Harry yelled. "You're dead!"

Eddie started to weep.

Harry bunched his hands into fists and clamped his eyes shut. They were both dead, that was the real truth. Harry opened his eyes, which felt hot and oddly heavy, and stared at his sobbing, red-smeared, useless little brother. "Blue rose," he said.

10

Little Eddie's hands fell to his sides. His chin dropped, and his mouth fell open. Blood ran in a smooth wide band down the left side of his face, dipped under the line of his jaw, and continued on down his neck and into his T-shirt. Pooled blood in his left eyebrow dripped steadily onto the floor, as if from a faucet.

"You are going deep *asleep*," Harry said. Where was the hat pin? He looked back to the single standing chair and saw the mother-of-pearl head glistening on the floor near it. "Your whole body is *numb*." He moved over to the pin, bent down, and picked it up. The metal shaft felt warm in his fingers. "You can feel no *pain*." He went back to Little Eddie. "Nothing can *hurt* you." Harry's breath seemed to be breathing itself, forcing itself into his throat in hot harsh shallow pants, then expelling itself out.

"Did you hear me, Little Eddie?"

In his gravelly, slow-moving hypnotized voice, Little Eddie said, "I heard you."

"And you can feel no *pain*?"

"I can feel no pain."

Harry drew his arm back, the point of the hat pin extending forward from his fist, and then jerked his hand forward as hard as he could and stuck the pin into Eddie's abdomen right through the blood-soaked T-shirt. He exhaled sharply, and tasted a sour misery on his breath.

"You don't feel a thing."

"I don't feel a thing."

Harry opened his right hand and drove his palm against the head of the pin, hammering it in another few inches. Little Eddie looked like a voodoo doll. A kind of sparkling light surrounded him. Harry gripped the head of the pin with his thumb and forefinger and yanked it out. He held it up and inspected it. Glittering light surrounded the pin, too. The long shaft was painted with blood. Harry slipped the point into his mouth and closed his lips around the warm metal.

He saw himself, a man in another life, standing in a row with men like himself in a bleak gray landscape defined by barbed wire. Emaciated people in rags shuffled up toward them and spat on their clothes. The smells of dead flesh and burning flesh hung in the air. Then the vision was gone, and Little Eddie stood before him again, surrounded by layers of glittering light.

Harry grimaced or grinned, he could not have told the difference, and drove his long spike deep into Eddie's stomach.

Eddie uttered a small *"Oof."*

"You don't feel anything, Eddie," Harry whispered. "You feel good all over. You never felt better in your life."

"Never felt better in my life."

Harry slowly pulled out the pin and cleaned it with his fingers.

He was able to remember every single thing anyone had ever told him about Tommy Golz.

"Now you're going to play a funny, funny game," he said. "This is called the Tommy Golz game because it's going to keep you safe from Mrs. Franken. Are you ready?" Harry carefully slid the pin into the fabric of his shirt collar, all the while watching Eddie's slack blood-streaked person. Vibrating bands of light beat rhythmically and steadily about Eddie's face.

"Ready," Eddie said.

"I'm going to give you your instructions now, Little Eddie. Pay attention to everything I say and it's all going to be okay. Everything's going to be okay—as long as you play the game exactly the way I tell you. You understand, don't you?"

"I understand."

"Tell me what I just said."

"Everything's going to be okay as long as I play the game exactly the way you tell me." A dollop of blood slid off Eddie's eyebrow and splashed onto his already soaked T-shirt.

"Good, Eddie. Now the first thing you do is fall down—not now, when I tell you. I'm going to give you all the instructions, and then I'm going to count backward from ten, and when I get to *one*, you'll start playing the game. Okay?"

"Okay."

"So first you fall down, Little Eddie. You fall down real hard. Then comes the fun part of the game. You bang your head on the floor. You start to go crazy. You twitch, and you bang your hands and feet on the floor. You do that for a long time. I guess you do that until you count to about a hundred. You foam at the mouth, you twist all over the place. You get real stiff, and then you get real loose, and then you get real stiff, and then real loose again, and all this time you're banging your head and your hands and feet on the floor, and you're twisting all over the place. Then when you finish counting to a hundred in your head, you do the last thing. You swallow your tongue. And that's the game. When you swallow your tongue you're the winner. And then nothing bad can ever happen to you, and Mrs. Franken won't be able to hurt you ever ever ever."

Harry stopped talking. His hands were shaking. After a second he realized that his insides were shaking too. His raised his trembling fingers to his shirt collar and felt the hat pin.

"Tell me how you win the game, Little Eddie. What is the last thing you do?"

"I swallow my tongue."

"Right. And then Mrs. Franken and Mom will never be able to hurt you, because you won the game."

"Good," said Little Eddie. The glittering light shimmered about him.

"Okay, we'll start playing right now," Harry said. "Ten." He went toward the attic steps. "Nine." He reached the steps. "Eight."

He went down one step. "Seven." Harry descended another two steps. "Six." When he went down another two steps, he called up in a slightly louder voice, "Five."

Now his head was beneath the level of the attic floor, and he could not see Little Eddie anymore. All he could hear was the soft, occasional plop of liquid hitting the floor.

"Four."

"Three."

"Two." He was now at the door to the attic steps. Harry opened the door, stepped through it, breathed hard, and shouted "One!" up the stairs.

He heard a thud, and then quickly closed the door behind him.

Harry went across the hall and into the "dormitory" bedroom. There seemed to be a strange absence of light in the hallway. For a second he saw—was sure he saw—a line of dark trees across a wall of barbed wire. Harry closed this door behind him too, and went to his narrow bed and sat down. He could feel blood beating in his face; his eyes seemed oddly warm, as if they were heated by filaments. Harry slowly, almost reverently, extracted the hat pin from his collar and set it on his pillow. "A hundred," he said. "Ninety-nine, ninety-eight, ninety-seven, ninety-six, ninety-five, ninety-four . . ."

When he had counted down to "one," he stood up and left the bedroom. He went quickly downstairs without looking at the door behind which lay the attic steps. On the ground floor he slipped into Maryrose's bedroom, crossed over to her desk, and slid open the bottom right-hand drawer. From the drawer he took a velvet-covered box. This he opened, and jabbed the hat pin into the ball of material, studded with pins of all sizes and descriptions, from which he had taken it. He replaced the box in the drawer, pushed the drawer into the desk, and quickly left the room and went upstairs.

Back in his own bedroom, Harry took off his clothes and climbed into his bed. His face still burned.

He must have fallen asleep very quickly, because the next thing he knew Albert was slamming his way into the bedroom and tossing his clothes and boots all over the place. "You asleep?" Albert asked. "You left the attic light on, you fuckin' dummies, but if you think I'm gonna save your fuckin' asses and go up and turn it off, you're even stupider than you look."

Harry was careful not to move a finger, not to move even a hair.

He held his breath while Albert threw himself onto his bed, and when Albert's breathing relaxed and slowed, Harry followed his big brother into sleep. He did not awaken again until he heard his father half-screeching, half-sobbing up in the attic, and that was very late at night.

11

Sonny came from Fort Sill, George all the way from Germany. Between them, they held up a sodden Edgar Beevers at the grave site while a minister Harry had never seen before read from a Bible as cracked and rubbed as an old brown shoe. Between his two older sons, Harry's father looked bent and ancient, a skinny old man only steps from the grave himself. Sonny and George despised their father, Harry saw— they held him up on sufferance, in part because they had chipped in thirty dollars apiece to buy him a suit and did not want to see it collapse with its owner inside onto the lumpy clay of the graves. His whiskers glistened in the sun, and moisture shone beneath his eyes and at the corners of his mouth. He had been shaking too severely for either Sonny or George to shave him, and had been capable of moving in a straight line only after George let him take a couple of long swallows from a leather-covered flask he took out of his duffel bag.

The minister uttered a few sage words on the subject of epilepsy.

Sonny and George looked as solid as brick walls in their uniforms, like prison guards or actual prisons themselves. Next to them, Albert looked shrunken and unfinished. Albert wore the green plaid sport jacket in which he had graduated from the eighth grade, and his wrists hung prominent and red four inches below the bottoms of the sleeves. His motorcycle boots were visible beneath his light gray trousers, but they, like the green jacket, had lost their flash. Like Albert, too: ever since the discovery of Eddie's body, Albert had gone around the house looking as if he'd just bitten off the end of his tongue and was trying to decide whether or not to spit it out. He never looked anybody in the eye, and he rarely spoke. Albert acted as though a gigantic padlock had been fixed to the middle of his chest and *he* was damned if he'd ever take it off. He had not asked Sonny or George a single question about the army. Every now and then he would utter a remark about the gas station so toneless that it suffocated any reply.

Harry looked at Albert standing beside their mother, kneading his hands together and keeping his eyes fixed as if by decree on the square foot of ground before him. Albert glanced over at Harry, he knew he was being looked at, and did what to Harry was an extraordinary thing. Albert *froze*. All expression drained out of his face, and his hands locked immovably together. *He's that way because he told Little Eddie that he wished he would die*, Harry thought for the tenth or eleventh time since he realized this, and with undiminished awe. Then was he lying? Harry wondered. And if he really did wish that Little Eddie would drop dead, why isn't he happy now? Didn't he get what he wanted? Albert would never spit out that piece of his tongue, Harry thought, watching his brother blink slowly and sightlessly toward the ground.

Harry shifted his gaze uneasily to his father, still propped up between George and Sonny, heard that the minister was finally reaching the end of his speech, and took a fast look at his mother. Maryrose was standing very straight in a black dress and black sunglasses, holding the straps of her bag in front of her with both hands. Except for the color of her clothes, she could have been a spectator at a tennis match. Harry knew by the way she was holding her face that she was wishing she could smoke. Dying for a cigarette, he thought, ha ha, the Monster Mash, it's a graveyard smash.

The minister finished speaking, and made a rhetorical gesture with his hands. The coffin sank on ropes into the rough earth. Harry's father began to weep loudly. First George, then Sonny, picked up large damp shovel-marked pieces of the clay and dropped them on the coffin. Edgar Beevers nearly fell in after his own tiny clod, but George contemptuously swung him back. Maryrose marched forward, bent and picked up a random piece of clay with thumb and forefinger as if using tweezers, dropped it, and turned away before it struck. Albert fixed his eyes on Harry—his own clod had split apart in his hand and crumbled away between his fingers. Harry shook his head *no*. He did not want to drop dirt on Eddie's coffin and make that noise. He did not want to look at Eddie's coffin again. There was enough dirt around to do the job without him hitting that metal box like he was trying to ring Eddie's doorbell. He stepped back.

"Mom says we have to get back to the house," Albert said.

Maryrose lit up as soon as they got into the single black car they had rented through the funeral parlor, and breathed out acrid smoke over everybody crowded into the backseat. The car reversed into a narrow graveyard lane, and turned down the main road toward the front gates.

In the front seat, next to the driver, Edgar Beevers drooped sideways and leaned his head against the window, leaving a blurred streak on the glass.

"How in the name of hell could Little Eddie have epilepsy without anybody knowing about it?" George asked.

Albert stiffened and stared out the window.

"Well, that's epilepsy," Maryrose said. "Eddie could have gone for years without having an attack." That she worked in a hospital always gave her remarks of this sort a unique gravity, almost as if she were a doctor.

"Must have been some fit," Sonny said, squeezed into place between Harry and Albert.

"Grand mal," Maryrose said, and took another hungry drag on her cigarette.

"Poor little bastard," George said. "Sorry, Mom."

"I know you're in the armed forces, and armed forces people speak very freely, but I wish you would not use that kind of language."

Harry, jammed into Sonny's rock-hard side, felt his brother's body twitch with a hidden laugh, though Sonny's face did not alter.

"I said I was sorry, Mom," George said.

"Yes. Driver! Driver!" Maryrose was leaning forward, reaching out one claw to tap the chauffeur's shoulder. "Livermore is the next street. Do you know South Sixth Street?"

"I'll get you there," the driver said.

This is not my family, Harry thought. I came from somewhere else and my rules are different from theirs.

His father mumbled something inaudible as soon as they got in the door, and disappeared into his curtained-off cubicle. Maryrose put her sunglasses in her purse and marched into the kitchen to warm the coffee cake and the macaroni casserole, both made that morning, in the oven. Sonny and George wandered into the living room and sat down on opposite ends of the couch. They did not look at each other— George picked up a *Reader's Digest* from the table and began leafing through it backward, and Sonny folded his hands in his lap and stared at his thumbs. Albert's footsteps plodded up the stairs, crossed the landing, and went into the dormitory bedroom.

"What's she in the kitchen for?" Sonny asked, speaking to his hands. "Nobody's going to come. Nobody ever comes here, because she never wanted them to."

"Albert's taking this kind of hard, Harry," George said. He propped the magazine against the stiff folds of his uniform and looked across the room at his little brother. Harry had seated himself beside the door, as out of the way as possible. George's attentions rather frightened him, though George had behaved with consistent kindness ever since his arrival two days after Eddie's death. His crew cut still bristled and he could still break rocks with his chin, but some violent demon seemed to have left him. "You think he'll be okay?"

"Him? Sure." Harry tilted his head, grimaced.

"He didn't see Little Eddie first, did he?"

"No, Dad did," Harry said. "He saw the light on in the attic when he came home, I guess. Albert went up there, though. I guess there was so much blood Dad thought somebody broke in and killed Eddie. But he just bumped his head, and that's where the blood came from."

"Head wounds bleed like bastards," Sonny said. "A guy hit me with a bottle once in Tokyo, I thought I was gonna bleed to death right there."

"And Mom's stuff got all messed up?" George asked quietly.

This time Sonny looked up.

"Pretty much, I guess. The dress rack got knocked down. Dad cleaned up what he could, the next day. One of the cane-back chairs got broke, and a hunk got knocked out of the teak table. And the mirror got broken into a million pieces."

Sonny shook his head, and made a soft whistling sound through his pursed lips.

"She's a tough old gal," George said. "I hear her coming though, so we have to stop, Harry. But we can talk tonight."

Harry nodded.

12

After dinner that night, when Maryrose had gone to bed—the hospital had given her two nights off—Harry sat across the kitchen table from a George who clearly had something to say. Sonny had polished off a six-pack by himself in front of the television and had gone up to the dormitory bedroom by himself. Albert had disappeared shortly after dinner, and their father had never emerged from his cubicle beside the junk room.

"I'm glad Pete Petrosian came over," George said. "He's a good old boy. Ate two helpings, too."

Harry was startled by George's use of their neighbor's first name—he was not even sure that he had ever heard it before.

Mr. Petrosian had been their only caller that afternoon. Harry had seen that his mother was grateful that someone had come, and despite her preparations wanted no more company after Mr. Petrosian had left.

"Think I'll get a beer, that is if Sonny didn't drink it all," George said, and stood up and opened the fridge. His uniform looked as if it had been painted on his body, and his muscles bulged and moved like a horse's. "Two left," he said. "Good thing you're underage." George popped the caps off both bottles and came back to the table. "So what the devil was Little Eddie doing up there, anyhow? Trying on dresses?"

"I don't know," Harry said. "I was asleep."

"Hell, I know I kind of lost touch with Little Eddie, but I got the impression he was scared of his own shadow. I'm surprised he had the nerve to go up there and mess around with Mom's precious stuff."

"Yeah," Harry said. "Me too."

"You didn't happen to go with him, did you?" George tilted the bottle to his mouth and winked at Harry.

Harry just looked back. He could feel his face getting hot.

"I was just thinking maybe you saw it happen to Little Eddie, and got too scared to tell anybody. Nobody would be mad at you, Harry. Nobody would blame you for anything. You couldn't know how to help someone who's having an epileptic fit. Little Eddie swallowed his tongue. Even if you'd been standing next to him when he did it and had the presence of mind to call an ambulance, he would have died before it got there. Unless you knew what was wrong and how to correct it. Which nobody would expect you to know, not in a million years. Nobody'd blame you for anything, Harry, not even Mom."

"I was asleep," Harry said.

"Okay, okay. I just wanted you to know."

They sat in silence for a time, then both spoke at once.

"Did you know—"

"We had this—"

"Sorry," George said. "Go on."

"Did you know that Dad used to be in the army? In World War II?"

"Yeah, I knew that. Of course I knew that."

"Did you know that he committed the perfect murder once?"

"*What?*"

"Dad committed the perfect murder. When he was at Dachau, that death camp."

"Oh, Christ, is that what you're talking about? You got a funny way of seeing things, Harry. He shot an enemy who was trying to escape. That's not murder, that's war. There's one hell of a big difference."

"I'd like to see war someday," Harry said. "I'd like to be in the army, like you and Dad."

"Hold your horses, hold your horses," George said, smiling now. "That's sort of one of the things I wanted to talk to you about." He set down his beer bottle, cradled his hands around it, and tilted his head to look at Harry. This was obviously going to be serious. "You know, I used to be crazy and stupid, that's the only way to put it. I used to look for fights. I had a chip on my shoulder the size of a house, and pounding some dipshit into a coma was my idea of a great time. The army did me a lot of good. It made me grow up. But I don't think you need that, Harry. You're too smart for that—if you have to go, you go, but out of all of us, you're the one who could really amount to something in this world. You could be a doctor. Or a lawyer. You ought to get the best education you can, Harry. What you have to do is stay out of trouble and get to college."

"Oh, college," Harry said.

"Listen to me, Harry. I make pretty good money, and I got nothing to spend it on. I'm not going to get married and have kids, that's for sure. So I want to make you a proposition. If you keep your nose clean and make it through high school, I'll help you out with college. Maybe you can get a scholarship—I think you're smart enough, Harry, and a scholarship would be great. But either way, I'll see you make it through." George emptied the first bottle, set it down, and gave Harry a quizzical look. "Let's get one person in this family off on the right track. What do you say?"

"I guess I better keep reading," Harry said.

"I hope you'll read your ass off, little buddy," George said, and picked up the second bottle of beer.

13

The day after Sonny left, George put all of Eddie's toys and clothes into a box and squeezed the box into the junk room; two days later, George took a bus to New York so he could get his flight to Munich from Idlewild. An hour before he caught his bus, George walked Harry up to Big John's and stuffed him full of hamburgers and french fries and said, "You'll probably miss Eddie a lot, won't you?" "I guess," Harry said, but the truth was that Eddie was now only a vacancy, a blank space. Sometimes a door would close and Harry would know that Little Eddie had just come in; but when he turned to look, he saw only emptiness. George's question, asked a week ago, was the last time Harry had heard anyone pronounce his brother's name.

In the seven days since the charmed afternoon at Big John's and the departure on a southbound bus of George Beevers, everything seemed to have gone back to the way it was before, but Harry knew that really everything had changed. They had been a loose, divided family of five, two parents and three sons. Now they seemed to be a family of three, and Harry thought that the actual truth was that the family had shrunk down to two, himself and his mother.

Edgar Beevers had left home—he too was an absence. After two visits from policemen who parked their cars right outside the house, after listening to his mother's muttered expressions of disgust, after the spectacle of his pale, bleary, but sober and clean-shaven father trying over and over to knot a necktie in front of the bathroom mirror, Harry finally accepted that his father had been caught shoplifting. His father had to go to court, and he was scared. His hands shook so uncontrollably that he could not shave himself, and in the end Maryrose had to knot his tie—doing it in one, two, three quick movements as brutal as the descent of a knife, never removing the cigarette from her mouth.

GRIEF-STRICKEN AREA MAN FORGIVEN OF SHOPLIFTING CHARGE, read the headline over the little story in the evening newspaper, which at least explained his father's crime. Edgar Beevers had been stopped on the sidewalk outside the Livermore Avenue National Tea, T-bone steaks hidden inside his shirt and a bottle of Rheingold beer in each of his front pockets. He had stolen two steaks! He had put beer bottles in his pockets! This made Harry feel like he was sweating inside. The judge had sent him home, but home was not where he went. For a short time, Harry thought, his father had hung out on Oldtown Road, Palmyra's skid row, and slept in vacant lots with winos and bums. (Then a woman was supposed to have taken him in.)

Albert was another mystery. It was as though a creature from outer space had taken him over and was using his body, like *Invasion of the Body Snatchers*. Albert looked like he thought somebody was always standing behind him, watching every move he made. He was still carrying around that piece of his tongue, and pretty soon, Harry thought, he'd get so used to it that he would forget he had it.

Three days after George left Palmyra, Albert actually tagged along after Harry on the way to Big John's. Harry turned around on the sidewalk and saw Albert in his black jeans and grease-blackened T-shirt halfway down the block, shoving his hands in his pockets and looking hard at the ground. That was Albert's way of pretending to be invisible. The next time he turned around, Albert growled, "Keep walking."

Harry went to work on the pinball machine as soon as he got inside Big John's. Albert slunk in a few minutes later and went straight to the counter. He took one of the stained paper menus from a stack squeezed in beside a napkin dispenser and inspected it as if he had never seen it before.

"Hey, let me introduce you guys," said Big John, leaning against the far side of the counter. Like Albert, he wore black jeans and motorcycle boots, but his dark hair, daringly for the 1950s, fell over his ears. Beneath his stained white apron he wore a long-sleeved black shirt with a pattern of tiny azure palm trees. "You two are the Beevers boys, Harry and Bucky. Say hello to each other, fellows."

Bucky Beaver was a toothy rodent in an Ipana television commercial. Albert blushed, still grimly staring at his menu sheet.

"Call me 'Beans,'" Harry said, and felt Albert's gaze shift wonderingly to him.

"Beans and Bucky, the Beevers boys," Big John said. "Well, Buck, what'll you have?"

"Hamburger, fries, shake," Albert said.

Big John half-turned and yelled the order through the hatch to Mama Mary's kitchen. For a time the three of them stood in uneasy silence. Then Big John said, "Heard your old man found a new place to hang his hat. His new girlfriend is a real pistol, I heard. Spent some time in County Hospital. On account of she picked up little messages from outer space on the good old Philco. You hear that?"

"He's gonna come home real soon," Harry said. "He doesn't have any new girlfriend. He's staying with an old friend. She's a rich lady and she wants to help him out because she knows he had a lot of trouble and she's going to get him a real good job, and then he'll come home, and we'll be able to move to a better house and everything."

He never even saw Albert move, but Albert had materialized beside him. Fury, rage, and misery distorted his face. Harry had time to cry out only once, and then Albert slammed a fist into his chest and knocked him backward into the pinball machine.

"I bet that felt real good," Harry said, unable to keep down his own rage. "I bet you'd like to kill me, huh? Huh, Albert? How about that?"

Albert moved backward two paces and lowered his hands, already looking impassive, locked into himself.

For a second in which his breath failed and dazzling light filled his eyes, Harry saw Little Eddie's slack, trusting face before him. Then Big John came up from nowhere with a big hamburger and a mound of french fries on his plate and said, "Down, boys. Time for Rocky here to tackle his dinner."

That night Albert did nothing at all to Harry as they lay in their beds. Neither did he fall asleep. Harry knew that for most of the night Albert just closed his eyes and faked it, like a possum in trouble. Harry tried to stay awake long enough to see when Albert's fake sleep melted into the real thing, but he sank into dreams long before that.

He was rushing down the stony corridor of a castle past suits of armor and torches guttering in sconces. His bladder was bursting, he had to let go, he could not hold it more than another few seconds . . . At last he came to the open bathroom door and ran into that splendid gleaming place. He began to tug at his zipper, and looked around for the butler and the row of marble urinals. Then he froze. Little Eddie was standing before him, not the uniformed butler. Blood ran in a gaudy streak from a gash high on his forehead over his cheek and right down his neck, neat as paint. Little Eddie was waving frantically at Harry, his eyes bright and hysterical, his mouth working soundlessly because he had swallowed his tongue.

Harry sat straight up in bed, about to scream, then realized that the bedroom was all around him and Little Eddie was gone. He hurried downstairs to the bathroom.

14

At two o'clock the next afternoon Harry Beevers had to pee again, and just as badly, but this time he was a long way from the bathroom across from the junk room and his father's old cubicle. Harry was standing in the humid sunlight across the street from 45 Oldtown Way. This short street connected the bums, transient hotels, bars, and seedy movie theaters of Oldtown Road with the more respectable hotels, department stores, and restaurants of Palmyra Avenue—the real downtown. Forty-five Oldtown Way was a four-story brick tenement with an exoskeleton of fire escapes. Black iron bars covered the ground-floor windows. On one side of 45 Oldtown Way were the large soap-smeared windows of a bankrupted shoe store, on the other a vacant lot where loose bricks and broken bottles nestled among dandelions and tall Queen Anne's lace. Harry's father lived in that building now. Everybody else knew it, and since Big John had told him, now Harry knew it too.

He jigged from leg to leg, waiting for a woman to come out through the front door. It was as chipped and peeling as his own, and a broken fanlight sat drunkenly atop it. Harry had checked the row of dented mailboxes on the brick wall just outside the door for his father's name, but none bore any names at all. Big John hadn't known the name of the woman who had taken Harry's father in, but he said that she was large, black-haired, and crazy, and that she had two children in foster care. About half an hour ago a dark-haired woman had come through the door, but Harry had not followed her because she had not looked especially large to him. Now he was beginning to have doubts. What did Big John mean by "large," anyhow? As big as he was? And how could you tell if someone was crazy? Did it show? Maybe he should have followed that woman. This thought made him even more anxious, and he squeezed his legs together.

His father was in that building now, he thought. Harry thought of his father lying on an unmade bed, his brown winter coat around him, his hat pulled low on his forehead like Lepke Buchalter's, drawing on a cigarette, looking moodily out the window.

Then he had to pee so urgently that he could not have held it in for more than a few seconds, and trotted across the street and into the vacant lot. Near the back fence the tall weeds gave him some shelter from the street. He frantically unzipped and let the braided yellow stream splash into a nest of broken bricks. Harry looked up at the side of the building beside him. It looked very tall, and seemed to be tilting toward him. The four blank windows on each floor looked back down at him. Just as he was tugging at his zipper, he heard the front door of the building slam shut.

His heart slammed too. Harry hunkered down behind the tall white weeds. Anxiety that she might walk the other way, toward downtown, made him twine his fingers together and bend them back. If he waited about five seconds, he figured, he'd know she was going toward Palmyra Avenue and would be able to get across the lot in time to see which way she turned. His knuckles cracked. He felt like a soldier hiding in a forest, like a murder weapon.

He raised up on his toes and got ready to dash back across the street, because an empty grocery cart, closely followed by a moving belly with a tiny head and basketball shoes, a cigar tilted in its mouth like a flag, appeared past the front of the building. He could go back and wait across the street. Harry settled down and watched the stomach go down the sidewalk past him. Then a shadow separated itself from the street side of the fat man, and the shadow became a black-haired woman in a long loose dress now striding past the grocery cart. She shook back her head, and Harry saw that she was tall as a queen and that her skin was darker than olive. Deep lines cut through her cheeks. It had to be the woman who had taken his father in. Her long rapid strides had taken her well past the fat man's grocery cart. Harry ran across the rubble of the lot and began to follow her up the sidewalk.

His father's woman walked in a hard, determined way. She stepped down into the street to get around groups too slow for her. At the Oldtown Road corner she wove her way through a group of saggy-bottomed men passing around a bottle in a paper bag and cut in front of two black children dribbling a basketball up the street. She was on the move, and Harry had to hurry along to keep her in sight.

"I bet you don't believe me," he said to himself, practicing, and skirted the group of winos on the corner. He picked up his speed until he was nearly trotting. The two black kids with the basketball ignored him as he kept pace with them, then went on ahead. Far up the block, the tall woman with the bouncing black hair marched right past a flashing neon sign in a bar window. Her bottom moved back and forth in the loose dress, surprisingly big whenever it bulged out the fabric of the dress; her back seemed as long as a lion's. "What would you say if I told you," Harry said to himself.

A block and a half ahead, the woman turned on her heel and went through the door of the A&P store. Harry sprinted the rest of the way, pushed the yellow wooden door marked ENTER, and walked into the dense, humid air of the grocery store. Other A&P stores may have been air-conditioned, but not the little shop on Oldtown Road.

What was foster care, anyway? Did you get money if you gave away your children?

A good person's children would never be in foster care, Harry thought. He saw the woman turning into the third aisle past the cash register. He took in with a small shock that she was taller than his father. *If I told you, you might not believe me.* He went slowly around the corner of the aisle. She was standing on the pale wooden floor about fifteen feet in front of him, carrying a wire basket in one hand. He stepped forward. *What I have to say might seem.* For good luck, he touched the hat pin inserted into the bottom of his collar. She was staring at a row of brightly colored bags of potato chips. Harry cleared his throat. The woman reached down and picked up a big bag and put it in the basket.

"Excuse me," Harry said.

She turned her head to look at him. Her face was as wide as it was long, and in the mellow light from the store's low-wattage bulbs her skin seemed a very light shade of brown. Harry knew he was meeting an equal. She looked like she could do magic, as if she could shoot fire and sparks out of her fierce black eyes.

"I bet you don't believe me," he said, "but a kid can hypnotize people just as good as an adult."

"What's that?"

His rehearsed words now sounded crazy to him, but he stuck to his script.

"A kid can hypnotize people. I can hypnotize people. Do you believe that?"

"I don't think I even care," she said, and wheeled away toward the rear of the aisle.

"I bet you don't think I could hypnotize you," Harry said.

"Kid, get lost."

Harry suddenly knew that if he kept talking about hypnotism the woman would turn down the next aisle and ignore him no matter what he said, or else begin to speak in a very loud voice about seeing the manager. "My name is Harry Beevers," he said to her back. "Edgar Beevers is my dad."

She stopped and turned around and looked expressionlessly into his face.

"I wonder if you maybe call him Beans," Harry said.

"Oh, great," she said. "That's just great. So you're one of his boys. Terrific. *Beans* wants potato chips, what do you want?"

"I want you to fall down and bang your head and swallow your tongue and *die* and get buried and have people drop dirt on you," Harry said. The woman's mouth fell open. "Then I want you to puff up with *gas*. I want you to *rot*. I want you to turn green and *black*. I want your *skin* to slide off your bones."

"You're crazy!" the woman shouted at him. "Your whole family's crazy! Do you think your mother wants him anymore?"

"My father shot us in the back," Harry said, and turned and bolted down the aisle for the door.

Outside, he began to trot down seedy Oldtown Road. At Oldtown Way he turned left. When he ran past number 45, he looked at every blank window. His face, his hands, his whole body felt hot and wet. Soon he had a stitch in his side. Harry blinked, and saw a dark line of trees, a wall of barbed wire before him. At the top of Oldtown Way he turned into Palmyra Avenue. From there he could continue running past Allouette's boarded-up windows, past all the stores old and new, to the corner of Livermore, and from there, he only now realized, to the little house that belonged to Mr. Petrosian.

15

On a sweltering mid-afternoon eleven years later at a camp in the central highlands of Vietnam, Lieutenant Harry Beevers closed the flap of his tent against the mosquitoes and sat on the edge of his temporary bunk to write a long-delayed letter to Pat Caldwell, the young woman he wanted to marry—and to whom he would be married for a time, after his return from the war to New York State.

This is what he wrote, after frequent crossings-out and hesitations. Harry later destroyed this letter.

Dear Pat:
   First of all I want you to know how much I miss you, my darling, and that if I ever get out of this beautiful and terrible country, which I am going to do, that I am going to chase you mercilessly

and unrelentingly until you say that you'll marry me. Maybe in the euphoria of relief (YES!!!), I have the future all worked out, Pat, and you're a big part of it. I have eighty-six days until DEROS, when they pat me on the head and put me on that big bird out of here. Now that my record is clear again, I have no doubts that Columbia Law School will take me in. As you know, my law board scores were pretty respectable (modest me!) when I took them at Adelphi. I'm pretty sure I could even get into Harvard Law, but I settled on Columbia because then we could both be in New York.

My brother George has already told me that he will help out with whatever money I—you and I—will need. George put me through Adelphi. I don't think you knew this. In fact, nobody knew this. When I look back, in college I was such a jerk. I wanted everybody to think my family was well-to-do, or at least middle-class. The truth is, we were damn poor, which I think makes my accomplishments all the more noteworthy, all the more loveworthy!

You see, this experience, even with all the ugly and self-doubting and humiliating moments, has done me a lot of good. I was right to come here, even though I had no idea what it was really like. I think I needed the experience of war to complete me, and I tell you this even though I know that you will detest any such idea. In fact, I have to tell you that a big part of me loves being here, and that in some way, even with all this trouble, this year will always be one of the high points of my life. Pat, as you see I'm determined to be honest—to be an honest man. If I'm going to be a lawyer, I ought to be honest, don't you think? (Or maybe the reverse is the reality!) One thing that has meant a lot to me here has been what I can only call the close comradeship of my friends and my men—I actually like the grunts more than the usual officer types, which of course means that I get more loyalty and better performance from my men than the usual lieutenant. Someday I'd like you to meet Mike Pole and Tim Underhill and Pumo the Puma and the most amazing of all, M.O. Dengler, who of course was involved with me in the Ia Thuc cave incident. These guys stuck by me. I even have a nickname, "Beans." They call me "Beans" Beevers, and I like it.

There was no way my court-martial could have really put me in any trouble, because all the facts, and my own men, were on my side. Besides, could you see me actually killing children? This is Vietnam and you kill people, that's what we're doing here—we kill Charlies.

But we don't kill babies and children. Not even in the heat of wartime—and Ia Thuc was pretty hot!

Well, this is my way of letting you know that at the court-martial of course I received a complete and utter vindication. Dengler did too. There were even unofficial mutterings about giving us medals for all the BS we put up with in the past six weeks—including that amazing story in Time *magazine. Before people start yelling about atrocities, they ought to have all the facts straight. Fortunately, last week's magazines go out with the rest of the trash.*

Besides, I already knew too much about what death does to people.

I never told you that I once had a little brother named Edward. When he was ten, my little brother wandered up into the top floor of our house one night and suffered a fatal epileptic fit. This event virtually destroyed my family. It led directly to my father's leaving home. (He had been a hero in WWII, something else I never told you.) It deeply changed, I would say even damaged, my older brother Albert. Albert tried to enlist in 1964, but they wouldn't take him because they said he was psychologically unfit. My mom too almost came apart for a while. She used to go up in the attic and cry and wouldn't come down. So you could say that my family was pretty well destroyed, or ruined, or whatever you want to call it, by a sudden death. I took it, and my dad's desertion, pretty hard myself. You don't get over these things easily.

The court-martial lasted exactly four hours. Big deal, hey?, as we used to say back in Palmyra. We used to have a neighbor named Pete Petrosian who said things like that, and against what must have been million-to-one odds, died exactly the same way my brother did, about two weeks after—lightning really did strike twice. I guess it's dumb to think about him now, but maybe one thing war does is to make you conversant with death. How it happens, what it does to people, what it means, how all the dead in your life are somehow united, joined, part of your eternal family. This is a profound feeling, Pat, and no damn whipped-up failed court-martial can touch it. If there were any innocent children in that cave, then they are in my family forever, like little Edward and Pete Petrosian, and the rest of my life is a poem to them. But the Army says there weren't, and so do I.

I love you and love you and love you. You can stop worrying now and start thinking about being married to a Columbia Law student with one hell of a good future. I won't tell you any more war stories than you want to hear. And that's a promise, whether the stories are about Nam or Palmyra.

Always yours,
Harry
(aka "Beans!")

In The Realm of Dreams

For a long time after the war, he dreamed about his childhood. He heard screams from the bedroom or the bathroom of the little duplex where they had lived when he was a small boy, and when he turned in panic to look out of the window, he knew that the street with its rising lawns and tall elms was only a picture over the face of a terrible fire. In the dreams, he knew that none of this had anything at all to do with the war. It had all happened before. Screams floated inside the brown and yellow house, and smoke and fire billowed up beneath the streets.

The screams would stop as soon as he touched the bathroom door-knob. When he opened the door, he would see the shower curtain pulled across the tub. It was splashed with blood, and curls and loops of blood lay scattered on the floor and the white toilet seat. The hard part was pushing back the shower curtain, but there was never anybody in the tub—only a big bloodstain moving toward the drain like a living thing. That was exactly what had happened, in and before the war.

The Juniper Tree

It is a school yard in my Midwest of empty lots, waving green and brilliant with tiger lilies, of ugly new "ranch" houses set down in rows in
glistening clay, of treeless avenues cooking in the sun. Our school yard
is black asphalt—on June days, patches of the asphalt loosen and stick
like gum to the soles of our high-top basketball shoes.

Most of the playground is black empty space from which heat radiates
up like the wavery images on the screen of a faulty television set. Tall
wire mesh surrounds it. A new boy named Paul is standing beside me.

Though it is now nearly the final month of the semester, Paul came
to us, carroty-haired, pale-eyed, too shy to ask even the whereabouts of
the lavatory, only six weeks ago. The lessons baffle him, and his Southern accent is a fatal error of style. The popular students broadcast in
hushed, giggling whispers the terrible news that Paul "talks like a nig-
ger." Their voices are *almost* awed—they are conscious of the enormity
of what they are saying, of the enormity of its consequences.

Paul is wearing a brilliant red shirt too heavy, too enveloping, for the
weather. He and I stand in the shade at the rear of the school, before
the cream-colored brick wall in which is placed at eye level a newly
broken window of pebbly green glass reinforced with strands of cop-
per wire. At our feet is a little scatter of green, edible-looking pebbles.
The pebbles dig into the soles of our shoes, too hard to shatter against
the softer asphalt. Paul is singing to me in his slow, lilting voice that
he will never have friends in this school. I put my foot down on one of
the green candy pebbles and feel it push up, hard as a bullet, against

my foot. "Children are so cruel," Paul casually sings. I think of sliding the pebble of broken glass across my throat, slicing myself wide open to let death in.

Paul did not return to school in the fall. His father, who had beaten a man to death down in Mississippi, had been arrested while leaving a movie theater near my house named the Orpheum-Oriental. Paul's father had taken his family to see an Esther Williams movie costar-ring Fernando Lamas, and when they came out, their mouths raw from salty popcorn, the baby's hands sticky with spilled Coca-Cola, the police were waiting for them. They were Mississippi people, and I think of Paul now, seated at a desk on a floor of an office building in Jackson filled with men like him at desks: his tie perfectly knot-ted, a good shine on his cordovan shoes, a necessary but unconscious restraint in the set of his mouth.

In those days I used to spend whole days in the Orpheum-Oriental.

I was seven. I held within me the idea of a disappearance like Paul's, of never having to be seen again. Of being an absence, a shadow, a place where something no longer visible used to be.

Before I met that young-old man whose name was "Frank" or "Stan" or "Jimmy," when I sat in the rapture of education before the movies at the Orpheum-Oriental, I watched Alan Ladd and Richard Widmark and Glenn Ford and Dane Clark. *Chicago Deadline*. Martin and Lewis, tangled up in some parachute in *At War with the Army*. William Boyd and Roy Rogers. Openmouthed, I drank down movies about spies and criminals, wanting the passionate and shadowy ones to fulfill them-selves, to gorge themselves on whatever they needed.

The feverish gaze of Richard Widmark, the anger of Alan Ladd, Berry Kroeger's sneaky eyes, girlish and watchful—vivid, total elegance.

—

When I was seven, my father walked into the bathroom and saw me looking at my face in the mirror. He slapped me, not with his whole strength, but hard, raging instantly. "What do you think you're looking at?" His hand cocked and ready. "What do you think you see?"

"Nothing," I said.

"Nothing is right."

A carpenter, he worked furiously, already defeated, and never had enough money—as if, permanently beyond reach, some quantity of money existed that would have satisfied him. In the mornings he went to the job site hardened like cement into anger he barely knew he had. Sometimes he brought men from the taverns home with him at night. They carried transparent bottles of Miller High Life in paper bags and set them down on the table with a bang that said: Men are here! My mother, who had returned from her secretary's job a few hours earlier, fed my brothers and me, washed the dishes, and put the three of us to bed while the men shouted and laughed in the kitchen.

He was considered an excellent carpenter. He worked slowly, patiently; and I see now that he spent whatever love he had in the rented garage that was his workshop. In his spare time he listened to baseball games on the radio. He had a professional, but not a personal, vanity, and he thought that a face like mine should not be examined.

Because I saw "Jimmy" in the mirror, I thought my father, too, had seen him.

One Saturday my mother took the twins and me on the ferry across Lake Michigan to Saginaw—the point of the journey was the journey, and at Saginaw the boat docked for twenty minutes before wallowing back out into the lake and returning. With us were women like my mother, her friends, freed by the weekend from their jobs, some of them accompanied by men like my father, with their felt hats and baggy weekend trousers flaring over their weekend shoes. The women wore blood-bright lipstick that printed itself onto their cigarettes and smeared across their front teeth. They laughed a great deal and repeated the words that had made them laugh. "Hot dog," "slippin' 'n' slidin'," "opera singer." Thirty minutes after departure, the men disappeared into the enclosed deck bar; the women, my mother among them, arranged deck chairs into a long oval tied together by laughter, attention, gossip. They waved their cigarettes in the air. My brothers raced around the deck, their shirts flapping, their hair glued to their skulls with sweat—when they squabbled, my mother ordered them into the empty deck chairs. I sat on the deck, leaning against the railings, quiet. If someone had asked me: What do you want to do this afternoon, what do you want to do for the rest of your life? I would have said, I want to stay right here, I want to stay here forever.

After a while I stood up and left the women. I went across the deck and stepped through a hatch into the bar. Dark, deeply grained imitation wood covered the walls. The odors of beer and cigarettes and the sound of men's voices filled the enclosed space. About twenty men stood at the bar, talking and gesturing with half-filled glasses. Then one man broke away from the others with a flash of dirty-blond hair. I saw his shoulders move, and my scalp tingled and my stomach froze and I thought: Jimmy. "Jimmy." But he turned all the way around, dipping his shoulders in some ecstasy of beer and male company, and I saw that he was a stranger, not "Jimmy," after all.

———

I was thinking: Someday when I am free, when I am out of this body and in some city whose name I do not even know now, I will remember this from beginning to end and I will be free of it.

The women floated over the empty lake, laughing out clouds of cigarette smoke; the men, too, as boisterous as the children on the sticky asphalt playground with its small green spray of glass like candy.

———

In those days I knew I was set apart from the rest of my family, an island between my parents and the twins. Those pairs that bracketed me slept in double beds in adjacent rooms at the back of the ground floor of the duplex owned by the blind man who lived above us. My bed, a cot coveted by the twins, stood in their room. An invisible line of great authority divided my territory and possessions from theirs.

———

This is what happened in the mornings in our half of the duplex. My mother got up first—we heard her showering, heard drawers closing, the sounds of bowls and milk being set out on the table. The smell of bacon frying for my father, who banged on the door and called out my brothers' names. "Don't you make me come in there, now!" The noisy, puppyish turmoil of my brothers getting out of bed. All three of us scramble into the bathroom as soon as my father leaves it. The bathroom was steamy, heavy with the odor of shit and the more piercing, almost palpable smell of shaving—lather and amputated whiskers. We all pee into the toilet at the same time. My mother frets and frets, pulling the twins into their clothes so that she can take them down the street to Mrs. Candee, who is given a five-dollar bill every week for taking care of them. I am supposed to be running back and forth on the playground in Summer Play School, supervised by two teenage girls who live a block away from us. (I went to Play School only twice.) After I dress myself in clean underwear and socks and put on my everyday shirt and pants, I come into the kitchen while my father finishes his breakfast. He is eating strips of bacon and golden-brown pieces of toast shiny with butter. A cigarette smolders in the ashtray before him. Everybody else has already left the house. My father and I can hear the blind man banging at the piano in his living room. I sit down before a bowl of cereal. My father looks at me, looks away. Angry at the blind man for banging at the piano this early in the morning, he is sweating already. His cheeks and forehead shine like the golden toast. My father glances at me, knowing he can postpone this no longer, and reaches wearily into his pocket and drops two quarters on the table. The high-school girls charge twenty-five cents a day, and the other quarter is for my lunch. "Don't lose that money," he says as I take the coins. My father dumps coffee into his mouth, puts the cup and his plate into the crowded sink, looks at me again, pats his pocket for his keys, and says, "Close the door behind you." I tell him that I will close the door. He picks up his gray toolbox and his black lunch pail, claps his hat on his head, and goes out, banging his toolbox against the door frame. It leaves a broad gray mark like a smear left by the passing of some angry creature's hide.

Then I am alone in the house. I go back to the bedroom, close the door and push a chair beneath the knob, and read *Blackhawk* and *Henry* and *Captain Marvel* comic books until at last it is time to go to the theater.

While I read, everything in the house seems alive and dangerous. I can hear the telephone in the hall rattling on its hook, the radio clicking as it tries to turn itself on and talk to me. The dishes stir and chime in the sink. At these times all objects, even the heavy chairs and sofa, become their true selves, violent as the fire that fills the sky I cannot see, and races through the secret ways and passages beneath the streets. At these times other people vanish like smoke.

When I pull the chair away from the door, the house immediately goes quiet, like a wild animal feigning sleep. Everything inside and out slips cunningly back into place, the fires bank, men and women reappear on the sidewalks. I must open the door and I do. I walk swiftly through the kitchen and living room to the front door, knowing that if I look too carefully at any one thing, I will wake it up again. My mouth is so dry, my tongue feels fat. "I'm leaving," I say to no one. Everything in the house hears me.

The quarter goes through the slot at the bottom of the window, the ticket leaps from its slot. For a long time, before "Jimmy," I thought that unless you kept your stub unfolded and safe in a shirt pocket, the usher could rush down the aisle in the middle of the movie, seize you, and throw you out. So into the pocket it goes, and I slip through the big doors into the cool, cross the lobby, and pass through a swinging door with a porthole window.

Most of the regular daytime patrons of the Orpheum-Oriental sit in the same seats every day—I am one of those who comes here every day. A small, talkative gathering of bums sits far to the right of the theater, in the rows beneath the sconces fastened like bronze torches to the walls. The bums choose these seats so they can examine their bits of paper, their "documents," and show them to each other during the movies. Always on their minds is the possibility that they might have lost one of these documents, and they frequently consult the tattered envelopes in which they are kept.

I take the end seat, left side of the central block of seats, just before the broad horizontal middle aisle. There I can stretch out. At other times I sit in the middle of the last row, or the first; sometimes when the balcony is open I go up and sit in its first row. From the first row of the balcony, seeing a movie is like being a bird and flying down into the movie from above. To be alone in the theater is delicious. The curtains hang heavy, red, anticipatory; the mock torches glow on the walls. Swirls of gilt wind through the red paint. On days when I sit near a wall, I reach out toward the red, which seems warm and soft, and find my fingers resting on chill dampness. The carpet of the Orpheum-Oriental must once have been a bottomlessly rich brown; now it is a dark noncolor, mottled with pink and gray smears, like melted Band-Aids, of chewing gum. From about a third of the seats dirty gray wool foams from slashes in the worn plush.

On an ideal day I sit through a cartoon, a travelogue, a sequence of previews, a movie, another cartoon, and another movie before anyone else enters the theater. This whole cycle is as satisfying as a meal. On other mornings, old women in odd hats and young women wearing scarves over their rollers, a few teenage couples are scattered throughout the theater when I come in. None of these people ever pays attention to anything but the screen and, in the case of the teenagers, each other.

Once, a man in his early twenties, hair like a haystack, sat up in the wide middle aisle when I took my seat. He groaned. Rusty-looking dried blood was spattered over his chin and his dirty white shirt. He groaned again and then got to his hands and knees. The carpet beneath him was spotted with what looked like a thousand red dots. The young man stumbled to his feet and began reeling up the aisle. A bright, depthless pane of sunlight surrounded him before he vanished into it.

At the beginning of July, I told my mother that the high-school girls had increased the hours of the Play School, because I wanted to be sure of seeing both features twice before I had to go home. After that I could learn the rhythms of the theater itself, which did not impress themselves on me all at once but revealed themselves gradually, so that by the middle of the first week, I knew when the bums would begin to move toward the seats beneath the sconces—they usually arrived on Tuesdays and Fridays shortly after eleven o'clock, when the liquor store down the block opened up to provide them with the pints and half-pints that nourished them. By the end of the second week, I knew when the ushers left the interior of the theater to sit on padded benches in the lobby and light up their Luckies and Chesterfields, when the old men and women would begin to appear. By the end of the third week, I felt like the merest part of a great, orderly machine. Before the beginning of the second showing of *Beautiful Hawaii* or *Curiosities Down Under*, I went out to the counter with my second quarter and purchased a box of popcorn or a packet of Good & Plenty candy.

In a movie theater nothing is random except the customers and hitches in the machine. Film strips break and lights fail; the projectionist gets drunk or falls asleep; and the screen presents a blank yellow face to the stamping, whistling audience. These inconsistencies are summer squalls, forgotten as soon as they have ended.

The occasion for the lights, the projectionist, the boxes of popcorn and packets of candy, the movies, enlarged when seen over and over. The truth gradually came to me that this deepening and widening out, this enlarging, was why movies were shown over and over all day long. The machine revealed itself most surely in the exact, limpid repetitions of the actors' words and gestures as they moved through the story. When Alan Ladd asked "Blacky Franchot," the dying gangster, "Who did it, Blacky?" his voice widened like a river, grew *sandier* with an almost unconcealed tenderness I had to learn to hear—the voice within the speaking voice.

———

Chicago Deadline was the exploration by a newspaper reporter named "Ed Adams" (Alan Ladd) of the tragedy of a mysterious young woman, "Rosita Jean d'Ur," who had died alone of tuberculosis in a shabby hotel room. The reporter soon learns that she had many names, many identities. She had been in love with an architect, a gangster, a crippled professor, a boxer, a millionaire, and had given a different facet of her being to each of them. Far too predictably, the adult me complains, the obsessed "Ed" falls in love with "Rosita." When I was seven, little was predictable—I had not yet seen *Laura*—and I saw a man driven by the need to understand, which became identical to the need to protect. "Rosita Jean d'Ur" was the embodiment of memory, which was mystery.

Through the sequences of her identities, the various selves shown to brother, boxer, millionaire, gangster, all the others, her memory kept her whole. I saw, twice a day, for two weeks, before and during "Jimmy," the machine deep within the machine. Love and memory were the same. Both love and memory accommodated us to death. (I did not understand this, but I saw it.) The reporter, Alan Ladd, with his dirty-blond hair, his perfect jawline, and brilliant, wounded smile, gave her life by making her memory his own.

"I think you're the only one who ever understood her," Arthur Kennedy—"Rosita's" brother—tells Alan Ladd.

Most of the world demands the kick of sensation, most of the world must gather and spend money, hunt for easier and more temporary forms of love, must feed itself, sell newspapers, destroy the enemy's plots with plots of its own . . .

"I don't know what you want," "Ed Adams" says to the editor of *The Journal*. "You got two murders . . ."

". . . and a mystery woman," I say along with him. His voice is tough and detached, the voice of a wounded man acting. The man beside me laughs. Unlike his normal voice, his laughter is breathless and high-pitched. It is the second showing today of *Chicago Deadline*, early afternoon—after the next showing of *At War with the Army* I will have to walk up the aisle and out of the theater. It will be twenty minutes to five, and the sun will still burn high over the cream-colored buildings across wide, empty Sherman Boulevard.

I met the man, or he met me, at the candy counter. He was at first only a tall presence, blond, dressed in dark clothing. I cared nothing for him, he did not matter. He was vague even when he spoke. "Good popcorn." I looked up at him—narrow blue eyes, bad teeth smiling at me. Stubble on his face. I looked away and the uniformed man behind the counter handed me popcorn. "Good for you, I mean. Good stuff in popcorn—comes right out of the ground. Grows on big plants tall as I am, just like other corn. You know that?"

When I said nothing, he laughed and spoke to the man behind the counter. "*He* didn't know that—the kid thought popcorn grew inside poppers." The counterman turned away. "You come here a lot?" the man asked me.

I put a few kernels of popcorn in my mouth and turned toward him. He was showing me his bad teeth.

"You do," he said. "You come here a lot."

I nodded.

"Every day?"

I nodded again.

"And we tell little fibs at home about what we've been doing all day, don't we?" he asked, and pursed his lips and raised his eyes like a comic butler in a movie. Then his mood shifted and everything about him became serious. He was looking at me, but he did not see me. "You got a favorite actor? I got a favorite actor. Alan Ladd."

And I saw—both saw and understood—that he thought he looked like Alan Ladd. He did, too, at least a little bit. When I saw the resemblance, he seemed like a different person, more glamorous. Glamour surrounded him, as though he were acting, impersonating a shabby young man with stained, irregular teeth.

"The name's Frank," he said, and stuck out his hand. "Shake?"

I took his hand.

"Real good popcorn," he said, and stuck his hand into the box. "Want to hear a secret?"

A secret.

"I was born twice. The first time, I died. It was on an army base. Everybody *told* me I should have joined the Navy, and everybody was right. So I just had myself get born somewhere else. Hey—the army's not for everybody, you know?" He grinned down at me. "Now I told you my secret. Let's go in—I'll sit with you. Everybody needs company, and I like you. You look like a good kid."

He followed me back to my seat and sat down beside me. When I quoted lines along with the actors, he laughed.

Then he said—

Then he leaned toward me and said—

He leaned toward me, breathing sour wine over me, and took—

No.

"I was just kidding out there," he said. "Frank ain't my real name. Well, it was my name. Before. See? Frank *used* to be my name for a while. But now my good friends call me Stan. I like that. Stanley the Steamer. Big Stan. Stan the Man. See? It works real good."

———

You'll never be a carpenter, he told me. You'll never be anything like that—because you got that look. I used to have that look, okay? So I know. I know about you just by looking at you.

He said he had been a clerk at Sears; after that he had worked as the custodian for a couple of apartment buildings owned by a guy who used to be a friend of his but was no longer. Then he had been a janitor at the high school where my grade school sent its graduates. "Good old booze got me fired, story of my life," he said. "Tight-ass bitches caught me drinking down in the basement, in a room I used there, and threw me out without a fare-thee-well. Hey, that was my *room*. My *place*. The best things in the world can do the worst things to you; you'll find that out someday. And when you go to that school, I hope you'll remember what they done to me there."

These days he was resting. He hung around, he went to the movies.

He said: You got something special in you. Guys like me, we're funny, we can tell.

We sat together through the second feature, Dean Martin and Jerry Lewis, comfortable and laughing. "Those guys are bigger bums than us," he said. I thought of Paul backed up against the school in his enveloping red shirt, imprisoned within his inability to be like anyone around him.

You coming back tomorrow? If I get here, I'll check around for you.

Hey. Trust me. I know you are.

You know that little thing you pee with? Leaning sideways and whispering into my ear. That's the best thing a man's got. Trust me.

The big providential park near our house, two streets past the Orpheum-Oriental, is separated into three different areas. Nearest the wide iron gates on Sherman Boulevard through which we enter was a wading pool divided by a low green hedge, so rubbery it seemed artificial, from a playground with a climbing frame, swings, and a row of seesaws. When I was a child of two and three, I splashed in a warm pool and clung to the chains of the swings, making myself go higher and higher, terror and joy and grim duty so woven together that no one could pull them apart.

Beyond the children's pool and playground was the zoo. My mother walked my brothers and me to the playground and wading pool and sat smoking on the bench while we played; both of my parents took us into the zoo. An elephant extended his trunk to my father's palm and delicately lipped peanuts toward his maw. The giraffe stretched toward the constantly diminishing supply of leaves, ever fewer and higher, above his cage. The lions drowsed on amputated branches and paced behind bars, staring out not at what was there but at the long, grassy plains imprinted on their memories. I knew the lions had the power not to see us, to look straight through us to Africa. But when they saw you instead of Africa, they looked right into your bones, they saw the blood traveling through your body. The lions were golden-brown, patient, green-eyed. They recognized me and could read thoughts. The lions neither liked nor disliked me, they did not miss me during their long weekdays, but they took me into the circle of known beings.

("You shouldn't have looked at me like that," June Havoc—"Leona"—tells "Ed Adams." She does not mean it, not at all.)

Past the zoo and across a narrow park road down which khaki-clothed park attendants pushed barrows heavy with flowers stood a wide, unexpected lawn bordered with flower beds and tall elms—open space hidden like a secret between the caged animals and the elm trees. Only my father brought me to this section of the park. Here he tried to make a baseball player of me.

"Get the bat off your shoulders," he says. "For God's sake, will you try to hit the ball, anyhow?"

When I fail once again to swing at his slow, perfect pitch, he spins around, raises his arm, and theatrically asks everyone in sight, "Whose kid is this, anyway? Can you answer me that?"

He has never asked me about the Play School I am supposed to be attending, and I have never told him about the Orpheum-Oriental—I will never come any closer to talking to him than now, for "Stan," "Stanley the Steamer," has told me things that cannot be true, that must be inventions and fables, part of the world of children wandering lost in the forest, of talking cats and silver boots filled with blood. In this world, dismembered children buried beneath juniper trees can rise and speak, made whole once again. Fables boil with underground explosions and hidden fires, and for this reason, memory rejects them, thrusts them out of its sight, and they must be repeated over and over. I cannot remember "Stan's" face—cannot even be sure I remember what he said. Dean Martin and Jerry Lewis are bums like us. I am certain of only one thing: tomorrow I am again going to see my newest, scariest, most interesting friend.

"When I was your age," my father says, "I had my heart set on playing pro ball when I grew up. And you're too damned scared or lazy to even take the bat off your shoulder. Kee-rist! I can't stand looking at you anymore."

He turns around and begins to move quickly toward the narrow park road and the zoo, going home, and I run after him. I retrieve the softball when he tosses it into the bushes.

"What the hell do you think you're going to do when you grow up?" my father asks, his eyes still fixed ahead of him. "I wonder what you think life is all *about*. I wouldn't trust you around carpenter tools, I wouldn't trust you to blow your nose right—to tell you the truth, I wonder if the hospital mixed up the goddamn babies."

I follow him, dragging the bat with one hand, the other cradling the softball in the pouch of my mitt.

At dinner my mother asks if Summer Play School is fun, and I say yes. I have already taken from my father's dresser drawer what "Stan" asked me to get for him, and it burns my pocket as if it were alight. I want to ask: Is it actually true and not a story? Does the worst thing always have to be the true thing? Of course, I cannot ask this. My father does not know about worse things—he sees what he wants to see, or he tries so hard, he thinks he does see it.

"I guess he'll hit a long ball someday. The boy just needs more work on his swing." He tries to smile at me, a boy who will someday learn to hit a long ball. The knife is upended in his fist—he is about to smear a pat of butter on his steak. He does not see me at all. My father is not a lion, he cannot make the switch to seeing what is really there in front of him.

—

Late at night Alan Ladd knelt beside my bed. He was wearing a neat gray suit, and his breath smelled like cloves. "You okay, son?" I nodded. "I just wanted to tell you that I like seeing you out there every day. That means a lot to me."

———

"Do you remember what I was telling you about?"

And I knew: it was true. He had said those things, and he would repeat them like a fairy tale, and the world was going to change because it would be seen through changed eyes. I felt sick—trapped in the theater as if in a cage.

"You think about what I told you?"

"Sure," I said.

"That's good. Hey, you know what? I feel like changing seats. You want to change seats too?"

"Where to?"

He tilted his head back, and I knew he wanted to move to the last row. "Come on. I want to show you something."

We changed seats.

For a long time we sat watching the movie from the last row, nearly alone in the theater. Just after eleven, three of the bums filed in and proceeded to their customary seats on the other side of the theater—a rumpled graybeard I had seen many times before; a fat man with a stubby, squashed face, also familiar; and one of the shaggy, wild-looking young men who hung around the bums until they became indistinguishable from them. They began passing a flat brown bottle back and forth. After a second I remembered the young man—I had surprised him awake one morning, passed out and spattered with blood, in the middle aisle.

Then I wondered if "Stan" was not the young man I had surprised that morning; they looked as alike as twins, though I knew they were not.

"Want a sip?" "Stan" said, showing me his own pint bottle. "Do you good."

Bravely, feeling privileged and adult, I took the bottle of Thunder-bird and raised it to my mouth. I wanted to like it, to share the pleasure of it with "Stan," but it tasted horrible, like garbage, and the little bit I swallowed burned all the way down my throat.

I made a face, and he said, "This stuff's really not so bad. Only one thing in the world can make you feel better than this stuff."

He placed his hand on my thigh and squeezed. "I'm giving you a head start, you know. Just because I liked you the first time I saw you." He leaned over and stared at me. "You believe me? You believe the things I tell you?"

I said I guessed so.

"I got proof. I'll show you it's true. Want to see my proof?"

When I said nothing, "Stan" leaned closer to me, inundating me with the stench of Thunderbird. "You know that little thing you pee with? Remember how I told you it gets real big when you're about thirteen? Remember how I told you about how incredible that feels? Well, you have to trust Stan now, because Stan's going to trust you." He put his face right beside my ear. "Then I'll tell you another secret."

He lifted his hand from my thigh and closed it around mine and pulled my hand down onto his crotch. "Feel anything?"

I nodded, but I could not have described what I felt any more than the blind men could describe the elephant.

"Stan" smiled tightly and tugged at his zipper in a way even I could tell was nervous. He reached inside his pants, fumbled, and pulled out a thick, pale club that looked like nothing human. I was so frightened I thought I would throw up, and I looked back up at the screen. Invisible chains held me to my seat.

"See? Now you understand me."

Then he noticed that I was not looking at him. "Kid. Look. I said, Look. It's not going to hurt you."

I could not look down at him. I saw nothing.

"Come on. Touch it, see what it feels like."

I shook my head.

"Let me tell you something. I like you a lot. I think the two of us are friends. This thing we're doing, it's unusual to you because this is your first time, but people do this all the time. Your mommy and daddy do it all the time, but they just don't tell you about it. We're pals, aren't we?"

I nodded dumbly. On the screen, Berry Kroeger was telling Alan Ladd, "Drop it, forget it, she's poison."

"Well, this is what friends do when they really like each other, like your mommy and daddy. Look at this thing, will you? Come on."

Did my mommy and daddy like each other? He squeezed my shoulder, and I looked.

Now the thing had folded up into itself and was drooping sideways against the fabric of his trousers. Almost as soon as I looked, it twitched and began to push itself out like the slide of a trombone.

"There," he said. "He likes you, you got him going. Tell me you like him too."

Terror would not let me speak. My brains had turned to powder.

"I know what—let's call him Jimmy. We'll say his name is Jimmy. Now that you've been introduced, say hi to Jimmy."

"Hi, Jimmy," I said, and despite my terror, could not keep myself from giggling.

"Now go on, touch him."

I slowly extended my hand and put the tips of my fingers on "Jimmy."

"Pet him. Jimmy wants you to pet him."

I tapped my fingertips against "Jimmy" two or three times, and he twitched up another few degrees, as rigid as a surfboard.

If I run, I thought, he'll catch me and kill me. If I don't do what he says, he'll kill me.

I rubbed my fingertips back and forth, moving the thin skin over the veins.

"Can't you imagine Jimmy going in a woman? Now you can see what you'll be like when you're a man. Keep on, but hold him with your whole hand. And give me what I asked you for."

I immediately took my hand from "Jimmy" and pulled my father's clean white handkerchief from my back pocket.

He took the handkerchief with his left hand and with his right guided me back to "Jimmy." "You're doing really great," he whispered.

In my hand "Jimmy" felt warm and slightly gummy. I could not join my fingers around its width. My head was buzzing. "Is Jimmy your secret?" I was able to say.

"My secret comes later."

"Can I stop now?"

"I'll cut you into little pieces if you do," he said, and when I froze, he stroked my hair and whispered, "Hey, can't you tell when a guy's kidding around? I'm really happy with you right now. You're the best kid in the world. You'd want this too, if you knew how good it felt."

After what seemed an endless time, while Alan Ladd was climbing out of a taxicab, "Stan" abruptly arched his back, grimaced, and whispered, "Look!" His entire body jerked, and too startled to let go, I held "Jimmy" and watched thick, ivory-colored milk spurt and drool almost unendingly onto the handkerchief. An odor utterly foreign but as familiar as the toilet or lakeshore rose from the thick milk. "Stan" sighed, folded the handkerchief, and pushed the softening "Jimmy" back into his trousers. He leaned over and kissed the top of my head. I think I nearly fainted. I felt lightly, pointlessly dead. I could still feel him pulsing in my palm and fingers.

When it was time for me to go home, he told me his secret—his own real name was Jimmy, not Stan. He had been saving his real name until he knew he could trust me.

"Tomorrow," he said, touching my cheek with his fingers. "We'll see each other again tomorrow. But you don't have anything to worry about. I trust you enough to give you my real name. You trusted me not to hurt you, and I didn't. We have to trust each other not to say anything about this, or both you and me'll be in a lot of trouble."

"I won't say anything," I said.

I love you.

I love you, yes I do.

Now *we're* a secret, he said, folding the handkerchief into quarters and putting it back in my pocket. A lot of love has to be a secret. Especially when a boy and a man are getting to know each other and learning how to make each other happy and be good, loving friends—not many people can understand that, so the friendship has to be protected. When you walk out of here, he said, you have to forget that this happened. Otherwise people will try to hurt us both.

—

Afterward I remember only the confusion of *Chicago Deadline*, how the story had abruptly surged forward, skipping over whole characters and entire scenes, how for long stretches the actors had moved their lips without speaking. I could see Alan Ladd stepping out of the taxicab, looking straight through the screen into my eyes, knowing me.

———

My mother said that I looked pale, and my father said that I didn't get enough exercise. The twins looked up from their plates, then went back to spooning macaroni and cheese into their mouths. "Were you ever in Chicago?" I asked my father, who asked what was it to me. "Did you ever meet a movie actor?" I asked, and he said, "This kid must have a fever." The twins giggled.

Alan Ladd and Donna Reed came into my bedroom together that night, moving with a brisk, cool theatricality, and kneeled down beside my cot. They smiled at me. Their voices were very soothing. I saw you missed a few things today, Alan said. Nothing to worry about. I'll take care of you. I know, I said, I'm your number-one fan.

Then the door cracked open, and my mother put her head inside the room. Alan and Donna smiled and stood up to let her pass between them and the cot. I missed them the second they stepped back. "Still awake?" I nodded. "Are you feeling all right, honey?" I nodded again, afraid that Alan and Donna would leave if she stayed too long. "I have a surprise for you," she said. "The Saturday after this, I'm taking you and the twins all the way across Lake Michigan on the ferry. There's a whole bunch of us. It'll be a lot of fun." Good, that's nice, I'll like that.

———

"I thought about you all last night and all this morning."

When I came into the lobby, he was leaning forward on one of the padded benches where the ushers sat and smoked, his elbows on his knees and his chin in his hand, watching the door. The metal tip of a flat bottle protruded from his side pocket. Beside him was a package rolled up in brown paper. He winked at me, jerked his head toward the door into the theater, stood up, and went inside in an elaborate charade of not being with me. I knew he would be just inside the door, sitting in the middle of the last row, waiting for me. I gave my ticket to the bored usher, who tore it in half and handed over the stub. I knew exactly what had happened yesterday, just as if I had never forgotten any of it, and my insides began shaking. All of the colors of the lobby, the red and the shabby gilt, seemed much brighter than I remembered them. I could smell the popcorn in the case and the oily butter heating in the machine. My legs moved me over a mile of sizzling brown carpet and past the candy counter.

Jimmy's hair gleamed in the empty, darkening theater. When I took the seat next to him, he ruffled my hair and grinned down and said he had been thinking about me all night and all morning. The package in the brown paper was a sandwich for my lunch—a kid had to eat more than popcorn.

The lights went all the way down as the series of curtains opened over the screen. Loud music, beginning in the middle of a note, suddenly jumped from the speakers, and the Tom and Jerry cartoon "Bull Dozing" began. When I leaned back, Jimmy put his arm around me. I felt sweaty and cold at the same time, and my insides were still shaking. I suddenly realized that part of me was glad to be in this place, and I shocked myself with the knowledge that all morning I had been looking forward to this moment as much as I had been dreading it.

"You want your sandwich now? It's liver sausage, because that was my personal favorite." I said no, thanks, I'd wait until the first movie was over. Okay, he said, just as long as you eat it. Then he said, Look at me. His face was right above mine, and he looked like Alan Ladd's twin brother. You have to know something, he said. You're the best kid I ever met. Ever. The man squeezed me up against his chest and into a dizzying funk of sweat and dirt and wine, along with a trace (imagined?) of that other, more animal odor that had come from him yesterday. Then he released me.

You want me to play with your little "Jimmy" today?
No.

Too small anyhow, he said with a laugh. He was in perfect good humor.

Bet you wish it was the same size as mine.

That wish terrified me, and I shook my head.

Today we're just going to watch the movies together, he said. I'm not greedy.

Except for when one of the ushers came up the aisle, we sat like that all day, his arm around my shoulders, the back of my neck resting in the hollow of his elbow. When the credits for *At War with the Army* rolled up the screen, I felt as though I had fallen asleep and missed everything. I couldn't believe that it was time to go home. Jimmy tightened his arm around me and in a voice full of amusement said, *Touch me.* I looked up into his face. Go on, he said, I want you to do that little thing for me. I prodded his fly with my index finger. "Jimmy" wobbled under the pressure of my fingers, seeming as long as my arm, and for a second of absolute wretchedness, I saw the other children running up and down the school playground behind the girls from the next block.

"Go on," he said.

———

Trust me, he said, investing "Jimmy" with an identity more concentrated, more focused, than his own. "Jimmy" wanted "to talk," "to speak his piece," "was hungry," "was dying for a kiss." All these words meant the same thing. *Trust me*: I trust you, so you must trust me. Have I ever hurt you? No. Didn't I give you a sandwich? Yes. Don't I love you? You know I won't tell your parents what you do—as long as you keep coming here, I won't tell your parents anything because I won't *have* to, see? And you love me too, don't you?

There. You see how much I love you?

I dreamed that I lived underground in a wooden room. I dreamed that my parents roamed the upper world, calling out my name and weeping because the animals had captured and eaten me. I dreamed that I was buried beneath a juniper tree, and the cut-off pieces of my body called out to each other and wept because they were separate. I dreamed that I ran down a dark forest path toward my parents, and when I finally reached the small clearing where they sat before a bright fire, my mother was Donna and Alan was my father. I dreamed that I could remember everything that was happening, every second of it, and that when the teacher called on me in class, when my mother came into my room at night, when the policeman went past me as I walked down Sherman Boulevard, I had to spill it out. But when I tried to speak, I could not remember what it was that I remembered, *only that there was something to remember,* and so I walked again and again toward my beautiful parents in the clearing, repeating myself like a fable, like the jokes of the women on the ferry.

Don't I love you? Don't I show you, can't you tell, that I love you? *Yes.* Don't you, can't you, love me too?

He stares at me as I stare at the movie. He could see me, the way I could see him, with his eyes closed. He has me memorized. He has stroked my hair, my face, my body into his memory, stroke after stroke, stealing me from myself. Eventually he took me in his mouth and his mouth memorized me too, and I knew that he wanted me to place my hands on that dirty-blond head resting so hugely in my lap, but I could not touch his head.

I thought: I have already forgotten this, I want to die, I am dead already, only death can make this not have happened.

When you grow up, I bet you'll be in the movies and I'll be your number-one fan.

———

By the weekend, those days at the Orpheum-Oriental seemed to have been spent underwater; or underground. The spiny anteater, the lyrebird, the kangaroo, the Tasmanian devil, the nun bat, and the frilled lizard were creatures found only in Australia. Australia was the world's smallest continent, its largest island. It was cut off from the earth's great landmasses. Beautiful girls with blond hair strutted across Australian beaches, and Australian Christmases were hot and sunbaked—everybody went outside and waved at the camera, exchanging presents from lawn chairs. The middle of Australia, its heart and gut, was a desert. Australian boys excelled at sports. Tom Cat loved Jerry Mouse, though he plotted again and again to murder him, and Jerry Mouse loved Tom Cat, though to save his life he had to run so fast, he burned a track through the carpet. Jimmy loved me and he would be gone some-day, and then I would miss him a lot. Wouldn't I? *Say you'll miss me.*

I'll—

I'll miss—

I think I'd go crazy without you.

When you're all grown up, will you remember me?

Each time I walked back out past the usher, who stood tearing in half the tickets of the people just entering, handing them the stubs, every time I pushed open the door and walked out onto the heat-filled side-walk of Sherman Boulevard and saw the sun on the buildings across the street, I lost my hold on what had happened inside the darkness of the theater. I didn't know what I wanted. I had two murders and a . . . My right hand felt as though I had been holding a smaller child's sticky hand very tightly between my palm and fingers. If I lived in Australia, I would have blond hair like Alan Ladd and run forever across tan beaches on Christmas Day.

———

I walked through high school in my sleep, reading novels, daydream-ing in classes I did not like but earning spuriously good grades; in the middle of my senior year Brown University gave me a full scholarship. Two years later I amazed and disappointed all my old teachers and my parents and my parents' friends by dropping out of school shortly before I would have failed all my courses but English and history, in which I was getting A's. I was certain that no one could teach anyone else how to write. I knew exactly what I was going to do, and all I would miss of college was the social life.

For five years I lived inexpensively in Providence, supporting myself by stacking books in the school library and by petty thievery. I wrote when I was not working or listening to the local bands; then I destroyed what I had written and wrote again. In this way I saw myself to the end of a novel, like walking through a park one way and then walking backward and forward through the same park, over and over, until every nick on every swing, every tawny hair on every lion's hide, had been witnessed and made to gleam or allowed to sink back into the importunate field of details from which it had been lifted. When this novel was rejected by the publisher to whom I had sent it, I moved to New York City and began another novel while I rewrote the first all over again at night. During this period an almost impersonal happiness, like the happiness of a stranger, lay beneath everything I did. I wrapped parcels of books at the Strand Book Store. For a short time, no more than a few months, I lived on shredded wheat and peanut butter. When my first book was accepted, I moved from a single room on the Lower East Side into another, larger single room, a "studio apartment," on Ninth Avenue in Chelsea, where I continue to live. My apartment is just large enough for my wooden desk, a convertible couch, two large crowded bookshelves, a shelf of stereo equipment, and dozens of cardboard boxes of records. In this apartment everything has its place and is in it.

My parents have never been to this enclosed, tidy space, though I speak to my father on the phone every two or three months. In the past ten years I have returned to the city where I grew up only once, to visit my mother in the hospital after her stroke. During the four days I stayed in my father's house I slept in my old room; my father slept upstairs. After the blind man's death my father bought the duplex—on my first night home he told me that we were both successes. Now when we speak on the telephone he tells me of the fortunes of the local baseball and basketball teams and respectfully inquires about my progress on "the new book." I think: This is not my father, he is not the same man.

My old cot disappeared long ago, and late at night I lay on the twins' double bed. Like the house as a whole, like everything in my old neighborhood, the bedroom was larger than I remembered it. I brushed the wallpaper with my fingers, then looked up to the ceiling. The image of two men tangled up in the ropes of the same parachute, comically berating each other as they fell, came to me, and I wondered if the image had a place in the novel I was writing, or if it was a gift from the as-yet-unseen novel that would follow it. I could hear the floor creak as my father paced upstairs in the blind man's former territory. My inner weather changed, and I began brooding about Mei-Mei Levitt, whom fifteen years earlier at Brown I had known as Mei-Mei Cheung.

Divorced, an editor at a paperback firm, she had called to congratulate me after my second novel was favorably reviewed in the *Times*, and on this slim but well-intentioned foundation we began to construct a long and troubled love affair. Back in the surroundings of my childhood, I felt profoundly uneasy, having spent the day beside my mother's hospital bed without knowing if she understood or even recognized me, and I thought of Mei-Mei with sudden longing. I wanted her in my arms, and yearned for my purposeful, orderly, dreaming, adult life in New York. I wanted to call Mei-Mei, but it was past midnight in the Midwest, an hour later in New York, and Mei-Mei, no owl, would have gone to bed hours earlier. Then I remembered my mother lying stricken in the narrow hospital bed, and suffered a spasm of guilt for thinking about my lover. For a deluded moment I imagined it was my duty to move back into the house and see if I could bring my mother back to life while I did what I could for my retired father. At that moment I remembered, as I often did, an orange-haired boy enveloped in a red wool shirt. Sweat poured from my forehead, my chest.

Then a terrifying thing happened to me. I tried to get out of bed to go to the bathroom and found that I could not move. My arms and legs were cast in cement; they were lifeless and *would not move*. I thought that I was having a stroke, like my mother. I could not even cry out—my throat, too, was paralyzed. I strained to push myself up off the double bed and smelled that someone very near, someone just out of sight or around the corner, was making popcorn and heating butter. Another wave of sweat gouted out of my inert body, turning the sheet and pillowcase slick and cold.

I saw—as if I were writing it—my seven-year-old self hesitating before the entrance of a theater a few blocks from this house. Hot, flat, yellow sunlight fell over everything, cooking the life from the wide boulevard. I saw myself turn away, felt my stomach churn with the smoke of underground fires, saw myself begin to run. Vomit backed up in my throat. My arms and legs convulsed, and I fell out of bed and managed to crawl out of the room and down the hall to throw up in the toilet behind the closed door of the bathroom.

———

My age, as I write these words, is forty-three. I have written five novels over a period of nearly twenty years, "only" five, each of them more difficult, harder to write than the one before. To maintain this hobbled pace of a novel every four years, I must sit at my desk at least six hours every day; I must consume hundreds of boxes of typing paper, scores of yellow legal pads, forests of pencils, miles of black ribbon. It is a fierce, voracious activity. Every sentence must be tested three or four ways, made to clear fences like a horse. The purpose of every sentence is to be an arrow into the secret center of the book. To find my way into the secret center I must hold the entire book, every detail and rhythm, in my memory. This comprehensive act of memory is the most crucial task of my life.

My books get flattering reviews, which usually seem to describe other, more linear novels, and they win occasional awards—I am one of those writers whose advances are funded by the torrents of money spun off by best-sellers. Lately I have had the impression that the general perception of me, to the extent that such a thing exists, is of a hermetic painter enscribing hundreds of tiny, grotesque, fantastic details over every inch of a large canvas. (My books are unfashionably long.) I teach writing at various colleges, give occasional lectures, am modestly enriched by grants. This is enough, more than enough. Now and then I am both dismayed and amused to discover that a young writer I have met at a PEN reception or workshop regards my life with envy. Envy misses the point completely.

"If you were going to give me one piece of advice," a young woman at a conference asked me, "I mean, *real* advice, not just the obvious stuff about keeping on writing, what would it be? What would you tell me to do?"

I won't tell you, but I'll write it out, I said, and picked up one of the conference flyers and printed a few words on its back. Don't read this until you are out of the room, I said, and watched while she folded the flyer into her bag.

What I had printed on the back of the flyer was: *Go to a lot of movies.*

———

On the Sunday after the ferry trip I could not hit a single ball in the park. My eyes kept closing, and as soon as my eyelids came down, visions started up like movies—quick, automatic dreams. My arms seemed too heavy to lift. After I had trudged home behind my dispirited father, I collapsed on the sofa and slept straight through to dinner. In a dream a spacious box confined me, and I drew colored pictures of elm trees, the sun, wide fields, mountains, and rivers on its wall. At dinner loud noises, never scarce around the twins, made me jump. That kid's not right, I swear to you, my father said. When my mother asked if I wanted to go to Play School on Monday, my stomach closed up like a fist. I have to, I said, I'm really fine, I have to go. Sentences rolled from my mouth, meaning nothing, or meaning the wrong thing. For a moment of confusion I thought that I really was going to the playground, and saw black asphalt, deep in a field, where a few children, diminished by perspective, clustered at the far end. I went to bed right after dinner. My mother pulled down the shades, turned off the light, and finally left me alone. From above came the sound, like a beast's approximation of music, of random notes struck on a piano. I knew only that I was scared, not why. The next day I had to go to a certain place, but I could not think where until my fingers recalled the velvety plush of the end seat on the middle aisle. Then black-and-white images, full of intentional menace, came to me from the previews I had seen for two weeks—*The Hitch-Hiker*, starring Edmond O'Brien. The spiny anteater and nun bat were animals found only in Australia.

I longed for Alan Ladd, "Ed Adams," to walk into the room with his reporter's notebook and pencil, and knew that I had *something to remember* without knowing what it was.

After a long time the twins cascaded into the bedroom, undressed, put on pajamas, brushed their teeth. The front door slammed—my father had gone out to the taverns. In the kitchen, my mother ironed shirts and talked to herself in a familiar, rancorous voice. The twins went to sleep. I heard my mother put away the ironing board and walk down the hall to the living room.

I saw "Ed Adams" calmly walking up and down on the sidewalk outside our house, as handsome as a god in his neat gray suit. "Ed" went all the way to the end of the block, put a cigarette in his mouth, and leaned into a sudden, round flare of brightness before exhaling smoke and walking away. I knew I had fallen asleep only when the front door slammed for the second time that night and woke me up.

In the morning my father struck his fist against the bedroom door and the twins jumped out of bed and began yelling around the bedroom, instantly filled with energy. As in a cartoon, into the bedroom drifted tendrils of the odor of frying bacon. My brothers jostled toward the bathroom. Water rushed into the sink and the toilet bowl, and my mother hurried in, her face tightened down over her cigarette, and began yanking the twins into their clothes. "You made your decision," she said to me, "now I hope you're going to make it to the playground on time." Doors opened, doors slammed shut. My father shouted from the kitchen, and I got out of bed. Eventually I sat down before my bowl of cereal. My father smoked and did not meet my eyes. The cereal tasted of dead leaves. "You look the way that asshole upstairs plays the piano," my father said. He dropped quarters on the table and told me not to lose that money.

After he left, I locked myself in the bedroom. The piano dully resounded overhead like a sound track. I heard the cups and dishes rattle in the sink, the furniture moving by itself, looking for something to hunt down and kill. *Love me, love me,* the radio called from beside a family of brown-and-white porcelain spaniels. I heard some light, whispery thing, a lamp or a magazine, begin to slide around the living room. *I am imagining all this,* I said to myself, and tried to concentrate on a *Blackhawk* comic book. The pictures jiggled and melted in their panels. *Love me,* Blackhawk cried out from the cockpit of his fighter as he swooped down to exterminate a nest of yellow, slant-eyed villains. Outside, fire raged beneath the streets, trying to pull the world apart. When I dropped the comic book and closed my eyes, the noises ceased and I could hear the hovering stillness of perfect attention. Even Blackhawk, belted into his airplane within the comic book, was listening to what I was doing.

———

In thick, hazy sunlight I went down Sherman Boulevard toward the Orpheum-Oriental. Around me the world was motionless, frozen like a frame in a comic strip. After a time, I noticed that the cars on the boulevard and the few people on the sidewalk had not actually frozen into place but instead were moving with great slowness. I could see men's legs advancing within their trousers, the knee coming forward to strike the crease, the cuff slowly lifting off the shoe, the shoe drifting up like Tom Cat's paw when he crept toward Jerry Mouse. The warm, patched skin of Sherman Boulevard . . . I thought of walking along Sherman Boulevard forever, moving past the nearly immobile cars and people, past the theater, past the liquor store, through the gates and past the wading pool and swings, past the elephants and lions reaching out to be fed, past the secret park where my father flailed in a rage of disappointment, past the elms and out the opposite gate, past the big houses on the opposite side of the park, past picture windows and past lawns with bikes and plastic pools, past slanting driveways and basketball hoops, past men getting out of cars, past playgrounds where children raced back and forth on a surface shining black. Then past fields and crowded markets, past high yellow tractors with mud dried like old wool inside the enormous hubs, past eloquent cats and fearful lions on wagons piled high with hay, past deep woods where lost children followed trails of bread crumbs to a gingerbread door, past other cities where nobody would see me because nobody knew my name, past everything, past everybody.

At the Orpheum-Oriental, I stopped still. My mouth was dry and my eyes would not focus. Everything around me, so quiet and still a moment earlier, jumped into life as soon as I stopped walking. Horns blared, cars roared down the boulevard. Beneath those sounds I heard the pounding of great machines, and the fires gobbling up the oxygen beneath the street. As if I had eaten them from the air, fire and smoke poured into my stomach. Flame slipped up my throat and sealed the back of my mouth. In my mind I saw myself taking the first quarter from my pocket, exchanging it for a ticket, pushing through the door, and moving into the cool air. I saw myself holding out the ticket to be torn in half, going over an endless brown carpet toward the inner door.

From the last row of seats on the other side of the inner door, inside the shadowy but not yet dark theater, a shapeless monster whose wet black mouth said *Love me, love me* stretched yearning arms toward me. Shock froze my shoes to the sidewalk, then shoved me firmly in the small of the back, and I was running down the block, unable to scream because I had to clamp my lips against the smoke and fire trying to explode from my mouth.

The rest of that afternoon remains vague. I wandered through the streets, not in the clean, hollow way I had imagined but almost blindly, hot and uncertain. I remember the taste of fire in my mouth and the loudness of my heart. After a time I found myself before the elephant enclosure in the zoo. A newspaper reporter in a neat gray suit passed through the space before me, and I followed him, knowing that he carried a notebook in his pocket, and that he had been beaten by gangsters, that he could locate the speaking secret that hid beneath the disconnected and dismembered pieces of the world. He would fire his pistol on an empty chamber and trick evil "Solly Wellman," Berry Kroeger, with his girlish, watchful eyes. And when "Solly Wellman" came gloating out of the shadows, the reporter would shoot him dead.

Dead.

Donna Reed smiled down from an upstairs window: has there ever been a smile like that? Ever? I was in Chicago, and behind a closed door "Blacky Franchot" bled onto a brown carpet. "Solly Wellman," something like "Solly Wellman," called and called to me from the decorated grave where he lay like a secret. The man in the gray suit finally carried his notebook and his gun through a front door, and I saw that I was only a few blocks from home.

———

Paul leans against the wire fence surrounding the playground, looking out, looking backward. Alan Ladd brushes off "Leona," for she has no history that matters and exists only in the world of work and pleasure, of cigarettes and cocktail bars. Beneath this world is another, and "Leona's" life is a blind, strenuous denial of that other world.

—

My mother held her hand to my forehead and declared that I not only had a fever but had been building up to it all week. I was not to go to the playground the next day; I had to spend the day lying down on Mrs. Candee's couch. When she lifted the telephone to call one of the high-school girls, I said not to bother, other kids were gone all the time, and she put down the receiver.

————

I lay on Mrs. Candee's couch staring up at the ceiling of her darkened living room. The twins squabbled outside, and maternal, slow-witted Mrs. Candee brought me an orange juice. The twins ran toward the sandbox, and Mrs. Candee groaned as she let herself fall into a wobbly lawn chair. The morning newspaper folded beneath the lawn chair said that *The Hitch-Hiker* and *Double Cross* had begun playing at the Orpheum-Oriental. *Chicago Deadline* had done its work and traveled on. It had broken the world in half and sealed the monster deep within. Nobody but me knew this. Up and down the block, sprinklers whirred, whipping loops of water onto the dry lawns. Men driving slowly up and down the street hung their elbows out of their windows. For a moment free of regret and nearly without emotion of any kind, I understood that I belonged utterly to myself. Like everything else, I had been torn asunder and glued back together with shock, vomit, and orange juice. "Stan," "Jimmy," whatever his name was, would never come back to the theater. He would be afraid that I had told my parents and the police about him. I knew that I had killed him by forgetting him, and then I forgot him again.

————

The next day I went back to the theater and went through the inner door and saw row after row of empty seats falling toward the curtained screen. I was all alone. The size and grandeur of the theater surprised me. I went down the long, descending aisle and took the last seat, left side, on the broad middle aisle. The next row seemed nearly a playground's distance away. The lights dimmed and the curtains rippled slowly away from the screen. Anticipatory music filled the air, and the first letters filled the screen.

—

What I am, what I do, why I do it. I am simultaneously a man in his early forties, that treacherous time, and a boy of seven before whose bravery I shall forever fall short. I live underground in a wooden room and patiently, in joyful concentration, decorate the walls. Before me, half unseen, hangs a large and appallingly complicated vision I must explore and memorize, must witness again and again in order to locate its hidden center. Around me, everything is in its proper place. My typewriter sits on the sturdy table. Beside the typewriter a cigarette smolders, raising a gray stream of smoke. A record revolves on the turntable, and my small apartment is dense with music. ("Bird of Prey Blues," with Coleman Hawkins, Buck Clayton, and Hank Jones.) Beyond my walls and windows is a world toward which I reach with outstretched arms and an ambitious and divided heart. As if "Bird of Prey Blues" has evoked them, the voices of sentences to be written this afternoon, tomorrow, or next month stir and whisper, beginning to speak, and I lean over the typewriter toward them, getting as close as I can.

Going Home

They had come back to their hometown to help her father move into a high-rise nursing home that looked like a luxury hotel. The rooms had a bland impersonality that made even the residents' old furniture look like it belonged in a hotel suite, and everybody liked the home a good deal. Most of the new residents experienced a period of euphoria after moving in. In the mornings, a girl at a desk pushed a button that set off a buzzer in every room, and if you did not answer your buzzer they sent a man up to see what had happened to you. The food was substantial and tasteless, and the large dining room was always crowded. There were prayer meetings and discussion groups. Everyone watched a lot of television. She and her husband sat in her father's new living room, on furniture she had known all her life, and listened to her father talk over the noise from the television.

One afternoon, they drove across town to her husband's old neighborhood—the neighborhood where he had been a small child, before his family had moved even farther away, to the suburbs. They got out of the car and walked up, then down the block, then crossed into the alley and walked up and down behind his old house. It looked as he remembered it—a two-story brown and yellow duplex with a small, patchy backyard. The house had been cared for. Yet the neighborhood was not what he remembered. All the elm trees had died, and the neighborhood was mysteriously larger—everything was bigger than he remembered, everything was cleaner and brighter. It was he who was smaller now. They walked a little bit away, into another of the little side streets that ran across a broad avenue, and here too everything was charged with a blazing, glowing familiarity. He felt a sudden emotion move into his chest like an alien force: a large, virtually featureless block of feeling that constricted his breathing and pushed tears into his eyes. He could not tell if this feeling were grief or joy or some unbearable mixture of the two. He had been a child right here, in this place, and the unbearable feeling came from the center of his childhood.

They returned to the car. She drove them back across town, and he cried the whole way, too deep inside the feeling to understand it or even identify it. When they left the city, he felt for the first time in his life that he was leaving his hometown, leaving home.

The Buffalo Hunter

For Rona Pondick

1

At the peasant's words . . . undefined but significant ideas
seemed to burst out as though they had been locked up,
and all striving toward one goal, they thronged whirling
through his head, blinding him with their light.
                    —LEO TOLSTOY, *Anna Karenina*

Bob Bunting's parents surprised him with a telephone call on the Sunday that was his thirty-fifth birthday. It was his first conversation with his parents in three years, though he had received a monthly letter from them during this period, along with cards on his birthdays. These usually reflected his father's abrasive comic style. Bunting had written back with the same frequency, and it seemed to him that he had achieved a perfect relationship with his parents. Separation was health; independence was health.

During his twenties, when he was sometimes between jobs and was usually short of money, he had flown from New York to spend Christmases with his parents in Michigan—Battle Creek, Michigan. Thanksgiving disappeared first, when Bunting finally got a job he liked, and in his thirtieth year Bunting had realized how he could avoid making the dreary Christmas journey into the dark and frigid Midwest. It was to his inspiration that his father referred after wishing him what sounded to Bunting like a perfunctory and insincere Happy Birthday and alluding to the rarity of their telephone conversations.

"I suppose Veronica keeps you pretty busy, huh? You guys go out a lot?"

"Oh, you know," Bunting said. "About the usual."

Veronica was entirely fictional. Bunting had not had a date with a member of the opposite sex since certain disastrous experiments in high school. Over the course of a great many letters, Veronica had evolved from a vaguely defined "friend" into a tall, black-haired, Swiss-born executive of DataComCorp, Bunting's employer. Still somewhat vague, she looked a little like Sigourney Weaver and a little like a woman in horn-rimmed eyeglasses he had twice seen on the M104 bus. "Well something's keeping you pretty busy, because you never answer your phone."

"Oh, Robert," said Bunting's mother, addressing her husband's implication more than his actual words. Bunting, who also had been named Robert, was supposed to be scattering some previously unsuspected wild oats.

"Sometimes I think you just lie there and listen to the phone ring," his father said, mollifying and critical at once.

"He's *busy,*" his mother breathed. "You know how they are in New York."

"Do I?" his father asked. "So you went to see *Cats,* hey, Bobby? You liked it?"

Bunting sighed. "We left at the intermission." This is what he had intended to write when the next letter came due. "I liked it okay, but Veronica thought it was terrible. Anyhow, some Swiss friends of hers were in town, and we had to go downtown to meet them."

His father asked, "Girls or boys?"

"A couple, a very good-looking young couple," Bunting said. "We went to a nice new restaurant called the Blue Goose."

"Is that a Swiss restaurant, Bobby?" his mother asked, and he glanced across the room to the mantel above the unusable fireplace of his single room, where the old glass baby bottle he had used in his childhood stood beside a thrift-shop mirror. He was used to inventing details about imaginary restaurants on paper, and improvisation made him uneasy.

"No, just an American sort of place," he said.

"While we're on the subject of Veronica, is there any chance you could bring her back here this Christmas? We'd sure like to meet the gal."

"No—no—no, Christmas is no good, you know that. She has to get back to Switzerland to see her family, it's a really big deal for her, they all troop down to the church in the snow—"

"Well, it's kind of a big deal for us, too," his father said.

Bunting's scalp grew sweaty. He unbuttoned his shirt collar and pulled down his tie, wondering why he had answered the telephone. "I know, but . . ."

None of them spoke for a moment.

"We're just grateful you write so often," his mother finally said.

"I'll get back home one of these days, you know I will. I'm just waiting for the right time."

"Well, I suggest you make it snappy," his father said. "We're both getting older."

"But thank God, you're both healthy."

"Your mother fainted in the Red Owl parking lot last week. Passed right out and banged her head. Racked up her knee, too."

"Fainted? Why did you faint?" Bunting said. He pictured his mother swaddled in bandages.

"Oh, I don't want to talk about it," she said. "It's not really serious. I can still get around, what with my cane."

"What do you mean, 'not really serious'?"

"I get a headache when I think of all those eggs I broke," she said. "You're not to worry about me, Bobby."

"You didn't even go to a doctor, did you?"

"Oh, hell, we don't need any *doctors*," said his father. "Charge you an arm and a leg for nothing. Neither one of us has been to a doctor in twenty years."

There was a silence during which Bunting could hear his father compute the cost of the call. "Well, let's wrap this up, all right?" his father said at last.

This conversation, with its unspoken insinuations, suspicions, and judgments, left Bunting feeling jittery and exhausted. He set down the telephone, rubbed his hands over his face, and stood up to pick his way through his crowded, untidy room to the mantel of the useless fireplace. He bent to look at himself in the mirror. His thinning hair stood up in little tufts where he had tortured it while talking to his parents. He pulled a comb from his jacket pocket and flattened the tufts over his scalp. His pink, inquisitive face looked reassuringly back at him from above the collar of his crisp white shirt. In honor of his birthday, he had put on a new tie and one of his best suits, a gray nail-head worsted that instantly made its wearer look like the CEO of a Fortune 500 company. He posed for a moment before the mirror, bending his knees to consult the image of his torso, neck, and boyish, balding head. Then he straightened up and looked at his watch. It was four-thirty, not too early for a birthday drink.

Bunting took his old baby bottle from the mantel and stepped over a pile of magazines to enter his tiny kitchen area and open the freezer compartment of his refrigerator. He set the baby bottle down on the meager counter beside the sink and removed a quart bottle of Popov vodka from the freezer, which he placed beside the baby bottle. Bunting unscrewed the nipple from the bottle, inspected the pink, chewed-looking nipple and the interior of the bottle for dust and foreign substances, blew into each, and then set down the bottle and the nipple. He removed the cap from the vodka and tilted it over the baby bottle. A stream of liquid like silvery treacle poured from one container into the other. Bunting half-filled the baby bottle with the frigid vodka, and then, because it was his birthday, added another celebratory gurgle that made it nearly three-quarters full. He capped the vodka bottle and put it back in the otherwise empty freezer. From the refrigerator he removed a plastic bottle of Schweppes tonic water, opened it, and added tonic until the baby bottle was full. He screwed the nipple back onto the neck of the bottle and gave it two hard shakes. A little of the mixture squirted through the opening of the nipple, which Bunting had enlarged with the tip of a silver pocketknife. The glass bottle grew cold in his hand.

Bunting skirted the wing chair that marked the boundary of his kitchen, stepped back over the mound of old newspapers, dropped the bottle on his hastily made bed, and shrugged off his suit jacket. He hung the jacket over the back of a wooden chair and sat down on the bed. There was a Luke Short novel on the rush seat of the wooden chair, and he picked it up and swung his legs onto the bed. When he leaned back into the pillows, the bottle tilted and expressed a transparent drop of vodka and tonic onto the rumpled blue coverlet. Bunting snatched up the bottle, awkwardly opened the book, and grunted with satisfaction as the words lifted, full of consolation and excitement, from the page. He brought the bottle to his mouth and began to suck cold vodka through the hole in the spongy pink nipple.

On one of his Christmas visits home, Bunting had unearthed the bottle while rummaging through boxes in the attic of his parents' house. He had not even seen it at first—a long glass shape at the bottom of a paper bag containing an empty wartime ration book, two small, worn pairs of moccasins, and a stuffed monkey, partially dismembered. He had gone upstairs to escape his father's questions and his mother's look of worry—Bunting at the time being employed in the mail room of a magazine devoted to masturbatory fantasies—and had become absorbed in the record of his family's past life which the attic contained. Here were piles of old winter coats, boxed photograph albums containing tiny pictures of strangers and empty streets and long-dead dogs, stacks of yellowed newspapers with giant wartime headlines (ROMMEL SMASHED! and VICTORY IN EUROPE!), paperback novels in rows against a slanting wall, bags of things swept from the backs of closets.

The monkey came firmly into this category, as did the shoes, though Bunting was not certain about the ration book. Wedged beneath the moccasins, the tubular glass bottle glinted up from the bottom of the bag. Bunting discarded the monkey, a barely remembered toy, and fished out the thick, surprisingly weighty baby bottle. An ivory-colored ring of plastic with a wide opening for a rubber nipple had been screwed down over the bottle's top. Bunting examined the bottle, realizing that once, in true helplessness, he had clutched this object to his infant chest. Once his own tiny fingers had spread over the thick glass while he had nursed. This proxy, this imitation and simulated breast had kept him alive; it was a period piece, it was something like an object of everyday folk art, and it had survived when his childhood—visible now only as a small series of static moments that seemed plucked from vast darkness—had not. Above all, it made him smile. He held on to it as he walked around the little attic—he did not want to let go of it—and when he came back downstairs, he hid it in his suitcase. And then he forgot it was there.

When he got home, the baby bottle's presence in his suitcase, wrapped in a coil of dirty shirts, startled him: it was as if the glass tube had followed him from Battle Creek to Manhattan by itself. Then he remembered wrapping it in the shirts on the night before his departure, a night when his father got drunk during dinner and said three times in succession, each time louder than the last, "I don't think you're ever going to amount to anything in the world, Bobby," and his mother started crying, and his father got disgusted with them and stomped outside to lurch around in the snow. His mother had gone upstairs to the bedroom, and Bunting had switched on the television and sat without feeling before depictions of other people's Christmases. Eventually his father had come back inside and joined him in front of the television without speaking to him or even looking at him. At the airport the next morning, his father had scratched his face in a whiskery embrace and said that it had been good to see him again, and his mother looked brave and stricken. They were two old people, and working-class Michigan seemed unbearably ugly, with an ugliness he remembered.

He put the bottle away in a cupboard on a high shelf and forgot about it again.

Over the following years, Bunting saw the bottle only on the few occasions he had to reach for something on its shelf. He either ate most of his meals in inexpensive neighborhood restaurants or ordered them from Empire Szechuan, so he had little use for the pots and pans that stood there. During these years he found the job in the mail room of DataComCorp, invented Veronica for his parents' pleasure and his own, reduced and then finally terminated his visits to Michigan, moved into his early thirties, and settled into what he imagined were the habits of his adult life.

He saved his money, having little to spend it on apart from his rent. Every autumn and every spring, he went to a good men's clothing store and bought two suits, several new shirts, and three or four neckties: these excursions were great adventures, and he prepared for them carefully, examining advertisements and comparing the merits of the goods displayed at Barneys, Paul Stuart, Polo, Armani, and two or three other shops he considered to be in their class. He read the same Westerns and mystery novels his father had once read. He ate his two meals a day in the fashion described. His hair was cut once every two weeks by a Japanese barber around the corner who remarked on the smoothness of his collar as he tucked the protective sheet next to his neck. He washed his dishes only when they were all used up, and once a month or so he swept the floor and put things into piles. He set out roach killer and mousetraps and closed his eyes when he disposed of the corpses. No one but himself ever entered his apartment, but at work he sometimes talked with Frank Herko, the man at the next word processor. Frank envied Bunting's wardrobe, and swapped tales of his own sex life, conducted in bars and discos, for Bunting's more sedate accounts of evenings with Veronica.

Bunting liked to read lying down, and liked to drink while he read. His little apartment was cold in the winter, and the only place to lie down in it was the bed, so for four months of every year, Bunting spent much of every weekend and most of his evenings wrapped up fully clothed in his blankets, a glass of cold vodka (without tonic, for this was after Labor Day) in one hand, a paperback book in the other. The only difficulty with this system, otherwise perfectly adapted to Bunting's desires and needs, had been the occasional spillage. There had been technical problems concerning the uprightness of the glass during the turning of the pages. One solution was to prop the glass against the side of his body as he turned the page, but this method met with frequent failure, as did the technique of balancing the glass on his chest. Had he cleared all the books, wads of Kleenex used and unused, pill bottles, cotton balls, ear cleaners, jars of Vaseline, and the hand mirror from the chair beside his bed, he could have placed the glass on the seat between sips; but he did not want to have to reach for his drink. Bunting wanted his satisfactions prompt and ready to hand.

Depending on the time of the day, the drink Bunting might choose to go with *New Gun in Town* or *Saddles and Sagebrush* could be herbal tea, orange juice, warm milk, Tab or Pepsi-Cola, mineral water; should he not be enabled to take in such pleasurable and harmless liquids without removing his eye from the page? Every other area of his life was filled with difficulty and compromise; this—bed and a book—should be pristine.

The solution came to him one November after a mysterious and terrifying experience that occurred as he was writing his monthly letter home.

Dear Mom and Dad,

Everything is still going so well I sometimes think I must be dreaming. Veronica says she has never seen any employee anywhere come so far so fast. We went dancing at the Rainbow Room last night following dinner at Quaglino's, a new restaurant all the critics are raving about. As I walked her back to Park Avenue through the well-dressed crowds on Fifth Avenue, she told me that she felt

she would once again really need me by her side in Switzerland this
Christmas, it's hard for her to defend herself against her brother's
charges that she has sold out her native country, and the local
aristocracy is all against her too . . .

The mention of Christmas caused him to see, as if printed on a postcard, the image of the dingy white house in Battle Creek, with his parents standing before the front steps, his father scowling beneath the bill of his plaid cap and his mother blinking with apprehension. They faced forward, like the couple in *American Gothic*. He stopped writing and his mind spun past them up the steps, through the door, up the stairs into a terrifying void. For a moment he thought he was going to faint, or that he *had* fainted. Distant white lights wheeled above him, and he was falling through space. Some massive knowledge moved within him, thrusting powerfully upward from the darkness where it had been jailed, and he understood that his life depended on keeping this knowledge locked inside him, in a golden casket within a silver casket within a leaden casket. It was a wild beast with claws and teeth, a tiger, and this tiger had threatened to surge into his conscious mind and destroy him. Bunting was panting from both the force and the threat of the tiger locked up within him, and he was looking at the white paper where his pen had made a little scratchy scrawl after the word *too*, aware that he had not fainted—but it was, just then and only for a second, as if his body had been hurled through some dark barrier.

Drained, he lay back against the headboard and tried to remember what had just happened. It was already blurred by distance. He had seen his parents and flown . . . ? He remembered the expression on his mother's face, the blinking, almost simian eyes and the deep parallel lines in her forehead, and felt his heart beating with the relief that he had escaped whatever it was that had surged up from within him. So thoroughly had he escaped that he now wondered about the reality of his experience. A thick shield had slammed back into place, where it emphatically belonged.

And then came Bunting's revelation.

He thought of the old baby bottle on its shelf and saw how he could use it. He set aside the letter and went across his room to take down the bottle from its high shelf. It came away from the shelf with a faint kissing sound.

The bottle was covered with fluffy gray dust, and a sticky brown substance from the shelf circled its base. Bunting squeezed dishwashing liquid into the bottle and held it under a stream of hot water. He scrubbed the bottom clean, unscrewed the plastic cap, and washed the grooves on the cap and neck of the bottle. As he dried the warm bottle with his clean dish towel, he saw his mother bent over the sink in her dark little kitchen, her arms sunk into soapy water and steam rising past her head.

Bunting thrust this image away and regarded the bottle. It seemed surprisingly beautiful for so functional an object. The bottle was a perfect cylinder of clear glass, which sparkled as it dried. Oddly, its smooth, caressing weight felt as comfortable in his adult hand as it must have in his childish one. The plastic cap twirled gracefully down over the molded O of the bottle's mouth. One tiny air bubble had been caught ascending from the thick rim at the bottom. The manufacturer's name, Prentiss, was spelled out in thick transparent letters circling the bottle's shoulders.

He placed it on the cleanest section of the counter and squatted to admire his work. The bottle was an obelisk made of a miraculous transparent skin. The wall behind it turned to a swarmy, elastic blur. For a moment Bunting wished that his two windows, which looked out onto a row of decrepit brownstones on the west side of Manhattan, were of the same thick, distorting glass.

He went out onto Eighth Avenue to search for nipples, and found them in a drugstore, hanging slightly above eye level, wrapped in packages of three like condoms, and surrounded by a display of bottles. He snatched the first pack of nipples off the hook and carried it to the register. He practiced what he would say if the sullen Puerto Rican girl asked him why he was buying baby bottle nipples—*Darn kid goes through these things in a hurry*—but she charged him ninety-six cents, pushed the package into a bag, took his dollar, and gave him change without comment or even a curious glance.

He carried the bag back to his building rejoicing, as if he had narrowly escaped some great danger. The ice had not broken beneath his feet; he was in command of his life.

At home, he drew the package of nipples from the bag and noticed first that they were stacked vertically, like the levels of a pagoda, secondly that they were Evenflo nipples, "designed especially for juice." That was all right, he was going to use them to get juiced.

Dear Parent, read the back of the package, *All babies are unique.*

Bunting cheered the wise patriarchs of the Evenflo Products Company. The Evenflo system let you adjust the flow rate to ensure that Baby always got a smooth, even flow. *Baby swallows less air, too.* Sure-Seal nipples had twin air valves. They were called the Pacers, as if they were members of a swift, confident family.

Bunting was warned not to put the nipples into microwave ovens, and cautioned that every nipple wore out. There was an 800 number to call, if you had questions.

He took his quart of Popov from the freezer and carefully decanted vodka into the sparkling bottle. The clear liquid sprang to the top and formed a trembling meniscus above the glass mouth. Bunting used his pocketknife to cut the nipples from the pack, taking care to preserve the instructions for their use, and removed the topmost level of the pagoda. The nipple felt surprisingly firm and resilient between his fingers. Impatiently, he fitted the nipple into the cap ring and screwed the ring down onto the bottle. Then he tilted it to his mouth and sucked.

The nipple met his teeth and tongue, which instantly accepted it, for what suits a mouth better than a nice new nipple? But a frustratingly thin stream of vodka came through the crosscut opening. Bunting sucked harder, working the nipple between his teeth like gum, but the vodka continued to stream through the opening at the same even, deliberate rate.

Now Bunting took his little silver knife, actually Frank Herko's, from his pocket. Bunting had seen it lying on Herko's desk for several days before borrowing it. He intended to give it back someday, but no one could dispute that the elegant knife suited someone like Bunting far more than Frank Herko—in fact, Herko had probably found it on a sidewalk, or beneath a table in a restaurant (for Frank Herko really did go to restaurants, the names of which Bunting appropriated for his tales of Veronica), and therefore it was as much Bunting's as his. Very cautiously, Bunting inserted the delicate blade into one of the smooth crosscut incisions. He lengthened the cut in the rubber by perhaps an eighth of an inch, then did the same to the other half of the crosscut. He replaced the nipple in the cap ring, tightened the ring onto the bottle, and tested his improvement. A mouthful of vodka slipped through the enlarged opening and chilled his teeth.

Bunting had taken his wonderful new invention directly to bed, shedding his tie and jacket as he went. He picked up his Luke Short novel and sucked vodka through the nipple. When he turned the page, he clamped the nipple between his teeth and let the bottle dangle, jutting downward past his lower lip like a monstrous cigar. A feeling of discontinuity, of unfinished business, troubled him. He was riding down onto a grassy plateau atop a dun horse named Shorty. He gazed out across a herd of grazing buffalo. The bottle dangled again as the bottom half of the letter to his parents slipped down his legs into the herd of buffalo. "Oh," he said. "Oh, yes."

The baby bottle, inspired by the event which had befallen him as he wrote the letter, had *replaced* it. All Bunting wanted to do was luxuriate in his bed, rolling atop old Shorty, clutching his trusty bottle in pursuit of buffalo hides, but more than a sense of duty compelled him to fold down the corner of the page and close the book on Shorty and the browsing herd. Bunting's heart had lightened. He picked up the pad on which he had been writing to faraway Battle Creek, found his pen in the folds of the blanket, and resumed writing.

So I'll have to go with her again, he wrote, then dropped down the page to begin a paragraph dictated from the center of his new satisfaction.

Have I ever really told you about Veronica, Mom and Dad? I mean, really told you about her? Do you know how beautiful she is, and how intelligent, and how successful? I bet not a day goes by that some photographer doesn't ask her to pose for him, or an editor doesn't stop her on the street to say that she has to be on the cover of his magazine. She has dark hair and high, wide cheekbones, and sometimes she looks like a great cat getting ready to spring. She has an MBA, and she reads a novel in one day. She does all the crossword puzzles in ink. And fashion sense! It's no wonder she looks like a model! You look at those top models in newspaper ads, the ones with long dark hair and full lips, and you'll see her, you'll see how graceful Veronica is. The way she bends, the way she moves, the way she holds her glasses in one hand, and how cute she looks when she looks out through them, just like a beautiful kitten. And she loves this country, Dad, you should hear her talk about the benefits America gives its people—honestly, there's never been a girl like this before, and I thank my stars I found her and won her love.

With this letter Bunting had come into his own. Despite all the lies he had told about her, lies that had become woven into his life so deeply that a beautiful shadow had seemed to accompany him on the bus back and forth to work, Veronica had never been so present to him, so visible. She had come out of the shadows.

He continued:

In fact, my relationship with Veronica is getting better and better. She gives me what I need, that comfort and stability you need when you come home from the business world, close your door behind you, and want to be free from the troubles and pressures of the day. Did I tell you about the way she'll pout at me in the middle of some big meeting with a DataComCorp client, just a little tiny movement that no one but me would possibly notice? It gives me the shivers, Mom and Dad. And she has shown me so much of the life and excitement of this town, the ins and outs of having fun in the Big Apple—I really think this is going to last, and one fine day I'll probably pop the question! I know, because she really does love me as much as I love her—

2

Bunting woke up with a hangover on the Monday after his birthday and immediately decided that it would not be necessary to go to work.

His room offered evidence of a disorderly night. The Popov bottle, nearly empty, stood on the counter beside the refrigerator, and one of his lamps had been on all night, shedding a yellow circle of light upon a mass of folds and wrinkles that resolved into his gray worsted suit from Paul Stuart. Evidently he had tossed aside the jacket, undone his belt, and stepped out of his trousers as he moved toward the bed. His shoes lay widely separated, as if he had torn them off his feet and tossed them away. Closer to the bed were his tie, yesterday's white shirt, and his underwear, all of which formed points on a line leading toward his poisoned body. Beside him lay the empty Prentiss baby bottle and a paperback copy of *The Buffalo Hunter*, splayed open on the sheet. Evidently he had tried to read after finally getting out of his clothes and making it to bed: his body had followed its habits although his mind had stopped working.

He moved his legs off the bed, and sudden nausea made him fear that he was going to vomit before he could get to the toilet. The clarity he had experienced on first waking vanished into the headache and other physical miseries. Some other, more decayed body had replaced the one he knew. The nausea ebbed away, and he pushed himself off the bed. He looked down at long white skinny legs. These certainly were not his. The legs took him to the bathroom, where he sat on the toilet. He heard himself moaning. Eventually he was able to get into the shower, where the hot water sizzled down the stranger's body. The stranger's wrinkled hands pushed soap across his white skin and rubbed shampoo into his lifeless hair.

Slowly, he dressed himself in a dark suit, a clean white shirt, and a navy blue necktie with white stripes, the clothes he would have worn to a funeral. His head seemed to float farther from the ground than he remembered, and his arms and legs were spindly and breakable. Bunting experienced a phantasmal happiness, a ghastly good cheer released by the disappearance of so much of his everyday self.

The mirror showed him a white, aged Bunting with sparkling eyes. He was still a little drunk, he realized, but did not remember why he'd had so much of the vodka—he wondered if there had been a reason and decided that he had simply celebrated his birthday too vigorously. "Thirty-five," he said to the white specter in the mirror. "Thirty-five and one day." Bunting was not accustomed to giving much attention to any birthdays or anniversaries, even his own, and only the call from Battle Creek had reminded him that anyone else knew that the day was anything but ordinary. He had not even given himself a present.

That was how he would spend this peculiar morning. He would buy himself a thirty-fifth birthday present. Then, if he felt more like himself, he would go in to work.

Bunting located his sunglasses on his dining table, pushed them into his breast pocket, and let himself out of his room. The corridor looked even shabbier than usual. Sections of wallpaper curled down from the seams and corners, and whole sections of the wall had been spray-painted with puffy, cartoonish nonsense words. BANGO SKANK. JEEPY. Bunting's feeling of breakability increased. He worked his way through the murk of the hallway to the elevator and pushed the button several times. A few minutes later, he stepped out of the elevator and permitted himself to breathe. After the elevator, the lobby smelled like a freshly mown hayfield. Two ripped couches of imitation leather faced each other across a dirty stone floor. A boxy wooden desk stood empty against a gray wall miraculously kept clean of graffiti. A six-foot fern was turning a crisp, pale brown in a pot beside the desk.

Bunting pushed his way through the smudgy glass doors, then the heavy wooden doors past the row of buzzers, and came out into the bright sunlight that instantly bounced into his eyes from the tops of a dozen cars, from clean shopwindows, from the steel wristbands of watches and glittering earrings, from a hundred bright things large and small. Bunting yanked his sunglasses from his pocket and put them on.

When he passed the drugstore, he remembered that he needed a new pack of nipples, and turned in. Inside, a slanted mirror gave him a foreshortened version of himself, all bulging forehead and sinister glasses. He looked like an alien being in disguise. Bunting walked through the glaring aisles to the back of the store and the displays of goods for infants.

Here were the wonderful siblings of the Pacer family, but as he reached for them, he saw what he had missed the first time. The drugstore carried not only the orange nipples with the special crosscut opening, but, in rows on both sides of the juice nipples, flesh-colored nipples for drinking formula, white nipples for drinking milk, and blue nipples for drinking water.

He took down packets of each kind of nipple, and then realized that perfect birthday presents were hanging all over the wall before him. On his first visit, he had not even noticed all the baby bottles displayed alongside the nipples; he had not been interested in baby bottles then, apart from his own. He had not imagined that he would ever be interested in other baby bottles. And in other ways also he had been mistaken. He had assumed that baby bottles remained the same over time, like white dress shirts and black business shoes and hardcover books, that the form had been perfected sometime early in the twentieth century and seventy or eighty years later was simply reproduced in larger numbers. This had been an error. Baby bottles were objects like automobiles and breakfast cereals, capable of astonishing variation.

Smiling with this astonished pleasure, Bunting walked up and down past the display, carrying his packets of white, orange, blue, and flesh-colored nipples. The first transformation in bottles had been in shape, the second in material, and the third in color. There had also been an unexplained change of manufacturers. None of these bottles before him were Prentiss baby bottles. Every single one was made either by

Evenflo or Playtex. What had happened to Prentiss? The manufacturers of his long-lasting, extremely serviceable bottle had gone out of business—skunked, flushed, busted.

Bunting felt a searing flash of shame for his parents: they had backed a loser.

Most baby bottles were not even round anymore. They were six-sided, except for those (Easy Hold) that looked like elongated doughnuts, with a long narrow oval in the middle through which a baby's fingers could presumably slide. And the round ones, the Playtex bottles, were nothing more than shells around collapsible plastic bags. These hybrid objects, redolent of menopausal old age, made Bunting shudder. Of the six-sided bottles—nursers, as they were now called—some were yellow, others orange, and some had a row of little smiling faces marching up the ounce markings on the side. Some of these new types of bottles were glass, but most were made of a thin transparent plastic.

Bunting instantly understood that, except for the ones that contained the collapsing breast, he had to have all of these bottles. Even his headache seemed to loosen its grip. He had found the perfect birthday present for himself. Now that he had seen them, it was not possible not to buy one of each of most of these varieties of "nursers." Another brilliant notion penetrated him, as if by arrow from a heavenly realm.

He saw lined up on the shelf beside the stove a bottle for coffee and one for tea, a bottle for cold vodka, another for nice warm milk, bottles for soft drinks and different kinds of beer and one for mineral water, a library of bottles. There could be morning bottles and evening bottles and late-night bottles. He'd need a lot more nipples, he realized, and began taking things down from their hooks.

Back in his apartment, Bunting washed his birthday presents and set them out on his counter. The row did not look as imposing as he'd envisioned it would—there were only seven bottles in all, his old Prentiss and six new ones. Seven seemed too few. He remembered all the bottles left on the wall. He should have bought more of them. A double row of bottles—"nursers"—would be twice as impressive. It was his birthday, wasn't it?

Still, he had a collection—a small collection. He ran his fingers over the row of bottles and selected one made of clear plastic, to sample the difference between it and the old round glass Prentiss. Because he felt a bit dehydrated, he filled it with tap water and pushed a blue Water

Nipple through the cap ring. The new nipple was deliciously slippery on his tongue. Bunting yawned, and half-consciously took the new blue-tipped bottle to his bed. He promised himself he would lie down for just a few minutes, and collapsed onto the unmade bed. He opened his book, and began to suck water through the new nipple, and fell asleep so immediately and thoroughly he might have been struck on the back of the head with a mallet.

When Bunting awoke two hours later, he could not remember exactly where, or even exactly who, he was. Nothing around him looked familiar. The light—more precisely, the relative quality of the darkness—was all wrong. He did not understand why he was wearing a suit, a shirt, a tie, and shoes, and he felt some deep, mysterious sense of shame. He had betrayed himself, he had been *found out*, and now he was in disgrace. His mouth tasted terrible. Gradually, his room took shape around him, but it was the wrong time for this room. Why wasn't he at work? His heart began to beat faster. Bunting sat up, groaning, and saw the rank of sparkling new baby bottles, each with its new nipple, beside his sink. The sense of shame and disgrace retreated. He remembered that he had taken the morning off, and for a moment thought that he really should write a letter to his parents as soon as his head cleared.

But he had just talked to his parents. He had escaped another Christmas, though this was balanced by some alarming news his father had given to him. The exact nature of this news would not yield itself: it felt like a large, tender bruise, and his mind recoiled from the memory of the injury.

He looked at his watch, and was surprised that it was only eleven-thirty.

Bunting got out of bed, thinking that he might as well go to work. In the bathroom, he splashed water on his face and brushed his teeth, taking care not to get water or toothpaste on his jacket and tie. While he gargled mouthwash, he remembered: his mother had fallen down in some supermarket parking lot. Had his father insinuated that he ought to come back to Battle Creek? No, there had been no such insinuation. He was sure of that. And what could he do to help his mother, even if he went back? She was all right—what she had really minded was breaking a lot of eggs.

3

An oddly energetic exhilaration, as if he had narrowly escaped some great danger, came to Bunting when he walked back out into the sunlight, and when his bus did not arrive immediately, he found himself walking to DataComCorp's offices. His body felt in some way still not his, but capable of moving at a good rate down the sidewalks toward Columbus Circle and then midtown. The mid-autumn air felt fresh and cool, and the memory of the six new baby bottles back in his apartment was a bubbling inner spring, surfacing in his thoughts, then disappearing underground before coming to the surface again.

Did ever a young mother go into a drugstore in search of a baby bottle for her new infant, and not find one?

Bunting arrived at the door of the Data Entry room just at the time that one of his fellow workers was leaving with orders for sandwiches and drinks. Few of Bunting's fellow workers chose to spend their salaries on restaurant lunches, and nearly all of them ate delicatessen sandwiches in a group by the coffee machine or alone at their desks. Bunting generally ate in his cubicle or in Frank Herko's, for Frank disdained most of their fellow clerks, as did Bunting. Though some of the other clerks had attended trade or technical schools, only Bunting and Frank Herko had been to college. Bunting had two years at Lansing College, Herko two at Yale. Frank Herko looked nothing like Bunting's idea of a Yale student. He was stocky and barrel-chested, with a black beard and long, curly black hair. He generally dressed in baggy trousers and shabby sweaters, some with actual holes in the wool. Neither did Herko behave like his office friend's idea of a Yalie, being aggressive, loud, and frank to the point of crudity. Bunting had been disturbed and annoyed by Herko during his first months in Data Entry, an attitude undermined and finally challenged by the other man's persistent, oddly delicate deference, friendliness, and curiosity. Herko seemed to decide that the older man was a sort of treasure, a real rara avis, deserving of special treatment.

Bunting asked the messenger to bring him a Swiss cheese and Black Forest ham sandwich on whole wheat, mustard and mayonnaise, lettuce and tomato. "Oh, and coffee," he said. "Black coffee."

Herko was winding his way to the door, beaming at him. "Uh-huh, black coffee," he said. "You *look* like black coffee today. Nice of you to make it in, Bunting, my man. I take it you had an unusually late night."

"You could say that."

"Oh yes, oh yes. And we show up for work right after getting out of bed, don't we? With our beautiful suit all over wrinkles from the night before."

"Well," Bunting said, looking down. Long pronounced wrinkles ran down the length of his suit jacket, intersecting longitudinal wrinkles that matched the other wrinkles in his tie. He had been too disoriented to notice them when he had awakened from his nap. "I did just get out of bed." He began trying to smooth out the wrinkles in his jacket.

Frank took a step nearer and sniffed the air. "A stench of alcohol is still oozing from the old pores. Had a little party, did we?" He bent toward Bunting and peered into his face. "My God. You really look like shit, you know that? Why'd you come to work anyhow, you dumb fuck? Why couldn't you take a day off?"

"I wanted to come to work," Bunting said. "I took the morning off, didn't I?"

"Rolling around in bed with the beautiful Veronica," Herko said. "Hurry up and get into your cubicle before one of the old cunts gets a whiff of you and keels over."

He propelled Bunting toward his row and cubicle. Bunting pushed open his door and fell into the chair facing his terminal. A stack of paper several inches high had been placed beside his keyboard.

Herko pulled a tube of Binaca from his trousers pocket. "For God's sake, give yourself a shot of this, will you?"

"I brushed my teeth," Bunting protested. "Twice."

"Use it anyhow. Keep it. You're going to need it."

Bunting dutifully squirted cinnamon-flavored vapor onto his tongue and put the tube in his jacket pocket.

"Bunting cuts loose," Herko said. "Bunting gets down and dirty. Bunting the party animal." He was grinning. "Did Veronica do a number on you, or did you do a number on her, man?"

Bunting rubbed his eyes.

"Hey, man, you can't just show up in last night's clothes, still wasted from the night before, on top of everything else three hours late!—and expect me not to be curious." He leaned forward and stretched out his arms, enlarging the baggy blue sweater. "Talk to me! What the hell happened? Did you and Veronica have an anniversary or a fight?"

"Neither one," said Bunting.

Herko put his hands on his hips and shook his head, silently plead-
ing for more of the story.

"Well, I was somewhere else," Bunting said.

"Obviously. You sure as hell didn't go *home* last night."

"Well, I was with someone else," Bunting said.

Herko crowed and balled his fist and pumped his arm, elbow bent.
"Attaboy. Attaway. Bunting's on a roll."

Again Bunting saw his parents posed before their peeling house like
the couple in *American Gothic*, his father on the verge of uttering some
banal heartlessness and his mother virtually twitching with anxiety.
They were small, Bunting realized, the size of dolls.

"I've been seeing a couple of new people. Now and then. Off and on."

"A couple of new people," Herko said.

"Two or three. Three, actually."

"What does Veronica have to say about that? Does she even know?"

"Veronica and I are cooling off a little bit. We're creating some space
between us. She's probably seeing other people too, but she says she
isn't." These inventions came easily to Bunting, and he propped his
chin in the palm of his hand and looked into Frank Herko's luminous
eyes. "I guess I was getting a little bored or something. I wanted some
variety. You don't want the same thing all the time, do you?"

"You don't want to be stultified," Herko said quickly. "You get stultified, going with the same person all the time."

"It was always hard for Veronica to relax. People like that don't ever
really slow down and take things easy. They're always thinking about
getting ahead, about how to make more money, get a little more
status."

"I didn't know Veronica was like that," Herko said. He had been
given a very different picture of Bunting's girlfriend.

"Believe me, it even took me a long time to see it. You don't want
to admit a kind of thing like that." He shrugged. "But once she starts
looking around, she'll find somebody more suitable. I mean, we still
love each other, but . . ."

"It wasn't working out, that's obvious," Herko supplied. "She wasn't
right for you, she didn't have the same values, it could never turn out
happily. You're doing the right thing. Besides, you're going out and having fun, aren't you? What more do you want?"

"I want my headache to go away," Bunting said. The sensation of a slight, suspended drunkenness had passed, and with it the feeling of inhabiting an unfamiliar body.

"Oh, for God's sake, why didn't you say so?" asked Herko, and disappeared into his own cubicle. Bunting could see the top of his head floating back and forth like a wig over the top of the partition. Desk drawers moved in and out. In a moment Herko was back with two aspirin, which he set atop Bunting's desk before going out to the water cooler. Bunting sat motionless as royalty. Herko returned with a conical paper cup brimming with water just as the woman came in with a cardboard box filled with the department's order from the deli.

"Hand over our wonderful four-star lunches and leave us alone," Herko said.

They unwrapped their sandwiches and began to eat, Herko casting eager and importunate looks toward the older man. Bunting ate with fussy deliberation, and Herko chomped. There was a long silence.

"This sandwich tastes good," Bunting said at last.

"Yeah, yeah," Herko said. "Right now, *Alpo* would taste good to you. What about the girl? Tell me about the girl."

"Oh, Carol?"

"What's this 'Oh, Carol?' shit, Bunting? You think I know the girl, or something? Tell me about her—where did you meet her, how old is she, what does she do for a living, does she have good legs and big tits, you know—*tell* me!"

Bunting chewed on slowly, deliberately, regarding Herko. The younger man looked like a large, shaggy puppy. "I met her in an art gallery."

"You devil."

"I was just walking past the place, and when I looked in the window I saw her sitting behind the desk. The next day when I walked past, she was there again, so I went in and walked around, pretending to look at the pictures. I started talking with her, and then I started coming back to the gallery, and after a while I asked her out."

"Those girls in art galleries are incredible," Herko said. "That's why they're working in art galleries. You can't have a dog selling beautiful pictures, right?" He shook his head. His sandwich oozed whitish liquid onto the thick white paper, and traces of the liquid clung to the side of his mouth. "You know what you are, Bunting? You're a secret weapon." A bit more white liquid squirted from the corner of his mouth. "You're a goddamned *missile silo*."

"Carol is more like my kind of person, that's all," Bunting said. Secretly, this description thrilled him. "She's more like an artistic kind of person, not so into her career and everything. She's willing to focus more on me."

"Which means she's a hundred percent better in bed, am I right?"

"Well," Bunting said, thinking vaguely that Veronica had after all been very good in bed.

"It's obvious, it goes without saying," Herko said. "You don't even have to tell me."

Bunting shrugged.

"What's her last name?"

"Even," Bunting said. "Carol Even. It's an English name."

"At least English is her first language. She's a product of your own culture, of course she's more your type than some Swiss money machine. Tell me about the other two."

"Oh, you know," Bunting said. He sipped from the Styrofoam container of coffee. "It's the usual kind of thing."

"Do they all work in art galleries? Do you boff 'em all at once, or do you just take them one by one? Where do you go? Do you make the club scene? Concerts? Or do you just invite them back to your place for a nice soulful *talk*?" He was chewing frantically as he talked, waving his free hand. A pink paste filled his mouth, a pulp of compressed roast beef, mayonnaise, and whole-grain bread. "You're a madman, Bunting, you're a stone wacko. I always knew it—I knew you were gonzo from the moment you first walked into this place. You can fool all these old ladies with your fancy clothes, but I can see your fangs, my friend, and they are long, long fangs." Herko swallowed the mess in his mouth and twinkled at Bunting.

"You could see that, huh?"

"First thing. Long fangs, my friend. Now tell me about these other women." He suppressed a burp. "Go on, we only got a couple of minutes."

Lunch ended twenty minutes later, and the day slid forward. Though Bunting felt tired, his odd exhilaration had returned—an exhilaration that seemed like a freedom from some heavy, painful responsibility— and as his fingers moved across the keyboard of his computer, he thought about the women he had described to Frank Herko. Images of the wonderful new baby bottles back in his room flowed in and out of his fantasies.

Late in the afternoon, Herko's head appeared over the top of the partition separating their two cubicles.

"How's it going?"

"Slowly," Bunting said.

"Forget about it, you're still convalescing. Listen, I had a great idea. You're not really going out with Veronica anymore, right?"

"I didn't say that," Bunting said.

"You know what I mean. You're basically a free man, aren't you? My friend Lindy has this girlfriend, Marty, who wants to go out with someone new. Marty's a great kid. You'd like her. That's a promise, man. If I could, I'd take her out myself, but Lindy would kill me if I did. No kidding—I wouldn't put you on about this, I think you'd like her a lot and you could have a good time with her, and if everything works out, which I don't see why it should not, the four of us could go out somewhere together."

"Marty?" Bunting asked. "You want me to go out with someone named Marty?"

Frank snickered. "Hey, she's really cute, don't act that way with me. This is actually Lindy's idea, I guess I talked about you with her, and she thought you sounded okay, you know, so when her friend Marty started saying this and that, she was breaking up with a guy, she asked me about you. And I said no way, this guy is all wrapped up. But since you're going wild, you really ought to check Marty out. I'm not kidding."

He was not. His head looked even bigger than usual, his beard seemed to jump out of his skin, his hair foamed down from his scalp, his eyes bulged. Bunting had a brief, unsettling image of what it would be to be a girl, fending off all this insistent male energy.

"I'll think about it," he said.

"Great. Do I have your phone number? I do, don't I?"

Bunting could not remember having given Herko his telephone number—he very rarely gave it out—but he recited it to the eager head looking down at him, and the head disappeared below the partition as Herko went to his desk to write down the number. A moment later, the head reappeared. "You're not going to be sorry about this. I promise!" Herko disappeared behind the partition.

Bunting's entire body went cold. "Now, wait just a second. What are you going to do?" He could feel his heart racing.

"What do you think I'm going to do?" Herko called over the partition.

"You can't give anybody my number," Bunting heard his own voice come up in a squeaky wail, and realized that everybody else in the Data Entry room had also heard him.

Herko's upper body appeared leaning around the door to Bunting's cubicle. He was frowning. "Hey, man. Did I say I was going to give anybody your number?"

"Well, don't," Bunting said. He felt as though he had been struck by a bolt of lightning a second ago. He looked down at his hands and saw that they, and presumably the rest of his body, had turned a curious lobster-red flecked with white spots.

"You're going to piss me off, man, because you ought to know you can trust me. I'm not just some jerk, Bunting. I'm trying to do something nice for you."

Bunting stared furiously down at his keyboard.

"You're starting to piss me off," Herko said in a low, quiet voice.

"Okay, I trust you," Bunting said, and continued staring at his keyboard until Herko retreated into his own cubicle.

At the end of the day Bunting left the office quickly and took the staircase to avoid having to wait for the elevator. When he reached the ground floor, he sensed two elevators opening simultaneously off to his right, and hurried toward the door, dreading that someone would call out his name. Bunting spun through the door and walked as quickly as he could to the corner, where he turned off on a deeply shadowed crosstown street. He pulled his sunglasses from his pocket and put them on. Strangers moved past him, and even the Oriental rug outlets and Indian restaurants that lined the street seemed interchangeable and anonymous. His pace slowed. It came to him that, without consciously planning to do so, he was walking away from his bus stop. Bunting experienced every sensation of running away from something, but had no clear idea of what he was running from. It was all an illusion; there was nothing to run from. Herko? The idea was absurd. He certainly did not have to run from fuzzy, noisy Frank Herko.

Bunting ambled along, too tired to walk all the way back up to his building but aware of some new dimension, an anticipatory expectancy, in his life that made it pleasant to walk along the crosstown street.

He crossed Broadway and kept walking, thinking that he might even try to figure out which subway could take him uptown. Bunting had taken the subway only once, shortly after his arrival in New York, and on the hot, crowded train he had felt in mortal danger. Every inch of the walls had been filled with lunatic scribbling; every other male on the subway had looked like a mugger. But Frank Herko took the subway in from Brooklyn every day. According to the newspapers, all the subway graffiti had been removed. Bunting had lived in New York for a decade without getting mugged, walked all alone down dark streets, the subway could not possibly be so threatening to him now. And it was much faster than the bus.

Bunting passed the entrance to a subway station just as he had these thoughts, and he paused to look at it. Stairs led down to a smoky blackness filled with noise; up the filthy steps floated a stench of zoo, of other people's private parts.

Bunting twitched away like a cat and kept walking west, committed now to walking to Eighth Avenue. He suddenly felt nearly bad enough to hail a cab and spend five dollars on the trip home. It had come to him that Frank Herko and his friend Lindy were going to set about making him go out on a date with a girl named Marty, and that this must have been the vague pleasure that had lightened his mood only minutes ago.

Nothing was right about this, the whole idea was nightmarishly grotesque.

But why did the idea of a date have to be grotesque? He was a well-dressed man with a steady job. His looks were okay—definitely on the okay side. Worse people had millions of dates. Above all, Veronica had given him a kind of history, a level of experience no other data clerk could claim. He had spent hundreds of hours talking to Veronica in restaurants, another hundred in airplanes. He had traveled to Switzerland and stayed in luxury hotel suites.

Bunting realized that if something happened in your mind, it had happened—you had a memory of it, you could talk about it. It changed you in the same way as an event in the world. In the long run, there was very little difference between events in the world and events in the mind, because one reality inhabited them both. He had been the lover of a sophisticated Swiss woman named Veronica, and he could certainly handle a date with a scruffy acquaintance of Frank Herko's. Named Marty.

In fact, he could see her. He could summon her up. Her name and friendship with Frank evoked a short, dark-haired, undemanding girl who liked to have a good time. She would be passably pretty, wear short skirts and fuzzy sweaters, and go to a lot of movies. A passive, good-hearted quality would balance her occasional crudeness. He would appear patrician, aloof, ironic to her—a sophisticated older man.

He would take her out once, in some indeterminate future time. The differences between them would speak for themselves, and he and Marty would part with a mixture of regret and relief. It was this infinitely postponable scenario that hovered about him with such delightful vagueness.

Bunting turned up Eighth Avenue smiling to himself. When he saw that he was walking past a drugstore he turned in and moved through the aisles until he came to a large display of baby bottles. Here beside the three kinds of Evenflo and Playtex hung bottles he had never heard of—no sturdy Prentisses, but squat little blue bottles and bottles with patterns and flags and teddy bears, a whole range of baby bottles made by a company named Ama. Bunting saw instantly that Ama was a wonderful company. They were located in Florida, and they had a sunny, inventive, Floridian sensibility. Bunting began scooping up bottles, and ended up carrying an awkward armful to the counter.

"How many babies you *got?*" the young woman behind the register asked him.

"These are for a project," Bunting said.

"Like a collection?" she asked. Her head tilted prettily in the dusty light through the big plate-glass window on Eighth Avenue.

"Yes, like a collection," Bunting said. "Exactly." He smiled at her bushy hair and puzzling eyes.

Outside the drugstore, he moved to the curb and raised his hand for a cab. With the same heightened sense of self that came when he bought his splendid suits, he rode back to his building in the ripped backseat of a jouncing, smelly taxi, splurging another fifteen cents every time the meter changed.

4

That night he ate a microwaved Lean Cuisine dinner and divided his attention between the evening news on his television set and the array of freshly washed bottles on both sides of it. The news seemed out-moded and repetitious, the bottles various and pristine. The news had happened before, the same murders and explosions and declarations and demonstrations had occurred yesterday and the day before and the week and month before that, but the bottles existed in present time, unprecedented and extraordinary. The news was routine, the bottles possessed wonder. It was difficult for him to take his eyes from them.

How many bottles, he wondered, would it take to fill up his table? Or his bed?

For an instant, he saw his entire room festooned, engorged with cylindrical glass and plastic bottles—blue bottles covering one wall, yellow ones another, a curving path between bottles on the floor, a smooth cushion of nippled bottles on his bed. Bunting blinked and smiled as he chewed on turkey. He sipped Spanish burgundy from one of the new glass Evenflos.

When he dumped the Lean Cuisine tray in the garbage and dropped his silverware in the sink, Bunting scrubbed out the bottle, rinsed the nipple, and set them on his draining board. He put a kettle of hot water on the stove, two teaspoons of instant coffee in one of the new bottles, and added boiling water and cold milk before screwing on the nipple. He poured a generous slug of cognac into another new bottle, a squat, pink, friendly-looking little Ama, and took both bottles to his bed along with a pen and a pad of paper.

Bunting pulled coffee, then cognac, into his mouth, and let the little pink Ama dangle from his mouth while he wrote.

Dear Mom and Dad,

  There have been some changes that I ought to tell you about. For some time there have been difficulties between Veronica and me which I haven't told you about because I didn't want you to worry about me. I guess what it boils down to is that I've been feeling you could say stultified by our relationship. This has been difficult for both of us, after all the time we've been together, but things are finally resolved, and Veronica and I are only distant friends now. Of course there has been some pain, but I felt that my freedom was worth that price.

  Lately I have been seeing a girl named Carol, who is really great. I met her in an art gallery where she works, and we hit it off right away. Carol makes me feel loved and cared for, and I love her already, but I'm not going to make the mistake of tying myself down so soon after breaking up with Veronica, and I'm going out with two other great girls too. I'll tell you about them in the weeks to come.

Unfortunately, I will still not be able to come for Christmas, since New York is getting so expensive, and my rent just went up to an astronomical sum . . .

If nobody hears the tree falling down in the forest, does it make any sound?

Does the air hear?

When his letter was done, Bunting folded it into an envelope and set it aside to be mailed in the morning. It was two hours to bedtime. He removed his jacket, loosened his tie, and slipped off his shoes. He thought of Veronica, sitting on the edge of a bed on the east side of town. A Merlin phone on a long cord sat beside her. Veronica's eyes were dark and hard, and a deep vertical line between her harsh thick eyebrows cut into her forehead. Bunting noticed for the first time that her calves were skinny, that the loose skin beneath her eyes was a shade darker than the rest of her face. Without his noticing it, Veronica had been getting old. She had been hardening and drying like something left out in the sun. It came to him that he had always been unsuitable for her, and that was why she had chosen him. In her personal life, she set up situations destined from the first to fail. He had spent years "with" Veronica, but he had never understood this before.

He had been an actor in a psychic drama, and he had done no more than to play his role.

It came to him that Veronica had deliberately introduced him to a way of life he could not afford by himself in order to deprive him of it later. If he had not broken off with her, she would have dropped him. Veronica was a poignant case. Those winks and flashes of leg in office meetings had simply been part of a larger plan unconsciously designed to leave him gasping in pain. Without Bunting, she would find someone else—an impoverished young poet, say—and do the whole thing over again, dinner at the Blue Goose and first-class trips to Switzerland (Bunting had not told his parents about traveling first class), orchestra seats at Broadway plays, until what was twisted in her made her discard him.

Bunting felt sort of . . . awed. He knew someone like that.

He washed the Evenflo, refilled the pink little bottle with cognac, and picked up his novel and went back to bed to read. For a moment he squirmed around on top of his sheets, getting into the right position. He sucked cognac into his mouth, swallowed, and opened the book.

The lines of print swam up to meet him, and instantly he was on top of a quick little gray horse named Shorty, looking down the brown sweep of a hill toward a herd of grazing buffalo. An enormous, nearly cloudless sky hung above him; far ahead, so distant they were color-less and vague, a bumpy line of mountains rose up from the yellow plain. Shorty began to pick his way down the hill, and Bunting saw that he was wearing stained leather chaps over his trousers, a dark blue shirt, a sheepskin vest, and muddy brown boots with tarnished spurs. Two baby bottles had been inserted, nipple-down, into holsters on his hips, and a rifle hung in a long sheath from the pommel of his saddle. Shorty's muscles moved beneath his legs, and a strong smell of horse came momentarily to Bunting, then was gone in a wave of fresh, liv-ing odors from the whole scene before him. A powerful smell of grass dominated, stronger than the faint, tangy smell of the buffalo. From a long way off, Bunting smelled fresh water. Off to the east, someone was burning dried sod in a fireplace. The strength and clarity of these odors nearly knocked Bunting off his horse, and Shorty stopped mov-ing and looked around at him with a large, liquid brown eye. Bunting smiled and prodded Shorty with his heels, and the horse continued walking quietly down the hill, and the astonishing freshness of the air sifted around and through him. It was the normal air of this world, the air he knew.

Shorty reached the bottom of the hill and began moving slowly alongside the great herd of buffalo. He wanted to move into a gal-lop, to cut toward the buffalo and divide them, but Bunting pulled back on the reins. Shorty's hide quivered, and the short coarse hairs scratched against Bunting's chaps. It was important to proceed slowly and get into firing range before scattering the buffalo. A few of the massive bearded heads swung toward Bunting and Shorty as they plod-ded west toward the front of the herd. One of the females snorted and pushed her way toward the center of the herd, and the others grunted and moved aside to let her pass. Bunting slipped his rifle from its case, checked to be sure it was fully loaded, and held it across his lap. He stuffed six extra shells in each pocket of the sheepskin vest.

Shorty was ambling away past the front of the herd now, something like fifty yards away from the nearest animals. A few more of the buffalo watched him. Their furry mouths drizzled onto the grass. When he passed out of their immediate field of vision, they did not turn their heads but went back to nuzzling the thick grass. Bunting kept moving until he was far past the front of the herd, and then cut Shorty back around in a wide circle behind them.

The herd moved very slightly apart; now the males had noticed him, and were watching to see what he would do. Bunting knew that if he got off the horse and stood in the sun for a few minutes the males would walk up to him and stand beside him and find on him the smell of every place he had ever been in his life. Then the ones who liked the smells would stay around him and the rest would wander off a little way. That was what buffalo did, and it was fine if you could stand their own smell.

Bunting cocked his rifle, and one big male raised his head and shook it, as if trying to get rid of a bad dream.

Bunting kept Shorty moving on a diagonal line toward the middle of the herd, and the buffalo began moving apart very slowly.

The big male who had been watching seemed to come all the way out of his dream, and started ambling toward him. Bunting was something like ten yards from the big male, and twenty yards from the rest of the herd. It wasn't too bad: it could have been better but it would do.

Bunting raised his rifle and aimed it at the center of the big male's forehead. The buffalo instantly stopped moving and uttered a deep sound of alarm that made the entire herd ripple. A single electrical impulse seemed to pass through all the animals ranged out before Bunting. Bunting squeezed the trigger, and the rifle made a flat cracking sound that instantly spread to all parts of the long grassy plain, and the big male went down on his front knees and then collapsed onto his side.

The rest of the herd exploded. Buffalo ran toward the hill and scattered across the plain. Bunting kicked Shorty into action and rode into their midst, shooting as he went. Two others fell instantly, then a third around whose body Shorty wheeled. Two of the fastest buffalo had reached the hill, and Bunting aimed and fired and brought them down. He reloaded as a line of panicked buffalo swung away from the hill and bolted deeper into the meadow. The leader fell and rolled, and Shorty carried Bunting up alongside the second in line. Bunting shot the second buffalo in the eye, and it shuddered and fell. He swiveled in the saddle and brought down two more that were pounding toward the opposite end of the meadow.

By now the grass was spattered with blood, and the air had become thick with the screams of dying animals and the buzzing of flies. Bunting's own hands were spotted with blood, and long smears of blood covered his chaps. He fired until the rifle was empty, and then he reloaded and fired again as Shorty charged and separated the stampeding buffalo, and in the end he thought that only a few of the fastest animals had escaped. Dead and dying buffalo like huge sacks of dark brown wool lay all over the meadow, males and females. A few infant buffalo who had been trampled in the panic lay here and there in the tall grass.

Bunting swung himself off Shorty and went moving among the prone buffalo, slitting open the bellies of the dead. A great rush of purple and silver entrails fell out of the dead buffalo's body cavities, and Bunting's arms grew caked with drying blood. At last he came to a young female that was struggling to get onto its feet. He took one of the baby bottles from his holster, put the barrel behind the animal's ear, and pulled the trigger. The female jerked forward and slammed its dripping muzzle into the grass. Bunting sliced open its belly.

He skinned the female, then moved to another. He managed to skin four of the buffalo, a third of all he had killed, before it grew too dark to work. His arms and shoulders ached from tearing the thick flesh away from the animals' fatty hides. The entire meadow reeked of blood and death. Bunting built a small fire and unrolled his pack beside it and lay down to doze until morning.

Then the meadow and the night and the piles of dead animals slid away into nothingness, into white space, and Bunting's head jerked up. He was lying in his bed, and there was no fire, and for a moment he did not understand why he could not see the sky. A close, stuffy odor, the odor of himself and his room, surrounded him. Bunting looked back at the book and saw that he had reached the end of a chapter. He shook his head, rubbed his face, and took in that he was wearing a shirt, a tie, the trousers to a good suit.

More than three hours had passed since he had picked up *The Buffalo Hunter*. He had been reading, and what he had read was a single chapter of a novel by Luke Short. The chapter seemed incomparably more real than his own life. Now Bunting regarded the book as though it were a bomb, a secret weapon—it had stolen him out of the world. While he had been in the book, he had been more purely alive than at any other time during the day.

Bunting could not keep himself from testing the book again. His mouth was dry, and his heart was thumping hard enough nearly to shake the bed. He picked up the book and sucked cognac, for courage, from the little pink bottle. The book opened in his hand to the words CHAPTER THREE. He looked down to the first line of print, saw the words "The sun awakened him . . ." and in an instant he was lying on a bed of thick grass beside a low, smoky fire. His horse whickered softly. The sun, already warm, slanted into his eyes and dazzled him, and he threw off his blanket and got to his feet. His hips ached. A thick mat of flies covered the heaps of entrails, dark blood glistened on the grass, and Bunting closed his eyes and *wrenched* himself out of the page and back into his own body. He was breathing hard. The world of the book still seemed to be present, just out of sight, calling him.

Hurriedly he put the book on the seat of his chair and stood up. The room swayed twice, right to left, left to right, and Bunting put out his hand to steady himself. He had been lost inside the book for only a few hours, but now it felt like he had spent an entire night asleep in a bloody meadow, keeping uneasy watch over a slaughtered herd. He turned the book over so that its cover was facedown on his chair, and carried the bottle to the counter. He refilled it with cognac and took two large swallows before screwing the nipple back on.

What had happened to him was both deeply disturbing and powerfully, seductively pleasurable. It was as if he had traveled backward in time, gone into a different body and a different life, and there lived at a pitch of responsiveness and openness not available to him in his real, daily life. Bunting began to tremble again, remembering the clarity and freshness of the air, the touch of Shorty's coarse hair against his legs, the way the big male buffalo had come slowly toward him as the others began to stir apart—in that world, everything had possessed consequence. No detail was wasted because every detail overflowed with meaning.

He sucked cognac into his mouth, troubled by something else that had just occurred to him.

Bunting had read *The Buffalo Hunter* three or four times before—he had a small shelf of Western and mystery novels, and he read them over and over. What troubled him was that there was no slaughter of buffalo in *The Buffalo Hunter*. Bunting could remember—vaguely, without any particularity—a few scenes in which the hunter rode down buffalo and killed them, but none in which he massacred great numbers and waded through their bloody entrails.

Bunting let the bottle hang down from the nipple in his teeth and looked around his cramped, disorderly little room. For a moment— less than that, for an almost imperceptible fraction of a second—his familiar squalor seemed almost to tremble with promise, like the lips of one on the verge of telling a story. Bunting had the sense of some unimaginable anticipation, and then it was gone, so quickly it barely had time to leave behind the trace of an astonished curiosity.

He wondered if he dared go back to *The Buffalo Hunter*, and then knew he could not resist it. He would give himself a few more hours' reading, then pull himself out of the book and make sure he got enough sleep.

Bunting took off the rest of his clothes and hung up the excellent suit. He brushed his teeth and ran hot water over the dishes in the sink to discourage the roaches. Then he turned off the overhead light and the other lamp and got into bed. His heart was beating fast again: he trembled with an almost sexual anticipation: and he licked his lips and took the book off the crowded seat of the chair. He nestled into the sheets and folded his pillow. Then at last Bunting opened the book once again.

5

When the white spaces came he held himself in suspension as he turned the page and in this way went without a break from waking in the morning and skinning the buffalo and rigging a sledge to drag them behind Shorty to selling them to a hide broker and being ambushed and nearly killed for the money. Bunting was thrown in jail and escaped, found Shorty tethered in a feedlot, and spent two nights sleeping in the open. He got a job as a ranch hand and overheard enough to learn that the hide broker ran the town: after that, Bunting shot a man in a gunfight, escaped arrest again, stole his hides back from a locked warehouse, killed two more men in a gunfight, faced down the crooked broker, and was offered and refused the position of town sheriff. He rode out of the town back toward the freedom he needed, and two days later he was looking again across a wide plain of grazing buffalo. Shorty began trotting toward them, moving at an angle that would take him past the top of the herd. Bunting patted the extra shells in the pockets of his sheepskin vest and slowly drew the rifle from its sheath. A muscle twitched in Shorty's flank. A shaggy female buffalo cocked her head and regarded Bunting without alarm. Something was coming to an end, Bunting knew, some way of life, some ordained, flawless narrative of what it meant to be alive at this moment. A cold breeze carried the strong aroma of buffalo toward him, and the sheer beauty and right-ness—a formal rightness—inescapable and exact—of who and where he was went through Bunting like music, and as he sailed off into the final, the most charged and pregnant white space, he could no longer keep himself from weeping.

Bunting let the book fall from his hands, back in a shrunken and diminished world. He experienced a long moment of pure loss from which only tremendous hunger and certain physical urgencies imper-fectly distracted him. He needed, with overpowering urgency, to get into the bathroom; his legs had fallen asleep, his neck ached, and his knees creaked with pain. When he finally sat down on the toilet he actually cried out—it was as if he had gone days without moving. He realized he was incredibly thirsty, and as he sat, he forced his arms to move to the sink, take up the glass, fill it with water. He swallowed, and the water forced its way down his throat and into his chest, break-ing passage for itself. The world of Shorty, the meadow of endless green, and the grazing buffalo were already swimming backward, like a long night's dream. He was left behind in this littler, less eloquent world.

He turned on his shower and stepped inside to soak away his pains.

When he dried himself off, he realized that he had no proper idea of the time. Nor was he really certain of what day it was. He remembered seeing gray darkness outside his windows, so presumably it would soon be time to go to work—Bunting always awakened at the same time every day, seven-thirty, and he had no need of an alarm: but suppose that he had read very late into the night, as on the night of his birth-day; had he really just finished reading the book? *Living in* the book, as it actually seemed? That would mean that he had not slept at all, though it seemed to Bunting that he'd had the *experience* of sleeping, in gullies and in a little jailhouse, in a bunkhouse and a tavern's back room, and beside a fire in a wide meadow with millions of pinpoint stars overhead.

He dressed in a fresh shirt, a glen plaid suit, and a pair of cracked, well-polished brown shoes. When he strapped on his watch, he saw that it was six-thirty. He had read all night long, or most of it: he supposed he must have slept now and then, and dreamed certain passages of the book. Hunger forced him out of his room as soon as he was dressed, although he was an hour early: Bunting supposed he could walk to work again and get there early enough to clean up everything from Monday. Now that he was no longer stiff, his body and his mind both felt, beneath a lingering layer of tiredness like that after a session of strenuous exercise, refreshed and energetic.

The light in the corridor seemed darker than it should have been, and in the lobby two teenage boys who had stayed up all night sucking on crack pipes and plotting crimes shared a thin hand-rolled cigarette beside the dying fern. Bunting hurried past them to the street. It was surprisingly crowded. He had gone halfway to the diner before the fact of the crowd, the darkness, and the whole feeling of the city combined into the recognition that it was evening, not morning. An entire day had disappeared.

Outside the diner, he bought a paper, looked at the date, and found that it was even worse than that. It was Thursday—not Tuesday: he had not left his apartment—not even his bed—for two and a half days. For something like sixty hours he had lived inside a book.

Bunting went into the bright diner, and the man behind the cash register, who had seen him at least four mornings a week for the past ten years, gave him an odd, apprehensive look. For a second or two the counterman also seemed wary of him. Then the man recognized him, and his face relaxed. Bunting tried to smile, and realized that he was still showing the shock he had felt at the loss of those sixty hours. His smile felt like a mask.

Bunting ordered a feta cheese omelette and a cup of coffee, and the counterman turned away toward the coffee machine. Headlines and rows of black print at Bunting's elbow seemed to lift up from the surface of the folded newspaper and blare out at him; the whole dazzle of the restaurant surged and chimed, as if saying *Wait for it, wait for it*: but the counterman turned carrying a white cup brimming with black coffee, the ink sifted down into the paper, and the sense of promise and anticipation faded back down into the general bright surface of things.

Bunting lifted the thick china cup. Its rim was chalky and abraded with use. He was at a counter where he had eaten a thousand meals; the people around him offered the combination of anonymity and familiarity that most represents safety in urban life; but Bunting wanted overwhelmingly to be in his crowded little room, flat on his unmade bed, with the nipple of a baby bottle clamped between his teeth and a book open in his hands. If there was a promised land—a Promised Land—he had lived in it from Monday night to Thursday evening.

He was still in shock, and still frightened by the intensity of what had happened to him, but he knew more than anything else that he wanted to go back there.

When his omelette came it was overcooked and too salty, but Bunting bolted it down so quickly he scarcely tasted it. "You were hungry," the counterman said, and gave him his check without coming any nearer than he had to.

Bunting came out of the restaurant into what at first looked like an utter darkness punctuated here and there by street lamps and the headlights of the cars streaming down upper Broadway. Red lights flashed off and on. A massive policeman motioned Bunting aside, away from some commotion in the middle of the sidewalk. Bunting glanced past him and saw a body curled on the pavement, another man lying almost serenely prone with his hands stapled into handcuffs. A sheet of smooth black liquid lay across half the sidewalk. The policeman moved toward him, and Bunting hurried away.

More shocks, more disturbance—savage, pale faces came out of the dark, and cars sizzled past, honking. The red of the traffic lights burned into his eyes. All about him were creatures of another species, more animal, more instinctual, more brutal than he. They walked past him, unnoticing, flaring their lips and showing their teeth. He heard steps behind him and imagined his own body limp on the pockmarked concrete, his empty wallet tossed into the pool of his blood. The footsteps accelerated, and a white frozen panic filled Bunting's body. He stepped sideways, and a hand fell on his shoulder.

Bunting jumped, and a deep voice said, "Just hold it, will you?"

Bunting looked over his shoulder at a wide brutal face filled with black dots—little holes full of darkness—and a black mustache. He nearly fainted.

"I just wanted to ask you some questions, sir."

Bunting took in the uniform at the same time as he saw the amusement on the policeman's face.

"You came out of the diner, didn't you, sir?"

Bunting nodded.

"Did you see what happened?"

"What?"

"The shooting, sir. Did you see a shooting?"

Bunting was trembling. "I saw—" He stopped talking, having become aware that he had intended to say *I saw myself shoot a man out west in a gunfight.* He looked wildly back toward the diner. A dozen policemen stood around a roped-off area of sidewalk, and red lights flashed and spun. "I really didn't see anything at all. I barely saw—" he gestured toward the confusion.

The man nodded wearily and folded his notebook with a contemptuous, disbelieving snap. "Yeah," he said. "You have a good night, sir."

"I didn't see—I didn't—"

The policeman had already turned away.

On Bunting's side of the avenue, the lobby of the bank offered access to their rows of cash machines; across it, the drugstore's windows blared out light through a display of stuffed cartoon characters. A cardboard cutout of a girl in a bathing suit held a camera. Bunting watched the policeman go back to his colleagues. Before they could begin talking about him, he ducked into the bank and removed a hundred dollars from his checking account.

When he came out again, he went to the corner, crossed the street without looking at the police cars lined up in front of the diner, and went into the drugstore. There he bought five tubes of epoxy glue and ninety dollars' worth of baby bottles and nipples, enough to fill a large box. He carried this awkwardly to his building, peering over the top to see where he was going.

Bunting had to set down the box to push his button in the elevator, and again to let himself into his apartment. When he was finally safe inside his room, with the police bolt pushed back in front of the door, his lights on, and a colorful little Ama filled with vodka in his hand, he felt his true self returning to him, ragged and shredded from his nightmare on the streets. Except for the curious tingle of anticipation that had come to him in the diner, everything since being driven from his room by hunger had been like being attacked and beaten. Bunting could not even remember buying all the bottles and nipples, which had taken place in a tense, driven flurry.

Bunting began unpacking the baby bottles from the giant box, now and then stopping to suck cold Popov from the Ama. When he got to sixty-five, he saw that he was only one layer from the bottom, and was immediately sorry that he had not taken another hundred from the cash machine. He was going to need at least twice as many bottles to fulfill his plan, unless he spaced them out. He did not want to space them out, he wanted a nice tight look. A nice tight look was essential: a kind of *blanketing* effect.

Bunting thought he would try to do as much this night as he could with what he had, then get more money from the bank tomorrow evening and see how far another seventy or eighty bottles got him. When he was done tonight, he would read some more, not *The Buffalo Hunter* again, but some other novel, to see if the same incredible state of grace, like the ultimate movie, would come to him.

Bunting did not understand how, but what he wanted to do with all the new baby bottles was tied to what had happened to him when he read the Luke Short novel. It had to do with . . . with *inwardness*. That was as close as he could come to defining the connection. They led him *inward*, and inward was where everything important lay. He felt that though his entire way of life could be seen as a demonstration of this principle, he had never really understood it before—never seen it clearly. And he thought that this insight must have been what he felt coming toward him in the coffee shop: what mattered about his life took place entirely in this room.

When all the bottles were out of the box, Bunting began slicing open the packages of nipples and attaching the nipples to the bottles. When this was done, he opened a tube of epoxy and put a few dots on the base of one of the bottles. Then he pressed the bottle to the corner of the blank wall and held it there until it stuck. At last he lowered his arm and stepped away. The pink-tipped bottle adhered to the wall and jutted out into the room like an illusion. It took Bunting's breath away. The bottle appeared to be on the point of shooting or dripping milk, juice, water, vodka, any sort of fluid onto anyone in front of it. He dotted epoxy onto the base of another bottle and held it to the wall snugly alongside the first.

An hour and a half later, when he ran out of new bottles, more than a third of the wall was covered: perfectly aligned horizontal bottles and jutting nipples marched along its surface from the entrance to the kitchen alcove to the door frame. Bunting's arms ached from holding the bottles to the wall, but he wished that he could finish the wall and go on to another. Beautiful now, the wall would be even more beautiful when finished.

Bunting stretched and yawned and went to the sink to wash his hands. A number of roaches ambled into their hiding places, and Bunting decided to wash the stacked dishes and glasses before the roaches started crowding each other out of the sink. He had his hands deep in soapy water when a thought disquieted him: he had not thought about the loss of all Tuesday, all Wednesday, and most of Thursday since buying the box of nipples and bottles, but what if his radical redecoration of his apartment was no more than a reaction to that loss?

But that was the viewpoint of another kind of mind. The world in which he went to work and came home was the world of public life. In that world, according to people like his father and Frank Herko, one "counted," "amounted to something," or did not. For a dizzy second, Bunting imagined himself entirely renouncing this worthless, superficial world to become a Magellan of the interior.

At that moment the telephone rang. Bunting dried his hands on the greasy dish towel, picked up the phone, and heard his father pronouncing his name as if he were grinding it to powder. Bunting's heart stopped. The world had heard him. This unnerving impression was strong enough to keep him from taking in the meaning of his father's first few sentences.

"She fell down again?" he finally said.

"Yeah, something wrong with your ears? I just *said* that."

"Did she hurt herself?"

"About the same as before," his father said. "Like I say, I just thought you ought to know about stuff like this, when it happens."

"Well, is she bruised? Is her knee injured?"

"No, she mainly fell on her face this time, but her knee's just the same. She wears that big bandage on it, you know, probably kept her from busting the knee all up."

"What's making her fall down?" Bunting asked. "What does the doctor say?"

"I don't know, he don't say much at all. We're taking her in for some tests Friday, probably find out something then."

"Can I talk to her?"

"Nah, she's down in the basement, washing clothes. That's why I could call—she didn't even want me to tell you about what happened. She's on this washing thing now, she does the wash two, three times a day. Once I caught her going downstairs with a dish towel, she was going to put it in the machine."

Bunting glanced at his own filthy dish towel. "Why does she—what is she trying to—?"

"She forgets," his father said. "That's it, pure and simple. She forgets."

"Should I come out there? Is there anything I could do?"

"You made it pretty clear you *couldn't* come here, Bobby. We got your letter, you know, about Veronica and Carol and the rent and everything else. You tell us you got a busy social life, you tell us you got a steady job but you don't have much extra money. That's your life. And what could you do anyhow?"

Bunting said, "Not much, I guess," feeling stung and dismissed by this summary.

"Nothing," his father said. "I can do everything that has to be done. If she does the wash twice a day, what's the big deal? That's okay with me. We got the doctor appointment Friday, that's all set. And what's he going to say? Take it easy, that's what, and it'll cost us thirty-five bucks to hear this guy telling your mother to take it easy. So as far as we know yet, everything's basically okay. I just wanted to keep you up to date. Glad I caught you in."

"Oh, sure. Me, too."

" 'Cause you must be out a lot these days, huh? You must get out even more than you used to, right?"

"I'm not sure," Bunting said.

"I never could get a straight answer out of you, Bobby," his father said. "Sometimes I wonder if you know how to give one. I been calling you for two days, and all you say is *I'm not sure*. Anyhow, keep in touch."

Bunting promised to keep in touch, and his father cleared his throat and hung up without actually saying good-bye.

Bunting sat staring at the telephone receiver for a long time, barely conscious of what he was doing, not thinking and not aware of not thinking. He could remember what he had been doing before the telephone rang: he had been puffed up with self-importance, it seemed to him now, as inflated as a bullfrog. He pictured his mother trotting down the basement stairs toward the washing machine with a single dish towel in her hands. Her bruised face was knotted with worry, and a thick white pad had been clamped to her knee with a tightly rolled Ace bandage. She looked as driven as if she held a dying baby. He saw her drop the cloth into the washing machine, pour in a cup of Oxydol, close the lid, and punch the starting button. Then what did she do? Nod and walk away, satisfied that one tiny scrap of the universe had been nailed into place? Go upstairs and wander around in search of another dishcloth, a single sock, a handkerchief?

Did she fall down inside the house?

He set the receiver back in its cradle and stood up. Before he knew he intended to go there, he was across the room and in front of the rows of bottles. He spread his arms and leaned forward. Rubber nipples pressed against his forehead, his closed eyes, cheeks, shoulders, and chest. He turned his face sideways, spread his arms, and moved in tighter. It was something like lying on a fakir's bed of nails, he thought. It was pretty good. It wasn't bad at all. He liked it. The nipples were harder than expected, but not painfully hard. Not a single bottle moved—the epoxy clamped them to the wall. Nothing would get these bottles off the wall, short of a blowtorch or a cold chisel. Bunting was slightly in awe of what he had done. He sighed. *She forgets. That's it, pure and simple.* Tough little nipples pressed lightly against the palms of his hands. He began to feel better. His father's voice and the image of his mother darting downstairs to drop a single cloth into the washing machine receded to a safe distance. He straightened up and passed his palms over the rows of nipples, which flattened against his skin and then bounced back into position. Tomorrow he would have to go to the bank and withdraw more money. Another hundred to hundred and fifty would finish the wall.

He couldn't go to Battle Creek, anyhow; it would be a waste of time. His mother already had an appointment with a doctor.

He backed away from the wall. The image of the fakir's bed resurfaced in his mind: nails, blood leaking from punctured skin. He shook it off by taking a long drink from the Ama. The vodka burned all the way down his throat. Bunting realized that he was slightly drunk.

He could do no more tonight; his arms and shoulders still ached from gluing bottles onto the wall; he would just tip a little more vodka into the Ama—another inch, for an hour's reading—and get into bed. He had to go to work tomorrow.

As he folded and hung up the day's clothes, Bunting looked over his row of books, wondering if the *Buffalo Hunter* experience would ever be given to him again, afraid that reading might just be reading again.

On the other hand, he was also afraid that it might not be. Did he want to jump down the rabbit hole every time he opened a book?

Bunting had been groping toward the clothes rail with the suit hanger in hand while looking down at his row of books, and finally he leaned into his closet and put the hook on the rail so that he could really inspect the books. There were thirty or forty, all of them dated to his first days in New York. All the paperbacks had curling covers, cracked spines, and pulpy pages that looked as if they had been dunked in a bathtub. Slightly more than half of these were Westerns, many of these taken from Battle Creek. Most of the others were mysteries. He finally selected one of these, *The Lady in the Lake*, by Raymond Chandler.

It would be a relatively safe book to see from the inside—it wasn't one of the books where Philip Marlowe got beaten up, shot full of drugs, or locked away in a mental hospital. As importantly, he had read it last year and remembered it fairly well. He would be able to see if any important details changed once he got inside the book.

Bunting carefully brushed his teeth and washed his face. He peered through his blinds and looked out at the dingy brownstones, wondering if any of the people who lived behind those lighted windows had ever felt anything like his fearful and impatient expectancy.

Bunting checked the level in his bottle and turned off his other lamp. Then he switched it on again and ducked into his closet to set an alarm clock that he had brought with him from Michigan but never needed. Bunting extracted the clock from a bag behind his shoes, set it to the proper time, shoved various things off the bedside chair to make room for it, and wound it up. After he set the alarm for seven-thirty he switched off the light near the sink. Now the only light burning in his room was the reading lamp at the head of his bed. He folded his pillow in half and wedged it behind his head. He licked his lips and opened *The Lady in the Lake* to the first chapter. Blood pounded in his temples, his fingertips, and at the back of his head. The first sentence swam up at him, and he was gone.

6

Nearly everything was different, the cloudy air, the loud ringing sounds, the sense of a wide heartbreak, his taller, more detached self, and one of the greatest differences was that this time he had a vast historical memory, comprehensive and investigatory—he knew that the city around him was changing, that its air was far more poisoned than the beautiful clean air of the meadow where the buffalo grazed but much cleaner than the air of New York City forty-five years hence: some aspect of himself was familiar with a future in which violence, ignorance, and greed had finally won the battle. He was walking through downtown Los Angeles, and men were tearing up a rubber sidewalk at Sixth and Olive. The world beat in on him, its sharp particulars urged him toward knowledge, and as he entered a building and was instantly in a seventh-floor office his eye both acknowledged and deflected that knowledge by assessing the constant stream of details—double-plate glass doors bound in platinum, Chinese rugs, a glass display case with tiers of creams and soaps and perfumes in fancy boxes. A man named Kingsley wanted him to find his mother. Kingsley was a troubled man of six-two, elegant in a chalk-striped gray flannel suit, and he moved around his office a lot as he talked. His mother and his stepfather had been in their cabin up in the mountains at Puma Point for most of the summer, and then had suddenly stopped communicating.

"Do you think they left the cabin?" Bunting asked.

Kingsley nodded.

"What have you done about it?"

"Nothing. Not a thing. I haven't even been up there." Kingsley waited for Bunting to ask why, and Bunting could smell the man's anger and impatience. He was like a cocked and loaded gun.

"Why?" he asked.

Kingsley opened a desk drawer and took out a telegraph form. He passed it over, and Bunting unfolded it under Kingsley's smoldering gaze. The wire had been sent to Derace Kingsley at a Beverly Hills address and said: I AM DIVORCING CHRIS STOP MUST GET AWAY FROM HIM AND THIS AWFUL LIFE STOP PROBABLY FOR GOOD STOP GOOD LUCK MOTHER.

When Bunting looked up, Kingsley was handing him an eight-by-ten glossy photograph of a couple in bathing suits sitting on a bench beneath a sun umbrella. The woman was a slim blonde in her sixties, smiling and still attractive. She looked like a good-looking widow on a cruise. The man was a handsome brainless animal with a dark tan, sleek black hair, and strong shoulders and legs.

"My mother," Kingsley said. "Crystal. And Chris Lavery. Former playmate. He's my stepfather."

"Playmate?" Bunting asked.

"To a lot of rich women. My mother was just the one who married him. He's a no-good son of a bitch, and there's never been any love lost between us."

Bunting asked if Lavery were at the cabin.

"He wouldn't stay a minute if my mother went away. There isn't even a telephone. He and my mother have a house in Bay City. Let me give you the address." He scribbled on a stiff sheet of stationery from the top of his desk—*Derace Kingsley, Gillerlain Company*—and folded the card in half and handed it to Bunting like a state secret.

"Were you surprised that your mother wanted out of the marriage?"

Kingsley considered the question while he took a panatela out of a copper-and-mahogany box and beheaded it with a silver guillotine. He took his time about lighting it. "I was surprised when she wanted *in*, but I wasn't surprised when she wanted to dump him. My mother has her own money, a lot of it, from her family's oil leases, and she always did as she pleased. I never thought her marriage to Chris Lavery would last. But I got that wire three weeks ago, and I thought I'd hear from her long before now. Two days ago a hotel in San Bernardino called me to say that my mother's Packard Clipper was unclaimed in their garage. It's been there for better than two weeks. I figured she was out of state, and sent them a check to hold the car. Yesterday I ran into Chris Lavery in front of the Athletic Club and he acted as if nothing had happened—when I confronted him with what I knew, he denied everything and said that as far as he knew, she was enjoying herself up at the cabin."

"So that's where she is," Bunting said.

"That bastard would lie just for the fun of it. But there's another angle here. My mother has had trouble with the police occasionally."

He looked genuinely uncomfortable now, and Bunting helped him out. "The police?"

"She helps herself to things from stores. Especially when she's had too many martinis at lunch. We've had some pretty nasty scenes in managers' offices. So far nobody's filed charges, but if something happened in a strange city where nobody knew her—" He lifted his hands and let them fall back onto the desk.

"Wouldn't she call you, if she got into trouble?"

"She might call Chris first," Kingsley admitted. "Or she might be too embarrassed to call anybody."

"Well, I think we can almost throw the shoplifting angle out of this," Bunting said. "If she'd left her husband and gotten into trouble, the police would be likely to get in touch with you."

Kingsley poured himself a drink to help himself with this worrying. "You're making me feel better."

"But a lot of other things could have happened. Maybe she ran away with some other man. Maybe she had a sudden loss of memory—maybe she fell down and hurt herself somewhere, and she can't remember her name or where she lives. Maybe she got into some jam we haven't thought of. Maybe she met foul play."

"Good God, don't say that," Kingsley said.

"You've got to consider it," Bunting told him. "All of it. You never know what's going to happen to a woman your mother's age. Plenty of them go off the rails, believe me—I've seen it again and again. They start washing dishcloths in the middle of the night. They fall down in parking lots and mess up their faces. They forget their own names."

Kingsley stared at him, horrified. He took another slug of his drink.

"I get a hundred dollars a day, and a hundred right now," Bunting said.

Bunting drove to an address in Bay City that Kingsley's secretary gave him. The bungalow where Kingsley's mother had lived with Chris Lavery lay on the edge of the V forming the inner end of a deep canyon. It was built downward, and the front door was slightly below street level. Patio furniture stood on the roof. The bedrooms would be in the basement, and lowest of all, like the corner pocket on a pool table, was the garage. Korean moss edged the flat stones of the front walk. An iron knocker hung on the narrow door below a metal grille.

Bunting pounded the knocker against the door. When nothing happened, he pushed the bell. Then he hammered on the knocker again. No one came to the door. He walked around the side of the house and lifted the garage door to eye level. A car with white sidewalls was inside the garage. He went back to the front door.

Bunting pushed the bell and banged on the door, thinking that Chris Lavery might have been sleeping off a hangover. When there was still no response, Bunting twisted back and forth in front of the door, uncertain of his next step. He would have to drive all day and get nowhere—at Puma Point there would be another empty building, and he would stand at another door, knocking and ringing, and nobody would ever let him in. He would stand outside in the dark, banging on a locked door.

How had he become a detective? What had made him do it? *That* was the mystery, it seemed to him, not the whereabouts of some rich idiot who had married a playboy. He touched the little pink Ama bottle in his shoulder holster, for comfort.

Bunting stepped off the porch and walked back around the side of the house to the garage. He swung up the door, went inside, and pulled the door down behind him. The car with whitewalls was a big roadster convertible that would gulp down gasoline like it was vodka and looked as if it could hit a hundred and twenty on the highway. Bunting realized that if he had the key, he could turn on the ignition, lean back in the car, stick his good old bottle in his mouth, and take the long, long ride. He could make the long good-bye, the one you never came back from.

But he did not have the key to the roadster, and even if he did, he had a business card with a tommy gun in the corner; he had to detect. At the back of the garage was a plywood door leading into the house. The door was locked with something the builder had bought at a five-and-dime, and Bunting kicked at the door until it broke open. Wooden splinters and tinny pieces of metal sprayed into the hallway.

Bunting stepped inside. His heart was beating fast, and he thought, with sudden clarity: *This is why I'm a detective.* It was not just the excitement, it was the sense of imminent discovery. The whole house lay above him like a beating heart, and he was in a passage *inside* that heart.

The hushed warm smell of late morning in a closed house came to him, along with the odor of Vat 69. Bunting began moving down the hall. He glanced into a guest bedroom with drawn blinds. At the end of the hall he stepped into an elaborately furnished bedroom where a crystal greyhound stood on a smeary mirror-top table. Two pillows lay side by side on the unmade bed, and a pink towel with lipstick smears hung over the side of the wastebasket. Red lipstick smears lay like slashes across one of the pillows. Some foul, emphatic perfume hung in the air.

Bunting turned to the bathroom door and put his hand on the knob.

No, he did not want to look in the bathroom—he suddenly realized that he wanted to be anyplace at all, a Sumatran jungle, a polar ice cap, rather than where he was. The lipstick stain on the towel dripped steadily on the carpet, turning into a squashy red mush. He looked at the bed, and saw that the second pillow glistened with red that had leaked onto the sheet.

No, he said inside himself, please no, not again. One of them is in there, or both of them are in there, and it'll look like a butcher shop, you don't want, you can't, it's too much . . .

He turned the knob and opened the door. His eyes were nearly closed. Drools and sprays of blood covered the floor. A fine spattering of blood misted the shower curtain.

It's only Bunting, finding another body. Body-a-day Bunting, they call him.

He walked through the blood and pushed back the shower curtain.

The tub was empty—only a thick layer of blood lay on the bottom of the tub, slowly oozing down the drain.

The hideous clanging of a bell came to him through the bathroom windows. A white space in the air filled with the sound of the bell. Bunting clapped his hands to his ears. His neck hurt, and his back ached. He turned to flee the bathroom, but the bathroom had disappeared into empty white space. His legs could not move. Pain encased his body like St. Elmo's fire, and he groaned aloud and closed his eyes and opened them to the unbearable enclosure of his room and the shrieking clock.

For a moment he knew that the walls of this room were splashed with someone's blood, and he dropped the book and scuttled off the bed, gasping in pain and terror. His legs cried out, his entire body cried out. He could not move. He began writhing toward the door, moaning, and stopped only when he realized that he was back in his room. He lay on his carpet, panting, until the blood had returned to his legs enough for him to stand up and go into the bathroom. He had a difficult moment when he had to pull back the shower curtain, but none of the numerous stains on the porcelain and the wall tiles were red, and hot water soon brought him back into his daily life.

7

The next significant event in Bunting's life followed the strange experience just described as if it had been rooted in or inspired by it, and began shortly after he left his building to go to work. He had a slight headache, and his hands trembled: it seemed to him while tying his necktie that his face had subtly altered in a way that the discolored bags under his eyes did not entirely account for. His cheeks looked sunken, and his skin was an almost unnatural white. He supposed that he had not slept at all. He looked as if he were still staring at the bloody bathtub.

A layer of skin had been peeled away from him. All the colors and noises on the street seemed brighter and louder, everything seemed several notches more alive—the cars streaming down the avenue, the men and women rushing along the sidewalk, the ragged bums holding their paper bags. Even the little pieces of grit and paper whirled by the wind seemed like messages. Although he was never truly conscious of this, Bunting usually tried to take in as little as possible on his way to work. He thought of himself as in a transparent bubble which protected him from unnecessary pain and distraction. That was how you lived in New York City—you moved around inside an envelope of tough resistant varnish. A crew of men in orange hard hats and jackets were taking up the concrete sidewalk down the block from his building, and the sound of a jackhammer pounded in Bunting's ears. For a second the world wobbled around him, and he was back in the Los Angeles of forty years before, on his way to see a man named Derace Kingsley. He shuddered, then remembered: in the first paragraph of *The Lady in the Lake*, he had seen workmen taking up a rubber sidewalk.

For a second the clouds parted, and bright sunlight fell upon Bunting and everything before him. Then the air went dark.

The sound of the jackhammers abruptly ceased, and the workmen behind Bunting began shouting indistinct, urgent words. They had found something under the sidewalk, and because Bunting had to get away from what they found, he took one quick step toward his bus stop. Then a thick wall of water smashed against his head—without any warning, a thick drenching rainfall had soaked his clothes, his hair, and everything and everybody around him. The air turned black in an instant, and a loud roll of thunder, followed immediately by a crack of lightning that illuminated the frozen street, obliterated the shouts of the workmen. The lightning turned the world white for a brief electric moment: Bunting could not move. His suit was a wet rag, his hair streamed down the sides of his face. The sudden rainfall and the lightning that illuminated the water bouncing crazily off the roof of the bus shelter threw Bunting right out of his frame. What had been promised for days had finally arrived. His eyes had been washed clean of habit, and he *saw*.

People thrust past him to get into doorways and beneath the roof of the bus shelter, but he neither could, nor wanted to, move. If he could have moved, he would have fallen to his knees with thanks. For long, long seconds after the lightning faded, everything blazed and burned with life. Being streamed from every particle of the world—wood, metal, glass, or flesh. Cars, fire hydrants, the concrete and crushed stones of the road, each individual raindrop, all contained the same living substance that Bunting himself contained—and this was what was significant about himself and them. If Bunting had been religious, he would have felt that he had been given a direct, unmediated vision of God; since he was not, his experience was of the sacredness of the world itself.

All of this took place in a few seconds, but those seconds were out of time altogether. When the experience began to fade, and Bunting began to slip out of eternity back into time, he wiped the mixture of rain and tears from his face and started to move toward the bus shelter. It seemed that he too had overflowed. He moved beneath the roof of the bus shelter. Several people were looking at him oddly. He wondered what his face looked like—it seemed to him that he might be glowing. The bus appeared in the rainy darkness up the avenue, lurching and rolling through the potholes like an ocean liner. What had happened to him—what he was already beginning to think of as his "experience"—was similar, he realized, to what he felt when he tumbled into *The Buffalo Hunter*.

He sighed loudly and wiped his eyes. The people nearest him moved away.

8

He arrived at DataComCorp soaked and irritable, not knowing why. He wanted to push people who got in his way, to yell at anyone who slowed him down. He blamed this feeling on having to arrive at the office in wet clothes. The truth was that discomfort caused only the smallest part of his anger. Bunting felt as if he had been forced into an enclosure too small for him; he had left a mansion and returned to a hovel. The glimpse of the mansion made the hovel unendurable.

He came stamping out of the elevator and scowled at the reception-ist. As soon as he was inside his cubicle, he ripped off his suit jacket and threw it at a chair. He yanked down his tie and rubbed his neck and forehead with his damp handkerchief. In a dull, ignorant fury he banged his fist against his computer's On switch and began punch-ing in data. If Bunting had been in a better mood, his natural cau-tion would have protected him from the mistake he made after Frank Herko appeared in his cubicle. As it was, he didn't have a chance—foolhardy anger spoke for him.

"The Great Lover returns at last," Herko said.

"Leave me alone," said Bunting.

"Bunting the Infallible shows up still drunk after partying with his lovely bimbo, misses work for two days, doesn't answer his phone, shows up half-drowned—"

"Get out, Frank," Bunting said.

"—and madder than a stuck bull, probably suffering from the flu if not your actual pneumonia—"

Bunting sneezed.

"—and expects the only person who really understands him to shut up and leave him alone. God, you're *soaked*. Don't you have any sense? Hold on, I'll be right back."

Bunting growled. Herko slipped out of the cubicle, and a minute later returned with both hands full of wadded brown paper napkins from the dispenser in the men's room. "Dry yourself off, will you?"

Bunting snarled and swabbed his face with some of the napkins. He scrubbed napkins in his hair, unbuttoned his shirt and rubbed napkins over his damp chest.

"So what were you doing?" Herko asked. "Coming down with double pneumonia?"

Herko was a hysterical fool. Also, he thought he owned Bunting. Bunting did not feel ownable. "Thanks for the napkins," he said. "Now get out of here."

Herko threw up his hands. "I just wanted to tell you that I set up your date with Marty for tonight. I suppose that's still all right, or do you want to kill me for that, too?"

Around Bunting the world went white. His blood stopped moving in his veins. "You set up my date?"

"Well, Marty was eager to meet you. Eight o'clock, at the bar at One Fifth Avenue. Then you're in the Village, you can go to eat at a million places right around there." Herko leaned forward to peer at Bunting's face. "What's the matter? You sick again? Maybe you should go home."

Bunting whirled to face his computer. "I'm okay. Will you get the hell out of here?"

"Jesus," Herko said. "How about some thanks?"

"Don't do me any more favors, okay?" Bunting did not take his eyes from the screen, and Herko retreated.

Late in the afternoon, Bunting put his head around the door of his friend's cubicle. Herko glanced up, frowning. "I'm sorry," Bunting said. "I was in a bad mood this morning. I know I was rude, and I want to apologize."

"Okay," Herko said. "That's all right." He was still a little stiff and wounded. "It's okay about the date, right?"

"Well," Bunting said, and saw Herko's face tighten. "No, it's fine. Sure. That's great. Thanks."

"You'll love the bar," Herko said. "And then you're right down there in the Village. Million restaurants, all around you."

Bunting had never been in Greenwich Village, and knew only of the restaurants, many of them invented, to which he had taken Veronica. Then something else occurred to him.

"You like Raymond Chandler, don't you?" he asked, having remembered an earlier conversation.

"Ray is my man, my *main* man."

"Do you remember that part in *The Lady in the Lake* where Marlowe first goes to Chris Lavery's house?"

Herko nodded, instantly in a better mood.

"What does he find?"

"Chris Lavery."

"Alive?"

"Well, how else could he talk to him?"

"He doesn't find a lot of blood splashed all over the bathroom, does he?"

"What's happening to you?" Herko asked. "You starting to put the great literature of our time through a mental shredder, or what?"

"Or what," Bunting said, though it seemed that he had certainly shuffled, if not actually shredded, the pages he had read. He backed out of the cubicle and disappeared into his own.

Herko sat quiet with surprise for a moment, then yelled, "Long fangs! Long, long fangs! Bunting's gone a-hunting!" He howled like a wolf.

Some of the ladies giggled, and one of them said that he shouldn't tease. Herko started laughing big chesty barrelhouse laughs.

Bunting sat behind his computer, trying to force himself to concentrate on his work. Herko gasped for breath, then went on rolling out laughter. The bubble of noise about him suddenly evoked the image of the workmen who had exclaimed, an instant before the sudden storm, over the hole they had made in the sidewalk: they had found a dead man in that hole.

Bunting knew this with a sudden and absolute certainty. The men working on the sidewalk had looked down into that hole and seen a rotting corpse, or a heap of bones and a skull in a dusty suit, or a body in some stage between those two. Bunting saw the open mouth, the matted hair, the staring eyes and the writhing maggots. He tried to wrench himself back into the present, where his own living body sat in a damp shirt before a computer terminal filled with what for the moment looked alarmingly like gibberish.

DATATRAX 30 CARTONS MONMOUTH NJ BLUE CODE RED CODE

Jesus stepped past the rock at the mouth of the tomb, spread his arms wide, and sailed off in his dusty white robe into a flawless blue sky.

That's my body, he thought. *My* body.

Something the size of a walnut rattled in his stomach, grew to the size of an apple, then developed a point that lengthened into a needle. Bunting held his hands to his stomach and rushed out of the Data Entry room into the corridor. He banged through the men's room door and entered a toilet stall not much smaller than his cubicle. He pressed his necktie to his chest to avoid spatter, bent over, and vomited.

In the middle of the afternoon, Bunting looked up from his screen and saw the flash of a green dress moving past the door of his cubicle. The color was a dark flat green that both stood out from the office's pale walls and harmonized with them, and for an instant it seemed to float toward Bunting, who had been daydreaming about nothing in particular. The flat green jumped into sharp focus; then it was gone. The air the woman had filled hummed with her absence, and suddenly all the world Bunting could see promised to overflow with sacred and eternal being, as it had that morning. Bunting braced himself and fought the rising sense of expectancy—he did not know why, but he had to resist. The world instantly lost the feeling of trembling anticipation that had filled it a moment before: every detail fell back onto itself. Jesus went back into his cave and rolled the rock back across the entrance. The workmen standing in the rain looked down into an empty hole. Bunting was still alive, or still dead. He had been saved. The tree had fallen in the deep forest, and no one had heard it, so it still stood.

————

That night Bunting again set his alarm and went back into *The Lady in the Lake*. He was driving into the mountains, and once he got to a place called Bubbling Springs, the air grew cool. Canoes and rowboats went back and forth on Puma Lake, and speedboats filled with squealing girls zipped past, leaving wide foamy wakes. Bunting drove through meadows dotted with white irises and purple lupines. He turned off at a sign for Little Fawn Lake and crawled past granite rocks. He drove past a waterfall and through a maze of black oak trees. Now everything about him sang with meaning, and he was alive within this meaning, as alive as he was supposed to be, equal to the significance of every detail of the landscape. A woodpecker peered around a tree trunk, an oval lake curled at the bottom of a valley, a small bark-covered cabin stood against a stand of oaks. This information came toward and into him in a steady stream, every glowing feather and shining outcropping of rock and inch of wood overflowing with its portion of being, and Bunting, the eye around which this speaking world cohered, moved through this stream of information undeflected and undisturbed.

He got out of his car and pounded on the cabin door, and a man named Bill Chess came limping into view. Bunting gave Bill Chess a drink from a pint of rye in his pocket and they sat on a flat rock and talked. Bill Chess's wife had left him and his mother had died. He was lonely in the mountains. He didn't know anything about Derace Kingsley's mother. Eventually, they went up the heavy wooden steps to Kingsley's cabin and Chess unlocked the door and they went inside to the hushed warmth. Bunting's heart was breaking. Everything he saw looked like a postcard from a world without grief. The floors were plain and the beds were neat. Bill Chess sat down on one of the cream-colored bedspreads while Bunting opened the door to the bathroom. The air was hot, and the stink of blood stopped him as soon as he stepped inside. Bunting moved to the shower curtain, knowing that what was left of Crystal Kingsley's body lay inside the tub. He held his breath and grasped the curtain. When he pushed it aside, Bill Chess cried out behind him. "Muriel, Sweet Christ, it's Muriel!" But there was no body in the tub, only a bloodstain hardening as it oozed toward the drain.

9

At seven-thirty on Friday night, Bunting sat at a table facing the entrance of One Fifth Avenue, alternately checking his watch and looking at the door. He had arrived fifteen minutes before, dressed in one of his best suits, showered, freshly shaved, black wingtips and teeth brushed, his mouth tingling with Binaca. To get to the bar, which was already crowded, you had to walk past the tables, and Bunting planned to get a good look at this woman before she saw him. After that he would know what to do. The waitress came around, and he ordered another vodka martini. Bunting thought he felt comfortable. His heart was beating fast, and his hands were sweaty, but that was okay, Bunting thought—after all, this was his first date, his first real date, since he had broken up with Veronica. In another sense, one he did not wish to consider, this was his first date in twenty years. Every couple of minutes, he went to the men's room and splashed water on his face. He fluffed up his hair and buffed his shoes with paper towels. Then he went back to his table and sipped his drink and watched the door.

He wished that he had thought of secreting an Ama in one of his pockets. Even a loose nipple would work: he could tuck it into his mouth whenever he felt anxious. Or just keep it in his pocket!

Bunting shot his cuffs, ran a hand over his hair, looked at his watch. He leaned on his elbows and stared at the people in the bar. Most of them were younger than himself, and all of them were talking and laughing. He checked the door again. A young woman with black hair and round glasses had just entered, but it was still only twenty minutes to eight—far too early for Marty. He pulled out his handkerchief and wiped his forehead, wondering if he ought to go back into the bathroom and splash more water on his face. He felt a little bit hot. Still okay, but just a tad hot. He advised himself to think about all those times he had gone to fancy places with Veronica, and shoved his hands in his pockets and tried to remember the exact feelings of walking into Quaglino's beside his tall, executive girlfriend . . .

"Bob? Bob Bunting?" someone said in his ear, and he jumped forward as if he had been jabbed with a fork. His chest struck the table, and his glass wobbled. He stabbed out a hand to grasp the drink and knocked it over. Clear liquid spilled out and darkened the tablecloth. Two large olives rolled across the table, and one of them fell to the floor. Bunting uttered a short, mortifying shriek. The woman who had spoken to him was laughing. She placed a hand on his arm. He whirled around on his chair, bumping his elbow on the table's edge, and found the black-haired woman who had just entered the restaurant staring down at him with a quizzical alarm.

"After all that, I hope you are Bob Bunting," she said.

Bunting nodded. "I hope I am, too," he said. "I don't seem to be too sure, do I? But who are you? Do we know each other?"

"I'm Marty," she said. "Weren't you waiting for me?"

"Oh," he said, understanding everything at last. She was a short, round-faced woman with a restless, energetic quality that made Bunting feel tired. Her eyes were very blue and her lipstick was very red. At the moment she seemed to be inwardly laughing at him. "Excuse me, my goodness," he said, "yes, of course, nice to meet you." He got to his feet and held out his hand.

She took it, not bothering to conceal her amusement. "You been here long?"

She had a strong New York accent.

"A little while," he confessed.

"You wanted to check me out, didn't you?"

"Well, no. Not really." He thought with longing of his room, his bed, his wall of bottles, and *The Lady in the Lake*. "How did you know who I was?"

"Frank described you, how else? He said you'd be dressed like a lawyer and that you looked a little shy. Do you want to have another drink here, now that I made you spill that one? I'll have one, too."

He took her coat to the checkroom, and when he returned he found a fresh martini at his place, a glass of white wine in front of Marty, and a clean tablecloth on the table. She was smiling at him. He could not decide if she was unusually pretty or just disconcerting.

"You did get here early to check me out, didn't you?" she asked. "If you didn't like the way I looked, you could duck out when I went into the bar."

"I'd never do that."

"Why not? I would. Why do you think I got here so early? I wanted to check you out. Blind dates make me feel funny. Anyhow, I knew who you were right away, and you didn't look so bad. I was afraid you might be real gonzo, from what Frank said about you, but I knew that anybody as nervous as you couldn't really be gonzo."

"I'm not nervous," Bunting said.

"Then why did you go off like a bomb when I said your name?"

"You startled me."

"Well, I couldn't have startled you if you weren't nervous. It's okay. You never saw me before either. So tell me the truth—if you saw me walk in the door, and if I didn't notice you, would you have cut out? Or would you have gone through with it?"

She raised her glass and sipped. Her eyes were so blue that the color had leaked into the whites, spreading a faint blue nimbus around the irises. He saw for the first time that she was wearing a black dress that fit her tightly, and that her eyebrows were firm black lines. She seemed exotic, almost mysterious, despite her forthright manner. She was, he realized, startlingly good-looking. Then he suddenly saw her naked, a vision of smooth white skin and large soft breasts.

"Oh," he said, "I would have gone through with it, of course."

"Why are you blushing? Your whole face just turned red."

He shrugged in an agony of embarrassment. He was certain that she knew what he had been thinking. He gulped at his drink.

"You're not exactly what I expected, Bob," she said in a very dry voice.

"Well, you're not quite what I expected, either," was all he could think to say. Unable to look at her, he was sitting straight upright on his chair and facing the happy crowd in the bar. How were those men able to be so casual? How did they think of things to say?

"How well do you know Frank and Lindy?" she asked.

"I work with Frank." He glanced over at her, then looked back at the happy, untroubled people in the bar. "We're in the same office."

"That's all? You don't see him after work?"

He shook his head.

"You made a big impression on Frank," she said. "He seems to think . . . Bob, would you mind looking at me, Bob? When I'm talking to you?"

Bunting cleared his throat and turned to face her. "Sorry."

"Is anything wrong? Anything I should know about? Do I look just like the person you hated most in the fourth grade?"

"No, I like the way you look," Bunting said.

"Frank acted like you were this real swinger. This wild man. 'Long fangs, Marty,' he says to me, 'this guy has got long, long fangs,' you know how Frank talks. This means he likes you. So I figured if Frank *Herko* liked you so much, how bad could you be? Because Frank Herko acts like a real asshole, but underneath, he's a sweetheart." She sipped her wine and continued looking at him coolly. "So I got all dolled up and took the train into Manhattan, figuring at least I might get some fun out of the evening, go to some clubs, maybe a good restaurant, meet this wild man, if I have to fight him off when it's all over, well, I can do that. But it's not like that, is it? You don't know any clubs—you don't really go out much, do you, Bobby?"

Bunting stood up and took a twenty out of his wallet. He was blushing so hard his ears felt twice their normal size. He put the money down on the table and said, "I'm sorry, I didn't mean to waste your time."

Marty grinned. "Hold on, will you?" She reached across the table and grabbed his wrist. "Don't act that way, I'm just saying you're different from what I expected. Sit down. Please. Don't be so . . ."

Bunting sat down, and she let go of his wrist. He could still feel her fingers around him. The sensation made him feel slightly dizzy. He was looking at her pale clever pretty face.

"So *scared*," she said. "There's no reason for that. Let's just sit here and talk. In a while, we can go out and eat somewhere. Or we could even eat here. Okay?"

"Sure," he said, recovering. "We can just sit here and talk."

"So say something," Marty said. She frowned. "Do you always sweat this much? Or is it just me?"

He wiped his forehead. "I, uh, had a kind of funny week. Things have been affecting me in an odd way. I broke up with somebody a little while ago."

"Frank told me. Me, too. That's why he thought we ought to meet each other. But I think you ought to think of another topic."

"I don't have any topics," Bunting said.

"Guys all talk about sports. I like sports. Honest, I really do. I'm a Yankee fan from way back. And I like Islanders games. But basketball is my favorite sport. Who do you like? Larry Bird, I bet—you look like a Larry Bird type. Guys who like Larry Bird never like Michael Jordan. I don't know why."

"Michael who?" Bunting said.

"Okay, football. Phil Simms. The Jets. The good old Giants. Lawrence Taylor."

"I hate football."

"Okay, what about music? What kind of music do you like? You ever hear house music?"

Bunting imagined a house like a child's drawing, two windows on either side of a simple door, dancing to notes spilling from the chimney attached to its pointed roof.

Marty tilted her head and smiled at him. "On second thought, I bet you like classical music. You sit around in your place and listen to symphonies and stuff like that. You make yourself a little martini and then you put on a little Beethoven, right? And then you're right in the groove. I like classical music sometimes too, I think it's good."

"People are too interested in sports and music," Bunting said. "All they talk about is some game they saw on television, or some series, or some record. It's like there isn't anything else."

"You forgot one," she said. "You forgot money."

"That's right—they pay too much attention to money."

"So what should they pay attention to?"

"Well . . ." He looked up, for the moment wholly distracted from his embarrassment and discomfort. It seemed to him that there existed an exact answer to this question, and that he knew it. "Well, more important things." He raised his hands, as if he could catch the answer while it flew past him.

"More important than sports, television, and music. Not to mention money."

"Yes. None of that is important at all—it's worthless, when you come right down to it."

"So what is important?" She looked at him with her eyes narrowed behind her big glasses. "I'm dying to hear about it."

"Um, what's inside us."

"What's *inside* us? What does that mean?"

Bunting made another large vague gesture with his hands. "I sort of think God is inside us." This sentence came out of his mouth by itself, and it startled him as much as it did Marty. "Something like God is inside us. Outside of us, too." Then he found a way to say it. "God is what lets us see."

"So, you're religious."

"No, the funny thing is, I'm not. I haven't gone to church in twenty-five years." He flattened his hands against his eyes for a moment, then took them away. His whole face had a naked look, as if he had just taken off a pair of eyeglasses. "Let's say you're just walking down the street. Let's say you're not thinking about anything in particular. You're trying to get to work, and you're even a little worried about something—the rent, or the way your boss is acting, or something. You're absolutely, completely, inside the normal world. And then something happens—a car backfires, or a woman with a gorgeous voice starts to sing behind you—and suddenly you see what's really there—that everything, absolutely everything is alive. The whole world is one living thing, and that living thing is just *beating* with life. Every rock, every blade of grass, every speck of dust, every raindrop, even the windshield wipers and the headlights, it's like you're floating in space, no, it's like you're gone, disappeared, like you don't really exist anymore in the old way at all because you're just the same as everything else, no more alive, no more conscious, *just* as alive, *just* as conscious, everything is overflowing, light streams and pours out of every little detail . . ." Bunting fought down the desire to cry.

"I'll give you one thing, it makes a double play against Los Angeles sound pretty small."

"The double play would be part of it too," he said, understanding that, too, now. "Us sitting here is part of it. We're talking, that's a big part of it. If churches were about what they're supposed to be about, they'd open their windows and concentrate on us sitting here. Look at that, they'd say, look at all that beauty and feeling, look at that radiance, that incredible radiance, that's what's holy. But do you know what they say instead?" He hitched his chair closer to her, and took another big gulp of his drink. "Maybe they really know all this, I think some of them must know it, it must be their secret, but instead, what they say is just the *opposite*. The world is evil and ugly, they say—turn your back on it. You need blood, they say—you need sacrifice. We're back to savages jumping around in front of a fire. Kill that child, kill that goat, the body is sinful and the world is bad. Ignore it long enough and you'll get a reward in heaven. People get old believing this, they get sick and forgetful, they begin to fade out of the world without ever having seen it."

Marty was looking at him intently, and her mouth was open. She blinked when he stopped talking. "I can see why Frank is impressed with you. He can go on like this for hours. You must have a great time at work."

"We never talk about this at work. I never talked about it with any-body until now." It came to Bunting that he was sitting at a table with a pretty woman. He was in the world and enjoying himself. He was on a date, talking. It was not a problem. He was like the men in the bar behind him, talking to their dates. He wondered if he could tell Marty about the baby bottles.

"Didn't you talk like this with your old girlfriend?"

Bunting shook his head. "She was only interested in her career. She would have thought I was crazy."

"Well, I think you're crazy too," Marty said. "But that's okay. Frank is crazy in another way, and among other, less harmless things, my old boyfriend was crazy about doo-wop music. Johnny Maestro? He wor-shipped Johnny Maestro. He thought it summed it all up."

"I suppose it did," Bunting said. "But no more than anything else."

"Do you get a lot of this stuff out of books? Do you read a lot?"

Another flare went off in Bunting's brain, and he took another gulp of his drink, waving his free hand in the air, semaphoring that she hadn't quite understood matters, but that he had plenty to say about her question. "Books!" he said after he had swallowed. "You wouldn't believe what I've . . ." He shook his head. She was smiling at him. "Think about what reading a book is really *like*. A novel, I mean—

you're reading a novel. What's happening? You're in another world, right? Somebody made it, somebody selected everything in it, and so suddenly you're not in your apartment anymore, you're walking along this mountain road, and you're sitting on top of a horse. You look out and see things. What you see is partly what the guy put there for you to see, and partly what you make up on the basis of that. Everything means something, because it was all chosen. Everything you see, touch, feel, smell, and everything you notice and everything you think, is organized to take you somewhere. Do you see? Everything *glows*! In paintings too, don't you suppose? There's some force pushing away at all the details, making them *bulge*, making them *sing*. Because the act of painting or writing about a leaf or a house or whatever, if the guy does it right, amounts to saying: I saw the amazing overflowing of life in this thing, and now you can see it too. So wake up!" He gestured with both arms, like a conductor calling for a great swell of sound.

"Have you ever thought about becoming a teacher?" Marty asked. "You get all fired up, Bobby, you'd be great in a classroom."

"I just want to say something." Bunting held his hands over his heart. "This is the greatest night of my life. I never really felt like this before. At least, not since I was really small, three or four, or something. I feel wonderful!"

"Well, you're certainly not nervous anymore," Marty said. "But I still say you're religious."

"I never heard of any religion that preaches about this, did you? If you hear of one, let me know and I'll sign up. It has to be a church that says, Don't come in here, stay outside in the weather. Wake up and open your eyes. What we do in here, with the crosses and stuff, that's just to remind you of what's *really* sacred."

"You're something else," she said, laughing. "You and Frank Herko are quite the pair. The two of you must get that office all stirred up."

"Maybe we should." For a giddy instant, Bunting saw himself and shaggy, overbearing Frank Herko conducting loud debates over the partition. He would speak as he was speaking now, and Frank would respond with delight and abandon, and the two of them would carry on their talks after work, in apartments and restaurants and bars. It was a vision of a normal and joyous life—he would call up Frank Herko at his apartment, and Frank would say, Why don't you come over? Bring Marty, we'll go out for dinner, have a little fun.

Bunting and Marty were smiling at each other.

"You're sort of like Frank, you know. You like saying outrageous things. You're not at all the way I thought you were when I came in. I mean, I liked you, and I thought you were interesting, but I thought it might be kind of a long evening. You don't mind my saying that now? I really don't want to hurt your feelings, and I shouldn't be, because you seem so different now. I never heard anybody talk that way before, even Frank. It might be crazy, but it's fascinating."

Nobody had ever told Bunting he was fascinating before this, especially not a young woman staring at him with wonderful blue eyes past a swerve of pure black hair. He realized, and this was one of the most triumphant moments of his life, that he could very likely bring this amazing young woman back to his apartment.

Then he remembered what his apartment—his room—actually looked like, and what he had done to it.

"Don't start blushing again," Marty said. "It's just a compliment. You're an interesting man, and you hardly know it." She reached across the table and rested her fingers lightly on the back of his hand. "Why don't we finish these drinks and order some food? It's Friday. We don't have to go anywhere else. This is fine. I'm enjoying myself."

Marty's light cool fingers felt as heavy as anvils on his skin. A wave of pure guilt made him pull his hand away. She was still smiling at him, but a shadow passed behind her wonderful eyes. "I have to do something," he said. "I shouldn't have let myself forget," he said. "There must be a telephone in this place somewhere." He began looking wildly around the restaurant.

"You have to call someone?"

"It's urgent, I'm sorry, I can't believe I've been acting like . . ." Bunting wiped his face and pushed himself away from the table and stood up. He moved clumsily toward the people standing at the bar.

"Like *what*?" she asked, but he was already pushing clumsily through the crowd.

Bunting found a pay telephone outside the men's room. He scooped change out of his pockets and stacked it up. Then he dialed the area code for Battle Creek and his parents' number. He dropped most of the money. The phone rang and rang, and Bunting fidgeted and cupped his ear against the roar of voices from the bar.

Finally his mother answered.

"Mom! How are you? How'd it go?"

"Yes, who is this?"

"Bobby. It's Bobby."

"Bobby isn't here," she said.

"No, *I'm* Bobby, Mom. How are you feeling?"

"Fine. Why wouldn't I feel fine?"

"Did you see the doctor today?"

"Why would I see him?" She sounded sharp, almost angry. "That was stupid. I don't have to see *him*, listen to your father gripe about the money for the rest of his life."

"Didn't you have an appointment?"

"Did I?"

"I think so," he said, feeling his grip on reality loosen.

"Well, what if I did? This isn't Russia. Your father wanted to bully me about the money, that's all it is. I pretended—just sat in my car, that's all I did. He wants to humiliate me, that's what it is, thirty-seven years of humiliation."

"He didn't go with you?"

"He *couldn't*, there wasn't any *appointment*. And when I came home, I drove and drove, I kept seeing Kellogg's and the sanitarium, but I never knew where I was and so I had to keep driving, and then, like a miracle, I saw I was turning into our street, and I was so mad at him I swore I'd never ever go to that doctor again."

"You got lost driving home?" His body felt hot all over.

"Now, you stop talking about that. You sound like him. I want to know about that beautiful girlfriend of yours. Tell me about Veronica. Someday you have to bring that girl home, Bobby. We want to meet her."

"I'm not going out with her anymore," Bunting said. "I wrote you."

"You're just like that horrible old crosspatch. 'Brutal' is the word for him. Brutal all his life, brutal brutal brutal. Says things just to confuse me, and then he gets upset when I want to do a little wash, acts as if I haven't been his punching bag for the past thirty years—"

Bunting heard only heavy breathing for a moment. "Mom?"

"I don't know who you are, and I wish you'd stop calling," she said. Bunting heard his father's voice, loud and indistinct, and his mother said, "Oh, you can leave me alone, too." Then he heard a startled outcry.

"Hello, what's going on?" Bunting said. All the sounds from Battle Creek had dwindled into a muffled silence overwhelmed by the din from the bar. His father had put his hand over the mouthpiece. This almost certainly meant he was yelling. "Someone talk to me!" Bunting shouted, and the yelling in the bar abruptly ceased. Bunting hunched his shoulders and tried to burrow into the hood over the telephone.

"All right, who is this?" his father asked.

"Bob, it's Bobby," he said.

"You've got some nerve, calling out of the blue, but you never did care much about what anybody else might be going through, did you? Look, I know you're sensitive and all that, but this isn't the best time to give us bullshit about your little girlfriends. You got your mother all upset, and she was upset enough already, believe me." He hung up.

Bunting replaced the receiver. He was not at all clear about what was going on in Battle Creek. It seemed that his mother had forgotten who he was during the course of their worrying conversation. He pushed his way through the men and women at the bar and came out into the restaurant where a young woman with a round face framed in black hair was looking at him curiously from one of the rear tables. It took him a moment to remember her name. He tried to smile at her, but his face would not work right.

"What happened to you?" she asked.

"This isn't . . . um, I can't, ah . . . I'm afraid that I have to go home."

Her face hardened with a recognition: in an instant, all the sympathy dropped away. "We were having a nice time, and you go make a phone call, and now everything's off?"

Bunting shrugged and looked at his feet. "It's a personal thing—I can't really explain it—but, uh—"

"But, *uh*, that's it? What happened to, 'This is the greatest night of my life'?" she squinted at him. "Oh, boy. I guess I get it. You ran out, didn't you? You thought you could get through an evening, and then you realized you can't, so you called your guy. And everything you said wasn't really you, it was just—that crap you take. You're pathetic."

"I don't know what you're talking about," Bunting said. His misery seemed to be compounding itself second by second.

"I know guys like you," she said, her eyes blazing at him. "One in particular." She held out an imperious hand for the checkroom ticket. "I know a few inadequate children who can't handle relationships, one in particular, but I thought I was all done hanging around a guy who spent half the night making phone calls and the other half in the bathroom—I guess I really am done! Because I'm going!" She retrieved her coat and shoved her arms into its sleeves. People at other tables were staring at them.

"You must have the wrong idea about something," Bunting said.

"Oh, that's good," she said. She buttoned her coat. Her small face seemed cold, a cold white stone with a red smear near the bottom. "Sleep on it, if you do sleep, see if you can come up with something a little snappier." Marty walked quickly through the tables, passed the lounging headwaiter, and went outside. Frigid air swept into the restaurant as the door closed on empty darkness.

Bunting paid for the drinks and noticed that the waitress would not look directly at him. An artificial quiet had settled on the bar. Bunting put on his coat and wandered outside, feeling lost and aimless. He had no appetite. He buttoned up his coat and watched cars stream toward him down the wide avenue. A short distance to his left, the avenue ended at a massive arch which stood at the entrance to a park. He had no idea where he was. That didn't matter: all places were the same place. Traffic continued to come toward him out of the dark, and he realized that he was in Battle Creek, Michigan—he was back in Battle Creek, downtown in the business district, a long way from home.

10

When Jesus flew to heaven he had wounds in his hands and feet, they had torn his flesh and killed him on a cross, there was blood on the ground, and when he rolled the rock away in his dusty robe he left bloody palm prints on the rock.

Jesus said, So you have some fucking doubts, Bobby? Take a look at this. And opened his clothes and showed Bunting the great open wound in his side. Go on, he said, stick your goddamned hand in it, stick your mitt in there, how about them goddamn apples, Bobby? You get it, you get it now, good buddy? This shit is for real.

And Jesus walked on his bleeding feet through Battle Creek, leaving his bloodstains on sidewalks unseen by assholes who had never been wounded by anything more serious than a third martini, and who had never wounded anyone else with a weapon deadlier than an insult. There was a savage grin on his face. He slammed the palm of a hand against the side of one of those little houses, and blood squirted onto the peeling paint. Holy holy holy. The palm print was holy, the flecks of paint were holy, the cries of pain and sorrow too.

Go home, you little asshole, said Jesus. You're never gonna get it, never. But neither do most people, so that part's okay. Go home and read a book. That'll do—it's a piss-poor way to get there, but I guess it's about the best you can do.

Suffer the little children, said Jesus, suffer everybody else, too. You think this shit is easy?

Still muttering to himself, Jesus turned off on a side street, his bloody footprints following after, his thin robe whipping around him in the wind, and Bunting saw the frame houses of working-class Battle Creek all around. Some were covered with hideous brick-face, some with grainy tar paper that peeled away from the seams around the window frames. Most of these houses had porches where skeletal furniture turned brittle in the cold, and birdbaths and shrines to Mary stood in a few tiny front yards. Before one of these unhappy two-story frame houses his parents had posed for the only photograph ever taken of the two of them together, a testament to ignorance, incompatibility, resentment, violence, and disorder. His father scowls out from under the brim of his hat, his mother twitches. Holy holy holy. From this chaos, from this riot, the overpowering sacred bounty. He was standing on his old street, Bunting realized, the ultimate sample in this dwindled and partial world of blazing real life. Jesus' bloody palm print shone from the ugly wall, even uglier now in winter when the dirty chipping paint looked like a skin disease. Here was his childhood, which he had not been intended to escape—its smallness and meanness had been supposed to accompany him always.

Bunting stared at the shabby building in which his childhood had happened, and heard the old screams, the grunts and shrieks of pain and passion, sail through the thin walls. This was the bedrock. His childhood reached forth and touched him with a cold, cold finger. He could not survive it now, he could not even bear to witness a tenth of it. But neither could he live without it.

He turned around and found that he had left Battle Creek and walked all the way from Washington Square to the Upper West Side. Across the street, on the other side of several hundred jostling, honking cars, stood his apartment building. Home again.

11

Bunting's weekend was glacial. He had trouble getting out of bed, and remembered to eat only when he realized that the sun had gone down. He felt so tired it was difficult to walk to the bathroom, and fell asleep in front of the television, watching programs that seemed without point or plot. It was all one great formless story, a story with no internal connections, and its incoherence made it watchable.

On Sunday afternoon Bunting scratched his face and remembered that he had not bathed or shaved since Friday evening. He took off the clothes he'd worn since Saturday morning, showered, shaved, and dressed in gray slacks and a sport jacket, put on his coat, and went around the corner through brittle wintry air to the diner. The man at the register and the counterman treated him normally. He ordered something from the enormous menu, ate what he ordered without tasting it, and forgot it as soon as he was done. When he walked back out into the cold he realized that he could buy more baby bottles. He had to finish the wall he had begun, and there was another wall he could cover with bottles, if he chose—he was under no real compulsion to do this, he knew, but it would be like finishing an old project. Bunting had always liked to complete his projects. There were several other things he could do with baby bottles, too, once he got started.

He walked to the cash machine and took out three hundred dollars, leaving only five hundred and change in his account. At the drugstore he bought a gross of mixed bottles and another gross of mixed nipples, and asked for them to be delivered. Then he walked again out into the cold and turned toward his building. His entire attitude toward the bottles, even the redecoration project, had changed—he could remember his first, passionate purchases, the haste and embarrassment, the sheer weight of the need. Bunting supposed that this calm, passive state was a dull version of what most people felt all the time. It was probably what they called sanity. Sanity was what took over when you got too tired for anything else.

He stopped off at the liquor store and bought two liters of vodka and a bottle of cognac.

This time when he walked out into the cold, it came to him that Veronica had never existed. Of course he had always known at some level that his executive, Swiss-born mistress was a fantasy, but it seemed to him that he had never quite admitted this to himself. He had lived with his stories for so long he had forgotten that they had begun as an excuse for not going back to Battle Creek.

Battle Creek had come to him instead, two nights ago. *Suffer the little children, suffer everybody, suffer suffer.* The furious, complaining Jesus had shown what was real. This dry, reduced world was what was left when he stormed back into his cave to lie down dead again.

Bunting walked past the leavings of BANGO SKANK and JEEPY and let himself back into his room. He switched on the television and poured cold vodka into an Ama. Words and phrases of unbelievable ugliness, language murdered by carelessness and indifference, dead bleeding language, came from the television. People all over the nation listened to stuff like this every day and heard nothing wrong with it. Bunting watched some of the action on the screen for a moment, trying to make at least some kind of primitive sense out of it. A blond man ran down a flight of stairs and punched another man in the face. The second man, taller and stronger than the first, collapsed and fell all the way down the stairs. A car sped down a highway, and lights flashed. Bunting sighed and snapped off the television.

Bunting wandered through the stacks of magazines and newspapers and picked up *The Lady in the Lake.* He wondered if the buzzing of the delivery boy would pull him out of the book and then remembered with a deepening sense of gloom—with something very close to despair—that he probably would not have to be pulled out of the book. He was sane now. Or, if that was an error in terminology, he was in the same relationship to the world that he had been in before everything changed.

Bunting held his breath and opened the book. He let his eyes drop to the lines of print, which resolutely stayed on the page. He sighed again and sat down on the bed to read until the new baby bottles arrived.

It was another book—the details were the same but all the essentials had changed. Chris Lavery was apparently still alive, and Muriel Chess had been found in Little Fawn Lake, not in the bathroom of a mountain cabin. Crystal Kingsley was Derace Kingsley's wife, not his mother. All the particulars of weather, appearances, and speech, the entire atmosphere of the book, came to Bunting in a flawed and ordinary way, sentence by sentence. For Bunting, this way of reading was like having lost the ability, briefly and mysteriously gained, of being able to fly. He stumbled along after the sentences, remembering what had been. When the buzzer rang he put the book down with relief, and spent the rest of the night gluing bottles to his walls.

On Monday morning, Frank Herko came into his cubicle even before going into his own. His eyes looked twice their normal size, and his forehead was still red from the cold. Static electricity had given his hair a lively, unbridled, but stiff look, as if it had been starched or deep-fried. "What the hell went on?" he yelled as soon as he came in. Bunting could feel the attention of everyone else in the Data Entry room focusing on his cubicle.

"I don't know what you mean," he said.

Herko actually bared his teeth at him. His eyes grew even larger. He unzipped his down jacket, ripped it off his body, and startled Bunting by throwing it to the floor. "Then I'll try to tell you," he said, speaking so softly he was nearly whispering. "My girlfriend Lindy has a girlfriend. A person named Marty. This is a person she likes. Particularly likes. You could even go so far as to say that Marty is a person very dear to my friend Lindy, and that what affects Marty affects my girlfriend Lindy. So the little ups and downs of this person Marty's life, who by the way is also kind of dear to me, though not of course to the extent that she is dear to my friend, these ups and downs affect my friend Lindy and therefore, in a roundabout sort of way, also affect me." Frank leaned forward from the waist and extended his arms. "SO! When Marty has a bad experience with a guy she calls a sleazeball and blames this experience on her friend Lindy Berman and Lindy Berman's friend Frank HERKO, then Frank HERKO winds up eating SHIT! Is this starting to fall into place, Bobby? Are you starting to get why I asked you what the HELL happened?" He planted his fists on his hips and glowered, then shook his head and made a gesture with one arm that implored the universe to witness his frustration.

"It just didn't work out," Bunting said.

"Oh, is that right? You don't suppose you could go into a little more detail on that, could you?"

Bunting tried to remember why his date had ended. "My mother didn't make her doctor's appointment."

Herko stared at him pop-eyed. "Your mother . . . Does that make sense to you? You're out with a girl, you're supposed to be having a good time, you say, Gee, Mom didn't get over to the doctor's, I guess I better SPLIT?"

"I'm sorry," Bunting said. "I'm not in a very good mood right now. I don't like it when you yell at me. That makes me feel very uneasy. I wish you'd leave me alone."

"Boy, you got it," Herko said. "You have got it, Bobby, in spades. But there are a few vital bits of information it has become extremely necessary for you to have in your possession, Bobby, and I'm going to give them to you."

He stepped backward and saw his down jacket on the floor. He raised his eyes as if the jacket had disobediently conjured itself off a hook and thrown itself on the carpet. He leaned over and picked it up, ostentatiously folded it in half, and draped it over one arm. All this reminded Bunting sharply, even sickeningly, of his father. The affectation of delicacy had been a crucial part of his father's arsenal of scorn. Herko had probably reminded him of his father from the beginning; he had just never noticed it.

"One," Frank said. "I assumed you were going to act like a man. Funny, huh? I thought you would know that a man remembers his friends, and a man is grateful to his friends. A man does not act like a goddamn loony and bring down trouble on his friends. Two. A man does not run out on a woman. A man does not leave a woman in the middle of a restaurant—he acts like a MAN, damn it, and conducts himself like he knows what he's doing. Three. She thought you were a drug addict, did that get through to you?"

"I didn't leave her alone, she left me alone," Bunting said.

"She thought you were a junkie!" Herko was yelling again. "She thought I fixed her up with a fucking cocaine freak, right after she broke up with a guy who put a restaurant, a house, and a car up his nose! That's . . ." Herko raised his arms and lifted his head, trying to find the right word. "That's . . . MISERABLE! DISGUSTING!"

Bunting stood up and grabbed his coat. His heart wanted to explode.

It was not possible to spend another second in his cubicle. Frank Herko had become ten feet tall, and every one of his breaths drained all the air from Bunting's own lungs. His screams bruised Bunting's ears. Bunting was buttoning up his coat before he realized that he was walking out of the cubicle and going home.

"Where the hell do you think you're going?" Herko yelled. "You can't leave!"

Unable to speak, nearly unable to see through the red mist that surrounded him, Bunting hurried out of the Data Entry room and fled down the corridor toward the elevator.

As soon as he got out of the building he felt a little better, but the woman who stood next to him on the uptown bus edged visibly away.

He could still hear Frank's huge, punishing voice. The world belonged to people like his father and Frank Herko, and people like himself lived in its potholes and corners.

Bunting got out of the bus and realized he was talking to himself only when he saw himself in a shopwindow. He blushed, and would have apologized, but no one around him met his eye.

He walked into the lobby of his apartment building and realized that it was not going to be possible for him to go back to work. He could never face Herko again, nor the other people who had overheard Frank's terrible yelling. That was finished. It was all over, like the fantasy of Veronica.

He got into the elevator, thinking that he seemed to be different from what he thought he was, though it was hard to tell if this was for the better or worse. In the old days, he would have been figuring out where to go to get another job, and now all he wanted to do was to get back into his room, pour himself a drink, and open a book. Of course all of these had also changed, room, drink, and book.

By the time he pushed his key into the lock he realized that he was no longer so frightened. In the psychic background, the waves of Frank Herko's voice crashed and rumbled on a distant beach. Bunting decided to give himself something like a week to recover from the events of the past few days, then to go out and look for another job. A week was a comfortable time. Monday to Monday. He hung up his coat and poured a drink into a clean Ama. Then he collapsed onto his bed and let his head fall back on the pillow. He groaned with satisfaction.

For a time he merely sucked at his bottle and let his body sink down into the wrinkled sheets. In a week, he told himself, he would get out of bed. He'd shave and dress in clean clothes and go outside and nail down a new job. He'd sit in front of another computer terminal and type in a lifetime's worth of mumbo jumbo. Soon there would be another Veronica or Carol, an Englishwoman or a Texan or a Cuban with an MBA from Wharton who was just finding her sea legs at Citibank. It would be the same thing all over again, and it would be terrible, but it would be okay. Sometimes it would even be sort of nice.

He sucked air, and lifted the bottle in surprise and found that it was empty. It seemed he had just declared a private holiday. Bunting rolled off the bed and went through the litter to the refrigerator. He dumped more vodka into the bottle. Vodka could get you through these little blue periods.

Bunting closed the freezer door, screwed the top onto the bottle, and held the nipple clenched between his teeth while he surveyed his room. One week, then back into the world. Bunting remembered his vision of the raging Jesus who had stormed through working-class Battle Creek. Suffer the little children.

He crossed to his bed and picked up the telephone. "Okay," he said, sucked from the bottle, and sat down. "Why not?"

"I ought to," he said.

He dialed the area code for Battle Creek, then the first three digits of his parents' number.

"Just thought I'd call," he said. He pulled more vodka into his mouth. "How are things? I don't want to upset anybody."

He dialed the last four numbers and listened to the phone ring in that little house so far away. Finally his father answered, not with "Hello," but with "Yeah."

"Hi, Dad, this is Bobby," he said. "Just thought I'd call. How are things?"

"Fine, why wouldn't they be?" his father said.

"Well, I didn't want to upset anybody."

"Why would we get upset? You know how your mother and I feel. We enjoy your calls."

"You do?"

"Well, sure. Don't get enough of 'em." There was a small moment of silence. "Got anything special on your mind, Bobby?"

It was as if the other night had never happened. This was how it went, Bunting remembered. If you forgot about something, it went away.

"I guess I was wondering about Mom," he said. "She sounded a little confused, the other night."

"Guess she was," his father said in an abrupt, dismissive voice. "She gets that way, now and then. I can't do anything about it, Bobby. How're things at work? Okay?"

"Things could be better," Bunting said, and immediately regretted it.

"Oh?" His father's voice was hard and biting. "What happened, you get fired? They fired you, didn't they? You screwed up and they fired you."

He could hear his father breathing hard, stoking himself up like a steam engine.

For a second it seemed that his father was right: he had screwed up, and they had fired him. "No," he said. "They didn't. I'm not fired."

"But you're not at work, either. It's nine o'clock in the morning here, so it's ten where you are, and Bobby Bunting is still in his apartment. So you lost your job. I knew it was gonna happen."

"No, it didn't," Bunting said. "I just left early."

"Sure. You left at eight-thirty on Monday morning. What do you call that, premature retirement? I call it getting fired. Just don't try to kid me about it, Bobby, I know what kind of person you are." He inhaled. "And don't expect any money from the old folks, okay? Remember all those meals at fancy restaurants and all those trips to Europe, and you'll know where your money went. If you ever had any, and if any of that stuff was true, which is something I have my doubts about."

"I took the day off," Bunting said. "Maybe I'll take off tomorrow, too. I'm taking care of a few details around here."

"Yeah, those kind of details are likely to take care of you, if you don't watch out."

"Look," said Bunting, stung. "I'm not fired. You hear me? Nobody fired me. I took the day off, because somebody got on my back. I don't know why you never believe me about anything."

"Do you want me to remind you about your whole life, back here? I know who you are, Bobby, let's leave it at that." His father inhaled again, so loudly it sounded as if he had put the telephone into his mouth. He was calming himself. "Don't get me wrong, you got your good points, same as everybody else. Maybe you ought to cut down on the wild social life, and stop trying to make up for never going out when you were a teenager, that's all. There's responsibilities. Responsibilities were never your strong point. But maybe you changed. Fine. Okay?"

Bunting felt as if he had been mugged on a dark street. It was like having Frank Herko yell at him about manhood all over again.

"Let me ask you something," he said, and pulled another mouthful of Popov out of the Ama. "Have you ever thought that you saw what reality really was?"

"Jesus wept."

"Wait. I mean something by that. Didn't you ever have a time when you saw that everything was alive?"

"Stop right there, Bobby, I don't want to hear this shit all over again. Just shut your trap, if you know what's good for you."

"What do you mean?" Bunting was almost yelling. "You mean I can't talk about it? Why can't I talk about it?"

"Because it's crazy, you dummy," his father said. "I want you to hear this, Bobby. You're nothing special. You got that? You worried your mother enough already, so keep your trap shut. For your own good."

Bunting felt astonishingly small. His father's voice had pounded him down into childhood, and he was now about three feet tall. "I can't talk anymore."

"Sleep it off and straighten up," his father said. "I mean it."

Bunting let the phone slide back into the cradle and grabbed for the Ama.

By the time he decided to get out of bed, he was so drunk that he had trouble navigating across the room and into the bathroom. As he peed, a phrase of his father's came back to him, and his urine splattered off the wall. *I don't want to hear this shit all over again.* All over again? If he weren't drunk, he thought, he would understand some fact he did not presently understand. But because he was drunk, he couldn't. Neither could he go outside. Bunting reeled back to his bed and passed out.

He woke up in the darkness with a headache and a vast, encompassing feeling of shame and sorrow. His life was nothing—it had always been nothing, it would always be nothing. There could be no release. The things he had seen, his experiences of ecstasy, the moment he had tried to describe to Marty, all were illusion. In a week he would go back to DataComCorp, and everything would return to normal. Probably they would just take him back—he wasn't important enough to fire. The only difference would be that Frank Herko would ignore him.

His whole problem was that he always forgot he was nothing special.

He promised himself that he would stop making things up. There would be no more imaginary love affairs. Bunting walked over to his window and looked down upon men and women in winter coats and hats who had normal, unglamorous, realistic lives. They looked cold. He got back into bed as if into a coffin.

12

The next morning, Bunting poured all of his vodka and cognac down the sink. He washed the dishes that had accumulated since his last washing. He looked at the sacks of garbage stowed away here and there, put the worst of them into large plastic bags, and took them all downstairs to the street. Back in his apartment, he swept and scrubbed for several hours. He changed his sheets and organized the magazines and newspapers into neat piles. Then he washed the bathroom floor and soaked in the tub for half an hour. He dried himself, brushed his teeth, combed his hair, and went straight back to bed. One of these days, he told himself, he would begin regular exercise.

The next day, he fought down the impulse to get another bottle of vodka and went to the supermarket on Broadway and bought a bag of carrots, a bag of celery, cartons of fruit juice and low-fat milk, a loaf of whole-grain bread, and a container of cholesterol-free margarine. Such a diet would keep the raging Jesus at bay.

Bunting spent most of Thursday lying down. He ate two carrots, three celery sticks, and one slice of dry bread. The bread tasted particularly good. He drank all of his fruit juice. In the evening, he tried switching on the television, but what came out was a stream of language so ugly it squeaked with pain. He fell soundly asleep at nine-thirty, was awakened by the sound of gunshots around three in the morning, and went promptly back to sleep.

On Friday he rose, showered, dressed in a conservative gray suit, ate a carrot and drank two or three ounces of papaya juice, put on his coat, and went outside for the first time since Monday morning. It was a bright brisk day, and the air, though not as fresh as that of the Montana plains in 1878 or Los Angeles in 1944, seemed startlingly clean and pure. Even on upper Broadway, Bunting thought he could smell the sea. The outline of a body had been chalked on a roped-off portion of the sidewalk, and as Bunting walked between two parked cars and stepped down onto unsanitary, untidy Broadway to walk alongside the traffic in the dazzling sunlight, he merely glanced at the white outline of the body and then firmly looked away and continued moving toward the traffic light and the open sidewalk.

Bunting walked for miles. He looked at the watches in Tourneau's windows, at the shoes in Church Brothers, the pocket calculators and compact disc players in a string of windows on lower Fifth Avenue. He came at length to Battery Park, and sat for a moment, looking out toward the Statue of Liberty. He was in the world, surrounded by people and things; the breeze that touched him touched everyone else, too. To Bunting, this world seemed new and almost undamaged, barren in a fashion only he had once known and now wished nearly to forget.

If a tree fell in the forest, it would not make a sound, no, none.

He began walking back uptown, remembering how he had once sat comfortably astride a horse named Shorty and how a worried perfume executive in a flannel suit had handed him a photograph of his mother. These experiences too could be sealed within a leaden casket and pushed overboard into the great psychic sea. They were aberrations: silent and weightless exceptions to a general rule. He would get old in his little room, drinking iced tea and papaya juice out of baby bottles. He would outlive his parents. Both of them. Everybody did that.

He took a bus up Broadway, and got off several blocks before his building because he wanted to walk a little more. On the corner a red-faced man in a shabby plaid coat sat on a camp chair behind a display of used paperback books. Bunting paused to look over the titles for Luke Short or a Max Brand, but saw mainly romance novels with titles like *Love's Savage Bondage* or *Sweet Merciless Kiss*. These titles, and the disturbing covers that came with them, threatened to remind Bunting of Marty seated across from him in a Greenwich Village restaurant, and he stepped back from the array to banish even the trace of this memory. A cover unlike the others met his eye, and he took in the title, *Anna Karenina*, and realized that he had heard of the book somewhere—of course he had never read it, it was nothing like the sort of books he usually read, but he was sure that it was supposed to be very good. He bent down and picked it up and opened it at random. He leaned toward the page in the light of the street lamp and read. *Before the early dawn all was hushed. Nothing was to be heard but the night sounds of the frogs that never ceased in the marsh, and the horses snorting in the mist that rose over the meadow before the morning.*

A thrill went through his body, and he turned the page and read another couple of sentences. *A slight wind rose, and the sky looked gray and sullen. The gloomy moment that usually precedes the dawn had come, the full triumph of light over darkness.*

Bunting felt a strange desire to weep: he wanted to stand there for a long time, leafing through this miraculous book.

A voice said, "World's greatest realistic novel, hands down."

Bunting looked up to meet the uncommonly intelligent gaze of the pudgy red-faced man in the camp chair. "That right?"

"Anybody says different, he's outta his fuckin' mind." He wiped his nose on his sleeve. "One dollar."

Bunting fished a dollar from his pocket and leaned over the rows of bright covers to give it to the man. "What makes it so great?" he asked.

"Understanding. *Depth* of understanding. Unbelievable responsiveness to detail linked to amazing clarity of vision."

"Yeah," Bunting said, "yeah, that's it." He clutched the book to his chest and turned away toward his apartment building.

He placed the book on his chair and sat on the bed and looked at its cover. In a few sentences, *Anna Karenina* had brought shining bits of the world to him—it was as close as you could get to the *Buffalo Hunter* experience and still be sane. Everything was so close that it was almost like being inside it. The two short passages he had read had brought the other world within him, which had once seemed connected to a great secret truth about the world as a whole, once again into being—had awakened it by touching it. Bunting was almost afraid of this power. He had to have the book, but he was not sure that he could read it.

Bunting jumped off the bed and ate two slices of whole-grain bread and a couple of carrots. Then he put his coat on and went back to the cash machine at the bank and to the drugstore across the street.

That night he lay in bed, enjoying the slight ache in his legs all the walking had given him and drinking warm milk from his old Prentiss. Beneath him, odd and uncomfortable but perfect all the same, was the construction he had made from eighty round plastic Evenflos and a tube of epoxy, a lumpy blanket of baby bottles that nestled into and warmed itself against his body. He had thought of making a sheet of baby bottles a long time ago, when he had been thinking about fakirs and beds of nails, and finally making the sheet now was a whimsical reference to that time when he had thought mainly about baby bottles. Bunting thought that sometime he could take off all the nipples and fill every one of the Evenflos beneath him with warm milk. It would be like going to bed with eighty little hot water bottles.

He held the slightly battered copy of *Anna Karenina* up before him and looked at the cover illustration of a train which had paused at a country station to take on fuel or food for its passengers. A snowstorm swirled around the front of the locomotive. The illustration seemed filled with the same luminous, almost alarming reality as the sentences he had found at random within the book, and Bunting knew that this sense of promise and immediacy came from the memory of those passages. Opening the book at all seemed to invoke a great risk, but if Bunting could have opened it to those sentences in which the horses snorted in the mist and the wind sprang up under a gray morning sky, he would have done so instantly. His eyes drooped, and the little train in the illustration threw upward a white flag of steam and jolted forward in the falling snow.

13

Monday morning the telephone rang with a fussy, importunate clamor that all but announced the presence of Frank Herko on the other end of the line—Bunting, who was in the fourth day of his sobriety, could imagine Herko grimacing and cursing as the phone went unanswered. Bunting continued chewing on a slice of dry bread, and looked at his watch. It was ten o'clock. Herko had finally admitted that he was not coming in again, and was trying to bully him back to DataComCorp. Bunting had no intention of answering the telephone. Frank Herko and the job in the Data Entry room dwindled as they shrank into the past. He swallowed the last of his papaya juice and reminded himself to pick up more fruit juices that morning. At last, on the thirteenth ring, the telephone fell silent.

Bunting thought of the horses snorting in the cold morning mist when everything else was silent but the frogs, and a shiver went through him.

He stood up from the table and looked around his room. It was pretty radical. He thought it might look a little better if he got rid of all the newspapers and magazines—his room would never look ordinary anymore, but what he had done would mean more if the whole room was a little cleaner. The nipples of baby bottles jutted out from two walls, and a blanket of baby bottles, like a sheet of chain mail, covered his bed. If there were very little else in the room, Bunting saw, it would be as purposeful as a museum exhibit. He could get rid of the television. His room would be stark as a monument. And the monument would be to everything that was missing, but he didn't think it could be summed up easily.

He washed his plate and glass and put them on the drying rack. Then he unplugged his television set, picked it up, unlocked his door, and carried the set out into the hall. He took it down past the elevators and set it on the floor. Then he turned around and hurried back into his apartment.

Bunting spent the morning stuffing the magazines and newspapers into black garbage bags and taking them downstairs to the sidewalk. On his fourth or fifth trip, he noticed that the television had disappeared from the hallway. Bango Skank or Jeepy had a new toy. Gradually, Bunting's room lost its old enclosed look. There were the two walls covered with jutting bottles, the wall with the windows that overlooked the brownstones, and the kitchen alcove. There was his bed and the bedside chair. He had uncovered another chair which had been concealed under a mound of papers, and this too he took out into the hallway for his neighbors.

When he came up from taking out the last of the garbage bags, he closed and locked the door behind him, pulled the police bar into its slot, and inspected his territory. A bare wooden floor, with dusty squares where stacks of newspapers had stood, extended toward him from the exterior wall. Without the newspapers, the distance between himself and the windows seemed immense. For the first time, Bunting noticed the streaks on the glass. The bright daylight turned them silver and cast long rectangles on the floor. Rigid baby bottles stuck out of the wall on both sides, to his right going toward the bathroom door and the kitchen alcove, and to his left, extending toward his bed. The wall above and beyond the bed was also covered with a mat of jutting baby bottles. A wide blanket of baby bottles, half-covering a flat pillow and a white blanket, lay across his bed.

After a lunch of carrots, celery, and bread, Bunting poured hot water and soap into a bucket and washed his floor. Then he poured out the filthy water, started again, and washed the table and the kitchen counters. After that he scrubbed even his bathroom—sink, toilet, floor, and tub. Large brown mildew stains blotted the shower curtain, and Bunting carefully unhooked it from the plastic rings, folded it into quarters, and took it downstairs and stuffed it into a garbage can.

He went to bed hungry but not painfully so, his back and shoulders tingling from the work, and his legs still aching from his long walk down the length of Manhattan. He lay atop the blanket of bottles, and pulled the sheet and woolen blanket over his body. He picked up the old paperback copy of *Anna Karenina* and opened it with trembling hands. For a second it seemed that the sentences were going to lift up off the page and claim him, and his heart tightened with both fear and some other, more anticipatory emotion. But his gaze met the page, and he stayed within his body and his room, and read. *And all at once she thought of the man crushed by the train the day she had first met Vronsky, and she knew what she had to do. With a light, rapid step she went down the steps that led from the water tank to the rails and stopped close to the approaching train.*

Bunting shuddered and fell into an exhausted sleep.

He was walking through a landscape of vacant lots and cement walls in a city street that might have been New York or Battle Creek. Broken bottles and pages from old newspapers lay in the street. Here and there across the weedy lots, tenements rose into the gray air. His legs ached, and his feet hurt, and it was difficult for him to follow the man walking along ahead of him, whose pale robe filled and billowed in the cold wind. The man was slightly taller than Bunting, and his dark hair blew about his head. Untroubled by the winter wind, the man strode along, increasing the distance between himself and Bunting with every step. Bunting did not know why he had to follow this strange man, but that was what he had to do. To lose him would be disaster—he would be lost in this dead, ugly world. Then he would be dead himself. His feet seemed to adhere to the gritty pavement, and a stiff wind held him back like a hand. As the man receded another several yards down the street, it came to Bunting that what he was following was an angel, not a man, and he cried out in terror. Instantly the being stopped moving and stood with his back to Bunting. The pale robe fluttered about him.

A certain word had to be spoken, or the angel would begin walking and leave Bunting in this terrible world. The word was essential, and Bunting did not know it, but he opened his mouth and shouted the first word that came to him. The instant it was spoken, Bunting knew that it was the correct word. He forgot it as soon as it left his throat. The angel slowly began to turn around. Bunting inhaled sharply. The front of the robe was red with blood, and when the angel held out the palms of his hands, they were bloody too. The angel's face was tired and dazed, and his eyes looked blind.

14

Tuesday morning, Bunting awoke with tears in his eyes for the wounded angel, the angel beyond help, and realized with a shock of alarm that he was in someone else's house. For a moment he was completely adrift in time and space, and thought he might actually be a prisoner in an attic—his room held no furniture except a table and chair, and the windows seemed barred. It came to him that he might have died. The afterlife contained a strong, pervasive odor of soap and disinfectant. Then the bars on the windows resolved into streaks and shadows, and he looked up to the bottles sticking straight out on the wall above his head, and remembered what he had done. The wounded angel slipped backward into the realm of forgotten things where so much of Bunting's life lay hidden, and Bunting moved his legs across the bumpy landscape of baby bottles, his fakir's bed of nails, and pulled himself out of bed. His legs, shoulders, back, and arms all ached.

Out on the street, Bunting realized that he was enjoying his unemployment. For days he had carried with him always a slight burn of hunger, and hunger was such a sharp sensation that there was a small quantity of pleasure in it. Sadness was the same, Bunting realized—if you could stand beside your own sadness, you could appreciate it. Maybe it was the same with the big emotions, love and terror and grief. Terror and grief would be the hardest, he thought, and for a moment uneasily remembered Jesus slapping a bloody palm against the side of his old house in Battle Creek. Holy holy holy.

The extremely uncomfortable thought came to him that maybe terror and grief were holy too, and that Jesus had appeared before him in a Battle Creek located somewhere north of Greenwich Village to convey this.

A white cloud of steam vaguely the size and shape of an adult woman rose up from a manhole in the middle of Broadway and by degrees vanished into transparency.

Bunting felt the world begin to shred around him and hurried into Fairway Fruits and Vegetables. He bought apples, bread, carrots, tangerines, and milk. At the checkout counter he imagined the little engine on the cover of the Tolstoy novel issuing white flags of steam and launching itself into the snowstorm. He had the strange sense, which he knew to be untrue, that someone was *watching* him, and this sense followed him back out onto the wide crowded street.

A woman-sized flag of white steam did not linger over Broadway, there was no sudden outcry, no chalked outline to show where a human being had died.

Bunting began walking up the street toward his building. Brittle pale light bounced from the roofs of cars, from thick gold necklaces, from sparkling shopwindows displaying compact discs. In all this brightness and activity lurked the mysterious sense that someone was still watching him—as if the entire street held its breath as it attended Bunting's progress up the block. He carried his bag of groceries through the cold bright air. Far down the block, someone called out in a belling tenor voice like a hunting horn, and the world's hovering attention warmed this beautiful sound so that it lingered in Bunting's ears. A taxi slid forward out of the shadows into a shower of light and revealed, in a sudden blaze of color, a pure and molten yellow. The white of a Chinese woman's eyes flashed toward Bunting, and her black hair swung lustrously about her head. A plume of white breath came from his mouth. It was as if someone had spoken secret words, instantly forgotten, and the words spoken had transformed him. The cold sidewalk beneath his feet seemed taut as a lion's hide, as resonant as a drum.

Even the lobby of his building was charged with anticipatory meaning.

He let himself into his bare room and carried the groceries to his bed and carefully took from the bag each apple and tangerine, the carrots, the milk. He balled up the bag and folded it neatly, and then poured the milk into three separate bottles. These he took back across his sparkling floor and set them beside the bed. Bunting took off his shoes, the suit he was wearing, his shirt and tie, and hung everything neatly in his closet. He returned to the bed in his underwear and socks. He turned back the bed and got in on top of the fakir's blanket of baby bottles and pulled the sheets and blanket up over his body without shaking off any of the objects on the bed. He doubled his pillow and switched on his lamp, though the cold light from outside still cast large bright rectangles on the floor. He leaned back under the reading light and arranged the fruit, carrots, bread, and bottles around him. He raised one of the bottles to his mouth and clamped the nipple between his teeth. There was a brisk pleasant coolness in the air that seemed to come from the world contained in the illustration on the cover of the book beside him.

Bunting drew in a mouthful of milk and picked up the copy of *Anna Karenina* from the bedside chair. He was trembling. He opened the book to the first page, and when he looked down at the lines of print, they rose to meet his eyes.

15

The super of the building looked down as he fit the key into the lock. He turned it, and both men heard the lock click open. The super kept looking at the floor. He was as heavy as Bunting's father, and the two sweaters he wore against the cold made him look pregnant. Bunting's father was wearing an overcoat, and his shoulders were hunched and his hands were thrust into its pockets. The breath of both men came out in clouds white as milk. Finally the super glanced up at Mr. Bunting.

"Go on, open it up," said Mr. Bunting.

"Okay, but there are some things you probably don't know," the super said.

"There's a lot I don't know," said Mr. Bunting. "Like what the hell happened, basically. And I guess you can't be too helpful on that issue, or am I wrong?"

"Well, there's other things, too," the super said, and opened the door at last. He stepped backward to let Mr. Bunting go into the room.

Bunting's father went about a yard and a half into the room, then stopped moving. The super stepped in behind him and closed the door.

"I fucking hate New York," said Mr. Bunting. "I hate the crap that goes on down here. Excuse me for getting personal, but you can't even keep the heat on in this dump." He was looking at the wall above the bed, where many of the bottles had been splashed, instead of directly at the bed itself. The bed had been cracked along a diagonal line, and the sheets, which were brown with dried blood, had hardened so that they would form a giant stiff V if you tried to take them off. Someone, probably the super's wife, had tried to mop up the blood alongside the cracked, folded bed. Chips of wood and bent, flattened bedsprings lay on the smeary floor.

"The tenants are all mad, but it's a good thing we got no heat," the super said. "I mean, we'll *get* it, when we get the new boiler, but he was here ten days before I found him. And I'll tell you something." He came cautiously toward Mr. Bunting, who took his eyes off the wall to scowl at him. "He made it easy for me. See that police bolt?"

The super gestured toward the long iron rod leaning against the wall beside the door frame. "He left it that way—unlocked. It was like he was doing me a favor. If he'd a pushed that sucker across the door, I'd a had to break down the door to get in. And I probably wouldn't have found him for two more weeks. At least."

"So maybe he made it easy for whoever did it," said Bunting's father. "Some favor."

"You saw him?"

Mr. Bunting turned back to look at the bottles above the bed. He turned slowly to look at the bottles on the front wall. "Sure I saw him. I saw his face. You want details? You can go fuck yourself, you want details. All they let me see was his face."

"It didn't look like anybody could have done that," the super said.

"That's real clever. Nobody did it." He saw something on the bed, and moved closer to it. "What's that?" He was looking at a shriveled red ball that had fallen into the bottom of the fold. A smaller, equally shriveled black ball had fallen a few feet from it.

"I think it's an apple," said the super. "He had some apples and tangerines, some bread. And if you look close, you can see little bits of paper stuck all over the place, like some book exploded. All the fruit dried out, but the book . . . I don't know what happened to the book. Maybe he tore it up."

"Could you maybe keep your trap shut?" Mr. Bunting took in the bottles above the bed for an entire minute. Then he turned and stared at the unstained bottles on the far wall. At last he said, "That is what I don't get. I don't get this with the baby bottles."

He glanced at the super, who quickly shook his head to indicate that he did not get it either.

"I mean, you ever get any other tenants down here who did this kind of thing?"

"I've never seen anyone do this before," said the super. "This is a new one. These bottles, I gotta take the walls down to get 'em off."

Mr. Bunting seemed not to have heard him. "First my wife dies— three weeks ago Tuesday. Then I hear about Bobby, who was always a fuckup, but who happens to be my only kid. When they decide to give it to you, they really give it to you good. They know how to do it. Now on top of everything else, here's this crap. Maybe I should of stayed away."

"You saw his face?" the super asked.

"Huh?"

"You said you saw his face."

Mr. Bunting gave the super the glance that one heavyweight gives another when they touch gloves.

"Well, I did too, when I found him," the super said. "I think you ought to know this. It's something, anyhow."

Mr. Bunting nodded, but did not alter his expression.

"When I came in . . . I mean, your son was dead, there was no doubt about that. I was in Korea, and I know what dead people look like. It looked like he got hit by a truck. It's crazy, but that's what I thought when I saw him. He was smashed up against the wall, and the bed was all smashed . . . Anyhow, what got me was the expression on his face. Whatever happened happened all right, and pardon me, but there's no way the police are ever going to arrest a couple of guys and get 'em on this, because no couple of guys could ever do what I saw in this room with my own eyes, believe me—"

He inhaled. Bunting's father was looking at him with flat impatient indifferent anger.

"But anyhow, the point is, the way your son looked. He looked happy. He looked like he saw the greatest goddamn thing in the world before *whatever* the hell it was happened to him."

"Oh, yeah," Mr. Bunting said. He was shaking his head. "Well, he didn't look that way when I saw him, but I'm not too surprised by what you say." He smiled for the first time since entering his son's room, and started shaking his head again. The smile made the other man's stomach feel small and cold. "His mother never understood it, but I sure did."

"What?" asked the super.

"He always thought he was some kind of a big deal." Mr. Bunting included the whole apartment in the gesture of his arm. "I couldn't see it."

"It's like that sometimes," the super said.

Bar Talk

It was an ordinary side-street bar, its only oddity being its placement on the second floor over an Indian restaurant. The patrons of the bar never entered the restaurant, and the customers and staff of the restaurant never came upstairs to the bar. The people who went there liked the long dark dull wood of the bar, the mirror, the wooden paneling and old beer signs on the walls. Few people bothered to look anymore at the photographs of poets and novelists who had been regular patrons once, or at the pictures of boxers and anonymous show-business people who had also been regulars, though at another time. Nobody ever looked out of the windows, which were the unremarkable windows of the apartment the bar had once been. It was as if the new regulars did not wish to be reminded they were above the street, once they had climbed the stairs.

These patrons were the people of the neighborhood, and they used the bar to escape from their apartments. None of them were young or rich, and most of them seemed to have settled into their various lives. They did not talk very much, except to Max, the bartender. Sometimes they seemed to be waiting for the bartender to return to them, so that they could continue their conversation, and to be impatient with the customer who had delayed him. Max was often the youngest person in the room—he wanted to be a stand-up comedian, and he liked to present his own experience in a comic, representative fashion.

In the autumn, nearly on the first cold day of the year, a new person started coming upstairs to the bar. He dressed in camouflage fatigues, a leather jacket, and worn black running shoes. The fatigues seemed faded from thousands of washings, and darker patches showed where tags and insignia had been torn off. He had long thick black hair, and he wore heavy round glasses. The man always carried a book with him, and he sat down at the far end of the bar, ordered a vodka on the rocks, and opened his book and read for a couple of hours. He had three or four drinks. Then he closed the book, paid up, and left. Pretty soon he was there every day. Some of the regulars started nodding hello to him, and he nodded back or smiled, but he never said anything, even to Max.

After a couple of weeks, he turned up one day in a black turtleneck and a pair of jeans so faded they were almost white. One of the regulars, a woman in her sixties named Jeannie, couldn't stand it anymore and went over to him when he opened his book. "What happened to the fatigues?" she asked. "You finally wash them?"

Max laughed.

"I have a lot of fatigues," the young man said.

"You must like to read," Jeannie said. "Every time I see you, you're reading something."

"I have a lot of books, too," he said, and laughed, startled by his own words.

Everybody else in the bar, even Max, was staring at them, and Jeannie inexplicably turned red. She stepped away from the young man, but he put his hand on hers, and she moved back beside him. Max drifted up the bar, and everybody else went back to their conversations or their silences. After a while Max began talking to an old merchant seaman named Billy Blue, and Billy began to laugh. Max turned to another of his regulars and told the same story, and both customers started laughing. Everybody forgot about Jeannie after a while. Then Max or someone else looked down at the end of the bar, and she was sitting there by herself. The man had dropped some bills on the bar and left without anybody noticing. Jeannie had a funny look on her face, as if she were remembering something she'd be happier to forget.

"That guy say something to you, Jeannie?" Max asked. "He get nasty?"

"No, nothing like that," Jeannie said. "He was fine. Really."

She stood up and carried her glass over to the window and looked down onto the street.

"He was fine?" Max said. "What the hell does that mean?"

"You wouldn't understand," Jeannie said. She turned away from all of them and looked down. Some of the regulars thought she might be crying, but they couldn't really tell. Everybody was sort of embarrassed for a little while, and then Jeannie finally turned away from the window and went back to her old place at the bar. The guy with the book never came back; after a couple of weeks, Jeannie began going to a bar further down the block.

A Short Guide to the City

The viaduct killer, named for the location where his victims' bodies have been discovered, is still at large. There have been six victims to date, found by children, people exercising their dogs, lovers or—in one instance—by policemen. The bodies lay sprawled, their throats slashed, partially sheltered by one or another of the massive concrete supports at the top of the slope beneath the great bridge. We assume that the viaduct killer is a resident of the city, a voter, a renter or property owner, a product of the city's excellent public school system, perhaps even a parent of children who even now attend one of its several elementary schools, three public high schools, two parochial schools, or single non-denominational private school. He may own a boat or belong to the Book-of-the-Month Club, he may frequent one or another of its many bars and taverns, he may have subscription tickets to the concert series put on by the city symphony orchestra. He may be a factory worker with a library ticket. He owns a car, perhaps two. He may swim in one of the city's public pools or the vast lake, punctuated with sailboats, during the hot moist August of the city.

For this is a Midwestern city, northern, with violent changes of season. The extremes of climate, from ten or twenty below zero to up around one hundred in the summer, cultivate an attitude of acceptance in its citizens, of insularity—it looks inward, not out, and few of its children leave for the more temperate, uncertain, and experimental cities of the eastern or western coasts. The city is proud of its modesty—it cherishes the ordinary, or what it sees as the ordinary, which is not. (It has had the same mayor for twenty-four years, a man of limited-to-average intelligence who has aged gracefully and has never had any other occupation of any sort.)

Ambition, the yearning for fame, position, and achievement, is discouraged here. One of its citizens became the head of a small foreign state, another a famous bandleader, yet another a Hollywood staple who for decades played the part of the star's best friend and confidant; this, it is felt, is enough, and besides, all of these people are now dead. The city has no literary tradition. Its only mirror is provided by its two newspapers, which have thick sports sections and are comfortable enough to be read in bed.

The city's characteristic mode is *denial*. For this reason, an odd fabulousness permeates every quarter of the city, a receptiveness to fable, to the unrecorded. A river runs through the center of the business district, as the Liffey runs through Dublin, the Seine through Paris, the Thames through London, and the Danube through Budapest, though our river is smaller and less consequential than any of these.

Our lives are ordinary and exemplary, the citizens would say. We take part in the life of the nation, history courses through us for all our immunity to the national illnesses: it is even possible that in our ordinary lives . . . We too have had our pulse taken by the great national seers and opinion-makers, for in us you may find . . .

Forty years ago, in winter, the body of a woman was found on the banks of the river. She had been raped and murdered, cast out of the human community—a prostitute, never identified—and the noises of struggle that must have accompanied her death went unnoticed by the patrons of the Green Woman Taproom, located directly above that point on the river where her body was discovered. It was an abnormally cold winter that year, a winter of shared misery, and within the Green Woman the music was loud, feverish, festive.

In that community, which is Irish and lives above its riverfront shops and bars, neighborhood children were supposed to have found a winged man huddling in a packing case, an aged man, half-starved, speaking a strange language none of the children knew. His wings were ragged and dirty, many of the feathers as cracked and threadbare as those of an old pigeon's, and his feet were dirty and swollen. *Ull! Li! Gack!* The children screamed at him, mocking the sounds that came from his mouth. They pelted him with rocks and snowballs, imagining that he had crawled up from that same river which sent chill damp—a damp as cold as cancer—into their bones and bedrooms, which gave them earaches and chilblains, which in summer bred rats and mosquitoes.

One of the city's newspapers is Democratic, the other Republican. Both papers ritually endorse the mayor, who though consummately political has no recognizable politics. Both of the city's newspapers also support the chief of police, crediting him with keeping the city free of the kind of violence that has undermined so many other American cities. None of our citizens goes armed, and our church attendance is still far above the national average.

We are ambivalent about violence.

We have very few public statues, mostly of Civil War generals. On the lakefront, separated from the rest of the town by a six-lane expressway, stands the cubelike structure of the Arts Center, otherwise called the War Memorial. Its rooms are hung with mediocre paintings before which schoolchildren are led on tours by their teachers, most of whom were educated in our local school system.

Our teachers are satisfied, decent people, and the statistics about alcohol and drug abuse among both students and teachers are very encouraging.

There is no need to linger at the War Memorial.

Proceeding directly north, you soon find yourself among the orderly, impressive precincts of the wealthy. It was in this sector of the town, known generally as the East Side, that the brewers and tanners who made our city's first great fortunes set up their mansions. Their houses have a northern, Germanic, even Baltic look which is entirely appropriate to our climate. Of gray stone or red brick, the size of factories or prisons, these stately buildings seem to conceal that vein of fantasy that is actually our most crucial inheritance. But it may be that the style of life—the invisible, hidden life—of these inbred merchants is itself fantastic: the multitude of servants, the maids and coachmen, the cooks and laundresses, the private zoos, the elaborate dynastic marriages and fleets of cars, the rooms lined with silk wallpaper, the twenty-course meals, the underground wine cellars and bomb shelters . . . Of course we do not know if all of these things are true, or even if some of them are true. Our society folk keep to themselves, and what we know of them we learn chiefly from the newspapers, where they are pictured at their balls, standing with their beautiful daughters before fountains of champagne. The private zoos have been broken up long ago. As citizens, we are free to walk down the avenues, past the magnificent houses, and to peer in through the gates at their coach houses and lawns. A uniformed man polishes a car, four tall young people in white play tennis on a private court.

The viaduct killer's victims have all been adult women.

While you continue moving north you will find that as the houses diminish in size the distance between them grows greater. Through the houses, now without gates and coach houses, you can glimpse a sheet of flat grayish-blue—the lake. The air is free, you breathe it in. That is freedom, breathing this air from the lake. Free people may invent themselves in any image, and you may imagine yourself a prince of the earth, walking with an easy stride. Your table is set with linen, china, crystal, and silver, and as you dine, as the servants pass among you with the serving trays, the talk is educated, enlightened, without prejudice of any sort. The table talk is mainly about ideas, it is true, ideas of a conservative cast. You deplore violence, you do not recognize it.

Further north lie suburbs, which are uninteresting.

If from the War Memorial you proceed south, you cross the viaduct. Beneath you is a valley—the valley is perhaps best seen in the dead of winter. All of our city welcomes winter, for our public buildings are gray stone fortresses which, on days when the temperature dips below zero and the old gray snow of previous storms swirls in the avenues, seem to blend with the leaden air and become dreamlike and cloudy. This is how they were meant to be seen. The valley is called . . . it is called the Valley. Red flames tilt and waver at the tops of columns, and smoke pours from factory chimneys. The trees seem to be black. In the winter, the smoke from the factories becomes solid, like dark gray glaciers, and hangs in the dark air in defiance of gravity, like wings that are a light feathery gray at their tips and darken imperceptibly toward black, toward pitchy black at the point where these great frozen glaciers, these dirigibles, would join the body at the shoulder. The bodies of the great birds to which these wings are attached must be imagined.

In the old days of the city, the time of the private zoos, wolves were bred in the Valley. Wolves were in great demand in those days. Now the wolf ranches have been entirely replaced by factories, by rough taverns owned by retired shop foremen, by spurs of the local railroad line, and by narrow streets lined with rickety frame houses and shoe-repair shops. Most of the old wolf-breeders were Polish, and though their kennels, grassy yards, and barbed-wire exercise runs have disappeared, at least one memory of their existence endures: the Valley's street signs are in the Polish language. Tourists are advised to skirt the Valley, and it is always recommended that photographs be confined to the interesting views obtained by looking down from the viaduct. The more courageous visitors, those in search of pungent experience, are cautiously directed to the taverns of the ex-foremen, in particular the oldest of these (the Rusty Nail and the Brace 'n' Bit), where the wooden floors have so softened and furred with lavings and scrubbings that the boards have come to resemble the pelts of long narrow short-haired animals. For the intrepid, these words of caution: do not dress conspicuously, and carry only small amounts of cash. Some working knowledge of Polish is also advised.

Continuing further south, we come to the Polish district proper, which also houses pockets of Estonians and Lithuanians. More than the city's sadly declining downtown area, this district has traditionally been regarded as the city's heart, and has remained unchanged for more than a hundred years. Here the visitor may wander freely among the markets and street fairs, delighting in the sight of well-bundled children rolling hoops, patriarchs in tall fur hats and long beards, and women gathering around the numerous communal water pumps. The sausages and stuffed cabbage sold at the food stalls may be eaten with impunity, and the local beer is said to be of an unrivaled purity. Violence in this district is invariably domestic, and the visitor may feel free to enter the frequent political discussions, which in any case partake of a nostalgic character. In late January or early February the "South Side" is at its best, with the younger people dressed in multilayered heavy woolen garments decorated with the "reindeer" or "snowflake" motif, and the older women of the community seemingly vying to see which of them can outdo the others in the thickness, blackness, and heaviness of her outergarments and in the severity of the traditional head scarf known as the babushka. In late winter the neatness and orderliness of these colorful folk may be seen at their best, for the wandering visitor will often see the bearded paterfamilias sweeping and shoveling not only his immaculate bit of sidewalk (for these houses are as close together as those of the wealthy along the lakefront, so near to one another that until very recently telephone service was regarded as an irrelevance), but his tiny front lawn as well, with its Marian shrines, crèches, ornamental objects such as elves, trolls, postboys, etc. It is not unknown for residents here to proffer the stranger an invitation to inspect their house, in order to display the immaculate condition of the kitchen with its well-blackened wood stove and polished ornamental tiles, and perhaps even extend a thimble-glass of their own peach or plum brandy to the thirsty visitor.

Alcohol, with its association of warmth and comfort, is ubiquitous here, and it is the rare family that does not devote some portion of the summer to the preparation of that winter's plenty.

For these people, violence is an internal matter, to be resolved within or exercised upon one's own body and soul or those of one's immediate family. The inhabitants of these neat, scrubbed little houses with their statues of Mary and cathedral tiles, the descendants of the hard-drinking wolf-breeders of another time, have long since abandoned the practice of crippling their children to ensure their continuing exposure to parental values, but self-mutilation has proved more difficult to eradicate. Few blind themselves now, but many a grandfather conceals a three-fingered hand within his embroidered mitten. Toes are another frequent target of self-punishment, and the prevalence of cheerful, even boisterous shops, always crowded with old men telling stories, which sell the hand-carved wood legs known as "pegs" or "dollies," speaks of yet another.

No one has ever suggested that the viaduct killer is a South Side resident.

The South Siders live in a profound relationship to violence, and its effects are invariably implosive rather than explosive. Once a decade, perhaps twice a decade, one member of a family will realize, out of what depths of cultural necessity the outsider can only hope to imagine, that the whole family must die—*be sacrificed*, to speak with great accuracy. Axes, knives, bludgeons, bottles, babushkas, ancient derringers, virtually every imaginable implement has been used to carry out this aim. The houses in which this act of sacrifice has taken place are immediately if not instantly cleaned by the entire neighborhood acting in concert. The bodies receive a Catholic burial in consecrated ground, and a mass is said in honor of both the victims and their murderer. A picture of the departed family is installed in the church which abuts Market Square, and for a year the house is kept clean and dust-free by the grandmothers of the neighborhood. Men young and old will quietly enter the house, sip the brandy of the "removed," as they are called, meditate, now and then switch on the wireless or the television set, and reflect on the darkness of earthly life. The departed are frequently said to appear to friends and neighbors, and often accurately predict the coming of storms and assist in the location of lost household objects, a treasured button or Mother's sewing needle. After the year has elapsed, the house is sold, most often to a young couple, a young blacksmith or market vendor and his bride, who find the furniture and even the clothing of the "removed" welcome additions to their small household.

Further south are suburbs and impoverished hamlets, which do not compel a visit.

Immediately west of the War Memorial is the city's downtown. Before its decline, this was the city's business district and administrative center, and the monuments of its affluence remain. Marching directly west on the wide avenue which begins at the expressway are the Federal Building, the Post Office, and the great edifice of City Hall. Each is an entire block long and constructed of granite blocks quarried far north in the state. Flights of marble stairs lead up to the massive doors of these structures, and crystal chandeliers can be seen through many of the windows. The facades are classical and severe, and create an architectural landscape of granite revetments and colonnades of pillars. (Within, these grand, inhuman buildings have long ago been carved and partitioned into warrens illuminated by bare lightbulbs or flickering fluorescent tubing, each tiny office with its worn counter for petitioners and a stamped sign proclaiming its function: TAX & EXCISE, DOG LICENSES, PASSPORTS, GRAPHS & CHARTS, REGISTRY OF NOTARY PUBLICS, and the like. The larger rooms with chandeliers which face the avenue, reserved for civic receptions and banquets, are seldom used.)

In the next sequence of buildings are the Hall of Records, the Police Headquarters, and the Criminal Courts Building. Again, wide empty marble steps lead up to massive bronze doors, rows of columns, glittering windows which on wintry days reflect back the gray empty sky. Local craftsmen, many of them descendants of the city's original French settlers, forged and installed the decorative iron bars and grilles on the facade of the Criminal Courts Building.

After we pass the massive, nearly windowless brick facades of the Gas and Electric buildings, we reach the arching metal drawbridge over the river. Looking downriver, we can see its muddy banks and the lights of the terrace of the Green Woman Taproom, now a popular gathering place for the city's civil servants. (A few feet further east is the spot from which a disgruntled lunatic attempted and failed to assassinate President Dwight D. Eisenhower.) Further on stand the high cement walls of several breweries. The drawbridge has not been raised since 1956, when a corporate yacht passed through.

Beyond the drawbridge lies the old mercantile center of the city, with its adult bookstores, pornographic theaters, coffee shops, and its rank of old department stores. These now house discount outlets selling roofing tiles, mufflers and other auto parts, plumbing equipment, and cut-rate clothing, and most of their display windows have been boarded or bricked-in since the civic disturbances of 1968. Various civic plans have failed to revive this area, though the cobblestones and gas street lamps installed in the optimistic mid-seventies can for the most part still be seen. Connoisseurs of the poignant will wish to take a moment to appreciate them, though they should seek to avoid the bands of ragged children that frequent this area at nightfall, for though these children are harmless they can become pressing in their pleas for small change.

Many of these children inhabit dwellings they have constructed themselves in the vacant lots between the adult bookstores and fast-food outlets of the old mercantile district, and the "tree houses" atop mounds of tires, most of them several stories high and utilizing fire escapes and flights of stairs scavenged from the old department stores, are of some architectural interest. The stranger should not attempt to penetrate these "children's cities," and on no account should offer them any more than the pocket change they request or display a camera, jewelry, or an expensive wristwatch. The truly intrepid tourist seeking excitement may hire one of these children to guide him to the diversions of his choice. Two dollars is the usual gratuity for this service.

It is not advisable to purchase any of the goods the children themselves may offer for sale, although they have been affected by the same self-consciousness evident in the impressive buildings on the other side of the river and do sell picture postcards of their largest and most eccentric constructions. It may be that the naive architecture of these tree houses represents the city's most authentic artistic expression, and the postcards, amateurish as most of them are, provide interesting, perhaps even valuable, documentation of this expression of what may be called folk art.

These industrious children of the mercantile area have ritualized their violence into highly formalized tattooing and "spontaneous" forays and raids into the tree houses of opposing tribes during which only superficial injuries are sustained, and it is not suspected that the viaduct killer comes from their number.

Further west are the remains of the city's museum and library, devastated during the civic disturbances, and beyond these picturesque, still-smoking hulls lies the ghetto. It is not advised to enter the ghetto on foot, though the tourist who has arranged to rent an automobile may safely drive through it after he has negotiated his toll at the gatehouse. The ghetto's residents are completely self-sustaining, and the attentive tourist who visits this district will observe the multitude of tents housing hospitals, wholesale food and drug warehouses, and the like. Within the ghetto are believed to be many fine poets, painters, and musicians, as well as the historians known as "memoirists," who are the districts' living encyclopedias and archivists. The "memoirist's" tasks include the memorization of the works of the area's poets, painters, etc., for the district contains no printing presses or art-supply shops, and these inventive and self-reliant people have devised this method of preserving their works. It is not believed that a people capable of inventing the genre of "oral painting" could have spawned the viaduct killer, and in any case no ghetto resident is permitted access to any other area of the city.

The ghetto's relationship to violence is unknown.

Further west the annual snowfall increases greatly, for several months of the year dropping an average of two-point-three feet of snow each month upon the shopping malls and paper mills which have concentrated here. Dust storms are common during the summers, and certain infectious viruses, to which the inhabitants have become immune, are carried in the water.

Still further west lies the Sports Complex.

The tourist who has ventured thus far is well advised to turn back at this point and return to our beginning, the War Memorial. Your car may be left in the ample and clearly posted parking lot on the Memorial's eastern side. From the Memorial's wide empty terraces, you are invited to look southeast, where a great unfinished bridge crosses half the span to the hamlets of Wyatt and Arnoldville. Construction was abandoned on this noble civic project, subsequently imitated by many cities in our western states and in Australia and Finland, immediately after the disturbances of 1968, when its lack of utility became apparent. When it was noticed that many families chose to eat their bag lunches on the Memorial's lakeside terraces in order to gaze silently at its great interrupted arc, the bridge was adopted as the symbol of the city, and its image decorates the city's many flags and medals.

The "Broken Span," as it is called, which hangs in the air like the great frozen wings above the Valley, serves no function but the symbolic. In itself and entirely by accident this great non-span memorializes violence, not only by serving as a reference to the workmen who lost their lives during its construction (its non-construction). It is not rounded or finished in any way, for labor on the bridge ended abruptly, even brutally, and from its truncated floating end dangle lengths of rusting iron webbing, thick wire cables weighted by chunks of cement, and bits of old planking material. In the days before access to the un-bridge was walled off by an electrified fence, two or three citizens each year elected to commit their suicides by leaping from the end of the span; and one must resort to a certain lexical violence when referring to it. Ghetto residents are said to have named it "Whitey," and the tree-house children call it "Ursula," after one of their own killed in the disturbances. South Siders refer to it as "The Ghost," civil servants "The Beast," and East Siders simply as "that thing." The "Broken Span" has the violence of all unfinished things, of everything interrupted or left undone. In violence there is often the quality of *yearning*—the yearning for completion. For closure. For that which is absent and would if present bring to fulfillment. For the body without which the wing is a useless frozen ornament. It ought not to go unmentioned that most of the city's residents have never seen the "bridge" except in its representations, and for this majority the "bridge" is little more or less than a myth, being without any actual referent. It is pure idea.

Violence, it is felt though unspoken, is the physical form of sensitivity. The city believes this. Incompletion, the lack of referent which strands you in the realm of pure idea, demands release from itself. We are above all an American city, and what we believe most deeply we . . .

The victims of the viaduct killer, that citizen who excites our attention, who makes us breathless with outrage and causes our police force to ransack the humble dwellings along the riverbank, have all been adult women. These women in their middle years are taken from their lives and set like statues beside the pillar. Each morning there is more pedestrian traffic on the viaduct, in the frozen mornings men (mainly men) come with their lunches in paper bags, walking slowly along the cement walkway, not looking at one another, barely knowing what they are doing, looking down over the edge of the viaduct, looking away, dawdling, finally leaning like fishermen against the railing, waiting until they can no longer delay going to their jobs.

The visitor who has done so much and gone so far in this city may turn his back on the "Broken Span," the focus of civic pride, and look in a southwesterly direction past the six lanes of the expressway, perhaps on tiptoe (children may have to mount one of the convenient retaining walls). The dull flanks of the viaduct should just now be visible, with the heads and shoulders of the waiting men picked out in the gray air like brush strokes. The quality of their yearning, its expectancy, is visible even from here.

From

Magic Terror

Ashputtle

People think that teaching little children has something to do with helping other people, something to do with service. People think that if you teach little children, you must love them. People get what they need from thoughts like this.

People think that if you happen to be very fat and are a person who acts happy and cheerful all the time, you are probably pretending to be that way in order to make them forget how fat you are, or cause them to forgive you for being so fat. They make this assumption, thinking you are so stupid that you imagine that you're getting away with this charade. From this assumption, they get confidence in the superiority of their intelligence over yours, and they get to pity you, too.

Those figments, those stepsisters, came to me and said, *Don't you know that we want to help you?* They came to me and said, *Can you tell us what your life is like?*

These moronic questions they asked over and over: *Are you all right? Is anything happening to you? Can you talk to us now, darling? Can you tell us about your life?*

I stared straight ahead, not looking at their pretty hair or pretty eyes or pretty mouths. I looked over their shoulders at the pattern on the wallpaper and tried not to blink until they stood up and went away.

What my *life* was like? What was *happening* to me?
Nothing was happening to me. I was *all right.*
They smiled briefly, like a twitch in their eyes and mouths, before they stood up and left me alone. I sat still on my chair and looked at the wallpaper while they talked to Zena.

The wallpaper was yellow, with white lines going up and down through it. The lines never touched—just when they were about to run into each other, they broke, and the fat thick yellow kept them apart.

I liked seeing the white lines hanging in the fat yellow, each one separate.

When the figments called me *darling*, ice and snow stormed into my mouth and went pushing down my throat into my stomach, freezing everything. They didn't know I was nothing, that I would never be like them, they didn't know that the only part of me that was not nothing was a small hard stone right at the center of me.

That stone has a name. MOTHER.

If you are a female kindergarten teacher in her fifties who happens to be very fat, people imagine that you must be truly dedicated to their children, because you cannot possibly have any sort of private life. If they are the parents of the children in your kindergarten class, they are almost grateful that you are so grotesque, because it means that you must really care about their children. After all, even though you couldn't possibly get any other sort of job, you can't be in it for the money, can you? Because what do people know about your salary? They know that garbage men make more money than kindergarten teachers. So at least you didn't decide to take care of their delightful, wonderful, lovable little children just because you thought you'd get rich, no no.

Therefore, even though they disbelieve all your smiles, all your pretty ways, even though they really do think of you with a mixture of pity and contempt, a little gratitude gets in there.

—

Sometimes when I meet with one of these parents, say a fluffy-haired young lawyer, say named Arnold Zoeller, Arnold and his wife, Kathi, Kathi with an *i*, mind you, sometimes when I sit behind my desk and watch these two slim handsome people struggle to keep the pity and contempt out of their well-cared-for faces, I catch that gratitude heating up behind their eyes.

Arnold and Kathi believe that a pathetic old lumpo like me must love their lovely little girl, a girl say named Tori, Tori with an *i* (for Victoria). And I think I do rather love little Tori Zoeller, yes I do think I love that little girl. My mother would have loved her, too. And that's the God's truth.

I can see myself in the world, in the middle of the world.

I can see that I am the same as all nature.

In our minds exists an awareness of perfection, but nothing on earth, nothing in all of nature, is perfectly conceived. Every response comes straight out of the person who is responding.

I have no responsibility to stimulate or satisfy your needs. All that was taken care of a long time ago. Even if you happen to be some kind of supposedly exalted person, like a lawyer. Even if your name is Arnold Zoeller, for example.

Once, briefly, there existed a golden time. In my mind existed an awareness of perfection, and all of nature echoed and repeated the awareness of perfection in my mind. My parents lived, and with them, I too was alive in the golden time. Our name was Asch, and in fact I am known now as Mrs. Asch, the "Mrs." being entirely honorific, no husband having ever been in evidence, nor ever likely to be. (To some sixth-graders, those whom I did not beguile and enchant as kindergartners, those before whose parents I did not squeeze myself into my desk chair and pronounce their dull, their dreary treasures delightful, wonderful, lovable, above all *intelligent*, I am known as Mrs. Fat-Asch. Of this I pretend to be ignorant.) Mr. and Mrs. Asch did dwell together in the golden time, and both mightily did love their girl-child. And then, whoops, the girl-child's mommy upped and died. The girl-child's daddy buried her in the estate's churchyard, with the minister and everything, in the coffin and everything, with hymns and talking and crying and the animals standing around, and Zena, I remember, Zena was already there, even then. So that was how things were, right from the start.

The figments came because of what I did later. They came from a long way away—the city, I think. We never saw city dresses like that, out where we lived. We never saw city hair like that, either. And one of those ladies had a veil!

One winter morning during my first year teaching kindergarten here, I got into my car—*shoved myself* into my car, I should explain; this is different for me than for you, I *rammed myself* between the seat and the steering wheel, and I drove forty miles east, through three different suburbs, until I got to the city, and thereupon I drove through the city to the slummiest section, where dirty people sit in their cars and drink right in the middle of the day. I went to the department store nobody goes to unless they're on welfare and have five or six kids all with different last names. I just parked on the street and sailed in the door. People like that, they never hurt people like me.

Down in the basement was where they sold the wallpaper, so I huffed and puffed down the stairs, smiling cute as a button whenever anybody stopped to look at me, and shoved myself through the aisles until I got to the back wall, where the samples stood in big books like the fairytale book we used to have. I grabbed about four of those books off the wall and heaved them over onto a table there in that section and perched myself on a little tiny chair and started flipping the pages.

A scared-looking black kid in a cheap suit mumbled something about helping me, so I gave him my happiest, most pathetic smile and said, well, I was here to get wallpaper, wasn't I? What color did I want, did I know? Well, I was thinking about yellow, I said. Uh-huh, he says, what kinda yellow you got in mind? Yellow with white lines in it. Uh-huh, says he, and starts helping me look through those books with all the samples in them. They have about the ugliest wallpaper in the world in this place, wallpaper likes sores on the wall, wallpaper that looks like it got rained on before you get it home. Even the black kid knows this crap is ugly, but he's trying his damnedest not to show it.

I bestow smiles everywhere. I'm smiling like a queen riding through her kingdom in a carriage, like a little girl who just got a gold and silver dress from a turtledove up in a magic tree. I'm smiling as if Arnold Zoeller himself and of course his lovely wife are looking across my desk at me while I drown, suffocate, stifle, bury their *lovely, intelligent* little Tori in golden words.

I think we got some more yellow in this book here, he says, and fetches down another big fairy-tale book and plunks it between us on the table. His dirty-looking hands turn those big stiff pages. And just as I thought, just as I knew would happen, could happen, probably would happen, but only here in this filthy corner of a filthy department store, this ignorant but helpful lad opens the book to my mother's wallpaper pattern.

I see the fat yellow and those white lines that never touch anything, and I can't help myself, sweat breaks out all over my body, and I groan so horribly that the kid actually backs away from me, lucky for him, because in the next second I'm bending over and throwing up interesting-looking reddish goo all over the floor of the wallpaper department. Oh God, the kid says, oh lady. I groan, and all the rest of the goo comes jumping out of me and splatters down on the carpet. Some older black guy in a clip-on bow tie rushes up toward us but stops short with his mouth hanging open as soon as he sees the mess on the floor. I take my hankie out of my bag and wipe off my mouth. I try to smile at the kid, but my eyes are too blurry. No, I say, I'm fine, I want to buy this wallpaper for my kitchen, this one right here. I turn over the page to see the name of my mother's wallpaper—Zena's wallpaper, too—and discover that this kind of wallpaper is called the "Thinking Reed."

You don't have to be religious to have inspirations.

An adventurous state of mind is like a great dwelling place.

To be lived truly, life must be apprehended with an adventurous state of mind.

But no one on earth can explain the lure of adventure.

—

Zena's example gives me two tricks that work in my classroom, and the reason they work is that they are not actually tricks!

The first of these comes into play when a particular child is disobedient or inattentive, which, as you can imagine, often occurs in a room full of kindergarten-age children. I deal with these infractions in this fashion. I command the child to come to my desk. (Sometimes I command two children to come to my desk.) I stare at the child until it begins to squirm. Sometimes it blushes or trembles. I await the physical signs of shame or discomfort. Then I pronounce the child's name. "Tori," I say, if the child is Tori. Its little eyes invariably fasten upon mine at this instant. "Tori," I say, "you know that what you did is wrong, don't you?" Ninety-nine times out of a hundred, the child nods its head. "And you will never do that wrong thing again, will you?" Most often the child can speak to say *No.* "Well, you'd better not," I say, and then I lean forward until the little child can see nothing except my enormous, inflamed face. Then in a guttural, lethal, rumble-whisper, I utter, "OR ELSE." When I say "OR ELSE," I am very emphatic. I am so very emphatic that I feel my eyes change shape. I am thinking of Zena the time she told me that weeping on my mother's grave wouldn't make a glorious wonderful tree grow there, it would just drown my mother in mud.

The attractiveness of teaching is that it is adventurous, as adventurous as life.

———

My mother did not drown in mud. She died some other way. She fell down in the middle of the downstairs parlor, the parlor where Zena sat on her visits. Zena was just another lady then, and on her visits, her "social calls," she sat on the best antique chair and held her hands in her lap like the most modest, innocent lady ever born. She was half Chinese, Zena, and I knew she was just like bright sharp metal inside of her, metal that could slice you but good. Zena was very adventurous, but not as adventurous as me. Zena never got out of that town. Of course, all that happened to Zena was that she got old, and everybody left her alone because she wasn't pretty anymore, she was just an old yellow widow-lady, and then I heard that she died pulling up weeds in her garden. I heard this from two different people. You could say that Zena got drowned in mud, which proves that everything spoken on this earth contains a truth not always apparent at the time.

The other trick I learned from Zena that is not a trick is how to handle a whole class that has decided to act up. These children come from parents who, thinking they know everything, in fact know less than nothing. These children will never see a classical manner demonstrated at home. You must respond in a way that demonstrates your awareness of perfection. You must respond in a way that will bring this awareness to the unruly children, so that they too will possess it.

It can begin in a thousand different ways. Say I am in conference with a single student—say I am delivering the great OR ELSE. Say that my attention has wandered off for a moment, and I am contemplating the myriad of things I contemplate when my attention is wandering free. My mother's grave, watered by my tears. The women with city hair who desired to give me help, but could not, so left to be replaced by others, who in turn were replaced by yet others. How it felt to stand naked and besmeared with my own feces in the front yard, moveless as a statue, the same as all nature, classical. The gradual disappearance of my father, like that of a figure in a cartoon who grows increasingly transparent until total transparency is reached. Zena facedown in her garden, snuffling dirt up into her nostrils. The resemblance of the city women to certain wicked stepsisters in old tales. Also their resemblance to handsome princes in the same tales.

She who hears the tale makes the tale.

Say therefore that I am no longer quite anchored within the classroom, but that I float upward into one, several, or all of these realms. People get what they need from their own minds. Certain places, you can get in there and rest. The classical was a cool period. I am floating within my cool realms. At that moment, one child pulls another's hair. A third child hurls a spitball at the window. Another falls to the floor, emitting pathetic and mechanical cries. Instantly, what was order is misrule. Then I summon up the image of one of my female angels and am on my feet before the little beasts even notice that I have left my desk. In a flash, I am beside the light switch. The Toris and Tiffanys, the Joshuas and Jeremys, riot on. I slap down the switch, and the room goes dark.

Result? Silence. Inspired action is destiny.

The children freeze. Their pulses race—veins beat in not a few little blue temples. I say four words. I say, "Think what this means." They know what it means. I grow to twice my size in the meaning of these words. I loom over them, and darkness pours out of me. Then I switch the lights back on, and smile at them until they get what they need from my smiling face. These children will never call me Mrs. Fat-Asch; these children know that I am the same as all nature.

Once upon a time a dying queen sent for her daughter, and when her daughter came to her bedside the queen said, "I am leaving you, my darling. Say your prayers and be good to your father. Think of me always, and I will always be with you." Then she died. Every day the little girl watered her mother's grave with her tears. But her heart was dead. You cannot lie about a thing like this. Hatred is the inside part of love. And so her mother became a hard cold stone in her heart. And that was the meaning of the mother, for as long as the little girl lived.

Soon the king took another woman as his wife, and she was most beautiful, with skin the color of gold and eyes as black as jet. She was like a person pretending to be someone else inside another person pretending she couldn't pretend. She understood that reality was contextual. She understood about the condition of the observer.

One day when the king was going out to be among his people, he asked his wife, "What shall I bring you?"

"A diamond ring," said the queen. And the king could not tell who was speaking, the person inside pretending to be someone else, or the person outside who could not pretend.

"And you, my daughter," said the king, "what would you like?"

"A diamond ring," said the daughter.

The king smiled and shook his head.

"Then nothing," said the daughter. "Nothing at all."

When the king came home, he presented the queen with a diamond ring in a small blue box, and the queen opened the box and smiled at the ring and said, "It's a very small diamond, isn't it?" The king's daughter saw him stoop forward, his face whitening, as if he had just lost half his blood. "I like my small diamond," said the queen, and the king straightened up, although he still looked white and shaken. He patted his daughter on the head on his way out of the room, but the girl merely looked forward and said nothing, in return for the nothing he had given her.

And that night, when the rest of the palace was asleep, the king's daughter crept to the kitchen and ate half of a loaf of bread and most of a quart of homemade peach ice cream. This was the most delicious food she had ever eaten in her whole entire life. The bread tasted like the sun on wheatfields, and inside the taste of the sun was the taste of the bursting kernels of the wheat, even of the rich dark crumbly soil that surrounded the roots of the wheat, even of the lives of the bugs and animals that had scurried through the wheat, even of the droppings of those foxes, beetles, and mice. And the homemade peach ice cream tasted overwhelmingly of sugar, cream, and peaches, but also of the bark and meat of the peach tree and the pink feet of the birds that had landed on it, and the sharp, brittle voices of those birds, also of the effort of the hand crank, of the stained, whorly wood of its sides, and of the sweat of the man who had worked it so long. Every taste should be as complicated as possible, every taste goes up and down at the same time: up past the turtledoves to the far reaches of the sky, so that one final taste in everything is *whiteness*, and down all the way to the mud at the bottom of graves, then to the mud beneath that mud, so that another final taste in everything, in even peach ice cream, is the taste of *blackness*.

From about this time, the king's daughter began to attract undue attention. From the night of the whiteness of turtledoves and the blackness of grave-mud to the final departure of the stepsisters was a period of something like six months.

I thought of myself as a work of art. I caused responses without being responsible for them. This is the great freedom of art.

They asked questions that enforced the terms of their own answers. *Don't you know we want to help you?* Such a question implies only two possible answers, 1: no, 2: yes. The stepsisters never understood the queen's daughter, therefore the turtledoves pecked out their eyes, first on the one side, then on the other. The correct answer—3: person to whom the question is directed is not the one in need of help—cannot be given. Other correct answers, such as 4: help shall come from other sources, and 5: neither *knowledge* nor *help* means what you imagine it means, are also forbidden by the form of the question.

Assignment for tonight: make a list of proper but similarly forbidden answers to the question *What is happening to you?* Note: be sure to consider conditions imposed by the use of the word *happening*.

The stepsisters arrived from the city in grand state. They resembled peacocks. The stepsisters accepted Zena's tea, they admired the house, the paintings, the furniture, just as if admiring these things, which everybody admired, meant that they, too, should be admired. The stepsisters wished to remove the king's daughter from this setting, but their power was not so great. Zena would not permit it, nor would the ailing king. (At night, Zena placed her subtle mouth over his sleeping mouth and drew breath straight out of his body.) Zena said that the condition of the king's daughter would prove to be temporary. The child was eating well. She was loved. In time, she would return to herself.

When the figments asked, *What is happening to you?* I could have answered, *Zena is happening to me.* This answer would not have been understood. Neither would the answer *My mother is happening to me.*

Undue attention came about in the following fashion. Zena knew all about my midnight feasts, but was indifferent to them. Zena knew that each person must acquire what she needs. This is as true for a king's daughter as for an ordinary commoner. But she was ignorant of what I did in the name of art. Misery and anger made me a great artist, though now I am a much greater artist. I think I was twelve. (The age of the artist is of no importance.) Both my mother and Zena were happening to me, and I was happening to them, too. Such is the world of women. My mother, deep in her mud-grave, hated Zena. Zena, second in the king's affections, hated my mother. Speaking from the center of the stone at the center of me, my mother frequently advised me on how to deal with Zena. Silently, speaking with her eyes, Zena advised me on how to deal with my mother. I, who had to deal with both of them, hated them both.

And I possessed an adventurous mind.

———

The main feature of adventure is that it goes forward into unknown country.

Adventure is filled with nameless joy.

Alone in my room in the middle of Saturday, on later occasions after my return from school, I removed my clothes and placed them neatly on my bed. (My *canopied* bed.) I had no feelings, apart from a sense of urgency, concerning the actions I was about to perform. Perhaps I experienced a nameless joy at this point. Later on, at the culmination of my self-display, I experienced a nameless joy. And later yet, I experienced the same nameless joy at the conclusions of my various adventures in art. In each of these adventures, as in the first, I created responses not traceable within the artwork, but which derived from the conditions, etc., of the audience. Alone and unclothed now in my room, ready to create responses, I squatted on my heels and squeezed out onto the carpet a long cylinder of fecal matter, the residue of, dinner not included, an entire loaf of seven-grain bread, a half a box of raisins, a can of peanuts, and a quarter pound of cervelat sausage, all consumed when everyone else was in bed and Zena was presumably leaning over the face of my sleeping father, greedily inhaling his life. I picked up the warm cylinder and felt it melt into my hands. I hastened this process by squeezing my palms together. Then I rubbed my hands over my body. What remained of the stinking cylinder I smeared along the walls of the bedroom. Then I wiped my hands on the carpet. (The *white* carpet.) My preparations concluded, I moved regally through the corridors until I reached the front door and let myself out.

I have worked as a certified grade-school teacher in three states. My record is spotless. I never left a school except by my own choice. When tragedies came to my charges or their parents, I invariably sent sympathetic notes, joined volunteer groups to search for bodies, attended funerals, etc., etc. Every teacher eventually becomes familiar with these unfortunate duties.

Outside, there was all the world, at least all of the estate, from which to choose. Two lines from Edna St. Vincent Millay best express my state of mind at this moment: *The world stands out on either side / No wider than the heart is wide.* I well remember the much-admired figure of Dave Garroway quoting those lovely words on his Sunday-afternoon television program, and I pass along this beautiful sentiment to each fresh class of kindergartners. They must start somewhere, and at other moments in their year with me they will have the opportunity to learn that nature never gives you a chance to rest. Every animal on earth is hungry.

Turning my back on the fields of grazing cows and sheep, ignoring the hills beyond, hills seething with coyotes, wildcats, and mountain lions, I moved with stately tread through the military rows of fruit trees and, with papery apple and peach blossoms adhering to my bare feet, passed into the expanse of the grass meadow where grew the great hazel tree. Had the meadow been recently mown, long green stalks the width of caterpillars leapt up from the ground to festoon my legs. (I often stretched out full-length and rolled in the freshly mown grass meadow.) And then, at the crest of the hill that marked the end of the meadow, I arrived at my destination. Below me lay the road to unknown towns and cities in which I hoped one day to find my complicated destiny. Above me stood the hazel tree.

I have always known that I could save myself by looking into my own mind.

I stood above the road on the crest of the hill and raised my arms. When I looked into my mind I saw two distinct and necessary states, one that of the white line, the other that of the female angels, akin to the turtledoves.

The white line existed in a calm rapture of separation, touching neither the sky nor meadow but suspended in the space between. The white line was silence, isolation, classicism. This state is one half of what is necessary in order to achieve the freedom of art, and it is called the Thinking Reed.

The angels and turtledoves existed in a rapture of power, activity, and rage. They were absolute whiteness and absolute blackness, gratification and gratification's handmaiden, revenge. The angels and turtledoves came streaming up out of my body and soared from the tips of my fingers into the sky, and when they returned they brought golden and silver dresses, diamond rings, and emerald tiaras.

I saw the figments slicing off their own toes, sawing off their heels, and stepping into shoes already slippery with blood. The figments were trying to smile, they were trying to stand up straight. They were like children before an angry teacher, a teacher transported by a righteous anger. Girls like the figments never did understand that what they needed, they must get from their own minds. Lacking this understanding, they tottered along, pretending that they were not mutilated, pretending that blood did not pour from their shoes, back to their pretend houses and pretend princes. The nameless joy distinguished every part of this process.

Lately, within the past twenty-four hours, a child has been lost.

A lost child lies deep within the ashes, her hands and feet mutilated, her face destroyed by fire. She has partaken of the great adventure, and now she is the same as all nature.

At night, I see the handsome, distracted, still hopeful parents on our local news programs. Arnold and Kathi, he as handsome as a prince, she as lovely as one of the figments, still have no idea of what has actually happened to them—they lived their whole lives in utter abysmal ignorance—they think of hope as an essential component of the universe. They think that other people, the people paid to perform this function, will conspire to satisfy their needs.

A child has been lost. Now her photograph appears each day on the front page of our sturdy little tabloid-style newspaper, beaming out with luminous ignorance beside the columns of print describing a sudden disappearance after the weekly Sunday school class at St.-Mary-in-the-Forest's Episcopal church, the deepening fears of the concerned parents, the limitless charm of the girl herself, the searches of nearby video parlors and shopping malls, the draggings of two adjacent ponds, the slow, painstaking inspections of the neighboring woods, fields, farms, and outbuildings, the shock of the child's particularly well-off and socially prominent relatives, godparents included.

A particular child has been lost. A certain combination of variously shaded blond hair and eyes the blue of early summer sky seen through a haze of cirrus clouds, of an endearingly puffy upper lip and a recurring smudge, like that left on corrasable bond typing paper by an unclean eraser, on the left side of the mouth, of an unaffected shyness and an occasional brittle arrogance destined soon to overshadow more attractive traits will never again be seen, not by parents, friends, teachers, or the passing strangers once given to spontaneous tributes to the child's beauty.

A child of her time has been lost. Of no interest to our local newspaper, unknown to the Sunday school classes at St.-Mary-in-the-Forest, were this moppet's obsession with the dolls Exercise Barbie and Malibu Barbie, her fanatical attachment to My Little Ponies Glory and Applejack, her insistence on introducing during classtime observations upon the cartoon family named Simpson, especially the "videos" featuring groups like Kris Kross and Boyz II Men. She was once observed holding hands with James Halliwell, a first-grade boy. Once, just before naptime, she turned upon a pudgy, unpopular girl of protosadistic tendencies named Deborah Monk and hissed, "Debbie, I hate to tell you this, but you *suck*."

A child of certain limitations has been lost. She could never learn to tie her cute but oddly blunt-looking size-1 running shoes and eventually had to become resigned to the sort fastened with Velcro straps. When combing her multishaded blond hair with her fingers, she would invariably miss a cobwebby patch located two inches aft of her left ear. Her reading skills were somewhat, though not seriously, below average. She could recognize her name, when spelled out in separate capitals, with narcissistic glee; yet all other words, save *and* and *the*, turned beneath her impatient gaze into random, Sanskrit-like squiggles and uprights. (This would soon have corrected itself.) She could recite the alphabet all in a rush, by rote, but when questioned was incapable of remembering if the *O* came before or after the *S*. I doubt that she would have been capable of mastering long division during the appropriate academic term.

Across the wide, filmy screen of her eyes would now and then cross a haze of indefinable confusion. In a child of more finely tuned sensibilities, this momentary slippage might have suggested a sudden sense of loss, even perhaps a premonition of the loss to come. In her case, I imagine the expression was due to the transition from the world of complete unconsciousness (Barbie and My Little Ponies) to a more fully socialized state (Kris Kross). Introspection would have come only late in life, after long exposure to experiences of the kind from which her parents most wished to shelter her.

An irreplaceable child has been lost. What was once in the land of the Thinking Reed has been forever removed, like others before it, like all others in time, to turtledove territory. This fact is borne home on a daily basis. Should some informed anonymous observer report that the child is all right, that nothing happened to her, the comforting message would be misunderstood as the prelude to a demand for ransom. The reason for this is that no human life can ever be truly substituted for another. The increasingly despairing parents cannot create or otherwise acquire a living replica, though they are certainly capable of reproducing again, should they stay married long enough to do so. The children in the lost one's class are reported to suffer nightmares and recurrent enuresis. In class, they exhibit lassitude, wariness, a new unwillingness to respond, like the unwillingness of the very old. At a schoolwide assembly where the little ones sat right up front, nearly every one expressed the desire for the missing one to return. Letters and cards to the lost one now form two large, untidy stacks in the principal's office and, with parental appeals to the abductor or abductors broadcast every night, it is felt that the school will accumulate a third stack before these tributes are offered to the distraught parents.

Works of art generate responses not directly traceable to the work itself. Helplessness, grief, and sorrow may exist simultaneously alongside aggressiveness, hostility, anger, or even serenity and relief. The more profound and subtle the work, the more intense and long-lasting the responses it evokes.

Deep, deep in her muddy grave, the queen and mother felt the tears of her lost daughter. *All will pass.* In the form of a turtledove, she rose from grave-darkness and ascended into the great arms of the hazel tree. *All will change.* From the topmost branch, the turtledove sang out her everlasting message. *All is hers, who will seek what is true.* "What is true?" cried the daughter, looking dazzled up. *All will pass, all will change, all is yours*, sang the turtledove.

In a recent private conference with the principal, I announced my decision to move to another section of the country after the semester's end.

The principal is a kindhearted, limited man still loyal, one might say rigidly loyal, to the values he absorbed from popular music at the end of the 1960s, and he has never quite been able to conceal the unease I arouse within him. Yet he is aware of the respect I command within every quarter of the school, and he has seen former kindergartners of mine, now freshmen in our trisuburban high school, return to my classroom and inform the awed children seated before them that Mrs. Asch placed them on the right path, that Mrs. Asch's lessons would be responsible for seeing them successfully through high school and on to college.

Virtually unable to contain the conflict of feelings my announcement brought to birth within him, the principal assured me that he would that very night compose a letter of recommendation certain to gain me a post at any elementary school, public or private, of my choosing.

After thanking him, I replied, "I do not request this kindness of you, but neither will I refuse it."

The principal leaned back in his chair and gazed at me, not unkindly, through his granny glasses. His right hand rose like a turtledove to caress his graying beard, but ceased halfway in its flight, and returned to his lap. Then he lifted both hands to the surface of his desk and intertwined the fingers, still gazing quizzically at me.

"Are you all right?" he inquired.

"Define your terms," I said. "If you mean, am I in reasonable health, enjoying physical and mental stability, satisfied with my work, then the answer is yes, I am all right."

"You've done a wonderful job dealing with Tori's disappearance," he said. "But I can't help but wonder if all that has played a part in your decision."

"My decisions make themselves," I said. "All will pass, all will change. I am a serene person."

He promised to get the letter of recommendation to me by lunchtime the next day, and as I knew he would, he kept his promise. Despite my serious reservations about his methods, attitude, and ideology—despite my virtual certainty that he will be unceremoniously forced from his job within the next year—I cannot refrain from wishing the poor fellow well.

Pork Pie Hat

If you know jazz, you know about him, and the title of this memoir tells you who he is. If you don't know the music, his name doesn't matter. I'll call him Hat. What does matter is what he meant. I don't mean what he meant to people who were touched by what he said through his horn. (His horn was an old Selmer Balanced Action tenor saxophone, most of its lacquer worn off.) I'm talking about the whole long curve of his life, and the way that what appeared to be a long slide from joyous mastery to outright exhaustion can be seen in another way altogether.

Hat did slide into alcoholism and depression. The last ten years of his life amounted to suicide by malnutrition, and he was almost transparent by the time he died in the hotel room where I met him. Yet he was able to play until nearly the end. When he was working, he would wake up around seven in the evening, listen to Frank Sinatra or Billie Holiday records while he dressed, get to the club by nine, play three sets, come back to his room sometime after three, drink and listen to more records (he was on a lot of those records), and finally go back to bed around the time day-people begin thinking about lunch. When he wasn't working, he got into bed about an hour earlier, woke up about five or six, and listened to records and drank through his long upside-down day.

It sounds like a miserable life, but it was just an unhappy one. The unhappiness came from a deep, irreversible sadness. Sadness is different from misery, at least Hat's was. His sadness seemed impersonal—it did not disfigure him, as misery can do. Hat's sadness seemed to be for the universe, or to be a larger than usual personal share of a sadness already existing in the universe. Inside it, Hat was unfailingly gentle, kind, even funny. His sadness seemed merely the opposite face of the equally impersonal happiness that shone through his earlier work.

In Hat's later years, his music thickened, and sorrow spoke through the phrases. In his last years, what he played often sounded like heartbreak itself. He was like someone who had passed through a great mystery, who *was passing* through a great mystery, and had to speak of what he had seen, what he was seeing.

2

I brought two boxes of records with me when I first came to New York from Evanston, Illinois, where I'd earned a B.A. in English at Northwestern, and the first thing I set up in my shoebox at the top of John Jay Hall in Columbia University was my portable record player. I did everything to music in those days, and I supplied the rest of my unpacking with a soundtrack provided by Hat's disciples. The kind of music I most liked when I was twenty-one was called "cool" jazz, but my respect for Hat, the progenitor of this movement, was almost entirely abstract. I didn't know his earliest records, and all I'd heard of his later style was one track on a Verve sampler album. I thought he must almost certainly be dead, and I imagined that if by some miracle he was still alive, he would have been in his early seventies, like Louis Armstrong. In fact, the man who seemed a virtual ancient to me was a few months short of his fiftieth birthday.

In my first weeks at Columbia I almost never left the campus. I was taking five courses, also a seminar that was intended to lead me to a Master's thesis, and when I was not in lecture halls or my room, I was in the library. But by the end of September, feeling less overwhelmed, I began to go downtown to Greenwich Village. The IRT, the only subway line I actually understood, described a straight north-south axis which allowed you to get on at 116th Street and get off at Sheridan Square. From Sheridan Square radiated out an unimaginable wealth (unimaginable if you'd spent the previous four years in Evanston, Illinois) of cafés, bars, restaurants, record shops, bookstores, and jazz clubs. I'd come to New York to get an M.A. in English, but I'd also come for this.

I learned that Hat was still alive about seven o'clock in the evening on the first Saturday in October when I saw a poster bearing his name on the window of a storefront jazz club near St. Mark's Place. My conviction that Hat was dead was so strong that I first saw the poster as an advertisement of past glory. I stopped to gaze longer at this relic of a historical period. Hat had been playing with a quartet including a bassist and drummer of his own era, musicians long associated with him. But the piano player had been John Hawes, one of *my* musicians—John Hawes was on half a dozen of the records back in John Jay Hall. He must have been about twenty at the time, I thought, convinced that the poster had been preserved as memorabilia. Maybe Hawes's first job had been with Hat—anyhow, Hat's quartet must have been one of Hawes's first stops on the way to fame. John Hawes was a great figure to me, and the thought of him playing with a back number like Hat was a disturbance in the texture of reality. I looked down at the date on the poster, and my snobbish and rule-bound version of reality shuddered under another assault of the unthinkable. Hat's engagement had begun on the Tuesday of this week—the first Tuesday in October, and its last night took place on the Sunday after next—the Sunday before Halloween. Hat was still alive, and John Hawes was playing with him. I couldn't have told you which half of this proposition was the more surprising.

To make sure, I went inside and asked the short, impassive man behind the bar if John Hawes were really playing there tonight. "He'd better be, if he wants to get paid," the man said.

"So Hat is still alive," I said.

"Put it this way," he said. "If it was you, you probably wouldn't be."

3

Two hours and twenty minutes later, Hat came through the front door, and I saw what he meant. Maybe a third of the tables between the door and the bandstand were filled with people listening to the piano trio. This was what I'd come for, and I thought that the evening was perfect. I hoped that Hat would stay away. All he could accomplish by showing up would be to steal soloing time from Hawes, who, apart from seeming a bit disengaged, was playing wonderfully. Maybe Hawes always seemed a bit disengaged. That was fine with me. Hawes was supposed to be cool. Then the bass player looked toward the door and smiled, and the drummer grinned and knocked one stick against the side of his snare drum in a rhythmic figure that managed both to suit what the trio was playing and serve as a half-comic, half-respectful greeting. I turned away from the trio and looked back toward the door. The bent figure of a light-skinned black man in a long, drooping, dark coat was carrying a tenor saxophone case into the club. Layers of airline stickers covered the case, and a black pork pie hat concealed most of the man's face. As soon as he got past the door, he fell into a chair next to an empty table—really fell, as if he would need a wheelchair to get any farther.

Most of the people who had watched him enter turned back to John Hawes and the trio, who were beginning the last few choruses of "Love Walked In." The old man laboriously unbuttoned his coat and let it fall off his shoulders onto the back of the chair. Then, with the same painful slowness, he lifted the hat off his head and lowered it to the table beside him. A brimming shotglass had appeared between himself and the hat, though I hadn't noticed any of the waiters or waitresses put it there. Hat picked up the glass and poured its entire contents into his mouth. Before he swallowed, he let himself take in the room, moving his eyes without changing the position of his head. He was wearing a dark gray suit, a blue shirt with a tight tab collar, and a black knit tie. His face looked soft and worn with drink, and his eyes were of no real color at all, as if not merely washed out but washed clean. He bent over, unlocked the case, and began assembling his horn. As soon as "Love Walked In" ended, he was on his feet, clipping the horn to his strap and walking toward the bandstand. There was some quiet applause.

Hat stepped neatly up onto the bandstand, acknowledged us with a nod, and whispered something to John Hawes, who raised his hands to the keyboard. The drummer was still grinning, and the bassist had closed his eyes. Hat tilted his horn to one side, examined the mouthpiece, and slid it a tiny distance down the cork. He licked the reed, tapped his foot twice, and put his lips around the mouthpiece.

What happened next changed my life—changed me, anyhow. It was like discovering that some vital, even necessary substance had all along been missing from my life. Anyone who hears a great musician for the first time knows the feeling that the universe has just expanded. In fact, all that happened was that Hat had started playing "Too Marvelous for

Words," one of the twenty-odd songs that were his entire repertoire at the time. Actually, he was playing some oblique, one-time-only melody of his own that floated above "Too Marvelous for Words," and this spontaneous melody seemed to me to comment affectionately on the song while utterly transcending it—to turn a nice little song into something profound. I forgot to breathe for a little while, and goosebumps came up on my arms. Halfway through Hat's solo, I saw John Hawes watching him and realized that Hawes, whom I all but revered, revered him. But by that time, I did, too.

I stayed for all three sets, and after my seminar the next day, I went down to Sam Goody's and bought five of Hat's records, all I could afford. That night, I went back to the club and took a table right in front of the bandstand. For the next two weeks, I occupied the same table every night I could persuade myself that I did not have to study— eight or nine, out of the twelve nights Hat worked. Every night was like the first: the same things, in the same order, happened. Halfway through the first set, Hat turned up and collapsed into the nearest chair. Unobtrusively, a waiter put a drink beside him. Off went the pork pie and the long coat, and out from its case came the horn. The waiter carried the case, pork pie, and coat into a back room while Hat drifted toward the bandstand, often still fitting the pieces of his saxophone together. He stood straighter, seemed almost to grow taller, as he got on the stand. A nod to his audience, an inaudible word to John Hawes. And then that sense of passing over the border between very good, even excellent music and majestic, mysterious art. Between songs, Hat sipped from a glass placed beside his left foot. Three forty-five-minute sets. Two half-hour breaks, during which Hat disappeared through a door behind the bandstand. The same twenty or so songs, recycled again and again. Ecstasy, as if I were hearing Mozart play Mozart.

One afternoon toward the end of the second week, I stood up from a library book I was trying to stuff whole into my brain—*Modern Approaches to Milton*—and walked out of my carrel to find whatever I could that had been written about Hat. I'd been hearing the sound of Hat's tenor in my head ever since I'd gotten out of bed. And in those days, I was a sort of apprentice scholar: I thought that real answers in the form of interpretations could be found in the pages of scholarly journals. If there were at least a thousand, maybe two thousand, articles concerning John Milton in Low Library, shouldn't there be at least a hundred about Hat? And out of the hundred shouldn't a dozen or so at least begin to explain what happened to me when I heard him play? I was looking for close readings of his solos, for analyses that would explain Hat's effects in terms of subdivided rhythms, alternate chords, and note choices, in the way that poetry critics parsed diction levels, inversions of meter, and permutations of imagery.

Of course I did not find a dozen articles that applied a musicological version of the New Criticism to Hat's recorded solos. I found six old concert write-ups in the *New York Times*, maybe as many record reviews in jazz magazines, and a couple of chapters in jazz histories. Hat had been born in Mississippi, played in his family band, left after a mysterious disagreement at the time they were becoming a successful "territory" band, then joined a famous jazz band in its infancy and quit, again mysteriously, just after its breakthrough into nationwide success. After that, he went out on his own. It seemed that if you wanted to know about him, you had to go straight to the music: there was virtually nowhere else to go.

I wandered back from the catalogs to my carrel, closed the door on the outer world, and went back to stuffing *Modern Approaches to Milton* into my brain. Around six o'clock, I opened the carrel door and realized that I could write about Hat. Given the paucity of criticism of his work—given the virtual absence of information about the man himself—I virtually had to write something. The only drawback to this inspiration was that I knew nothing about music. I could not write the sort of article I had wished to read. What I could do, however, would be to interview the man. Potentially, an interview would be more valuable than analysis. I could fill in the dark places, answer the unanswered questions—Why had he left both bands just as they began to do well? I wondered if he'd had problems with his father, and then transferred these problems to his next bandleader. There had to be some kind of story. Any band within smelling distance of its first success would be more than reluctant to lose its star soloist—wouldn't they beg him, bribe him, to stay? I could think of other questions no one had ever asked: Who had influenced him? What did he think of all those tenor players whom he had influenced? Was he friendly with any of his artistic children? Did they come to his house and talk about music?

Above all, I was curious about the texture of his life—I wondered what his life, the life of a genius, tasted like. If I could have put my half-formed fantasies into words, I would have described my naive, uninformed conceptions of Leonard Bernstein's surroundings. Mentally, I equipped Hat with a big apartment, handsome furniture, advanced stereo equipment, a good but not flashy car, paintings . . . the surroundings of a famous American artist, at least by the standards of John Jay Hall and Evanston, Illinois. The difference between Bernstein and Hat was that the conductor probably lived on Fifth Avenue, and the tenor player in the Village.

I walked out of the library humming "Love Walked In."

4

The dictionary-sized Manhattan telephone directory chained to the shelf beneath the pay telephone on the ground floor of John Jay Hall failed to provide Hat's number. Moments later, I met similar failure back in the library after having consulted the equally impressive directories for Brooklyn, Queens, and the Bronx, as well as the much smaller volume for Staten Island. But of course Hat lived in New York: where else would he live? Like other celebrities, he avoided the unwelcome intrusions of strangers by going unlisted. I could not explain his absence from the city's five telephone books in any other way. Of course Hat lived in the Village—that was what the Village was for.

Yet even then, remembering the unhealthy-looking man who each night entered the club to drop into the nearest chair, I experienced a wobble of doubt. Maybe the great man's life was nothing like my imaginings. Hat wore decent clothes, but did not seem rich—he seemed to exist at the same oblique angle to worldly success that his nightly variations on "Too Marvelous for Words" bore to the original melody. For a moment, I pictured my genius in a slum apartment where roaches scuttled across a bare floor and water dripped from a rip in the ceiling. I had no idea of how jazz musicians actually lived. Hollywood, unafraid of cliché, surrounded them with squalor. On the rare moments when literature stooped to consider jazz people, it, too, served up an ambience of broken bedsprings and peeling walls. And literature's bohemians— Rimbaud, Jack London, Kerouac, Hart Crane, William Burroughs— had often inhabited mean, unhappy rooms. It was possible that the great man was not listed in the city's directories because he could not afford a telephone.

This notion was unacceptable. There was another explanation—Hat could not live in a tenement room without a telephone. The man still possessed the elegance of his generation of jazz musicians, the generation that wore good suits and highly polished shoes, played in big bands, and lived on buses and in hotel rooms.

And there, I thought, was my answer. It was a comedown from the apartment in the Village with which I had supplied him, but a room in some "artistic" hotel like the Chelsea would suit him just as well, and probably cost a lot less in rent. Feeling inspired, I looked up the Chelsea's number on the spot, dialed, and asked for Hat's room. The clerk told me that he wasn't registered in the hotel. "But you know who he is," I said. "Sure," said the clerk. "Guitar, right? I know he was in one of those San Francisco bands, but I can't remember which one."

I hung up without replying, realizing that the only way I was going to discover Hat's telephone number, short of calling every hotel in New York, was by asking him for it.

5

This was on a Monday, and jazz clubs were closed. On Tuesday, Professor Marcus told us to read all of *Vanity Fair* by Friday; on Wednesday, after I'd spent a nearly sleepless night with Thackeray, my seminar leader asked me to prepare a paper on James Joyce's "Two Gallants" for the Friday class. Wednesday and Thursday nights I spent in the library. On Friday I listened to Professor Marcus being brilliant about *Vanity Fair* and read my laborious and dim-witted Joyce paper, on each of the five pages of which the word "epiphany" appeared at least twice, to my fellow scholars. The seminar leader smiled and nodded throughout my performance and when I sat down metaphorically picked up my little paper between thumb and forefinger and slit its throat. "Some of you students are so certain about things," he said. The rest of his remarks disappeared into a vast, horrifying sense of shame. I returned to my room, intending to lie down for an hour or two, and woke up ravenous ten hours later, when even the West End bar, even the local Chock Full O' Nuts, were shut for the night.

On Saturday night, I took my usual table in front of the bandstand and sat expectantly through the piano trio's usual three numbers. In the middle of "Love Walked In" I looked around with an insider's foreknowledge to enjoy Hat's dramatic entrance, but he did not appear, and the number ended without him. John Hawes and the other two musicians seemed untroubled by this break in the routine, and went on to play "Too Marvelous for Words" without their leader. During the next three songs, I kept turning around to look for Hat, but the set ended without him. Hawes announced a short break, and the musicians stood up and moved toward the bar. I fidgeted at my table, nursing my second beer of the night and anxiously checking the door. The minutes trudged by. I feared he would never show up. He had passed out in his room. He'd been hit by a cab, he'd had a stroke, he was already lying dead in a hospital room—and just when I was going to write the article that would finally do him justice!

Half an hour later, still without their leader, John Hawes and other sidemen went back on the stand. No one but me seemed to have noticed that Hat was not present. The other customers talked and smoked— this was in the days when people still smoked—and gave the music the intermittent and sometimes ostentatious attention they allowed it even when Hat was on the stand. By now, Hat was an hour and a half late, and I could see the gangsterish man behind the bar, the owner of the club, scowling as he checked his wristwatch. Hawes played two originals I particularly liked, favorites of mine from his Contemporary records, but in my mingled anxiety and irritation I scarcely heard them.

Toward the end of the second of these songs, Hat entered the club and fell into his customary seat a little more heavily than usual. The owner motioned away the waiter, who had begun moving toward him with the customary shot glass. Hat dropped the pork pie on the table and struggled with his coat buttons. When he heard what Hawes was playing, he sat listening with his hands still on a coat button, and I listened, too—the music had a tighter, harder, more modern feel, like Hawes's records. Hat nodded to himself, got his coat off, and struggled with the snaps on his saxophone case. The audience gave Hawes unusually appreciative applause. It took Hat longer than usual to fit the horn together, and by the time he was up on his feet, Hawes and the other two musicians had turned around to watch his progress as if they feared he would not make it all the way to the bandstand. Hat wound through the tables with his head tilted back, smiling to himself. When he got close to the stand, I saw that he was walking on his toes like a small child. The owner crossed his arms over his chest and glared. Hat seemed almost to float onto the stand. He licked his reed. Then he lowered his horn and, with his mouth open, stared out at us for a moment. "Ladies, ladies," he said in a soft, high voice. These were the first words I had ever heard him speak. "Thank you for your appreciation of our pianist, Mr. Hawes. And now I must explain my absence during the first set. My son passed away this afternoon, and I have been . . . busy . . . with details. Thank you."

With that, he spoke a single word to Hawes, put his horn back in his mouth, and began to play a blues called "Hat Jumped Up," one of his twenty songs. The audience sat motionless with shock. Hawes, the bassist, and the drummer played on as if nothing unusual had happened—they must have known about his son, I thought. Or maybe they knew that he had no son, and had invented a grotesque excuse for turning up ninety minutes late. The club owner bit his lower lip and looked unusually introspective. Hat played one familiar, uncomplicated figure after another, his tone rough, almost coarse. At the end of his solo, he repeated one note for an entire chorus, fingering the key while staring out toward the back of the club. Maybe he was watching the customers leave—three couples and a couple of single people walked out while he was playing. But I don't think he saw anything at all. When the song was over, Hat leaned over to whisper to Hawes, and the piano player announced a short break. The second set was over.

Hat put his tenor on top of the piano and stepped down off the bandstand, pursing his mouth with concentration. The owner had come out from behind the bar and moved up in front of him as Hat tiptoed around the stand. The owner spoke a few quiet words. Hat answered. From behind, he looked slumped and tired, and his hair curled far over the back of his collar. Whatever he had said only partially satisfied the owner, who spoke again before leaving him. Hat stood in place for a moment, perhaps not noticing that the owner had gone, and resumed his tiptoe glide toward the door. Looking at his back, I think I took in for the first time how genuinely strange he was. Floating through the door in his gray flannel suit, hair dangling in ringlet-like strands past his collar, leaving in the air behind him the announcement about a dead son, he seemed absolutely separate from the rest of humankind, a species of one.

I turned as if for guidance to the musicians at the bar. Talking, smiling, greeting a few fans and friends, they behaved just as they did on every other night. Could Hat really have lost a son earlier today? Maybe this was the jazz way of facing grief—to come back to work, to carry on. Still it seemed the worst of all times to approach Hat with my offer. His playing was a drunken parody of itself. He would forget anything he said to me; I was wasting my time.

On that thought, I stood up and walked past the bandstand and opened the door—if I was wasting my time, it didn't matter what I did.

He was leaning against a brick wall about ten feet up the alleyway from the club's back door. The door clicked shut behind me, but Hat did not open his eyes. His face tilted up, and a sweetness that might have been sleep lay over his features. He looked exhausted and insubstantial, too frail to move. I would have gone back inside the club if he had not produced a cigarette from a pack in his shirt pocket, lit it with a match, and then flicked the match away, all without opening his eyes. At least he was awake. I stepped toward him, and his eyes opened. He glanced at me and blew out white smoke. "Taste?" he said.

I had no idea what he meant. "Can I talk to you for a minute, sir?" I asked.

He put his hand into one of his jacket pockets and pulled out a half-pint bottle. "Have a taste." Hat broke the seal on the cap, tilted it into his mouth, and drank. Then he held the bottle out toward me.

I took it. "I've been coming here as often as I can."

"Me too," he said. "Go on, do it."

I took a sip from the bottle—gin. "I'm sorry about your son."

"Son?" He looked upward, as if trying to work out my meaning. "I got a son—out on Long Island. With his momma." He drank again and checked the level of the bottle.

"He's not dead, then."

He spoke the next words slowly, almost wonderingly. "Nobody—told—me—if—he—is." He shook his head and drank another mouthful of gin. "Damn. Wouldn't that be something, boy dies and nobody tells me? I'd have to think about that, you know, have to really think about that one."

"I'm just talking about what you said on stage."

He cocked his head and seemed to examine an empty place in the dark air about three feet from his face. "Uh-huh. That's right. I did say that. Son of mine passed."

It was like dealing with a sphinx. All I could do was plunge in. "Well, sir, actually there's a reason I came out here," I said. "I'd like to interview you. Do you think that might be possible? You're a great artist, and there's very little about you in print. Do you think we could set up a time when I could talk to you?"

He looked at me with his bleary, colorless eyes, and I wondered if he could see me at all. And then I felt that, despite his drunkenness, he saw everything—that he saw things about me that I couldn't see.

"You a jazz writer?" he asked.

"No, I'm a graduate student. I'd just like to do it. I think it would be important."

"Important." He took another swallow from the half-pint and slid the bottle back into his pocket. "Be nice, doing an important interview."

He stood leaning against the wall, moving further into outer space with every word. Only because I had started, I pressed on: I was already losing faith in this project. The reason Hat had never been interviewed was that ordinary American English was a foreign language to him. "Could we do the interview after you finish up at this club? I could meet you anywhere you like." Even as I said these words, I despaired. Hat was in no shape to know what he had to do after this engagement finished. I was surprised he could make it back to Long Island every night.

Hat rubbed his face, sighed, and restored my faith in him. "It'll have to wait a little while. Night after I finish here, I go to Toronto for two nights. Then I got something in Hartford on the thirtieth. You come see me after that."

"On the thirty-first?" I asked.

"Around nine, ten, something like that. Be nice if you brought some refreshments."

"Fine, great," I said, wondering if I would be able to take a late train back from wherever he lived. "But where on Long Island should I go?"

His eyes widened in mock-horror. "Don't go nowhere on Long Island. You come see me. In the Albert Hotel, Forty-ninth and Eighth. Room 821."

I smiled at him—I had guessed right about one thing, anyhow. Hat did not live in the Village, but he did live in a Manhattan hotel. I asked him for his phone number, and wrote it down, along with the other information, on a napkin from the club. After I folded the napkin into my jacket pocket, I thanked him and turned toward the door.

"Important as a motherfucker," he said in his high, soft, slurry voice.

I turned around in alarm, but he had tilted his head toward the sky again, and his eyes were closed.

"Indiana," he said. His voice made the word seem sung. "Moonlight in Vermont. I Thought About You. Flamingo."

He was deciding what to play during his next set. I went back inside, where twenty or thirty new arrivals, more people than I had ever seen in the club, waited for the music to start. Hat soon reappeared through the door, the other musicians left the bar, and the third set began. Hat played all four of the songs he had named, interspersing them through his standard repertoire during the course of an unusually long set. He was playing as well as I'd ever heard him, maybe better than I'd heard on all the other nights I had come to the club. The Saturday night crowd applauded explosively after every solo. I didn't know if what I was seeing was genius or desperation.

An obituary in the Sunday *New York Times*, which I read over breakfast the next morning in the John Jay cafeteria, explained some of what had happened. Early Saturday morning, a thirty-eight-year-old tenor saxophone player named Grant Kilbert had been killed in an automobile accident. One of the most successful jazz musicians in the world, one of the few jazz musicians known outside of the immediate circle of fans, Kilbert had probably been Hat's most prominent disciple. He had certainly been one of my favorite musicians. More importantly, from his first record, *Cool Breeze*, Kilbert had excited respect and admiration. I looked at the photograph of the handsome young man beaming out over the neck of his saxophone and realized that the first four songs on *Cool Breeze* were "Indiana," "Moonlight in Vermont," "I Thought About You," and "Flamingo." Sometime late Saturday afternoon, someone had called up Hat to tell him about Kilbert. What I had seen had not merely been alcoholic eccentricity, it had been grief for a lost son. And when I thought about it, I was sure that the lost son, not himself, had been the important motherfucker he'd apotheosized. What I had taken for spaciness and disconnection had all along been irony.

PART TWO

1

On the thirty-first of October, after calling first to make sure he remembered our appointment, I did go to the Albert Hotel, room 821, and interview Hat. That is, I asked him questions and listened to the long, rambling, often obscene responses he gave them. During the long night I spent in his room, he drank the fifth of Gordon's gin, the "refreshments" I brought with me—all of it, an entire bottle of gin, without tonic, ice, or other dilutants. He just poured it into a tumbler and drank, as if it were water. (I refused his single offer of a "taste.") I made frequent checks to make sure that the tape recorder I'd borrowed from a business student down the hall from me was still working, I changed tapes until they ran out, I made detailed backup notes with a ballpoint pen in a stenographic notebook. A couple of times, he played me sections of records that he wanted me to hear, and now and then he sang a couple of bars to make sure that I understood what he was telling me. He sat me in his only chair, and during the entire night stationed himself, dressed in his pork pie hat, a dark blue chalk-stripe suit, and white button-down shirt with a black knit tie, on the edge of his bed. This was a formal occasion. When I arrived at nine o'clock, he addressed me as "Mr. Leonard Feather" (the name of a well-known jazz critic), and when he opened his door at six-thirty the next morning, he called me "Miss Rosemary." By then, I knew that this was an allusion to Rosemary Clooney, whose singing I had learned that he liked, and that the nickname meant he liked me, too. It was not at all certain, however, that he remembered my actual name.

I had three 60-minute tapes and a notebook filled with handwriting that gradually degenerated from my usual scrawl into loops and wiggles that resembled Arabic more than English. Over the next month, I spent whatever spare time I had transcribing the tapes and trying to decipher my own handwriting. I wasn't sure that what I had was an interview. My carefully prepared questions had been met either with evasions or blank, silent refusals to answer—he had simply started talking about something else. After about an hour, I realized that this was his interview, not mine, and let him roll.

After my notes had been typed up and the tapes transcribed, I put everything in a drawer and went back to work on my M.A. What I had was even more puzzling than I'd thought, and straightening it out would have taken more time than I could afford. So the rest of that academic year was a long grind of studying for the comprehensive exam and getting a thesis ready. Until I picked up an old *Time* magazine in the John Jay lounge and saw his name in the "Milestones" column, I didn't even know that Hat had died.

Two months after I'd interviewed him, he had begun to hemorrhage on a flight back from France; an ambulance had taken him directly from the airport to a hospital. Five days after his release from the hospital, he had died in his bed at the Albert.

After I earned my degree, I was determined to wrestle something usable from my long night with Hat—I owed it to him. During the first seven weeks of that summer, I wrote out a version of what Hat had said to me, and sent it to the only publication I thought would be interested in it. *Downbeat* accepted the interview, and it appeared there about six months later. Eventually, it acquired some fame as the last of his rare public statements. I still see lines from the interview quoted in the sort of pieces about Hat never printed during his life. Sometimes they are lines he really did say to me; sometimes they are stitched together from remarks he made at different times; sometimes, they are quotations I invented in order to be able to use other things he did say.

But one section of that interview has never been quoted, because it was never printed. I never figured out what to make of it. Certainly I could not believe all he had said. He had been putting me on, silently laughing at my credulity, for he could not possibly believe that what he was telling me was literal truth. I was a white boy with a tape recorder, it was Halloween, and Hat was having fun with me. He was jiving me.

Now I feel different about his story, and about him, too. He was a great man, and I was an unworldly kid. He was drunk, and I was priggishly sober, but in every important way, he was functioning far above my level. Hat had lived forty-nine years as a black man in America, and I'd spent all of my twenty-one years in white suburbs. He was an immensely talented musician, a man who virtually thought in music, and I can't even hum in tune. That I expected to understand anything at all about him staggers me now. Back then, I didn't know anything about grief, and Hat wore grief about him daily, like a cloak. Now that I am the age he was then, I see that most of what is called information is interpretation, and interpretation is always partial.

Probably Hat was putting me on, jiving me, though not maliciously.

He certainly was not telling me the literal truth, though I have never been able to learn what was the literal truth of this case. It's possible that even Hat never knew what was the literal truth behind the story he told me—possible, I mean, that he was still trying to work out what the truth was, forty years after the fact.

2

He started telling me the story after we heard what I thought were gunshots from the street. I jumped from the chair and rushed to the windows, which looked out onto Eighth Avenue. "Kids," Hat said. In the hard yellow light of the street lamps, four or five teenage boys trotted up the avenue. Three of them carried paper bags. "Kids shooting?" I asked. My amazement tells you how long ago this was.

"Fireworks," Hat said. "Every Halloween in New York, fool kids run around with bags full of fireworks, trying to blow their hands off."

Here and in what follows, I am not going to try to represent the way Hat actually spoke. I cannot represent the way his voice glided over certain words and turned others into mushy growls, though he expressed more than half of his meaning by sound; and I don't want to reproduce his constant, reflexive obscenity. Hat couldn't utter four words in a row without throwing in a "motherfucker." Mostly, I have replaced his obscenities with other words, and the reader can imagine what was really said. Also, if I tried to imitate his grammar, I'd sound racist and he would sound stupid. Hat left school in the fourth grade, and his language, though precise, was casual. To add to these difficulties, Hat employed a private language of his own, a code to ensure that he would be understood only by the people he wished to understand him. I have replaced most of his code words with their equivalents.

It must have been around one in the morning, which means that I had been in his room about four hours. Until Hat explained the "gunshots," I had forgotten that it was Halloween night, and I told him this as I turned away from the window.

"I never forget about Halloween," Hat said. "If I can, I stay home on Halloween. Don't want to be out on the street, that night."

He had already given me proof that he was superstitious, and as he spoke he glanced almost nervously around the room, as if looking for sinister presences.

"You'd feel in danger?" I asked.

He rolled gin around in his mouth and looked at me as he had in the alley behind the club, taking note of qualities I myself did not yet perceive. This did not feel at all judgmental. The nervousness I thought I had seen had disappeared, and his manner seemed marginally more concentrated than earlier in the evening. He swallowed the gin and looked at me without speaking for a couple of seconds.

"No," he finally said. "Not exactly. But I wouldn't feel safe, either."

I sat with my pen half an inch from the page of my notebook, uncertain whether or not to write this down.

"I'm from Mississippi, you know."

I nodded.

"Funny things happen down there. Whole different world. Back when I was a little kid, it was really a different world. Know what I mean?"

"I can guess," I said.

He nodded. "Sometimes people just disappeared. They'd be gone. All kinds of stuff used to happen, stuff you wouldn't even believe in now. I met a witch-lady once, a real one, who could put curses on you, make you go blind and crazy. I saw a dead man walk. Another time, I saw a mean, murdering son of a bitch named Eddie Grimes die and come back to life—he got shot to death at a dance we were playing, he was dead, and a woman went down and whispered to him, and Eddie Grimes stood right back up on his feet. The man who shot him took off double-quick and he must have kept on going, because we never saw him after that."

"Did you start playing again?" I asked, taking notes as fast as I could.

"We never stopped," Hat said. "You let the people deal with what's going on, but you gotta keep on playing."

"Did you live in the country?" I asked, thinking that all of this sounded like Dogpatch—witches and walking dead men.

He shook his head. "I was brought up in town, Woodland, Mississippi. On the river. Where we lived was called Darktown, you know, but most of Woodland was white, with nice houses and all. Lots of our people did the cooking and washing in the big houses on Miller's Hill, that kind of work. In fact, we lived in a pretty nice house, for Darktown—the band always did well, and my father had a couple of other jobs on top of that. He was a good piano player, mainly, but he could play any kind of instrument. And he was a big, strong guy, nice-looking, real light-complected, so he was called Red, which was what that meant in those days. People respected him."

Another long, rattling burst of explosions came from Eighth Avenue. I wanted to ask him again about leaving his father's band, but Hat once more gave his little room a quick inspection, swallowed another mouthful of gin, and went on talking.

"We even went out trick-or-treating on Halloween, you know, just like the white kids. I guess our people didn't do that everywhere, but we did. Naturally, we stuck to our neighborhood, and probably we got a lot less than the kids from Miller's Hill, but they didn't have anything up there that tasted as good as the apples and candy we brought home in our bags. Around us, folks made instead of bought, and that's the difference." He smiled at either the memory or the unexpected sentimentality he had just revealed—for a moment, he looked both lost in time and uneasy with himself for having said too much. "Or maybe I just remember it that way, you know? Anyhow, we used to raise some hell, too. You were supposed to raise hell, on Halloween."

"You went out with your brothers?" I asked.

"No, no, they were—" He flipped his hand in the air, dismissing whatever it was that his brothers had been. "I was always apart, you dig? Me, I was always into my own little things. I was that way right from the beginning. I play like that—never play like anyone else, don't even play like myself. You gotta find new places for yourself, or else nothing's happening, isn't that right? Don't want to be a repeater pencil." He saluted this declaration with another swallow of gin. "Back in those days, I used to go out with a boy named Rodney Sparks—we called him Dee, short for 'Demon,' 'cause Dee Sparks would do anything that came into his head. That boy was the bravest little bastard I ever knew. He'd wrassle a mad dog. He was just that way. And the reason was, Dee was the preacher's boy. If you happen to be the preacher's boy, seems like you gotta prove every way you can that you're no Buster Brown, you know? So I hung with Dee, because I wasn't any Buster Brown, either. This is all when we were eleven, around then—the time when you talk about girls, you know, but you still aren't too sure what that's about. You don't know what anything's about, to tell the truth. You along for the ride, you trying to pack in as much fun as possible. So Dee was my right hand, and when I went out on Halloween in Woodland, I went out with him."

He rolled his eyes toward the window and said, "Yeah." An expression I could not read at all took over his face. By the standards of ordinary people, Hat almost always looked detached, even impassive, tuned to some private wavelength, and this sense of detachment had intensified. I thought he was changing mental gears, dismissing his childhood, and opened my mouth to ask him about Grant Kilbert. But he raised his glass to his mouth again and rolled his eyes back to me, and the quality of his gaze told me to keep quiet.

"I didn't know it," he said, "but I was getting ready to stop being a little boy. To stop believing in little boy things and start seeing like a grown-up. I guess that's part of what I liked about Dee Sparks—he seemed like he was a lot more grown-up than I was, shows you what my head was like. The age we were, this would have been the last time we actually went out on Halloween to get apples and candy. From then on, we would have gone out mainly to raise hell. Smash in a few windows. Bust up somebody's wagon. Scare the shit out of little kids. But the way it turned out, it was the last time we ever went out on Halloween."

He finished off the gin in his glass and reached down to pick the bottle off the floor and pour another few inches into the tumbler. "Here I am, sitting in this room. There's my horn over there. Here's this bottle. You know what I'm saying?"

I didn't. I had no idea what he was saying. The hint of fatality clung to his earlier statement, and for a second I thought he was going to say that he was here but Dee Sparks was nowhere because Dee Sparks had died in Woodland, Mississippi, at the age of eleven on Halloween night. Hat was looking at me with a steady curiosity which compelled a response. "What happened?" I asked.

Now I know that he was saying, It has come down to just this, my room, my horn, my bottle. My question was as good as any other response.

"If I was to tell you everything that happened, we'd have to stay in this room for a month." He smiled and straightened up on the bed. His ankles were crossed, and for the first time I noticed that his feet, shod in dark suede shoes with crepe soles, did not quite touch the floor. "And, you know, I never tell anybody everything, I always have to keep something back for myself. Things turned out all right. Only thing I mind is, I should have earned more money. Grant Kilbert, he earned a lot of money, and some of that was mine, you know."

"Were you friends?" I asked.

"I knew the man." He tilted his head and stared at the ceiling for so long that eventually I looked up at it too. It was not a remarkable ceiling. A circular section near the center had been replastered not long before.

"No matter where you live, there are places you're not supposed to go," he said, still gazing up. "And sooner or later, you're gonna wind up there." He smiled at me again. "Where we lived, the place you weren't supposed to go was called the Backs. Out of town, stuck in the woods on one little path. In Darktown, we had all kinds from preachers on down. We had washerwomen and blacksmiths and carpenters, and we had some no-good thieving trash, too, like Eddie Grimes, that man who came back from being dead. In the Backs, they started with trash like Eddie Grimes, and went down from there. Sometimes, some of our people went out there to buy a jug, and sometimes they went there to get a woman, but they never talked about it. The Backs was rough. What they had was rough." He rolled his eyes at me and said, "That witch-lady I told you about, she lived in the Backs." He snickered. "Man, they were a mean bunch of people. They'd cut you, you looked at 'em bad. But one thing funny about the place, white and colored lived there just the same—it was integrated. Backs people were so evil, color didn't make no difference to them. They hated everybody anyhow, on principle." Hat pointed his glass at me, tilted his head, and narrowed his eyes. "At least, that was what everybody said. So this particular Halloween, Dee Sparks says to me after we finish with Darktown, we ought to head out to the Backs and see what the place is really like. Maybe we can have some fun.

"Well, that sounded fine to me. The idea of going out to the Backs kind of scared me, but being scared was part of the fun—Halloween, right? And if anyplace in Woodland was perfect for all that Halloween shit, you know, someplace where you might really see a ghost or a goblin, the Backs was better than the graveyard." Hat shook his head, holding the glass out at a right angle to his body. A silvery amusement momentarily transformed him, and it struck me that his native elegance, the product of his character and bearing much more than of the handsome suit and the suede shoes, had in effect been paid for by the surviving of a thousand unimaginable difficulties, each painful to a varying degree. Then I realized that what I meant by "elegance" was really dignity, that for the first time I had recognized actual dignity in another human being, and that dignity was nothing like the self-congratulatory superiority people usually mistook for it.

"We were just little babies, and we wanted some of those good old Halloween scares. Like those dumbbells out on the street, tossing firecrackers at each other." Hat wiped his free hand down over his face and made sure that I was prepared to write down everything he said. (The tapes had already been used up.) "When I'm done, tell me if we found it, okay?"

"Okay," I said.

3

"Dee showed up at my house just after dinner, dressed in an old sheet with two eye-holes cut in it and carrying a paper bag. His big old shoes stuck out underneath the sheet. I had the same costume, but it was the one my brother used the year before, and it dragged along the ground and my feet got caught in it. The eye-holes kept sliding away from my eyes. My mother gave me a bag and told me to behave myself and get home before eight. It didn't take but half an hour to cover all the likely houses in Darktown, but she knew I'd want to fool around with Dee for an hour or so afterwards.

"Then up and down the streets we go, knocking on the doors where they'd give us stuff and making a little mischief where we knew they wouldn't. Nothing real bad, just banging on the door and running like hell, throwing rocks on the roof, little stuff. A few places, we plain and simple stayed away from—the places where people like Eddie Grimes lived. I always thought that was funny. We knew enough to steer clear of those houses, but we were still crazy to get out to the Backs.

"Only way I can figure it is, the Backs was forbidden. Nobody had to tell us to stay away from Eddie Grimes's house at night. You wouldn't even go there in the daylight, 'cause Eddie Grimes would get you and that would be that.

"Anyhow, Dee kept us moving along real quick, and when folks asked us questions or said they wouldn't give us stuff unless we sang a song, he moaned like a ghost and shook his bag in their faces, so we could get away faster. He was so excited, I think he was almost shaking.

"Me, I was excited too. Not like Dee—sort of sick-excited, the way people must feel the first time they use a parachute. Scared-excited.

"As soon as we got away from the last house, Dee crossed the street and started running down the side of the little general store we all used. I knew where he was going. Out behind the store was a field, and on the other side of the field was Meridian Road, which took you out into the woods and to the path up to the Backs. When he realized that I wasn't next to him, he turned around and yelled at me to hurry up. No, I said inside myself, I ain't gonna jump outta of this here airplane, I'm not dumb enough to do that. And then I pulled up my sheet and scrunched up my eye to look through the one hole close enough to see through, and I took off after him.

"It was beginning to get dark when Dee and I left my house, and now it was dark. The Backs was about a mile and a half away, or at least the path was. We didn't know how far along that path you had to go before you got there. Hell, we didn't even know what it was—I was still thinking the place was a collection of little houses, like a sort of shadow-Woodland. And then, while we were crossing the field, I stepped on my costume and fell down flat on my face. Enough of this stuff, I said, and yanked the damned thing off. Dee started cussing me out, I wasn't doing this stuff the right way, we had to keep our costumes on in case anybody saw us, did I forget that this is Halloween, on Halloween a costume protected you. So I told him I'd put it back on when we got there. If I kept on falling down, it'd take us twice as long. That shut him up.

"As soon as I got that blasted sheet over my head, I discovered that I could see at least a little ways ahead of me. The moon was up, and a lot of stars were out. Under his sheet, Dee Sparks looked a little bit like a real ghost. It kind of glimmered. You couldn't really make out its edges, so the darn thing like floated. But I could see his legs and those big old shoes sticking out.

"We got out of the field and started up Meridian Road, and pretty soon the trees came up right to the ditches alongside the road, and I couldn't see too well anymore. The road looked like it went smack into the woods and disappeared. The trees looked taller and thicker than in the daytime, and now and then something right at the edge of the woods shone round and white, like an eye—reflecting the moonlight, I guess. Spooked me. I didn't think we'd ever be able to find the path up to the Backs, and that was fine with me. I thought we might go along the road another ten-fifteen minutes, and then turn around and go home. Dee was swooping around up in front of me, flapping his sheet and acting bughouse. He sure wasn't trying too hard to find that path.

"After we walked about a mile down Meridian Road, I saw head-lights like yellow dots coming toward us fast—Dee didn't see anything at all, running around in circles the way he was. I shouted at him to get off the road, and he took off like a rabbit—disappeared into the woods before I did. I jumped the ditch and hunkered down behind a pine about ten feet off the road to see who was coming. There weren't many cars in Woodland in those days, and I knew every one of them. When the car came by, it was Dr. Garland's old red Cord—Dr. Garland was a white man, but he had two waiting rooms and took colored patients, so colored patients was mostly what he had. And the man was a heavy drinker, heavy drinker. He zipped by, goin' at least fifty, which was mighty fast for those days, probably as fast as that old Cord would go. For about a second, I saw Dr. Garland's face under his white hair, and his mouth was wide open, stretched like he was screaming. After he passed, I waited a long time before I came out of the woods. Turning around and going home would have been fine with me. Dr. Garland changed everything. Normally, he was kind of slow and quiet, you know, and I could still see that black screaming hole opened up in his face—he looked like he was being tortured, like he was in Hell. I sure as hell didn't want to see whatever he had seen.

"I could hear the Cord's engine after the taillights disappeared. I turned around and saw that I was all alone on the road. Dee Sparks was nowhere in sight. A couple of times, real soft, I called out his name. Then I called his name a little louder. Away off in the woods, I heard Dee giggle. I said he could run around all night if he liked but I was going home, and then I saw that pale silver sheet moving through the trees, and I started back down Meridian Road. After about twenty paces, I looked back, and there he was, standing in the middle of the road in that silly sheet, watching me go. Come on, I said, let's get back. He paid me no mind. Wasn't that Dr. Garland? Where was he going, as fast as that? What was happening? When I said the doctor was prob-ably out on some emergency, Dee said the man was going home—he lived in Woodland, didn't he?

"Then I thought maybe Dr. Garland had been up in the Backs. And Dee thought the same thing, which made him want to go there all the more. Now he was determined. Maybe we'd see some dead guy. We stood there until I understood that he was going to go by himself if I didn't go with him. That meant that I had to go. Wild as he was, Dee'd get himself into some kind of mess for sure if I wasn't there to hold him down. So I said okay, I was coming along, and Dee started swooping along like before, saying crazy stuff. There was no way we were going to be able to find some little old path that went up into the woods. It was so dark, you couldn't see the separate trees, only giant black walls on both sides of the road.

"We went so far along Meridian Road I was sure we must have passed it. Dee was running around in circles about ten feet ahead of me. I told him that we missed the path, and now it was time to get back home. He laughed at me and ran across to the right side of the road and disappeared into the darkness.

"I told him to get back, damn it, and he laughed some more and said I should come to him. Why? I said, and he said, Because this here is the path, dummy. I didn't believe him—came right up to where he disappeared. All I could see was a black wall that could have been trees or just plain night. Moron, Dee said, look down. And I did. Sure enough, one of those white things like an eye shone up from where the ditch should have been. I bent down and touched cold little stones, and the shining dot of white went off like a light—a pebble that caught the moonlight just right. Bending down like that, I could see the hump of grass growing up between the tire tracks that led out onto Meridian Road. He'd found the path, all right.

"At night, Dee Sparks could see one hell of a lot better than me. He spotted the break in the ditch from across the road. He was already walking up the path in those big old shoes, turning around every other step to look back at me, make sure I was coming along behind him. When I started following him, Dee told me to get my sheet back on, and I pulled the thing over my head even though I'd rather have sucked the water out of a hollow stump. But I knew he was right—on Halloween, especially in a place like where we were, you were safer in a costume.

"From then on in, we were in no-man's-land. Neither one of us had any idea how far we had to go to get to the Backs, or what it would look like once we got there. Once I set foot on that wagon track I knew for sure the Backs wasn't anything like the way I thought. It was a lot more primitive than a bunch of houses in the woods. Maybe they didn't even have houses! Maybe they lived in caves!

"Naturally, after I got that blamed costume over my head, I couldn't see for a while. Dee kept hissing at me to hurry up, and I kept cussing him out. Finally I bunched up a couple handfuls of the sheet right under my chin and held it against my neck, and that way I could see pretty well and walk without tripping all over myself. All I had to do was follow Dee, and that was easy. He was only a couple of inches in front of me, and even through one eye-hole, I could see that silvery sheet moving along.

"Things moved in the woods, and once in a while an owl hooted. To tell you the truth, I never did like being out in the woods at night. Even back then, give me a nice warm barroom instead, and I'd be happy. Only animal I ever liked was a cat, because a cat is soft to the touch, and it'll fall asleep on your lap. But this was even worse than usual, because of Halloween, and even before we got to the Backs, I wasn't sure if what I heard moving around in the woods was just a possum or a fox or something a lot worse, something with funny eyes and long teeth that liked the taste of little boys. Maybe Eddie Grimes was out there, looking for whatever kind of treat Eddie Grimes liked on Halloween night. Once I thought of that, I got so close to Dee Sparks I could smell him right through his sheet.

"You know what Dee Sparks smelled like? Like sweat, and a little bit like the soap the preacher made him use on his hands and face before dinner, but really like a fire in a junction box. A sharp, kind of bitter smell. That's how excited he was.

"After a while we were going uphill, and then we got to the top of the rise, and a breeze pressed my sheet against my legs. We started going downhill, and over Dee's electrical fire I could smell woodsmoke. And something else I couldn't name. Dee stopped moving so sudden, I bumped into him. I asked him what he could see. Nothing but the woods, he said, but we're getting there. People are up ahead somewhere. And they got a still. We got to be real quiet from here on out, he told me, as if he had to, and to let him know I understood I pulled him off the path into the woods.

"Well, I thought, at least I know what Dr. Garland was after.

"Dee and I went snaking through the trees—me holding that blamed sheet under my chin so I could see out of one eye, at least, and walk without falling down. I was glad for that big fat pad of pine needles on the ground. An elephant could have walked over that stuff as quiet as a beetle. We went along a little further, and it got so I could smell all kinds of stuff—burned sugar, crushed juniper berries, tobacco juice, grease. And after Dee and I moved a little bit along, I heard voices, and that was enough for me. Those voices sounded angry.

"I yanked at Dee's sheet and squatted down—I wasn't going any farther without taking a good look. He slipped down beside me. I pushed the wad of material under my chin up over my face, grabbed another handful, and yanked that up too, to look out under the bottom of the sheet. Once I could actually see where we were, I almost passed out. Twenty feet away through the trees, a kerosene lantern lit up the greasepaper window cut into the back of a little wooden shack, and a big raggedy guy carrying another kerosene lantern came stepping out of a door we couldn't see and stumbled toward a shed. On the other side of the building I could see the yellow square of a window in another shack, and past that, another one, a sliver of yellow shining out through the trees. Dee was crouched next to me, and when I turned to look at him, I could see another chink of yellow light from some way off in the woods over that way. Whether he knew it or not, he'd just about walked us straight into the middle of the Backs.

"He whispered for me to cover my face. I shook my head. Both of us watched the big guy stagger toward the shed. Somewhere in front of us, a woman screeched, and I almost dumped a load in my pants. Dee stuck his hand out from under his sheet and held it out, as if I needed him to tell me to be quiet. The woman screeched again, and the big guy sort of swayed back and forth. The light from the lantern swung around in big circles. I saw that the woods were full of little paths that ran between the shacks. The light hit the shack, and it wasn't even wood, but tarpaper. The woman laughed or maybe sobbed. Whoever was inside the shack shouted, and the raggedy guy wobbled toward the shed again. He was so drunk he couldn't even walk straight. When he got to the shed, he set down the lantern and bent to get in.

"Dee put his mouth up to my ear and whispered, Cover up—you don't want these people to see who you are. Rip the eye-holes, if you can't see good enough.

"I didn't want anyone in the Backs to see my face. I let the costume drop down over me again, and stuck my fingers in the nearest eye-hole and pulled. Every living thing for about a mile around must have heard that cloth ripping. The big guy came out of the shed like someone pulled him out on a string, yanked the lantern up off the ground, and held it in our direction. Then we could see his face, and it was Eddie Grimes. You wouldn't want to run into Eddie Grimes anywhere, but the Backs was the last place you'd want to come across him. I was afraid he was going to start looking for us, but that woman started making stuck-pig noises, and the man in the shack yelled something, and Grimes ducked back into the shed and came out with a jug. He lumbered back toward the shack and disappeared around the front of it. Dee and I could hear him arguing with the man inside.

"I jerked my thumb toward Meridian Road, but Dee shook his head. I whispered, Didn't you already see Eddie Grimes, and isn't that enough for you? He shook his head again. His eyes were gleaming behind that sheet. So what do you want, I asked, and he said, I want to see that girl. We don't even know where she is, I whispered, and Dee said, All we got to do is follow her sound.

"Dee and I sat and listened for a while. Every now and then, she let out a sort of whoop, and then she'd sort of cry, and after that she might say a word or two that sounded almost ordinary before she got going again on crying or laughing, the two all mixed up together. Sometimes we could hear other noises coming from the shacks, and none of them sounded happy. People were grumbling and arguing or just plain talking to themselves, but at least they sounded normal. That lady, she sounded like Halloween—like something that came up out of a grave.

"Probably you're thinking what I was hearing was sex—that I was too young to know how much noise ladies make when they're having fun. Well, maybe I was only eleven, but I grew up in Darktown, not Miller's Hill, and our walls were none too thick. What was going on with this lady didn't have anything to do with fun. The strange thing is, Dee didn't know that—he thought just what you were thinking. He wanted to see this lady getting humped. Maybe he even thought he could sneak in and get some for himself, I don't know. The main thing is, he thought he was listening to some wild sex, and he wanted to get close enough to see it. Well, I thought, his daddy was a preacher, and maybe preachers didn't do it once they got kids. And Dee didn't have an older brother like mine, who sneaked girls into the house whenever he thought he wouldn't get caught.

"He started sliding sideways through the woods, and I had to follow him. I'd seen enough of the Backs to last me the rest of my life, but I couldn't run off and leave Dee behind. And at least he was going at it the right way, circling around the shacks sideways, instead of trying to sneak straight through them. I started off after him. At least I could see a little better ever since I ripped at my eye-hole, but I still had to hold my blasted costume bunched up under my chin, and if I moved my head or my hand the wrong way, the hole moved away from my eye and I couldn't see anything at all.

"So naturally, the first thing that happened was that I lost sight of Dee Sparks. My foot came down in a hole and I stumbled ahead for a few steps, completely blind, and then I hit a tree. I just came to a halt, sure that Eddie Grimes and a few other murderers were about to jump on me. For a couple of seconds I stood as still as a wooden Indian, too scared to move. When I didn't hear anything, I hauled at my costume until I could see out of it. No murderers were coming toward me from the shack beside the still. Eddie Grimes was saying, You don't understand, over and over, like he was so drunk that one phrase got stuck in his head, and he couldn't say or hear anything else. That woman yipped, like an animal noise, not a human one—like a fox barking. I sidled up next to the tree I'd run into and looked around for Dee. All I could see was dark trees and that one yellow window I'd seen before. To hell with Dee Sparks, I said to myself, and pulled the costume off over my head. I could see better, but there wasn't any glimmer of white over that way. He'd gone so far ahead of me I couldn't even see him.

"So I had to catch up with him, didn't I? I knew where he was going—the woman's noises were coming from the shack way up there in the woods—and I knew he was going to sneak around the outside of the shacks. In a couple of seconds, after he noticed I wasn't there, he was going to stop and wait for me. Makes sense, doesn't it? All I had to do was keep going toward that shack off to the side until I ran into him. I shoved my costume inside my shirt, and then I did something else—set my bag of candy down next to the tree. I'd clean forgotten about it ever since I saw Eddie Grimes's face, and if I had to run, I'd go faster without holding onto a lot of apples and chunks of taffy.

"About a minute later, I came out into the open between two big old chinaberry trees. There was a patch of grass between me and the next stand of trees. The woman made a gargling sound that ended in one of those fox-yips, and I looked up in that direction and saw that the clearing extended in a straight line up and down, like a path. Stars shone out of the patch of darkness between the two parts of the woods.

And when I started to walk across it, I felt a grassy hump between two beaten tracks. The path into the Backs off Meridian Road curved around somewhere up ahead and wound back down through the shacks before it came to a dead end. It had to come to a dead end, because it sure didn't join back up with Meridian Road.

"And this was how I'd managed to lose sight of Dee Sparks. Instead of avoiding the path and working his way north through the woods, he'd just taken the easiest way toward the woman's shack. Hell, I'd had to pull him off the path in the first place! By the time I got out of my sheet, he was probably way up there, out in the open for anyone to see and too excited to notice that he was all by himself. What I had to do was what I'd been trying to do all along, save his ass from anybody who might see him.

"As soon as I started going as soft as I could up the path, I saw that saving Dee Sparks's ass might be a tougher job than I thought—maybe I couldn't even save my own. When I first took off my costume, I'd seen lights from three or four shacks. I thought that's what the Backs was—three or four shacks. But after I started up the path, I saw a low square shape standing between two trees at the edge of the woods and realized that it was another shack. Whoever was inside had extinguished his kerosene lamp, or maybe wasn't home. About twenty-thirty feet on, there was another shack, all dark, and the only reason I noticed that one was, I heard voices coming from it, a man and a woman, both of them sounding drunk and slowed-down. Deeper in the woods past that one, another greasepaper window gleamed through the trees like a firefly. There were shacks all over the woods. As soon as I realized that Dee and I might not be the only people walking through the Backs on Halloween night, I bent down low to the ground and damn near slowed to a standstill. The only thing Dee had going for him, I thought, was good night vision—at least he might spot someone before they spotted him.

"A noise came from one of those shacks, and I stopped cold, with my heart pounding away like a bass drum. Then a big voice yelled out, Who's that?, and I just lay down in the track and tried to disappear. Who's there? Here I was calling Dee a fool, and I was making more noise than he did. I heard that man walk outside his door, and my heart pretty near exploded. Then the woman moaned up ahead, and the man who'd heard me swore to himself and went back inside. I just lay there in the dirt for a while. The woman moaned again, and this time it sounded scarier than ever, because it had a kind of a chuckle in it. She was crazy. Or she was a witch, and if she was having sex, it was with the devil. That was enough to make me start crawling along, and I kept on crawling until I was long past the shack where the man had heard me. Finally I got up on my feet again, thinking that if I didn't see Dee Sparks real soon, I was going to sneak back to Meridian Road by myself. If Dee Sparks wanted to see a witch in bed with the devil, he could do it without me.

"And then I thought I was a fool not to ditch Dee, because hadn't he ditched me? After all this time, he must have noticed that I wasn't with him anymore. Did he come back and look for me? The hell he did.

"And right then I would have gone back home, but for two things. The first was that I heard that woman make another sound—a sound that was hardly human, but wasn't made by any animal. It wasn't even loud. And it sure as hell wasn't any witch in bed with the devil. It made me want to throw up. That woman was being hurt. She wasn't just getting beat up—I knew what that sounded like—she was being hurt bad enough to drive her crazy, bad enough to kill her. Because you couldn't live through being hurt bad enough to make that sound. I was in the Backs, sure enough, and the place was even worse than it was supposed to be. Someone was killing a woman, everybody could hear it, and all that happened was that Eddie Grimes fetched another jug back from the still. I froze. When I could move, I pulled my ghost costume out from inside my shirt, because Dee was right, and for certain I didn't want anybody seeing my face out there on this night. And then the second thing happened. While I was pulling the sheet over my head, I saw something pale lying in the grass a couple of feet back toward the woods I'd come out of, and when I looked at it, it turned into Dee Sparks's Halloween bag.

"I went up to the bag and touched it to make sure about what it was. I'd found Dee's bag, all right. And it was empty. Flat. He had stuffed the contents into his pockets and left the bag behind. What that meant was, I couldn't turn around and leave him—because he hadn't left me after all. He waited for me until he couldn't stand it anymore, and then he emptied his bag and left it behind as a sign. He was counting on me to see in the dark as well as he could. But I wouldn't have seen it at all if that woman hadn't stopped me cold.

"The top of the bag was pointing north, so Dee was still heading toward the woman's shack. I looked up that way, and all I could see was a solid wall of darkness underneath a lighter darkness filled with stars. For about a second, I realized, I had felt pure relief. Dee had ditched me, so I could ditch him and go home. Now I was stuck with Dee all over again.

"About twenty feet ahead, another surprise jumped up at me out of the darkness. Something that looked like a little tiny shack began to take shape, and I got down on my hands and knees to crawl toward the path when I saw a long silver gleam along the top of the thing. That meant it had to be metal—tar paper might have a lot of uses, but it never yet reflected starlight. Once I realized that the thing in front of me was metal, I remembered its shape and realized it was a car. You wouldn't think you'd come across a car in a down-and-out rathole like the Backs, would you? People like that, they don't even own two shirts, so how do they come by cars? Then I remembered Dr. Garland speeding away down Meridian Road, and I thought, You don't have to live in the Backs to drive there. Someone could turn up onto the path, drive around the loop, pull his car off onto the grass, and no one would ever see it or know that he was there.

"And this made me feel funny. The car probably belonged to someone I knew. Our band played dances and parties all over the county and everywhere in Woodland, and I'd probably seen every single person in town, and they'd seen me, too, and knew me by name. I walked closer to the car to see if I recognized it, but it was just an old black Model T. There must have been twenty cars just like it in Woodland. Whites and coloreds, the few coloreds that owned cars, both had them. And when I got right up beside the Model T, I saw what Dee had left for me on the hood—an apple.

"About twenty feet further along, there was an apple on top of a big old stone. He was putting those apples where I couldn't help but see them. The third one was on top of a post at the edge of the woods, and it was so pale it looked almost white. Next to the post one of those paths running all through the Backs led back into the woods. If it hadn't been for that apple, I would have gone right past it.

"At least I didn't have to worry so much about making noise once I got back into the woods. Must have been six inches of pine needles and fallen leaves underfoot, and I walked so quiet I could have been floating—tell you the truth, I've worn crepe soles ever since then, and for the same reason. You walk soft. But I was still plenty scared—back in the woods there was a lot less light, and I'd have to step on an apple to see it. All I wanted was to find Dee and persuade him to leave with me.

"For a while, all I did was keep moving between the trees and try to make sure I wasn't coming up on a shack. Every now and then, a faint, slurry voice came from somewhere off in the woods, but I didn't let it spook me. Then, way up ahead, I saw Dee Sparks. The path didn't go in a straight line, it kind of angled back and forth, so I didn't have a good clear look at him, but I got a flash of that silvery-looking sheet way off through the trees. If I sped up I could get to him before he did anything stupid. I pulled my costume up a little further toward my neck and started to jog.

"The path started dipping downhill. I couldn't figure it out. Dee was in a straight line ahead of me, and as soon as I followed the path down-hill a little bit, I lost sight of him. After a couple more steps, I stopped. The path got a lot steeper. If I kept running, I'd go ass over teakettle. The woman made another terrible sound, and it seemed to come from everywhere at once. Like everything around me had been hurt. I damn near came unglued. Seemed like everything was dying. That Hallow-een stuff about horrible creatures wasn't any story, man, it was the way things really were—you couldn't know anything, you couldn't trust anything, and you were surrounded by death. I almost fell down and cried like a baby boy. I was lost. I didn't think I'd ever get back home.

"Then the worst thing of all happened.

"I heard her die. It was just a little noise, more like a sigh than any-thing, but that sigh came from everywhere and went straight into my ear. A soft sound can be loud, too, you know, be the loudest thing you ever heard. That sigh about lifted me up off the ground, about blew my head apart.

"I stumbled down the path, trying to wipe my eyes with my costume, and all of a sudden I heard men's voices from off to my left. Someone was saying a word I couldn't understand over and over, and someone else was telling him to shut up. Then, behind me, I heard running—heavy running, a man. I took off, and right away my feet got tangled up in the sheet and I was rolling downhill, hitting my head on rocks and bouncing off trees and smashing into stuff I didn't have any idea what it was. *Biff bop bang slam smash clang crash ding dong.* I hit some-thing big and solid and wound up half-covered in water. Took me a long time to get upright, twisted up in the sheet the way I was. My ears buzzed, and I saw stars—yellow and blue and red stars, not real ones. When I tried to sit up, the blasted sheet pulled me back down, so I got a faceful of cold water. I scrambled around like a fox in a trap, and when I finally got so I was at least sitting up, I saw a slash of real sky out the corner of one eye, and I got my hands free and ripped that hole in the sheet wide enough for my whole head to fit through it.

"I was sitting in a little stream next to a fallen tree. The tree was what had stopped me. My whole body hurt like the dickens. No idea where I was. Wasn't even sure I could stand up. Got my hands on the top of the fallen tree and pushed myself up with my legs—blasted sheet ripped in half, and my knees almost bent back the wrong way, but I got up on my feet. And there was Dee Sparks, coming toward me through the woods on the other side of the stream.

"He looked like he didn't feel any better than I did, like he couldn't move in a straight line. His silvery sheet was smearing through the trees. Dee got hurt too, I thought—he looked like he was in some total panic. The next time I saw the white smear between the trees it was twisting about ten feet off the ground. No, I said to myself, and closed my eyes. Whatever that thing was, it wasn't Dee. An unbearable feeling, an absolute despair, flowed out from it. I fought against this wave of despair with every weapon I had. I didn't want to know that feeling. I couldn't know that feeling—I was eleven years old. If that feeling reached me when I was eleven years old, my entire life would be changed, I'd be in a different universe altogether.

"But it did reach me, didn't it? I could say no all I liked, but I couldn't change what had happened. I opened my eyes, and the white smear was gone.

"That was almost worse—I wanted it to be Dee after all, doing something crazy and reckless, climbing trees, running around like a wild man, trying to give me a big whopping scare. But it wasn't Dee Sparks, and it meant that the worst things I'd ever imagined were true. Everything was dying. You couldn't know anything, you couldn't trust anything, we were all lost in the midst of the death that surrounded us.

"Most people will tell you growing up means you stop believing in Halloween things—I'm telling you the reverse. You start to grow up when you understand that the stuff that scares you is part of the air you breathe.

"I stared at the spot where I'd seen that twist of whiteness, I guess trying to go back in time to before I saw Dr. Garland fleeing down Meridian Road. My face looked like his, I thought—because now I knew that you really could see a ghost. The heavy footsteps I'd heard before suddenly cut through the buzzing in my head, and after I turned around and saw who was coming at me down the hill, I thought it was probably my own ghost I'd seen.

"Eddie Grimes looked as big as an oak tree, and he had a long knife in one hand. His feet slipped out from under him, and he skidded the last few yards down to the creek, but I didn't even try to run away. Drunk as he was, I'd never get away from him. All I did was back up alongside the fallen tree and watch him slide downhill toward the water. I was so scared I couldn't even talk. Eddie Grimes's shirt was flapping open, and big long scars ran all across his chest and belly. He'd been raised from the dead at least a couple of times since I'd seen him get killed at the dance. He jumped back up on his feet and started coming for me. I opened my mouth, but nothing came out.

"Eddie Grimes took another step toward me, and then he stopped and looked straight at my face. He lowered the knife. A sour stink of sweat and alcohol came off him. All he could do was stare at me. Eddie Grimes knew my face all right, he knew my name, he knew my whole family—even at night, he couldn't mistake me for anyone else. I finally saw that Eddie was actually afraid, like he was the one who'd seen a ghost. The two of us just stood there in the shallow water for a couple more seconds, and then Eddie Grimes pointed his knife at the other side of the creek.

"That was all I needed, baby. My legs unfroze, and I forgot all my aches and pains. Eddie watched me roll over the fallen tree and lowered his knife. I splashed through the water and started moving up the hill, grabbing at weeds and branches to pull me along. My feet were frozen, and my clothes were soaked and muddy, and I was trembling all over. About halfway up the hill, I looked back over my shoulder, but Eddie Grimes was gone. It was like he'd never been there at all, like he was nothing but the product of a couple of good raps to the noggin.

"Finally, I pulled myself shaking up over the top of the rise, and what did I see about ten feet away through a lot of skinny birch trees but a kid in a sheet facing away from me into the woods, and hopping from foot to foot in a pair of big clumsy shoes? And what was in front of him but a path I could make out from even ten feet away? Obviously, this was where I was supposed to turn up, only in the dark and all I must have missed an apple stuck onto a branch or some blasted thing, and I took that little side trip downhill on my head and wound up throwing a spook into Eddie Grimes.

"As soon as I saw him, I realized I hated Dee Sparks. I wouldn't have tossed him a rope if he was drowning. Without even thinking about it, I bent down and picked up a stone and flung it at him. The stone bounced off a tree, so I bent down and got another one. Dee turned around to find out what made the noise, and the second stone hit him right in the chest, even though it was really his head I was aiming at.

"He pulled his sheet up over his face like an Arab and stared at me with his mouth wide open. Then he looked back over his shoulder at the path, as if the real me might come along at any second. I felt like pegging another rock at his stupid face, but instead I marched up to him. He was shaking his head from side to side. Jim Dawg, he whispered, what happened to you? By way of answer, I hit him a good hard knock on the breastbone. What's the matter? he wanted to know. After you left me, I say, I fell down a hill and ran into Eddie Grimes.

"That gave him something to think about, all right. Was Grimes coming after me, he wanted to know? Did he see which way I went? Did Grimes see who I was? He was pulling me into the woods while he asked me these dumb-ass questions, and I shoved him away. His sheet flopped back down over his front, and he looked like a little boy. He couldn't figure out why I was mad at him. From his point of view, he'd been pretty clever, and if I got lost, it was my fault. But I wasn't mad at him because I got lost. I wasn't even mad at him because I'd run into Eddie Grimes. It was everything else. Maybe it wasn't even him I was mad at.

"I want to get home without getting killed, I whispered. Eddie ain't gonna let me go twice. Then I pretended he wasn't there anymore and tried to figure out how to get back to Meridian Road. It seemed to me that I was still going north when I took that tumble downhill, so when I climbed up the hill on the other side of the creek I was still going north. The wagon track that Dee and I took into the Backs had to be off to my right. I turned away from Dee and started moving through the woods. I didn't care if he followed me or not. He had nothing to do with me anymore, he was on his own. When I heard him coming along after me, I was sorry. I wanted to get away from Dee Sparks. I wanted to get away from everybody.

"I didn't want to be around anybody who was supposed to be my friend. I'd rather have had Eddie Grimes following me than Dee Sparks.

"Then I stopped moving, because through the trees I could see one of those greasepaper windows glowing up ahead of me. That yellow light looked evil as the devil's eye—everything in the Backs was evil, poisoned, even the trees, even the air. The terrible expression on Dr. Garland's face and the white smudge in the air seemed like the same thing—they were what I didn't want to know.

"Dee shoved me from behind, and if I hadn't felt so sick inside I would have turned around and punched him. Instead, I looked over my shoulder and saw him nodding toward where the side of the shack would be. He wanted to get closer! For a second, he seemed as crazy as everything else out there, and then I got it: I was all turned around, and instead of heading back to the main path, I'd been taking us toward the woman's shack. That was why Dee was following me.

"I shook my head. No, I wasn't going to sneak up to that place. Whatever was inside there was something I didn't have to know about. It had too much power—it turned Eddie Grimes around, and that was enough for me. Dee knew I wasn't fooling. He went around me and started creeping toward the shack.

"And damnedest thing, I watched him slipping through the trees for a second, and started following him. If he could go up there, so could I. If I didn't exactly look at whatever was in there myself, I could watch Dee look at it. That would tell me most of what I had to know. And anyways, probably Dee wouldn't see anything anyhow, unless the front door was hanging open, and that didn't seem too likely to me. He wouldn't see anything, and I wouldn't either, and we could both go home.

"The door of the shack opened up, and a man walked outside. Dee and I freeze, and I mean freeze. We're about twenty feet away, on the side of this shack, and if the man looked sideways, he'd see our sheets. There were a lot of trees between us and him, and I couldn't get a very good look at him, but one thing about him made the whole situation a lot more serious. This man was white, and he was wearing good clothes—I couldn't see his face, but I could see his rolled-up sleeves, and his suit jacket slung over one arm, and some kind of wrapped-up bundle he was holding in his hands. All this took about a second. The white man started carrying his bundle straight through the woods, and in another two seconds he was out of sight.

"Dee was a little closer than I was, and I think his sight line was a little clearer than mine. On top of that, he saw better at night than I did. Dee didn't get around like me, but he might have recognized the man we'd seen, and that would be pure trouble. Some rich white man, killing a girl out in the Backs? And us two boys close enough to see him? Do you know what would have happened to us? There wouldn't be enough left of either one of us to make a decent shadow.

"Dee turned around to face me, and I could see his eyes behind his costume, but I couldn't tell what he was thinking. He just stood there, looking at me. In a little bit, just when I was about to explode, we heard a car starting up off to our left. I whispered at Dee if he saw who that was. Nobody, Dee said. Now, what the hell did that mean? Nobody? You could say Santa Claus, you could say J. Edgar Hoover, it'd be a better answer than Nobody. The Model T's headlights shone through the trees when the car swung around the top of the path and started going toward Meridian Road. Nobody I ever saw before, Dee said. When the headlights cut through the trees, both of us ducked out of sight. Actually, we were so far from the path, we had nothing to worry about. I could barely see the car when it went past, and I couldn't see the driver at all.

"We stood up. Over Dee's shoulder I could see the side of the shack where the white man had been. Lamplight flickered on the ground in front of the open door. The last thing in the world I wanted to do was to go inside that place—I didn't even want to walk around to the front and look in the door. Dee stepped back from me and jerked his head toward the shack. I knew it was going to be just like before. I'd say no, he'd say yes, and then I'd follow him wherever he thought he had to go. I felt the same way I did when I saw that white smear in the woods—hopeless, lost in the midst of death. You go, if you have to, I whispered to him, it's what you wanted to do all along. He didn't move, and I saw that he wasn't too sure about what he wanted anymore.

"Everything was different now, because the white man made it different. Once a white man walked out that door, it was like raising the stakes in a poker game. But Dee had been working toward that one shack ever since we got into the Backs, and he was still curious as a cat about it. He turned away from me and started moving sideways in a straight line, so he'd be able to peek inside the door from a safe distance.

"After he got about halfway to the front, he looked back and waved me on, like this was still some great adventure he wanted me to share. He was afraid to be on his own, that was all. When he realized I was going to stay put, he bent down and moved real slow past the side. He still couldn't see more than a sliver of the inside of the shack, and he moved ahead another little ways. By then, I figured, he should have been able to see about half of the inside of the shack. He hunkered down inside his sheet, staring in the direction of the open door. And there he stayed.

"I took it for about half a minute, and then I couldn't anymore. I was sick enough to die and angry enough to explode, both at the same time. How long could Dee Sparks look at a dead whore? Wouldn't a couple of seconds be enough? Dee was acting like he was watching a god-damn Hopalong Cassidy movie. An owl screeched, and some man in another shack said, Now that's over, and someone else shushed him. If Dee heard, he paid it no mind. I started along toward him, and I don't think he noticed me, either. He didn't look up until I was past the front of the shack, and had already seen the door hanging open, and the lamplight spilling over the plank floor and onto the grass outside.

"I took another step, and Dee's head snapped around. He tried to stop me by holding out his hand. All that did was make me mad. Who was Dee Sparks to tell me what I couldn't see? All he did was leave me alone in the woods with a trail of apples, and he didn't even do that right. When I kept on coming, Dee started waving both hands at me, looking back and forth between me and the inside of the shack. Like something was happening in there that I couldn't be allowed to see. I didn't stop, and Dee got up on his feet and skittered toward me.

"We gotta get out of here, he whispered. He was close enough so I could smell that electrical fire stink. I stepped to his side, and he grabbed my arm. I yanked my arm out of his grip and went forward a little ways and looked through the door of the shack.

"A bed was shoved up against the far wall, and a woman lay naked on the bed. There was blood all over her legs, and blood all over the sheets, and big puddles of blood on the floor. A woman in a raggedy robe, hair stuck out all over her head, squatted beside the bed, holding the other woman's hand. She was a colored woman—a Backs woman— but the other one, the one on the bed, was white. Probably she was pretty, when she was alive. All I could see was white skin and blood, and I near fainted.

"This wasn't some white-trash woman who lived out in the Backs, she was brought there, and the man who brought her had killed her. More trouble was coming down than I could imagine, trouble enough to kill lots of our people. And if Dee and I said a word about the white man we'd seen, the trouble would come right straight down on us.

"I must have made some kind of noise, because the woman next to the bed turned halfways around and looked at me. There wasn't any doubt about it—she saw me. All she saw of Dee was a dirty white sheet, but she saw my face, and she knew who I was. I knew her, too, and she wasn't any Backs woman. She lived down the street from us. Her name was Mary Randolph, and she was the one who came up to Eddie Grimes after he got shot to death and brought him back to life. Mary Randolph followed my dad's band, and when we played roadhouses or colored dance halls, she'd be likely to turn up. A couple of times she told me I played good drums—I was a drummer back then, you know, switched to saxophone when I turned twelve. Mary Randolph just looked at me, her hair stuck out straight all over her head like she was already inside a whirlwind of trouble. No expression on her face except that look you get when your mind is going a mile a minute and your body can't move at all. She didn't even look surprised. She almost looked like she wasn't surprised, like she was expecting to see me. As bad as I'd felt that night, this was the worst of all. I liked to have died. I'd have disappeared down an anthill, if I could. I didn't know what I had done—just be there, I guess—but I'd never be able to undo it.

"I pulled at Dee's sheet, and he tore off down the side of the shack like he'd been waiting for a signal. Mary Randolph stared into my eyes, and it felt like I had to pull myself away—I couldn't just turn my head, I had to disconnect. And when I did, I could still feel her staring at me. Somehow I made myself go down past the side of the shack, but I could still see Mary Randolph inside there, looking out at the place where I'd been.

"If Dee said anything at all when I caught up with him, I'd have knocked his teeth down his throat, but he just moved fast and quiet through the trees, seeing the best way to go, and I followed after. I felt like I'd been kicked by a horse. When we got on the path, we didn't bother trying to sneak down through the woods on the other side, we lit out and ran as hard as we could—like wild dogs were after us. And after we got onto Meridian Road, we ran toward town until we couldn't run anymore.

"Dee clamped his hand over his side and staggered forward a little bit. Then he stopped and ripped off his costume and lay down by the side of the road, breathing hard. I was leaning forward with hands on my knees, as winded as he was. When I could breathe again, I started walking down the road. Dee picked himself up and got next to me and walked along, looking at my face and then looking away, and then looking back at my face again.

"So? I said.

"I know that lady, Dee said.

"Hell, that was no news. Of course he knew Mary Randolph—she was his neighbor too. I didn't bother to answer, I just grunted at him. Then I reminded him that Mary hadn't seen his face, only mine.

"Not Mary, he said. The other one.

"He knew the dead white woman's name? That made everything worse. A lady like that shouldn't be in Dee Sparks's world, especially if she's going to wind up dead in the Backs. I wondered who was going to get lynched, and how many.

"Then Dee said that I knew her too. I stopped walking and looked him straight in the face.

"Miss Abbey Montgomery, he said. She brings clothes and food down to our church, Thanksgiving and Christmas.

"He was right—I wasn't sure if I'd ever heard her name, but I'd seen her once or twice, bringing baskets of ham and chicken and boxes of clothes to Dee's father's church. She was about twenty years old, I guess, so pretty she made you smile just to look at. From a rich family in a big house right at the top of Miller's Hill. Some man didn't think a girl like that should have any associations with colored people, I guess, and decided to express his opinion about as strong as possible. Which meant that we were going to take the blame for what happened to her, and the next time we saw white sheets, they wouldn't be Halloween costumes.

"He sure took a long time to kill her, I said.

"And Dee said, She ain't dead.

"So I asked him, What the hell did he mean by that? I saw the girl. I saw the blood. Did he think she was going to get up and walk around? Or maybe Mary Randolph was going to tell her that magic word and bring her back to life?

"You can think that if you want to, Dee said. But Abbey Montgomery ain't dead.

"I almost told him I'd seen her ghost, but he didn't deserve to hear about it. The fool couldn't even see what was right in front of his eyes. I couldn't expect him to understand what happened to me when I saw that miserable . . . that thing. He was rushing on ahead of me anyhow, like I'd suddenly embarrassed him or something. That was fine with me. I felt the exact same way. I said, I guess you know neither one of us can ever talk about this, and he said, I guess you know it too, and that was the last thing we said to each other that night. All the way down Meridian Road, Dee Sparks kept his eyes straight ahead and his mouth shut. When we got to the field, he turned toward me like he had something to say, and I waited for it, but he faced forward again and ran away. Just ran. I watched him disappear past the general store, and then I walked home by myself.

"My mom gave me hell for getting my clothes all wet and dirty, and my brothers laughed at me and wanted to know who beat me up and stole my candy. As soon as I could, I went to bed, pulled the covers up over my head, and closed my eyes. A little while later, my mom came in and asked if I was all right. Did I get into a fight with that Dee Sparks? Dee Sparks was born to hang, that was what she thought, and I ought to have a better class of friends. I'm tired of playing those drums, Momma, I said, I want to play the saxophone instead. She looked at me surprised, but said she'd talk about it with Daddy, and that it might work out.

"For the next couple days, I waited for the bomb to go off. On that Friday, I went to school, but couldn't concentrate for beans. Dee Sparks and I didn't even nod at each other in the hallways—just walked by like the other guy was invisible. On the weekend I said I felt sick and stayed in bed, wondering when that whirlwind of trouble would come down. I wondered if Eddie Grimes would talk about seeing me—once they found the body, they'd get around to Eddie Grimes real quick.

"But nothing happened that weekend, and nothing happened all the next week. I thought Mary Randolph must have hid the white girl in a grave out in the Backs. But how long could a girl from one of those rich families go missing without investigations and search parties? And, on top of that, what was Mary Randolph doing there in the first place? She liked to have a good time, but she wasn't one of those wild girls with a razor under her skirt—she went to church every Sunday, was good to people, nice to kids. Maybe she went out to comfort that poor girl, but how did she know she'd be there in the first place? Misses Abbey Montgomerys from the hill didn't share their plans with Mary Randolphs from Darktown. I couldn't forget the way she looked at me, but I couldn't understand it, either. The more I thought about that look, the more it was like Mary Randolph was saying something to me, but what? Are you ready for this? Do you understand this? Do you know how careful you must be?

"My father said I could start learning the C-melody sax, and when I was ready to play it in public, my little brother wanted to take over the drums. Seems he always wanted to play drums, and in fact he's been a drummer ever since, a good one. So I worked out how to play my little sax, I went to school and came straight home after, and everything went on like normal, except Dee Sparks and I weren't friends anymore. If the police were searching for a missing rich girl, I didn't hear anything about it.

"Then one Saturday I was walking down our street to go to the general store, and Mary Randolph came through her front door just as I got to her house. When she saw me, she stopped moving real sudden, with one hand still on the side of the door. I was so surprised to see her that I was in a kind of slow motion, and I must have stared at her. She gave me a look like an X-ray, a look that searched around down inside me. I don't know what she saw, but her face relaxed, and she took her hand off the door and let it close behind her, and she wasn't looking inside me anymore. Miss Randolph, I said, and she told me she was looking forward to hearing our band play at a Beergarden dance in a couple of weeks. I told her I was going to be playing the saxophone at that dance, and she said something about that, and all the time it was like we were having two conversations, the top one about me and the band, and the one underneath about her and the murdered white girl in the Backs. It made me so nervous, my words got all mixed up.

Finally she said, You make sure you say hello to your daddy from me, now, and I got away.

"After I passed her house, Mary Randolph started walking down the street behind me. I could feel her watching me, and I started to sweat. Mary Randolph was a total mystery to me. She was a nice lady, but probably she buried that girl's body. I didn't know but that she was going to come and kill me, one day. And then I remembered her kneeling down beside Eddie Grimes at the roadhouse. She had been dancing with Eddie Grimes, who was in jail more often than he was out. I wondered if you could be a respectable lady and still know Eddie Grimes well enough to dance with him. And how did she bring him back to life? Or was that what happened at all? Hearing that lady walk along behind me made me so uptight, I crossed to the other side of the street.

"A couple days after that, when I was beginning to think that the trouble was never going to happen after all, it came down. We heard police cars coming down the street right when we were finishing supper. I thought they were coming for me, and I almost lost my chicken and rice. The sirens went right past our house, and then more sirens came toward us from other directions—the old klaxons they had in those days. It sounded like every cop in the state was rushing into Darktown. This was bad, bad news. Someone was going to wind up dead, that was certain. No way all those police were going to come into our part of town, make all that commotion, and leave without killing at least one man. That's the truth. You just had to pray that the man they killed wasn't you or anyone in your family. My daddy turned off the lamps, and we went to the window to watch the cars go by. Two of them were state police. When it was safe, Daddy went outside to see where all the trouble was headed. After he came back in, he said it looked like the police were going toward Eddie Grimes's place. We wanted to go out and look, but they wouldn't let us, so we went to the back windows that faced toward Grimes's house. Couldn't see anything but a lot of cars and police standing all over the road back there. Sounded like they were knocking down Grimes's house with sledgehammers. Then a whole bunch of cops took off running, and all I could see was the cars spread out across the road. About ten minutes later, we heard lots of gunfire coming from a couple of streets further back. It like to have lasted forever. Like hearing the Battle of the Bulge. My momma started to cry, and so did my little brother. The shooting stopped. The police shouted to each other, and then they came back and got in their cars and went away.

"On the radio the next morning, they said that a known criminal, a Negro man named Edward Grimes, had been killed while trying to escape arrest for the murder of a white woman. The body of Eleanore Monday, missing for three days, had been found in a shallow grave by Woodland police searching near an illegal distillery in the region called the Backs. Miss Monday, the daughter of grocer Albert Monday, had been in poor mental and physical health, and Grimes had apparently taken advantage of her weakness either to abduct or lure her to the Backs, where she had been savagely murdered. That's what it said on the radio—I still remember the words. In poor mental and physical health. Savagely murdered.

"When the paper finally came, there on the front page was a picture of Eleanore Monday, a girl with dark hair and a big nose. She didn't look anything like the dead woman in the shack. She hadn't even disappeared on the right day. Eddie Grimes was never going to be able to explain things, because the police had finally cornered him in the old jute warehouse just off Meridian Road next to the general store. I don't suppose they even bothered trying to arrest him—they weren't interested in arresting him. He killed a white girl. They wanted revenge, and they got it.

"After I looked at the paper, I got out of the house and ran between the houses to get a look at the jute warehouse. Turned out a lot of folks had the same idea. A big crowd strung out in a long line in front of the warehouse, and cars were parked all along Meridian Road. Right up in front of the warehouse door was a police car, and a big cop stood in the middle of the big doorway, watching people file by. They were walking past the doorway one by one, acting like they were at some kind of exhibit. Nobody was talking. It was a sight I never saw before in that town, whites and colored all lined up together. On the other side of the warehouse, two groups of men stood alongside the road, one colored and one white, talking so quietly you couldn't hear a word.

"Now, I was never one who liked standing in lines, so I figured I'd just dart up there, peek in, and save myself some time. I came around the end of the line and ambled toward the two bunches of men, like I'd already had my look and was just hanging around to enjoy the scene. After I got a little past the warehouse door, I sort of drifted up alongside it. I looked down the row of people, and there was Dee Sparks, just a few yards away from being able to see in. Dee was leaning forward, and when he saw me he almost jumped out of his skin. He looked away as fast as he could. His eyes turned as dead as stones. The cop at the door yelled at me to go to the end of the line. He never would have noticed me at all if Dee hadn't jumped like someone just shot off a firecracker behind him.

"About halfway down the line, Mary Randolph was standing behind some of the ladies from the neighborhood. She looked terrible. Her hair stuck out in raggedy clumps, and her skin was all ashy, like she hadn't slept in a long time. I sped up a little, hoping she wouldn't notice me, but after I took one more step, Mary Randolph looked down and her eyes hooked into mine. I swear, what was in her eyes almost knocked me down. I couldn't even tell what it was, unless it was just pure hate. Hate and pain. With her eyes hooked into mine like that, I couldn't look away. It was like I was seeing that miserable, terrible white smear twisting up between the trees on that night in the Backs. Mary let me go, and I almost fell down all over again.

"I got to the end of the line and started moving along regular and slow with everybody else. Mary Randolph stayed in my mind and blanked out everything else. When I got up to the door, I barely took in what was inside the warehouse—a wall full of bullet holes and bloodstains all over the place, big slick ones and little drizzly ones. All I could think of was the shack and Mary Randolph sitting next to the dead girl, and I was back there all over again.

"Mary Randolph didn't show up at the Beergarden dance, so she didn't hear me play saxophone in public for the first time. I didn't expect her, either, not after the way she looked out at the warehouse. There'd been a lot of news about Eddie Grimes, who they made out to be less civilized than a gorilla, a crazy man who'd murder anyone as long as he could kill all the white women first. The paper had a picture of what they called Grimes's 'lair,' with busted furniture all over the place and holes in the walls, but they never explained that it was the police tore it up and made it look that way.

"The other thing people got suddenly all hot about was the Backs. Seems the place was even worse than everybody thought. Seems white girls besides Eleanore Monday had been taken out there—according to some, there was even white girls living out there, along with a lot of bad coloreds. The place was a nest of vice, Sodom and Gomorrah. Two days before the town council was supposed to discuss the problem, a gang of white men went out there with guns and clubs and torches and burned every shack in the Backs clear down to the ground. While they were there, they didn't see a single soul, white, colored, male, female, damned or saved. Everybody who lived in the Backs had skedaddled. And the funny thing was, long as the Backs had existed right outside of Woodland, no one in Woodland could recollect the name of anyone who had ever lived there. They couldn't even recall the name of anyone who had ever gone there, except for Eddie Grimes. In fact, after the place got burned down, it appeared that it must have been a sin just to say its name, because no one ever mentioned it. You'd think men so fine and moral as to burn down the Backs would be willing to take the credit, but none ever did.

"You could think they must have wanted to get rid of some things out there. Or wanted real bad to forget about things out there. One thing I thought, Dr. Garland and the man I saw leaving that shack had been out there with torches.

"But maybe I didn't know anything at all. Two weeks later, a couple things happened that shook me good.

"The first one happened three nights before Thanksgiving. I was hurrying home, a little bit late. Nobody else on the street, everybody inside either sitting down to dinner or getting ready for it. When I got to Mary Randolph's house, some kind of noise coming from inside stopped me. What I thought was, it sounded exactly like somebody trying to scream while someone else was holding a hand over their mouth. Well, that was plain foolish, wasn't it? How did I know what that would sound like? I moved along a step or two, and then I heard it again. Could be anything, I told myself. Mary Randolph didn't like me too much, anyway. She wouldn't be partial to my knocking on her door. Best thing I could do was get out. Which was what I did. Just went home to supper and forgot about it.

"Until the next day, anyhow, when a friend of Mary's walked in her front door and found her lying dead with her throat cut and a knife in her hand. A cut of fatback, we heard, had boiled away to cinders on her stove. I didn't tell anybody about what I heard the night before. Too scared. I couldn't do anything but wait to see what the police did.

"To the police, it was all real clear. Mary killed herself, plain and simple.

"When our minister went across town to ask why a lady who

intended to commit suicide had bothered to start cooking her supper, the chief told him that a female bent on killing herself probably didn't care what happened to the food on her stove. Then I suppose Mary Randolph nearly managed to cut her own head off, said the minister. A female in despair possesses a god-awful strength, said the chief. And asked, wouldn't she have screamed if she'd been attacked? And added, couldn't it be that maybe this female here had secrets in her life connected to the late savage murderer named Eddie Grimes? We might all be better off if these secrets get buried with your Mary Randolph, said the chief. I'm sure you understand me, Reverend. And yes, the Reverend did understand, he surely did. So Mary Randolph got laid away in the cemetery, and nobody ever said her name again. She was put away out of mind, like the Backs.

"The second thing that shook me up and proved to me that I didn't know anything, that I was no better than a blind dog, happened on Thanksgiving Day. My daddy played piano in church, and on special days we played our instruments along with the gospel songs. I got to church early with the rest of my family, and we practiced with the choir. Afterwards, I went to fooling around outside until the people came, and saw a big car come up into the church parking lot. Must have been the biggest, fanciest car I'd ever seen. Miller's Hill was written all over that vehicle. I couldn't have told you why, but the sight of it made my heart stop. The front door opened, and out stepped a colored man in a fancy gray uniform with a smart cap. He didn't so much as dirty his eyes by looking at me, or at the church, or at anything around him. He stepped around the front of the car and opened the rear door on my side. A young woman was in the passenger seat, and when she got out of the car, the sun fell on her blond hair and the little fur jacket she was wearing. I couldn't see more than the top of her head, her shoulders under the jacket, and her legs. Then she straightened up, and her eyes lighted right on me. She smiled, but I couldn't smile back. I couldn't even begin to move.

"It was Abbey Montgomery, delivering baskets of food to our church, the way she did every Thanksgiving and Christmas. She looked older and thinner than the last time I'd seen her alive—older and thinner, but more than that, like there was no fun at all in her life anymore. She walked to the trunk of the car, and the driver opened it up, leaned in, and brought out a great big basket of food. He took it into the church by the back way and came back for another one. Abbey Montgomery just stood still and watched him carry the baskets. She looked—she looked like she was just going through the motions, like going through the motions was all she was ever going to do from now on, and she knew it. Once she smiled at the driver, but the smile was so sad that the driver didn't even try to smile back. When he was done, he closed the trunk and let her into the passenger seat, got behind the wheel, and drove away.

"I was thinking, Dee Sparks was right, she was alive all the time. Then I thought, No, Mary Randolph brought her back, too, like she did Eddie Grimes. But it didn't work right, and only part of her came back.

"And that's the whole thing, except that Abbey Montgomery didn't deliver food to our church that Christmas—she was traveling out of the country, with her aunt. And she didn't bring food the next Thanksgiving, either, just sent her driver with the baskets. By that time, we didn't expect her, because we'd already heard that, soon as she got back to town, Abbey Montgomery stopped leaving her house. That girl shut herself up and never came out. I heard from somebody who probably didn't know any more than I did that she eventually got so she wouldn't even leave her room. Five years later, she passed away. Twenty-six years old, and they said she looked to be at least fifty."

4

Hat fell silent, and I sat with my pen ready over the notebook, waiting for more. When I realized that he had finished, I asked, "What did she die of?"

"Nobody ever told me."

"And nobody ever found who had killed Mary Randolph."

The limpid, colorless eyes momentarily rested on me. "Was she killed?"

"Did you ever become friends with Dee Sparks again? Did you at least talk about it with him?"

"Surely did not. Nothing to talk about."

This was a remarkable statement, considering that for an hour he had done nothing but talk about what had happened to the two of them, but I let it go. Hat was still looking at me with his unreadable eyes. His face had become particularly bland, almost immobile. It was not possible to imagine this man as an active eleven-year-old boy. "Now you heard me out, answer my question," he said.

I couldn't remember the question.

"Did we find what we were looking for?"

Scares—that was what they had been looking for. "I think you found a lot more than that," I said.

He nodded slowly. "That's right. They was more."

Then I asked him some question about his family's band, he lubricated himself with another swallow of gin, and the interview returned to more typical matters. But the experience of listening to him had changed. After I had heard the long, unresolved tale of his Halloween night, everything Hat said seemed to have two separate meanings, the daylight meaning created by sequences of ordinary English words, and another, nighttime meaning, far less determined and knowable. He was like a man discoursing with eerie rationality in the midst of a particularly surreal dream: like a man carrying on an ordinary conversation with one foot placed on solid ground and the other suspended above a bottomless abyss. I focused on the rationality, on the foot placed in the context I understood; the rest was unsettling to the point of being frightening. By six-thirty, when he kindly called me "Miss Rosemary" and opened his door, I felt as if I'd spent several weeks, if not whole months, in his room.

PART THREE
1

Although I did get my M.A. at Columbia, I didn't have enough money to stay on for a Ph.D., so I never became a college professor. I never became a jazz critic, either, or anything else very interesting. For a couple of years after Columbia, I taught English in a high school until I quit to take the job I have now, which involves a lot of traveling and pays a little bit better than teaching. Maybe even quite a bit better, but that's not saying much, especially when you consider my expenses. I own a nice little house in the Chicago suburbs, my marriage held up against everything life did to it, and my twenty-two-year-old son, a young man who never once in his life for the purpose of pleasure read a novel, looked at a painting, visited a museum, or listened to anything but the most readily available music, recently announced to his mother and myself that he has decided to become an artist, actual type of art to be determined later, but probably to include aspects of photography, videotape, and the creation of "installations." I take this as proof that he was raised in a manner that left his self-esteem intact.

I no longer provide my life with a perpetual sound track (though my son, who has moved back in with us, does), in part because my income does not permit the purchase of a great many compact discs. (A friend presented me with a CD player on my forty-fifth birthday.) And these days, I'm as interested in classical music as in jazz. Of course, I never go to jazz clubs when I am home. Are there still people, apart from New Yorkers, who patronize jazz nightclubs in their own hometowns? The concept seems faintly retrograde, even somehow illicit. But when I am out on the road, living in airplanes and hotel rooms, I often check the jazz listings in the local papers to see if I can find some way to fill my evenings. Many of the legends of my youth are still out there, in most cases playing at least as well as before. Some months ago, while I was in San Francisco, I came across John Hawes's name in this fashion. He was working in a club so close to my hotel that I could walk to it.

His appearance in any club at all was surprising. Hawes had ceased performing jazz in public years before. He had earned a great deal of fame (and, undoubtedly, a great deal of money) writing film scores, and in the past decade he had begun to appear in swallowtail coat and white tie as a conductor of the standard classical repertoire. I believe he had a permanent post in some city like Seattle, or perhaps Salt Lake City. If he was spending a week playing jazz with a trio in San Francisco, it must have been for the sheer pleasure of it.

I turned up just before the beginning of the first set, and got a table toward the back of the club. Most of the tables were filled—Hawes's celebrity had guaranteed him a good house. Only a few minutes after the announced time of the first set, Hawes emerged through a door at the front of the club and moved toward the piano, followed by his bassist and drummer. He looked like a more successful version of the younger man I had seen in New York, and the only indication of the extra years were his silver-gray hair, still abundant, and a little paunch. His playing, too, seemed essentially unchanged, but I could not hear it in the way I once had. He was still a good pianist—no doubt about that—but he seemed to be skating over the surface of the songs he played, using his wonderful technique and good time merely to decorate their melodies. It was the sort of playing that becomes less impressive the more attention you give it—if you were listening with half an ear, it probably sounded like Art Tatum. I wondered if John Hawes had always had this superficial streak in him, or if he had lost a certain necessary passion during his years away from jazz. Certainly he had not sounded superficial when I had heard him with Hat.

Hawes, too, might have been thinking about his old employer, because in the first set he played "Love Walked In," "Too Marvelous for Words," and "Up Jumped Hat." In the last of these, inner gears seemed to mesh, the rhythm simultaneously relaxed and intensified, and the music turned into real, not imitation, jazz. Hawes looked pleased with himself when he stood up from the piano bench, and half a dozen fans moved to greet him as he stepped off the bandstand. Most of them were carrying old records they wished him to sign.

A few minutes later, I saw Hawes standing by himself at the end of the bar, drinking what appeared to be club soda, in proximity to his musicians but not actually speaking with them. Wondering if his allusions to Hat had been deliberate, I left my table and walked toward the bar. Hawes watched me approach out of the side of his eye, neither encouraging nor discouraging me to approach him. When I introduced myself, he smiled nicely and shook my hand and waited for whatever I wanted to say to him.

At first, I made some inane comment about the difference between playing in clubs and conducting in concert halls, and he replied with the noncommittal and equally banal agreement that yes, the two experiences were very different.

Then I told him that I had seen him play with Hat all those years ago in New York, and he turned to me with genuine pleasure in his face. "Did you? At that little club on St. Mark's Place? That was the only time I ever worked with him, but it sure was fun. What an experience. I guess I must have been thinking about it, because I played some of those songs we used to do."

"That was why I came over," I said. "I guess that was one of the best musical experiences I ever had."

"You and me both." Hawes smiled to himself. "Sometimes, I just couldn't believe what he was doing."

"It showed," I said.

"Well." His eyes slid away from mine. "Great character. Completely otherworldly."

"I saw some of that," I said. "I did that interview with him that turns up now and then, the one in *Downbeat*."

"Oh!" Hawes gave me his first genuinely interested look so far. "Well, that was him, all right."

"Most of it was, anyhow."

"You cheated?" Now he was looking even more interested.

"I had to make it understandable."

"Oh, sure. You couldn't put in all those ding-dings and bells and Bob Crosbys." These had been elements of Hat's private code. Hawes laughed at the memory. "When he wanted to play a blues in G, he'd lean over and say, 'Gs, please.'"

"Did you get to know him at all well, personally?" I asked, thinking that the answer must be that he had not—I didn't think that anyone had ever really known Hat very well.

"Pretty well," Hawes said. "A couple of times, around '54 and '55, he invited me home with him, to his parents' house, I mean. We got to be friends on a Jazz at the Phil tour, and twice when we were in the South, he asked me if I wanted to eat some good home cooking."

"You went to his hometown?"

He nodded. "His parents put me up. They were interesting people. Hat's father, Red, was about the lightest black man I ever saw, and he could have passed for white anywhere, but I don't suppose the thought ever occurred to him."

"Was the family band still going?"

"No, to tell you the truth, I don't think they were getting much work up toward the end of the forties. At the end, they were using a tenor player and a drummer from the high school band. And the church work got more and more demanding for Hat's father."

"His father was a deacon, or something like that?"

He raised his eyebrows. "No, Red was the Baptist minister. The Reverend. He ran that church. I think he even started it."

"Hat told me his father played piano in church, but . . ."

"The Reverend would have made a hell of a blues piano player, if he'd ever left his day job."

"There must have been another Baptist church in the neighborhood," I said, thinking this the only explanation for the presence of two Baptist ministers. But why had Hat not mentioned that his own father, like Dee Sparks's, had been a clergyman?

"Are you kidding? There was barely enough money in that place to keep one of them going." He looked at his watch, nodded at me, and began to move closer to his sidemen.

"Could I ask you one more question?"

"I suppose so," he said, almost impatiently.

"Did Hat strike you as superstitious?"

Hawes grinned. "Oh, he was superstitious, all right. He told me he never worked on Halloween—he didn't even want to go out of his room on Halloween. That's why he left the big band, you know. They were starting a tour on Halloween, and Hat refused to do it. He just quit." He leaned toward me. "I'll tell you another funny thing. I always had the feeling that Hat was terrified of his father—I thought he invited me to Hatchville with him so I could be some kind of buffer between him and his father. Never made any sense to me. Red was a big strong old guy, and I'm pretty sure a long time ago he used to mess around with the ladies, Reverend or not, but I couldn't ever figure out why Hat should be afraid of him. But whenever Red came into the room, Hat shut up. Funny, isn't it?"

I must have looked very perplexed. "Hatchville?"

"Where they lived. Hatchville, Mississippi—not too far from Biloxi."

"But he told me—"

"Hat never gave too many straight answers," Hawes said. "And he didn't let the facts get in the way of a good story. When you come to think of it, why should he? He was Hat."

After the next set, I walked back uphill to my hotel, wondering again about the long story Hat had told me. Had there been any truth in it at all?

2

Three weeks later I found myself released from a meeting at our Midwestern headquarters in downtown Chicago earlier than I had expected, and, instead of going to a bar with the other wandering corporate ghosts like myself, made up a story about a relative I had promised to visit. I didn't want to admit to my fellow employees, committed like all male businesspeople to aggressive endeavors such as racquetball, drinking, and the pursuit of women, that I intended to visit the library. Short of a trip to Mississippi, a good periodical room offered the most likely means of finding out once and for all how much truth had been in what Hat had told me.

I hadn't forgotten everything I had learned at Columbia—I still knew how to look things up.

In the main library, a boy set me up with a monitor and spools of microfilm representing the complete contents of the daily newspapers from Biloxi and Hatchville, Mississippi, for Hat's tenth and eleventh years. That made three papers, two for Biloxi and one for Hatchville, but all I had to examine were the issues dating from the end of October through the middle of November—I was looking for references to Eddie Grimes, Eleanore Monday, Mary Randolph, Abbey Montgomery, Hat's family, the Backs, and anyone named Sparks.

The *Hatchville Blade*, a gossipy daily printed on peach-colored paper, offered plenty of references to each of these names and places, and the papers from Biloxi contained nearly as many—Biloxi could not conceal the delight, disguised as horror, aroused in its collective soul by the unimaginable events taking place in the smaller, supposedly respectable town ten miles west. Biloxi was riveted, Biloxi was superior, Biloxi was virtually intoxicated with dread and outrage. In Hatchville, the press maintained a persistent optimistic dignity: when wickedness had appeared, justice official and unofficial had dealt with it. Hatchville was shocked but proud (or at least pretended to be proud), and Biloxi all but preened. The *Blade* printed detailed news stories, but the Biloxi papers suggested implications not allowed by Hatchville's version of events. I needed Hatchville to confirm or question Hat's story, but Biloxi gave me at least the beginning of a way to understand it.

A black ex-convict named Edward Grimes had in some fashion persuaded or coerced Eleanore Monday, a retarded young white woman, to accompany him to an area variously described as "a longstanding local disgrace" (the *Blade*) and "a haunt of deepest vice" (Biloxi), and after "the perpetration of the most offensive and brutal deeds upon her person" (the *Blade*) or "acts which the judicious commentator must decline to imagine, much less describe" (Biloxi) murdered her, presumably to ensure her silence, and then buried the body near the "squalid dwelling" where he made and sold illegal liquor. State and local police departments acting in concert had located the body, identified Grimes as the fiend, and, after a search of his house, had tracked him to a warehouse where the murderer was killed in a gun battle. The *Blade* covered half its front page with a photograph of a gaping double door and a bloodstained wall. All Mississippi, both Hatchville and Biloxi declared, now could breathe more easily.

The *Blade* gave the death of Mary Randolph a single paragraph on its back page, the Biloxi papers nothing.

In Hatchville, the raid on the Backs was described as a heroic assault on a dangerous criminal encampment which had somehow come to flourish in a little-noticed section of the countryside. At great risk to themselves, anonymous citizens of Hatchville had descended like the army of the righteous and driven forth the hidden sinners from their dens. Troublemakers, beware! The Biloxi papers, while seeming to endorse the action in Hatchville, actually took another tone altogether. Can it be, they asked, that the Hatchville police had never before noticed the existence of a Sodom and Gomorrah so close to the town line? Did it take the savage murder of a helpless woman to bring it to their attention? Of course Biloxi celebrated the destruction of the Backs, such vileness must be eradicated, but it wondered what else had been destroyed along with the stills and the mean buildings where loose women had plied their trade. Men ever are men, and those who have succumbed to temptation may wish to remove from the face of the earth any evidence of their lapses. Had not the police of Hatchville ever heard the rumor, vague and doubtless baseless, that operations of an illegal nature had been performed in the selfsame Backs? That in an atmosphere of drugs, intoxication, and gambling, the races had mingled there, and that "fast" young women had risked life and honor in search of illicit thrills? Hatchville may have rid itself of a few buildings, but Biloxi was willing to suggest that the problems of its smaller neighbor might not have disappeared with them.

As this campaign of innuendo went on in Biloxi, the *Blade* blandly reported the ongoing events of any smaller American city. Miss Abigail Montgomery sailed with her aunt, Miss Lucinda Bright, from New Orleans to France for an eight-week tour of the Continent. The Reverend Jasper Sparks of the Miller's Hill Presbyterian Church delivered a sermon on the subject "Christian Forgiveness." (Just after Thanksgiving, the Reverend Sparks's son, Rodney, was sent off with the blessings and congratulations of all Hatchville to a private academy in Charleston,

South Carolina.) There were bake sales, church socials, and costume parties. A saxophone virtuoso named Albert Woodland demonstrated his astonishing wizardry at a well-attended recital presented in Temperance Hall.

Well, I knew the name of at least one person who had attended the recital. If Hat had chosen to disguise the name of his hometown, he had done so by substituting for it a name that represented another sort of home.

But, although I had more ideas about this than before, I still did not know exactly what Hat had seen or done on Halloween night in the Backs. It seemed possible that he had gone there with a white boy of his age, a preacher's son like himself, and had the wits scared out of him by whatever had happened to Abbey Montgomery—and after that night, Abbey herself had been sent out of town, as had Dee Sparks. I couldn't think that a man had murdered the young woman, leaving Mary Randolph to bring her back to life. Surely whatever had happened to Abbey Montgomery had brought Dr. Garland out to the Backs, and what he had witnessed or done there had sent him away screaming. And this event—what had befallen a rich young white woman in the shadiest, most criminal section of a Mississippi county—had led to the slaying of Eddie Grimes and the murder of Mary Randolph. Because they knew what had happened, they had to die.

I understood all this, and Hat had understood it too. Yet he had introduced needless puzzles, as if embedded in the midst of this unresolved story were something he wished either to conceal or not to know. And concealed it would remain; if Hat did not know it, I never would. Whatever had really happened in the Backs on Halloween night was lost for good.

On the *Blade*'s entertainment page for a Saturday in the middle of November I had come across a photograph of Hat's family's band, and when I reached this hopeless point in my thinking, I spooled back across the pages to look at it again. Hat, his two brothers, his sister, and his parents stood in a straight line, tallest to smallest, in front of what must have been the family car. Hat held a C-melody saxophone, his brothers a trumpet and drumsticks, his sister a clarinet. As the piano player, the Reverend carried nothing at all—nothing except for what came through even a grainy, sixty-year-old photograph as a powerful sense of self. Hat's father had been a tall, impressive man, and in the photograph he looked as white as I did. But what was impressive was not the lightness of his skin, or even his striking handsomeness: what impressed was the sense of authority implicit in his posture, his straightforward gaze, even the dictatorial set of his chin. In retrospect, I was not surprised by what John Hawes had told me, for this man could easily be frightening. You would not wish to oppose him, you would not elect to get in his way. Beside him, Hat's mother seemed vague and distracted, as if her husband had robbed her of all certainty. Then I noticed the car, and for the first time realized why it had been included in the photograph. It was a sign of their prosperity, the respectable status they had achieved—the car was as much an advertisement as the photograph. It was, I thought, an old Model T Ford, but I didn't waste any time speculating that it might have been the Model T Hat had seen in the Backs.

And that would be that—the hint of an absurd supposition—except for something I read a few days ago in a book called *Cool Breeze: The Life of Grant Kilbert.*

There are few biographies of any jazz musicians apart from Louis Armstrong and Duke Ellington (though one does now exist of Hat, the title of which was drawn from my interview with him), and I was surprised to see *Cool Breeze* at the B. Dalton in our local mall. Biographies have not yet been written of Art Blakey, Clifford Brown, Ben Webster, Art Tatum, and many others of more musical and historical importance than Kilbert. Yet I should not have been surprised. Kilbert was one of those musicians who attract and maintain a large personal following, and twenty years after his death, almost all of his records have been released on CD, many of them in multidisc boxed sets. He had been a great, great player, the closest to Hat of all his disciples. Because Kilbert had been one of my early heroes, I bought the book (for $35!) and brought it home.

Like the lives of many jazz musicians, I suppose of artists in general, Kilbert's had been an odd mixture of public fame and private misery. He had committed burglaries, even armed robberies, to feed his persistent heroin addiction; he had spent years in jail; his two marriages had ended in outright hatred; he had managed to betray most of his friends. That this weak, narcissistic louse had found it in himself to create music of real tenderness and beauty was one of art's enigmas, but not actually a surprise. I'd heard and read enough stories about Grant Kilbert to know what kind of man he'd been.

But what I had not known was that Kilbert, to all appearances an American of conventional northern European, perhaps Scandinavian or Anglo-Saxon, stock, had occasionally claimed to be black. (This claim had always been dismissed, apparently, as another indication of Kilbert's mental aberrancy.) At other times, being Kilbert, he had denied ever making this claim.

Neither had I known that the received versions of his birth and upbringing were in question. Unlike Hat, Kilbert had been interviewed dozens of times both in *Downbeat* and in mass-market weekly newsmagazines, invariably to offer the same story of having been born in Hattiesburg, Mississippi, to an unmusical, working-class family (a plumber's family), of knowing virtually from infancy that he was born to make music, of begging for and finally being given a saxophone, of early mastery and the dazzled admiration of his teachers, then of dropping out of school at sixteen and joining the Woody Herman band. After that, almost immediate fame.

Most of this, the Grant Kilbert myth, was undisputed. He had been raised in Hattiesburg by a plumber named Kilbert, he had been a prodigy and high-school dropout, he'd become famous with Woody Herman before he was twenty. Yet he told a few friends, not necessarily those to whom he said he was black, that he'd been adopted by the Kilberts, and that once or twice, in great anger, either the plumber or his wife had told him that he had been born into poverty and disgrace and that he'd better by God be grateful for the opportunities he'd been given. The source of this story was John Hawes, who'd met Kilbert on another long JATP tour, the last he made before leaving the road for film scoring.

"Grant didn't have a lot of friends on that tour," Hawes told the biographer. "Even though he was such a great player, you never knew what he was going to say, and if he was in a bad mood, he was liable to put down some of the older players. He was always respectful around Hat, his whole style was based on Hat's, but Hat could go days without saying anything, and by those days he certainly wasn't making any new friends. Still, he'd let Grant sit next to him on the bus, and nod his head while Grant talked to him, so he must have felt some affection for him. Anyhow, eventually I was about the only guy on the tour that was willing to have a conversation with Grant, and we'd sit up in the bar late at night after the concerts. The way he played, I could forgive him a lot of failings. One of those nights, he said that he'd been adopted, and that not knowing who his real parents were was driving him crazy. He didn't even have a birth certificate. From a hint his mother once gave him, he thought one of his birth parents was black, but when he asked them directly, they always denied it. These were white Mississippians, after all, and if they had wanted a baby so bad that they had taken in a child who looked completely white but maybe had a drop or two of black blood in his veins, they weren't going to admit it, even to themselves."

In the midst of so much supposition, here is a fact. Grant Kilbert was exactly eleven years younger than Hat. The jazz encyclopedias give his birth date as November 1, which instead of his actual birthday may have been the day he was delivered to the couple in Hattiesburg.

I wonder if Hat saw more than he admitted to me of the man leaving the shack where Abbey Montgomery lay on bloody sheets; I wonder if he had reason to fear his father. I don't know if what I am thinking is correct—I'll never know that—but now, finally, I think I know why Hat never wanted to go out of his room on Halloween nights. The story he told me never left him, but it must have been most fully present on those nights. I think he heard the screams, saw the bleeding girl, and saw Mary Randolph staring at him with displaced pain and rage. I think that in some small closed corner deep within himself, he knew who had been the real object of these feelings, and therefore had to lock himself inside his hotel room and gulp gin until he obliterated the horror of his own thoughts.

Mr. Clubb and Mr. Cuff

1

I never intended to go astray, nor did I know what that meant. My journey began in an isolated hamlet notable for the piety of its inhabitants, and when I vowed to escape New Covenant I assumed that the values instilled within me there would forever be my guide. And so, with a depth of paradox I still only begin to comprehend, they have been. My journey, so triumphant, also so excruciating, is both *from* my native village and *of* it. For all its splendor, my life has been that of a child of New Covenant.

When in my limousine I scanned *The Wall Street Journal*, when in the private elevator I ascended to the rosewood-paneled office with harbor views, when in the partners' dining room I ordered squab on a mesclun bed from a prison-rescued waiter known to me alone as Charlie-Charlie, also when I navigated for my clients the complex waters of financial planning, above all when before her seduction by my enemy Graham Leeson I returned homeward to luxuriate in the attentions of my stunning Marguerite, when transported within the embraces of my wife, even then I carried within the frame houses dropped like afterthoughts down the streets of New Covenant, the stiff faces and suspicious eyes, the stony cordialities before and after services in the grim great Temple, the blank storefronts along Harmony Street—tattooed within me was the ugly, enigmatic beauty of my birthplace. Therefore I believe that when I strayed, and stray I did, make no mistake, it was but to come home, for I claim that the two strange gentlemen who beckoned me into error were the night of its night, the dust of its dust. In the period of my life's greatest turmoil—the month of my exposure to Mr. Clubb and Mr. Cuff, "Private Detectives Extraordinaire," as their business card described them—in the midst of the uproar I felt that I saw *the contradictory dimensions of . . .*

of . . .

I felt I saw . . . had seen, had at least glimpsed . . . what a wiser man might call . . . try to imagine the sheer difficulty of actually writing these words . . . the Meaning of Tragedy. You smirk; I don't blame you: in your place I'd do the same, but I assure you I saw *something*.

I must sketch in the few details necessary for you to understand my story. A day's walk from New York State's Canadian border, New Covenant was (and still is, really still *is*) a town of just under a thousand inhabitants united by the puritanical Protestantism of the Church of the New Covenant, whose founders had broken away from the even more puritanical Saints of the Covenant. (The Saints had proscribed sexual congress in the hope of hastening the Second Coming.) The village flourished during the end of the nineteenth century and settled into its permanent form around 1920.

To wit: Temple Square, where the Temple of the New Covenant and its bell tower, flanked left and right by the Youth Bible Study Center and the Combined Boys and Girls Elementary and Middle School, dominate a modest greensward. Southerly stand the shop fronts of Harmony Street, the bank, also the modest placards indicating the locations of New Covenant's doctor, lawyer, and dentist; south of Harmony Street lie the two streets of frame houses sheltering the town's clerks and artisans, beyond these the farms of the rural faithful, beyond the farmland deep forest. North of Temple Square is Scripture Street, two blocks lined with the residents of the Reverend and his Board of Brethren, the aforementioned doctor, dentist, and lawyer, the president and vice president of the bank, also the families of some few wealthy converts devoted to Temple affairs. North of Scripture Street are more farms, then the resumption of the great forest, in which our village described a sort of clearing.

My father was New Covenant's lawyer, and to Scripture Street I was born. Sundays I spent in the Youth Bible Study Center, weekdays in the Combined Boys and Girls Elementary and Middle School. New Covenant was my world, its people all I knew of the world. Three-fourths of all mankind consisted of gaunt, bony, blond-haired individuals with chiseled features and blazing blue eyes, the men six feet or taller in height, the women some inches shorter—the remaining fourth being the Racketts, Mudges, and Blunts, our farm families, who after generations of intermarriage had coalesced into a tribe of squat, black-haired, gap-toothed, moonfaced males and females seldom taller than five feet, four or five inches. Until I went to college I thought that all people were divided into the races of town and barn, fair and dark, the spotless and the mud-spattered, the reverential and the sly.

Though Racketts, Mudges, and Blunts attended our school and worshipped in our Temple, though they were at least as prosperous as we in town, we knew them tainted with essential inferiority. Rather than intelligent they seemed *crafty*; rather than spiritual, *animal*. Both in classrooms and Temple, they sat together, watchful as dogs compelled for the nonce to be "good," now and then tilting their heads to pass a whispered comment. Despite Sunday baths and Sunday clothes, they bore an unerasable odor redolent of the barnyard. Their public self-effacement seemed to mask a peasant amusement, and when they separated into their wagons and other vehicles, they could be heard to share a rough peasant laughter.

I found this mysterious race unsettling, in fact profoundly annoying. At some level they frightened me—I found them compelling. Oppressed from my earliest days by life in New Covenant, I felt an inadmissible fascination for this secretive brood. Despite their inferiority, I wished to know what they knew. Locked deep within their shabbiness and shame I sensed the presence of a freedom I did not understand but found *thrilling*.

Because town never socialized with barn, our contacts were restricted to places of education, worship, and commerce. It would have been as unthinkable for me to take a seat beside Delbert Mudge or Charlie-Charlie Rackett in our fourth-grade classroom as for Delbert or Charlie-Charlie to invite me for an overnight in their farmhouse bedrooms. Did Delbert and Charlie-Charlie actually have bedrooms, where they slept alone in their own beds? I recall mornings when the atmosphere about Delbert and Charlie-Charlie suggested nights spent in close proximity to the pigpen, others when their worn dungarees exuded a freshness redolent of sunshine, wildflowers, and raspberries.

During recess an inviolable border separated the townies at the northern end of our play area from the barnies at the southern. Our play, superficially similar, demonstrated essential differences, for we could not cast off the unconscious stiffness resulting from constant adult measurement of our spiritual worthiness. In contrast, the barnies did not play at playing but actually *played*, plunging back and forth across the grass, chortling over victories, grinning as they muttered what must have been jokes. (We were not adept at jokes.) When school closed at end of day, I tracked the homebound progress of Delbert, Charlie-Charlie, and clan with envious eyes and a divided heart.

Why should they have seemed in possession of a liberty I desired? After graduation from middle school, we townies progressed to Shady Glen's Consolidated High, there to monitor ourselves and our fellows while encountering the temptations of the wider world, in some cases then advancing into colleges and universities. Having concluded their educations with the seventh grade's long division and "Hiawatha" recitations, the barnies one and all returned to their barns. Some few, some very few of *us*, among whom I had determined early on to be numbered, left for good, thereafter to be celebrated, denounced, or mourned. One of *us*, Caleb Thurlow, violated every standard of caste and morality by marrying Munna Blunt and vanishing into barnie-dom. A disgraced, disinherited pariah during my childhood, Thurlow's increasingly pronounced stoop and decreasing teeth terrifyingly mutated him into a blond, wasted barnie-parody on his furtive annual Christmas appearances at Temple. One of *them*, one only, my old classmate Charlie-Charlie Rackett, escaped his ordained destiny in our twentieth year by liberating a plow horse and Webley-Vickers pistol from the family farm to commit serial armed robbery upon Shady Glen's George Washington Inn, Town Square Feed & Grain, and Allsorts Emporium. Every witness to his crimes recognized what, if not who, he was, and Charlie-Charlie was apprehended while boarding the Albany train in the next village west. During the course of my own journey from and of New Covenant, I tracked Charlie-Charlie's gloomy progress through the way stations of the penal system until at last I could secure his release at a parole hearing with the offer of a respectable job in the financial-planning industry.

I had by then established myself as absolute monarch of three floors in a Wall Street monolith. With my two junior partners, I enjoyed the services of a fleet of paralegals, interns, analysts, investigators, and secretaries. I had chosen these partners carefully, for as well as the usual expertise, skill, and dedication, I required other, less conventional qualities.

I had sniffed out intelligent but unimaginative men of some slight moral laziness; capable of cutting corners when they thought no one would notice; controlled drinkers and secret drug takers: juniors with reason to be grateful for their positions. I wanted no *zealousness*. My employees were to be steadfastly incurious and able enough to handle their clients satisfactorily, at least with my paternal assistance.

My growing prominence had attracted the famous, the established, the notorious. Film stars and athletes, civic leaders, corporate pashas, and heirs to long-standing family fortunes regularly visited our offices, as did a number of conspicuously well-tailored gentlemen who had accumulated their wealth in a more colorful fashion. To these clients I suggested financial stratagems responsive to their labyrinthine needs. I had not schemed for their business. It simply *came to me*, willy-nilly, as our Temple held that salvation came to the elect. One May morning, a cryptic fellow in a pinstriped suit appeared in my office to pose a series of delicate questions. As soon as he opened his mouth, the cryptic fellow summoned irresistibly from memory a dour, squinting member of the Board of Brethren of New Covenant's Temple. I *knew* this man, and instantly found the tone most acceptable to him. Tone is all to such people. After our interview he directed others of his kind to my office, and by December my business had tripled. Individually and universally these gentlemen pungently reminded me of the village I had long ago escaped, and I cherished my suspicious buccaneers even as I celebrated the distance between my moral life and theirs. While sheltering these self-justifying figures within elaborate trusts, while legitimizing subterranean floods of cash, I immersed myself within a familiar atmosphere of pious denial. Rebuking home, I *was* home.

Life had not yet taught me that revenge inexorably exacts its own revenge.

My researches eventually resulted in the hiring of two junior partners known privately to me as Gilligan and the Skipper. The first, a short, trim fellow with a comedian's rubber face and disheveled hair, brilliant with mutual funds but an ignoramus at estate planning, each morning worked so quietly as to become invisible. To Gilligan I had referred many of our actors and musicians, and those whose schedules permitted them to attend meetings before the lunch hour met their soft-spoken adviser in a dimly lighted office with curtained windows. After lunch, Gilligan tended toward the vibrant, the effusive, the extrovert. Red-faced and sweating, he loosened his tie, turned on a powerful sound system, and ushered emaciated musicians with haystack hair into the atmosphere of a backstage party. Morning Gilligan spoke in whispers; Afternoon Gilligan batted our secretaries' shoulders as he bounced officeward down the corridors. I snapped him up as soon as one of my competitors let him go, and he proved a perfect complement to the Skipper. Tall, plump, silver-haired, this gentleman had come to me from a specialist in estates and trusts discomfited by his tendency to become pugnacious when outraged by a client's foul language, improper dress, or other offense against good taste. Our tycoons and inheritors of family fortunes were in no danger of arousing the Skipper's ire, and I myself handled the unshaven film stars' and heavy metalists' estate planning. Neither Gilligan nor the Skipper had any contact with the cryptic gentlemen. Our office was an organism balanced in all its parts. Should any mutinous notions occur to my partners, my spy the devoted Charlie-Charlie Rackett, known to them as Charles the Perfect Waiter, every noon silently monitored their every utterance while replenishing Gilligan's wineglass. My marriage of two years seemed blissfully happy, my reputation and bank account flourished alike, and I anticipated perhaps another decade of labor followed by luxurious retirement. I could not have been less prepared for the disaster to come.

Mine, as disasters do, began at home. I admit my contribution to the difficulties. While immersed in the demands of my profession, I had married a beautiful woman twenty years my junior. It was my understanding that Marguerite had knowingly entered into a contract under which she enjoyed the fruits of income and social position while postponing deeper marital communication until I cashed in and quit the game, at which point she and I could travel at will, occupying grand hotel suites and staterooms while acquiring every adornment that struck her eye. How could an arrangement so harmonious have failed to satisfy her? Even now I feel the old rancor. Marguerite had come into our office as a faded singer who wished to invest the remaining proceeds from a five- or six-year-old "hit," and after an initial consultation Morning Gilligan whispered her down the corridor for my customary lecture on estate tax, trusts, so forth and so on, in her case due to the modesty of the funds in question mere show. (Since during their preliminary discussion she had casually employed the Anglo-

Saxon monosyllable for excrement, Gilligan dared not subject her to the Skipper.) He escorted her into my chambers, and I glanced up with the customary show of interest. You may imagine a thick bolt of lightning slicing through a double-glazed office window, sizzling across the width of a polished teak desk, and striking me in the heart.

Already I was lost. Thirty minutes later I violated my most sacred edict by inviting a female client to a dinner date. She accepted, damn her. Six months later, Marguerite and I were married, damn us both. I had attained everything for which I had abandoned New Covenant, and for twenty-three months I inhabited a paradise of fools.

I need say only that the usual dreary signals, matters like unexplained absences, mysterious telephone calls abruptly terminated upon my appearance, and visitations of a melancholic, distracted *daemon* forced me to set one of our investigators on Marguerite's trail, resulting in the discovery that my wife had been two-backed-beasting it with my sole professional equal, the slick, the smooth Graham Leeson, to whom I, swollen with uxorious pride a year after our wedding day, had introduced her during a function at the Waldorf-Astoria hotel. I know what happened. I don't need a map. Exactly as I had decided to win her at our first meeting, Graham Leeson vowed to steal Marguerite from me the instant he set his handsome blue eyes on her between the fifty-thousand-dollar tables on the Starlight Roof.

My enemy enjoyed a number of natural advantages. Older than she by but ten years to my twenty, at six-four three inches taller than I, this reptile had been blessed with a misleadingly winning Irish countenance and a full head of crinkly red-blond hair. (In contrast, my white tonsure accentuated the severity of the all-too-Cromwellian townie face.) I assumed her immune to such obvious charms, and I was wrong. I thought Marguerite could not fail to see the meagerness of Leeson's inner life, and I was wrong again. I suppose he exploited the inevitable temporary isolation of any spouse to a man in my position. He must have played upon her grudges, spoken to her secret vanities. Cynically, I am sure, he encouraged the illusion that she was an "artist." He flattered, he very likely wheedled. By every shabby means at his disposal he had overwhelmed her, most crucially by screwing her brains out three times a week in a corporate suite at a Park Avenue hotel.

After I had examined the photographs and other records arrayed before me by the investigator, an attack of nausea brought my dizzied head to the edge of my desk; then rage stiffened my backbone and induced a moment of hysterical blindness. My marriage was dead, my wife a repulsive stranger. Vision returned a second or two later. The checkbook floated from the desk drawer, the Waterman pen glided into position between thumb and forefinger, and while a shadow's efficient hand inscribed a check for ten thousand dollars, a disembodied voice informed the hapless investigator that the only service required of him henceforth would be eternal silence.

For perhaps an hour I sat alone in my office, postponing appointments and refusing telephone calls. In the moments when I had tried to envision my rival, what came to mind was some surly drummer or guitarist from her past, easily intimidated and readily bought off. In such a case, I should have inclined toward mercy. Had Marguerite offered a sufficiently self-abasing apology, I would have slashed her clothing allowance in half, restricted her public appearances to the two or three most crucial charity events of the year and perhaps as many dinners at my side in restaurants where one is "seen," and ensured that the resultant mood of sackcloth and ashes prohibited any reversion to bad behavior by intermittent use of another investigator.

No question of mercy, now. Staring at the photographs of my life's former partner entangled with the man I detested most in the world, I shudder with a combination of horror, despair, loathing, and— appallingly—an urgent spasm of sexual arousal. I unbuttoned my trousers, groaned in ecstatic torment, and helplessly ejaculated over the images on my desk. When I had recovered, weak-kneed and trembling, I wiped away the evidence, closed the hateful folders, and picked up the telephone to request Charlie-Charlie Rackett's immediate presence in my office.

The cryptic gentlemen, experts in the nuances of retribution, might have seemed more obvious sources of assistance, but I could not afford obligations in that direction. Nor did I wish to expose my humiliation to clients for whom the issue of respect was all-important. Devoted Charlie-Charlie's years in the jug had given him an extensive acquaintanceship among the dubious and irregular, and I had from time to time commandeered the services of one or another of his fellow yardbirds. My old companion sidled around my door and posted himself before me, all dignity on the outside, all curiosity within.

"I have been dealt a horrendous blow, Charlie-Charlie," I said, "and as soon as possible I wish to see one or two of the best."

Charlie-Charlie glanced at the folders. "You want serious people," he said, speaking in code. "Right?"

"I must have men who can be serious when seriousness is necessary," I said, replying in the same code.

While my lone surviving link to New Covenant struggled to understand this directive, it came to me that Charlie-Charlie had now become my only true confidant, and I bit down on an upwelling of fury. I realized that I had clamped shut my eyes, and opened them upon an uneasy Charlie-Charlie.

"You're sure," he said.

"Find them," I said. Then, to restore some semblance of our conventional atmosphere, I asked, "The boys still okay?"

Telling me that the juniors remained content, he said, "Fat and happy. I'll find what you want, but it'll take a couple of days."

I nodded, and he was gone.

For the remainder of the day I turned in an inadequate impersonation of the executive who usually sat behind my desk, and after putting off the moment as long as reasonably possible, buried the awful files in a bottom drawer and returned to the town house I had purchased for my bride-to-be and which, I remembered with an unhappy pang, she had once in an uncharacteristic moment of cuteness called "our town home."

Since I had been too preoccupied to telephone wife, cook, or butler with the information that I would be staying late at the office, when I walked into our dining room the table had been laid with our china and silver, flowers arranged in the centerpiece, and, in what I took to be a new dress, Marguerite glanced mildly up from her end of the table and murmured a greeting. Scarcely able to meet her eyes, I bent to bestow the usual homecoming kiss with a mixture of feelings more painful than I previously would have imagined myself capable. Some despicable portion of my being responded to her beauty with the old husbandly appreciation even as I went cold with the loathing I could not permit myself to show. I hated Marguerite for her treachery, her beauty for its falsity, myself for my susceptibility to what I knew was treacherous and false. Clumsily, my lips brushed the edge of an azure eye, and it came to me that she may well have been with Leeson while the investigator was displaying the images of her degradation. Through me coursed an involuntary moment of revulsion with, strange to say, at its center a molten erotic core. Part of my extraordinary pain was the sense that I too had been contaminated: a layer of illusion had been peeled away, revealing monstrous blind groping slugs and maggots.

Having heard voices, Mr. Moncrieff, the butler I had employed upon the abrupt decision of the Duke of Denbigh to cast off worldly ways and enter an order of Anglican monks, came through from the kitchen and awaited orders. His bland, courteous manner suggested as usual that he was making the best of having been shipwrecked on an island populated by illiterate savages. Marguerite said that she had been worried when I had not returned home at the customary time.

"I'm fine," I said. "No, I'm not fine. Distinctly unwell. Grave difficulties at the office." With that I managed to make my way up the table to my chair, along the way signaling to Mr. Moncrieff that the Lord of the Savages wished him to bring in the predinner martini and then immediately begin serving whatever the cook had prepared. I took my seat at the head of the table, and Mr. Moncrieff removed the floral centerpiece to the sideboard. Marguerite regarded me with the appearance of probing concern. This was false, false, false. Unable to meet her eyes, I raised mine to the row of Canalettos along the wall, then the intricacies of the plaster molding above the paintings, at last to the chandelier depending from the central rosette on the ceiling. More had changed than my relationship with my wife. The molding, the blossoming chandelier, even Canaletto's Venice resounded with a cold, selfish lovelessness.

Marguerite remarked that I seemed agitated.

"No, I am not," I said. The butler placed the ice-cold drink before me, and I snatched up the glass and drained half its contents. "Yes, I am agitated, terribly," I said. "The difficulties at the office are more far-reaching than I intimated." I polished off the martini and tasted only glycerin. "It is a matter of betrayal and treachery made all the more wounding by the closeness of my relationship with the traitor."

I lowered my eyes to measure the effect of this thrust to the vitals on the traitor in question. She was looking back at me with a flawless imitation of wifely concern. For a moment I doubted her unfaithfulness. Then the memory of the photographs in my bottom drawer once again brought crawling into view the slugs and maggots. "I am sickened unto rage," I said, "and my rage demands vengeance. Can you understand this?"

Mr. Moncrieff carried into the dining room the tureens or serving dishes containing whatever it was we were to eat that night, and my wife and I honored the silence that had become conventional during the presentation of our evening meal. When we were alone again, she nodded in affirmation.

I said, "I am grateful, for I value your opinions. I should like you to help me reach a difficult decision."

She thanked me in the simplest of terms.

"Consider this puzzle," I said. "Famously, vengeance is the Lord's, and therefore it is often imagined that vengeance exacted by anyone other is immoral. Yet if vengeance is the Lord's, then a mortal being who seeks it on his own behalf has engaged in a form of worship, even an alternate version of prayer. Many good Christians regularly pray for the establishment of justice, and what lies behind an act of vengeance but a desire for justice? God tells us that eternal torment awaits the wicked. He also demonstrates a pronounced affection for those who prove unwilling to let Him do all the work."

Marguerite expressed the opinion that justice was a fine thing indeed, and that a man such as myself would always labor in its behalf. She fell silent and regarded me with what on any night previous I would have seen as tender concern. Though I had not yet so informed her, she declared, the Benedict Arnold must have been one of my juniors, for no other employee could injure me so greatly. Which was the traitor?

"As yet I do not know," I said. "But once again I must be grateful for your grasp of my concerns. Soon I will put into position the bear-traps that will result in the fiend's exposure. Unfortunately, my dear, this task will demand all of my energy over at least the next several days. Until the task is accomplished, it will be necessary for me to camp out in the —— Hotel." I named the site of her assignations with Graham Leeson.

A subtle, momentary darkening of the eyes, her first genuine response of the evening, froze my heart as I set the bear-trap into place. "I know, the ——'s vulgarity deepens with every passing week, but Gilligan's apartment is only a few doors north, the Skipper's one block south. Once my investigators have installed their electronic devices, I shall be privy to every secret they possess. Would you enjoy spending several days at Green Chimneys? The servants have the month off, but you might enjoy the solitude there more than you would being alone in town."

Green Chimneys, our country estate on a bluff above the Hudson River, lay two hours away. Marguerite's delight in the house had inspired me to construct on the grounds a fully equipped recording studio, where she typically spent days on end, trying out new "songs."

Charmingly, she thanked me for my consideration and said that she would enjoy a few days' seclusion at Green Chimneys. After I had exposed the traitor, I was to telephone her with the summons home. Accommodating on the surface, vile beneath, these words brought an anticipatory tinge of pleasure to her face, a delicate heightening of her beauty I would have, very like *had*, misconstrued on earlier occasions. Any appetite I might have had disappeared before a visitation of nausea, and I announced myself exhausted. Marguerite intensified my discomfort by calling me her poor darling. I staggered to my bedroom, locked the door, threw off my clothes, and dropped into bed to endure a sleepless night. I would never see my wife again.

2

Sometime after first light I had attained an uneasy slumber; finding it impossible to will myself out of bed on awakening, I relapsed into the same restless sleep. By the time I appeared within the dining room, Mr. Moncrieff, as well-chilled as a good Chardonnay, informed me that Madame had departed for the country some twenty minutes before. Despite the hour, did Sir wish to breakfast? I consulted, trepidatiously, my wristwatch. It was ten-thirty: my unvarying practice was to arise at six, breakfast soon after, and arrive in my office well before seven. I rushed downstairs, and as soon as I slid into the backseat of the limousine forbade awkward queries by pressing the button to raise the window between the driver and myself.

No such mechanism could shield me from Mrs. Rampage, my secretary, who thrust her head around the door a moment after I had expressed my desire for a hearty breakfast of poached eggs, bacon, and whole-wheat toast from the executive dining room. All calls and appointments were to be postponed or otherwise put off until the completions of my repast. Mrs. Rampage had informed me that two men without appointments had been awaiting my arrival since 8:00 a.m. and asked if I would consent to see them immediately. I told her not to be absurd. The door to the outer world swung to admit her beseeching head. "Please," she said. "I don't know who they are, but they're *frightening* everybody."

This remark clarified all. Earlier than anticipated, Charlie-Charlie Rackett had deputized two men capable of seriousness when seriousness was called for. "I beg your pardon," I said. "Send them in."

Mrs. Rampage withdrew to lead into my chambers two stout, stocky, short, dark-haired men. My spirits had taken wing the moment I beheld these fellows shouldering through the door, and I rose smiling to my feet. My secretary muttered an introduction, baffled as much by my cordiality as by her ignorance of my visitors' names.

"It is quite all right," I said. "All is in order, all is in train." New Covenant had just entered the sanctum.

Barnie-slyness, barnie-freedom shone from their great, round gap-toothed faces: in precisely the manner I remembered, these two suggested mocking peasant violence scantily disguised by an equally mocking impersonation of convention. Small wonder that they had intimidated Mrs. Rampage and her underlings, for their nearest exposure to a like phenomenon had been with our musicians, and when offstage they were pale, emaciated fellows of little physical vitality. Clothed in black suits, white shirts, and black neckties, holding their black derbies by their brims and turning their gappy smiles back and forth between Mrs. Rampage and myself, these barnies had evidently been loose in the world for some time. They were perfect for my task. *You will be irritated by their country manners, you will be annoyed by their native insubordination,* I told myself, *but you will never find men more suitable, so grant them what latitude they need.* I directed Mrs. Rampage to cancel all telephone calls and appointments for the next hour.

The door closed, and we were alone. Each of the black-suited darlings snapped a business card from his right jacket pocket and extended it to me with a twirl of the fingers. One card read:

MR. CLUBB AND MR. CUFF
Private Detective Extraordinaire
MR. CLUBB

and the other:

MR. CLUBB AND MR. CUFF
Private Detective Extraordinaire
MR. CUFF

I inserted the cards into a pocket and expressed my delight at making their acquaintance.

"Becoming aware of your situation," said Mr. Clubb, "we preferred to report as quickly as we could."

"Entirely commendable," I said. "Will you gentlemen please sit down?"

"We prefer to stand," said Mr. Clubb.

"I trust you will not object if I again take my chair," I said, and did so. "To be honest, I am reluctant to describe the whole of my problem. It is a personal matter, therefore painful."

"It is a domestic matter," said Mr. Cuff.

I stared at him. He stared back with the sly imperturbability of his kind.

"Mr. Cuff," I said, "you have made a reasonable and, as it happens, an accurate supposition, but in the future you will please refrain from speculation."

"Pardon my plain way of speaking, sir, but I was not speculating," he said. "Marital disturbances are domestic by nature."

"All too domestic, one might say," put in Mr. Clubb. "In the sense of pertaining to the home. As we have so often observed, you find your greatest pain right smack-dab in the living room, as it were."

"Which is a somewhat politer fashion of naming another room altogether." Mr. Cuff appeared to suppress a surge of barnie-glee.

Alarmingly, Charlie-Charlie had passed along altogether too much information, especially since the information in question should not have been in his possession. For an awful moment I imagined that the dismissed investigator had spoken to Charlie-Charlie. The man may have broadcast my disgrace to every person encountered on his final journey out of my office, inside the public elevator, thereafter even to the shoeshine "boys" and cup-rattling vermin lining the streets. It occurred to me that I might be forced to have the man silenced. Symmetry would then demand the silencing of valuable Charlie-Charlie. The inevitable next step would resemble a full-scale massacre.

My faith in Charlie-Charlie banished these fantasies by suggesting an alternate scenario, and enabled me to endure the next utterance.

Mr. Clubb said, "Which in plainer terms would be to say the bedroom."

After speaking to my faithful spy, the Private Detectives Extraordinaire had taken the initiative by acting as if *already employed* and following Marguerite to her afternoon assignation at the —— Hotel. Here, already, was the insubordination I had foreseen, but instead of the expected annoyance I felt a thoroughgoing gratitude for the two men leaning slightly toward me, their animal senses alert to every nuance of my response. That they had come to my office armed with the essential secret absolved me from embarrassing explanations; blessedly, the hideous photographs would remain concealed in the bottom drawer.

"Gentlemen," I said, "I applaud your initiative."

They stood at ease. "Then we have an understanding," said Mr. Clubb. "At various times, various matters come to our attention. At these times we prefer to conduct ourselves according to the wishes of our employer, regardless of difficulty."

"Agreed," I said. "However, from this point forward I must insist—"

A rap at the door cut short my admonition. Mrs. Rampage brought in a coffeepot and cup, a plate beneath a silver cover, a rack with four slices of toast, two jam pots, silverware, a linen napkin, and a glass of water, and came to a halt some five or six feet short of the barnies. A sinfully arousing smell of butter and bacon emanated from the tray. Mrs. Rampage deliberated between placing my breakfast on the table to her left or venturing into proximity to my guests by bringing the tray to my desk. I gestured her forward, and she tacked wide to port and homed in on the desk. "All is in order, all is in train," I said. She nodded and backed out—literally walked backward until she reached the door, groped for the knob, and vanished.

I removed the cover from the plate containing two poached eggs in a cup-sized bowl, four crisp rashers of bacon, and a mound of home fried potatoes all the more welcome for being a surprise gift from our chef.

"And now, fellows, with your leave I shall—"

For the second time my sentence was cut off midflow. A thick barnie-hand closed upon the handle of the coffeepot and proceeded to fill the cup. Mr. Clubb transported my coffee to his lips, smacked appreciatively at the taste, then took up a toast slice and plunged it like a dagger into my egg cup, releasing a thick yellow suppuration. He crunched the dripping toast between his teeth.

At that moment, when mere annoyance passed into dumbfounded ire, I might have sent them packing despite my earlier resolution, for

Mr. Clubb's violation of my breakfast was as good as an announcement that he and his partner respected none of the conventional boundaries and would indulge in boorish, even disgusting behavior. I very nearly did send them packing, and both of them knew it. They awaited my reaction, whatever it should be. Then I understood that I was being tested, and half of my insight was that ordering them off would be a failure of imagination. I had asked Charlie-Charlie to send me serious men, not Boy Scouts, and in the rape of my breakfast were depths and dimensions of seriousness I had never suspected. In that instant of comprehension, I believe, I virtually knew all that was to come, down to the last detail, and gave a silent assent.

"Here are our methods in action," he said. "We prefer not to go hungry while you gorge yourself, speaking freely, for the one reason that all of this stuff represents what you ate every morning when you were a kid." Leaving me to digest this shapeless utterance, he bit into his impromptu sandwich and sent golden-brown crumbs showering to the carpet.

"For as the important, abstemious man you are now," said Mr. Clubb, "what do you eat in the mornings?"

"Toast and coffee," I said. "That's about it."

"But in childhood?"

"Eggs," I said. "Scrambled or fried, mainly. And bacon. Home fries, too." Every fatty, cholesterol-crammed ounce of which, I forbore to add, had been delivered by barnie-hands directly from barnie-farms. I looked at the rigid bacon, the glistening potatoes, the mess in the egg cup. My stomach lurched.

"We prefer," Mr. Clubb said, "that you follow your true preferences instead of muddying mind and stomach by gobbling this crap in search of an inner peace that never existed in the first place, if you can be honest with yourself." He leaned over the desk and picked up the plate. His partner snatched a second piece of bacon and wrapped it within a second slice of toast. Mr. Clubb began working on the eggs, and Mr. Cuff grabbed a handful of home fried potatoes. Mr. Clubb dropped the empty egg cup, finished his coffee, refilled the cup, and handed it to Mr. Cuff, who had just finished licking the residue of fried potato from his free hand.

I removed the third slice of toast from the rack. Forking home fries into his mouth, Mr. Clubb winked at me. I bit into the toast and considered the two little pots of jam, greengage, I think, and rosehip. Mr.

Clubb waggled a finger. I contented myself with the last of the toast. After a while I drank from the glass of water. All in all I felt reasonably satisfied and, but for the deprivation of my customary cup of coffee, content with my decision. I glanced in some irritation at Mr. Cuff. He drained his cup, then tilted into it the third and final measure from the pot and offered it to me. "Thank you," I said. Mr. Cuff picked up the pot of greengage jam and sucked out its contents, loudly. Mr. Clubb did the same with the rosehip. They sent their tongues into the corners of the jam pots and cleaned out whatever adhered to the side. Mr. Cuff burped. Overlappingly, Mr. Clubb burped.

"Now, that is what I call by the name of breakfast, Mr. Clubb," said Mr. Cuff. "Are we in agreement?"

"Deeply," said Mr. Clubb. "That is what I call by the name of breakfast now, what I have called by the name of breakfast in the past, and what I shall continue to call by that sweet name on every morning in the future." He turned to me and took his time, sucking first one tooth, then another. "Our morning meal, sir, consists of that simple fare with which we begin the day, except when in all good faith we wind up sitting in a waiting room with our stomachs growling because our future client has chosen to skulk in late for work." He inhaled. "Which was for the same exact reason that brought him to our attention in the first place and for which we went without in order to offer him our assistance. Which is, begging your pardon, sir, the other reason for which you ordered a breakfast you would ordinarily rather starve than eat, and all I ask before we get down to the business at hand is that you might begin to entertain the possibility that simple men like ourselves might possibly understand a thing or two."

"I see that you are faithful fellows," I began.

"Faithful as dogs," broke in Mr. Clubb.

"And that you understand my position," I continued.

"Down to its smallest particulars," he interrupted again. "We are on a long journey."

"And so it follows," I pressed on, "that you must also understand that no further initiatives may be taken without my express consent."

These last words seemed to raise a disturbing echo—of what I could not say, but an echo nonetheless, and my ultimatum failed to achieve the desired effect. Mr. Clubb smiled and said, "We intend to follow your inmost desires with the faithfulness, as I have said, of trusted dogs, for one of our sacred duties is that bringing these to fulfillment, as evidenced, begging your pardon, sir, in the matter of the breakfast our actions spared you from gobbling up and sickening yourself with. Before you protest, sir, please let me put to you the question of how you think you would be feeling right now if you had eaten that greasy stuff all by yourself?"

The straightforward truth announced itself and demanded utterance. "Poisoned," I said. After a second's pause, I added, "Disgusted."

"Yes, for you are a better man than you know. Imagine the situation. Allow yourself to picture what would have transpired had Mr. Cuff and myself not acted on your behalf. As your heart throbbed and your veins groaned, you would have taken in that while you were stuffing yourself the two of us stood hungry before you. You would have remembered that good woman informing you that we had patiently awaited your arrival since eight this morning, and at that point sir, you would have experienced a self-disgust that would forever have tainted our relationship. From that point forth, sir, you would have been incapable of receiving the full benefits of our services."

I stared at the twinkling barnie. "Are you saying that if I had eaten my breakfast you would have refused to work for me?"

"You did eat your breakfast. The rest was ours."

This statement was so literally true that I burst into laughter. "Then I must thank you for saving me from myself. Now that you may accept employment, please inform me of the rates for your services."

"We have no rates," said Mr. Clubb.

"We prefer to leave compensation to the client," said Mr. Cuff.

This was crafty by even barnie-standards, but I knew a countermove. "What is the greatest sum you have ever been awarded for a single job?"

"Six hundred thousand dollars," said Mr. Clubb.

"And the smallest?"

"Nothing, zero, nada, zilch," said the same gentleman.

"And your feelings as to the disparity?"

"None," said Mr. Clubb. "What we are given is the correct amount. When the time comes, you shall know the sum to the penny."

To myself I said, *So I shall, and it shall be nothing*; to them, "We must devise a method by which I may pass along suggestions as I monitor your ongoing progress. Our future consultations should take place in anonymous public places on the order of street corners, public parks, diners, and the like. I must never be seen in your office."

"You must not, you could not," said Mr. Clubb. "We would prefer to install ourselves here within the privacy and seclusion of your own beautiful office."

"Here?" He had once again succeeded in dumbfounding me.

"Our installation within the client's work space proves so advantageous as to overcome all initial objections," said Mr. Cuff. "And in this case, sir, we would occupy but the single corner behind me where the table stands against the window. We would come and go by means of your private elevator, exercise our natural functions in your private bathroom, and have our simple meals sent in from your kitchen. You would suffer no interference or awkwardness in the course of your business. So we prefer to do our job here, where we can do it best."

"You prefer," I said, giving equal weight to every word, "to move in with me."

"Prefer it to declining the offer of our help, thereby forcing you, sir, to seek the aid of less reliable individuals."

Several factors, first among them being the combination of delay, difficulty, and risk involved in finding replacements for the pair before me, led me to give further thought to this absurdity. Charlie-Charlie, a fellow of wide acquaintance among society's shadow side, had sent me his best. Any others would be inferior. It was true that Mr. Clubb and Mr. Cuff could enter and leave my office unseen, granting us a greater degree of security than possible in diners and public parks. There remained an insuperable problem.

"All you say may be true, but my partners and clients alike enter this office daily. How do I explain the presence of two strangers?"

"That is easily done, Mr. Cuff, is it not?" said Mr. Clubb.

"Indeed it is," said his partner. "Our experience has given us two infallible and complementary methods. The first of these is the installation of a screen to shield us from the view of those who visit this office."

I said, "You intend to hide behind a screen."

"During those periods when it is necessary for us to be on-site."

"Are you and Mr. Clubb capable of perfect silence? Do you never shuffle your feet, do you never cough?"

"You could justify our presence within these sacrosanct confines by the single manner most calculated to draw over Mr. Clubb and myself a blanket of respectable, anonymous impersonality."

"You wish to be introduced as my lawyers?" I asked.

"I invite you to consider a word," said Mr. Cuff. "Hold it steadily in your mind. Remark the inviolability that distinguishes those it identifies, measure its effect upon those who hear it. The word of which I speak, sir, is this: *consultant*."

I opened my mouth to object and found I could not.

Every profession occasionally must draw upon the resources of impartial experts—consultants. Every institution of every kind has known the visitations of persons answerable only to the top and given access to all departments—consultants. Consultants are *supposed* to be invisible. Again I opened my mouth, this time to say, "Gentlemen, we are in business." I picked up my telephone and asked Mrs. Rampage to order immediate delivery from Bloomingdale's of an ornamental screen and then to remove the breakfast tray.

Eyes agleam with approval, Mr. Clubb and Mr. Cuff stepped forward to clasp my hand.

"We are in business," said Mr. Clubb.

"Which is by way of saying," said Mr. Cuff, "jointly dedicated to a sacred purpose."

Mrs. Rampage entered, circled to the side of my desk, and gave my visitors a glance of deep-dyed wariness. Mr. Clubb and Mr. Cuff looked heavenward. "About the screen," she said. "Bloomingdale's wants to know if you would prefer one six feet high in a black and red Chinese pattern or one ten feet high, Art Deco, in ochers, teals, and taupes."

My barnies nodded together at the heavens. "The latter, please, Mrs. Rampage," I said. "Have it delivered this afternoon, regardless of the cost, and place it beside the table for the use of these gentlemen, Mr. Clubb and Mr. Cuff, highly regarded consultants to the financial industry. That table shall be their command post."

"Consultants," she said. "Oh."

The barnies dipped their heads. Much relaxed, Mrs. Rampage asked if I expected great changes in the future.

"We shall see," I said. "I wish you to extend every cooperation to these gentlemen. I need not remind you, I know, that change is the first law of life."

She disappeared, no doubt on a beeline for her telephone.

Mr. Clubb stretched his arms above his head. "The preliminaries are out of the way, and we can move to the job at hand. You, sir, have been most *exceedingly*, most *grievously* wronged. Do I overstate?"

"You do not," I said.

"Would I overstate to assert that you have been injured, that you have suffered a devastating wound?"

"No, you would not," I responded, with some heat.

Mr. Clubb settled a broad haunch upon the surface of my desk. His face had taken on a grave, sweet serenity. "You seek redress. Redress, sir, is a *correction*, but it is nothing more. You imagine that it restores a lost balance, but it does nothing of the kind. A crack has appeared on the earth's surface, causing widespread loss of life. From all sides are heard the cries of the wounded and dying. It is as though the earth itself has suffered an injury akin to yours, is it not?"

He had expressed a feeling I had not known to be mine until that moment, and my voice trembled as I said, "It is exactly."

"Exactly," he said. "For that reason I said *correction* rather than *restoration*. Restoration is never possible. Change is the first law of life."

"Yes, of course," I said, trying to get down to brass tacks.

Mr. Clubb hitched his buttock more comprehensively onto the desk. "What will happen will indeed happen, but we prefer our clients to acknowledge from the first that, apart from human desires being a messy business, outcomes are full of surprises. If you choose to repay one disaster with an equal and opposite disaster, we would reply, in our country fashion, There's a calf that won't suck milk."

I said, "I know I can't pay my wife back in kind, how could I?"

"Once we begin," he said, "we cannot undo our actions."

"Why should I want them undone?" I asked.

Mr. Clubb drew up his legs and sat cross-legged before me. Mr. Cuff placed a meaty hand on my shoulder. "I suppose there is no dispute," said Mr. Clubb, "that the injury you seek to redress is the adulterous behavior of your spouse."

Mr. Cuff's hand tightened on my shoulder.

"You wish that my partner and myself punish your spouse."

"I didn't hire you to read her bedtime stories," I said.

Mr. Cuff twice smacked my shoulder, painfully, in what I took to be approval.

"Are we assuming that her punishment is to be of a physical nature?" asked Mr. Clubb. His partner gave my shoulder another all-too-hearty squeeze.

"What other kind is there?" I asked, pulling away from Mr. Cuff's hand.

The hand closed on me again, and Mr. Clubb said, "Punishment of a mental or psychological nature. We could, for example, torment her with mysterious phone calls and anonymous letters. We could use any of a hundred devices to make it impossible for her to sleep. Threatening incidents could be staged so often as to put her in a permanent state of terror."

"I want physical punishment," I said.

"That is our constant preference," he said. "Results are swifter and more conclusive when physical punishment is used. But again, we have a wide spectrum from which to choose. Are we looking for mild physical pain, real suffering, or something in between, on the order of, say, broken arms or legs?"

I thought of the change in Marguerite's eyes when I named the ——— Hotel. "Real suffering."

Another bone-crunching blow to my shoulder from Mr. Cuff and a wide, gappy smile from Mr. Clubb greeted this remark. "You, sir, are our favorite type of client," said Mr. Clubb. "A fellow who knows what he wants and is unafraid to put it into words. This suffering, now, did you wish it in brief or extended form?"

"Extended," I said. "I must say that I appreciate your thoughtfulness in consulting with me like this. I was not quite sure what I wanted of you when first I requested your services, but you have helped me become perfectly clear about it."

"That is our function," he said. "Now, sir. The extended form of real suffering permits two different conclusions, gradual cessation or termination. What is your preference?"

I opened my mouth and closed it. I opened it again and stared at the ceiling. Did I want these men to murder my wife? No. Yes. No. Yes, but only after making sure that the unfaithful trollop understood exactly why she had to die. No, surely an extended term of excruciating torture would restore the world to proper balance. Yet I wanted the witch dead. But then I would be ordering these barnies to kill her. "At the moment I cannot make that decision," I said. Irresistibly, my eyes found the bottom drawer containing the files of obscene photographs. "I'll let you know my decision after we have begun."

Mr. Cuff dropped his hand, and Mr. Clubb nodded with exaggerated, perhaps ironic slowness. "And what of your rival, the seducer, sir? Do we have any wishes in regard to that gentleman, sir?"

The way these fellows could sharpen one's thinking was truly remarkable. "I most certainly do," I said. "What she gets, he gets. Fair is fair."

"Indeed, sir," said Mr. Clubb, "and, if you will permit me, sir, only fair is fair. And fairness demands that before we go any deeper into the particulars of the case we must examine the evidence as presented to yourself, and when I speak of fairness, sir, I refer to fairness particularly to yourself, for only the evidence seen by your own eyes can permit us to view this matter through them."

Again, I looked helplessly down at the bottom drawer. "That will not be necessary. You will find my wife at our country estate, Green . . ."

My voice trailed off as Mr. Cuff's hand ground into my shoulder while he bent down and opened the drawer.

"Begging to differ," said Mr. Clubb, "but we are now and again in a better position than the client to determine what is necessary. Remember, sir, that while shame unshared is toxic to the soul, shame shared is the beginning of health. Besides, it only hurts for a little while."

Mr. Cuff drew the files from the drawer.

"My partner will concur that your inmost wish is that we examine the evidence," said Mr. Clubb. "Else you would not have signaled its location. We would prefer to have your explicit command to do so, but in the absence of explicit, implicit serves just about as well."

I gave an impatient, ambiguous wave of the hand, a gesture they cheerfully understood.

"Then all is . . . how do you put it, sir? 'All is . . .' "

"All is in order, all is in train," I muttered.

"Just so. We have even found it beneficial to establish a common language with our clients, in order to conduct ourselves within terms enhanced by their constant usage in the dialogue between us." He took the files from Mr. Cuff's hands. "We shall examine the contents of these folders at the table across the room. After the examination has been completed, my partner and I shall deliberate. And then, sir, we shall return for further instructions."

They strolled across the office and took adjoining chairs on the near side of the table, presenting me with two identical wide, black-clothed backs. Their hats went to either side, the files between them. Attempting unsuccessfully to look away, I lifted my receiver and asked my secretary who, if anyone, had called in the interim and what appointments had been made for the day.

Mr. Clubb opened a folder and leaned forward to inspect the topmost photograph.

My secretary informed me that Marguerite had telephoned from the road with an inquiry concerning my health. Mr. Clubb's back and shoulders trembled with what I assumed was the shock of disgust. One of the scions was due at 2:00 p.m., and at 4:00 a cryptic gentleman would arrive. By their works shall ye know them, and Mrs. Rampage proved herself to be a diligent soul by asking if I wished her to place a call to Green Chimneys at three o'clock. "I think not," I said. "Anything else?" She told me that Gilligan had expressed a desire to see me privately—meaning, without the Skipper—sometime during the morning. A murmur came from the table. "Gilligan can wait," I said, and the murmur, expressive, I had thought, of dismay and sympathy, rose in volume and revealed itself as amusement.

They were chuckling—even chortling!

I replaced the telephone and said, "Gentlemen, your laughter is insupportable." The potential effect of this remark was undone by its being lost within a surge of coarse laughter. I believe that something else was at that moment lost . . . some dimension of my soul . . . an element akin to pride . . . akin to dignity . . . but whether the loss was for good or ill, then I could not say. For some time, in fact an impossibly lengthy time, they found cause for laughter in the wretched photographs. My occasional attempts to silence them went unheard as they passed the dread images back and forth, discarding some instantly and to others returning for a second, a third, even a fourth and fifth perusal.

At last the barnies reared back, uttered a few nostalgic chirrups of laughter, and returned the photographs to the folders. They were still twitching with remembered laughter, still flicking happy tears from their eyes, as they sauntered, grinning, back across the office and tossed the files onto my desk. "Ah me, sir, a delightful experience," said Mr. Clubb. "Nature in all her lusty romantic splendor, one might say. Remarkably stimulating, I could add. Correct, sir?"

"I hadn't expected you fellows to be stimulated to mirth," I grumbled, ramming the foul things into the drawer and out of view.

"Laughter is merely a portion of the stimulation to which I refer," he said. "Unless my sense of smell has led me astray, a thing I fancy it has yet to do, you could not but feel another sort of arousal altogether before these pictures, am I right?"

I refused to respond to this sally but felt the blood rising in my cheeks. Here they were again, the slugs and maggots.

"We are all brothers under the skin," said Mr. Clubb. "Remember my words. Shame unshared poisons the soul. And besides, it only hurts for a little while."

Now I could not respond. What was the "it" that hurt only for a little while—the pain of cuckoldry, the mystery of my shameful response to the photographs, or the horror of the barnies knowing what I had done?

"You will find it helpful, sir, to repeat after me: *It only hurts for a little while.*"

"It only hurts for a little while," I said, and the naive phrase reminded me that they were only barnies after all.

"Spoken like a child," Mr. Clubb most annoyingly said, "in, as it were, the tones and accents of purest innocence," and then righted matters by asking where Marguerite might be found. Had I not mentioned a country place named Green . . . ?

"Green Chimneys," I said, shaking off the unpleasant impression that the preceding few seconds had made upon me. "You will find it at the end of —— Lane, turning right off —— Street just north of the town of ——. The four green chimneys easily visible above the hedge along —— Lane are your landmark, though as it is the only building in sight you can hardly mistake it for another. My wife left our place in the city just after ten this morning, so she should be getting there . . ." I looked at my watch. ". . . in thirty to forty-five minutes. She will unlock the front gate, but she will not relock it once she has passed through, for she never does. The woman does not have the self-preservation of a sparrow. Once she has entered the estate, she will travel up the drive and open the door of the garage with an electronic device. This door, I assure you, will remain open, and the door she will take into the house will not be locked."

"But there are maids and cooks and laundresses and bootboys and suchlike to consider," said Mr. Cuff. "Plus a majordomo to conduct the entire orchestra and go around rattling the doors to make sure they're locked. Unless all of these parties are to be absent on account of the annual holiday."

"My servants have the month off," I said.

"A most suggestive consideration," said Mr. Clubb. "You possess a devilish clever mind, sir."

"Perhaps," I said, grateful for the restoration of the proper balance. "Marguerite will have stopped along the way for groceries and other essentials, so she will first carry the bags into the kitchen, which is the first room to the right off the corridor from the garage. Then I suppose she will take the staircase upstairs and air out the bedroom." I took pen and paper from my topmost drawer and sketched the layout of the house. "She may go around to the library, the morning room, and the drawing room, opening the shutters and a few windows. Somewhere during this process, she is likely to use the telephone. After that, she will leave the house by the rear entrance and take the path along the top of the bluff to a long, low building that looks like this."

I drew in the outlines of the studio in its nest of trees above the Hudson. "It is a recording studio I had built for her convenience. She may well plan to spend the entire afternoon inside it. You will know if she is there by the lights." I saw Marguerite smiling to herself as she fit the key into the lock on the studio door, saw her let herself in and reach for the light switch. A wave of emotion rendered me speechless.

Mr. Clubb rescued me by asking. "It is your feeling, sir, that when the lady stops to use the telephone she will be placing a call to that energetic gentleman?"

"Yes, of course," I said, only barely refraining from adding *you dolt*. "She will seize the earliest opportunity to inform him of their good fortune."

He nodded with an extravagant caution I recognized from my own dealings with backward clients. "Let us pause to see all 'round the matter, sir. Would the lady wish to leave a suspicious entry in your telephone records? Isn't it more likely that the person she telephones will be you, sir? The call to the athletic gentleman will already have been placed, according to my way of seeing things, either from the roadside or the telephone in the grocery where you have her stop to pick up her essentials."

Though disliking these references to Leeson's physical condition, I admitted that he might have a point.

"In that case, sir, and I know that a mind as quick as yours has already overtaken mine, you would want to express yourself with the utmost cordiality when the missus calls again, so as not to tip your hand in even the slightest way. But that, I'm sure, goes without saying, after all you have been through, sir."

Without bothering to acknowledge this, I said, "Shouldn't you fellows be leaving? No sense in wasting time, after all."

"Precisely why we shall wait here until the end of the day," said Mr. Clubb. "In cases of this unhappy sort, we find it more effective to deal with both parties at once, acting in concert when they are in prime condition to be taken by surprise. The gentleman is liable to leave his place of work at the end of the day, which implies to me that he is unlikely to appear at your lovely country place at any time before seven this evening or, which is more likely, eight. At this time of year, there is still enough light at nine o'clock to enable us to conceal our vehicle on the grounds, enter the house, and begin our business. At eleven o'clock, sir, we shall call with our initial report and request additional instructions."

I asked the fellow if he meant to idle away the entire afternoon in my office while I conducted my business.

"Mr. Cuff and I are never idle, sir. While you conduct your business, we will be doing the same, laying out our plans, refining our strategies, choosing our methods and the order of their use."

"Oh, all right," I said, "but I trust you'll be quiet about it."

At that moment, Mrs. Rampage buzzed to say that Gilligan was before her, requesting to see me immediately, proof that bush telegraph is a more efficient means of spreading information than a newspaper. I told her to send him in, and a second later Morning Gilligan, pale of face, dark hair tousled but not as yet completely wild, came treading softly toward my desk. He pretended to be surprised that I had visitors and pantomimed an apology which incorporated the suggestion that he depart and return later. "No, no," I said, "I am delighted to see you, for this gives me the opportunity to introduce you to our new consultants, who will be working closely with me for a time."

Gilligan swallowed, glanced at me with the deepest suspicion, and extended his hand as I made the introductions. "I regret that I am unfamiliar with your work, gentlemen," he said. "Might I ask the name of your firm? Is it Locust, Bleaney, Burns or Charter, Carter, Maxton, and Coltrane?"

By naming the two most prominent consultancies in our industry, Gilligan was assessing the thinness of the ice beneath his feet. LBB specialized in investments, CCM&C in estates and trusts. If my visitors worked for the former, he would suspect that a guillotine hung above his neck; if the latter, the Skipper was liable for the chop. "Neither," I said. "Mr. Clubb and Mr. Cuff are the directors of their own concern, which covers every aspect of the trade with such tactful professionalism that it is known to but the few for whom they will consent to work."

"Excellent," Gilligan whispered, gazing in some puzzlement at the map and floor plan atop my desk. "Tip-top."

"When their findings are given to me, they shall be given to all. In the meantime, I would prefer that you say as little as possible about the matter. Though change is a law of life, we wish to avoid unnecessary alarm."

"You know that you can depend on my silence," said Morning Gilligan, and it was true, I did know that. I also knew that his alter ego, Afternoon Gilligan, would babble the news to everyone who had not already heard it from Mrs. Rampage. By 6:00 p.m., our entire industry would be pondering the information that I had called in a consultancy team of such rarified accomplishments *that they chose to remain unknown but to the very few.* None of my colleagues could dare admit to an ignorance of Clubb & Cuff, and my reputation, already great, would increase exponentially.

To distract him from the floor plan of Green Chimneys and the rough map of my estate, I said, "I assume that some business brought you here, Gilligan."

"Oh! Yes—yes—of course," he said, and with a trace of embarrassment brought to my attention the pretext for his being there, the ominous plunge in value of an overseas fund in which we had advised one of his musicians to invest. Should we recommend selling the fund before more money was lost, or was it wisest to hold on? Only a minute was required to decide that the musician should retain his share of the fund until next quarter, when we anticipated a general improvement, but both Gilligan and I were aware that this recommendation call could easily have been handled by telephone. Soon he was moving toward the door, smiling at the barnies in a pathetic display of false confidence.

The telephone rang a moment after the detectives had returned to the table. Mr. Clubb said, "Your wife, sir. Remember: the utmost cordiality." Here was false confidence, I thought, of an entirely different sort. I picked up the receiver to hear Mrs. Rampage tell me that my wife was on the line.

What followed was a banal conversation of the utmost *duplicity.*

Marguerite pretended that my sudden departure from the dinner table and my late arrival at the office had caused her to fear for my health. I pretended that all was well, apart from a slight indigestion. Had the drive up been peaceful? Yes. How was the house? A little musty, but otherwise fine. She had never quite realized, she said, how very large Green Chimneys was until she walked around in it, knowing she was going to be there alone. Had she been out to the studio? No, but she was looking forward to getting a lot of work done over the next three or four days and thought she would be working every night, as well. (Implicit in this remark was the information that I should be unable to reach her, the studio being without a telephone.) After a moment of awkward silence, she said, "I suppose it is too early for you to have identified your traitor." It was, I said, but the process would begin that evening. "I'm so sorry you have to go through this," she said. "I know how painful the discovery was for you, and I can only begin to imagine how angry you must be, but I hope you will be merciful. No amount of punishment can undo the damage, and if you try to exact retribution you will only injure yourself. The man is going to lose his job and his reputation. Isn't that punishment enough?" After a few meaningless pleasantries the conversation had clearly come to an end, although we still had yet to say good-bye. Then an odd thing happened to me. I nearly said, *Lock all the doors and windows tonight and let no one in.* I nearly said, *You are in grave danger and must come home.* With these words rising in my throat, I looked across the room at Mr. Clubb and Mr. Cuff. Mr. Clubb winked at me. I heard myself bidding Marguerite farewell, and then heard her hang up her telephone.

"Well done, sir," said Mr. Clubb. "To aid Mr. Cuff and myself in the preparation of our inventory, can you tell us if you keep certain staples at Green Chimneys?"

"Staples?" I said, thinking he was referring to foodstuffs.

"Rope?" he asked. "Tools, especially pliers, hammers, and screwdrivers? A good saw? A variety of knives? Are there by any chance firearms?"

"No firearms," I said. "I believe all the other items you mention can be found in the house."

"Rope and tool chest in the basement, knives in the kitchen?"

"Yes," I said, "precisely." I had not ordered these barnies to murder my wife, I reminded myself; I had drawn back from that precipice. By the time I went into the executive dining room for my luncheon, I felt sufficiently restored to give Charlie-Charlie that ancient symbol of approval, the thumbs-up sign.

3

When I returned to my office the screen had been set in place, shielding from view the detectives in their preparations but in no way muffling the rumble of comments and laughter they brought to the task. "Gentlemen," I said in a voice loud enough to be heard behind the screen—a most unsuitable affair decorated with a pattern of ocean liners, martini glasses, champagne bottles, and cigarettes—"you must modulate your voices, as I have business to conduct here as well as you." There came a somewhat softer rumble of acquiescence. I took my seat to discover my bottom desk drawer pulled out, the folders absent. Another roar of laughter jerked me once again to my feet.

I came around the side of the screen and stopped short. The table lay concealed beneath drifts and mounds of legal paper covered with lists of words and drawings of stick figures in varying stages of dismemberment. Strewn through the yellow pages were the photographs, loosely divided into those which either Marguerite or Graham Leeson provided the principal focus. Crude genitalia had been drawn, without reference to either party's actual gender, over and atop both of them. Aghast, I began gathering up the defaced photographs. "I must insist . . ." I said. "I really must insist, you know . . ."

Mr. Clubb immobilized my wrist with one hand and extracted the photographs with the other. "We prefer to work in our time-honored fashion," he said. "Our methods may be unusual, but they are ours. But before you take up the afternoon's occupations, sir, can you tell us if items of the handcuff order might be found in the house?"

"No," I said. Mr. Cuff pulled a yellow page before him and wrote *handcuffs*.

"Chains?" asked Mr. Clubb.

"No chains," I said, and Mr. Cuff added *chains* to his list.

"That is all for the moment," said Mr. Clubb, and released me.

I took a step backward and massaged my wrist, which stung as if from a rope burn. "You speak of your methods," I said, "and I understand that you have them. But what can be the purpose of defacing my photographs in this grotesque fashion?"

"Sir," said Mr. Clubb in a stern, teacherly voice, "where you speak of defacing, we use the term 'enhancement.' Enhancement is a tool we find vital to the method known by the name of Visualization."

I retired defeated to my desk. At five minutes before 2:00, Mrs. Rampage informed me that the Skipper and our scion, a thirty-year-old inheritor of a great family fortune named Mr. Chester Montfort de M——, awaited my pleasure. Putting Mrs. Rampage on hold, I called out, "Please do give me absolute quiet, now. A client is on his way in."

First to appear was the Skipper, his tall, rotund form as alert as a pointer's in a grouse field as he led in the taller, inexpressibly languid figure of Mr. Chester Montfort de M——, a person marked in every inch of his being by great ease, humor, and stupidity. The Skipper froze to gape horrified at the screen, but Montfort de M—— continued around him to shake my hand and say, "Have to tell you, I like that thingamabob over there immensely. Reminds me of a similar thing-amabob at the Beeswax Club a few years ago, whole flocks of girls used to come tumbling out. Don't suppose we're in for any unicycles and trumpets today, eh?"

The combination of the raffish screen and our client's unbridled memories brought a dangerous flush to the Skipper's face, and I hastened to explain the presence of top-level consultants who preferred to pitch tent on-site, as it were, hence the installation of a screen, all the above in the service of, well, *service*, an all-important quality we . . .

"By Kitchener's mustache," said the Skipper. "I remember the Beeswax Club. Don't suppose I'll ever forget the night Little Billy Pegleg jumped up and . . ." The color darkened on his cheeks, and he closed his mouth.

From behind the screen, I heard Mr. Clubb say, "Visualize *this*." Mr. Cuff chuckled.

The Skipper recovered himself and turned his sternest glare upon me. "Superb idea, consultants. A white-glove inspection tightens up any ship." His veiled glance toward the screen indicated that he had known of the presence of our "consultants" but, unlike Gilligan, had restrained himself from thrusting into my office until given legitimate reason. "That being the case, is it still quite proper that these people remain while we discuss Mr. Montfort de M——'s confidential affairs?"

"Quite proper, I assure you," I said. "The consultants and I prefer to work in an atmosphere of complete cooperation. Indeed, this arrangement is a condition of their accepting our firm as their client."

"Indeed," said the Skipper.

"Top of the tree, are they?" said Mr. Montfort de M———. "Expect no less of you fellows. Fearful competence. *Terrifying* competence."

Mr. Cuff's voice could be heard saying, "Okay, visualize *this*." Mr. Clubb uttered a high-pitched giggle.

"Enjoy their work," said Mr. Montfort de M———.

"Shall we?" I gestured to their chairs. As a young man whose assets equaled two to three billion dollars (depending on the condition of the stock market, the value of real estate in half a dozen cities around the world, global warming, forest fires, and the like), our client was as catnip to the ladies, three of whom he had previously married and divorced after siring a child upon each, resulting in a great interlocking complexity of trusts, agreements, and contracts, all of which had to be reexamined on the occasion of his forthcoming wedding to a fourth young woman, named like her predecessors after a semiprecious stone. Due to the perspicacity of the Skipper and myself, each new nuptial altered the terms of those previous so as to maintain our client's liability at an unvarying level. Our computers had enabled us to generate the documents well before his arrival, and all Mr. Montfort de M——— had to do was listen to the revised terms and sign the papers, a task that generally induced a slumberous state except for those moments when a prized asset was in transition.

"Hold on, boys," he said ten minutes into our explanations, "you mean Opal has to give the racehorses to Garnet, and in return she gets the teak plantation from Turquoise, who gets Garnet's ski resort in Aspen? Opal is crazy about those horses."

I explained that his second wife could easily afford the purchase of a new stable with the income from the plantation. He bent to the task of scratching his signature on the form. A roar of laughter erupted behind the screen. The Skipper glanced sideways in displeasure, and our client looked at me blinking. "Now to the secondary trusts," I said. "As you will recall, three years ago—"

My words were cut short by the appearance of a chuckling Mr. Clubb clamping an unlighted cigar in his mouth, a legal pad in his hand, as he came toward us. The Skipper and Mr. Montfort de M——— goggled at him, and Mr. Clubb nodded. "Begging your pardon, sir, but some queries cannot wait. Pickax, sir? Dental floss? Awl?"

"No, yes, no," I said, and then introduced him to the other two men. The Skipper appeared stunned, Mr. Montfort de M——— cheerfully puzzled.

"We would prefer the existence of an attic," said Mr. Clubb.

"An attic exists," I said.

"I must admit my confusion," said the Skipper. "Why is a consultant asking about awls and attics? What is dental floss to a consultant?"

"For the nonce, Skipper," I said, "these gentlemen and I must communicate in a form of cipher or code, of which these are examples, but soon—"

"Plug your blowhole, Skipper," broke in Mr. Clubb. "At the moment you are as useful as wind in an outhouse, always hoping you will excuse my simple way of expressing myself."

Sputtering, the Skipper rose to his feet, his face rosier by far than during his involuntary reminiscence of what Little Billy Pegleg had done one night at the Beeswax Club.

"Steady on," I said, fearful of the heights of choler to which indignation could bring my portly, white-haired, but still powerful junior.

"Not on your life," bellowed the Skipper. "I cannot brook . . . cannot tolerate . . . If this ill-mannered dwarf imagines excuse is possible after . . ." He raised a fist. Mr. Clubb said, "Pish tosh," and placed a hand on the nape of the Skipper's neck. Instantly, the Skipper's eyes rolled up, the color drained from his face, and he dropped like a sack into his chair.

"Hole in one," marveled Mr. Montfort de M——. "Old boy isn't dead, is he?"

The Skipper exhaled uncertainly and licked his lips.

"With my apologies for the unpleasantness," said Mr. Clubb, "I have only two more queries at this juncture. Might we locate bedding in the aforesaid attic, and have you an implement such as a match or lighter?"

"There are several old mattresses and bed frames in the attic," I said, "but as to matches, surely you do not . . ."

Understanding the request better than I, Mr. Montfort de M—— extended a golden lighter and applied an inch of flame to the tip of Mr. Clubb's cigar. "Don't think that part was code," he said. "Rules have changed? Smoking allowed?"

"From time to time during the workday my colleague and I prefer to smoke," said Mr. Clubb, expelling a reeking miasma across the desk. I had always found tobacco nauseating in every form, and in all parts of our building smoking had, of course, long been prohibited.

"Three cheers, my man, plus three more after that," said Mr. Montfort de M——, extracting a ridged case from an inside pocket, an absurdly phallic cigar from the case. "I prefer to smoke too, you know, especially during these deadly conferences about who gets the pincushions and who gets the snuffboxes." He submitted the object to a circumcision, *snick-snick*, and to my horror set it alight. "Ashtray?" I dumped paper clips from a crystal oyster shell and slid it toward him. "Mr. Clubb, is it? Mr. Clubb, you are a fellow of wonderful accomplishments, still can't get over that marvelous whopbopaloobop on the Skipper, and I'd like to ask if we could get together some evening, cigars and cognac and that kind of thing."

"We prefer to undertake one matter at a time," said Mr. Clubb. Mr. Cuff appeared beside the screen. He, too, was lighting up eight or nine inches of brown rope. "However, we welcome your appreciation and would be delighted to swap tales of derring-do at a later date."

"Very, very cool," said Mr. Montfort de M——, "especially if you could teach me how to do the whopbopaloobop."

"This is a world full of hidden knowledge," Mr. Clubb said. "My partner and I have chosen as our sacred task the transmission of that knowledge."

"Amen," said Mr. Cuff.

Mr. Clubb bowed to my awed client and sauntered off. The Skipper shook himself, rubbed his eyes, and took in the client's cigar. "My goodness," he said. "I believe . . . I can't imagine . . . Heavens, is smoking permitted again? What a blessing." With that, he fumbled a cigarette from his shirt pocket, accepted a light from Mr. Montfort de M——, and sucked in the fumes. Until that moment I had not known that the Skipper was an addict of nicotine.

For the remainder of the hour a coiling layer of smoke like a low-lying cloud established itself beneath the ceiling and increased in density as it grew toward the floor while we extracted Mr. Montfort de M——'s careless signature on the transfers and assignments. Now and again the Skipper displaced one of a perpetual chain of cigarettes from his mouth to remark upon the peculiar pain in his neck. Finally I was able to send client and junior partner on their way with those words of final benediction, "All is in order, all is in train," freeing me at last to stride about my office flapping a copy of *Institutional Investor* at the cloud, a remedy our fixed windows made more symbolic than actual. The barnies further defeated the effort by wafting ceaseless billows of cigar effluvia over the screen, but as they seemed to be conducting their business in a conventionally businesslike manner I made no objection and retired in defeat to my desk for the preparations necessitated by the arrival in an hour of my next client, Mr. Arthur "This Building Is Condemned" C———, the most cryptic of all the cryptic gentlemen.

So deeply was I immersed in these preparations that only a polite cough and the supplication of "Begging your pardon, sir" brought to my awareness the presence of Mr. Clubb and Mr. Cuff before my desk. "What is it now?" I asked.

"We are, sir, in need of creature comforts," said Mr. Clubb. "Long hours of work have left us exceeding dry in the region of mouth and throat, and the pressing sensation of thirst has made it impossible for us to maintain the concentration required to do our best."

"Meaning a drink would be greatly appreciated, sir," said Mr. Cuff.

"Of course, of course," I said. "I'll have Mrs. Rampage bring in a couple of bottles of water. We have San Pellegrino and Evian. Which would you prefer?"

With a smile almost menacing in its intensity, Mr. Cuff said, "We prefer drinks when we drink. *Drink* drinks, if you take my meaning."

"For the sake of the refreshment found in them," said Mr. Clubb, ignoring my obvious dismay. "I speak of refreshment in its every aspect, from relief of the parched tongue, taste to the ready palate, warmth to the inner man, and to the highest of refreshments, that of the mind and soul. We prefer bottles of gin and bourbon, and while almost any decent gargle would be gratefully received, we have, like all men who partake of grape and grain, our favorite tipples. Mr. Cuff is partial to J. W. Dant bourbon, and I enjoy a drop of Bombay gin. A bucket of ice would not go amiss, and I could say the same for a case of ice-cold Old Bohemian beer. As a chaser."

"You consider it a good idea to consume alcohol before embarking on . . ." I sought for the correct phrase. "A mission so delicate?"

"We consider it an essential prelude. Alcohol inspires the mind and awakens the imagination. A fool dulls both by overindulgence, but up to that point, which is a highly individual matter, there is only enhancement. Through history, alcohol has been known for its sacred properties, and the both of us know that during the sacrament of Holy Communion, priests and reverends happily serve as bartenders, passing out free drinks to all comers, children included."

"Besides that," I said after a pause, "I suppose you would prefer not to be compelled to quit my employment after we have made such strides together."

"We are on a great journey," he said.

I placed the order with Mrs. Rampage, and thirty minutes later into my domain entered two ill-dressed youths laden with the requested liquors and a metal bucket, in which the necks of beer bottles protruded from a bed of ice. I tipped the louts a dollar apiece, which they accepted with a boorish lack of grace. Mrs. Rampage took in this activity with none of the revulsion for the polluted air and spirituous liquids I had anticipated.

The louts slouched away; the chuckling barnies disappeared from view with their refreshments; and, after fixing me for a moment of silence, her eyes alight with an expression I had never before observed in them, Mrs. Rampage ventured the amazing opinion that the recent relaxation of formalities should prove beneficial to the firm as a whole and added that, were Mr. Clubb and Mr. Cuff responsible for the reformation, they had already justified their reputation and would assuredly enhance my own.

"You believe so," I said, noting with momentarily delayed satisfaction that the effects of Afternoon Gilligan's indiscretions had already begun to declare themselves.

Employing the tactful verbal formula for *I wish to speak exactly half my mind and no more*, Mrs. Rampage said, "May I be frank, sir?"

"I depend on you to do no less," I said.

Her carriage and face became what I can only describe as girlish— years seemed to drop away from her. "I don't want to say too much, sir, and I hope you know how much everyone understands what a privilege it is to be a part of this firm." Like the Skipper but more attractively, she blushed. "Honest, I really mean that. Everybody knows that we're one of the two or three companies best at what we do."

"Thank you," I said.

"That's why I feel I can talk like this," said my ever-less-recognizable Mrs. Rampage. "Until today, everybody thought if they acted like themselves, the way they really were, you'd fire them right away. Because, and maybe I shouldn't say this, maybe I'm way out of line, sir, but it's because you always seem, well, so proper you could never forgive a person for not being as dignified as you are. Like the Skipper is a heavy smoker and everybody knows it's not supposed to be permitted in this building, but a lot of companies here let their top people smoke in their offices as long as they're discreet because it shows that if you get to the top you can be appreciated, too, but here the Skipper has to go all the way to the elevator and stand outside with the file clerks if he wants a cigarette. And in every other company I know the partners and important clients sometimes have a drink together and nobody thinks they're committing a terrible sin. You're a religious man, sir, we look up to you so much, but I think you're going to find that people will respect you even more once it gets out that you've loosened the rules a little bit." She gave me a look in which I read that she feared having spoken too freely. "I just wanted to say that I think you're doing the right thing, sir."

What she was saying, of course, was that I was widely regarded as pompous, remote, and out of touch. "I had not known that my employees regarded me as a religious man," I said.

"Oh, we all do," she said with an almost touching earnestness. "Because of the hymns."

"The hymns?"

"The ones you hum to yourself when you're working."

"Do I, indeed? Which ones?"

" 'Jesus Loves Me,' 'The Old Rugged Cross,' 'Abide with Me,' and 'Amazing Grace,' mostly. Sometimes 'Onward, Christian Soldiers.' "

Here, with a vengeance, were Temple Square and Scripture Street! Here was the Youth Bible Study Center, where the child-me had hours on end sung these same hymns during our Sunday school sessions! I did not know what to make of the knowledge that I hummed them to myself at my desk, but it was some consolation that this unconscious habit had at least partially humanized me to my staff.

"You didn't know you did that? Oh, sir, that's so *cute*!"

Sounds of merriment from the far side of the office rescued Mrs. Rampage from the fear that this time she had truly overstepped the bounds, and she made a rapid exit. I stared after her for a moment, at first unsure how deeply I ought to regret a situation in which my secretary found it possible to describe myself and my habits as *cute*, then resolved that it probably was, or eventually would be, for the best. "All is in order, all is in train," I said to myself. "It only hurts for a little while." With that, I took my seat once more to continue delving into the elaborations of Mr. "This Building Is Condemned" C——'s financial life.

Another clink of bottle against glass and ripple of laughter brought with them the recognition that this particular client would never consent to the presence of unknown "consultants." Unless the barnies could be removed for at least an hour, I should face the immediate loss of a substantial portion of my business.

"Fellows," I cried, "come up here now. We must address a serious problem."

Glasses in hand, cigars nestled into the corners of their mouths, Mr. Clubb and Mr. Cuff sauntered into view. Once I had explained the issue in the most general terms the detectives readily agreed to absent themselves for the required period. Where might they install themselves? "My bathroom," I said. "It has a small library attached, with a desk, a worktable, leather chairs and sofa, a billiard table, a large-screen television set, and a bar. Since you have not yet had your luncheon, you may wish to order whatever you like from the kitchen."

Five minutes later, bottles, glasses, hats, and mounds of paper arranged on the bathroom table, the bucket of beer beside it, I exited through the concealed door as Mr. Clubb ordered up from my doubtless astounded chef a meal of chicken wings, french fries, onion rings, and T-bone steaks, medium well. With plenty of time to spare, I immersed myself again in details, only to be brought up short by the recognition that I was humming, none too quietly, the most innocent of hymns, "Jesus Loves Me." Then, precisely at the appointed hour, Mrs. Rampage informed me of the arrival of my client and his associates, and I bade her bring them through.

A sly, slow-moving whale encased in an exquisite double-breasted black pinstripe, Mr. "This Building Is Condemned" C—— advanced into my office with his customary hauteur and offered me the customary nod of the head while his three "associates" formed a human breakwater in the center of the room. Regal to the core, he affected not to notice Mrs. Rampage sliding a black leather chair out of the middle distance and around the side of the desk until it was in position, at which point he sat himself in it without looking down. Then he inclined his slablike head and raised a small pallid hand. One of the "associates" promptly moved to hold the door for Mrs. Rampage's departure. At this signal, I sat down, and the two remaining henchmen separated themselves by a distance of perhaps eight feet. The third closed the door and stationed himself by his general's right shoulder. These formalities complete, my client shifted his close-set obsidian eyes to mine and said, "You well?"

"Very well, thank you," I replied, according to ancient formula. "And you?"

"Good," he said. "But things could be better." This, too, followed a long-established formula. His next words were a startling deviation. He took in the stationary cloud and the corpse of Montfort de M——'s cigar rising like a monolith from the reef of cigarette butts in the crystal shell and, with the first genuine smile I had ever seen on his pock-marked, small-featured face, said, "I can't believe it, but one thing just got better already. You eased up on the stupid no-smoking rule which is poisoning this city, good for you."

"It seemed," I said, "a concrete way in which to demonstrate our appreciation for the smokers among those clients we most respect." When dealing with the cryptic gentlemen, one must not fail to offer intervallic allusions to the spontaneous respect in which they are held.

"Deacon," he said, employing the sobriquet he had given me on our first meeting, "you being one of a kind at your job, the respect you speak of is mutual, and besides that, all surprises should be as pleasant as this here." With that, he snapped his fingers at the laden shell, and as he produced a ridged case similar to but more capacious than Mr. Montfort de M——'s, the man at his shoulder whisked the impromptu ashtray from the desk, deposited its contents in the *poubelle*, and repositioned it at a point on the desk precisely equidistant from us. My client opened the case to expose the six cylinders contained within, removed one, and proffered the remaining five to me. "Be my guest, Deacon," he said. "Money can't buy better Havanas."

"Your gesture is much appreciated," I said. "However, with all due respect, at the moment I shall choose not to partake."

Distinct as a scar, a vertical crease of displeasure appeared on my client's forehead, and the ridged case and its five inhabitants advanced an inch toward my nose. "Deacon, you want me to smoke alone?" asked Mr. "This Building Is Condemned" C——. "This stuff, if you were ever lucky enough to find it at your local cigar store, which that lucky believe me you wouldn't be, is the best of the best, straight from me to you as what you could term a symbol of the cooperation and respect between us, and at the commencement of our business today it would please me greatly if you would do me the honor of joining me in a smoke."

As they say, or, more accurately, as they used to say, needs must when the devil drives, or words to that effect. "Forgive me," I said, and drew one of the fecal things from the case. "I assure you, the honor is all mine."

Mr. "This Building Is Condemned" C—— snipped the rounded end from his cigar, plugged the remainder in the center of his mouth, then subjected mine to the same operation. His henchman proffered a lighter, and Mr. "This Building Is Condemned" C—— bent forward and surrounded himself with clouds of smoke, in the manner of Bela Lugosi materializing before the brides of Dracula. The henchman moved the flame toward me, and for the first time in my life I inserted in my mouth an object that seemed as large around as the handle of a baseball bat, brought it to the dancing flame, and drew in that burning smoke from which so many other men before me had derived pleasure.

Legend and common sense alike dictated that I should sputter and cough in an attempt to rid myself of the noxious substance. Nausea was in the cards, also dizziness. It is true that I suffered a degree of initial discomfort, as if my tongue had been lightly singed or seared, and the sheer unfamiliarity of the experience—the thickness of the tobacco tube, the texture of the smoke, as dense as chocolate—led me to fear for my well-being. Yet, despite the not altogether unpleasant tingling on the upper surface of my tongue, I expelled my first mouthful of cigar smoke with the sense of having sampled a taste every bit as delightful as the first sip of a properly made martini. The thug whisked away the flame, and I drew in another mouthful, leaned back, and released a wondrous quantity of smoke. Of a surprising smoothness, in some sense almost cool rather than hot, the delightful taste defined itself as heather, loam, morel mushrooms, venison, and some distinctive spice akin to coriander. I repeated the process, with results even more pleasurable—this time I tasted a hint of black butter sauce. "I can truthfully say," I told my client, "that never have I met a cigar as fine as this one."

"You bet you haven't," said Mr. "This Building Is Condemned" C——, and on the spot presented me with three more of the precious objects. With that, we turned to the tidal waves of cash and the interlocking corporate shells, each protecting another series of interconnected shells that concealed yet another, like Chinese boxes.

The cryptic gentlemen one and all appreciated certain ceremonies, such as the appearance of espresso coffee in thimble-sized porcelain cups and an accompanying assortment of biscotti at the halfway point of our meditations. Matters of business being forbidden while coffee and cookies were dispatched, the conversation generally turned to the conundrums posed by family life. Since I had no family to speak of, and, like most of his kind, Mr. "This Building Is Condemned" C—— was richly endowed with grandparents, parents, uncles, aunts, sons, daughters, nephews, nieces, and grandchildren, these remarks on the genealogical tapestry tended to be monologic in nature, my role in them limited to nods and grunts. Required as they were more often by the business of the cryptic gentlemen than was the case in other trades or professions, funerals were also an ongoing topic. Taking tiny sips of his espresso and equally maidenish nibbles from his favorite sweet-meats (Hydrox and Milano), my client favored me with the expected praises of his son, Arthur Jr. (Harvard graduate school, English Lit), lamentations of his daughter, Fidelia (thrice-married, never wisely), hymns to his grandchildren (Cyrus, Thor, and Hermione, respectively the genius, the dreamer, and the despot), and then proceeded to link his two unfailing themes by recalling the unhappy behavior of Arthur Jr. at the funeral of my client's uncle and a principal figure in his family's rise to an imperial eminence, Mr. Vincente "Waffles" C——.

This anecdote called for the beheading and ignition of another magnificent stogie, and I greedily followed suit.

"Arthur Jr.'s got his head screwed on right, and he's got the right kinda family values," said my client. "Straight A's all through school, married a stand-up dame with money of her own, three great kids, makes a man proud. Hard worker. Got his head in a book morning to night, human-encyclopedia-type guy, up there at Harvard, those professors, they love him. Kid knows how you're supposed to act, right?"

I nodded and filled my mouth with another fragrant draft.

"So he comes to my Uncle Vincente's funeral all by himself, which troubles me. On top of it doesn't show the proper respect to old Waffles, who was one hell of a man, there's guys still pissing blood on account of they looked at him wrong forty years ago, on top of that, I don't have the good feeling I get from taking his family around to my friends and associates and saying, So look here, this here is Arthur Jr., my Harvard guy, plus his wife, Hunter, whose ancestors I think got here even before that rabble on the *Mayflower*, plus his three kids—Cyrus, the little bastard's even smarter than his dad, Thor, the one's got his head in the clouds, which is okay because we need people like that, too, and Hermione, who you can tell just by looking at her she's mean as a snake and is gonna wind up running the world someday. So I say, Arthur Jr., what the hell happened, everybody else get killed in a train wreck or something? He says, No, Dad, they just didn't wanna come, these big family funerals, they make 'em feel funny, they don't like having their pictures taken so they show up on the six o'clock news. Didn't wanna come, I say back, what kinda shit is that, you shoulda made 'em come, and if anyone took their pictures when they didn't want, we can take care of that, no trouble at all. I go on like this, I even say, What good is Harvard and all those books if they don't make you any smarter than this, and finally Arthur Jr.'s mother tells me, Put a cork in it, you're not exactly helping the situation here.

"So what happens then? Insteada being smart like I should, I go nuts on account of I'm the guy who pays the bills, that Harvard up there pulls in the money better than any casino I ever saw, and you wanna find a real good criminal, get some Boston WASP in a bow tie, and all of a sudden nobody listens to me! I'm seeing red in a big way here, Deacon, this is my uncle Vincente's funeral, and insteada backing me up his mother is telling me I'm not *helping*. I yell, You wanna help? Go up there and bring back his wife and kids, or I'll send Carlo and Tommy to do it. All of a sudden I'm so mad I'm thinking these people are insulting me, and how can they think they can get away with that, people who insult me don't do it twice—and then I hear what I'm thinking, and I do what she said and put a cork in it, but it's too late, I went way over the top and we all know it.

"Arthur Jr. takes off, and his mother won't talk to me for the whole rest of the day. Only thing I'm happy about is I didn't blow up where anyone else could see it. Deacon, I know you're the type guy wouldn't dream of threatening his family, but if the time ever comes, do yourself a favor and light up a Havana instead."

"I'm sure that is excellent advice," I said.

"Anyhow, you know what they say, it only hurts for a little while, which is true as far as it goes, and I calmed down. Uncle Vincente's funeral was beautiful. You woulda thought the Pope died. When the people are going out to the limousines, Arthur Jr. is sitting in a chair at the back of the church reading a book. Put that in your pocket, I say, wanna do homework, do it in the car. He tells me it isn't homework, but he puts the book in his pocket and we go out to the cemetery. His mother looks out the window the whole time we're driving to the cemetery, and the kid starts reading again. So I ask what the hell is it, this book he can't put down? He tells me but it's like he's speaking some foreign language, only word I understand is 'the,' which happens a lot when your kid reads a lot of fancy books, half the titles make no sense to an ordinary person. Okay, we're out there in Queens, god-damn graveyard the size of Newark, FBI and reporters all over the place, and I'm thinking maybe Arthur Jr. wasn't so wrong after all, Hunter probably hates having the FBI take her picture, and besides that little Hermione probably woulda mugged one of 'em and stole his wallet. So I tell Arthur Jr. I'm sorry about what happened. I didn't really think you were going to put me in the same grave as Uncle Waf-fles, he says, the Harvard smart-ass. When it's all over, we get back in the car, and out comes the book again. We get home, and he disap-pears. We have a lot of people over, food, wine, politicians, old-timers from Brooklyn, Chicago people, Detroit people, L.A. people, movie directors, cops, actors I never heard of, priests, bishops, the guy from the Cardinal. Everybody's asking me, Where's Arthur Jr.? I go upstairs to find out. He's in his old room, and he's still reading that book. I say, Arthur Jr., people are asking about you, I think it would be nice if you mingled with our guests. I'll be right down, he says, I just finished what I was reading. Here, take a look, you might enjoy it. He gives me the book and goes out of the room. So I'm wondering—what the hell *is* this, anyhow? I take it into the bedroom, toss it on the table. About ten-thirty, eleven, everybody's gone, kid's on the shuttle back to Boston, house is cleaned up, enough food in the refrigerator to feed the whole bunch all over again, I go up to bed. Arthur Jr.'s mother still isn't talk-ing to me, so I get in and pick up the book. Herman Melville is the name of the guy who wrote it. The story the kid was reading is called 'Bartleby the Scrivener.' I decide I'll try it. What the hell, right? You're an educated guy, you ever read that story?"

"A long time ago," I said. "A bit . . . *odd*, isn't it?"

"Odd? That's the most terrible story I ever read in my whole life! This dud gets a job in a law office and decides he doesn't want to work. Does he get fired? He does not. This is a story? You hire a guy who won't do the job, what do you do, pamper the asshole? At the end, the dud ups and disappears and you find out he used to work in the dead-letter office. Is there a point here? The next day I call up Arthur Jr., say could he explain to me please what that story is supposed to mean? Dad, he says, it means what it says. Deacon, I just about pulled the plug on Harvard right then and there. I never went to any college, but I do know that nothing means what it says, not on this planet."

This reflection was accurate when applied to the documents on my desk, for each had been encoded in a systematic fashion that rendered their literal contents deliberately misleading. Another code had informed both of my recent conversations with Marguerite. "Fiction is best left to real life," I said.

"Someone shoulda told that to Herman Melville," said Mr. Arthur "This Building Is Condemned" C——.

Mrs. Rampage buzzed me to advise that I was running behind schedule and inquire about removing the coffee things. I invited her to gather up the debris. A door behind me opened, and I assumed my secretary had responded to my request with an alacrity remarkable even for her. The first sign of my error was the behavior of the three other men in the room, until this moment no more animated than marble statues. The thug at my client's side stepped forward to stand behind me, and his fellows moved to the front of my desk. "What the hell is this shit?" said the client, unable, because of the man in front of him, to see Mr. Clubb and Mr. Cuff. Holding a pad bearing one of his many lists, Mr. Clubb gazed in mild surprise at the giants flanking my desk and said, "I apologize for the intrusion, sir, but our understanding was that your appointment would be over in an hour, and by my simple way of reckoning you should be free to answer a query as to steam irons."

"What the hell *is* this shit?" said my client, repeating his original question with a slight tonal variation expressive of gathering dismay.

I attempted to salvage matters. "Please allow me to explain the interruption. I have employed these men as consultants, and as they prefer to work in my office, a condition I of course could not permit during our business meeting, I temporarily relocated them to my washroom, outfitted with a library adequate to their needs."

"Fit for a king, in my opinion," said Mr. Clubb.

At that moment the other door into my office, to the left of my desk, opened to admit Mrs. Rampage, and my client's guardians inserted their hands into their suit jackets and separated with the speed and precision of a dance team.

"Oh, my," said Mrs. Rampage. "*Excuse* me. Should I come back later?"

"Not on your life, my darling," said Mr. Clubb. "Temporary misunderstanding of the false-alarm sort. Please allow us to enjoy the delightful spectacle of your feminine charms."

Before my wondering eyes, Mrs. Rampage curtsied and hastened to my desk to gather up the wreckage.

I looked toward my client and observed a detail of striking peculiarity, that although his half-consumed cigar remained between his lips, four inches of cylindrical ash had deposited a gray smear on his necktie before coming to rest on the shelf of his belly. He was staring straight ahead with eyes grown to the size of quarters. His face had become the color of raw piecrust.

Mr. Clubb said, "Respectful greetings, sir."

The client gargled and turned upon me a look of unvarnished horror.

Mr. Clubb said, "Apologies to all." Mrs. Rampage had already bolted. From unseen regions came the sound of a closing door.

Mr. "This Building Is Condemned" C—— blinked twice, bringing his eyes to something like their normal dimensions. With an uncertain hand but gently, as if it were a tiny but much-loved baby, he placed his cigar in the crystal shell. He cleared his throat; he looked at the ceiling. "Deacon," he said, gazing upward. "Gotta run. My next appointment musta slipped my mind. What happens when you start to gab. I'll be in touch." He stood, dislodging the ashen cylinder to the carpet, and motioned his goons to the outer office.

4

Of course at the earliest opportunity I interrogated my detectives about this turn of events, and while they moved their mountains of paper, bottles, buckets, glasses, hand-drawn maps, and other impedimenta back behind the screen, I continued the questioning. No, they averred, the gentleman at my desk was not a gentleman whom previously they had been privileged to look upon, acquaint themselves with, or encounter in any way whatsoever. They had never been employed in any capacity by the gentleman. Mr. Clubb observed that the unknown gentleman had been wearing a conspicuously handsome and well-tailored suit.

"That is his custom," I said.

"And I believe he smokes, sir, a noble high order of cigar," said Mr.

Clubb with a glance at my breast pocket. "Which would be the sort of item customarily beyond the dreams of honest laborers such as ourselves."

"I trust that you will permit me," I said with a sigh, "to offer you the pleasure of two of the same." No sooner had the offer been accepted, the barnies back behind their screen, than I buzzed Mrs. Rampage with the request to summon by instant delivery from the most distinguished cigar merchant in the city a box of his finest. "Good for you, boss!" whooped the new Mrs. Rampage.

I spent the remainder of the afternoon brooding upon the reaction of Mr. Arthur "This Building Is Condemned" C—— to my "consultants." I could not but imagine that his hasty departure boded ill for our relationship. I had seen terror on his face, and he knew that *I* knew what I had seen. An understanding of this sort is fatal to that nuance-play critical alike to high-level churchmen and their outlaw counterparts, and I had to confront the possibility that my client's departure had been of a permanent nature. Where Mr. "This Building Is Condemned" C—— went, his colleagues of lesser rank, Mr. Tommy "I Believe in Rainbows" B——, Mr. Anthony "Moonlight Becomes You" M——, Mr. Bobby "Total Eclipse" G——, and their fellow archbishops, cardinals, and papal nuncios would assuredly follow. Before the close of the day, I would send a comforting fax informing Mr. "This Building Is Condemned" C—— that the consultants had been summarily released from employment. I would be telling only a "white" or provisional untruth, for Mr. Clubb and Mr. Cuff's task would surely be completed long before my client's return. All was in order, all was in train, and as if to put the seal upon the matter, Mrs. Rampage buzzed to inquire if she might come through with the box of cigars. Speaking in a breathy timbre I had never before heard from anyone save Marguerite in the earliest, most blissful days of our marriage, Mrs. Rampage added that she had some surprises for me, too. "By this point," I said, "I expect no less." Mrs. Rampage *giggled*.

The surprises, in the event, were of reassuring practicality. The good woman had wisely sought the advice of Mr. Montfort de M——, who, after recommending a suitably aristocratic cigar emporium and a favorite cigar, had purchased for me a rosewood humidor, a double-bladed cigar cutter, and a lighter of antique design. As soon as Mrs. Rampage had been instructed to compose a note of gratitude embellished in whatever fashion she saw fit, I arrayed all but one of the cigars in the humidor, decapitated that one, and set it alight. Beneath a fair touch of fruitiness like the aroma of a blossoming pear tree, I met in successive layers the tastes of black olives, aged Gouda cheese, pine needles, new leather, miso soup, either sorghum or brown sugar, burning pear, library paste, and myrtle leaves. The long finish intriguingly combined Bible paper and sunflower seeds. Mr. Montfort de M—— had chosen well, though I regretted the absence of black butter sauce.

Feeling comradely, I strolled across my office toward the merriment emanating from the far side of the screen. A superior cigar should be complemented by a worthy liquor, and in light of what was to transpire during the evening I considered a snifter of Mr. Clubb's Bombay gin not inappropriate. "Fellows," I said, tactfully announcing my presence, "are preparations nearly completed?"

"That, sir, they are," said one or another of the pair.

"Welcome news," I said, and stepped around the screen. "But I must be assured—"

It was as if the detritus of New York City's half dozen filthiest living quarters had been scooped up, shaken, and dumped into my office. Heaps of ash, bottles, shoals of paper, books with stained covers and broken spines, battered furniture, broken glass, refuse I could not identify, refuse I could not even *see*, undulated from the base of the screen, around and over the table, heaping itself into landfill-like piles here and there, and washed against the plate-glass window. A jagged, five-foot opening gaped in a smashed pane. Their derbies perched on their heads, islanded in their chairs, Mr. Clubb and Mr. Cuff leaned back, feet up on what must have been the table.

"You'll join us in a drink, sir," said Mr. Clubb, "by way of wishing us success and adding to the pleasure of that handsome smoke." He extended a stout leg and kicked rubble from a chair. I sat down. Mr. Clubb plucked an unclean glass from the morass and filled it with Dutch gin, or *jenever*, from one of the minaret-shaped stone flagons I had observed upon my infrequent layovers in Amsterdam, the Netherlands. Mrs. Rampage had been variously employed during the barnies' sequestration. Then I wondered if Mrs. Rampage might not have shown signs of intoxication during our last encounter.

"I thought you drank Bombay," I said.

"Variety is, as they say, life's condiment," said Mr. Clubb, and handed me the glass.

I said, "You have made yourselves quite at home."

"I thank you for your restraint," said Mr. Clubb. "In which sentiment my partner agrees, am I correct, Mr. Cuff?"

"Entirely," said Mr. Cuff. "But I wager you a C-note to a see-gar that a word or two of explanation is in order."

"How right that man is," said Mr. Clubb. "He has a genius for the truth I have never known to fail him. Sir, you enter our work space to come upon the slovenly, the careless, the unseemly, and your response, which we comprehend in every particular, is to recoil. My wish is that you take a moment to remember these two essentials: one, we have, as aforesaid, our methods, which are ours alone, and two, having appeared fresh on the scene, you see it worse than it is. By morning tomorrow, the cleaning staff shall have done its work."

"I suppose you have been Visualizing." I quaffed *jenever*.

"Mr. Cuff and I," he said, "prefer to minimize the risk of accidents, surprises, and such by the method of rehearsing our, as you might say, performances. These poor sticks, sir, are easily replaced, but our work once under way demands completion and cannot be duplicated, redone, or undone."

I recalled the all-important guarantee. "I remember your words," I said, "but I must be assured that you remember mine. I did not request termination. During the course of the day my feelings on the matter have intensified. Termination, if by that term you meant—"

"Termination is termination," said Mr. Clubb.

"*Ex*termination," I said. "Cessation of life due to external forces. It is not my wish, it is unacceptable, and I have even been thinking that I overstated the degree of physical punishment appropriate to this matter."

"'Appropriate'?" said Mr. Clubb. "When it comes to desire, 'appropriate' is a concept without meaning. In the sacred realm of desire, 'appropriate,' being meaningless, does not exist. We speak of your inmost wishes, sir, and desire is an extremely *thingy* sort of thing."

I looked at the hole in the window, the broken bits of furniture and ruined books. "I think," I said, "that permanent injury is all I wish. Something on the order of blindness or the loss of a hand."

Mr. Clubb favored me with a glance of humorous irony. "It goes, sir, as it goes, which brings to mind that we have but an hour more, a period of time to be splendidly improved by a superior Double Corona such as the fine example in your hand."

"Forgive me," I said. "And might I then request . . . ?" I extended the nearly empty glass, and Mr. Clubb refilled it. Each received a cigar, and I lingered at my desk for the required term, sipping *jenever* and pretending to work until I heard sounds of movement. Mr. Clubb and Mr. Cuff approached. "So you are off," I said.

"It is, sir, to be a long and busy night," said Mr. Clubb. "If you take my meaning."

With a sigh I opened the humidor. They reached in, snatched a handful of cigars apiece, and deployed them into various pockets. "Details at eleven," said Mr. Clubb.

A few seconds after their departure, Mrs. Rampage informed me that she would be bringing through a fax communication just received.

The fax had been sent me by Chartwell, Munster, and Stout, a legal firm with but a single client, Mr. Arthur "This Building Is Condemned" C——. Chartwell, Munster, and Stout regretted the necessity to inform me that their client wished to seek advice other than my own in his financial affairs. A sheaf of documents binding me to silence as to all matters concerning the client would arrive for my signature the following day. All records, papers, computer disks, and other data were to be referred posthaste to their office. I had forgotten to send my intended note of client-saving reassurance.

5

What an abyss of shame I must now describe, at every turn what humiliation. It was at most five minutes past 6:00 p.m. when I learned of the desertion of my most valuable client, a turn of events certain to lead to the loss of his cryptic fellows and some 40 percent of our annual business. Gloomily I consumed my glass of Dutch gin without noticing that I had already far exceeded my tolerance. I ventured behind the screen and succeeded in unearthing another stone flagon, poured another measure, and gulped it down while attempting to demonstrate numerically that (a) the anticipated drop in annual profit could not be as severe as feared and (b) if it were, the business could continue as before, without reductions in salary, staff, or benefits. Despite ingenious feats of juggling, the numbers denied (a) and mocked (b), suggesting that I should be fortunate to retain, not lose, 40 percent of present business. I lowered my head to the desk and tried to regulate my breathing. When I heard myself rendering an off-key version of "Abide with Me," I acknowledged that it was time to go home, got to my feet, and made the unfortunate decision to exit through the general offices on the theory that a survey of my presumably empty realm might suggest the sites of pending amputations.

I tucked the flagon under my elbow, pocketed the five or six cigars remaining in the humidor, and passed through Mrs. Rampage's chamber. Hearing the abrasive music of the cleaners' radios, I moved with exaggerated care down the corridor, darkened but for the light spilling from an open door thirty feet before me. Now and again, finding myself unable to avoid striking my shoulder against the wall, I took a medicinal swallow of *jenever*. I drew up to the open door and realized that I had come to Gilligan's quarters. The abrasive music emanated from his sound system. *We'll get rid of that, for starters*, I said to myself, and straightened up for a dignified navigation past his doorway. At the crucial moment I glanced within to observe my jacketless junior partner sprawled, tie undone, on his sofa beside a scrawny ruffian with a quiff of lime-green hair and attired for some reason in a skintight costume involving zebra stripes and many chains and zippers. Disreputable creatures male and female occupied themselves in the background. Gilligan shifted his head, began to smile, and at the sight of me turned to stone.

"Calm down, Gilligan," I said, striving for an impression of sober paternal authority. I had recalled that my junior had scheduled a late appointment with his most successful musician, a singer whose band sold millions of records year in and year out despite the absurdity of their name, the Dog Turds or the Rectal Valves, something of that sort. My calculations had indicated that Gilligan's client, whose name I recalled as Cyril Futch, would soon become crucial to the maintenance of my firm, and as the beaky little rooster coldly took me in I thought to impress upon him the regard in which he was held by his chosen financial-planning institution. "There is, I assure you, no need for alarm, no, certainly not, and in fact, Gilligan, you know, I should be honored to seize this opportunity of making the acquaintance of your guest, whom it is our pleasure to assist and advise and whatever."

Gilligan reverted to flesh and blood during the course of this utterance, which I delivered gravely, taking care to enunciate each syllable clearly in spite of the difficulty I was having with my tongue. He noted the bottle nestled into my elbow and the lighted cigar in the fingers of my right hand, a matter of which until that moment I had been imperfectly aware. "Hey, I guess the smoking lamp is lit," I said. "Stupid rule, anyhow. How about a little drink on the boss?"

Gilligan lurched to his feet and came reeling toward me.

All that followed is a montage of discontinuous imagery. I recall Cyril Futch propping me up as I communicated our devotion to the safeguarding of his wealth, also his dogged insistence that his name was actually Simon Gulch or Sidney Much or something similar before he sent me toppling onto the sofa; I see an odd little fellow with a tattooed head and a name like Pus (there was a person named Pus in attendance, though he may not have been the one) accepting one of my cigars and eating it; I remember inhaling from smirking Gilligan's cigarette and drinking from a bottle with a small white worm lying dead at its bottom and snuffling up a white powder recommended by a female Turd or Valve; I remember singing "The Old Rugged Cross" in a state of partial undress. I told a face brilliantly lacquered with makeup that I was "getting a feel" for "this music." A female Turd or Valve, not the one who had recommended the powder but one in a permanent state of hilarity I found endearing, assisted me into my limousine and on the homeward journey experimented with its many buttons and controls. Atop the town-house steps, she removed the key from my fumbling hand gleefully to insert it into the lock. The rest is welcome darkness.

6

A form of consciousness returned with a slap to my face, the muffled screams of the woman beside me, a bowler-hatted head thrusting into view and growling, "The shower for you, you damned idiot." As a second assailant whisked her away, the woman, whom I thought to be Marguerite, wailed. I struggled against the man gripping my shoulders, and he squeezed the nape of my neck.

When next I opened my eyes, I was naked and quivering beneath an onslaught of cold water within the marble confines of my shower cabinet. Charlie-Charlie Rackett leaned against the open door of the cabinet and regarded me with ill-disguised impatience. "I'm freezing, Charlie-Charlie," I said. "Turn off the water."

Charlie-Charlie thrust an arm into the cabinet and became Mr.

Clubb. "I'll warm it up, but I want you sober," he said. I drew myself up into a ball.

Then I was on my feet and moaning while I massaged my forehead. "Bath time all done now," called Mr. Clubb. "Turn off the wa-wa." I did as instructed. The door opened, and a bath towel unfurled over my left shoulder.

Side by side on the bedroom sofa and dimly illuminated by the lamp, Mr. Clubb and Mr. Cuff observed my progress toward the bed. A black leather satchel stood on the floor between them. "Gentlemen," I said, "although I cannot presently find words to account for the condition in which you found me, I trust that your good nature will enable you to overlook . . . or ignore . . . whatever it was that I must have done . . . I cannot quite recall the circumstances."

"The young woman has been dispatched," said Mr. Clubb, "and you need never fear any trouble from that direction, sir."

"The young woman?" I remembered a hyperactive figure playing with the controls in the back of the limousine. A fragmentary memory of the scene in Gilligan's office returned to me, and I moaned aloud.

"None too clean, but pretty enough in a ragamuffin way," said Mr. Clubb. "The type denied the proper education in social graces. Rough about the edges. Intemperate in language. A stranger to discipline."

I groaned—to have introduced such a creature to my house!

"A stranger to honesty, too, sir, if you'll permit me," said Mr. Cuff. "It's addiction turns them into thieves. Give them half a chance, they'll steal the brass handles off their mothers' coffins."

"Addiction?" I said. "Addiction to what?"

"Everything, from the look of the bint," said Mr. Cuff. "Before Mr. Clubb and I sent her on her way, we retrieved these items doubtless belonging to you, sir." While walking toward me he removed from his pockets the following articles: my wristwatch, gold cuff links, wallet, the lighter of antique design given me by Mr. Montfort de M——, likewise the cigar cutter and the last of the cigars I had purchased the day before. "I thank you most gratefully," I said, slipping the watch onto my wrist and all else save the cigar into the pockets of my robe. It was, I noted, just past four o'clock in the morning. The cigar I handed back to him with the words "Please accept this as a token of my gratitude."

"Gratefully accepted," he said. Mr. Cuff bit off the end, spat it onto the carpet, and set the cigar alight, producing a nauseating quantity of fumes.

"Perhaps," I said, "we might postpone our discussion until I have had time to recover from my ill-advised behavior. Let us reconvene at . . ." A short period was spent pressing my hands to my eyes while rocking back and forth. "Four this afternoon?"

"Everything in its own time is a principle we hold dear," said Mr. Clubb. "And this is the time for you to down aspirin and Alka-Seltzer, and for your loyal assistants to relish the hearty breakfasts the thought of which sets our stomachs to growling. A man of stature and accomplishment like yourself ought to be able to overcome the effects of too much booze and attend to business, on top of the simple matter of getting his flunkies out of bed so they can whip up the bacon and eggs."

"Because a man such as that, sir, keeps ever in mind that business faces the task at hand, no matter how lousy it may be," said Mr. Cuff.

"The old world is in flames," said Mr. Clubb, "and the new one is just being born. Pick up the phone."

"All right," I said, "but Mr. Moncrieff's going to *hate* this. He worked for the Duke of Denbigh, and he's a terrible snob."

"All butlers are snobs," said Mr. Clubb. "Three fried eggs apiece, likewise six rashers of bacon, home fries, toast, hot coffee, and for the sake of digestion a bottle of your best cognac."

Mr. Moncrieff picked up his telephone, listened to my orders, and informed me in a small, cold voice that he would speak to the cook. "Would this repast be for the young lady and yourself, sir?"

With a wave of guilty shame that intensified my nausea, I realized that Mr. Moncrieff had observed my unsuitable young companion accompanying me upstairs to the bedroom. "No, it would not," I said. "The young lady, a client of mine, was kind enough to assist me when I was taken ill. The meal is for two male guests." Unwelcome memory returned the spectacle of a scrawny girl pulling my ears and screeching that a useless old fart like me didn't deserve her band's business.

"The phone," said Mr. Clubb. Dazedly I extended the receiver.

"Moncrieff, old man," he said, "amazing good luck, running into you again. Do you remember that trouble the Duke had with Colonel Fletcher and the diary? . . . Yes, this is Mr. Clubb, and it's delightful to hear your voice again . . . He's here too, couldn't do anything without him . . . I'll tell him . . . Much the way things went with the Duke, yes, and we'll need the usual supplies . . . Glad to hear it . . . The dining room in half an hour." He handed the telephone back to me and said to Mr. Cuff, "He's looking forward to the pinochle, and there's a first-rate Pétrus in the cellar he knows you're going to enjoy."

I had purchased six cases of 1928 Château Pétrus at an auction some years before and was holding it while its already immense value doubled, then tripled, until perhaps a decade hence, when I would sell it for ten times its original cost.

"A good drop of wine sets a man right up," said Mr. Cuff. "Stuff was meant to be drunk, wasn't it?"

"You know Mr. Moncrieff?" I asked. "You worked for the Duke?"

"We ply our humble trade irrespective of nationality and borders," said Mr. Clubb. "Go where we are needed, is our motto. We have fond memories of the good old Duke, who showed himself to be quite a fun-loving, spirited fellow, sir, once you got past the crust as it were. Generous, too."

"He gave until it hurt," said Mr. Cuff. "The old gentleman cried like a baby when we left."

"Cried a good deal before that, too," said Mr. Clubb. "In our experience, high-spirited fellows spend a deal more tears than your gloomy customers."

"I do not suppose you shall see any tears from me," I said. The brief look that passed between them reminded me of the complicitous glance I had once seen fly like a live spark between two of their New Covenant forebears, one gripping the hind legs of a pig, the other its front legs and a knife, in the moment before the knife opened the pig's throat and an arc of blood threw itself high into the air. "I shall heed your advice," I said, "and locate my analgesics." I got on my feet and moved slowly to the bathroom. "As a matter of curiosity," I said, "might I ask if you have classified me into the high-spirited category, or into the other?"

"You are a man of middling spirit," said Mr. Clubb. I opened my mouth to protest, and he went on, "But something may be made of you yet."

I disappeared into the bathroom. *I have endured these moonfaced yokels long enough*, I told myself. *Hear their story, feed the bastards, then kick them out.*

In a condition more nearly approaching my usual self, I brushed my teeth and splashed water on my face before returning to the bedroom.

I placed myself with a reasonable degree of executive command in a wing chair, folded my pinstriped robe about me, inserted my feet into velvet slippers, and said, "Things got a bit out of hand, and I thank you for dealing with my young client, a person with whom in spite of appearances I have a professional relationship only. Now let us turn to our real business. I trust you found my wife and Leeson at Green Chimneys. Please give me an account of what followed."

"Things got a bit out of hand," said Mr. Clubb. "Which is a way of describing something that can happen to us all, and for which no one can be blamed. Especially Mr. Cuff and myself, who are always careful to say right smack at the beginning, as we did with you, sir, what ought to be so obvious as to not need saying at all, that our work brings about permanent changes which can never be undone. Especially in the cases when we specify a time to make our initial report and the client disappoints us at the said time. When we are let down by our client, we must go forward and complete the job to our highest standards with no rancor or ill will, knowing that there are many reasonable explanations of a man's inability to get to a telephone."

"I don't know what you mean by this self-serving double-talk," I said. "We had no arrangement of the sort, and your effrontery forces me to conclude that you failed in your task."

Mr. Clubb gave me the grimmest possible suggestion of a smile. "One of the reasons for a man's failure to get to a telephone is a lapse of memory. You have forgotten my informing you that I would give you my initial report at eleven. At precisely eleven o'clock I called, to no avail. I waited through twenty rings, sir, before I abandoned the effort. If I had waited through a hundred, sir, the result would have been the same, on account of your decision to put yourself into a state where you would have had trouble remembering your own name."

"That is a blatant lie," I said, then remembered. The fellow had in fact mentioned in passing something about reporting to me at that hour, which must have been approximately the time when I was regaling the Turds or Valves with "The Old Rugged Cross." My face grew pink. "Forgive me," I said. "I am in error, it is just as you say."

"A manly admission, sir, but as for forgiveness, we extended that quantity from the get-go," said Mr. Clubb. "We are your servants, and your wishes are our sacred charge."

"That's the whole ball of wax in a nutshell," said Mr. Cuff, giving a fond glance to the final inch of his cigar. He dropped the stub onto my carpet and ground it beneath his shoe. "Food and drink to the fibers, sir," he said.

"Speaking of which," said Mr. Clubb. "We will continue our report in the dining room, so as to dig into the feast ordered up by that wondrous villain Reggie Moncrieff."

Until that moment it had never quite occurred to me that my butler possessed, like other men, a Christian name.

7

"A great design directs us," said Mr. Clubb, expelling morsels of his cud. "We poor wanderers, you and me and Mr. Cuff and the milkman too, only see the little portion right in front of us. Half the time we don't even see that in the right way. For sure we don't have a Chinaman's chance of understanding it. But the design is ever present, sir, a truth I bring to your attention for the sake of the comfort in it. Toast, Mr. Cuff."

"Comfort is a matter cherished by all parts of a man," said Mr. Cuff, handing his partner the toast rack. "Most particularly that part known as his soul, which feeds upon the nutrient adversity."

I was seated at the head of the table, flanked by Mr. Clubb and Mr. Cuff. The salvers and tureens before us overflowed, for Mr. Moncrieff, who after embracing each barnie in turn and entering into a kind of conference or huddle, had summoned from the kitchen a banquet far surpassing their requests. Besides several dozen eggs and perhaps two packages of bacon, he had arranged a mixed grill of kidneys, lambs' livers and lamb chops, and strip steaks, as well as vats of oatmeal and a pasty concoction he described as "kedgeree—as the old Duke fancied it."

Sickened by the odors of the food, also by the mush visible in my companions' mouths, I tried again to extract their report. "I don't believe in the grand design," I said, "and I already face more adversity than my soul finds useful. Tell me what happened at the house."

"No mere house, sir," said Mr. Clubb. "Even as we approached along —— Lane, Mr. Cuff and I could not fail to respond to its magnificence."

"Were my drawings of use?" I asked.

"Invaluable." Mr. Clubb speared a lamb chop and raised it to his mouth. "We proceeded through the rear door into your spacious

kitchen or scullery. Wherein we observed evidence of two persons having enjoyed a dinner enhanced by a fine wine and finished with a noble
champagne."

"Aha," I said.

"By means of your guidance, Mr. Cuff and I located the lovely staircase and made our way to the lady's chamber. We effected an entry of
the most praiseworthy silence, if I may say so."

"That entry was worth a medal," said Mr. Cuff.

"Two figures lay slumbering upon the bed. In a blamelessly professional manner we approached, Mr. Cuff on one side, I on the other. In
the fashion your client of this morning called the whopbopaloobop, we
rendered the parties in question even more unconscious than previous,
thereby giving ourselves a good fifteen minutes for the disposition of
instruments. We take pride in being careful workers, sir, and like all
honest craftsmen we respect our tools. We bound and gagged both
parties in timely fashion. Is the male party distinguished by an athletic
past?" Alight with barnieish glee, Mr. Clubb raised his eyebrows and
washed down the last of his chop with a mouthful of cognac.

"Not to my knowledge," I said. "I believe he plays a little racquetball
and squash, that kind of thing."

He and Mr. Cuff experienced a moment of mirth. "More like weight
lifting and football, is my guess," he said. "Strength and stamina. To a
remarkable degree."

"Not to mention considerable speed," said Mr. Cuff with the air of
one indulging a tender reminiscence.

"Are you telling me that he got away?" I asked.

"No one gets away," said Mr. Clubb. "That, sir, is gospel. But you
may imagine our surprise when for the first time in the history of our
consultancy"—and here he chuckled—"a gentleman of the civilian per-
suasion managed to break his bonds and free himself of his ropes whilst
Mr. Cuff and I were engaged in the preliminaries."

"Naked as jaybirds," said Mr. Cuff, wiping with a greasy hand a tear
of amusement from one eye. "Bare as newborn lambie-pies. There
I was, heating up a steam iron I'd just fetched from the kitchen, sir,
along with a selection of knives I came across in exactly the spot you
described, most grateful was I, too, squatting on my haunches without
a care in the world and feeling the first merry tingle of excitement in
my little soldier—"

"What?" I said. "You were naked? And what's this about your little soldier?"

"Hush," said Mr. Clubb, his eyes glittering. "Nakedness is a precaution against fouling our clothing with blood and other bodily products, and men like Mr. Cuff and myself take pleasure in the exercise of our skills. In us, the inner and the outer man are one and the same."

"Are they now?" I said, marveling at the irrelevance of this last remark. It then occurred to me that the remark might have been relevant after all—most unhappily so.

"At all times," said Mr. Cuff, amused by my having missed the point. "If you wish to hear our report, sir, reticence will be helpful."

I gestured for him to go on.

"As said before, I was squatting in my birthday suit by the knives and the steam iron, not a care in the world, when I heard from behind me the patter of little feet. *Hello*, I say to myself, *what's this?* and when I look over my shoulder here is your man, bearing down on me like a steam engine. Being as he is one of your big, strapping fellows, sir, it was a sight to behold, not to mention the unexpected circumstances. I took a moment to glance in the direction of Mr. Clubb, who was busily occupied in another quarter, which was, to put it plain and simple, the bed."

Mr. Clubb chortled and said, "By way of being in the line of duty."

"So in a way of speaking I was in the position of having to settle this fellow before he became a trial to us in the performance of our duties. He was getting ready to tackle me, sir, which was what put us in mind of football being in his previous life, tackle the life out of me before he rescued the lady, and I got hold of one of the knives. Then, you see, when he came flying at me that way all I had to do was give him a good jab in the bottom of the throat, a matter which puts the fear of God into the bravest fellow. It concentrates all their attention, and after that they might as well be little puppies for all the harm they're likely to do. Well, this boy was one for the books, because for the first time in I don't know how many similar efforts, a hundred—"

"I'd say double at least, to be accurate," said Mr. Clubb.

"—in at least a hundred, anyhow, avoiding immodesty, I underestimated the speed and agility of the lad, and instead of planting my weapon at the base of his neck stuck him in the side, a manner of wound which in the case of your really *aggressive* attacker, who you come across in about one out of twenty, is about as effective as a slap with a powder puff. Still, I put him off his stride, a welcome sign to me that he had gone a bit loosey-goosey over the years. Then, sir, the advantage was mine, and I seized it with a grateful heart. I spun him over, dumped him on the floor, and straddled his chest. At which point I thought to settle him down for the evening by taking hold of a cleaver and cutting off his right hand with one good blow.

"Ninety-nine times out of a hundred, sir, chopping off a hand will take the starch right out of a man. He settled down pretty well. It's the shock, you see, shock takes the mind that way, and because the stump was bleeding like a bastard, excuse the language, I did him the favor of cauterizing the wound with the steam iron because it was good and hot, and if you sear a wound there's no way that bugger can bleed anymore. I mean, the *problem* is *solved*, and that's a fact."

"It has been proved a thousand times over," said Mr. Clubb.

"Shock being a healer," said Mr. Cuff. "Shock being a balm like salt water to the human body, yet if you have too much of shock or salt water, the body gives up the ghost. After I seared the wound, it looked to me like he and his body got together and voted to take the next bus to what is generally considered a better world." He held up an index finger and stared into my eyes while forking kidneys into his mouth. "This, sir, is a *process*. A *process* can't happen all at once, and every reasonable precaution was taken. Mr. Clubb and I do not have, nor ever have had, the reputation for carelessness in our undertakings."

"And never shall." Mr. Clubb washed down whatever was in his mouth with a half glass of cognac.

"Despite the *process* under way," said Mr. Cuff, "the gentleman's left wrist was bound tightly to the stump. Rope was again attached to the areas of the chest and legs, a gag went back into his mouth, and besides all that I had the pleasure of whapping my hammer once and only once on the region of his temple, for the purpose of keeping him out of action until we were ready for him in case he was not boarding the bus. I took a moment to turn him over and gratify my little soldier, which I trust was in no way exceeding our agreement, sir." He granted me a look of purest innocence.

"Continue," I said, "although you must grant that your tale is utterly without verification."

"Sir," said Mr. Clubb, "we know one another better than that." He bent over so far that his head disappeared beneath the table, and I heard the undoing of a clasp. Resurfacing, he placed between us on the table an object wrapped in one of the towels Marguerite had purchased for Green Chimneys. "If verification is your desire, and I intend no reflection, sir, for a man in your line of business has grown out of the habit of taking a fellow at his word, here you have wrapped up like a birthday present the finest verification of this portion of our tale to be found in all the world."

"And yours to keep, if you're taken that way," said Mr. Cuff.

I had no doubts whatsoever concerning the nature of the trophy set before me, and therefore I deliberately composed myself before pulling away the folds of toweling. Yet for all my preparations the spectacle of the actual trophy itself affected me more greatly than I would have thought possible, and at the very center of the nausea rising within me I experienced the first faint stirrings of enlightenment. *Poor man*, I thought, *poor mankind*.

I refolded the material over the crablike thing and said, "Thank you. I meant to imply no reservations concerning your veracity."

"Beautifully said, sir, and much appreciated. Men like ourselves, honest at every point, have found that persons in the habit of duplicity often cannot understand the truth. Liars are the bane of our existence. And yet, such is the nature of this funny old world, we'd be out of business without them."

Mr. Cuff smiled up at the chandelier in rueful appreciation of the world's contradictions. "When I replaced him on the bed, Mr. Clubb went hither and yon, collecting the remainder of the tools for the job at hand."

"When you say you replaced him on the bed," I broke in, "is it your meaning—"

"Your meaning might differ from mine, sir, and mine, being that of a fellow raised without the benefits of a literary education, may be simpler than yours. But bear in mind that every guild has its legacy of customs and traditions which no serious practitioner can ignore without thumbing his nose at all he holds dear. For those brought up in our trade, physical punishment of a female subject invariably begins with the act most associated in the feminine mind with humiliation of the most rigorous sort. With males the same is generally true. Neglect this step, and you lose an advantage which can never be regained. It is the foundation without which the structure cannot stand, and the foundation must be set in place even when conditions make the job distasteful, which is no picnic, take my word for it." He shook his head and fell silent.

"We could tell you stories to curl your hair," said Mr. Clubb. "Matter for another day. It was on the order of nine-thirty when our materials had been assembled, the preliminaries taken care of, and business could begin in earnest. This is a moment, sir, ever cherished by professionals such as ourselves. It is of an eternal freshness. You are on the brink of testing yourself against your past achievements and those of masters gone before. Your skill, your imagination, your timing and resolve will be called upon to work together with your hard-earned knowledge of the human body, because it is a question of being able to sense when to press on and when to hold back, of, I can say, having that instinct for the right technique at the right time you can acquire only through experience. During this moment you hope that the subject, your partner in the most intimate relationship which can exist between two people, owns the spiritual resolve and physical capacity to inspire your best work. The subject is our instrument, and the nature of the instrument is vital. Faced with an out-of-tune, broken-down piano, even the greatest virtuoso is up so to speak Shit Creek without so to speak a ping-pong paddle. Sometimes, sir, our work has left us tasting ashes for weeks on end, and when you're tasting ashes in your mouth you have trouble remembering the grand design and your wee part in that majestical pattern."

As if to supplant the taste in question and without benefit of a knife and fork, Mr. Clubb bit off a generous portion of steak and moistened it with a gulp of cognac. Chewing with loud smacks of the lips and tongue, he thrust a spoon into the kedgeree and began moodily slapping it onto his plate while seeming for the first time to notice the Canalettos on the wall.

"We started off, sir, as well as we ever have," said Mr. Cuff, "and better than most times. The fingernails was a thing of rare beauty, sir, the fingernails was prime. And the hair was on the same transcendent level."

"The fingernails?" I asked. "The hair?"

"Prime," said Mr. Clubb with a melancholy spray of food. "If they could be done better, which they could not, I should like to be there as to applaud with my own hands."

I looked at Mr. Cuff, and he said, "The fingernails and the hair might appear to be your traditional steps two and three, but they are in actual fact steps one and two, the first procedure being more like basic groundwork than part of the performance work itself. Doing the fingernails and the hair tells you an immense quantity about the subject's pain level, style of resistance, and aggression/passivity balance, and that information, sir, is your virtual bible once you go past step four or five."

"How many steps are there?" I asked.

"A novice would tell you fifteen," said Mr. Cuff. "A competent journeyman would say twenty. Men such as us know there to be at least a hundred, but in their various combinations and refinements they come out into the thousands. At the basic kindergarten level, they are, after the first two: foot soles; teeth; fingers and toes; tongue; nipples; rectum; genital area; electrification; general piercing; specific piercing; small amputation; damage to inner organs; eyes, minor; eyes, major; large amputation; local flaying; and so forth."

At the mention of "tongue," Mr. Clubb had shoved a spoonful of kedgeree into his mouth and scowled at the paintings directly across from him. At "electrification," he had thrust himself out of his chair and crossed behind me to scrutinize them more closely. While Mr. Cuff continued my education, he twisted in his chair to observe his partner's actions, and I did the same.

After "and so forth," Mr. Cuff fell silent. The two of us watched Mr. Clubb moving back and forth in evident agitation before the paintings. He settled at last before a depiction of a regatta on the Grand Canal and took two deep breaths. Then he raised his spoon like a dagger and drove it into the painting to slice beneath a handsome ship, come up at its bow, and continue cutting until he had deleted the ship from the painting. "Now that, sir, is local flaying," he said. He moved to the next picture, which gave a view of the Piazzetta. In seconds he had sliced all the canvas from the frame. "And that, sir, is what is meant by general flaying." He crumpled the canvas in his hands, threw it to the ground, and stamped on it.

"He is not quite himself," said Mr. Cuff.

"Oh, but I am, I am myself to an alarming degree, I am," said Mr. Clubb. He tromped back to the table and bent beneath it. Instead of the second folded towel I had anticipated, he produced his satchel and used it to sweep away the plates and serving dishes in front of him. He reached within and slapped down beside me the towel I had expected.

"Open it," he said. I unfolded the towel. "Are these not, to the last particular, what you requested, sir?"

It was, to the last particular, what I had requested. Marguerite had not thought to remove her wedding band before her assignation, and her . . . I cannot describe the other but to say that it lay like the egg perhaps of some small shore bird in the familiar palm. Another portion of my eventual enlightenment moved into place within me, and I thought: *Here we are, this is all of us, this crab and this egg.* I bent over and vomited beside my chair. When I had finished, I grabbed the cognac bottle and swallowed greedily, twice. The liquor burned down my throat, struck my stomach like a branding iron, and rebounded. I leaned sideways and, with a dizzied spasm of throat and guts, expelled another reeking contribution to the mess on the carpet.

"It is a Roman conclusion to a meal, sir," said Mr. Cuff.

Mr. Moncrieff opened the kitchen door and peeked in. He observed the mutilated paintings and the objects nested in the striped towel and watched me wipe a string of vomit from my mouth. He withdrew for a moment and reappeared holding a tall can of ground coffee, wordlessly sprinkled its contents over the evidence of my distress, and vanished back into the kitchen. From the depths of my wretchedness, I marveled at the perfection of this display of butler decorum.

I draped the toweling over the crab and egg. "You are conscientious fellows," I said.

"Conscientious to a fault, sir," said Mr. Cuff, not without a touch of kindness. "For a person in the normal way of living cannot begin to comprehend the actual meaning of that term, nor is he liable to understand the fierce requirements it puts on a man's head. And so it comes about that persons in the normal way of living try to back out long after backing out is possible, even though we explain exactly what is going to happen in the very beginning. They listen, but they do not hear, and it's the rare civilian who has the common sense to know that if you stand in a fire you must be burned. And if you turn the world upside down, you're standing on your head with everybody else."

"Or," said Mr. Clubb, calming his own fires with another deep draft of cognac, "as the Golden Rule has it, what you do is sooner or later done back to you."

Although I was still one who listened but could not hear, a tingle of premonition went up my spine. "Please go on with your report," I said.

"The responses of the subject were all one could wish," said Mr.

Clubb. "I could go so far as to say that her responses were a thing of beauty. A subject who can render one magnificent scream after another while maintaining a basic self-possession and not breaking down is a subject highly attuned to her own pain, sir, and one to be cherished. You see, there comes a moment when they understand that they are changed for good, they have passed over the border into another realm, from which there is no return, and some of them can't handle it and turn, you might say, sir, to mush. With some it happens right at the foundation stage, a sad disappointment because thereafter the rest of the work could be done by the crudest apprentice. It takes some at the nipples stage, and at the genital stage quite a few more. Most of them comprehend irreversibility during the piercings, and by the stage of small amputation ninety percent have shown you what they are made of. The lady did not come to the point until we had begun the eye work, and she passed with flying colors, sir. But it was then the male upped and put his foot in it."

"And eye work is delicate going," said Mr. Cuff. "Requiring two men, if you want it done even close to right. But I couldn't have turned my back on the fellow for more than a minute and a half."

"Less," said Mr. Clubb. "And him lying there in the corner meek as a baby. No fight left in him at all, you would have said. You would have said, That fellow is not going to risk so much as opening his eyes until his eyes are opened for him."

"But up he gets, without a rope on him, sir," said Mr. Cuff, "which you would have said was beyond the powers of a fellow who recently lost a hand."

"Up he gets and on he comes," said Mr. Clubb. "In defiance of all of Nature's mighty laws. Before I know what's what, he has his good arm around Mr. Cuff's neck and is earnestly trying to snap that neck while beating Mr. Cuff about the head with his stump, a situation which compels me to set aside the task at hand and take up a knife and ram it into his back a fair old number of times. The next thing I know, he's on *me*, and it's up to Mr. Cuff to peel him off and set him on the floor."

"And then, you see, your concentration is gone," said Mr. Cuff. "After something like that, you might as well be starting all over again at the beginning. Imagine if you are playing a piano about as well as ever you did in your life, and along comes another piano with blood in its eye and jumps on your back. It was pitiful, that's all I can say about it. But

I got the fellow down and jabbed him here and there until he was still, and then I got the one item we count on as a surefire last resort for incapacitation."

"What is that item?" I asked.

"Dental floss," said Mr. Clubb. "Dental floss cannot be overestimated in our line of work. It is the razor wire of everyday life, and fishing line cannot hold a candle to it, for fishing line is dull, but dental floss is both *dull* and *sharp*. It has a hundred uses, and a book should be written on the subject."

"What do you do with it?" I asked.

"It is applied to a male subject," he said. "Applied artfully and in a manner perfected only over years of experience. The application is of a lovely *subtlety*. During the process, the subject must be in a helpless, preferably an unconscious, position. When the subject regains the first fuzzy inklings of consciousness, he is aware of no more than a vague discomfort like unto a form of tingling, similar to when a foot has gone to sleep. In a wonderfully short period of time, that discomfort builds itself up, ascending to mild pain, *severe* pain, and outright agony. Then it goes past agony. The final stage is a mystical condition I don't think there is a word for which, but it closely resembles ecstasy. Hallucinations are common. Out-of-body experiences are common. We have seen men speak in tongues, even when tongues were, strictly speaking, organs they no longer possessed. We have seen wonders, Mr. Cuff and I."

"That we have," said Mr. Cuff. "The ordinary civilian sort of fellow can be a miracle, sir."

"Of which the person in question was one, to be sure," said Mr. Clubb. "But he has to be said to be in a category all by himself, a man in a million you could put it, which is the cause of my mentioning the grand design ever a mystery to us who glimpse but a part of the whole. You see, the fellow refused to play by the time-honored rules. He was in an awesome degree of suffering and torment, sir, but he would not do us the favor to lie down and quit."

"The mind was not right," said Mr. Cuff. "Where the proper mind goes to the spiritual, sir, as just described, this was that one mind in *ten* million, I'd estimate, which moves to the animal at the reptile level. If you cut off the head of a venomous reptile and detach it from the body, that head will still attempt to strike. So it was with our boy. Bleeding from a dozen wounds. Minus one hand. Seriously concussed. The dental floss murdering all possibility of thought. Every nerve in his body howling like a banshee. Yet up he comes with his eyes red and the foam dripping from his mouth. We put him down again, and I did what I hate, because it takes all feeling away from the body along with the motor capacity, and cracked his spine right at the base of the head. Or would have, if his spine had been a normal thing instead of solid steel in a thick india-rubber case. Which is what put us in mind of weight lifting, sir, and activity resulting in such development about the top of the spine you need a hacksaw to get even close to it."

"We were already behind schedule," said Mr. Clubb, "and with the time required to get back into the proper frame of mind, we had at least seven or eight hours of work ahead of us. And you had to double that, because while we could knock the fellow out, he wouldn't have the decency to stay out more than a few minutes at a time. The natural thing, him being only the secondary subject, would have been to kill him outright so we could get on with the real job, but improving our working conditions by that fashion would require an amendment to our contract. Which comes under the heading of 'Instructions from the Client.'"

"And it was eleven o'clock," said Mr. Cuff.

"The exact time we scheduled for our conference," said Mr. Clubb. "My partner was forced to clobber the fellow into senselessness, how many times was it, Mr. Cuff, while I prayed for our client to do us the grace of answering his phone during twenty rings?"

"Three times, Mr. Clubb, three times exactly," said Mr. Cuff. "The blow each time more powerful than the last, which combined with his having a skull made of granite, led to a painful swelling of my hand."

"The dilemma stared us in the face," said Mr. Clubb. "Client unreachable. Impeded in the performance of our duties. State of mind, very foul. In such a pickle, we could do naught but obey instructions given us by our hearts. *Remove the gentleman's head*, I told my partner, *and take care not to be bitten once it's off.* Mr. Cuff took up an ax. Some haste was called for, the fellow just beginning to stir again. Mr. Cuff moved into position. Then from the bed, where all had been lovely silence but for soft moans and whimpers, we hear a god-awful yowling ruckus of the most desperate and importunate protest. It was of a sort to melt the heart, sir. Were we not experienced professionals who enjoy pride in our work, I believe we might have been persuaded almost to grant the fellow mercy, despite his being a pest of the first water. But now those heart-melting screeches reach the ears of the pest and rouse him into movement just at the moment Mr. Cuff lowers the boom, so to speak."

"Which was an unfortunate bit of business," said Mr. Cuff. "Causing me to catch him in the shoulder, causing him to rear up, causing me to lose my footing what with all the blood on the floor, then causing a tussle for possession of the ax and myself suffering several kicks to the breadbasket. I'll tell you, sir, we did a good piece of work when we took off his hand, for without the nuisance of a stump really being useful only for leverage, there's no telling what that fellow might have done. As it was, I had the devil's own time getting the ax free and clear, and once I had done, any chance of making a neat, clean job of it was long gone. It was a slaughter and an act of butchery with not a bit of finesse or sophistication to it, and I have to tell you, such a thing is both an embarrassment and an outrage to men like ourselves. Turning a subject into hamburger by means of an ax is a violation of all our training, and it is not why we went into this business."

"No, of course not, you are more like artists than I had imagined," I said. "But in spite of your embarrassment, I suppose you went back to work on . . . on the female subject."

"We are not *like* artists," said Mr. Clubb, "we *are* artists, and we know how to set our feelings aside and address our chosen medium of expression with a pure and patient attention. In spite of which we discovered the final and insurmountable frustration of the evening, and that discovery put paid to all our hopes."

"If you discovered that Marguerite had escaped," I said, "I believe I might almost, after all you have said, be—"

Glowering, Mr. Clubb held up his hand. "I beg you not to insult us, sir, as we have endured enough misery for one day. The subject had escaped, all right, but not in the simple sense of your meaning. She had escaped for all eternity, in the sense that her soul had taken leave of her body and flown to those realms at whose nature we can only make our poor, ignorant guesses."

"She died?" I asked. "In other words, in direct contradiction of my instructions, you two fools killed her. You love to talk about your expertise, but you went too far, and she died at your hands. Begone. Depart. This minute."

Mr. Clubb and Mr. Cuff looked into each other's eyes, and in that moment of private communication I saw an encompassing sorrow that utterly turned the tables on me: before I was made to understand how it was possible, I saw that the only fool present was myself. And yet the sorrow included all three of us, and more besides.

"The subject died, but we did not kill her," said Mr. Clubb. "We did not go, nor have we ever gone, too far. The subject chose to die. The subject's death was an act of suicidal will. While you are listening, sir, is it possible, sir, for you to open your ears and hear what I am saying? She who might have been in all of our long experiences the noblest, most courageous subject we ever will have the good fortune to be given witnessed the clumsy murder of her lover and decided to surrender her own life."

"Quick as a shot," said Mr. Cuff. "The simple truth, sir, is that otherwise we could have kept her alive for about a year."

"And it would have been a rare privilege to do so," said Mr. Clubb. "It is time for you to face facts, sir."

"I am facing them about as well as one could," I said. "Please tell me where you disposed of the bodies."

"Within the house," said Mr. Clubb. Before I could protest, he said, "Under the wretched circumstances, sir, including the continuing unavailability of the client and the enormity of the personal and professional letdown felt by my partner and myself, we saw no choice but to dispose of the house along with the telltale remains."

"Dispose of Green Chimneys?" I said, aghast. "How could you dispose of Green Chimneys?"

"Reluctantly, sir," said Mr. Clubb. "With heavy hearts and an equal anger. With the same degree of professional unhappiness experienced previous. In workaday terms, by means of combustion. Fire, sir, is a substance like shock and salt water, a healer and a cleanser, though more drastic."

"But Green Chimneys has not been healed," I said. "Nor has my wife."

"You are a man of wit, sir, and have provided Mr. Cuff and myself many moments of precious amusement. True, Green Chimneys has not been healed, but cleansed it has been, root and branch. And you hired us to punish your wife, not heal her, and punish her we did, as well as possible under very trying circumstances indeed."

"Which circumstances include our feeling that the job ended before its time," said Mr. Cuff. "Which circumstance is one we cannot bear."

"I regret your disappointment," I said, "but I cannot accept that it was necessary to burn down my magnificent house."

"Twenty, even fifteen years ago, it would not have been," said Mr. Clubb. "Nowadays, however, that contemptible alchemy known as Police Science has fattened itself up into such a gross and distorted breed of sorcery that a single drop of blood can be detected even after you scrub and scour until your arms hurt. It has reached the hideous point that if a constable without a thing in his head but the desire to imprison honest fellows employed in an ancient trade finds two hairs at what is supposed to be a crime scene, he waddles along to the labora-tory and instantly a loathsome sort of wizard is popping out to tell him that those same two hairs are from the heads of Mr. Clubb and Mr. Cuff, and I exaggerate, I know, sir, but not by much."

"And if they do not have our names, sir," said Mr. Cuff, "which they do not and I pray they never will, they ever after have our particulars, to be placed in a great universal file against the day when they might have our names, so as to look back into that cruel file and commit the monstrosity of unfairly increasing the charges against us. It is a malig-nant business, and all sensible precautions must be taken."

"A thousand times I have expressed the conviction," said Mr. Clubb, "that an ancient art ought not be against the law, nor its practitioners described as criminals. Is there a name for our so-called crime? There is not. GBH they call it, sir, for Grievous Bodily Harm, or even worse, Assault. We do not Assault. We induce, we instruct, we instill. Properly speaking, these cannot be crimes, and those who do them cannot be criminals. Now I have said it a thousand times and one."

"All right," I said, attempting to speed this appalling conference to its end, "you have described the evening's unhappy events. I appreciate your reasons for burning down my splendid property. You have enjoyed a lavish meal. All remaining is the matter of your remuneration, which demands considerable thought. This night has left me exhausted, and after all your efforts, you, too, must be in need of rest. Communicate with me, please, in a day or two, gentlemen, by whatever means you choose. I wish to be alone with my thoughts. Mr. Moncrieff will show you out."

The maddening barnies met this plea with impassive stares and stoic silence, and I renewed my silent vow to give them nothing—not a penny. For all their pretensions, they had accomplished naught but the death of my wife and the destruction of my country house. Rising to my feet with more difficulty than anticipated, I said, "Thank you for your efforts on my behalf."

Once again, the glance that passed between them implied that I had failed to grasp the essentials of our situation.

"Your thanks are gratefully accepted," said Mr. Cuff, "though, dispute it as you may, they are premature, as you know in your soul. Yesterday morning we embarked upon a journey of which we have yet more miles to go. In consequence, we prefer not to leave. Also, setting aside the question of your continuing education, which if we do not address will haunt us all forever, residing here with you for a sensible period out of sight is the best protection from law enforcement we three could ask for."

"No," I said, "I have had enough of your education, and I need no protection from officers of the law. Please, gentlemen, allow me to return to my bed. You may take the rest of the cognac with you as a token of my regard."

"Give it a moment's reflection, sir," said Mr. Clubb. "You have announced the presence of high-grade consultants and introduced these same to staff and clients both. Hours later, your spouse meets her tragic end in a conflagration destroying your upstate manor. On the very same night also occurs the disappearance of your greatest competitor, a person certain to be identified before long by a hotel employee as a fellow not unknown to the late spouse. Can you think it wise to have the high-grade consultants vanish right away?"

I did reflect, then said, "You have a point. It will be best if you continue to make an appearance in the office for a time. However, the proposal that you stay here is ridiculous." A wild hope, utterly irrational in the face of the grisly evidence, came to me in the guise of doubt. "If Green Chimneys had been destroyed by fire, I should have been informed long ago. I am a respected figure in the town of ———, personally acquainted with its chief of police, Wendall Nash. Why has he not called me?"

"Oh, sir, my goodness," said Mr. Clubb, shaking his head and smiling inwardly at my folly, "for many reasons. A small town is a beast slow to move. The available men have been struggling throughout the night to rescue even a jot or tittle portion of your house. They will fail, they have failed already, but the effort will keep them busy past dawn. Wendall Nash will not wish to ruin your night's sleep until he can make a full report." He glanced at his wristwatch. "In fact, if I am not mistaken . . ." He tilted his head, closed his eyes, and raised an index finger. The telephone in the kitchen began to trill.

"He has done it a thousand times, sir," said Mr. Cuff, "and I have yet to see him strike out."

Mr. Moncrieff brought the instrument through from the kitchen, said, "For you, sir," and placed the receiver in my waiting hand. I uttered the conventional greeting, longing to hear the voice of anyone but—

"Wendall Nash, sir," came the chief's raspy, high-pitched drawl. "Calling from up here in ——. I hate to tell you this, but I have some awful bad news. Your place Green Chimneys started burning sometime around midnight last night, and every man jack we had got put on the job and the boys worked like dogs to save what they could, but sometimes you can't win no matter what you do. Me personally, I feel terrible about this, but, tell you the truth, I never saw a fire like it. We nearly lost two men, but it looks like they're going to come out of it okay. The rest of our boys are still out there trying to save the few trees you got left.

"Dreadful," I said. "Please permit me to speak to my wife."

A speaking silence followed. "The missus is not with you, sir? You're saying she was inside there?"

"My wife left for Green Chimneys yesterday morning. I spoke to her there in the afternoon. She intended to work in her studio, a separate building at some distance from the house, and it is her custom to sleep in the studio when working late." Saying these things to Wendall Nash, I felt almost as though I were creating an alternative world, another town of —— and another Green Chimneys, where Marguerite had busied herself in the studio, and there gone to bed to sleep through the commotion. "Have you checked the studio? You are certain to find her there."

"Well, I have to say we didn't, sir," he said. "The fire took that little building pretty good, too, but the walls are still standing and you can tell what used to be what, furnishingwise and equipmentwise. If she was inside it, we'd of found her."

"Then she got out in time," I said, and instantly it was the truth: the other Marguerite had escaped the blaze and now stood, numb with shock and wrapped in a blanket, unrecognized amidst the voyeuristic crowd always drawn to disasters.

"It's possible, but she hasn't turned up yet, and we've been talking to everybody at the site. Could she have left with one of the staff?"

"All the help is on vacation," I said. "She was alone."

"Uh-huh," he said. "Can you think of anyone with a serious grudge against you? Any enemies? Because this was not a natural-type fire, sir. Someone set it, and he knew what he was doing. Anyone come to mind?"

"No," I said. "I have rivals, but no enemies. Check the hospitals and anything else you can think of, Wendall, and I'll be there as soon as I can."

"You can take your time, sir," he said. "I sure hope we find her, and by late this afternoon we'll be able to go through the ashes." He said he would give me a call if anything turned up in the meantime.

"Please, Wendall," I said, and began to cry. Muttering a consolation I did not quite catch, Mr. Moncrieff vanished with the telephone in another matchless display of butler politesse.

"The practice of hoping for what you know you cannot have is a worthy spiritual exercise," said Mr. Clubb. "It brings home the vanity of vanity."

"I beg you, leave me," I said, still crying. "In all decency."

"Decency lays heavy obligations on us all," said Mr. Clubb. "And no job is decently done until it is done completely. Would you care for help in getting back to the bedroom? We are ready to proceed."

I extended a shaky arm, and he assisted me through the corridors. Two cots had been set up in my room, and a neat array of instruments— "staples"—formed two rows across the bottom of the bed. Mr. Clubb and Mr. Cuff positioned my head on the pillows and began to disrobe.

8

Ten hours later, the silent chauffeur aided me in my exit from the limousine and clasped my left arm as I limped toward the uniformed men and official vehicles on the far side of the open gate. Blackened sticks that had been trees protruded from the blasted earth, and the stench of wet ash saturated the air. Wendall Nash separated from the other men, approached, and noted without comment my garb of gray homburg hat, pearl-gray cashmere topcoat, heavy gloves, woolen charcoal-gray pinstriped suit, sunglasses, and malacca walking stick. Then he looked more closely at my face. "Are you, uh, are you sure you're all right, sir?"

"In a manner of speaking," I said, and saw him blink at the oozing gap left in the wake of an incisor. "I slipped at the top of a marble staircase and tumbled down all forty-six steps, resulting in massive bangs and bruises, considerable physical weakness, and the persistent sensation of being uncomfortably cold. No broken bones, at least nothing major." Over his shoulder I stared at four isolated brick towers rising from an immense black hole in the ground, all that remained of Green Chimneys. "Is there news of my wife?"

"I'm afraid, sir, that—" Nash placed a hand on my shoulder, causing me to stifle a sharp outcry. "I'm sorry, sir. Shouldn't you be in the hospital? Did your doctors say you could come all this way?"

"Knowing my feelings in this matter, the doctors insisted I make the journey." Deep within the black cavity, men in bulky orange space suits and space helmets were sifting through the soggy ashes, now and then dropping unrecognizable nuggets into heavy bags of the same color. "I gather that you have news for me, Wendall," I said.

"Unhappy news, sir," he said. "The garage went up with the rest of the house, but we found some bits and pieces of your wife's little car. This here was one hot fire, sir, and by hot I mean *hot*, and whoever set it was no garden-variety firebug."

"You found evidence of the automobile," I said. "I assume you also found evidence of the woman who owned it."

"They came across some bone fragments, plus a small portion of a skeleton," he said. "This whole big house came down on her, sir. Those boys are experts at their job, and they don't hold out hope of finding a whole lot more. So if your wife was the only person inside . . ."

"I see, yes, I understand," I said, staying on my feet only with the support of the malacca cane. "How horrid, how hideous that it should all be true, that our lives should prove such a *littleness* . . ."

"I'm sure that's true, sir, and that wife of yours was a, was what I have to call a special kind of person who gave pleasure to us all, and I hope you know that we all wish things could of turned out different, same as you."

For a moment I imagined that he was talking about her recordings. Then I understood that he was laboring to express the pleasure he and others had taken in what they, no less than Mr. Clubb and Mr. Cuff but much, much more than I, had perceived as her essential character.

"Oh, Wendall," I said into the teeth of my sorrow, "it is not possible, not ever, for things to turn out different."

He refrained from patting my shoulder and sent me back to the rigors of my education.

9

A month—four weeks—thirty days—seven hundred and twenty hours—forty-three thousand, two hundred minutes—two million, five hundred, and ninety-two thousand seconds—did I spend under the care of Mr. Clubb and Mr. Cuff, and I believe I proved in the end to be a modestly, moderately, middlingly satisfying subject, a matter in which I take an immodest and immoderate pride. "You are little in comparison to the lady, sir," Mr. Clubb once told me while deep in his ministrations, "but no one could say that you are nothing." I, who had countless times put the lie to the declaration that they should never see me cry, wept tears of gratitude. We ascended through the fifteen stages known to the novice, the journeyman's further five, and passed, with frequent repetitions and backward glances appropriate for the slower pupil, into the artist's upper eighty, infinitely expandable by grace of the refinements of his art. We had the little soldiers. We had *dental floss*. During each of those forty-three thousand, two hundred minutes, through all the two million and nearly six hundred thousand seconds, it was always deepest night. We made our way through perpetual darkness, and the utmost darkness of the utmost night yielded an infinity of textural variation, cold slick dampness to velvety softness to leaping flame, for it was true that no one could say I was nothing.

Because I was not nothing, I glimpsed the Meaning of Tragedy.

Each Tuesday and Friday of these four sunless weeks, my consultants and guides lovingly bathed and dressed my wounds, arrayed me in my warmest clothes (for I never after ceased to feel the blast of arctic wind against my flesh), and escorted me to my office, where I was presumed much reduced by grief as well as by certain household accidents attributed to grief.

On the first of these Tuesdays, a flushed-looking Mrs. Rampage offered her consolations and presented me with the morning newspapers, an inch-thick pile of faxes, two inches of legal documents, and a tray filled with official-looking letters. The newspapers described the fire and eulogized Marguerite; the increasingly threatening faxes declared Chartwell, Munster, and Stout's intention to ruin me professionally and personally in the face of my continuing refusal to return the accompanying documents along with all records having reference to their client; the documents were those in question; the letters, produced by the various legal firms representing all my other cryptic gentlemen, deplored the (unspecified) circumstances necessitating their clients' universal desire for change in re financial management. These lawyers also desired all relevant records, disks, etc., etc., urgently. Mr. Clubb and Mr. Cuff roistered behind their screen. I signed the documents in a shaky hand and requested Mrs. Rampage to have these shipped with the desired records to Chartwell, Munster, and Stout. "And dispatch all these other records, too," I said, handing her the letters. "I am now going in for my lunch."

Tottering toward the executive dining room, now and then I glanced into smoke-filled offices to observe my much-altered underlings. Some of them appeared, after a fashion, to be working. Several were reading paperback novels, which might be construed as work of a kind. One of the Skipper's assistants was unsuccessfully lofting paper airplanes toward his wastepaper basket. Gilligan's secretary lay asleep on her office couch, and a records clerk lay sleeping on the file room floor. In the dining room, Charlie-Charlie Rackett hurried forward to assist me to my accustomed chair. Gilligan and the Skipper gave me sullen looks from their usual lunchtime station, an unaccustomed bottle of Scotch whisky between them. Charlie-Charlie lowered me into my seat and said, "Terrible news about your wife, sir."

"More terrible than you know," I said.

Gilligan took a gulp of whisky and displayed his middle finger, I gathered to me rather than Charlie-Charlie.

"Afternoonish," I said.

"Very much so, sir," said Charlie-Charlie, and bent closer to the brim of the homburg and my ear. "About that little request you made the other day. The right men aren't nearly so easy to find as they used to be, sir, but I'm still on the job."

My laughter startled him. "No squab today, Charlie-Charlie. Just bring me a bowl of tomato soup."

I had partaken of no more than two or three delicious mouthfuls when Gilligan lurched up beside me. "Look here," he said, "it's too bad about your wife and everything, I really mean it, honest, but that drunken act you put on in my office cost me my biggest client, not to forget that you took his girlfriend home with you."

"In that case," I said, "I have no further need of your services. Pack your things and be out of here by three o'clock."

He listed to one side and straightened himself up. "You can't mean that."

"I can and do," I said. "Your part in the grand design at work in the universe no longer has any connection with my own."

"You must be as crazy as you look," he said, and unsteadily departed.

I returned to my office and gently lowered myself into my seat. After I had removed my gloves and accomplished some minor repair work to the tips of my fingers with the tape and gauze pads thoughtfully inserted by the detectives into the pockets of my coat, I slowly drew the left glove over my fingers and became aware of feminine giggles amid the coarser sounds of male amusement behind the screen. I coughed into the glove and heard a tiny shriek. Soon, though not immediately, a blushing Mrs. Rampage emerged from cover, patting her hair and adjusting her skirt. "Sir, I'm so sorry, I didn't expect . . ." She was staring at my right hand, which had not yet been inserted into its glove.

"Lawn mower accident," I said. "Mr. Gilligan has been released, and I should like you to prepare the necessary papers. Also, I want to see all of our operating figures for the past year, as significant changes have been dictated by the grand design at work in the universe."

Mrs. Rampage flew from the room. For the next several hours, as for nearly every remaining hour I spent at my desk on the Tuesdays and Fridays thereafter, I addressed with a carefree spirit the details involved in shrinking the staff to the smallest number possible and turning the entire business over to the Skipper. Graham Leeson's abrupt disappearance greatly occupied the newspapers, and when not occupied as described I read that my archrival and competitor had been a notorious Don Juan, i.e., a compulsive womanizer, a flaw in his otherwise immaculate character held by some to have played a substantive role in his sudden absence. As Mr. Clubb had predicted, a clerk at the —— Hotel revealed Leeson's sessions with my late wife, and for a time professional and amateur gossipmongers alike speculated that he had caused the disastrous fire. This came to nothing. Before the month had ended, Leeson sightings were reported in Monaco, the Swiss Alps, and Argentina, locations accommodating to sportsmen—after four years of varsity football at the University of Southern California, Leeson had won an Olympic silver medal in weight lifting while earning his M.B.A. at Wharton.

In the limousine at the end of each day, Mr. Clubb and Mr. Cuff braced me in happy anticipation of the lessons to come as we sped back through illusory sunlight toward the real darkness.

10

THE MEANING OF TRAGEDY

Everything, from the designs of the laughing gods down to the lowliest cells in the human digestive tract, is changing all the time, every particle of being large and small is eternally in motion, but this simple truism, so transparent on its surface, evokes immediate headache and stupefaction when applied to itself, not unlike the sentence "Every word that comes out of my mouth is a bald-faced lie." The gods are ever laughing while we are always clutching our heads and looking for a soft place to lie down, and what I beheld in my momentary glimpses of the meaning of tragedy preceding, during, and after the experience of *dental floss* was so composed of paradox that I can state it only in cloud or vapor form, as:

The meaning of tragedy is: *All is in order, all is in train.*
The meaning of tragedy is: *It only hurts for a little while.*
The meaning of tragedy is: *Change is the first law of life.*

11

So it took place that one day their task was done, their lives and mine were to move forward into separate areas of the grand design, and all that was left before preparing my own departure was to stand, bundled up against the nonexistent arctic wind, on the bottom step and wave farewell with my remaining hand while shedding buckets and bathtubs of tears with my remaining eye. Chaplinesque in their black suits and

bowlers, Mr. Clubb and Mr. Cuff ambled cheerily toward the glittering avenue and my bank, where arrangements had been made for the
transfer into their hands of all but a small portion of my private fortune
by my private banker, virtually his final act in that capacity. At a distant corner, Mr. Clubb and Mr. Cuff, by then only tiny figures blurred
by my tears, turned, ostensibly to bid farewell, actually, as I knew, to
watch as I mounted my steps and went back within the house, and with
a salute I honored this last painful agreement between us.

A more pronounced version of the office's metamorphosis had taken
place inside my town house, but with the relative ease practice gives
to one whose step is halting, whose progress is interrupted by frequent
pauses for breath and the passing of certain shooting pains, I skirted
the mounds of rubble, the dangerous loose tiles, more dangerous open
holes in the floor, and the regions submerged under water and toiled
up the resilient staircase, moved with infinite care across the boards
bridging the former landing, and made my way into the former kitchen,
where broken pipes and limp wires protruding from the lathe marked
the sites of those appliances rendered pointless by the gradual disappearance of the household staff. (In a voice choked with feeling, Mr.
Moncrieff, Reggie Moncrieff, Reggie, the last to go, had informed me
that his final month of service had been "as fine as my days with the
Duke, sir, every bit as noble as ever it was with that excellent old gentleman.") The remaining cupboard yielded a flagon of *jenever*, a tumbler,
and a Monte Cristo torpedo, and with the tumbler filled and the cigar
alight I hobbled through the devastated corridors toward my bed, there
to gather my strength for the ardors of the coming day.

In good time, I arose to observe the final appointments of the life
soon to be abandoned. It is possible to do up one's shoelaces and knot
one's necktie as neatly with a single hand as with two, and shirt buttons
eventually become a breeze. Into my traveling bag I folded a few modest
essentials atop the flagon and cigar box, and into a pad of shirts nestled
the black Lucite cube prepared at my request by my instructor-guides
and containing, mingled with the ashes of the satchel and its contents,
the few bony nuggets rescued from Green Chimneys. The traveling bag
accompanied me first to my lawyer's office, where I signed papers making over the wreckage of the town house to the European gentleman
who had purchased it sight unseen as a "fixer-upper" for a fraction of its
(considerably reduced) value. Next I visited the melancholy banker and
withdrew the pittance remaining in my accounts. And then, glad of

heart and free of all unnecessary encumbrance, I took my place in the sidewalk queue to await transportation by means of a kindly kneeling bus to the great terminus where I should employ the ticket reassuringly lodged within my breast pocket.

Long before the arrival of the bus, a handsome limousine crawled past in the traffic, and glancing idly within, I observed Mr. Chester Montfort de M—— smoothing the air with a languid gesture while in conversation with the two stout, bowler-hatted men on his either side. Soon, doubtless, he would begin his instructions in the whopbop-aloobop.

12

What is a pittance in a great city may be a modest fortune in a hamlet, and a returned prodigal might be welcomed far in excess of his true deserts. I entered New Covenant quietly, unobtrusively, with the humility of a new convert uncertain of his station, inwardly rejoicing to see all unchanged from the days of my youth. When I purchased a dignified but unshowy house on Scripture Street, I announced only that I had known the village in my childhood, had traveled far, and now in my retirement wished no more than to immerse myself in the life of the community, exercising my skills only inasmuch as they might be requested of an elderly invalid. How well the aged invalid had known the village, how far and to what end had he traveled, and the nature of his skills remained unspecified. Had I not attended the daily services at the Temple, the rest of my days might have passed in pleasant anonymity and frequent perusals of a little book I had obtained at the terminus, for while my surname was so deeply of New Covenant that it could be read on a dozen headstones in the Temple graveyard, I had fled so early in life and so long ago that my individual identity had been entirely forgotten. New Covenant is curious—intensely curious—but it does not wish to pry. One fact and one only led to the metaphoric slaughter of the fatted calf and the prodigal's elevation. On the day when, some five or six months after his installation on Scripture Street, the afflicted newcomer's faithful attendance was rewarded with an invitation to read the Lesson for the Day, Matthew 5:43–48, seated amid numerous offspring and offspring's offspring in the barnie-pews for the first time since an unhappy tumble from a hayloft was Delbert Mudge.

My old classmate had weathered into a white-haired, sturdy replica of his own grandfather, and although his hips still gave him considerable difficulty his mind had suffered no comparable stiffening. Delbert knew my name as well as his own, and though he could not connect it to the wizened old party counseling him from the lectern to embrace his enemies, the old party's face and voice so clearly evoked the deceased lawyer who had been my father that he recognized me before I had spoken the whole of the initial verse. The grand design at work in the universe once again could be seen at its mysterious business: unknown to me, my entirely selfish efforts on behalf of Charlie-Charlie Rackett, my representation to his parole board and his subsequent hiring as my spy, had been noted by all of barnie-world. I, a child of Scripture Street, had become a hero to generations of barnies! After hugging me at the conclusion of the fateful service, Delbert Mudge implored my assistance in the resolution of a fiscal imbroglio that threatened his family's cohesion. I of course assented, with the condition that my services should be free of charge. The Mudge imbroglio proved elementary, and soon I was performing similar services for other barnie-clans. After listening to a half dozen accounts of my miracles while setting broken barnie-bones, New Covenant's physician visited my Scripture Street habitation under cover of night, was prescribed the solution to his uncomplicated problem, and sang my praises to his fellow townies. Within a year, by which time all New Covenant had become aware of my "tragedy" and consequent "reawakening," I was managing the Temple's funds as well as those of barn and town. Three years later, our reverend having in his ninety-first year, as the Racketts and Mudges put it, "woke up dead," I submitted by popular acclaim to appointment in his place.

Daily, I assume the honored place assigned me. Ceremonious vestments assure that my patchwork scars remain unseen. The Lucite box and its relics are interred deep within the sacred ground beneath the Temple where I must one day join my predecessors—some bony fragments of Graham Leeson reside there too, mingled with Marguerite's more numerous specks and nuggets. Eye patch elegantly in place, I lean forward upon the malacca cane and, while flourishing the stump of my right hand as if in demonstration, with my ruined tongue whisper what I know none shall understand, the homily beginning, "It *only* . . ." To this I append in silent exhalation the two words concluding that little book brought to my attention by an agreeable murderer and purchased at the great grand station long ago, these: *Ah, humanity!*

From

5 Stories

Little Red's Tango

Little Red Perceived as a Mystery

What a mystery is Little Red! How he sustains himself, how he lives, how he gets through his days, what passes through his mind as he endures that extraordinary journey . . . Is not mystery precisely that which does not yield, does not give access?

Little Red, His Wife, His Parents, His Brothers

Little is known of the woman he married. Little Red seldom speaks of her, except now and then to say, "My wife was half Sicilian," or "All you have to know about my wife is that she was half Sicilian." Some have speculated, though not in the presence of Little Red, that the long-vanished wife was no more than a fictional or mythic character created to lend solidity to his otherwise amorphous history. Years have been lost. Decades have been lost. (In a sense, an entire life has been lost, some might say Little Red's.) The existence of a wife, even an anonymous one, does lend a semblance of structure to the lost years.

Half of her was Sicilian; the other half may have been Irish. "People like that you don't mess with," says Little Red. "Even when you mess with them, you don't *mess* with them, know what I mean?"

The parents are likewise anonymous, though no one has ever speculated that they may have been fictional or mythic. Even anonymous parents must be of flesh and blood. Since Little Red has mentioned, in his flat, dry Long Island accent, a term in the Uniondale High School jazz ensemble, we can assume that for a substantial period his family resided in Uniondale, Long Island. There were, apparently, two brothers, both older. The three boys grew up in circumstances modest but otherwise unspecified. A lunch counter, a diner, a small mom-and-pop grocery may have been in the picture. Some connection with food, with nourishment.

Little Red's long years spent waiting on tables, his decades as a "waiter," continue this nourishment theme, which eventually becomes inseparable from the very conception of Little Red's existence. In at least one important way, *nourishment* lies at the heart of the mystery. Most good mysteries are rooted in the question of nourishment. As concepts, nourishment and sacrifice walk hand in hand, like old friends everywhere. Think of Judy Garland. The wedding at Cana. Think of the fish grilled at night on the Galilean shore. A fire, the fish in the simple pan, the flickeringly illuminated men.

The brothers have not passed through the record entirely unremarked, nor are they anonymous. In the blurry comet-trail of Little Red's history, the brothers exist as sparks, embers, brief coruscations. Blind, unknowing, they shared his early life, the life of Uniondale. They were, categorically, brothers, intent on their bellies, their toys, their cars, and their neuroses, all of that, and attuned not at all to the little red-haired boy who stumbled wide-eyed in their wake. Kyle, the recluse; Ernie, the hopeless. These are the names spoken by Little Red. After graduation from high school, the recluse lived one town over with a much older woman until his aging parents bought a trailer and relocated to rural Georgia, whereupon he moved into a smaller trailer on the same lot. When his father died, Kyle sold the little trailer and settled in with his mother. The hopeless brother, Ernie, followed Kyle and parents to Georgia within six weeks of their departure from Suffolk County. He soon found both a custodial position in a local middle school and a girlfriend, whom he married before the year was out. Ernie's weight, 285 pounds on his wedding day, ballooned to 350 soon after. No longer capable of fulfilling his custodial duties, he went on welfare. Kyle, though potentially a talented musician, experienced nausea and an abrupt surge in blood pressure at the thought of performing in public, so that source of income was forever closed to him. Fortunately, his only other talent, that of putting elderly women at their ease, served him well—his mother's will left him her trailer and the sum of $40,000, twice the amount bequested to her other two sons.

We should note that, before Kyle's windfall, Little Red periodically mailed him small sums of money—money he could ill afford to give away—and that he did the same for brother Ernie, although Ernie's most useful talent was that of attracting precisely the amount of money he needed at exactly the moment he needed it. While temporarily separated from his spouse, between subsistence-level jobs and cruelly hungry, Ernie waddled a-slouching past an abandoned warehouse, was tempted by the presence of a paper sack placed on the black leather passenger seat of an aubergine Lincoln Town Car, tested the door, found it open, snatched up the sack, and rushed Ernie-style into the cobweb-strewn shelter of the warehouse. An initial search of the bag revealed two foil-wrapped cheeseburgers, still warm. A deeper investigation uncovered an eight-ounce bottle of Poland Spring water and a green plastic-wrap-covered brick comprised of $2,300 in new fifties and twenties.

Although Ernie described this coup in great detail to his youngest brother, he never considered, not for a moment, sharing the booty.

These people are his immediate family. Witnesses to the trials, joys, despairs, and breakthroughs of his childhood, they noticed nothing. Of the actualities of his life, they knew less than nothing, for what they imagined they knew was either peripheral or inaccurate. Kyle and Ernie mistook the tip for the iceberg. And deep within herself, their mother had chosen, when most she might have considered her youngest son's life, to avert her eyes.

Little Red carries these people in his heart. He grieves for them; he forgives them everything.

What He Has Been

Over many years and in several cities, a waiter and a bartender; a bass player, briefly; a husband, a son, a nephew; a dweller in caves; an adept of certain magisterial substances; a friend most willing and devoted; a reader, chiefly of crime, horror, and science fiction; an investor and day trader; a dedicated watcher of cable television, especially the History, Discovery, and Sci-Fi channels; an intimate of nightclubs, joints, dives, and after-hour shebeens, also of restaurants, cafés, and diners; a purveyor of secret knowledge; a photographer; a wavering candle flame;

a voice of conundrums; a figure of steadfast loyalty; an intermittent beacon; a path beaten through the undergrowth.

THE BEATITUDES OF LITTLE RED, I

Whatsoever can be repaid, should be repaid with kindness.
Whatsoever can be borrowed, should be borrowed modestly.
Tip extravagantly, for they need the money more than you do.
You can never go wrong by thinking of God as Louis Armstrong.
Those who swing, should swing some more.
Something always comes along. It really does.
Cleanliness is fine, as far as it goes.
Remember—even when you are alone, you're in the middle of a
    party.
The blues ain't nothin' but a feeling, but *what* a feeling.
What goes up sometimes just keeps right on going.
Try to eat solid food at least once a day.
There is absolutely nothing wrong with television.
Anybody who thinks he sees everything around him isn't looking.
When you get your crib the way you like it, stay there.
Order can be created in even the smallest things, but that doesn't
    mean you have to create it.
Clothes are for sleeping in, too. The same goes for chairs.
Everyone makes mistakes, including deities and higher powers.
Avoid the powerful, for they will undoubtedly try to hurt you.
Doing one right thing in the course of a day is good enough.
Stick to beer, mainly.
Pay attention to musicians.
Accept your imperfections, for they can bring you to Paradise.
No one should ever feel guilty about fantasies, no matter how
    shameful they may be, for a thought is not a deed.
Sooner or later, jazz music will tell you everything you need to
    know.
There is no significant difference between night and day.
Immediately after death, human beings become so beautiful you
    can hardly bear to look at them.
To one extent or another, all children are telepathic.
If you want to sleep, sleep. Simple as that.

Do your absolute best to avoid saying bad things about people,
  especially those you dislike.
In the long run, grasshoppers and ants all wind up in the same
  place.

Little Red, His Appearance

When you meet Little Red for the first time, what do you see?

He will be standing in the doorway of his ground-floor apartment
on West Fifty-fifth Street, glancing to one side and backing away to
give you entry. The atmosphere, the tone created by these gestures,
will be welcoming and gracious in an old-fashioned, even almost rural,
manner.

He will be wearing jeans and an old T-shirt, or a worn gray bath-
robe, or a chain-store woolen sweater and black trousers. Black, rubber-
soled Chinese slippers purchased from a sidewalk vendor will cover his
narrow feet. Very slightly, his high, pale forehead will bulge forward
beneath his long red hair, which will have been pulled back from his
face and fastened into a ragged ponytail by means of a twisted rubber
band. An untrimmed beard, curled at the bottom like a giant ruff, will
cover much of his face. When he speaks, the small, discolored pegs of
his teeth will flicker beneath the fringe of his mustache.

Little Red will strike you as gaunt, in fact nearly haggard. He will
seem detached from the world beyond the entrance of his apartment
building. West Fifty-fifth Street and the rest of Manhattan will fade
from consciousness as you step through the door and move past your
host, who, still gazing to one side, will be gesturing toward the empty
chair separated from his recliner by a small, round, marble-topped
table or nightstand heaped with paperback books, pads of paper, ballpoint pens upright in a cup.

When first you enter Little Red's domain, and every subsequent time
thereafter, he will suggest dignity, solicitude, and pleasure in the fact
of your company. Little Red admits only those from whom he can be
assured of at least some degree of acknowledgment of that which they
will receive from him. People who have proven themselves indifferent
to the rewards of Little Red's hospitality are forbidden return, no matter how many times they press his buzzer or rap a quarter against his
big, dusty front window. He can tell them by their buzzes, their rings,

their raps: he knows the identities of most of his callers well before he glances down the corridor to find them standing before his building's glass entrance. (Of course nearly all of Little Red's visitors take the precaution of telephoning him before they venture to West Fifty-fifth Street, both for the customary reason of confirming his availability and for one other reason, which shall be disclosed in good time.)

Shortly after your entrance into his domain, his den, his consulting room, his confessional, Little Red will tender the offer of a bottle of Beck's beer from the Stygian depths of his kitchen. On the few occasions when his refrigerator is empty of Beck's beer, he will have requested that you purchase a six-pack on your way, and will reimburse you for the purchase upon your arrival.

His hands will be slim, artistic, and often in motion.

He will sometimes appear to stoop, yet at other times, especially when displeased, will adopt an almost military posture. A mild rash, consisting of a scattering of welts a tad redder than his hair and beard, will now and then constellate the visible areas of his face. From time to time, he will display the symptoms of pain, of an affliction or afflictions not readily diagnosed. These symptoms may endure for weeks. Such is his humanity, Little Red will often depress his buzzer (should the buzzer be operational) and admit his guests, his supplicants, when in great physical discomfort.

He will not remind you of anyone you know. Little Red is not a *type*.

The closest you will come to thinking that someone has reminded you of Little Red will occur in the midst of a movie seen late in a summer afternoon on which you have decided to use a darkened theater to walk away from your troubles for a couple of hours. As you sit surrounded by empty seats in the pleasant murk, watching a scene depicting a lavish party or a crowded restaurant, an unnamed extra will move through the door and depart, and at first you will feel no more than a mild tingle of recognition all the more compelling for having no obvious referent. *Someone is going, someone has gone*, that is all you will know. Then the tilt of the departing head or the negligent gesture of a hand will return to you a quality more closely akin to the emotional context of memory than to memory itself, and with the image of Little Red rising into your mind, you will find yourself pierced by an unexpected sense of loss, longing, and sweetness, as if someone had just spoken the name of a long-vanished, once-dear childhood friend.

Little Red, His Dwelling Place

He came to West Fifty-fifth Street in his early thirties, just at the final
cusp of his youth, after the years of wandering. From Long Island he
had moved into Manhattan, no one now knows where—Little Red
himself may have forgotten the address, so little had he come into his
adult estate. To earn his keep, he "waited." Kyle's small collection of
jazz records, also Kyle's enthusiasm for Count Basie, Maynard Fergu-
son, and Ella Fitzgerald, had given direction to his younger brother's
yearnings, and it was during this period that Little Red made his initial
forays into the world of which he would later become so central an element.

Photographs were taken, and he kept them. Should you be privileged to enter Little Red's inmost circle of acquaintances, he will one
night fetch from its hidey-hole an old album of cross-grained fabric
and display its treasures: snapshots of the boyish, impossibly youthful,
impossibly fresh Little Red, his hair short and healthy, his face shining, his spirit fragrant, in the company of legendary heroes. The album
contains no photographs of other kinds. Its centerpiece is a three-by-
five, taken outside a sun-drenched tent during a mid-sixties Newport
Jazz Festival, of a dewy Little Red leaning forward and smiling at the
camera as Louis Armstrong, horn tucked beneath his elbow, imparts a
never-to-be-forgotten bit of wisdom. On Armstrong's other side, grinning broadly, hovers a bearded man in his mid-forties. This is John
Elder, who has been called "the first Little Red." Little Red was sixteen,
already on his way.

From New York he wandered, "waiting," from city to city. A hidden design guided his feet, represented by an elderly, dung-colored
Volkswagen Beetle with a retractable sunroof and a minimum of trunk
space. Directed by the design, the VW brought him to New Orleans,
birthplace of Mighty Pops, and there he began his true instruction in
certain sacred mysteries. New Orleans was *instructive*, New Orleans
left a mark. And his journey through the kitchens and dining rooms of
great restaurants, his tutelage under their pitiless taskmasters, insured
that henceforth he would never have to go long without remunerative
employment.

It was in New Orleans that small groups of people, almost always
male, began to visit Little Red at all hours of day or night. Some stayed

half an hour; others lingered for days, participating in the simple, modest life of the apartment. John Elder is said to have visited the young couple. In those days, John Elder criss-crossed the country, staying with friends, turning up in jazz clubs to be embraced between sets by the musicians. Sometimes late at night, he spoke in a low voice to those seated on the floor around his chair. During these gatherings, John Elder oft-times mentioned Little Red, referring to him as his *son*.

Did John Elder precede Little Red to Aspen, Colorado? Although we have no documentation, the evidence suggests he did. An acquaintance of both men can recall Zoot Sims, the late tenor saxophonist, mentioning strolling into the kitchen of the Red Onion, Aspen's best jazz club, late on an afternoon in the spring of 1972 and finding John Elder deep in conversation with the owner over giant bowls of pasta. If this memory is accurate, John Elder was *preparing the way*—six months later, Little Red began working at the Red Onion.

He lived above a garage in a one-bedroom apartment accessible only by an exterior wooden staircase. As in New Orleans, individuals and small groups of men called upon him, in nearly every case having telephoned beforehand, to share his company for an hour or a span of days. Up the staircase they mounted, in all sorts of weather, to press the buzzer and await admittance. Little Red entertained his visitors with records and television programs; he invited them to partake of the Italian meals prepared by his wife, who always made herself scarce on these occasions. He produced bottles of Beck's beer from the refrigerator. Late at night, he spoke softly and without notes for an hour or two, no more. It was enough.

And too much for his wife, however, for she vanished from his life midway through his residency in Aspen. Single once more, pulling behind the VW a small U-Haul trailer filled with records, Little Red returned to Manhattan in the summer of 1973 and proceeded directly to the apartment on West Fifty-fifth Street then occupied by his old friend and mentor, John Elder, who unquestioningly turned over to his new guest the large front room of his long, railroad-style apartment.

The dwelling place Little Red has inhabited alone since 1976, when John Elder retired into luxurious seclusion, parses itself as three good-sized rooms laid end-to-end. Between the front room with its big shielded window and the sitting room lies a semi-warren of two small chambers separated by a door.

These chambers, the first containing a sink and shower stall, the second a toilet, exist in a condition of perpetual chiaroscuro, perhaps to conceal the stains encrusted on the fittings, especially the shower stall and curtain. Those visitors to Little Red's realm who have been compelled to wash their hands after the ritual of defecation generally glance at the shower arrangement, which in the ambient darkness at first tends to resemble a hulking stranger more than it does a structure designed for bodily cleansing, shudder at what they think, what they fear they may have seen there, then execute a one-quarter turn of the entire body before groping for the limp, threadbare towels drooping from a pair of hooks.

Beyond the sitting room and reached via a doorless opening in the wall is the kitchen.

Oh the kitchen, oh me oh my.

The kitchen has devolved into a progressive squalor. Empty bottles of Beck's in six-pack configurations piled chest-high dominate something like three-fourths of the grubby floor. Towers of filthy dishes and smeared glasses loom above the sink. The dirty dishes and beer bottles appear organic, as if they have grown untouched here in the gloom over the decades of Little Red's occupancy, producing bottle after bottle and plate after plate of the same ancient substance.

Heavy shades, the dusty tan of nicotine, conceal the kitchen's two windows, and a single 40-watt bulb dangles from a fraying cord over the landscape of stacked empties.

In the sitting room, a second low-wattage bulb of great antiquity oversees the long shelves, the two chairs, and the accumulation of goods before them. Not the only source of light in this barely illuminated chamber, the bulb has been in place, off and on but for several years mostly off, during the entire term of Little Red's occupancy of the apartment. "John Elder was using that lightbulb when I moved in," he says. "When you get that old, you'll need a lot of rest too." Two ornate table lamps, one beside the command post and the other immediately to the visitor's right, shed a ghostlike yellow pall. Little Red has no intrinsic need of bright light, including that of the sun. Shadow and relative darkness ease the eyes, calm the soul. The images on the rectangular screen burn more sharply in low light, and the low, moving banner charting the moment-by-moment activity of the stock market marches along with perfect clarity, every encoded symbol crisp as a snap-bean.

A giant shelving arrangement blankets the wall facing the two chairs, and Little Red's beloved television set occupies one of its open cabinets. Another black shelf, located just to the right of the television, holds his audio equipment—a CD player, a tape recorder, a tuner, a turntable, an amplifier, as well as the machines they have superseded, which are stacked beneath them, as if beneath headstones. A squat black speaker stands at either end of the topmost shelf. A cabinet located beneath the right-hand speaker houses several multivolume discographies, some so worn with use they are held together with rubber bands. All the remaining shelves support ranks of long-playing records. Records also fill the lower half of the freestanding bookshelf in front of the narrow wall leading from the small foyer area into the sitting room. Little Red must strain to reach the LPs located on the highest shelf; cardboard boxes of yet more jazz records stand before the ground-level shelves, their awkwardness and weight blocking access to the LPs arrayed behind them. Sometimes Little Red will wish to play a record hidden behind one of the boxes, then pause to consider the problems involved—the bending, the shoving, the risk to his lower back, the high concentration of dust likely to be disturbed—and will decide to feature another artist, one situated in a more convenient portion of the alphabet.

The records were alphabetized long ago. Two or three years after the accomplishment of the stupendous task, Little Red further refined the system by placing the records in alpha-chronological order, so that they stood not only in relation to the artists' placement in the alphabet, but also by date of recording, running from earliest to latest, oldest to newest, in each individual case. This process took him nearly a year to complete and occupied most of his free time—the time not given to his callers—during that period. For the callers kept coming, so they did, in numbers unceasing.

Actually, the alpha-chronologicalization process has not yet reached total completion, nor will it, nor can it, for reasons to be divulged in the next section of this account. Alpha-chronologicalization is an endless labor.

What occupies the territory between the chairs and the bookshelves constitutes the grave, grave problem of this room. The territory in question makes up the central portion of Little Red's sitting room, which under optimum conditions would provide a companionable open space for passage to and from the kitchen, to and from the bathroom and the front door, modest exercise, pacing, and for those so disposed, floor-sitting. Such a space would grant Little Red unimpeded access to the thousands of records packed onto the heavily laden shelves (in some cases so tightly that the withdrawal of a single LP involves pulling out an extra three or four on either side).

Once, a table of eccentric design was installed in the middle of the sitting room. At the time, it would have been a considerable amenity, with its broad, flat top for the temporary disposal of the inner and outer sleeves of the record being played, perhaps as well the sleeves containing those records to be played after that one. A large, square table it was, roughly the size of two steamer trunks placed side by side, and trunklike in its solidity from top to bottom, for its flanks contained a clever nest of drawers for the disposition of magazines, gewgaws, and knickknacks. It is believed that Little Red found this useful object on the street, the source of a good deal of his household furnishings, but it is possible that John Elder found it on the street, and that the table was already in place when Little Red was welcomed within.

Large as it was, the table offered no obstacle to a gaunt, red-haired individual moving from the command post to the records, or from any particular shelf of records to the cabinetlike space housing the turntable and other sound equipment. The table *cooperated*, it must have done. At one time—shortly after Little Red or John Elder managed to get the unwieldy thing off the sidewalk and into the sitting room—the table must have functioned properly, that is as a literal support system. The table undoubtedly performed this useful function for many months. After that . . . entropy took over, and the literal support system began to disappear beneath the mass and quantity of material it was required literally to support. In time, the table *vanished*, as an old car abandoned in a field gradually vanishes beneath and into the mound of weeds that overtakes it, or as the genial scientist who became ferocious Swamp Thing vanished beneath and into the vegetation that had surrounded, supported, nourished his wounded body. Little Red's is the Swamp Thing of the table family.

From the command post and the guest's chair, the center of the sitting room can be seen to be dominated by a large, unstable mound rising from the floor to a height of something like three and a half feet and comprised in part of old catalogs from Levenger, Sharper Image, and Herrington; copies of *Downbeat, Jazz Times,* and *Biblical Archaeology Review*; record sleeves and CD jewel boxes; takeout menus; flyers distributed on behalf of drugstores; copies of *Life* magazine containing particularly eloquent photographs of Louis Armstrong or Ella Fitzgerald; books about crop circles and alien visitations; books about miracles; concert programs of considerable sentimental value; sheets of notepaper scribbled over with cryptic messages (What in the world does *mogrom* mean? Or *rambichure*?); the innards of old newspapers; photographs of jazz musicians purchased from a man on the corner of West Fifty-seventh Street and Eighth Avenue; posters awaiting reassignment to the walls; and other suchlike objects submerged too deeply to be identified. Like the dishes in the sink, the mound seems to be increasing in size through a version of parthenogenesis.

Leaning against the irregular sides of Swamp Thing are yet more records, perhaps as few as fifty, perhaps as many as a hundred, already alphabetized; and around the listing, accordion-shaped constructions formed by propped-up records sit a varying number of cardboard boxes filled with still *more* records, these newly acquired from a specialist dealer or at a vintage record show. (John Elder, who in his luxurious seclusion possesses eighty to ninety thousand records stored on industrial metal shelves, annually attends a record fair in Newark, New Jersey, where he allows Little Red a corner at his lavish table.)

Long-playing records may be acquired virtually anywhere: in little shops tucked into obscure byways; from remote bins in vast retail outlets; from boxes carelessly arranged on the counters of small-town Woolworth's stores; within the outer circles of urban flea markets located in elementary-school playgrounds; from boxes, marked $1 EACH, displayed by unofficial sidewalk vendors who with their hangers-on lounge behind their wares on lawn furniture, smoking cigars and muffled up against the cold.

So Little Red gets and he spends, but when it comes to records he gets a lot more than he spends. His friends and followers occasionally give him CDs, and Little Red enjoys the convenience of compact discs; however, as long as they do not skip, he much prefers the sound of LPs, even scratchy ones. They are warmer and more resonant: the atmosphere of *distant places, distant times* inhabits long-playing vinyl records, whereas CDs are always in the here and now.

And what Little Red gets must in time be accommodated within his vast system, and a new old Duke Ellington record will eventually have to find its correct alpha-chronological position.

The word Little Red uses for this placement process is "filing." "Filing" records has become his daily task, his joy, his curse, his primary occupation.

Little Red, His Filing

Should you telephone Little Red and should he answer, you, like numerous others, might ask, with a hopeful lilt in your voice, what he has been up to lately.

"Nothing much," Little Red will answer. "Doing a lot of filing."

"Ah," you say.

"Got started yesterday afternoon around three, right after S—— and G—— G—— left. They were here since about ten o'clock the night before—we played some cards. Between three and six I filed at least two hundred records. Something like that, anyhow. Then I was thinking about going out and having dinner somewhere, but R—— was coming over at eight, and I looked at the boxes on the floor, and I just kept on filing. R—— left an hour ago, and I went right back into it. Got a lot of work done, man. The next time you come over, you'll see a big difference."

This assertion means only that *Little Red* sees a great difference. Nine times out of ten, you won't have a prayer. Swamp Thing will seem no less massive than on your previous visit; the boxes of records and accordion shapes will appear untouched.

Of course, time-lapse photography would prove you wrong, for Little Red's collection, filed and unfiled, is in constant motion. Occasionally, as in the case of the Japanese Gentleman, or during one of Little Red's visits to the record fair, albums are sold, leaving gaps on the shelves. These gaps are soon filled with the new old records from the accordions, which have already been alphabetized, and from the boxes, which have not. The customary progress of an album is from box to accordion, then finally to the shelf, after a consultation of the discographical record has pinned down its chronological moment. (Those discographies are in constant use, and their contents heavily annotated, underlined, and highlighted in a variety of cheerful colors.)

The quantity of rearrangement necessitated by the box-accordion-shelf progression would be daunting, exhausting, unbearable to anyone but Little Red. The insertion onto the proper shelf of four recently acquired Roy Eldridge LPs could easily involve redistributing two or three hundred records over four long shelves, so that a three-inch gap at the beginning of the Monk section might be transferred laterally and up to the midst of the Roys. The transferal of this gap requires twenty minutes of shifting and moving, not counting the time previously spent in chronologicizing the new acquisitions with the aid of the (sometimes warring) discographies. It's surprisingly dirty work, too. After ten or twelve hours of unbroken filing, Little Red resembles a coal miner at shift's end, grubby from head to foot, with grime concentrated on his face and hands, bleary-eyed, his hair in wisps and tangles.

At the end of your conversation, Little Red will say, "You can come over tonight, if you feel like it. It doesn't matter how late it is. I'll be up."

None of Little Red's friends, followers, or acquaintances has ever seen him in the act of filing his records. He files only when alone.

Miracles Attributed to Little Red

1. The Miracle of the Japanese Gentleman

The Japanese people include a surprising number of record collectors, a good half of whom specialize in jazz. Japanese collectors are famous for the purity of their standards, also for their willingness to expend great sums in pursuit of the prizes they desire. One of these gentlemen, a Kyoto businessman named Mr. Yoshi, learned of Little Red's collection from John Elder, with whom he had done business for many years. By this time, Mr. Yoshi's collection nearly equaled John Elder's in size, though only in the numbers of LP, EP, and 78 records it contained. In memorabilia, Mr. Yoshi lagged far behind his friend: when it comes to items like plaster or ceramic effigies of Louis Armstrong, signed photos of Louis Armstrong, and oversized white handkerchiefs once unfurled onstage by Louis Armstrong, John Elder is and always will be in a class by himself.

Little Red knew that the Japanese Gentleman had a particular interest in Blue Note and Riverside recordings from the 1950s, especially those by Sonny Clark and Kenny Dorham. Mr. Yoshi would accept only records in or near mint condition and in their original state—original cover art and record label, as if they had been issued yesterday and were essentially unplayed.

Little Red's monthly rent payment of $980 was coming due, and his bank balance stood at a dismal $205.65. The sale of two mint-condition records to Mr. Yoshi could yield the amount needed, but Little Red faced the insurmountable problem of not owning any mint-condition Sonny Clark or Kenny Dorham records on the Blue Note or Riverside labels. He had, it is true, a dim memory of once seeing *The Sonny Clark Trio*, the pianist's first recording as a leader for Blue Note and an object greatly coveted by Japanese collectors, pass through his hands, but that was the entire content of the memory: the record's shiny sleeve passing into and then out of his hands. He had not been conscious of its value on the collector's market; Sonny Clark had never been one of his favorites. However, he *knew* that he had once purchased a nice copy of Kenny Dorham's *Una Mas*, maybe not in mint condition but Excellent, at least Very Good anyhow, A to A–, worth perhaps $150 to $200 to a fanatical Japanese collector who did not already own one.

Little Red scanned the spines of his Kenny Dorham records without finding a single original 1963 copy of *Una Mas*. He had a Japanese reissue, but imagine offering a Japanese reissue to a Japanese collector!

Yet if he had neither of the most desired records, he did have a good number of consolation prizes, Blue Notes and Riversides maybe not exactly unplayed but certainly eminently playable and with sleeves in Fine to Very Fine condition. These twenty records he coaxed from the shelves and stacked on a folding chair for immediate viewing. With luck, he imagined, they could go for $30 to $40 apiece—he had seen them listed at that price in the catalogs. If he sold them all, he would make about $700, leaving him only a few dollars short of his rent.

Mr. Yoshi appeared at precisely the designated hour and wasted no time before examining the records set aside for him. Five-seven, with a severe face and iron-gray hair, he wore a beautiful dark blue pin-striped suit and gleaming black loafers. His English was rudimentary, but his tact was sublime. He had to pick his way around Swamp Thing to reach the folding chair, but the Japanese Gentleman acknowledged its monstrous presence by not so much as a raised eyebrow. For him,

Swamp Thing did not exist. All that existed, all that deserved notice, was the stack of records passed to him, two at a time, by Little Red.

"No good," he said. "Not for me."

"That's a shame," said his host, hiding his disappointment. "I hope your trip hasn't been wasted."

Mr. Yoshi ignored this remark and turned to face the crowded shelves. "Many records," he said. "Many, many." Little Red understood it was a show of politeness, and he appreciated the gesture.

"For sale?"

"Some, I guess," said Little Red. "Take a look."

The Japanese Gentleman cautiously made his way around the accordions and through the boxes on Swamp Thing's perimeter. When he stood before the shelves, he clasped his hands behind his back. "You have Blue Note?"

"Sure," said Little Red. "All through there. Riverside, too."

"You have Sonny Clark, Kenny Dorham?"

"Some Kenny, yeah," said Little Red, pointing to a shelf. "Right there."

"Aha," said Mr. Yoshi, moving closer. "I have funny feeling . . ."

Little Red clasped his own hands behind his back, and the Japanese Gentleman began to brush the tip of his index finger against the spines of the Dorham records. "Here is reason for funny feeling," he said, and extracted a single record. "*Una Mas*. Blue Note, 1963. Excellent condition."

"Yeah, well," said Little Red.

But the record in Mr. Yoshi's right hand was not the Japanese reissue. The Japanese Gentleman was holding, in a state akin to reverence, exactly what he had said it was, the original Blue Note issue from 1963, in immaculate condition.

"Huh!" said Little Red.

"Must look," said Mr. Yoshi, and slid the record from its sleeve. No less than his shoes, the grooved black vinyl shone.

"You try to keep this one for yourself," Mr. Yoshi teased. "Suppose I give you five hundred dollars, would you sell?"

"Uh, sure," said Little Red.

"What else you hiding here?" asked Mr. Yoshi, more to the intoxicating shelves than to Little Red. He picked his way along, flicking his fingers on the spines. "Uh-huh. Uh-huh. Not bad. Uh-oh, *very* bad. Poor, poor condition. Should throw out, no good anymore to listen."

Little Red said he would think about it.

"I have funny feeling again." Mr. Yoshi stiffened his spine and glared at the spines of the records. "Oh yes, *very* funny feeling."

Little Red came closer.

"Something here."

The Japanese Gentleman leaned forward and pushed two B– Sonny Clark Trio records on Savoy as far apart as they would go, about a quarter of an inch. A collector's instincts are not those of an ordinary man. He twitched out the Sonny Clark Trio records and passed them to Little Red without turning his head. His hand slid into the widened gap, his head moved nearer. "Aha."

Very gently, Mr. Yoshi pulled out his arm from between the records. A fine layer of dust darkened his white, elegant cuff. When his hand cleared the shelf, it brought into view two LPs which had been shoved into an opening once occupied by John Elder's long-departed reel-to-reel tape recorder. On the albums' identical covers, staggered red, blue, green, and yellow bars formed keyboard patterns. *The Sonny Clark Trio*, Blue Note, 1957, still in their plastic wrappers.

"You hide, I find," said the Japanese Gentleman. "This the Sonny Clark mother lode!"

"Sure looks like it," said dumbfounded Little Red.

"All three records, I give two thousand dollars. Right now. In cash."

"Talked me into it," said Little Red, and the Japanese Gentleman counted out two months' rent in new, sequentially numbered $100 bills and pressed them into his host's waiting hand. Little Red threw in a plastic LP carrier that looked a bit like a briefcase, and Dr. Yoshi left beaming.

After the departure of the Japanese Gentleman, Little Red remembered the wad of bills remaining in his guest's wallet after the removal of twenty hundreds and realized that he could have asked for and received another ten.

Don't be greedy, he told himself. *Be grateful.*

2. *The Miracle of the Weeping Child*

Late on a winter night, Little Red emerged from stuporous slumber and observed that he was fully dressed and seated at his command post in the freezing semidarkness. Across the room, the twinkling screen displayed in black and white a fly-like Louis Jourdan scaling down the facade of a hideous castle. (He had thought to enjoy the BBC's '70s *Dracula* as a reward for long hours of filing.) By the dim lamplight he saw that the time was 3:25. He had been asleep for about an hour and a half. His arms ached from the evening's labor; the emptiness in his stomach reminded him that he had failed to eat anything during the course of the busy day. Little Red's hands and feet were painfully cold. He reached down for the plaid blanket strewn at the left-hand side of his recliner. Even in his state of mild befuddlement, Little Red wondered what had pulled him so urgently into wakefulness.

How many days had passed without the refreshment of sleep? Two? Three? When deprived so long of sleep, the rebelling body and mind yield to phantoms. Elements of the invisible world take on untrustworthy form and weight, and their shapes speak in profoundly ambiguous voices. Little Red had been in this condition many times before; now he wished only to return to the realm from which he had been torn.

A push on the lever tilted the back of the chair to an angle conducive to slumber. Little Red draped the blanket over his legs and drew its upper portion high upon his chest.

Faintly but clearly, from somewhere in his apartment came the sound of a child weeping in either pain or despair. As soon as Little Red heard the sound, he knew that this was what had awakened him: a dream had rippled and broken beneath its pressure. He had been pulled upward, drawn *up* into the cold.

It came again, this time it seemed from the kitchen: a hiccup of tears, a muffled sob.

"Anybody there?" asked Little Red in a blurry voice. Wearily, he turned his head toward the kitchen and peered at the nothing he had expected to see. Of course no distraught child sat weeping in his kitchen. Little Red supposed that it had been two or three years since he had even *seen* a child.

He dropped his head back into the pillowy comfort of the recliner and heard it again—the cry of a child in misery. This time it seemed not to come from the kitchen but from the opposite end of his apartment, either the bathroom or the front room that served as storage shed and bedroom. Although Little Red understood that the sound was a hallucination and the child did not exist, that the sound should seem to emanate from the bedroom disturbed him greatly. He kept his bedroom to himself. Only in extreme cases had he allowed a visitor entrance to this most private of his chambers.

He closed his eyes, but the sound continued. False, false perception! He refused to be persuaded. There was no child; the misery was his own, and it derived from exhaustion. Little Red nearly arose from his command post to unplug his telephone, but his body declined to cooperate.

The child fell silent. Relieved, Little Red again closed his eyes and folded his hands beneath the rough warmth of the woolen blanket. A delightful rubbery sensation overtook the length of his body, and his mind lurched toward a dream. A series of sharp cries burst like tracers within his skull, startling him back into wakefulness.

Little Red cursed and raised his head. He heard another flaring outcry, then another, and the sound subsided back into pathetic weeping. "Go to sleep!" he yelled, and at that moment realized what had happened: a woman, not a child, was standing distressed on the sidewalk outside his big front window, crying loudly enough to be audible deep within. A woman sobbing on West Fifty-fifth Street at 3:30 in the morning, no remedy existed for a situation like that. He could do nothing but wait for her to leave. An offer of assistance or support would earn only rebuff, vituperation, insults, and the threat of criminal charges. Nothing could be done, Little Red advised himself. *Leave well enough alone, stay out.* He shut his eyes and waited for quiet. At least he had identified the problem, and sooner or later the problem would take care of itself. Tired as he was, he thought he might fall asleep before the poor creature moved on. He might, yes, for he felt the gravity of approaching unconsciousness slip into his body's empty spaces despite the piteous noises floating through his window.

Then he opened his eyes again and swung his legs from beneath the blanket's embrace and out of the chair, for he was Little Red and could not do otherwise. The woman's misery was intolerable, how could he pretend not to hear it? Thinking to peek around the side of the front window's shade, Little Red pushed himself out of the command center and marched stiff-legged into the toilet.

As if the woman had heard his footsteps, the noise cut off. He paused, took a slow step forward. *Just let me get a look at you*, he thought. *If you don't look completely crazy, I'll give you whatever help you can accept.* In a moment he had passed through the bathroom and was opening the door to his bedroom, the only section of the apartment we have not as yet seen.

The weeping settled into a low, steady, fearful wail. The woman must have heard him, he thought, but was too frightened to leave the window. "Can't be as bad as that," he said, making his slow way down the side of the bed toward the far wall, where an upright piano covered half of the big window. Now the wailing seemed very close at hand. Little Red imagined the woman huddled against his building, her head bent to his window. Her mechanical cries pierced his heart. He almost felt like going outside immediately.

Little Red reached the right edge of the window and touched the stiff, dark material of the shade. Unraised for nearly forty years, it smelled like a sick animal. A pulse of high-pitched keening filled his ears, and a dark shape that huddled beside the piano moved nearer the wall. Little Red dropped his hand from the shade and stepped back, fearing that he had come upon a monstrous rat. His heart pounded, and his breath caught in his throat. Even the most ambitious rat could not grow so large; Little Red quieted his impulse to run from the room and looked down at the being crouching beside the piano.

A small dark head bent over upraised knees tucked under a white stretched-out T-shirt. Two small feet shone pale in the darkness. Little Red stared at the creature before him, which appeared to tighten down into itself, as if trying to disappear. A choked sound of combined misery and terror came from the little being. It was a child after all: he had been right the first time.

"How did you get in here?" Little Red asked.

The child hugged its knees and buried its face. The sound it made went up in pitch and became a fast, repeated *ih ih ih*.

Little Red lowered himself to the floor beside the child. "You don't have to be so afraid," he said. "I'm not going to hurt you."

A single eye peeked at him, then dropped back to the T-shirt and the bent knees. The boy was about five or six, with short brown hair and thin arms and legs. He shivered from the cold. Little Red patted him lightly on the back and was surprised by the relief aroused in him by the solidity of what he touched.

"Do you have a name?"

The boy shook his head.

"No?"

"No." It was the smallest whisper.

"That's too bad. I bet you have a name, really."

No response, except that the shivering child had stopped whimpering *ih ih ih*.

"Can you tell me what you're doing here?"

"I'm *cold*," the boy whispered.

"Well, sure you are," said Little Red. "Here we are in the middle of winter, and all you have on is a T-shirt. Hold on, I'm going to get you a blanket."

Little Red pushed himself to his feet and went quickly to the sitting room, fearing that the child might vanish before his return. *But why do I want him to stay?* he asked himself, and had no answer.

When he came back, the child was still huddled alongside the piano. Little Red draped the blanket over his shoulders and once again sat beside him.

"Better?"

"A little." His teeth made tiny clicking noises.

Little Red rubbed a hand on the boy's blanket-covered arms and back.

"I want to lie down," the child said.

"Will you tell me your name now?"

"I don't have a name."

"Do you know where you are?"

"Where I am? I'm here."

"Where do you live? What's your address? Or how about your phone number? You're old enough to know your phone number."

"I want to lie down," the boy said. "Put me on the bed. Please." He nodded at Little Red's bed, in the darkness seemingly buried beneath the rounded bodies of many sleeping animals. These were the mounds of T-shirts, underpants, socks, sweatshirts, and jeans Little Red had taken, the previous night, to the twenty-four-hour Laundromat on the corner of Fifty-fifth Street and Ninth Avenue. He had filled five washers, then five dryers, with his semiannual wash, taken the refreshed clothing home in black garbage bags, and sorted it all on his bed, where it was likely to remain for the entirety of the coming month, if not longer.

"Whatever you say," said Little Red, and lifted the child in his arms and carried him to the bed. The boy seemed to weigh no more than a handful of kitchen matches. He leaned over the bed and nestled the child between a pile of balled socks and a heap of folded jazz festival T-shirts. "You can't stay here, you know, little boy," he said.

The child said, "I'm not going to stay here. This is just where I *am*."

"You don't have to be scared anymore."

"I thought you were going to hurt me." For a second his eyes narrowed, and his skin seemed to shrink over his skull. He was actually a very unattractive little boy, thought Little Red. The child looked devious and greedy, like an urchin who had lived too long by its wits. In some ways, he had the face of a sour, bad-tempered old man. Little Red felt as though he had surrendered his bed to a beast like a weasel, a coyote.

But he's only a little boy, Little Red told Little Red, who did not believe him. This was not a child—this was something that had come in from the freezing night. "Do you think you can go to sleep now?"

But the child—the being—had slipped into unconsciousness before Little Red asked the question.

What to *do* with him? The ugly little thing asleep in the midst of Little Red's laundry was never going to produce an address or a telephone number, that was certain. Probably it was telling the truth about not having a name.

But that was crazy—he had gone too long without sleep, and his mind could no longer work right. A wave of deep weariness rolled through him, bringing with it the recognition that his mind could no longer work at all, at least not rationally. If he did not lie down, he was going to fall asleep standing up. So Little Red got his knees up on the mattress, pushed aside some heaps of clothing, stretched out, and watched his eyes close by themselves.

Asleep, he inhaled the scent of clean laundry, which seemed the most beautiful odor in the world. Clean laundry smelled like sunshine, fresh air, and good health. This lovely smell contained a hint of the celestial, of the better world that heaven is said to be. It would be presumptuous to speak of angels, but if angels wore robes, those robes would smell like the clean, fluffy socks and underwear surrounding Little Red and his nameless guest. The guest's own odor now and then came to Little Red. Mingled with the metallic odor of steam vented from underground regions, the sharp, gamy tang of fox sometimes cut through the fragrance of the laundry, for in his sleep Little Red had shifted nearer to the child.

To sleeping Little Red, the two scents twisted together and became a single thing, an odor of architectural complexity filled with wide plazas and long colonnades, also with certain cramped, secret dens and cells. And from the hidden dens and cells a creature came in pursuit of him, whether for good or ill he did not know. But in pursuit it came: Little Red felt the displacement of the air as it rushed down long corridors, and there were times when he spun around a corner an instant before his pursuer would have caught sight of him. And though he continued to run as if for his life, Little Red still did not know if the creature meant him well or meant to do him harm.

He twisted and squirmed in imitation of the motions of his dream-body, and it so fell out that eventually he had folded his body around that of his little guest, and the animal smell became paramount.

During what happened next, Little Red could not make out whether he was asleep and dreaming of being half awake, or half awake and still dreaming of being asleep. He seemed to pass back and forth between two states of being with no registration of their boundaries. His hand had fallen on the child's chest—he remembered that, for instantly he had thought to snatch it back from this accidental contact. Yet in pulling back his hand he had somehow succeeded in pulling the child with it, though his hand was empty and his fingers open. The child, the child-*thing*, floated up from the rumpled blanket and the disarranged piles of laundry, clinging to Little Red's hand as metal clings to a magnet. That was how it seemed to Little Red: the boy *adhered* to his raised hand, the boy *followed* the hand to his side, and when the boy-thing came to rest beside him, the boy-thing smiled a wicked smile and bit him in the neck.

The gamy stink of fox streamed into his nostrils, and he cried out in pain and terror . . . and in a moment the child-thing was stroking his head and telling him he had nothing to fear, and the next moment he dropped through the floor of sleep into darkness and knew nothing.

Little Red awakened in late afternoon of the following day. He felt wonderfully rested and restored. A decade might have been subtracted from his age, and he become a lad of forty once again. Two separate mental events took place at virtually the same moment, which came as he sat up and stretched out his arms in a tremendous yawn. He remembered the weeping child he had placed in this bed; and he noticed that one of his arms was spattered with drying blood.

He gasped and looked down at his chest, his waist, his legs. Bloodstains covered his clothes like thrown paint. The blanket and the folded clothing littered across the bed were drenched in blood. There were feathery splashes of blood on the dusty floor. Spattered bloodstains mounted the colorless wall.

For a moment, Little Red's heart stopped moving. His breathing was harsh and shallow. Gingerly, he swung his legs to the floor and got out of bed. First he looked at the blanket, which would have to be thrown out, then, still in shock, down at his own body. Red blotches bloomed on his shirt. The bottom of his shirt and the top of his jeans were sodden, too soaked in blood to have dried.

Little Red peeled the shirt off over his head and dropped it to the floor. His chest was irregularly stained with blood but otherwise undamaged. He saw no wounds on his arms. His fingers unbuckled his belt and undid his zipper, and he pushed his jeans down to his ankles. The Chinese slippers fell off his feet when he stepped out of the wet jeans. From mid-thigh to feet he was unmarked; from navel to mid-thigh he was solid red.

Yet he felt no pain. The blood could not be his. Had something terrible happened to the child? Moaning, Little Red scattered the clothing across the bed, looked in the corners of the room, and went as far as the entrance to the sitting room, but saw no trace of his guest. Neither did he see further bloodstains. The child, the *thing*, had disappeared.

When Little Red stood before his bathroom mirror, he remembered the dream, if it had been a dream, and leaned forward to inspect the side of his neck. The skin was pale and unbroken. So it had been a dream, all of it.

Then he remembered the sounds of weeping that had awakened him at his command post, and *ih ih ih*, and he remembered the weight of the child in his arms and his foxy smell. Little Red turned on his shower and stepped into the stall. Blood sluiced down his body, his groin, his legs to the drain. He remembered the blissful fragrance of his clean laundry. That magnificent odor, containing room upon room. Thinking to aid a distressed woman, he had discovered a terrified child, or something that looked like a child, and had given it a night's shelter and a bed of socks and underwear. Standing in the warm spray of the shower, Little Red said, "In faith, a miracle."

3. The Miracle of C—— M—— and Vic Dickenson

Late one summer afternoon, C—— M——, a young trombonist of growing reputation, sat in Little Red's guest chair listening to *Very Saxy* and bemoaning the state of his talent.

"I feel stuck," he said. "I'm playing pretty well . . ."

"You're playing great," said Little Red.

"Thanks, but I feel like there's some direction I ought to go, but I can't figure out what it is. I keep doing the same things over and over. It's like, I don't know, like I have to wash my ears before I'll be able to make any progress."

"Ah," said Little Red. "Let me play something for you." He rose from his chair.

"What?"

"Just listen."

"I don't need this jive bullshit, Little Red."

"I said, just *listen*."

"Okay, but if you were a musician, you'd know this isn't how it works."

"Fine," said Little Red, and placed on the turntable a record by the Vic Dickenson Trio—trombone, bass, and guitar—made in 1949. "I'm going to my bedroom for a few minutes," he said. "Something screwy happened to my laundry a while ago, and I have to throw about half of it away."

C—— M—— leaned forward to rest his forearms on his knees, the posture in which he listened most carefully.

Little Red disappeared through the door to the toilet and went to his bedroom. Whatever he did there occupied him for approximately twenty minutes, after which he returned to the sitting room.

His face wet with tears, C—— M—— was leaning far back in his chair, looking as though he had just been dropped from a considerable height. "God bless you," he said. "God bless you, Little Red!"

4. The Miracle of the Blind Beggar-Man

He had been seeing the man for the better part of the year, seated on a wooden box next to the flowers outside the Korean deli on the corner of Fifty-fifth Street and Eighth Avenue, shaking a white paper cup salted with coins. Tall, heavy, dressed always in a double-breasted dark blue pinstriped suit of wondrous age, his skin a rich chocolate brown, the

man was at his post four days every week from about nine in the morning to well past midnight. Whatever the weather, he covered his head
with an ancient brown fedora, and he always wore dark glasses with
lenses the size of quarters.

He was present on days when it rained and days when it snowed. On
sweltering days, he never removed his hat to wipe his forehead, and
on days when the temperature dropped into the teens he wore neither
gloves nor overcoat. Once he had registered the man's presence, Little
Red soon observed that he took in much more money than the other
panhandlers who worked Hell's Kitchen. The reason for his success,
Little Red surmised, was that his demeanor was as unvarying as his
wardrobe.

He was a beggar who did not beg. Instead, he allowed you to give
him money. Enthroned on his box, elbows planted on his knees, cup
upright in his hand, he offered a steady stream of greetings, compli-
ments, and benedictions to those who walked by.

*You're sure looking fine today, Miss . . . God bless you, son . . . You make
sure to have a good day today, sir . . . God bless you, ma'am . . . Honey, you
make me happy every time you come by . . . God bless you . . . God bless . . .
God bless . . .*

And so it happened that one day Little Red dropped a dollar bill into
the waiting cup.

"God bless," the man said.

On the following day, Little Red gave him another dollar.

"Thank you and God bless you, son," the man said.

The next day, Little Red put two dollars in the cup.

"Thank you, Little Red, God bless you," said the man.

"How did you learn my name?" asked Little Red. "And how did you
know it was me?"

"I hear they come to you, the peoples," the man said. "Night and day,
they come. Ain't that the righteous truth? Night *and* day."

"They come, each in his own way," said Little Red. "But how do you
know my name?"

"I always knew who you were," said the man. "And now I know what
you are."

Little Red placed another dollar in his cup.

"Maybe I come see you myself, one day."

"Maybe you will," said Little Red.

5. *The Miracle of the Greedy Demon (from Book I,* Little Red, His Trials)

The greedy demons were everywhere. He saw them in the patrons' eyes—the demons, glaring out, saying *more, more.* While Little Red dressed to go to work, while he laced up his sturdy shoes, while taking the crosstown bus, as he opened the door to the bar and the head-waiter's desk, his stomach tightened at the thought of the waiting demons. Where demons reign, all joy is hollow, all happiness is pain in disguise, all pleasure merely the product of gratified envy. Daily, as he padded to the back of the restaurant to don his bow tie and white jacket, he feared he would be driven away by the flat, toxic stench of evil.

This occurred in the waning days of Little Red's youth, when he had not as yet entered fully into his adult estate.

The demons gathered here because they enjoyed each other's company. Demons can always recognize other demons, but the human beings they inhabit are ignorant of their possession and don't have a clue what is going on. They suppose they simply enjoy going to certain restaurants, or, say, a particular restaurant, because the food is decent and the atmosphere pleasant. The human beings possessed by demons fail to notice that while the prices have gone up a bit, the food has slipped and the atmosphere grown leaden, sour, stale. The headwaiter notices only that a strange languor has taken hold of the service staff, but he feels too languid himself to get excited about it. Ninety-nine percent of the waiters fail to notice that they seldom wish to look their patrons in the eye and record only that the place seems rather *dimmer* than it once was. Only Little Red sees the frantic demons jigging in the eyes of the torpid diners; only Little Red understands, and what he understands sickens him.

There came a day when a once-handsome gentleman in a blue blazer as taut as a sausage casing waved Little Red to his table and ordered a second 16-oz. rib eye steak, rare, and a second order of onion rings, and oh yeah, might as well throw in a second bottle of that Napa Valley cabernet.

"I won't do that," said Little Red.

"Kid, you gotta be shitting me," said the patron. His face shone a hectic pink. "I ordered another rib eye, more onion rings, and a fresh bottle of wine."

"You don't want any more food," said Little Red. He bent down and gazed into the man's eyes. "Something inside you wants it, but you don't."

The man gripped his wrist and moved his huge head alongside Little Red's. "You act that way with me, kid, and one cold night you could wake up and find me in your room, wearing nothing but a T-shirt."

"Then let it be so," said Little Red.

6. *The Miracle of the Murdered Cat*

Years after he had come into his adult estate, Little Red one day left his apartment to replenish his stock of Beck's beer. It was just before 6:00 a.m. on a Saturday morning in early June. Two trumpet players and a petty thief who had dropped in late Thursday night were scattered around the sitting room, basically doing nothing but waiting for him to come back with their breakfasts.

The Koreans who owned the deli on the corner of Fifty-fifth and Eighth lately had been communicating some kind of weirdness, so he turned the corner, intending to walk past the front of their shop and continue north to the deli on the corner of Fifty-sixth Street, where the Koreans were still sane. The blind beggar startled him by stepping out of the entrance and saying, "My man, Little Red Man! Good morning to you, son. Seems to me you ought to be thinkin' about getting more sleep one of these days."

"Morning to you, too," said Little Red. "Early for you to be getting to work, isn't it?"

"Somethin' big's gonna happen today," said the beggar-man. "Wanted to make sure I didn't miss out." He set down his box, placed himself on it, and opened the 12-oz. bottle of Dr Pepper he had just purchased.

Only a few taxicabs moved up wide Eighth Avenue, and no one else was on the sidewalk on either side. Iron shutters protected the windows of most of the shops.

As he moved up the block, Little Red looked across the street and saw a small shape leave the shelter of a rank of garbage cans and dart into the avenue. It was a little orange cat, bony with starvation.

The cat had raced to within fifteen feet of the western curb when a taxi rocketing north toward Columbus Circle swerved toward it. The cat froze, eyed the taxi, then gathered itself into a ball and streaked forward.

Little Red stood openmouthed on the sidewalk. "You worthless little son of a bitch," he said. "Get moving!"

As the cat came nearly within leaping distance of the curb, the cab picked up speed and struck it. Little Red heard a muffled sound, then saw the cat roll across the surface of the road and come to rest in the gutter.

"Damn," he said, and glanced back at the beggar-man. He sat on his box, gripping his bottle of Dr Pepper and staring straight ahead at nothing. Little Red came up to the lifeless cat and lowered himself to the sidewalk. "You just get on now," he said. "Get going, little cat."

The lump of fur in the gutter twitched, twitched again, and struggled to its feet. It turned its head to Little Red and regarded him with opaque, suspicious eyes.

"Git," said Little Red.

The cat wobbled up onto the sidewalk, sat to drag its tongue over an oily patch of fur, and limped off into the shelter of a doorway.

Little Red stood up and glanced back down the street. The blind man cupped his hands around his mouth and called out something. Little Red could not quite make out his words, but they sounded approving.

7. The Miracle of the Kitchen Mouse

On a warm night last year, Little Red awakened in his command center to a silent apartment. His television set was turned off, and a single red light burned in the control panel of his CD player, which, having come to the end of *The Count on the Coast, Vol. II*, awaited further instructions.

Little Red rubbed his hands over his face and sat up, trying to decide whether or not to put on a new CD before falling back asleep. Before he could make up his mind, a small gray mouse slipped from between two six-packs of Beck's empties and hesitated at the edge of the sitting room. The mouse appeared to be looking at him.

"You go your way, and I'll go mine," said Little Red.

"God bless you, Little Red," said the mouse. Its voice was surprisingly deep.

"Thank you," said Little Red, and lapsed back into easy-breathing slumber.

THE BEATITUDES OF LITTLE RED, II

Over the long run, staying on good terms with your dentist really pays off.

Bargain up, not down.

When you're thinking about sex, the only person you have to please is yourself.

At least once a day, think about the greatest performance you ever heard.

Every now and then, remember Marilyn Monroe.

Put your garbage in the bin.

When spring comes, *notice* it.

Taste what you eat, dummy.

God pities demons, but He does not love them.

No matter how poor you are, put a little art up on your walls.

Let other people talk first. Your turn will come.

Wealth is measured in books and records.

All leases run out, sorry.

Every human being is beautiful, especially the ugly ones.

Resolution and restitution exist only in fantasy.

Learn to live *broken*. It's the only way.

Dirty dishes are just as sacred as clean ones.

In the midst of death, we are in life.

If some miserable bastard tries to cheat you, you might as well let the sorry piece of shit get away with it.

As soon as possible, move away from home.

Don't buy shoes that hurt your feet.

We are all walking through fire, so keep walking.

Never tell other people how to raise their children.

The truth not only hurts, it's unbearable. You have to live with it anyway.

Don't reject what you don't understand.

Simplicity works.

Only idiots boast, and only fools believe in "bragging rights."

You are *not* better than anyone else.

Cherish the dents in your armor.

Always look for the *source*.

Rhythm is repetition, repetition, repetition.

Snobbery is a disease of the imagination.

Happiness is primarily for children.

When it's time to go, that's what time it is.

Little Red, His Hobbies and Amusements

Apart from music, books, and television, he has no hobbies or amusements.

Epistle of C—— M——to R—— B——, Concerning Little Red

Dear R——,

Have you heard of the man, if he is a man, called Little Red? Has the word reached you? Okay, I know how that sounds, but don't start getting worried about me, because I haven't flipped out or lost my mind or anything, and I'm not trying to convert you to anything. I just want to describe something to you, that's all. You can make up your own mind about it afterward. Whatever you think will be okay with me. I guess I'm still trying to make up my own mind—probably that's one reason why I'm writing you this letter.

I told you that before I left Chicago the last time, I took some lessons from C—— F——, right? What a great player that cat is. Well, you know. The year we got out of high school, we must have listened to Live in Las Vegas *at least a thousand times. Man, he really opened our eyes, didn't he? And not just about the trombone, as amazing as that was, but about music in general, remember? So he was playing in town, and I went every night and stayed for every set, and before long he noticed I was there all the time, and on the third night I bought him a drink, and we got talking, and he found out I played trombone, and when and where and all that, and he asked me if I would sit in during the second set the next night. So I brought my horn and I sat in, and he was amazing. I guess I did okay, because he said, "That was nice, kid." Which made me feel very very good, as you can imagine. I asked could he give me some lessons while he was in town. Know what he told me? "I can probably show you some things, sure."*

*We met four times in his hotel room, besides spending an hour or
two together after the gig, most nights. Mainly, he worked on my
breathing and lip exercises, but apart from that the real education
was just listening to him talk, man. Crazy shit that happened on
the road with Kenton and Woody Herman, stories about the guys
who could really cut it and the guys who couldn't but got over
anyhow, all kinds of great stories. And one day he says to me, When
you get to New York, kid, you should look up this guy Little Red,
and tell him I said you were okay.*

"What is he," I asked, "a trombone player?"

*Nah, he said, just a guy he thought I should know. Maybe he
could do me some good. "Little Red, he's hard to describe if you
haven't met him," he said. "Being with the guy is sort of like doing
the tango." Then he laughed.*

"The tango?" I asked.

*"Yeah," he said. "You might wind up with your head up your ass,
but you know you had a hell of a time anyway."*

*So when I got to New York I asked around about this Little Red,
and plenty of people knew him, it turned out, musicians especially,
but nobody could tell me exactly what the guy did, or what made
him so special. It was like—if you know, then there's no point in
talking about it, and if you don't, you can't talk about it at all, you
can't even begin. Because I met a couple of guys like that, when
Little Red's name came up they just shrugged their shoulders and
shook their heads. One guy even walked out of the room we were in!*

*Eventually I decided I had to see for myself, and I called him up.
He acted sort of cagey. How did I hear about him, who did I know?
"C—— F—— said to tell you I was okay," I said. All right, he said,
come on over later, around 10, when he'd be free.*

*About 10:30, I got to his building—55th off 8th, an easy walk
from my room on 44th and 9th. I buzz his apartment, he buzzes
me in. And here he is, opening the door to his apartment, this
skinny guy with a red beard and long red hair tied back in a
ponytail. His face looks sad, and he looks pretty tired, but he gives
me a beer right away and sits me down in his incredibly messy room,
stuff piled up in front of a wall of about a million records, and asks
me what I'd like to hear. I dunno, I say, I'm a trombone player, is
it possible he has some good stuff I maybe don't know about? And*

we're off! The guy has hundreds of great things I'd never heard before, some I never heard of at all, and before I know it five or six hours have gone by and I have to get back to my room before I pass out in his chair. He says he'll make me a tape of the best stuff we heard, and I go home. In all that time, I realized, Little Red said maybe a dozen words altogether. I felt like something tremendously important had happened to me, but I couldn't have told you what it was.

The third time I went back to Little Red's, I started complaining about feeling stuck in my playing, and he put on an old Vic Dickenson record that made my head spin around on my shoulders. It was exactly what I needed, and he knew it! He understood.

After that, I started spending more and more time at his place. Winter had ended, but spring hadn't come yet. When I walked up 9th Avenue, the air was bright and cold. Little Red seemed not to notice how frigid his apartment was, and after a while, I forgot all about it. The sunlight burned around the edges of the shades in his kitchen and his living room, and as the time went by it faded away and turned to utter darkness, and sometimes I thought of all the stars filling the sky over 55th Street, even though we wouldn't be able to see them if we went outside.

Usually, we were alone. He talked to me—he spoke. There were times when other people came in, said a few things, then left us alone again.

Often, he let his words drift away into silence, brought some fresh bread in from his kitchen, and shared it with me. That bread had a wonderful, wonderful taste. I've never managed to find that taste again.

A couple of times he poured out wine for me instead of beer, and that wine seemed extraordinary. It tasted like sunshine, like sunshine on rich farmland.

Once, he asked me if I knew anything about a woman named something like Simone Vey. When I said I'd never heard of her, he said that was all right, he was just asking. Later he wrote out her name for me, and it was spelled W-E-I-L, not V-E-Y. Who is this woman? What did she do? I can't find out anything about her.

After a couple of weeks, I got out of the habit of going home when it was time to sleep, and I just stretched out on the floor and slept until I woke up again. Little Red almost always went to sleep in his chair, and when I woke up I would see him, tilted back, his eyes closed, looking like the most peaceful man in the world.

He talked to me, but it wasn't as though he was teaching me anything, exactly. We talked back and forth, off and on, during the days and nights, in the way friends do, and to me everything seemed comfortable, familiar, as it should be.

One morning he told me that I had to go, it was time. "You're kidding," I said. "This is perfect. I don't really have to leave, do I?"

"You must go," he said. I wanted to fall to the floor and beg, I wanted to clutch the cuffs of his trousers and hang on until he changed his mind.

He shoved me out into the hallway and locked the door behind me. I had no choice but to leave. I stumbled down the hall and wandered into the streets, remembering a night when I'd seen a mouse creep out of his kitchen, bless him by name, and receive his blessing in return. When I had staggered three or four blocks south on 8th Avenue, I realized that I could never again go back.

It was a mistake that I had been there in the first place—he had taken me in by mistake, and my place was not in that crowded apartment. My place might be anywhere, a jail cell, a suburban bedroom with tacky paintings on the wall, a bench in a subway station, anywhere but in that apartment.

I often try to remember the things he said to me. My heart thickens, my throat constricts, a few words come back, but how can I know if they are the right words? He can never tell me if they are.

I think: some kind of love did pass between us. But how could Little Red have loved me? He could not, it is impossible. And yet, R——, a fearful, awkward bit of being, a particle hidden deep within myself, has no choice but to think that maybe, just maybe, in spite of everything, he does after all love me.

So tell me, old friend, have you ever heard of Little Red?

Yours,

C——

Lapland, or Film Noir

A GENERAL INTRODUCTION

Our initial purpose is to discuss the effect, the *feeling tone* of headlights reflected on wet urban streets in Lapland, Florida. This is central to our discourse, the feeling tone of those reflections. By implication, then, rain; cars veering at great speed around sharp corners; unholstered pistols, brandished; desperate men; a sick, thrilled sense of impendingness. The immediate historical context plays a central role, as does a profound national sense of the shameful, the squalid, matters never acknowledged in the golden but streaky Florida light. You'd need a spotlight and a truncheon to beat it out of these people. Florida, it will be remembered, tends toward the hot, the dark, the needy, the rotting, the "sultry." The stunted and unnatural. Lapland, i.e., someone's (theoretically) warm yet not really comfortable, in fact impossibly dispossessing . . .

Steam rises through the grates.

We are in . . . . Gulf Coast . . . . semipiternal darkness . . . . without surcease, without hope for Silky's . . . .

—

In Lapland, all the women are always awake. Even your *mother* lies awake all the night through, drawing essential feminine nourishment from the bottomless communal well. Headlights shine in long streaks on the rain-soaked streets. Just outside the city limits, a gas station attendant named Bud Forrester rolls on his side in bed, thinking of a woman named Carole Chandler. Carole Chandler is his boss's wife, and she has no conscience whatsoever. Bud does possess a conscience, rudimentary though it is. He wishes he could amputate it, without pain, like a sixth finger no thicker around than a twig. In Bud Forrester's past lies a tremendous crime for which his simple duties at the gas station represent a conscious and ongoing penance.

During the commission of the crime, Frank Bigelow took two rounds in the gut, and he will never again void his bowels without whimpering, cursing, sweating. He walks with a limp, Frank. He isn't the kind of guy who can accept stuff like the whimpering, the sweating, the limping with every step of his beautifully shod feet. And when everything depended on where the money was, the money was lifting and blowing all across the tarmac, jittering through the air, like leaves, falling earthward in zigzags, like leaves. Bud Forrester always had a little tingle of a premonition that it was going to end this way. The other guys, they didn't want to hear about it. Bradford Galt and Tom Jardine, Bigelow had them hypnotized, *in thrall*. If Bud had tried to tell them about his little tingle, Galt and Jardine would have taped his mouth shut, bound his arms and legs, and locked him in a closet. That's the way these boys operate—on only a couple of very simple levels.

Frank Bigelow, though, is another matter. One night, over a lamplit table littered with charts and maps, he had observed a certain shine in the whites of Bud's eyes, and immediately he had known of his underling's traitorous misgivings.

One more detail, essential to the coils of the plot: Frank Bigelow also thinks endlessly and without . . . . upon Carole Chandler. These thoughts, alas, have darkened since he wound up impotent. Deep in his heart what he'd like to do is sic Tom Jardine on Carole; brutal, stupid Jardine is hung like a stallion (off-camera, the guy is always inventing excuses for showing off his tool), and while Tom makes Carole Chandler beg for more like the bitch she is, Frank would like to be watching through a kind of peephole arrangement. Trouble is, after that he would have to murder Tom Jardine, and Tom is one of his main guys, he's like one of the family, so that's out.

Every film noir has one impossible plot convenience, in this instance: despite his frustrated passion for wicked Carole Chandler, Frank Bigelow has no idea that Bud Forrester is employed at her husband's Shell station, because he sees her only at the Black Swan, the gambling club of which he is part-owner with Nicky Drake, a smooth, smooth operator. In Lapland, one always finds gambling clubs; also, drunken or corrupt night watchmen; a negligee; a ditch; a running man; a number of raincoats and hats; a man named "Johnny"; a man named "Doc," sometimes varied to "Dad"; an alcoholic; a penthouse; a beach shack; a tavern full of dumbbells; an armored car; a racetrack; a . . . . ; a shadowy staircase. These elements commonly participate in and enhance the effect of headlights reflected on wet urban streets.

THE WOMEN OF LAPLAND

When young, remarkably beautiful. When aged, negligible. This disparity passes without notice because few of the women of Lapland outlive their youth. They often hiss when they speak, or exhibit some other charming speech defect. Their reflections can be seen in rearview mirrors, the windows of apartments at night, the surfaces of slick wooden bars, the surfaces of lakes and pools, in the eyes of dead men. Carole Chandler likes the look of Bud Forrester, she "fancies" the "cut of his jib," but he strikes her as strangely inert, withdrawn, passive. Of course Carole takes these qualities both at face value and as a personal challenge. Nicky Drake wouldn't fuck this dame for, oh, a hundred million bucks, and his partner's obsession with her makes him . . . . When Carole slinks into the Black Swan, handsome Nicky looks away and frowns in disgust.

Having the life expectancy of mayflies, these women dress like dragonflies, for like cigarette-smoking and cocktail-drinking the wearing of dragonfly attire is a means of slowing time. The most gifted women in Lapland live in virtual dog years, or on a 7:1 ratio. Time is astonishingly relative for everyone in Lapland. That it is especially so for the women allows them a tremendous advantage. They can outthink any man who wanders into their crosshairs because they have a great deal more time to do their thinking in.

In Lapland, no woman ever speaks to another woman, there'd be no point in wasting valuable time like that. What would they talk about, their feelings? They already understand everything they have to know about their feelings. In Lapland, no woman ever speaks to a child, for they are all barren, although some may now and again pretend to be pregnant. It follows that there are no children in Lapland. However, in a location error that went largely unnoticed, Frank Bigelow once drove past an elementary school. In Lapland, women speak only to men, and these interchanges are deeply codified. The soundtrack (see below) becomes especially intrusive at such moments. It is understood that the woman is motivated by a private scheme, of which the man is entirely ignorant, though he may be suspicious, and it's always better, more dramatic, if he is.

Lapland women all have at least two names, the old one that got used up, and the new one, which gets a little more tarnished every day. Carole Chandler used to be Dorothy Lyons, back when she lived in Center City and engineered the moral ruin and financial collapse of Nicky Drake's best friend, Rip Murdock, the owner of the Orchid Club, a gambling establishment with a private membership.

Rip, a dandy at the time, used to . . . . , and Carol/ Dorothy, then a cocktail waitress at his club, ...
. . . .
. . . .
. . . .
. . . . his   beach   shack . .
. . . .
. . . . a moue . . . .
. . . . a
stranger with a gun . . . .
. . . .
. . . .
. . . . bloody rags . . . .
. . . .
. . . .
. . . . off the cliff . . . .
. . . .
. . . .
. . . .
. . . .
arched an eyebrow.

Once in her life, every woman in Lapland gazes through lowered eyelids at a man like Nicky, or Frank, or Rip, or even Doc/Dad (but never at a man like Bud), and says, "You and me, we're the same—a no-good piece of trash." In every case, this declaration is meant as, and is taken to be, a compliment.

SOCIAL CRITICISM

In Lapland, the spectator observes a world characterized by deliberate dislocations, complex and indirect narratives, flawed protagonists, ambiguous motives and resolutions, a fascination with death . . . . "the blood in her hair, the blood on the floor, the blood in her hair" . . . . and an atmosphere of nightmare.

When Rusty Fontaine blew into town, he took a room at the Mandarin hotel and started spreading his money around. He was so successful at exploiting middle-class greed and venality that in six months every square in Lapland owed him a fortune. To get out of debt, a consortium of the squares lured a banker, Chalmers Vermilyea, into an abandoned warehouse and, assisted by Rusty's luscious and treacherous female sidekick, Marie Gardner, persuaded him to embezzle . . . . sprinkled gasoline over the corpse . . . . off the cliff.

To the extent that Lapland is a style and not a genre, the vertiginous camera angles, broken shadows, neon-lit interiors, hairpin staircases, extreme high-angle long shots, graphics specific to entrapment, represent a radically disenchanted vision of postwar American life and values.

PSYCHOPATHS

Because paranoia is always justified in Lapland, psychopathology becomes an adaptive measure. Johnny O'Clock runs a gambling casino, the Velvet Deuce. He knew Bud Forrester in the war, when they fought across France, killing hundreds of Krauts in one bombed-out village

after another. Forrester was his sergeant, and he always respected the man. When one day O'Clock stops for gas at a Shell station on the edge of town, he recognizes his old friend in the station attendant and, acting on impulse, offers him a job in the casino. Forrester accepts, thinking that he might escape his obsession with Carole Chandler. Unknown to Forrester, Johnny O'Clock was unable to stop killing after returning to civilian life and now, under the cover of his job at the Velvet Deuce, hires himself out as a contract killer. He intends to recruit his old sergeant into . . . . velvet gloves, his trademark . . . .
. . . .
. . . .
. . . .
. . . Frank Bigelow . . . .
. . . . steam rising through the grates . . . .
. . . .
. . . .
. . . . to the beach shack . . . .
with the alcoholic security guard in a stupor . . . .
. . . .
. . . . aflame, the Dodge . . . .
. . . . two corpses in the back-seat and six thousand dollars in cash.

World War II, it must be remembered, serves as the unspoken background for these films and defines their emotional context. Eight percent of adult males in Lapland served as snipers in the war, and a good twelve percent have metal plates in their heads. These men drink too much and mutter to themselves. Because it gives them red-rimmed headaches, they detest big-band jazz, which they refer to as "that monkey music." They are prone to blackouts and spells of amnesia. They often marry blind women and/or nymphomaniacs. Unlike them, the former snipers display no visible emotion of any kind. The men with plates in their heads are completely devoted to the ex-snipers, who reward their loyalty with . . . .
. . . . with onions . . . .

Brace Bannister threw an old woman down the stairs. For pleasure, Johnny O'Clock shot Nelle Marchetti, a prostitute, in the head, and got clean away with it. Norman Clyde existed entirely in flashbacks.

Old Man Tierney poisoned a girl visiting from California and kept her severed hand in his pocket. Carole Chandler's husband, Smokey Chandler, molests small boys on "business trips" to Center City. Nicky Drake has assigned a number to everyone in the world. Carter Carpenter, the vice-mayor of Lapland, sleeps on a mattress stuffed with human hair.

PRIVATE EYES

Most noncriminal adult males in Lapland, apart from the doomed squares, are either policemen or private eyes. It is the job of the policemen to accept bribes and arrest the innocent. It is the job of the private investigators to discover bodies, to be interrogated, to drink from the bottle, to wear trench coats, to smoke all the time, to rebuff sexual invitations from females with charming lisps and hair that hangs, fetchingly, over one eye. The private eyes distrust authority, even their own. Nick Cochran is a rich private eye, and Eddie Willis, Mike Lane, and Tony Burke struggle to make the rent on their ugly little offices, where they sleep on . . . . Frank Bigelow hired Eddie Willis to find Bud Forrester, but Johnny O'Clock followed Eddie into an alley behind the Black Swan and shot him dead. In Nick Cochran's penthouse, Nicky Drake persuaded Rusty Fontaine to . . . . , but Marie Gardner, who was hiding on the . . . . , overheard and . . . . with Chalmers Vermilyea. Esther Vermilyea (no relation) made an anonymous call to Nick Cochran and . . . . two corpses in the backseat and a man with a plate in his head . . . . screaming and sobbing in the dark and rainy street.

Six thousand dollars blew away in the wind, and Tom Jardine . . . . for the first time since the landing at Anzio. Frank Bigelow could protect him no longer.

The armored car left the racetrack. The wrinkled old criminal mas-

termind known as Dad, whose . . . .
. . . . had never left him, led Carole Chandler up the shadowy stair-
case and . . . .
. . . . with a new negligee from the Smart
Shoppe.

THE ROLE OF ALAN LADD

Alan Ladd attracts the light.

THE OTHER ROLE OF ALAN LADD

He hovers at the edge of the screen, reminding you that you are, after
all, in Lapland, and in some sense always will be. When he smiles, his
hair gleams. The smile of Alan Ladd is both tough and wounded, an
effect akin to that of headlights reflected on a dark, rain-wet street in
downtown Lapland, his turf, his home territory. A sick, shameful nos-
talgia leaks from every frame, and it is abetted, magnified, amplified
by the swooning strings on the sound track. The sound track clings to
you like grease. You carry it with you out of the theater, and it swells
between the parked cars baking in the sunlight, indistinguishable from
the sounds in your head.

ALAN LADD CONSIDERED AS EXTENSION OF THE SOUND TRACK

His name is . . . . , says Alan Ladd, whose
name is Ed Adams, or Johnny Morrison. *That man's name is* . . . .
. . . . *He is known as Slim Dundee and Johnny O'Clock, also* . . .
. . . . *and* . . . . *His names surround him
like a cloud of flies. At the center of his names, he* . . . .
. . *and* . . . . A speaking shadow rises from between
the parked cars, and you wish for it to follow you home.

. . . . , Alan says in musical italics, coming along steadily behind. Sirens flare. A man with a gun flees into a
dark, sunlit alley. The hot white stripes of headlights reflected on rainy
asphalt shine and shine and shine on the street. Beneath a car further
down the block an oily shadow moves, and the name of that shadow
is . . . .

Forget him, Alan says. *Forget IT.* Underneath his warm deep grainy voice, that of a tender and exhausted god, a hundred stringed instruments swoop and twirl, following its music. *Do it for my sake. If not for . . . . . . sake, for mine. I know . . . . . . can hear me, kid. Kiddo. Little guy.*

I always liked . . . . . . , did you know that?

And at night, when . . . . lie in the bottom bunk with your face to the onyx window, only . . . . awake in all the house, a streak of blond hair shines in the corner of the window frame, the music stirs like the sound of death and heartbreak, and when his wounded face slips into view, he says, *A lot of this is gonna disappear forever. If you remember anything, remember that it's . . . . fault . . . . mber that. Little guy. If you can't remember that, remember me.*

Mr. Aickman's Air Rifle

1

On the twenty-first, or "Concierge," floor of New York's Governor General Hospital, located just south of midtown on Seventh Avenue, a glow of recessed lighting and a rank of framed, eye-level graphics (Twombly, Shapiro, Marden, Warhol) escort visitors from a brace of express elevators to the reassuring spectacle of a graceful cherrywood desk occupied by a red-jacketed gatekeeper named Mr. Singh. Like a hand cupped beneath a waiting elbow, this gentleman's enquiring yet deferential appraisal and his stupendous display of fresh flowers nudge the visitor over hushed beige carpeting and into the wood-paneled realm of Floor 21 itself.

First to appear is the nursing station, where in a flattering chiaroscuro efficient women occupy themselves with charts, telephones, and the ever-changing patterns traversing their computer monitors; directly ahead lies the first of the great, half-open doors of the residents' rooms or suites, each with its brass numeral and discreet nameplate. The great hallway extends some sixty yards, passing seven named and numbered doors on its way to a bright window with an uptown view. To the left, the hallway passes the front of the nurses' station and the four doors directly opposite, then divides. The shorter portion continues on to a large, south-facing window with a good prospect of the Hudson River, the longer defines the southern boundary of the station. Hung with an Elizabeth Murray lithograph and a Robert Mapplethorpe calla lily, an ochre wall then rises up to guide the hallway over another carpeted fifty feet to a long, narrow room. The small brass sign beside its wide, pebble-glass doors reads SALON.

The Salon is not a salon but a lounge, a rather makeshift lounge at that. At one end sits a good-sized television set; at the other, a green fabric sofa with two matching chairs. Midpoint in the room, which was intended for the comfort of stricken relatives and other visitors but has always been patronized chiefly by Floor 21's more ambulatory patients, stands a white-draped table equipped with coffee dispensers, stacks of cups and saucers, and cut-glass containers for sugar and artificial sweeteners. In the hours from four to six in the afternoon, platters laden with pastries and chocolates from the neighborhood's gourmet specialty shops appear, as if delivered by unseen hands, upon the table.

On an afternoon early in April, when during the hours in question the long window behind the table of goodies registered swift, unpredictable alternations of light and dark, the male patients who constituted four-fifths of the residents of Floor 21, all of them recent victims of atrial fibrillation or atrial flutter, which is to say sufferers from that dire annoyance in the life of a busy American male, nonfatal heart failure, the youngest a man of fifty-eight and the most senior twenty-two years older, found themselves once again partaking of the cream cakes and petit fours and reminding themselves that they had not, after all, undergone heart attacks. Their recent adventures had aroused in them an indulgent fatalism. After all, should the worst happen, which of course it would not, they were already at the epicenter of a swarm of cardiologists!

To varying degrees, these were men of accomplishment and achievement in their common profession, that of letters.

In descending order of age, the four men enjoying the amenities of the Salon were Max Baccarat, the much respected former president of Gladstone Books, the acquisition of which by a German conglomerate had lately precipitated his retirement; Anthony Flax, a self-described "critic" who had spent the past twenty years as a full-time book reviewer for a variety of periodicals and journals, a leisurely occupation he could afford due to his having been the husband, now for three years the widower, of a sugar-substitute heiress; William Messinger, a writer whose lengthy backlist of horror/mystery/suspense novels had been kept continuously in print for twenty-five years by the biannual appearance of yet another new astonishment; and Charles Chipp Traynor, child of a wealthy New England family, Harvard graduate, self-declared veteran of the Vietnam conflict, and author of four nonfiction books, also (alas) a notorious plagiarist.

The connections between these four men, no less complex and multi-layered than one would gather from their professional circumstances, had inspired some initial awkwardness on their first few encounters in the Salon, but a shared desire for the treats on offer had encouraged these gentlemen to reach the accommodation displayed on the afternoon in question. By silent agreement, Max Baccarat arrived first, a few minutes after opening, to avail himself of the greatest possible range of selection and the most comfortable seating position, which was on that end side of the sofa nearest the pebble-glass doors, where the cushion was a touch more yielding than its mate. Once the great publisher had installed himself to his satisfaction, Bill Messenger and Tony Flax happened in to browse over the day's bounty before seating themselves at a comfortable distance from each other. Invariably the last to arrive, Traynor edged around the door sometime around 4:15, his manner suggesting that he had wandered in by accident, probably in search of another room altogether. The loose, patterned hospital gown he wore fastened at neck and backside added to his air of inoffensiveness, and his round glasses and stooped shoulders gave him a generic resemblance to a creature from *The Wind in the Willows*.

Of the four, the plagiarist alone had surrendered to the hospital's tacit wishes concerning patients' in-house mode of dress. Over silk pajamas of a glaring, Greek-village white, Max Baccarat wore a dark, dashing navy blue dressing gown, reputedly a Christmas present from Graham Greene, which fell nearly to the tops of his velvet fox-head slippers. Over his own pajamas, of fine-combed baby-blue cotton instead of white silk, Tony Flax had buttoned a lightweight tan trench coat, complete with epaulettes and grenade rings. With his extra chins and florid complexion, he looked like a correspondent from a war conducted well within striking distance of hotel bars. Bill Messenger had taken one look at the flimsy shift offered him by the hospital staff and decided to stick, for as long as he could get away with it, to the pinstriped Armani suit and black loafers he had worn into the ER. His favorite men's stores delivered fresh shirts, socks, and underwear.

When Messenger's early, less successful books had been published by Max's firm, Tony Flax had given him consistently positive reviews; after Bill's defection to a better house and larger advances for more ambitious books, Tony's increasingly bored and dismissive reviews accused him of hubris, then ceased altogether. Messenger's last three novels had not been reviewed anywhere in the *Times*, an insult he attributed to Tony's malign influence over its current editors. Likewise, Max had published Chippie Traynor's first two anecdotal histories of World War I, the second of which had been considered for a Pulitzer Prize, then lost him to a more prominent publisher whose shrewd publicists had placed him on NPR, *The Today Show*, and—after the film deal for his third book—*Charlie Rose*. Bill had given blurbs to Traynor's first two books, and Tony Flax had hailed him as a great vernacular historian. Then, two decades later, a stunned graduate student in Texas discovered lengthy, painstakingly altered parallels between Traynor's books and the contents of several Ph.D. dissertations containing oral histories taken in the 1930s. Beyond that, the student found that perhaps a third of the personal histories had been invented, simply made up, like fiction.

Within days, the graduate student had detonated Chippie's reputation. One week after the detonation, his university placed him "on leave," a status assumed to be permanent. He had vanished into his family's Lincoln Log compound in Maine, not to be seen or heard from until the moment when Bill Messenger and Tony Flax, who had left open the Salon's doors the better to avoid conversation, had witnessed his sorry, supine figure being wheeled past. Max Baccarat was immediately informed of the scoundrel's arrival, and before the end of the day the legendary dressing gown, the trench coat, and the pinstriped suit had overcome their mutual resentments to form an alliance against the disgraced newcomer. There was nothing, they found, like a common enemy to smooth over complicated, even difficult relationships.

Chippie Traynor had not found his way to the lounge until the following day, and he had been accompanied by a tremulous elderly woman who with equal plausibility could have passed for either his mother or his wife. Sidling around the door at 4:15, he had taken in the trio watching him from the green sofa and chairs, blinked in disbelief and recognition, ducked his head even closer to his chest, and permitted his companion to lead him to a chair located a few feet from the television set. It was clear that he was struggling with the impulse to scuttle out of the room, never to reappear. Once deposited in the chair, he tilted his head upward and whispered a few words into the woman's ear. She moved toward the pastries, and at last he eyed his former compatriots.

"Well, well," he said. "Max, Tony, and Bill. What are you in for, anyway? Me, I passed out on the street in Boothbay Harbor and had to be airlifted in. Medevaced, like back in the day."

"These days, a lot of things must remind you of Vietnam, Chippie," Max said. "We're heart failure. You?"

"Atrial fib. Shortness of breath. Weaker than a baby. Fell down right in the street, boom. As soon as I get regulated, I'm supposed to have some sort of echo scan."

"Heart failure, all right," Max said. "Go ahead, have a cream cake. You're among friends."

"Somehow, I doubt that," Traynor said. He was breathing hard, and he gulped air as he waved the old woman further down the table, toward the chocolate slabs and puffs. He watched carefully as she selected a number of the little cakes. "Don't forget the decaf, will you, sweetie?"

The others waited for him to introduce his companion, but he sat in silence as she placed a plate of cakes and a cup of coffee on a stand next to the television set, then faded backward into a chair that seemed to have materialized, just for her, from the ether. Traynor lifted a forkful of shiny brown goo to his mouth, sucked it off the fork, and gulped coffee. Because of his long, thick nose and recessed chin, first the fork, then the cup seemed to disappear into the lower half of his face. He twisted his head in the general direction of his companion and said, "Health food, yum yum."

She smiled vaguely at the ceiling. Traynor turned back to face the other three men, who were staring open-eyed, as if at a performance of some kind.

"Thanks for all the cards and letters, guys. I loved getting your phone calls, too. Really meant a lot to me. Oh, sorry, I'm not being very polite, am I?"

"There's no need to be sarcastic," Max said.

"I suppose not. We were never friends, were we?"

"You were looking for a publisher, not a friend," Max said. "And we did quite well together, or so I thought, before you decided you needed greener pastures. Bill did the same thing to me, come to think of it. Of course, Bill actually wrote the books that came out under his name. For a publisher, that's quite a significant difference." (Several descendants of the Ph.D.s from whom Traynor had stolen material had initiated suits against his publishing houses, Gladstone House among them.)

"Do we have to talk about this?" asked Tony Flax. He rammed his hands in the pockets of his trench coat and glanced from side to side. "Ancient history, hmmm?"

"You're just embarrassed by the reviews you gave him," Bill said. "But everybody did the same thing, including me. What did I say about *The Middle of the Trenches*? 'The . . .' The what? 'The most truthful, in a way the most visionary book ever written about trench warfare.'"

"Jesus, you remember your *blurbs*?" Tony asked. He laughed and tried to draw the others in.

"I remember everything," said Bill Messenger. "Curse of being a novelist—great memory, lousy sense of direction."

"You always remembered how to get to the bank," Tony said.

"Lucky me, I didn't have to marry it," Bill said.

"Are you accusing me of marrying for money?" Tony said, defending himself by the usual tactic of pretending that what was commonly accepted was altogether unthinkable. "Not that I have any reason to defend myself against you, Messenger. As that famous memory of yours should recall, I was one of the first people to support your work."

From nowhere, a reedy English female voice said, "I did enjoy reading your reviews of Mr. Messenger's early novels, Mr. Flax. I'm sure that's why I went round to our little bookshop and purchased them. They weren't at all my usual sort of *thing*, you know, but you made them sound . . . I think the word would be *imperative*."

Max, Tony, and Bill peered past Charles Chipp Traynor to get a good look at his companion. For the first time, they took in that she was wearing a long, loose collection of elements that suggested feminine literary garb of the 1920s: a hazy, rather shimmery woolen cardigan over a white, high-buttoned blouse, pearls, an ankle-length heather skirt, and low-heeled black shoes with laces. Her long, sensitive nose pointed up, exposing the clean line of her jaw; her lips twitched in what might have been amusement. Two things struck the men staring at her: that this woman looked a bit familiar, and that in spite of her age and general oddness, she would have to be described as beautiful.

"Well, yes," Tony said. "Thank you. I believe I was trying to express something of the sort. They were books . . . well. Bill, you never understood this, I think, but I felt they were books that deserved to be read. For their workmanship, their modesty, what I thought was their actual decency."

"You mean they did what you expected them to do," Bill said.

"Decency is an uncommon literary virtue," said Traynor's companion.

"Thank you, yes," Tony said.

"But not a very interesting one, really," Bill said. "Which probably explains why it isn't all that common."

"I think you are correct, Mr. Messenger, to imply that decency is more valuable in the realm of personal relations. And for the record, I do feel your work since then has undergone a general improvement. Perhaps Mr. Flax's limitations do not permit him to appreciate your progress." She paused. There was a dangerous smile on her face. "Of course you can hardly be said to have improved to the extent claimed in your latest round of interviews."

In the moment of silence that followed, Max Baccarat looked from one of his new allies to the other and found them in a state too reflective for commentary. He cleared his throat. "Might we have the honor of an introduction, Madame? Chippie seems to have forgotten his manners."

"My name is of no importance," she said, only barely favoring him with the flicker of a glance. "And Mr. Traynor has a thorough knowledge of my feelings on the matter."

"There's two sides to every story," Chippie said. "It may not be grammar, but it's the truth."

"Oh, there are many more than that," said his companion, smiling again.

"Darling, would you help me return to my room?"

Chippie extended an arm, and the Englishwoman floated to her feet, cradled his root-like fist against the side of her chest, nodded to the gaping men, and gracefully conducted her charge from the room.

"So who the fuck was *that*?" said Max Baccarat.

2

Certain rituals structured the nighttime hours on Floor 21. At 8:30 p.m., blood pressure was taken and evening medications administered by Tess Corrigan, an Irish softie with a saggy gut, an alcoholic, angina-ridden husband, and an understandable tolerance for misbehavior. Tess herself sometimes appeared to be mildly intoxicated. Class resentment caused her to treat Max a touch brusquely, but Tony's trench coat amused her to wheezy laughter. After Bill Messenger had signed two books for her niece, a devoted fan, Tess had allowed him to do anything he cared to, including taking illicit journeys downstairs to the gift shop. "Oh, Mr. Messenger," she had said, "a fella with your gifts, the books you could write about this place." Three hours after Tess's departure, a big, heavily dreadlocked nurse with an island accent surged into the patients' rooms to awaken them for the purpose of distributing tranquilizers and knockout pills. Because she resembled a greatly inflated, ever-simmering Whoopi Goldberg, Max, Tony, and Bill referred to this terrifying and implacable figure as "Molly." (Molly's real name, printed on the ID card attached to a sash used as a waistband, was permanently concealed behind beaded swags and little hanging pouches.) At six in the morning, Molly swept in again, wielding the blood-pressure mechanism like an angry deity maintaining a good grip on a sinner. At the end of her shift, she came wrapped in a strong, dark scent, suggestive of forest fires in underground crypts. The three literary gentlemen found this aroma disturbingly erotic.

On the morning after the appearance within the Salon of Charles Chipp Traynor and his disconcerting muse, Molly raked Bill with a look of pity and scorn as she trussed his upper arm and strangled it by pumping a rubber bulb. Her crypt-fire odor seemed particularly smoky.

"What?" he asked.

Molly shook her massive head. "Toddle, toddle, toddle, you must believe you're the new postman in this beautiful neighborhood of ours."

Terror seized his gut. "I don't think I know what you're talking about."

Molly chuckled and gave the bulb a final squeeze, causing his arm to go numb from bicep to his fingertips. "Of course not. But you do know that we have no limitations on visiting hours up here in our paradise, don't you?"

"Um," he said.

"Then let me tell you something you do not know, Mr. Postman. Miz LaValley in 21R-12 passed away last night. I do not imagine you ever took it upon yourself to pay the poor woman a social call. And *that*, Mr. Postman, means that you, Mr. Baccarat, Mr. Flax, and our new addition, Mr. Traynor, are now the only patients on Floor 21."

"Ah," he said.

As soon as she left his room, he showered and dressed in the previous day's clothing, eager to get out into the corridor and check on the

conditions in 21R-14, Chippie Traynor's room, for it was what he had
seen there in the hours between Tess Corrigan's florid departure and
Molly Goldberg's first drive-by shooting that had led to his becoming
the floor's postman.

It had been just before nine in the evening, and something had
urged him to take a final turn around the floor before surrendering
himself to the hateful "gown" and turning off his lights. His route took
him past the command center, where the Night Visitor, scowling over
a desk too small for her, made grim notations on a chart, and down
the corridor toward the window looking out toward the Hudson River
and the great harbor. Along the way he passed 21R-14, where muffled
noises had caused him to look in. From the corridor, he could see the
bottom third of the plagiarist's bed, on which the sheets and blanket
appeared to be writhing, or at least shifting about in a conspicuous
manner. Messenger noticed a pair of black, lace-up women's shoes on
the floor near the bottom of the bed. An untidy heap of clothing lay
beside the inturned shoes. For a few seconds ripe with shock and envy,
he had listened to the soft noises coming from the room. Then he
whirled around and rushed toward his allies' chambers.

"Who *is* that dame?" Max Baccarat had asked, essentially repeating
the question he had asked earlier that day. "*What* is she? That miserable
Traynor, God damn him to hell, may he have a heart attack and die. A
woman like that, who cares how old she is?"

Tony Flax had groaned in disbelief and said, "I swear, that woman
is either the ghost of Virginia Woolf or her direct descendant. All my
life, I had the hots for Virginia Woolf, and now she turns up with that
ugly crook, Chippie Traynor? Get out of here, Bill, I have to strategize."

3

At 4:15, the three conspirators pretended not to notice the plagiarist's
furtive, animal-like entrance to the Salon. Max Baccarat's silvery hair,
cleansed, stroked, clipped, buffed, and shaped during an emergency
session with a hair therapist named Mr. Keith, seemed to glow with
a virile inner light as he settled into the comfortable part of the sofa
and organized his decaf cup and plate of chocolates and little cakes
as if preparing soldiers for battle. Tony Flax's rubber chins shone a
twice-shaved red, and his glasses sparkled. Beneath the hem of the

trench coat, which appeared to have been ironed, colorful argyle socks descended from just below his lumpy knees to what seemed to be a pair of nifty two-tone shoes. Beneath the jacket of his pinstriped suit, Bill Messenger sported a brand-new, high-collared black silk T-shirt delivered by courier that morning from Sixty-fifth and Madison. Thus attired, the longer-term residents of Floor 21 seemed lost as much in self-admiration as in the political discussion under way when at last they allowed themselves to acknowledge Chippie's presence. Max's eye skipped over Traynor and wandered toward the door.

"Will your lady friend be joining us?" he asked. "I thought she made some really very valid points yesterday, and I'd enjoy hearing what she has to say about our situation in Iraq. My two friends here are simple-minded liberals, you can never get anything sensible out of them."

"You wouldn't like what she'd have to say about Iraq," Traynor said. "And neither would they."

"Know her well, do you?" Tony asked.

"You could say that." Traynor's gown slipped as he bent over the table to pump coffee into his cup from the dispenser, and the three other men hastily turned their glances elsewhere.

"Tie that up, Chippie, would you?" Bill asked. "It's like a view of the Euganean Hills."

"Then look somewhere else. I'm getting some coffee, and then I have to pick out a couple of these yum-yums."

"You're alone today, then?" Tony asked.

"Looks like it."

"By the way," Bill said, "you were entirely right to point out that nothing is really as simple as it seems. There *are* more than two sides to every issue. I mean, wasn't that the point of what we were saying about Iraq?"

"To you, maybe," Max said. "You'd accept two sides as long as they were both printed in *The Nation*."

"Anyhow," Bill said, "please tell your friend that the next time she cares to visit this hospital, we'll try to remember what she said about decency."

"What makes you think she's going to come here again?"

"She seemed very fond of you," Tony said.

"The lady mentioned your limitations." Chippie finished assembling his assortment of treats and at last refastened his gaping robe. "I'm surprised you have any interest in seeing her again."

Tony's cheeks turned a deeper red. "All of us have limitations, I'm sure. In fact, I was just remembering . . ."

"Oh?" Chippie lifted his snout and peered through his little lenses. "Were you? What, specifically?"

"Nothing," said Tony. "I shouldn't have said anything. Sorry."

"Did any of you know Mrs. LaValley, the lady in 21R-12?" Bill asked. "She died last night. Apart from us, she was the only other person on the floor."

"I knew Edie LaValley," Chippie said. "In fact, my friend and I dropped in and had a nice little chat with her just before dinnertime last night. I'm glad I had a chance to say goodbye to the old girl."

"Edie LaValley?" Max said. "Hold on. I seem to remember . . ."

"Wait, I do too," Bill said. "Only . . ."

"I know, she was that girl who worked for Nick Wheadle over at Viking, thirty years ago, back when Wheadle was everybody's golden boy," Tony said. "Stupendous girl. She got married to him and was Edith Wheadle for a while, but after the divorce she went back to her old name. We went out for a couple of months in 1983, '84. What happened to her after that?"

"She spent six years doing research for me," Traynor said. "She wasn't my *only* researcher, because I generally had three of them on the payroll, not to mention a couple of graduate students. Edie was very good at the job, though. Extremely conscientious."

"And knockout, drop-dead gorgeous," Tony said. "At least before she fell into Nick Wheadle's clutches."

"I didn't know you used so many researchers," Max said. "Could that be how you wound up quoting all those . . . ?"

"Deliberately misquoting, I suppose you mean," Chippie said. "But the answer is no." A fat, sugarcoated square of sponge cake disappeared beneath his nose.

"But Edie Wheadle," Max said in a reflective voice. "By God, I think I . . ."

"Think nothing of it," Traynor said. "That's what she did."

"Edie must have looked very different toward the end," said Tony. He sounded almost hopeful. "Twenty years, illness, all of that."

"My friend and I thought she looked much the same." Chippie's mild, creaturely face swung toward Tony Flax. "Weren't you about to tell us something?"

Tony flushed again. "No, not really."

"Perhaps an old memory resurfaced. That often happens on a night when someone in the vicinity dies—the death seems to awaken something."

"Edie's death certainly seemed to have awakened you," Bill said. "Didn't you ever hear of closing your door?"

"The nurses waltz right in anyhow, and there are no locks," Traynor said. "Better to be frank about matters, especially on Floor 21. It looks as though Max has something on his mind."

"Yes," Max said. "If Tony doesn't feel like talking, I will. Last night, an old memory of mine resurfaced, as Chippie puts it, and I'd like to get it off my chest, if that's the appropriate term."

"Good man," Traynor said. "Have another of those delicious little yummies and tell us all about it."

"This happened back when I was a little boy," Max said, wiping his lips with a crisp linen handkerchief.

Bill Messenger and Tony Flax seemed to go very still.

"I was raised in Pennsylvania, up in the Susquehanna Valley area. It's strange country, a little wilder and more backward than you'd expect, a little hillbillyish, especially once you get back in the Endless Mountains. My folks had a little store that sold everything under the sun, it seemed to me, and we lived in the building next door, close to the edge of town. Our town was called Manship, not that you can find it on any map. We had a one-room schoolhouse, an Episcopalian church and a Unitarian church, a feed and grain store, a place called the Lunch Counter, a Tract House, and a tavern called the Rusty Dusty, where, I'm sad to say, my father spent far too much of his time.

"When he came home loaded, as happened just about every other night, he was in a foul mood. It was mainly guilt, d'you see, because my mother had been slaving away in the store for hours, plus making dinner, and she was in a rage, which only made him feel worse. All he really wanted to do was to beat himself up, but I was an easy target, so he beat me up instead. Nowadays, we'd call it child abuse, but back then, in a place like Manship, it was just normal parenting, at least for a drunk. I wish I could tell you fellows that everything turned out well, and that my father sobered up, and we reconciled, and I forgave him, but none of that happened. Instead, he got meaner and meaner, and we got poorer and poorer. I learned to hate the old bastard, and I still hated him when a traveling junk wagon ran over him, right there in front of the Rusty Dusty, when I was eleven years old. 1935, the height of the Great Depression. He was lying passed out in the street, and the junkman never saw him.

"Now, I was determined to get out of that godforsaken little town, and out of the Susquehanna Valley and the Endless Mountains, and obviously I did, because here I am today, with an excellent place in the world, if I might pat myself on the back a little bit. What I did was, I managed to keep the store going even while I went to the high school in the next town, and then I got a scholarship to U. Penn., where I waited on tables and tended bar and sent money back to my mother. Two days after I graduated, she died of a heart attack. That was her reward.

"I bought a bus ticket to New York. Even though I was never a great reader, I liked the idea of getting into the book business. Everything that happened after that you could read about in old copies of *Publishers Weekly*. Maybe one day I'll write a book about it all.

"If I do, I'll never put in what I'm about to tell you now. It slipped my mind completely—the whole thing. You'll realize how bizarre that is after I'm done. I forgot all about it! Until about three this morning, that is, when I woke up too scared to breathe, my heart going *bump bump*, and the sweat pouring out of me. Every little bit of this business just came *back* to me, I mean everything, every goddamned little tiny detail . . ."

He looked at Bill and Tony. "What? You two guys look like you should be back in the ER."

"Every detail?" Tony said. "It's . . ."

"You woke up then too?" Bill asked him.

"Are you two knotheads going to let me talk, or do you intend to keep interrupting?"

"I just wanted to ask this one thing, but I changed my mind," Tony said. "Sorry, Max. I shouldn't have said anything. It was a crazy idea. Sorry."

"Was your Dad an alcoholic too?" Bill asked Tony Flax.

Tony squeezed up his face, said, "Aaaah," and waggled one hand in the air. "I don't like the word 'alcoholic.' "

"Yeah," Bill said. "All right."

"I guess the answer is, you're going to keep interrupting."

"No, please, Max, go on," Bill said.

Max frowned at both of them, then gave a dubious glance to Chippie Traynor, who stuffed another tiny cream cake into his maw and smiled around it.

"Fine. I don't know why I want to tell you about this anyhow. It's not like I actually *understand* it, as you'll see, and it's kind of ugly and kind of scary—I guess what amazes me is that I just remembered it all, or that I managed to put it out of my mind for nearly seventy years, one or the other. But you know? It's like, it's real even if it never happened, or even if I dreamed the whole thing."

"This story wouldn't happen to involve a house, would it?" Tony asked.

"Most goddamned stories involve houses," Max said. "Even a lousy book critic ought to know that."

"Tony knows that," Chippie said. "See his ridiculous coat? That's a house. Isn't it, Tony?"

"You know what this is," Tony said. "It's a *trench coat*, a real one. Only from World War II, not World War I. It used to belong to my father. He was a hero in the war."

"As I was about to say," Max said, looking around and continuing only when the other three were paying attention, "when I woke up in the middle of the night I could remember the feel of the old blanket on my bed, the feel of pebbles and earth on my bare feet when I ran to the outhouse, I could remember the way my mother's scrambled eggs tasted. The whole anxious thing I had going on inside me while my mother was making breakfast.

"I was going to go off by myself in the woods. That was all right with my mother. At least it got rid of me for the day. But what she didn't know was that I had decided to steal one of the guns in the case at the back of the store.

"And you know what? She didn't pay any attention to the guns. About half of them belonged to people who swapped them for food because guns were all they had left to barter with. My mother hated the whole idea. And my father was in a fog until he could get to the tavern, and after that he couldn't think straight enough to remember how many guns were supposed to be back in that case. Anyhow, for the past few days, I'd had my eye on an over-under shotgun that used to belong to a farmer called Hakewell, and while my mother wasn't watching I nipped in back and took it out of the case. Then I stuffed my pockets with shells, ten of them. There was something going on way back in the woods, and while I wanted to keep my eye on it, I wanted to be able to protect myself, too, in case anything got out of hand."

Bill Messenger jumped to his feet and for a moment seemed pre-occupied with brushing what might have been pastry crumbs off the bottom of his suit jacket. Max Baccarat frowned at him, then glanced down at the skirts of his dressing gown in a brief inspection. Bill con-tinued to brush off imaginary particles of food, slowly turning in a circle as he did so.

"There is something you wish to communicate," Max said. "The odd thing, you know, is that for the moment, you see, I thought communi-cation was in my hands."

Bill stopped fiddling with his jacket and regarded the old publisher with his eyebrows tugged toward the bridge of his nose and his mouth a thin, downturned line. He placed his hands on his hips. "I don't know what you're doing, Max, and I don't know where you're getting this. But I certainly wish you'd stop."

"What are you talking about?"

"He's right, Max," said Tony Flax.

"You jumped-up little fop," Max said, ignoring Tony. "You damned little show pony. What's your problem? You haven't told a good story in the past ten years, so listen to mine, you might learn something."

"You know what you are?" Bill asked him. "Twenty years ago, you used to be a decent second-rate publisher. Unfortunately, it's been all downhill from there. Now you're not even a third-rate publisher, you're a sellout. You took the money and went on the lam. Morally, you don't exist at all. You're a fancy dressing gown. And by the way, Graham Greene didn't give it to you, because Graham Greene wouldn't have given you a glass of water on a hot day."

Both of them were panting a bit and trying not to show it. Like a dog trying to choose between masters, Tony Flax swung his head from one to the other. In the end, he settled on Max Baccarat. "I don't really get it either, you know, but I think you should stop, too."

"Nobody cares what you think," Max told him. "Your brain dropped dead the day you swapped your integrity for a mountain of coffee sweetener."

"You did marry for money, Flax," Bill Messinger said. "Let's try being honest, all right? You sure as hell didn't fall in love with her beautiful face."

"And how about you, Traynor?" Max shouted. "I suppose you think I should stop, too."

"Nobody cares what I think," Chippie said. "I'm the lowest of the low. People despise me."

"First of all," Bill said, "if you want to talk about details, Max, you ought to get them *right*. It wasn't an 'over-under shotgun,' whatever the hell that is, it was a—"

"His name wasn't Hakewell," Tony said. "It was Hackman, like the actor."

"It wasn't Hakewell or Hackman," Bill said. "It started with an A."

"But there was a *house*," Tony said. "You know, I think my father probably was an alcoholic. His personality never changed, though. He was always a mean son of a bitch, drunk or sober."

"Mine, too," said Bill. "Where are you from, anyhow, Tony?"

"A little town in Oregon, called Milton. How about you?"

"Rhinelander, Wisconsin. My dad was the chief of police. I suppose there were lots of woods around Milton."

"We might as well have been in a forest. You?"

"The same."

"I'm from Boston, but we spent the summers in Maine," Chippie said. "You know what Maine is? Eighty percent woods. There are places in Maine, the roads don't even have names."

"There was a *house*," Tony Flax insisted. "Back in the woods, and it didn't belong there. Nobody builds houses in the middle of the woods, miles away from everything, without even a road to use, not even a road without a name."

"This can't be real," Bill said. "I had a house, you had a house, and I bet Max had a house, even though he's so long-winded he hasn't gotten to it yet. I had an air rifle, Max had a shotgun, what did you have?"

"My dad's .22," Tony said. "Just a little thing—around us, nobody took a .22 all that seriously."

Max was looking seriously disgruntled. "What, we all had the same *dream*?"

"You said it wasn't a dream," said Chippie Traynor. "You said it was a memory."

"It felt like a memory, all right," Tony said. "Just the way Max described it—the way the ground felt under my feet, the smell of my mother's cooking."

"I wish your lady friend was here now, Traynor," Max said. "She'd be able to explain what's going on, wouldn't she?"

"I have a number of lady friends," Chippie said, calmly stuffing a little glazed cake into his mouth.

"All right, Max," Bill said. "Let's explore this. You come across this big house, right? And there's someone in it?"

"Eventually, there is," Max said, and Tony Flax nodded.

"Right. And you can't even tell what age he is—or even if it *is* a he, right?"

"It was hiding in the back of a room," Tony says. "When I thought it was a girl, it really scared me. I didn't want it to be a girl."

"I didn't, either," Max said. "Oh—imagine how that would feel, a girl hiding in the shadows at the back of a room."

"Only this never happened," Bill said. "If we all seem to remember this bizarre story, then none of us is really remembering it."

"Okay, but it was a boy," Tony said. "And he got older."

"Right there in that house," said Max. "I thought it was like watching my damnable father grow up right in front of my eyes. In what, six weeks?"

"About that," Tony said.

"And him in there all alone," said Bill. "Without so much as a stick of furniture. I thought that was one of the things that made it so frightening."

"Scared the shit out of me," Tony said. "When my dad came back from the war, sometimes he put on his uniform and tied us to the chairs. Tied us to the chairs!"

"I didn't think it was really going to injure him," Bill said.

"I didn't even think I'd hit him," Tony said.

"I knew damn well I'd hit him," Max said. "I wanted to blow his head off. But my dad lived another three years, and then the junkman finally ran him over."

"Max," Tony said, "you mentioned there was a Tract House in Manship. What's a Tract House?"

"It was where they printed the religious tracts, you ignoramus. You could go in there and pick them up for free. All of this was like child abuse, I'm telling you. Spare-the-rod stuff."

"It was like his eye exploded," Bill said. Absentmindedly, he took one of the untouched pastries from Max's plate and bit into it.

Max stared at him.

"They didn't change the goodies this morning," Bill said. "This thing is a little stale."

"I prefer my pastries stale," said Chippie Traynor.

"I prefer to keep mine for myself, and not have them lifted off my plate," said Max, sounding as though something were caught in his throat.

"The bullet went straight through the left lens of his glasses and right into his head," said Tony. "And when he raised his head, his eye was full of blood."

"Would you look out that window?" Max said in a loud voice.

Bill Messenger and Tony Flax turned to the window, saw nothing special—perhaps a bit more haze in the air than they expected—and looked back at the old publisher.

"Sorry," Max said. He passed a trembling hand over his face. "I think I'll go back to my room."

4

"Nobody visits me," Bill Messenger said to Tess Corrigan. She was taking his blood pressure, and appeared to be having a little trouble getting accurate numbers. "I don't even really remember how long I've been here, but I haven't had a single visitor."

"Haven't you now?" Tess squinted at the blood pressure tube, sighed, and once again pumped the ball and tightened the band around his arm. Her breath contained a pure, razor-sharp whiff of alcohol.

"It makes me wonder, do I have any friends?"

Tess grunted with satisfaction and scribbled numbers on his chart. "Writers lead lonely lives," she told him. "Most of them aren't fit for human company, anyhow." She patted his wrist. "You're a lovely specimen, though."

"Tess, how long have I been here?"

"Oh, it was only a little while ago," she said. "And I believe it was raining at the time."

After she left, Bill watched television for a little while, but television, a frequent and dependable companion in his earlier life, seemed to have become intolerably stupid. He turned it off and for a time flipped through the pages of the latest book by a highly regarded contemporary novelist several decades younger than himself. He had bought the book before going into the hospital, thinking that during his stay he would have enough uninterrupted time to dig into the experience so many others had described as rich, complex, and marvelously nuanced, but he was having problems getting through it. The book bored him. The people were loathsome and the style was gelid. He kept wishing he had brought along some uncomplicated and professional trash he could use as a palate cleanser. By 10:00, he was asleep.

At 11:30, a figure wrapped in cold air appeared in his room, and he woke up as she approached. The woman coming nearer in the darkness must have been Molly, the Jamaican nurse who always charged in at this hour, but she did not give off Molly's arousing scent of fires in underground crypts. She smelled of damp weeds and muddy riverbanks. Bob did not want this version of Molly to get any closer to him than the end of his bed, and with his heart beating so violently that he could feel the limping rhythm of his heart, he commanded her to stop. She instantly obeyed.

He pushed the button to raise the head of his bed and tried to make her out as his body folded upright. The river smell had intensified, and cold air streamed toward him. He had no desire at all to turn on any of the three lights at his disposal. Dimly, he could make out a thin, tallish figure with dead hair plastered to her face, wearing what seemed to be a long cardigan sweater, soaked through and (he thought) dripping onto the floor. In this figure's hands was a fat, unjacketed book stained dark by her wet fingers.

"I don't want you here," he said. "And I don't want to read that book, either. I've already read everything you ever wrote, but that was a long time ago."

The drenched figure glided forward and deposited the book between his feet. Terrified that he might recognize her face, Bill clamped his eyes shut and kept them shut until the odors of river water and mud had vanished from the air.

When Molly burst into the room to gather the new day's information the next morning, Bill Messenger realized that his night's visitation could have occurred only in a dream. Here was the well-known, predictable world around him, and every inch of it was a profound relief to him. Bill took in his bed, the little nest of monitors ready to be called upon should an emergency take place, his television and its remote control device, the door to his spacious bathroom, the door to the hallway, as ever half-open. On the other side of his bed lay the long window, now curtained for the sake of the night's sleep. And here, above all, was Molly, a one-woman Reality Principle, exuding the rich odor of burning graves as she tried to cut off his circulation with a blood-pressure machine. The bulk and massivity of her upper arms suggested that Molly's own blood pressure would have to be read by means of some other technology, perhaps steam gauge. The whites of her eyes shone with a faint trace of pink, leading Bill to speculate for a moment of wild improbability if the ferocious night nurse indulged in marijuana.

"You're doing well, Mr. Postman," she said. "Making good progress."

"I'm glad to hear it," he said. "When do you think I'll be able to go home?"

"That is for the doctors to decide, not me. You'll have to bring it up with them." From a pocket hidden beneath her swags and pouches, she produced a white paper cup half-filled with pills and capsules of varying sizes and colors. She thrust it at him. "Morning meds. Gulp them down like a good boy, now." Her other hand held out a small plastic bottle of Poland Spring water, the provenance of which reminded Messenger of what Chippie Traynor had said about Maine. Deep woods, roads without names . . .

He upended the cup over his mouth, opened the bottle of water, and managed to get all his pills down at the first try.

Molly whirled around to leave with her usual sense of having had more than enough of her time wasted by the likes of him, and was halfway to the door before he remembered something that had been on his mind for the past few days.

"I haven't seen the *Times* since I don't remember when," he said. "Could you please get me a copy? I wouldn't even mind one that's a couple of days old."

Molly gave him a long, measuring look, then nodded her head. "Because many of our people find them so upsetting, we tend not to get the newspapers up here. But I'll see if I can locate one for you." She moved ponderously to the door and paused to look back at him again just before she walked out. "By the way, from now on you and your friends will have to get along without Mr. Traynor's company."

"Why?" Bill asked. "What happened to him?"

"Mr. Traynor is . . . gone, sir."

"Chippie died, you mean? When did that happen?" With a shudder, he remembered the figure from his dream. The smell of rotting weeds and wet riverbank awakened within him, and he felt as if she were once again standing before him.

"Did I say he was dead? What I said was, he is . . . *gone.*"

For reasons he could not identify, Bill Messenger did not go through the morning's rituals with his usual impatience. He felt slow-moving, reluctant to engage the day. In the shower, he seemed barely able to raise his arms. The water seemed brackish, and his soap all but refused to lather. The towels were stiff and thin, like the cheap towels he remembered from his youth. After he had succeeded in drying off at least most of the easily reachable parts of his body, he sat on his bed and listened to the breath laboring in and out of his body. Without him noticing, the handsome pinstriped suit had become as wrinkled and tired as he felt himself to be, and besides that he seemed to be out of clean shirts. He pulled a dirty one from the closet. His swollen feet took some time to ram into his black loafers.

Armored at last in the costume of a great worldly success, Bill stepped out into the great corridor with a good measure of his old dispatch. He wished Max Baccarat had not called him a "jumped-up little fop" and a "damned little show pony" the other day, for he genuinely enjoyed good clothing, and it hurt him to think that others might take this simple pleasure, which after all did contain a moral element, as a sign of vanity. On the other hand, he should have thought twice before telling Max that he was a third-rate publisher and a sellout. Everybody knew that robe hadn't been a gift from Graham Greene, though. That myth represented nothing more than Max Baccarat's habit of portraying and presenting himself as an old-line publishing grandee, like Alfred Knopf.

The nursing station—what he liked to think of as "the command center"—was oddly understaffed this morning. In a landscape of empty desks and unattended computer monitors, Molly sat on a pair of stools she had placed side by side, frowning as ever down at some form she was obliged to work through. Bill nodded at her and received the non-response he had anticipated. Instead of turning left toward the Salon as he usually did, Bill decided to stroll over to the elevators and the cherrywood desk where diplomatic, red-jacketed Mr. Singh guided newcomers past his display of Casablanca lilies, tea roses, and lupines. On his perambulations through the halls, he often passed through Mr. Singh's tiny realm, and he found the man a kindly, reassuring presence.

Today, though, Mr. Singh seemed not to be on duty, and the great glass vase had been removed from his desk. OUT OF ORDER signs had been taped to the elevators.

Feeling a vague sense of disquiet, Bill retraced his steps and walked past the side of the nursing station to embark upon the long corridor that led to the north-facing window. Max Baccarat's room lay down this corridor, and Bill thought he might pay a call on the old gent. He could apologize for the insults he had given him, and perhaps receive an apology in return. Twice, Baccarat had thrown the word "little" at him, and Bill's cheeks stung as if he had been slapped. About the story, or the memory, or whatever it had been, however, Bill intended to say nothing. He did not believe that he, Max, and Tony Flax had dreamed of the same bizarre set of events, nor that they had experienced these decidedly dreamlike events in youth. The illusion that they had done so had been inspired by proximity and daily contact. The world of Floor 21 was as hermetic as a prison.

He came to Max's room and knocked at the half-open door. There was no reply. "Max?" he called out. "Feel like having a visitor?"

In the absence of a reply, he thought that Max might be asleep. It would do no harm to check on his old acquaintance. How odd, it occurred to him, to think that he and Max had both had relations with little Edie Wheadle. And Tony Flax, too. And that she should have died on this floor, unknown to them! *There* was someone to whom he rightly could have apologized—at the end, he had treated her quite badly. She had been the sort of girl, he thought, who almost expected to be treated badly. But far from being an excuse, that was the opposite, an indictment.

Putting inconvenient Edie Wheadle out of his mind, Bill moved past the bathroom and the "reception" area into the room proper, there to find Max Baccarat not in bed as he had expected, but beyond it and seated in one of the low, slightly cantilevered chairs, which he had turned to face the window.

"Max?"

The old man did not acknowledge his presence in any way. Bill noticed that he was not wearing the splendid blue robe, only his white pajamas, and his feet were bare. Unless he had fallen asleep, he was staring at the window and appeared to have been doing so for some time. His silvery hair was mussed and stringy. As Bill approached, he took in the rigidity of Max's head and neck, the stiff tension in his shoulders. He came around the foot of the bed and at last saw the whole of the old man's body, stationed sideways to him as it faced the window. Max was gripping the arms of the chair and leaning forward. His mouth hung open, and his lips had been drawn back. His eyes, too, were open, hugely, as they stared straight ahead.

With a little thrill of anticipatory fear, Bill glanced at the window. What he saw, haze shot through with streaks of light, could hardly have brought Max Baccarat to this pitch. His face seemed rigid with terror. Then Bill realized that this had nothing to do with terror, and Max had suffered a great, paralyzing stroke. That was the explanation for the pathetic scene before him. He jumped to the side of the bed and pushed the call button for the nurse. When he did not get an immediate response, he pushed it again, twice, and held the button down for several seconds. Still no soft footsteps came from the corridor.

A folded copy of the *Times* lay on Max's bed, and with a sharp, almost painful sense of hunger for the million vast and minuscule dramas taking place outside Governor General, he realized that what he had said to Molly was no more than the literal truth: it seemed weeks since he had seen a newspaper. With the justification that Max would have no use for it, Bill snatched up the paper and felt, deep in the core of his being, a real greed for its contents—devouring the columns of print would be akin to gobbling up great bits of the world. He tucked the neat, folded package of the *Times* under his arm and left the room.

"Nurse," he called. It came to him that he had never learned the real name of the woman they called Molly Goldberg. "Hello? There's a man in trouble down here!"

He walked quickly down the hallway in what he perceived as a deep, unsettling silence. "Hello, nurse!" he called, at least in part to hear at least the sound of his own voice.

When Bill reached the deserted nurses' station, he rejected the impulse to say, "Where is everybody?" The Night Visitor no longer occupied her pair of stools, and the usual chiaroscuro had deepened into a murky darkness. It was as though they had pulled the plugs and stolen away.

"I don't get this," Bill said. "*Doctors* might bail, but nurses don't."

He looked up and down the corridor and saw only a gray carpet and a row of half-open doors. Behind one of those doors sat Max Baccarat, who had once been something of a friend. Max was destroyed, Bill thought; damage so severe could not be repaired. Like a greasy film, the sense descended upon him that he was wasting his time. If the doctors and nurses were elsewhere, as seemed the case, nothing could be done for Max until their return. Even after that, in all likelihood very little could be done for poor old Max. His heart failure had been a symptom of a wider systemic distress.

But still. He could not just walk away and ignore Max's plight. Messenger turned around and paced down the corridor to the door where the nameplate read ANTHONY FLAX. "Tony," he said. "Are you in there? I think Max had a stroke."

He rapped on the door and pushed it all the way open. Dreading what he might find, he walked into the room. "Tony?" He already knew the room was empty, and when he was able to see the bed, all was as he had expected: an empty bed, an empty chair, a blank television screen, and blinds pulled down to keep the day from entering.

Bill left Tony's room, turned left, then took the hallway that led past the Salon. A man in an unclean janitor's uniform, his back to Bill, was removing the Mapplethorpe photographs from the wall and loading them facedown onto a wheeled cart.

"What are you doing?" he asked.

The man in the janitor's uniform looked over his shoulder and said, "I'm doing my job, that's what I'm doing." He had dull hair, a low forehead, and an acne-scarred face with deep furrows in the cheeks.

"But why are you taking down those pictures?"

The man turned around to face him. He was strikingly ugly, and his ugliness seemed part of his intention, as if he had chosen it. "Gee, buddy, why do you suppose I'd do something like that? To upset *you*? Well, I'm sorry if you're upset, but you had nothing to do with this. They tell me to do stuff like this, I do it. End of story." He pushed his face forward, ready for the next step.

"Sorry," Bill said. "I understand completely. Have you seen a doctor or a nurse up here in the past few minutes? A man on the other side of the floor just had a stroke. He needs medical attention."

"The man I deal with is a supervisor. Supervisors don't wear white coats, and they don't carry stethoscopes. Now if you'll excuse me, I'll be on my way."

"But I need a doctor!"

"You look okay to me," the man said, turning away. He took the last photograph from the wall and pushed his cart through the metal doors that marked the boundary of the realm ruled by Tess Corrigan, Molly Goldberg, and their colleagues. Bill followed him through, and instantly found himself in a functional, green-painted corridor lit by fluorescent lighting and lined with locked doors. The janitor pushed his trolley around a corner and disappeared.

"Is anybody here?" Bill's voice carried through the empty hallways. "A man here needs a doctor!"

The corridor he was in led to another, which led to another, which went past a small, deserted nurses' station and ended at a huge, flat door with a sign that said MEDICAL PERSONNEL ONLY. Bill pushed at the door, but it was locked. He had the feeling that he could wander through these corridors for hours and find nothing but blank walls and locked doors. When he returned to the metal doors and pushed through to the private wing, relief flooded through him, making him feel light-headed.

The Salon invited him in—he wanted to sit down, he wanted to catch his breath and see if any of the little cakes had been set out yet. He had forgotten to order breakfast, and hunger was making him weak. Bill put his hand on one of the pebble-glass doors and saw an indistinct figure seated near the table. For a moment, his heart felt cold, and he hesitated before he opened the door.

Tony Flax was bent over in his chair, and what Bill Messenger noticed first was that the critic was wearing one of the thin hospital gowns that tied at the neck and the back. His trench coat lay puddled on the floor. Then he saw that Flax appeared to be weeping. His hands were clasped to his face, and his back rose and fell with jerky, uncontrolled movements.

"Tony?" he said. "What happened to you?"

Flax continued to weep silently, with the concentration and selfishness of a small child.

"Can I help you, Tony?" Bill asked.

When Flax did not respond, Bill looked around the room for the source of his distress. Half-filled coffee cups stood on the little tables, and petits fours lay jumbled and scattered over the plates and the white table. As he watched, a cockroach nearly two inches long burrowed out of a little square of white chocolate and disappeared around the back of a Battenburg cake. The cockroach looked as polished as a new pair of shoes.

Something was moving on the other side of the window, but Bill Messenger wanted nothing to do with it. "Tony," he said, "I'll be in my room."

Down the corridor he went, the tails of his suit jacket flapping behind him. A heavy, liquid pressure built up in his chest, and the lights seemed to darken, then grow brighter again. He remembered Max, his mind gone, staring openmouthed at his window: what had he seen?

Bill thought of Chippie Traynor, one of his mole-like eyes bloodied behind the shattered lens of his glasses.

At the entrance to his room, he hesitated once again as he had outside the Salon, fearing that if he went in, he might not be alone. But of course he would be alone, for apart from the janitor no one else on Floor 21 was capable of movement. Slowly, making as little noise as possible, he slipped around his door and entered his room. It looked exactly as it had when he had awakened that morning. The younger author's book lay discarded on his bed, the monitors awaited an emergency, the blinds covered the long window. Bill thought the wildly alternating pattern of light and dark that moved across the blinds proved nothing. Freaky New York weather, you never knew what it was going to do. He did not hear odd noises, like half-remembered voices, calling to him from the other side of the glass.

As he moved nearer to the foot of the bed, he saw on the floor the bright jacket of the book he had decided not to read, and knew that in the night it had fallen from his movable tray. The book on his bed had no jacket, and at first he had no idea where it came from. When he remembered the circumstances under which he had seen this book—or one a great deal like it—he felt revulsion, as though it were a great slug.

Bill turned his back on the bed, swung his chair around, and plucked the newspaper from under his arm. After he had scanned the headlines without making much effort to take them in, habit led him to the obituaries on the last two pages of the financial section. As soon as he had folded the pages back, a photograph of a sly, mild face with a recessed chin and tiny spectacles lurking above an overgrown nose levitated up from the columns of newsprint. The headline announced CHARLES CHIPP TRAYNOR, POPULAR WAR HISTORIAN, TARRED BY SCANDAL.

Helplessly, Bill read the first paragraph of Chippie's obituary. Four days past, this once-renowned historian whose career had been destroyed by charges of plagiarism and fraud had committed suicide by leaping from the window of his fifteenth-story apartment on the Upper West Side.

Four days ago? Bill thought. It seemed to him that was when Chippie Traynor had first appeared in the Salon. He dropped the paper, with the effect that Traynor's fleshy nose and mild eyes peered up at him from the floor. The terrible little man seemed to be everywhere, despite having *gone*. He could sense Chippie Traynor floating outside his window like a small, inoffensive balloon from Macy's Thanksgiving Day Parade. Children would say, "Who's that?" and their parents would look up, shield their eyes, shrug, and say, "I don't know, hon. Wasn't he in a Disney cartoon?" Only he was not in a Disney cartoon, and the children and their parents could not see him, and he wasn't at all cute. One of his eyes had been injured. This Chippie Traynor, not the one that had given them a view of his backside in the Salon, hovered outside Bill Messenger's window, whispering the wretched and insinuating secrets of the despised, the contemptible, the rejected and fallen from grace.

Bill turned from the window and took a single step into the nowhere that awaited him. He had nowhere to go, he knew, so nowhere had to be where he was going. It was probably going to be a lot like this place, only less comfortable. Much, *much* less comfortable. With nowhere to go, he reached out his hand and picked up the dull brown book lying at the foot of his bed. Bringing it toward his body felt like reeling in some monstrous fish that struggled against the line. There were faint water marks on the front cover, and it bore a faint, familiar smell. When he had it within reading distance, Bill turned the spine up and read the title and author's name: *In the Middle of the Trenches*, by Charles Chipp Traynor. It was the book he had blurbed. Max Baccarat had published it, and Tony Flax had rhapsodized over it in the *Sunday Times* book review section. About a hundred pages from the end, a bookmark in the shape of a thin silver cord with a hook at one end protruded from the top of the book.

Bill opened the book at the place indicated, and the slender bookmark slithered downwards like a living thing. Then the hook caught the top of the pages, and its length hung shining and swaying over the bottom edge. No longer able to resist, Bill read some random sentences, then two long paragraphs. This section undoubtedly had been lifted from the oral histories, and it recounted an odd event in the life of a young man who, years before his induction into the Armed Forces, had come upon a strange house deep in the piney woods of East Texas and been so unsettled by what he had seen through its windows that he brought a rifle with him on his next visit. Bill realized that he had never read this part of the book. In fact, he had written his blurb after merely skimming through the first two chapters. He thought Max had read even less of the book than he had. In a hurry to meet his deadline, Tony Flax had probably read the first half.

At the end of his account, the former soldier said, "In the many times over the years when I thought about this incident, it always seemed to me that the man I shot was myself. It seemed my own eye I had destroyed, my own socket that bled."

Uncollected Stories

Mallon the Guru

Near the end of what he later called his "developmental period," the American guru Spencer Mallon spent four months traveling through India with his spiritual leader, Urdang, a fearsome German with a deceptively mild manner. In the third of these months, they were granted an audience with a yogi, a great holy man who lived in the village of Sankwal. However, an odd, unsettling thing happened as soon as Mallon and Urdang reached the outskirts of the village. A carrion crow plummeted out of the sky and landed, with an audible thump and a skirl of feathers, dead on the dusty ground immediately in front of them. Instantly, villagers began streaming toward them, whether because of the crow or because he and Urdang were fair-skinned strangers, Mallon did not know. He fought the uncomfortable feeling of being surrounded by strangers gibbering away in a language he would never understand, and in the midst of this great difficulty tried to find the peace and balance he sometimes experienced during his almost daily, generally two-hour meditations.

An unclean foot with tuberous three-inch nails flipped aside the dead bird. The villagers drew closer, close enough to touch, and leaning in and jabbering with great intensity, urged them forward by tugging at their shirts and waistbands. They, or perhaps just he, Spencer Mallon, was being urged, importuned, begged to execute some unimaginable service. They wished him to perform some kind of *task*, but the task remained mysterious. The mystery became clearer only after a rickety hut seemed almost to materialize mirage-like from the barren scrap of land where it squatted. One of the men urging Mallon along yanked his sleeve more forcefully and implored him, with flapping, birdlike gestures, to go into the hut, evidently his, to enter it and *see* something— the man indicated the necessity for vision by jabbing a black fingernail at his protuberant right eye.

I have been chosen, Mallon thought. *I, not Urdang, have been elected by these ignorant and suffering people.*

Within the dim, hot enclosure, he was invited to gaze at a small child with huge, impassive eyes and limbs like twigs. The child appeared to be dying. Dark yellow crusts ringed its nostrils and its mouth.

Staring at Mallon, the trembling villager raised one of his own hands and brushed his fingertips gently against the boy's enormous forehead. Then he waved Mallon closer to the child's pallet.

"Don't you get it?" Urdang said. "You're supposed to touch the boy."

Reluctantly, unsure of what he was actually being asked to do and fearful of contracting some hideous disease, Mallon lowered his extended fingers toward the skeletal head as if he were about to dip them into a pail of reeking fluid drawn from the communal cesspit.

Kid, he thought, *I sure as hell hope we're going to see a miracle cure.*

At the moment of contact a tiny particle of energy, a radiant erg as quick and flowing as mercury, passed directly from his hand through the fragile wall of the boy's skull.

In the midst of this extremely interesting phenomenon, the father collapsed to his knees and began to croon in gratitude.

"How do these people know about me?" he asked.

"The real question is, what do they think you did?" Urdang said. "And how do they think they know it? Once we have had our audience, I suggest we put on our skates."

Urdang, Mallon realized, had no idea of what had just happened. It was the restoration of a cosmic balance: a bird died, and a child was saved. He had been the fulcrum between death and the restoration. A perfect Indian experience had been given to him. The great yogi would embrace him as he would a son, he would open his house and his ashram and welcome him as a student of unprecedented capabilities.

Proceeding down a narrow lane in the village proper, Mallon carelessly extended two fingers and ran them along a foot or two of the mud-plastered wall at his side. He had no plan, no purpose beyond just seeing what was going to happen, for he knew that in some fashion his touch would alter the universe. The results of his test were deeply gratifying: on the wall, the two lines traced by his fingers glowed a brilliant neon blue that brightened and intensified until it threatened to sear the eyes. The villagers spun around and waved their arms, releasing an ecstatic babble threaded with high-pitched cries of joy. Along with everybody else, Mallon had stopped moving to look at the marvelous, miraculous wall. An electrical buzz and hum filled all the spaces within his body; he felt as though he could shoot sparks from his fingers.

I should touch that kid all over again, he thought. *He'd zoom right up off the bed.*

In seconds, the vibrant blue lines cooled, shrank, and faded back into the dull khaki of the wall. The villagers thrust forward, rubbed the wall, flattened themselves against it, spoke to it in whispers. Those who kissed the wall came away with mouths and noses painted white with dust. Only Mallon, and perhaps Urdang, had been chagrined to see the evidence of his magic vanish so quickly from the world.

The babbling crowd, not at all disappointed, clustered again around him and pushed him forward. Their filthy, black-nailed hands gave him many a fond pat and awed, stroking caress. Eventually they came to a high yellow wall and an iron gate. Urdang pushed himself through the crowd and opened the gate upon a long, lush flower garden. At the distant end of the garden stood a graceful terra-cotta building with a row of windows on both sides of its elaborately tiled front door. The dark heads of young women appeared in the windows. Giggling, the women retreated backward.

The villagers thrust Mallon and Urdang forward. The gates clanged behind them. Far away, an ox-cart creaked. Cattle lowed from behind the creamy-looking terra-cotta building.

I am in love with all of India! Mallon thought.

"Come nearer," said a dry, penetrating voice.

A small man in a dhoti of dazzling white sat in the lotus position just in front of a fountain placed in the middle of the garden. A moment before, Mallon had noticed neither the man nor the fountain.

"I believe that you, sir, are Urdang," the man said. "But who is your most peculiar follower?"

"His name is Spencer Mallon," Urdang said. "But, Master, with all due respect, he is not peculiar."

"This man is a peculiarity entire unto himself," said the little man. "Please sit down."

They sat before him, adjusting themselves into the lotus position as well as they could, Urdang easily and perfectly, Mallon less so. He considered it extremely likely that in some deeply positive way he actually was peculiar. Peculiarity of his kind amounted to a great distinction, as the Master understood and poor Urdang did not.

Before them, the great holy man contemplated them in a silence mysteriously shaped by the harsh angles and shining curves of his shaven head and hard, nutlike face. Mallon gathered from the quality of the silence that the yogi was after all not unreservedly pleased by the homage of their visit. Of course the difficult element had to be Urdang—the presence of Urdang in this sacred place. After something like nine or ten minutes, the yogi turned his head to one side and, speaking either to the flowers or the splashing fountain, ordered sweet tea and honey cakes. These delights were delivered by two of the dark-haired girls, who wore beautiful, highly colored saris and sandals with little bells on the straps.

"Is it true that when you came into our village, a carrion crow came toppling dead from the sky?" asked the holy man.

Urdang and Mallon nodded.

"That is a sign, Urdang. We must consider the meaning of this sign."

"Let us do so, then," Urdang said. "I believe the sign to be auspicious. That which eats death is itself devoured by it."

"Yet death comes tumbling into our village."

"Immediately afterward, this young man touched the forehead of a dying child and restored him to good health."

"No one of this young man's age and position can do this," said the yogi. "Such a feat requires great holiness, but even great holiness is not sufficient. One must have spent decades in study and meditation."

"And yet it happened. Death was banished."

"Death is never banished, it merely travels elsewhere. Your student greatly distresses me."

"Dear Master, as the villagers led us toward your house, this man I have brought to you extended one arm and—"

The yogi silenced him with a wave of the hand. "I am not concerned with such displays. Fireworks do not impress me. Yes, they indicate the presence of a gift, but of what use is this gift, to what purposes will it be turned?"

Mallon had touched a dying child, the Master said, yet had he restored it to health? Even if he had, was the healing truly his work?

Mere belief could heal as successfully as other forces, temporarily. Was Mallon well schooled in the Sutras? How great was his knowledge of Buddhist teachings?

Urdang replied that Mallon was not a Buddhist.

"Then why have you come?"

Mallon spoke from his heart. "I come for your blessing, dear Master."

"You cannot have my blessing. I ask for yours instead." The holy man spoke as if to an ancient enemy.

"*My* blessing?" Mallon asked.

"Render it unto me as you did to the child."

Confused and irritated, Mallon scooted forward and extended a hand. Almost, he wished to withhold his blessing as had the yogi, but he could not behave so childishly in front of Urdang. The holy man leaned forward and permitted his brow to be brushed. If any molten particle of energy flew from his hand into the yogi's brainpan, Mallon did not feel its passage.

The Master's face contracted, no mean trick, and for a moment he closed his eyes.

"Well?" Mallon said. Urdang gasped at his rudeness.

"It is very much as I thought," said the Master, opening his eyes. "I cannot be responsible for your Spencer Mallon, and you must not request any more of me. I see it all very clearly. Already, this most peculiar, this most dangerously peculiar man has awakened disorder within our village. He must leave Sankwal immediately, and you who brought him here, Urdang, you must leave with him."

"If that is your wish, Master," Urdang said. "But perhaps—"

"No. No more. You would be wise to separate yourself from this student as soon as you can do so honorably. And as for you, young man . . ."

He turned his sorrowful eyes upon Mallon, and Mallon could feel his spirit hovering near, irate and fearful.

"I advise you to take great, great care in everything you do. But it would be wisest if you did nothing at all."

"Master, why are you afraid of me?" Mallon asked. "I want only to love you." In truth, he had wished to love the Master before he met him. Now, he wanted only to leave the village and its frightened, envious yogi far behind him. And, he realized, if Urdang wanted to leave him, that would be fine, too.

"I am grateful you do not," the Master said. "You will go from my village now, both of you."

When Urdang opened the gates, the lanes were empty. The villagers had fled back to their homes. The air darkened, and rain began to fall. Before they reached open ground, the earth had been churned to mud. A loud cry came from the hut of the poor man with the sick child, whether of joy or pain they could not say.

The Ballad of Ballard and Sandrine

1997

"So, do we get lunch again today?" Ballard asked. They had reached the steaming, humid end of November.

"We got fucking lunch yesterday," replied the naked woman splayed on the long table: knees bent, one hip elevated, one boneless-looking arm draped along the curves of her body, which despite its hidden scars appeared to be at least a decade younger than her face. "Why should today be different?"

After an outwardly privileged childhood polluted by parental misconduct, a superior education, and two failed marriages, Sandrine Loy had evolved into a rebellious, still-exploratory woman of forty-three. At present, her voice had a well-honed edge, as if she were explaining something to a person of questionable intelligence.

Two days before joining Sandrine on this river journey, Ballard had celebrated his sixty-fifth birthday at a dinner in Hong Kong, one of the cities where he conducted his odd business. Sandrine had not been invited to the dinner and would not have attended if she had. The formal, ceremonious side of Ballard's life, which he found so satisfying, interested her not at all.

Without in any way adjusting the facts of the extraordinary body she had put on display, Sandrine lowered her eyes from the ceiling and examined him with a glance brimming with false curiosity and false innocence. The glance also contained a flicker of genuine irritation.

Abruptly and with vivid recall, Ballard found himself remembering the late afternoon in 1969 when, nine floors above Park Avenue, upon a carpet of almost unutterable richness in a room hung with paintings by Winslow Homer and Albert Pinkham Ryder, he had stood with a rich scapegrace and client named Lauritzen Loy, his host, to greet Loy's daughter on her return from another grueling day at Dalton School, then observed the sidelong, graceful, slightly miffed entrance of a fifteen-year-old girl in pigtails and a Jackson Brown sweatshirt two sizes too large, met her gray-green eyes, and felt the very shape of his universe alter in some drastic way, either expanding a thousand times or contracting to a pinpoint, he could not tell. The second their eyes met, the girl blushed, violently.

She hadn't liked that, not at all.

"I didn't say it was going to be different, and I don't think it will." He turned to look at her, making sure to meet her gaze before letting his eye travel down her neck, over her breasts, the bowl of her belly, the slope of her pubis, the length of her legs. "Are you in a more than ordinarily bad mood?"

"You're snapping at me."

Ballard sighed. "You gave me that *look*. You said, 'Why should today be different?' "

"Have it your way, old man. But as a victory, it's fucking pathetic. It's hollow."

She rolled onto her back and gave her body a firm little shake that settled it more securely onto the steel surface of the table. The metal, only slightly cooler than her skin, felt good against it. In this climate, nothing not on ice or in a freezer, not even a corpse, could ever truly get cold.

"Most victories are hollow, believe me."

Ballard wandered over to the brassbound porthole on the deck side of their elaborate, many-roomed suite. Whatever he saw caused him momentarily to stiffen and take an involuntary step backward.

"What's the view like?"

"The so-called view consists of the filthy Amazon and a boring, muddy bank. Sometimes the bank is so far away it's out of sight."

He did not add that a Ballard approximately twenty years younger, the Ballard of, say, 1976, dressed in a handsome dark suit and brilliantly white shirt, was leaning against the deck rail, unaware of being under the eye of his twenty-years-older self. Young Ballard, older Ballard observed, did an excellent job of concealing his dire internal condition beneath a mask of deep, already well-weathered urbanity: the same performance, enacted day after day before an audience unaware of being an audience and never permitted backstage.

Unlike Sandrine, Ballard had never married. "Poor Ballard, stuck on the *Endless Night* with a horrible view and only his aging, moody girlfriend for company."

Smiling, he returned to the long steel table, ran his mutilated right hand over the curve of her belly, and cupped her navel. "This is exactly what I asked for. You're wonderful."

"But isn't it funny to think—everything could have been completely different."

Ballard slid the remaining fingers of his hand down to palpate, lightly, the springy black shrublike curls of her pubic bush.

"Everything is completely different right now."

"So take off your clothes and fuck me," Sandrine said. "I can get you hard again in a minute. In thirty seconds."

"I'm sure you could. But maybe you should put some clothes *on*, so we could go in to lunch."

"You prefer to have sex in our bed."

"I do, yes. I don't understand why you wanted to get naked and lie down on this thing, anyhow. Now, I mean."

"It isn't cold, if that's what you're afraid of." She wriggled her torso and did a snow-angel movement with her legs.

"Maybe this time we could catch the waiters."

"Because we'd be early?"

Ballard nodded. "Indulge me. Put on that sleeveless white French thing."

"Aye-aye, *mon capitain*." She sat up and scooted down the length of the table, pushing herself along on the raised vertical edges. These were of dark green marble, about an inch thick and four inches high. On both sides, round metal drains abutted the inner side of the marble. At the end of the table, Sandrine swung her legs down and straightened her arms, like a girl sitting on the end of a diving board. "I know why, too."

"Why I want you to wear that white thing? I love the way it looks on you."

"Why you don't want to have sex on this table."

"It's too narrow."

"You're thinking about what this table is for. Right? And you don't want to combine sex with *that*. Only I think that's exactly why we *should* have sex here."

"Everything we do, remember, is done by mutual consent. Our Golden Rule."

"Golden Spoilsport," she said. "Golden Shower of Shit."

"See? Everything's different already."

Sandrine levered herself off the edge of the table and faced him like a strict schoolmistress who happened momentarily to be naked. "I'm all you've got, and sometimes even I don't understand you."

"That makes two of us."

She wheeled around and padded into the bedroom, displaying her plush little bottom and sacral dimples with an absolute confidence Ballard could not but admire.

Although Sandrine and Ballard burst, in utter defiance of a direct order, into the dining room a full nine minutes ahead of schedule, the unseen minions had already done their work and disappeared. On the gleaming rosewood table two formal place settings had been laid, the plates topped with elaborately chased silver covers. Fresh irises brushed blue and yellow filled a tall, sparkling crystal vase.

"I swear, they must have a greenhouse on this yacht," Ballard said.

"Naked men with muddy hair row the flowers out in the middle of the night."

"I don't even think irises grow in the Amazon basin."

"Little guys who speak bird language can probably grow anything they like."

"That's only one tribe, the Pirahā. And all those bird sounds are actual words. It's a human language." Ballard walked around the table and took the seat he had claimed as his. He lifted the intricate silver cover. "Now what is that?" He looked across at Sandrine, who was prodding at the contents of her bowl with a fork.

"Looks like a cut-up sausage. At least I hope it's a sausage. And something like broccoli. And a lot of orangey-yellowy goo." She raised her fork and licked the tines. "Um. Tastes pretty good, actually. But . . ."

For a moment, she appeared to be lost in time's great forest.

"I know this doesn't make sense, but if we ever did this before, *exactly* this, with you sitting over there and me here, in this same room, well, wasn't the food even better, I mean a *lot* better?"

"I can't say anything about that," Ballard said. "I really can't. There's just this vague . . ." The vagueness disturbed him far more than seemed quite rational. "Let's drop that subject and talk about bird language. Yes, let's. And the wine." He picked up the bottle. "Yet again a very nice Bordeaux," Ballard said, and poured for both of them. "However. What you've been hearing are real birds, not the Pirahã."

"But they're talking, not just chirping. There's a difference. These guys are saying things to each other."

"Birds talk to one another. I mean, they sing."

She was right about one thing, though: in a funky, down-home way, the stewlike dish was delicious. He thrust away the feeling that it should have been a hundred, a thousand times more delicious: that once it, or something rather like it, had been paradisal.

"Birds don't sing in sentences. Or in paragraphs, like these guys do."

"They still can't be the Pirahã. The Pirahã live about five hundred miles away, on the Peruvian border."

"Your ears aren't as good as mine. You don't really hear them."

"Oh, I hear plenty of birds. They're all over the place."

"Only we're not talking about *birds*," Sandrine said.

1982

On the last day of November, Sandrine Loy, who was twenty-eight, constitutionally ill-tempered, and startlingly good-looking (wide eyes, long mouth, black widow's peak, columnar legs), formerly of Princeton and Clare College, Cambridge, glanced over her shoulder and said, "Please tell me you're kidding. I just showered. I put on this nice white frock you bought me in Paris. And I'm *hungry*." Relenting a bit, she let a playful smile warm her face for nearly a second. "Besides that, I want to catch sight of our invisible servants."

"I'm hungry, too."

"Not for food, unfortunately." She spun from the porthole and its ugly view—a mile of brown rolling river and low muddy banks where squat, sullen natives tended to melt back into the bushes when the *Sweet Delight* went by—to indicate the evidence of Ballard's arousal, which stood up, darker than the rest of him, as straight as a flagpole.

"Let's have sex on this table. It's a lot more comfortable than it looks."

"Kind of defeats the fucking purpose, wouldn't you say? Comfort's hardly the point."

"Might as well be as comfy as we can, I say." He raised his arms to let his hands drape from the four-inch marble edging on the long steel table. "There's plenty of space on this thing, you know. More than in your bed at Clare."

"Maybe you're not as porky as I thought you were."

"Careful, careful. If you insult me, I'll make you pay for it."

At fifty Ballard had put on some extra weight, but it suited him. His shoulders were still wider far than his hips, and his belly more nascent than actual. His hair, longer than that of most men his age and just beginning to show threads of gray within the luxuriant brown, framed his wide brow and executive face. He looked like an actor who had made a career of playing senators, doctors, and bankers. Ballard's real profession was that of fixer to an oversized law firm in New York with a satellite office in Hong Kong, where he had grown up. The weight of muscle in his arms, shoulders, and legs reinforced the hint of stubborn determination, even perhaps brutality, in his face: the suggestion that if necessary he would go a great distance and perform any number of grim deeds to do what was needed. Scars both long and short, scars like snakes, zippers, and tattoos bloomed here and there on his body.

"Promises, promises," she said. "But just for now, get up and get dressed, please. The sight of you admiring your own dick doesn't do anything for me."

"Oh, really?"

"Well, I do like the way you can still stick straight up into the air like a happy little soldier—at your age! But men are so soppy about their penises. You're all queer for yourselves. You more so than most, Ballard."

"Ouch," he said, and sat up. "I believe I'll put my clothes on now, Sandrine."

"Don't take forever, all right? I know it's only the second day, but I'd like to get a look at them while they're setting the table. Because someone, maybe even two someones, does set that table."

Ballard was already in the bedroom, pulling from their hangers a pair of white linen slacks and a thick, long-sleeved white cotton T-shirt. In seconds, he had slipped into these garments and was sliding his suntanned feet into rope-soled clogs.

"So let's move," he said, coming out of the bedroom with a long stride, his elbows bent, his forearms raised.

From the dining room came the sharp, distinctive chirping of a bird. Two notes, the second one higher, both clear and as insistent as the call of a bell. Ballard glanced at Sandrine, who seemed momentarily shaken.

"I'm not going in there if one of those awful jungle birds got in. They have to get rid of it. We're paying them, aren't we?"

"You have no idea," Ballard said. He grabbed her arm and pulled her along with him. "But that's no bird, it's *them*. The waiters. The staff."

Sandrine's elegant face shone with both disbelief and disgust.

"Those chirps and whistles are how they talk. Didn't you hear them last night and this morning?"

When he pulled again at her arm, she followed along, reluctance visible in her stance, her gait, the tilt of her head.

"I'm talking about birds, and they weren't even on the yacht. They were on shore. They were up in the air."

"Let's see what's in here." Six or seven minutes remained until the official start of dinnertime, and they had been requested never to enter the dining room until the exact time of the meal.

Ballard threw the door open and pulled her into the room with him. Silver covers rested on the Royal Doulton china, and an uncorked bottle of a distinguished Bordeaux stood precisely at the midpoint between the two place settings. Three inches to its right, a navy-blue-and-royal-purple orchid thick enough to eat leaned, as if languishing, against the side of a small square crystal vase. The air seemed absolutely unmoving. Through the thumb holes at the tops of the plate covers rose a dense, oddly meaty odor of some unidentifiable food.

"Missed 'em again, damn it." Sandrine pulled her arm from Ballard's grasp and moved a few steps away.

"But you have noticed that there's no bird in here. Not so much as a feather."

"So it got out—I know it was here, Ballard."

She spun on her four-inch heels, giving the room a fast 360-degree inspection. Their dining room, roughly oval in shape, was lined with glassed-in bookshelves of dark-stained oak containing perhaps five hundred books, most of them mid-to-late nineteenth and early twentieth century novels ranked alphabetically by author, regardless of genre. The jackets had been removed, which Ballard minded, a bit. Three feet in front of the bookshelves on the deck side, which yielded space to two portholes and a door, stood a long wooden table with a delicately inlaid top—a real table, unlike the one in the room they had just left, which was more like a workstation in a laboratory. The real one was presumably for setting out buffets.

The first door opened out onto the deck; another at the top of the oval led to their large and handsomely furnished sitting room, with reading chairs and lamps, two sofas paired with low tables, a bar with a great many bottles of liquor, two red-lacquered cabinets they had as yet not explored, and an air of many small precious things set out to gleam under the parlor's low lighting. The two remaining doors in the dining room were on the interior side. One opened into the spacious corridor that ran the entire length of their suite and gave access to the deck on both ends; the other revealed a gray passageway and a metal staircase that led up to the Captain's deck and cabin and down into the engine room, galley, and quarters for the yacht's small, unseen crew.

"So it kept all its feathers," said Sandrine. "If you don't think that's possible, you don't know doodley-squat about birds."

"What isn't possible," said Ballard, "is that some giant parrot got out of here without opening a door or a porthole."

"One of the waiters let it out, dummy. One of those handsome *Spanish-speaking* waiters."

They sat on opposite sides of the stately table. Ballard smiled at Sandrine, and she smiled back in rage and distrust. Suddenly and without warning, he remembered the girl she had been on Park Avenue at the end of the sixties, gawky-graceful, brilliantly surly, her hair and wardrobe goofy, claiming him as he had claimed her, with a glance. He had rescued her father from ruinous shame and a long jail term, but as soon as he had seen her he understood that his work had just begun, and that it would demand restraint, sacrifice, patience, and adamantine caution.

"A three-count?" he asked.

She nodded.

"One," he said. "Two." They put their thumbs into the round holes at the tops of the covers. "Three." They raised their covers, releasing steam and smoke and a more concentrated, powerful form of the meaty odor.

"Wow. What is that?"

Yellow-brown sauce or gravy covered a long, curved strip of foreign matter. Exhausted vegetables that looked a little like okra and string beans but were other things altogether lay strewn in limp surrender beneath the gravy.

"All of a sudden I'm really hungry," said Sandrine. "You can't tell what it is either?"

Ballard moved the strip of unknown meat back and forth with his knife. Then he jabbed his fork into it. A watery yellow fluid oozed from the punctures.

"God knows what this is."

He pictured some big reptilian creature sliding down the riverbank into the meshes of a native net, then being hauled back up to be pierced with poison-tipped wooden spears. Chirping like birds, the diminutive men rioted in celebration around the corpse, which was now that of a hideous insect the size of a pony, its shell a poisonous green.

"I'm not even sure it's a mammal," he said. "Might even be some organ. Anaconda liver. Crocodile lung. Tarantula heart."

"You first."

Ballard sliced a tiny section from the curved meat before him. He half-expected to see valves and tubes, but the slice was a dense light brown all the way through. Ballard inserted the morsel into his mouth, and his taste buds began to sing.

"My god. Amazing."

"It's good?"

"Oh, this is way beyond 'good.'"

Ballard cut a larger piece off the whole and quickly bit into it. Yes, there it was again, but more sumptuously, almost floral in its delicacy and grounded in some profoundly satisfactory flavor, like that of a great single-barrel bourbon laced with a dark, subversive French chocolate. Subtlety, strength, sweetness. He watched Sandrine lift a section of the substance on her fork and slip it into her mouth. Her face went utterly still, and her eyes narrowed. With luxuriant slowness, she began to chew. After perhaps a second, Sandrine closed her eyes. Eventually, she swallowed.

"Oh, yes," she said. "My, my. Yes. Why can't we eat like this at home?"

"Whatever kind of animal this is, it's probably unknown everywhere but here. People like J. Paul Getty might get to eat it once a year, at some secret location."

"I don't care what it is, I'm just extraordinarily happy that we get to have it today. It's even a little bit sweet, isn't it?"

A short time later, Sandrine said, "Amazing. Even these horrible-looking vegetables spill out amazing flavors. If I could eat like this every day, I'd be perfectly happy to live in a hut, walk around barefoot, bathe in the Amazon, and wash my rags on the rocks."

"I know exactly what you mean," said Ballard. "It's like a drug. Maybe it is a drug."

"Do the natives really eat this way? Whatever this animal was, before they serve it to us, they have to hunt it down and kill it. Wouldn't they keep half of it for themselves?"

"Be a temptation," Ballard said. "Maybe they lick our plates, too."

"Tell me the truth now, Ballard. If you know it. Okay?"

Chewing, he looked up into her eyes. Some of the bliss faded from his face. "Sure. Ask away."

"Did we ever eat this stuff before?"

Ballard did not answer. He sliced a quarter-sized piece off the meat and began to chew, his eyes on his plate.

"I know I'm not supposed to ask."

He kept chewing and chewing until he swallowed. He sipped his wine. "No. Isn't that strange? How we know we're not supposed to do certain things?"

"Like see the waiters. Or the maids, or the Captain."

"Especially the Captain, I think."

"Let's not talk anymore, let's just eat for a little while."

Sandrine and Ballard returned to their plates and glasses, and for a time made no noise other than soft moans of satisfaction.

When they had nearly finished, Sandrine said, "There are so many books on this boat! It's like a big library. Do you think you've ever read one?"

"Do you?"

"I have the feeling . . . well, of course that's the reason I'm asking. In a way, I mean in a *real* way, we've never been here before. On the Amazon? Absolutely not. My husband, besides being continuously unfaithful, is a total asshole who never pays me any attention at all unless he's angry with me, but he's also tremendously jealous and possessive. For me to get here to be with you required an amazing amount of secret organization. D-Day didn't take any more planning than this trip. On the other hand, I have the feeling I once read at least one of these books."

"I have the same feeling."

"Tell me about it. I want to read it again and see if I remember anything."

"I can't. But . . . well, I think I might have once seen you holding a copy of *Little Dorrit*. The Dickens novel."

"I went to Princeton and Cambridge, I know who wrote *Little Dorrit*," she said, irritated. "Wait. Did I ever throw a copy of that book overboard?"

"Might've."

"Why would I do that?"

Ballard shrugged. "To see what would happen?"

"Do you remember that?"

"It's tough to say what I remember. Everything's always different, but it's different *now*. I sort of remember a book, though—a book from this library. *Tono Bungay*. H. G. Wells. Didn't like it much."

"Did you throw it overboard?"

"I might've. Yes, I actually might have." He laughed. "I think I did. I mean, I think I'm throwing it overboard right now, if that makes sense."

"Because you didn't—don't—like it?"

Ballard laughed and put down his knife and fork. Only a few bits of the vegetables and a piece of meat the size of a knuckle sliced in half remained on his plate. "Stop eating and give me your plate." It was almost exactly as empty as his, though Sandrine's plate still had two swirls of the yellow sauce.

"Really?"

"I want to show you something."

Reluctantly, she lowered her utensils and handed him her plate. Ballard scraped the contents of his plate onto hers. He got to his feet and picked up a knife and the plate that had been Sandrine's. "Come out on deck with me."

When she stood up, Sandrine glanced at what she had only briefly and partially perceived as a hint of motion at the top of the room, where for the first time she took in a dun-colored curtain hung two or three feet before the end of the oval. What looked to be a brown or suntanned foot, smaller than a normal adult's and perhaps a bit grubby, was just now vanishing behind the curtain. Before Sandrine had deciphered what she thought she had seen, it was gone.

"Just see a rat?" asked Ballard.

Without intending to assent, Sandrine nodded.

"One was out on deck this morning. Disappeared as soon as I spotted it. Don't worry about it, though. The crew, whoever they are, will get rid of them. At the start of the cruise, I think there are always a few rats around. By the time we really get in gear, they're gone."

"Good," she said, wondering: *If the waiters are these really, really short Indian guys, would they hate us enough to make us eat rats?*

She followed him through the door between the two portholes into pitiless sunlight and crushing heat made even less comfortable by the dense, invasive humidity. The invisible water saturating the air pressed against her face like a steaming washcloth, and moisture instantly coated her entire body. Leaning against the rail, Ballard looked cool and completely at ease.

"I forgot we had air conditioning," she said.

"We don't. Vents move the air around somehow. Works like magic, even when there's no breeze at all. Come over here."

She joined him at the rail. Fifty yards away, what might have been human faces peered at them through a dense screen of jungle—weeds with thick, vegetal leaves of a green so dark it was nearly black. The half-seen faces resembled masks, empty of feeling.

"Remember saying something about being happy to bathe in the Amazon? About washing your clothes in the river?"

She nodded.

"You never want to go into this river. You don't even want to stick the tip of your finger in that water. Watch what happens, now. Our native friends came out to see this—you should, too."

"The Indians knew you were going to put on this demonstration? How could they?"

"Don't ask me, ask them. *I* don't know how they do it."

Ballard leaned over the railing and used his knife to scrape the few things on the plate into the river. Even before the little knuckles of meat and gristle, the shreds of vegetables, and liquid strings of gravy landed in the water, a six-inch circle of turbulence boiled up on the slow-moving surface. When the bits of food hit the water, the boiling circle widened out into a three-foot thrashing chaos of violent little fishtails and violent little green shiny fish backs with violent tiny green fins, all in furious motion. The fury lasted about thirty seconds, then disappeared back under the river's sluggish brown face.

"Like Christmas dinner with my husband's family," Sandrine said.

"When we were talking about throwing *Tono Bungay* and *Little Dorrit* into the river to see what would happen—"

"The fish ate the books?"

"They'll eat anything that isn't metal."

"So our little friends don't go swimming all that often, do they?"

"They never learn how. Swimming is death, it's for people like us. Let's go back in, okay?"

She whirled around and struck his chest, hard, with a pointed fist. "I want to go back to the room with the table in it. *Our* table. And this time, you can get as hard as you like."

"Don't I always?" he asked.

"Oh," Sandrine said, "I like that 'always.'"

"And yet, it's always different."

"I bet *I'm* always different," said Sandrine. "You, you'd stay pretty much the same."

"I'm not as boring as all that, you know," Ballard said, and went on, over the course of the long afternoon and sultry evening, to prove it.

After breakfast the next morning, Sandrine, hissing with pain, her skin clouded with bruises, turned on him with such fury that he gasped in joy and anticipation.

1976

End of November, hot sticky muggy, a vegetal stink in the air. Motionless tribesmen four feet tall stared out from the overgrown bank over twenty yards of torpid river. They held, seemed to hold, bows without arrows, though the details swam backward into the layers of folded green.

"Look at those little savages," said Sandrine Loy, twenty-two years old and already contemplating marriage to handsome, absurdly wealthy Antonio Barban, who had proposed to her after a chaotic Christmas dinner at his family's vulgar pile in Greenwich, Connecticut. That she knew marriage to Antonio would prove to be an error of sublime proportions gave the idea most of its appeal. "We're putting on a traveling circus for their benefit. Doesn't that sort of make you detest them?"

"I don't detest them at all," Ballard said. "Actually, I have a lot of respect for those people. I think they're mysterious. So much gravity. So much *silence*. They understand a million things we don't, and what we do manage to get they know about in another way, a more profound way."

"You're wrong. They're too stupid to understand anything. They have mud for dinner. They have mud for brains."

"And yet . . ." Ballard said, smiling at her.

As if they knew they had been insulted, and seemingly without moving out of position, the river people had begun to fade back into the network of dark, rubbery leaves in which they had for a long moment been framed.

"And yet what?"

"They knew what we were going to do. They wanted to see us throwing those books into the river. So out of the bushes they popped, right at the time we walked out on deck."

Her conspicuous black eyebrows slid nearer each other, creating a furrow. She shook her beautiful head and opened her mouth to disagree.

"Anyway, Sandrine, what did you think of what happened just now? Any responses, reflections?"

"What do I think of what happened to the books? What do I think of the fish?"

"Of course," Ballard said. "It's not *all* about us."

He leaned back against the rail, communicating utter ease and confidence. He was forty-four, attired daily in dark tailored suits and white shirts that gleamed like a movie star's smile, the repository of a thousand feral secrets, at home everywhere in the world, the possessor of an understanding it would take him a lifetime to absorb. Sandrine often seemed to him the center of his life. He knew exactly what she was going to say.

"I think the fish are astonishing," she said. "I mean it. Astonishing. Such concentration, such power, such complete *hunger*. It was breathtaking. Those books didn't last more than five or six seconds. All that thrashing! My book lasted longer than yours, but not by much."

"*Little Dorrit* is a lot longer than *Tono Bungay*. More paper, more thread, more glue. I think they're especially hot for glue."

"Maybe they're just hot for Dickens."

"Maybe they're speed readers," said Sandrine. "What do we do now?"

"What we came here to do," Ballard said, and moved back to swing open the dining room door, then froze in mid-step.

"Forget something?"

"I was having the oddest feeling, and I just now realized what it was.

You read about it all the time, so you think it must be pretty common, but until a second ago I don't think I'd ever before had the feeling that I was being watched. Not really."

"But now you did."

"Yes." He strode up to the door and swung it open. The table was bare, and the room was empty.

Sandrine approached and peeked over his shoulder. He had both amused and dismayed her. "The great Ballard exhibits a moment of paranoia. I think I've been wrong about you all this time. You're just another boring old creep who wants to fuck me."

"I'd admit to being a lot of things, but paranoid isn't one of them." He gestured her back through the door. That Sandrine obeyed him seemed to take both of them by surprise.

"How about being a boring old creep? I'm not really so sure I want to stay here with you. For one thing, and I know this is not related, the birds keep waking me up. If they are birds."

He cocked his head, interested. "What else could they be? Please tell me. Indulge a boring old creep."

"The maids and the waiters and the sailor guys. The cook. The woman who arranges the flowers."

"You think they belong to that tribe that speaks in birdcalls? Actually, how did *you* ever hear about them?"

"My anthropology professor was one of the people who first discovered that tribe. The Piranhas. Know what they call themselves? 'The tall people.' Not very observant, are they? According to the professor, they worshipped a much older tribe that had disappeared many generations back—miracle people, healers, shamans, warriors. The Old Ones, they called them, but the Old Ones called themselves 'WE,' you always have to put it in boldface. My professor couldn't stop talking about these tribes—he was so full of himself. *Sooo* vain. Kept staring at me. Vain, ugly, and lecherous, my favorite trifecta!"

The memory of her anthropology professor, with whom she had clearly gone through the customary adoration-boredom-disgust cycle of student-teacher love affairs, had put Sandrine in a sulky, dissatisfied mood. "You made a lovely little error about thirty seconds ago. The tribe is called the Pirahã, not the Piranhas. Piranhas are the fish you fell in love with."

"Ooh," she said, brightening up. "So the Pirahã eat piranhas?"

"Other way around, more likely. But the other people on the *Blinding Light* can't be Pirahã, we're hundreds of miles from their territory."

"You *are* tedious. Why did I ever let myself get talked into coming here, anyhow?"

"You fell in love with me the first time you saw me—in your father's living room, remember? And although it was tremendously naughty of me, in fact completely wrong and immoral, I took one look at your stupid sweatshirt and your stupid pigtails and fell in love with you on the spot. You were perfect—you took my breath away. It was like being struck by lightning."

He inhaled, hugely.

"And here I am, forty-four years of age, height of my powers, capable of performing miracles on behalf of our clients, exactly as I pulled off, not to say any more about this, a considerable miracle for your father, plus I am a fabulously eligible man, a tremendous catch, but what do you know, still unmarried. Instead of a wife or even a steady girlfriend, there's this succession of inane young women from twenty-five to thirty, these Heathers and Ashleys, these Morgans and Emilys, who much to their dismay grow less and less infatuated with me the more time we spend together. 'You're always so distant,' one of them said, 'you're never really *with* me.' And she was right, I couldn't really be with her. Because I wanted to be with you. I wanted us to be *here*."

Deeply pleased, Sandrine said, "You're such a pervert."

Yet something in what Ballard had evoked was making the handsome dining room awkward and dark. She wished he wouldn't stand still; there was no reason why he couldn't go into the living room, or the other way, into the room where terror and fascination beckoned. She wondered why she was waiting for Ballard to decide where to go, and as he spoke of seeing her for the first time, was assailed by an uncomfortably precise echo from the day in question.

Then, as now, she had been rooted to the floor: in her family's living room, beyond the windows familiar Park Avenue humming with the traffic she only in that moment became aware she heard, Sandrine had been paralyzed. Every inch of her face had turned hot and red. She felt intimate with Ballard before she had even begun to learn what intimacy meant. Before she had left the room, she waited for him to move between herself and her father, then pushed up the sleeves of the baggy sweatshirt and revealed the inscriptions of self-loathing, self-love, desire, and despair upon her pale forearms.

"You're pretty weird too. You'd just had your fifteenth birthday, and here you were, gobsmacked by this old guy in a suit. You even showed me your arms!"

"I could tell what made *you* salivate." She gave him a small, lopsided smile. "So why were you there, anyhow?"

"Your father and I were having a private celebration."

"Of what?"

Every time she asked this question, he gave her a different answer. "I made the fearsome problem of his old library fines disappear. *Poof!*, no more late-night sweats." Previously, Ballard had told her that he'd gotten her father off jury duty, had canceled his parking tickets, retro-actively upgraded his B– in Introductory Chemistry to an A.

"Yeah, what a relief. My father never walked into a library his whole life."

"You can see why the fine was so great." He blinked. "I just had an idea." Ballard wished her to cease wondering, to the extent this was possible, about the service he had rendered for her father. "How would you like to take a peek at the galley? Forbidden fruit, all that kind of thing. Aren't you curious?"

"You're suggesting we go down those stairs? Wasn't *not* doing that one of our most sacred rules?"

"I believe we were given those rules in order to make sure we broke them."

Sandrine considered this proposition for a moment, then nodded her head.

That's my girl, he thought.

"You may be completely perverted, Ballard, but you're pretty smart." A discordant possibility occurred to her. "What if we catch sight of our extremely discreet servants?"

"Then we know for good and all if they're little tribesmen who chirp like bobolinks or handsome South American yacht bums. But that won't happen. They may, in fact they undoubtedly do, see us, but we'll never catch sight of them. No matter how brilliantly we try to outwit them."

"You think they watch us?"

"I'm sure that's one of their main jobs."

"Even when we're in bed? Even when we . . . you know."

"Especially then," Ballard said.

"What do we think about that, Ballard? Do we love the whole idea, or does it make us sick? You first."

"Neither one. We can't do anything about it, so we might as well forget it. I think being able to watch us is one of the ways they're paid—these tribes don't have much use for money. And because they're always there, they can step in and help us when we need it, at the end."

"So it's like love," said Sandrine.

"Tough love, there at the finish. Let's go over and try the staircase."

"Hold on. When we were out on deck, you told me that you felt you were being watched, and that it was the first time you'd ever had that feeling."

"Yes, that was different—I don't *feel* the natives watching me, I just assume they're doing it. It's the only way to explain how they can stay out of sight all the time."

As they moved across the dining room to the inner door, for the first time Sandrine noticed a curtain the color of a dark camel-hair coat hanging up at the top of the room's oval. Until that moment, she had taken it for a wall too small and oddly shaped to be covered with bookshelves. The curtain shifted a bit, she thought: a tiny ripple occurred in the fabric, as if it had been breathed upon.

There's one of them now, she thought. *I bet they have their own doors and their own staircases.*

For a moment, she was disturbed by a vision of the yacht honeycombed with narrow passages and runways down which beetled small red-brown figures with matted black hair and faces like dull, heavy masks. Now and then the little figures paused to peer through chinks in the walls. It made her feel violated, a little, but at the same time immensely proud of the body at which the unseen and silent attendants were privileged to gaze. The thought of these mysterious little people watching what Ballard did to that body, and she to his, caused a thrill to course upward through her body.

"Stop daydreaming, Sandrine, and get over here." Ballard held the door that led to the gray landing and the metal staircase.

"You go first," she said, and Ballard moved through the frame while still holding the door. As soon as she was through, he stepped around her to grasp the gray metal rail and begin moving down the stairs.

"What makes you so sure the galley's downstairs?"

"Galleys are always downstairs."

"And why do you want to go there, again?"

"One: because they ordered us not to. Two: because I'm curious about what goes on in that kitchen. And three: I also want to get a look at the wine cellar. How can they keep giving us these amazing wines? Remember what we drank with lunch?"

"Some stupid red. It tasted good, though."

"That stupid red was a '55 Château Petrus. Two years older than you."

Ballard led her down perhaps another dozen steps, arrived at a landing, and saw one more long staircase leading down to yet another landing.

"How far down can this galley be?" she asked.

"Good question."

"This boat has a bottom, after all."

"It has a hull, yes."

"Shouldn't we actually have gone past it by now? The bottom of the boat?"

"You'd think so. Okay, maybe this is it."

The final stair ended at a gray landing that opened out into a narrow gray corridor leading to what appeared to be a large, empty room. Ballard looked down into the big space, and experienced a violent reluctance, a mental and physical refusal, to go down there and look further into the room: it was prohibited by an actual taboo. That room was not for him, it was none of his business, period. Chilled, he turned from the corridor and at last saw what was directly before him. What had appeared to be a high gray wall was divided in the middle and bore two brass panels at roughly chest height. The wall was a doorway.

"What do you want to do?" Sandrine asked.

Ballard placed a hand on one of the panels and pushed. The door swung open, revealing a white tile floor, metal racks filled with cast-iron pans, steel bowls, and other cooking implements. The light was a low, diffused dimness. Against the side wall, three sinks of varying sizes bulged downward beneath their faucets. He could see the inner edge of a long, shiny metal counter. Far back, a yellow propane tank clung to a range with six burners, two ovens, and a big griddle. A faint mewing, a tiny *skritch skritch skritch* came to him from the depths of the kitchen.

"Look, is there any chance . . . ?" Sandrine whispered.

In a normal voice, Ballard said, "No. They're not in here right now, whoever they are. I don't think they are, anyhow."

"So does that mean we're supposed to go inside?"

"How would I know?" He looked over his shoulder at her. "Maybe we're not *supposed* to do anything, and we just decide one way or the other. But here we are, anyhow. I say we go in, right? If it feels wrong, smells wrong, whatever, we boogie on out."

"You first," she said.

Without opening the door any wider, Ballard slipped into the kitchen. Before he was all the way in, he reached back and grasped Sandrine's wrist.

"Come along now."

"You don't have to drag me, I was right behind you. You bully."

"I'm not a bully, I just don't want to be in here by myself."

"All bullies are cowards, too."

She edged in behind him and glanced quickly from side to side. "I didn't think you could have a kitchen like this on a yacht."

"You can't," he said. "Look at that gas range. It must weigh a thousand pounds."

She yanked her wrist out of his hand. "It's hard to see in here, though. Why is the light so fucking weird?"

They were edging away from the door, Sandrine so close behind that Ballard could feel her breath on his neck.

"There aren't any light fixtures, see? No overhead lights, either."

He looked up and saw, far above, only a dim white-gray ceiling that stretched away a great distance on either side. Impossibly, the "galley" seemed much wider than the *Blinding Light* itself.

"I don't like this," he said.

"Me neither."

"We're really not supposed to be here," he said, thinking of that other vast room down at the end of the corridor, and said to himself, *That's what they call the "engine room," we absolutely can't even glance that way again, can't can't can't, the "engines" would be way too much for us.*

The mewing and skritching, which had momentarily fallen silent, started up again, and in the midst of what felt and tasted to him like panic, Ballard had a vision of a kitten trapped behind a piece of kitchen equipment. He stepped forward and leaned over to peer into the region beyond the long counter and beside the enormous range. Two funny striped cabinets about five feet tall stood there side by side.

"Do you hear a cat?" he asked.

"If you think that's a cat . . ." Sandrine said, a bit farther behind him than she had been at first.

The cabinets were cages, and what he had seen as stripes were their bars. "Oh," Ballard said, and sounded as though he had been punched in the stomach.

"Damn you, you started to bleed through your suit jacket," Sandrine whispered. "We have to get out of here, fast."

Ballard scarcely heard her. In any case, if he were bleeding, it was of no consequence. They knew what to do about bleeding. Here on the other hand, perhaps sixty feet away in this preposterous "galley," was a phenomenon he had never before witnessed. The first cage contained a thrashing beetle-like insect nearly too large for it. This gigantic insect was the source of the mewing and scratching. One of its mandibles rasped at a bar as the creature struggled to roll forward or back, producing noises of insect distress. Long smeary wounds in the wide middle area between its scrabbling legs oozed a yellow ichor.

Horrified, Ballard looked hastily into the second cage, which he had thought empty but for a roll of blankets, or towels, or the like, and discovered that the blankets or towels were occupied by a small boy from one of the river tribes who was gazing at him through the bars. The boy's eyes looked hopeless and dead. Half of his shoulder seemed to have been sliced away, and a long, thin strip of bone gleamed white against a great scoop of red. The arm half-extended through the bars concluded in a dark, messy stump.

The boy opened his mouth and released, almost too softly to be heard, a single high-pitched musical note. Pure, accurate, well defined, clearly a word charged with some deep emotion, the note hung in the air for a brief moment, underwent a briefer half-life, and was gone.

"What's that?" Sandrine said.

"Let's get out of here."

He pushed her through the door, raced around her, and began charging up the stairs. When they reached the top of the steps and threw themselves into the dining room, Ballard collapsed onto the floor, then rolled onto his back, heaving in great quantities of air. His chest rose and fell, and with every exhalation he moaned. A portion of his left side, pulsing with pain, felt warm and wet. Sandrine leaned against the wall, breathing heavily in a less convulsive way. After perhaps thirty seconds, she managed to say, "I trust that was a bird down there."

"Um. Yes." He placed his hand on his chest, then held it up like a stop sign, indicating that he would soon have more to say. After a few more great heaving lungfuls of air, he said, "Toucan. In a big cage."

"You were that frightened by a kind of parrot?"

He shook his head slowly from side to side on the polished floor. "I didn't want them to catch us down there. It seemed dangerous, all of a sudden. Sorry."

"You're bleeding all over the floor."

"Can you get me a new bandage pad?"

Sandrine pushed herself off the wall and stepped toward him. From his perspective, she was as tall as a statue. Her eyes glittered. "Screw you, Ballard. I'm not your servant. You can come with me. It's where we're going, anyhow."

He pushed himself upright and peeled off his suit jacket before standing up. The jacket fell to the floor with a squishy thump. With blood-dappled fingers, he unbuttoned his shirt and let that, too, fall to the floor.

"Just leave those things there," Sandrine said. "The invisible crew will take care of them."

"I imagine you're right." Ballard managed to get to his feet without staggering. Slow-moving blood continued to ooze down his left side.

"We have to get you on the table," Sandrine said. "Hold this over the wound for right now, okay?"

She handed him a folded white napkin, and he clamped it over his side. "Sorry. I'm not as good at stitches as you are."

"I'll be fine," Ballard said, and began moving, a bit haltingly, toward the next room.

"Oh, sure. You always are. But you know what I like about what we just did?"

For once he had no idea what she might say. He waited for it.

"That amazing food we loved so much was Toucan! Who would've guessed? You'd think Toucan would taste sort of like chicken, only a lot worse."

"Life is full of surprises."

In the bedroom, Ballard kicked off his shoes, pulled his trousers down over his hips, and stepped out of them.

"You can leave your socks on," said Sandrine, "but let's get your undies off, all right?"

"I need your help."

Sandrine grasped the waistband of his boxers and pulled them down, but they snagged on his penis. "Ballard is aroused, surprise number two." She unhooked his shorts, let them drop to the floor, batted his erection down, and watched it bounce back up. "Barkis is willin', all right."

"Let's get into the workroom," he said.

"Aye-aye, *mon capitain*." Sandrine closed her hand on his erection and said, "Want to go there on-deck, give the natives a look at your magnificent manliness? Shall we increase the index of penis envy among the river tribes by a really big factor?"

"Let's just get in there, okay?"

She pulled him into the workroom and only then released his erection.

A wheeled aluminum tray had been rolled up beside the worktable. Sometimes it was not given to them, and they were forced to do their work with their hands and whatever implements they had brought with them. Today, next to the array of knives of many kinds and sizes, cleavers, wrenches, and hammers lay a pack of surgical thread and a stainless steel needle still warm from the autoclave.

Ballard sat down on the worktable, pushed himself along until his heels had cleared the edge, and lay back. Sandrine threaded the needle and, bending over to get close to the wound, began to do her patient, expert stitching.

1982

"Oh, here you are," said Sandrine, walking into the sitting room of their suite to find Ballard lying on one of the sofas, reading a book whose title she could not quite make out. Because both of his hands were heavily bandaged, he was having some difficulty turning the pages. "I've been looking all over for you."

He glanced up, frowning. "All over? Does that mean you went down the stairs?"

"No, of course not. I wouldn't do anything like that alone, anyhow."

"And just to make sure . . . You didn't go up the stairs, either, did you?"

Sandrine came toward him, shaking her head. "No, I'd never do that, either. But I want to tell you something. I thought *you* might have decided to take a look upstairs. By yourself, to sort of protect me in a way I never want to be protected."

"Of course," Ballard said, closing his book on an index finger that protruded from the bulky white swath of bandage. "You'd hate me if I ever tried to protect you, especially by doing something sneaky. I knew that about you when you were fifteen years old."

"When I was fifteen, you did protect me."

He smiled at her. "I exercised an atypical amount of restraint."

His troublesome client, Sandrine's father, had told him one summer day that a business venture required him to spend a week in Mexico City. Could he think of anything acceptable that might occupy his daughter during that time, she being a teenager a bit too prone to independence and exploration? Let her stay with me, Ballard had said. The guest room has its own bathroom and a TV. I'll take her out to theaters at night, and to the Met and MoMA during the day when I'm not doing my job. When I *am* doing my job, she can bat around the city by herself the way she does now. Extraordinary man you are, the client had said, and allow me to reinforce that by letting you know that about a month ago my daughter just amazed me one morning by telling me that she liked you. You have no idea how goddamned fucking unusual that is. That she talked to me at all is staggering, and that she actually announced that she liked one of my friends is stupefying. So yes, please, thank you, take Sandrine home with you, please do, escort her hither and yon.

When the time came, he drove a compliant Sandrine to his house in Harrison, where he explained that although he would not have sex with her until she was at least eighteen, there were many other ways they could express themselves. And although it would be years before they could be naked together, for the present they would each be able to be naked before the other. Fifteen-year-old Sandrine, who had been expecting to use all her arts of bad temper, insult, duplicity, and evasiveness to escape ravishment by this actually pretty interesting old guy, responded to these conditions with avid interest. Ballard announced another prohibition no less serious, but even more personal.

"I can't cut myself anymore?" she asked. "Fuck you, Ballard, you loved it when I showed you my arm. Did my father put you up to this?" She began looking frantically for her bag, which Ballard's valet had already removed to the guest rooms.

"Not at all. Your father would try to kill me if he knew what I was going to do to you. And you to me, when it's your turn."

"So if I can't cut myself, what exactly happens instead?"

"*I* cut you," Ballard said. "And I do it a thousand times better than you ever did. I'll cut you so well, no one will ever be able to tell it happened, unless they're right on top of you."

"You think I'll be satisfied with some wimpy little cuts no one can even see? Fuck you all over again."

"Those cuts no one can see will be incredibly painful. And then I'll take the pain away, so you can experience it all over again."

Sandrine found herself abruptly caught up by a rush of feelings that seemed to originate in a deep region located just below her ribcage. At least for the moment, this flood of unnameable emotions blotted out her endless grudges and frustrations, also the chronic bad temper they engendered.

"And during this process, Sandrine, I will become deeply familiar, profoundly familiar with your body, so that when at last we are able to enjoy sex with each other, I will know how to give you the most amazing pleasure. I'll know every inch of you, I'll have your whole gorgeous map in my head. And you will do the same with me."

Sandrine had astonished herself by agreeing to this program on the spot, even to abstain from sex until she turned eighteen. Denial, too, was a pain she could learn to savor. At that point Ballard had taken her upstairs to show her the guest suite, and soon after down the hallway to what he called his "workroom."

"Oh my God," she said, taking it in, "I can't believe it. This is real. And you, you're real, too."

"During the next three years, whenever you start hating everything around you and feel as though you'd like to cut yourself again, remember that I'm here. Remember that this room exists. There'll be many days and nights when we can be here together."

In this fashion had Sandrine endured the purgatorial remainder of her days at Dalton. And when she and Ballard at last made love, pleasure and pain had become presences nearly visible in the room at the moment she screamed in the ecstasy of release.

"You dirty, dirty, dirty old man," she said, laughing.

A few years after that, Ballard overheard some Chinese bankers, clients of his firm for whom he had several times rendered his services, speaking in soft Mandarin about a yacht anchored in the Amazon Basin; he needed no more.

"I want to go off the boat for a couple of hours when we get to Manaus," Sandrine said. "I feel like getting back in the world again, at least for a little while. This little private bubble of ours is completely cut off from everything else."

"Which is why—"

"Which is why it works, and why we like it, I understand, but half the time I can't stand it, either. I don't live the way you do, always flying off to interesting places to perform miracles . . ."

"Try spending a rainy afternoon in Zurich holding some terminally anxious banker's hand."

"Not that it matters, especially, but you don't mind, do you?"

"Of course not. I need some recuperation time, anyhow. This was a little severe." He held up one thickly bandaged hand. "Not that I'm complaining."

"You'd better not!"

"I'll only complain if you stay out too late—or spend too much of your father's money!"

"What could I buy in Manaus? And I'll make sure to be back before dinner. Have you noticed? The food on this weird boat is getting better and better every day?"

"I know, yes, but for now I seem to have lost my appetite," Ballard said. He had a quick mental vision of a metal cage from which something hideous was struggling to escape. It struck an oddly familiar note, as of something half-remembered, but Ballard was made so uncomfortable by the image in his head that he refused to look at it any longer.

"Will they just know that I want to dock at Manaus?"

"Probably, but you could write them a note. Leave it on the bed. Or on the dining room table."

"I have a pen in my bag, but where can I find some paper?"

"I'd say, look in any drawer. You'll probably find all the paper you might need."

Sandrine went to the little table beside him, pulled open its one drawer, and found a single sheet of thick, cream-colored stationery headed *sweet delight*. An Omas Rollerball pen, much nicer than the Pilot she had liberated from their hotel in Rio, lay angled atop the sheet of stationery. In her formal, almost italic handwriting, Sandrine wrote: *Please dock at Manaus. I would like to spend two or three hours ashore.*

"Should I sign it?"

Ballard shrugged. "There's just the two of us. Initial it."

She drew a graceful, looping *S* under her note and went into the dining room, where she squared it off in the middle of the table. When she returned to the sitting room, she asked, "And now I just wait? Is that how it works? Just because I found a piece of paper and a pen, I'm supposed to trust this crazy system?"

"You know as much as I do, Sandrine. But I'd say yes, just wait a little while, yes, that's how it works, and yes, you might as well trust it. There's no reason to be bitchy."

"I have to stay in practice," she said, and lurched sideways as the yacht bumped against something hard and came to an abrupt halt.

"See what I mean?"

When he put the book down in his lap, Sandrine saw that it was *Tono Bungay*. She felt a hot, rapid flare of irritation that the book was not something like *The Women's Room*, which could teach him things he needed to know: and hadn't he already read *Tono Bungay*?

"Look outside, try to catch them tying us up and getting out that walkway thing."

"You think we're in Manaus already?"

"I'm sure we are."

"That's ridiculous. We scraped against a barge or something."

"Nonetheless, we have come to a complete halt."

Sandrine strode briskly to the on-deck door, threw it open, gasped, then stepped outside. The yacht had already been tied up at a long yellow dock at which two yachts smaller than theirs rocked in a desultory brown tide. No crewmen were in sight. The dock led to a wide concrete apron across which men of European descent and a few natives pushed wheelbarrows and consulted clipboards and pulled on cigars while pointing out distant things to other men. It looked false and stagy, like the first scene in a bad musical about New Orleans. An avenue began in front of a row of warehouses, the first of which was painted with the slogan MANAUS AMAZONA. The board walkway with rope handrails had been set in place.

"Yeah, okay," she said. "We really do seem to be docked at Manaus."

"Don't stay away too long."

"I'll stay as long as I like," she said.

The avenue leading past the facades of the warehouses seemed to run directly into the center of the city, visible now to Sandrine as a gathering of tall office buildings and apartment blocks that thrust upward from the jumble of their surroundings like an outcropping of mountains. The skyscrapers were blue-gray in color, the lower surrounding buildings a scumble of brown, red, and yellow that made Sandrine think of Cézanne, even of Seurat: dots of color that suggested walls and roofs. She thought she could walk to the center of the city in no more than forty-five minutes, which left her about two hours to do some exploring and have lunch.

Nearly an hour later, Sandrine trudged past the crumbling buildings and broken windows on crazed, tilting sidewalks under a domineering sun. Sweat ran down her forehead and cheeks and plastered her dress to her body. The air seemed half water, and her lungs strained to draw in oxygen. The office buildings did not seem any nearer than at the start of her walk. If she had seen a taxi, she would have taken it back to the port, but only a few cars and pickups rolled along the broad avenue. The dark, half-visible men driving these vehicles generally leaned over their steering wheels and stared at her, as if women were rare in Manaus. She wished she had thought to cover her hair, and was sorry she had left her sunglasses behind.

Then she became aware that a number of men were following her, how many she could not tell, but more than two. They spoke to each other in low, hoarse voices, now and then laughing at some remark sure to be at Sandrine's expense. Although her feet had begun to hurt, she began moving more quickly. Behind her, the men kept pace with her, neither gaining nor falling back. After another two blocks, Sandrine gave in to her sense of alarm and glanced over her shoulder. Four men in dark hats and shapeless, slept-in suits had ranged themselves across the width of the sidewalk. One of them called out to her in a language she did not understand; another emitted a wet, mushy laugh. The man at the curb jumped down into the street, trotted across the empty avenue, and picked up his pace on the sidewalk opposite until he had drawn a little ahead of Sandrine.

She felt utterly alone and endangered. And because she felt in danger, a scorching anger blazed up within her: at herself for so stupidly putting herself at risk, at the men behind her for making her feel frightened, for ganging up on her. She did not know what she was going to have to do, but she was not going to let those creeps get any closer to her than they were now. Twisting to her right, then to her left, Sandrine removed her shoes and rammed them into her bag. They were watching her, the river scum; even the man on the other side of the avenue had stopped moving and was staring at her from beneath the brim of his hat.

Literally testing the literal ground, Sandrine walked a few paces over the paving stones, discovered that they were at any rate not likely to cut her feet, gathered herself within, and, like a race horse bursting from the gate, instantly began running as fast as she could. After a moment in which her pursuers were paralyzed with surprise, they too began to run. The man on the other side of the street jumped down from the curb and began sprinting toward her. His shoes made a sharp *tick-tick* sound when they met the stony asphalt. As the ticks grew louder, Sandrine heard him inhaling great quantities of air. Before he could reach her, she came to a cross street and wheeled in, her bag bouncing at her hip, her legs stretching out to devour yard after yard of stony ground.

Unknowingly, she had entered a slum. The structures on both sides of the street were half-collapsed huts and shanties made of mismatched wooden planks, metal sheeting, and tar paper. She glimpsed faces peering out of greasy windows and sagging, cracked-open doors. Some of the shanties before her were shops with soft drink cans and bottles of beer arrayed on the windowsills. People were spilling from little tar paper and sheet-metal structures out into the street already congested with abandoned cars, empty pushcarts, and cartons of fruit for sale. Garbage lay everywhere. The women who watched Sandrine streak by displayed no interest in her plight.

Yet the slum's chaos was a blessing, Sandrine thought: the deeper she went, the greater the number of tiny narrow streets sprouting off the one she had taken from the avenue. It was a feverish, crowded warren, a favela, the kind of place you would never escape had you the bad luck to have been born there. And while outside this rat's nest the lead man chasing her had been getting dangerously near, within its boundaries the knots of people and the obstacles of cars and carts and mounds of garbage had slowed him down. Sandrine found that she could dodge all of these obstacles with relative ease. The next time she spun around a corner, feet skidding on a slick pad of rotting vegetables, she saw what looked to her like a miracle: an open door revealing a hunched old woman draped in black rags, beckoning her in.

Sandrine bent her legs, called on her youth and strength, jumped off the ground, and sailed through the open door. The old woman only just got out of the way in time to avoid being knocked down. She was giggling, either at Sandrine's athleticism or because she had rescued her from the pursuing thugs. When Sandrine had cleared her doorway and was scrambling to avoid ramming into the wall, the old woman darted forward and slammed her door shut. Sandrine fell to her knees in a small room suddenly gone very dark. A slanting shaft of light split the murk and illuminated a rectangular space on the floor covered by a threadbare rug no longer of any identifiable color. Under the light, the rug seemed at once utterly worthless and extraordinarily beautiful.

The old woman shuffled into the shaft of light and uttered an incomprehensible word that sounded neither Spanish nor Portuguese. A thousand wayward wrinkles like knife cuts, scars, and stitches had been etched into her white, elongated face. Her nose had a prominent hook, and her eyes shone like dark stones at the bottom of a fast, clear stream. Then she laid an upright index finger against her sunken lips and with her other hand gestured toward the door. Sandrine listened. In seconds, multiple footsteps pounded past the old woman's little house. Leading the pack was *tick tick tick*. The footsteps clattered up the narrow street and disappeared into the ordinary clamor.

Hunched over almost parallel to the ground, the old woman mimed hysterical laughter. Sandrine mouthed Thank you, thank you, thinking that her intention would be clear if the words were not. Still mock-laughing, her unknown savior shuffled closer, knitting and folding her long, spotted hands. She had the ugliest hands Sandrine had ever seen, knobbly arthritic fingers with filthy, ragged nails. She hoped the woman was not going to stroke her hair or pat her face: she would have to let her do it, however nauseated she might feel. Instead, the old woman moved right past her, muttering what sounded like Munna, munna, num.

Outside on the street, the ticking footsteps once again became audible. Someone began knocking, hard, on an adjacent door.

Only half-visible at the rear of the room, the old woman turned toward Sandrine and beckoned her forward with an urgent gesture of her bony hand. Sandrine moved toward her, uncertain of what was going on.

In an urgent, raspy whisper: *Munna! Num!*

The old woman appeared to be bowing to the baffled Sandrine, whose sense of peril had begun again to boil up within her. A pane of greater darkness slid open behind the old woman, and Sandrine finally understood that her savior had merely bent herself more deeply to turn a doorknob.

Num! Num!

Sandrine obeyed orders and *nummed* past her beckoning hostess. Almost instantly, instead of solid ground, her foot met a vacancy, and she nearly tumbled down what she finally understood to be a staircase. Only her sense of balance kept her upright: she was grateful she still had all of her crucial toes. Behind her, the door slammed shut. A moment later, she heard the clicking of a lock.

Back on the yacht, Ballard slipped a bookmark into *Tono Bungay* and for the first time, at least for what he thought was the first time, regarded the pair of red-lacquered cabinets against the wall beside him. Previously, he had taken them in, but never really examined them. About four feet high and three feet wide, they appeared to be Chinese and were perhaps moderately valuable. Brass fittings with latch pins held them closed in front, so they could be easily opened.

The thought of lifting the pins and opening the cabinets aroused both curiosity and an odd dread in Ballard. For a moment, he had a vision of a great and forbidden room deep in the bowels of the yacht where enormous spiders ranged across rotting, heaped-up corpses. (With wildly variant details, visions of exactly this sort had visited Ballard ever since his adolescence.) He shook his head to clear it of this vision, and when that failed, struck his bandaged left hand against the padded arm of the sofa. Bright, rolling waves of pain forced a gasp from him, and the forbidden room with its spiders and corpses zipped right back to wherever had given it birth.

Was this the sort of dread he was supposed to obey, or the sort he was supposed to ignore? Or, if not ignore, because that was always unwise and in some sense dishonorable, acknowledge but persist in the face of anyway? Cradling his throbbing hand against his chest, Ballard let the book slip off his lap and got to his feet, eyeing the pair of shiny cabinets. If asked to inventory the contents of the sitting room, he would have forgotten to list them. Presumably that meant he was supposed to overlook his foreboding and investigate the contents of these vertical little Chinese chests. *They* wanted him to open the cabinets, if *he* wanted to.

Still holding his electrocuted left hand to his chest, Ballard leaned over and brought his exposed right index finger in contact with the box on the left. No heat came from it, and no motion. It did not hum, it did not quiver, however delicately. At least six or seven coats of lacquer had been applied to the thing—he felt as though he were looking into a deep red river.

Ballard hunkered and used his index finger to push the brass latch pin up and out of the ornate little lock. It swung down on an intricate little cord he had not previously noticed. The door did not open by itself, as he had hoped. Once again, he had to make a choice, for it was not too late to drop the brass pin back into its latch. He could choose not to look; he could let the *Sweet Delight* keep its secrets. But as before, Ballard acknowledged the dread he was feeling, then dropped his hip to the floor, reached out, and flicked the door open with his fingernail. Arrayed on the cabinet's three shelves were what appeared to be photographs in neat stacks. Polaroids, he thought. He took the first stack of photos from the cabinet and looked down at the topmost one. What Ballard saw there had two contradictory effects on him. He became so light-headed he feared he might faint; and he almost ejaculated into his trousers.

Taking care not to tumble, Sandrine moved in the darkness back to the top of the staircase, found the door with her fingertips, and pounded. The door rattled in its frame but did not give. "Open up, lady!" she shouted. "Are you *kidding*? Open this door!" She banged her fists against the unmoving wood, thinking that although the old woman undoubtedly did not speak English, she could hardly misunderstand what Sandrine was saying. When her fists began to hurt and her throat felt ragged, the strangeness of what had just happened opened before her: it was like . . . like a fairy tale! She had been duped, tricked, flummoxed; she had been trapped. The world had closed on her, as a steel trap snaps shut on the leg of a bear.

"Please!" she yelled, knowing it was useless. She would not be able to beg her way out of this confinement. Here, the Golden Shower of Shit did not apply. "Please let me out!" A few more bangs of her fist, a few more shouted pleas to be set free, to be *let go, released*. She thought she heard her ancient captor chuckling to herself.

Two possibilities occurred to her: that her pursuers had driven her to this place and the old woman was in league with them; and that they had not and she was not. The worse by far of these options was the second, that to escape her rapists she had fled into a psychopath's dungeon. Maybe the old woman wanted to starve her to death. Maybe she wanted to soften her up so she'd be easy to kill. Or maybe she was just keeping her as a snack for some monstrous get of hers, some overgrown loony-tunes son with pinwheel eyes and horrible teeth and a vast appetite for stray women.

More to exhaust all of her possibilities than because she imagined they possessed any actual substance, Sandrine turned carefully around, planted a hand on the earthen wall beside her, and began making her way down the stairs in the dark. It would lead to some spider-infested cellar, she knew, a foul-smelling hole where ugly, discarded things waited thuglike in the seamless dark to inflict injury upon anyone who entered their realm. She would grope her way from wall to wall, feeling for another door, for a high window, for any means to escape, knowing all the while that earthen cellars in shabby slum dwellings never had separate exits.

Five steps down, it occurred to Sandrine that she might not have been the first woman to be locked into this awful basement, and that instead of broken chairs and worn-out tools she might find herself knocking against a ribcage or two, a couple of femurs, that her foot might land on the jawbone, that she might step on somebody's forehead! Her body all of a sudden shook, and her mind went white, and for a few moments Sandrine was on the verge of coming unglued: she pictured herself drawn up into a fetal ball, shuddering, weeping, whimpering. For a moment this dreadful image seemed unbearably tempting.

Then she thought, *Why the FUCK isn't Ballard here?*

Ballard was one hell of a tricky dude, he was full of little surprises, you could never really predict what he'd feel like doing, and he was a brilliant problem solver. That's what Ballard did for a living, he flew around the world mopping up other people's messes. The only reason Sandrine knew him at all was that Ballard had materialized in a New Jersey motel room where good old Dad, Lauritzen Loy, had been dithering over the corpse of a strangled whore, then caused the whore to vanish, the bloody sheets to vanish, and for all she knew the motel to vanish also. Two hours later a shaken but sober Lauritzen Loy reported to work in an immaculate and spotless Armani suit and Brioni tie. (Sandrine had known the details of her father's vile little peccadillo for years.) Also—and this quality meant that his presence would have been particularly valuable down in the witch-hag's cellar—although Ballard might have looked as though he had never picked up anything heavier than a briefcase, he was in fact astonishingly strong, fast, and smart. If you were experiencing a little difficulty with a dragon, Ballard was the man for you.

While meditating upon the all-around excellence of her longtime lover and wishing for him more with every fresh development of her thought, Sandrine had been continuing steadily on her way down the stairs. When she reached the part about the dragon, it came to her that she had been on these earthen stairs far longer than she had expected. Sandrine thought she was now actually beneath the level of the cellar she had expected to enter. The fairy tale feeling came over her again, of being held captive in a world without rational rules and orders, subject to deep patterns unknown to or rejected in the daylit world. In a flash of insight, it came to her that this fairy-tale world had much in common with her childhood.

To regain control of herself, perhaps most of all to shake off the sense of gloom-laden helplessness evoked by thoughts of childhood, Sandrine began to count the steps as she descended. Down into the earth they went, the dry firm steps that met her feet, twenty more, then forty, then fifty. At a hundred and one, she felt light-headed and weary, and sat down in the darkness. She felt like weeping. The long stairs were a grave, leading nowhere but to itself. Hope, joy, and desire had fled, even boredom and petulance had fled, hunger, lust, and anger were no more. She felt tired and empty. Sandrine leaned a shoulder against the earthen wall, shuddered once, and realized she was crying only a moment before she fled into unconsciousness.

In that same instant she passed into an ongoing dream, as if she had wandered into the middle of a story, more accurately a point far closer to its ending. Much, maybe nearly everything of interest, had already happened. Sandrine lay on a mess of filthy blankets at the bottom of a cage. The Golden Shower of Shit had sufficiently relaxed, it seemed, as to permit the butchering of entire slabs of flesh from her body, for much of the meat from her right shoulder had been sliced away. The wound reported a dull, wavering ache that spoke of those wonderful objects, Ballard's narcotic painkillers. So close together were the narrow bars, she could extend only a hand, a wrist, an arm. In her case, an arm, a wrist, and a stump. The hand was absent from the arm Sandrine had slipped through the bars, and someone had cauterized the wounded wrist.

The Mystery of the Missing Hand led directly to Cage Number One, where a giant bug-creature sat crammed in at an angle, filling nearly the whole of the cage, mewing softly, and trying to saw through the bars with its remaining mandible. It had broken the left one on the bars, but it was not giving up, it was a bug, and bugs don't quit. Sandrine was all but certain that when in possession of both mandibles, that is to say before capture, this huge *thing* had used them to saw off her hand, which it had then promptly devoured. The giant bugs were the scourge of the river tribes. However, the Old Ones, the Real People, the Cloud Huggers, the Tree Spirits, the archaic Sacred Ones who spoke in birdsong and called themselves WE had so shaped the River and the Forest, which had given them birth, that the meat of the giant bugs tasted exceptionally good, and a giant bug guilty of eating a person or parts of a person became by that act overwhelmingly delicious, like manna, like the food of paradise for human beings. WE were feeding bits of Sandrine to the captured bug that it might yield stupendous meals for the Sandrine and Ballard upstairs.

Sandrine awakened crying out in fear and horror, scattering tears she could not see.

Enough of that. Yes, quite enough of quivering; it was time to decide what to do next. Go back and try to break down the door, or keep going down and see what happens? Sandrine hated the idea of giving up and going backward. She levered herself upright and resumed her descent with stair number one hundred and two.

At stair three hundred she passed through another spasm of weepy trembling, but soon conquered it and moved on. By the four hundredth stair she was hearing faint carnival music and seeing sparkly light-figments flit through the darkness like illuminated moths. Somewhere around stair five hundred she realized that the numbers had become mixed up in her head, and stopped counting. She saw a grave that wasn't a grave, merely darkness, and she saw her old tutor at Clare, a cool, detached don named Quentin Jester who said things like "If I had a lifetime with you, Miss Loy, we'd both know a deal more than we do at present," but she closed her eyes and shook her head and sent him packing.

Many stairs later, Sandrine's thigh muscles reported serious aches, and her arms felt extraordinarily heavy. So did her head, which kept lolling forward to rest on her chest. Her stomach complained, and she said to herself, *Wish I had a nice big slice of sautéed giant bug right about now*, and chuckled at how crazy she had become in so short a time. Giant bug! Even good old Dad, old LL, who often respected sanity in others but wished for none of it himself, drew the line at dining on giant insects. And here came yet another proof of her deteriorating mental condition, that despite her steady progress deeper and deeper underground, Sandrine could almost sort of half-persuade herself that the darkness before her seemed weirdly less dark than only a moment ago. This lunatic delusion clung to her step after step, worsening as she went. She said to herself, I'll hold up my hand, and if I think I see it, I'll know it's good-bye, real world, pack Old Tillie off to Bedlam. She stopped moving, closed her eyes, and raised her hand before her face. Slowly, she opened her eyes, and beheld . . . her hand!

The problem with the insanity defense lay in the irrevocable truth that it was really her hand before her, not a mad vision from Gothic literature but her actual, entirely earthly hand, at present crusted with dirt from its long contact with the wall. Sandrine turned her head and discovered that she could make out the wall, too, with its hard-packed earth showing here and there the pale string of a severed root, at times sending in her direction a little spray or shower of dusty particulate. Sandrine held her breath and looked down to what appeared to be the source of the illumination. Then she inhaled sharply, for it seemed to her that she could see, dimly and a long way down, the bottom of the stairs. A little rectangle of light burned away down there, and from it floated the luminous translucency that made it possible for her to see.

Too shocked to cry, too relieved to insist on its impossibility, Sandrine moved slowly down the remaining steps to the rectangle of light. Its warmth heated the air, the steps, the walls, and Sandrine herself, who only now registered that for most of her journey she had been half paralyzed by the chill leaking from the earth. As she drew nearer to the light, she could finally make out details of what lay beneath her. She thought she saw a strip of concrete, part of a wooden barrel, the bottom of a ladder lying on the ground: the intensity of the light surrounding these enigmatic objects shrank and dwindled them, hollowed them out even as it drilled painfully into her eyes. Beneath her world existed another, its light a blinding dazzle.

When Sandrine had come within thirty feet of the blazing underworld, her physical relationship to it mysteriously altered. It seemed she no longer stepped downward, but moved across a slanting plane that leveled almost imperceptibly off. The dirt walls on either side fell back and melted to ghostly gray air, to nothing solid, until all that remained was the residue of dust and grime plastered over Sandrine's white dress, her hands and face, her hair. Heat reached her, the real heat of an incendiary sun, and human voices, and the clang and bang and underlying susurrus of machinery. She walked toward all of it, shading her eyes as she went.

Through the simple opening before her Sandrine moved, and the sun blazed down upon her, and her own moisture instantly soaked her filthy dress, and sweat turned the dirt in her hair to muddy trickles. She knew this place; the dazzling underworld was the world she had left. From beneath her shading hand Sandrine took in the wide concrete apron, the equipment she had noticed all that harrowing time ago and the equipment she had not, the men posturing for the benefit of other men, the sense of falsity and stagecraft and the incipient swelling of a banal unheard melody. The long yellow dock where on a sluggish umber tide three yachts slowly rocked, one of them the *Sweet Delight*.

In a warm breeze that was not a breeze, a soiled-looking scrap of paper flipped toward Sandrine over the concrete, at the last lifting off the ground to adhere to her leg. She bent down to peel it off and release it, and caught a strong, bitter whiff, unmistakably excremental, of the Amazon. The piece of paper wished to cling to her leg, and there it hung until the second tug of Sandrine's dirty fingers, when she observed that she was gripping not a scrap of paper but a Polaroid, now a little besmudged by contact with her leg. When she raised it to her face, runnels of dirt obscured portions of the image. She brushed away much of the dirt, but could still make no sense of the photograph, which appeared to depict some piglike animal.

In consternation, she glanced to one side and found there, lounging against bollards and aping the idleness of degenerates and river louts, two of the men in shabby suits and worn-out hats who had pursued her into the slum. She straightened up in rage and terror, and to confirm what she already knew to be the case, looked to her other side and saw their companions. One of them waved to her. Sandrine's terror cooled before her perception that these guys had changed in some basic way. Maybe they weren't idle, exactly, but these men were more relaxed, less predatory than they had been on the avenue into Manaus.

They had their eyes on her, though, they were interested in what she was going to do. Then she finally got it: they were different because now she was where they had wanted her to be all along. They didn't think she would try to escape again, but they wanted to make sure. Sandrine's whole long adventure, from the moment she noticed she was being followed to the present, had been designed to funnel her back to the dock and the yacht. The four men, who were now smiling at her and nodding their behatted heads, had pushed her toward the witch-hag, for they were all in it together! Sandrine dropped her arms, took a step backward, and in amazement looked from side to side, taking in all of them. It had all been a trick; herded like a cow, she had been played. Falsity again; more stagecraft.

One of the nodding, smiling men held his palm up before his face, and the man beside him leaned forward and laughed into his fist, as if shielding a sneeze. Grinning at her, the first man went through his meaningless mime act once again, lifting his left hand and staring into its palm. Grinning even more widely, he pointed at Sandrine and shouted, *"Munna!"*

The man beside him cracked up, *Munna!*, what a wit, then whistled an odd little four-note melody that might have been a birdcall.

Experimentally, Sandrine raised her left hand, regarded it, and realized that she was still gripping the dirty little Polaroid photograph of a pig. Those two idiots off to her left waved their hands in ecstasy. She was doing the right thing, so *Munna!* right back atcha, buddy. She looked more closely at the Polaroid and saw that what it pictured was not actually a pig. The creature in the photo had a head and a torso, but little else. The eyes, nose, and ears were gone. A congeries of scars like punctuation marks, like snakes, like words in an unknown language, decorated the torso.

I know what Munna *means, and* Num, thought Sandrine, and for a moment experienced a spasm of stunning, utterly sexual warmth before she fully understood what had been given her: that she recognized the man in the photo. The roar of oceans, of storm-battered leaves, filled her ears and caused her head to spin and wobble. Her fingers parted, and the Polaroid floated off in an artificial, wind-machine breeze that spun it around a couple of times before lifting it high above the port and winking it out of sight, lost in the bright hard blue above the *Sweet Delight*.

Sandrine found herself moving down the yellow length of the long dock.

Tough love, Ballard had said. To be given and received, at the end perfectly repaid by that which she had perhaps glimpsed but never witnessed, the brutal, exalted, slow-moving force that had sometimes rustled a curtain, sometimes moved through this woman, her hair and body now dark with mud, had touched her between her legs, Sandrine, poor profane lost deluded most marvelously fated Sandrine.

1997

From the galley they come, from behind the little dun-colored curtain in the dining room, from behind the bookcases in the handsome sitting room, from beneath the bed and the bloodstained metal table, through wood and fabric and the weight of years, WE come, the Old Ones and Real People, the Cloud Huggers, WE process slowly toward the center of the mystery WE understand only by giving it unquestioning service. What remains of the clients and patrons lies, still breathing though without depth or force, upon the metal work-table. It was always going to end this way, it always does, it can no other. Speaking in the high-pitched, musical language of birds that WE taught the Pirahã at the beginning of time, WE gather at the site of these ruined bodies, WE worship their devotion to each other and the Great Task that grew and will grow on them, WE treat them with grave tenderness as WE separate what can and must be separated. Notes of the utmost liquid purity float upward from the mouths of WE and print themselves upon the air. WE know what they mean, though they have long since passed through the realm of words and gained again the transparency of music. WE love and accept the weight and the weightlessness of music. When the process of separation is complete, through the old sacred inner channels WE transport what the dear, still-living man and woman have each taken from the other's body down down down to the galley and the ravening hunger that burns ever within it.

Then. Then. With the utmost tenderness, singing the deep tuneless music at the heart of the ancient world, WE gather up what remains of Ballard and Sandrine, armless and legless trunks, faces without features, their breath clinging to their mouths like wisps, carry them (in our arms, in baskets, in once-pristine sheets) across the deck and permit them to roll from our care, as they have always longed to do, and into that of the flashing furious little river-monarchs. WE watch the water boil in a magnificence of ecstasy, and WE sing for as long as it lasts.

The Collected Short Stories of Freddie Prothero

Introduction by Torless Magnussen, Ph.D.

The present volume presents in chronological order every known short story written by Frederick "Freddie" Prothero. Of causes that must ever remain obscure, he died "flying solo," his expression for venturing out in search of solitude, in a field two blocks from his house in Prospect Fair, Connecticut. His death took place in January 1988, nine months before his ninth birthday. It was a Sunday. At the hour of his death, approximately four o'clock of a bright, cold, snow-occluded day, the writer was wearing a hooded tan snowsuit he had in fact technically outgrown; a red woolen scarf festooned with "pills"; an imitation Aran knit sweater, navy blue with cables; a green-and-blue plaid shirt from Sam's; dark green corduroys with cuffs beginning to grow ragged; a shapeless white Jockey T-shirt also worn the day previous; Jockey briefs, once white, now stained lemon yellow across the Y-front; white tube socks; Tru-Value Velcro sneakers, so abraded as nearly to be threadbare; and black calf-high rubber boots with six metal buckles.

The inscription on the toaster-sized tombstone in Prospect Fair's spacious Gullikson & Son Cemetery reads FREDERICK MICHAEL PROTHERO, 1979–1988. A NEW ANGEL IN HEAVEN. In that small span of years, really in a mere three of those not-yet eight-and-a-half years, Freddie Prothero went from apprenticeship to mastery with unprecedented speed, in the process authoring ten of the most visionary short stories in the English language. It is my belief that this collection will now stand as a definitive monument to the unique merits—and difficulties!—presented by the only genuine prodigy in American literature.

That Prothero's fiction permits a multiplicity of interpretations supplies a portion, though scarcely all, of its interest to both the academic and the general reader. Beginning in 1984 with childish, nearly brutal simplicity and evolving toward the more polished (though still in fact unfinished) form of expression seen in the work of his later years, these stories were apparently presented to his mother, Varda Prothero, née Barthelmy. (*Baathy, baathy, momma sai.*) In any case, Momma Baathy Prothero preserved them (perhaps after the fact?) in individual manila files within a snug, smoothly mortised and sanded cherrywood box.

As the above example demonstrates, the earliest Prothero, the stories written from his fifth to seventh years, displays the improvised variant spelling long encouraged by American primary schools. The reader will easily decipher the childish code, although I should perhaps explain that *bood gig* stands for "bad guy."

From first to last, the stories demonstrate the writer's awareness of the constant presence of a bood gig. A threatening, indeterminate figure, invested with all the terrifying power and malignity of the monster beneath a child's bed, haunts this fiction. Prothero's "monster" figure, however, is not content to confine itself to the underside of his bed. It roams the necessarily limited map of the writer's forays both within and outside of his house: that is, across his front yard; down Gerhardie Street, which runs past his house; through the supermarket he, stroller-bound, visits with his mother; and perhaps above all in the shadowy, clamorous city streets he is forced to traverse with his father on the few occasions when R(andolph) Sullivan "Sully" Prothero brought him along to the law office where he spent sixty hours a week in pursuit of the partnership attained in 1996, eight years after his son's death and two prior to his own unexplained disappearance. The commuter train from Prospect Fair to Penn Station was another location favored by the omniscient shadow figure.

Though these occasions were in fact no more than an annual event (more specifically, on the Take Your Son to Work Days of 1985–86), they had a near-traumatic, no, let us face the facts and say traumatic, effect on Prothero. He pleaded, he wept, he screamed, he cowered gibbering in terror. One imagines the mingled disdain and distress of the fellow passengers, the unsympathetic conductor. The journey through the streets to Fifty-fourth and Madison was a horrifying trek, actually heroic on the boy's part.

A high-functioning alcoholic chronically unfaithful to his spouse, "Sully" was an absent, at best an indifferent, father. In her role as mother, Varda, about whom one has learned so much in recent years, can be counted, alas, as no better. The Fair Haven pharmacists open to examination of their records by a scholar of impeccable credentials have permitted us to document Varda's reliance upon the painkillers Vicodin, Percodan, and Percocet. Those seeking an explanation for her son's shabby, ill-fitting wardrobe need look no further. (One wishes almost to weep. His poor little snowsuit too tight for his growing body! And his autopsy, conducted in a completely up-to-date facility in Norwalk, Connecticut, revealed that, but for a single slice of bread lightly smeared with oleomargarine, Prothero had eaten nothing at all that day. Imagine.)

In some quarters, the four stories of 1984, his fifth year, are not thought to belong in a collection of his work, being difficult to decode from their primitive spelling and level of language. Absent any narrative sense whatsoever, these very early works perhaps ought to be considered poetry rather than prose. Prothero would not be the first author of significant fiction to begin by writing poems. The earliest works do, however, present the first form of this writer's themes and perhaps offer (multiple) suggestions of their emotional and intellectual significance.

Among the small number of we dedicated Protherians, considerable disagreement exists over the meaning and identification of the "Mannotmann," sometimes "Monnuttmonn." "Man not man" is one likely decipherment of the term, "Mammoth man" another. In the first of these works, "Te Styree Uboy F-R-E-D-D-I-E," or "The Story about Freddie," Prothero writes, *Ay am nott F-R-E-D-D-I-E*, and we are told that Freddie, a scaredy-cat, needs him precisely because Freddie is *not* "Mannotmann." *Can you hear me, everybody?* he asks: for this is a central truth.

The precocious child is self-protectively separating from himself within the doubled protection of art, the only realm available to the sane mind in which such separation is possible. In story after story, we are at first informed then reminded that this literal child, our author, had entered into an awareness of self-exile so profound and insistent, so inherent to the very act of expression, as to remind us of Fernando Pessoa. *Ol droo*, he tells us: It is all true. *Ol droo*, indeed.

It should go without saying, though unhappily it cannot, that the author's statement, in the more mature spelling and diction of his sixth year, that a man *came from the sky* does not refer to the appearance of an extraterrestrial. Some of my colleagues in Prothero studies strike one as nearly as juvenile as, though rather less savvy than, the doomed, hungry little genius who so commands all of us.

1984
Te Styree Uboy F-R-E-D-D-I-E

Ay am nott F-r-e-d-d-i-e. F-R-E-D-D-I-E nott be mee
Hah hah
F-R-E-D-D-I-E iss be nyce, tooo Cin yoo her mee, evvrrie
F-r-e-d-d-i-e iss scarrdiecutt fradydiecutt, nott mee Hee neid mee.
Mannnuttmonn hah scir him hah hah
Bcayuzz Monnntmonn hee eezzz naytt
BOOOO
Ol droo

Ta Sturree Ubot Monnnuttmonn

Baathy baathy momma sai baathy mi nom mommnas sai in gd dyz id wuzz Baaaathy
Monnoittmoon be lissen yz hee lizzen oh ho
Tnbur wz a boi nommed F-r-e-d-d-i-e sai Monnuttmon he sai evvrwhy inn shaar teevee taybbull rug ayr

F-r-e-d-d-i-e un Monnuttmin

Monnuttmoon sai gud boi F-r-e-d-d-i-e god boi
En niht sai SKRREEEEAAAKKKK her wz da bood gig
SKREEEEAAAAKK mummay no heer onny F-r-e-d-d-i-e
Ta bood gig smylz smylz smilez hippi bood gig SKKRREEEEE-AAAAAKK att niht
Hi terz mi ert appurt id hertz my ert mi ert pur erzees
Bugg flyes in skie bugg waks on gras
Whi nutt F-r-e-d-d-i-e kann bee bugg
oho ha ha F-r-e-d-d-i-e pur boi pour boi

Ta Struuyrie Abot Dadddi

Wee go in trauyhn sai Dudddi wee wuk striits sai Duddi noon ooh sai F-r-e-d-d-i-e

Bood gig lissen bood gig lisen an laff yu cribbabby cri al yu went sai Mannuttmon

Daddi sai sit heir siitt doon sunn and te boi satt dunn onb triyn wiff Mannnottmonn ryt bezyd hum te biu wuzz escayrt att nite nooo hee sai nooo mummma nut trayn

Hah hah

Dyddi be nutt Mannuttmon F-r-e-d-d-i-e be nott Mannuttmon Mummna be nott Mannuttmon hah no Cus Mannotttmon izz mee Aruynt de Kernerr duywn de strittt ever evverweaur

Deddi sai Wak Faysterr Wak Fayster Whatt ur yu affraitt ovv WhATT

De kerner de strett F-r-e-d-d-i-e sai

1985
The Cornoo

The boy waz standing. He waz standing in the cornoo. There waz a man who caym from the sky. The sky was al blakk. I ate the starz sed the man around the cornoo. The boy cloused his eyz. I ate the stars I ate the moon and the sunn now I eat the wrld. And yu in it. He laft. Yu go playe now he sed. If play yu can. Hah hah he laft. Freddie waked until he ran. That waz suun. I waz in my cornoo and I saw that, I saw him runn. Runn, Freddie. Runn, lettul boy.

Wher iz F-R-E-D-D-I-E ??

He waz not in the bed. He was not in the kishen he was not in the living roome. The Mumma could not find littl Freddie. The man from the blakk sky came and tuke the boy to the ruume in the sky. The Mumma calld the Duddah and she sed are you takng the boy??? Giv him bakk, she sed. This iz my sunn she sed and the Duddah said cam down ar yu craazie?? Becus rembur this is my sunn to onnlee I doin havv him. I saw from the rome in the sky. I herd. They looked soo lidl. And small. And teenie tinee downn thur small as the bugs. Ar you

F-R-E-D-D-I-E ?? ast the man of the ruume. No he sed. I waz nevrr him. Now I am the blakk sky and I waz alws the blakk sky.

F-R-E-D-D-I-E Is Lahst

The Mumma the Duddah they sed Were Culd Hee Bee? It waz funnee. They cri they cri OUT hiz namm Freddie Freddie you are lahst. Cann you here us?? No and yes he sed you woodunt Now. The Onne who cumms for mee sum tymes is in Feeldss somme tymes in grasse or rode or cite farr awii. He sed Boi yuu ar nott Freeddie an Freddie iz nott yuu Hee sed Boi Mannuttman iuz whutt yuu cal mee Mannuttmonn is my namm. Mannuttmonn ius for-evv-err.

The boi went dun Gurrhurrdee Streeyt and lookt for his fayce. It waz thurr on the streyt al ruff. The boi mad it smuuf wuth hiz ohn hanns. Wenm hee treyd ut onn itt futt purfuct onn hiz fayce. Hiz fayce fiutt onn hiz fayce. It waz wurm frum the sunn. Wurm Fayce is guud it is luyke Mumma Baathy and Duddah Jymm longg aggoo.

I luv yuur fayce Mumma sed your swite faycce thuer is onnye wann lyke itt in the wrld. Soo I cuuyd nott staye inn mye huis. Itt waz nutt my huis anny moire. It waz Leev Freddiue leeve boi for mee. Thenn hee the boi cam bayck and sed I went Nooweehre Noowehre thads wehre. Noo he sed I dudd nott go to the Citty no I did nutt go to the wood. I went to Noowehre thats wehre. It waz all tru. Aall tru it was sed the boi whooz fayce wuz neoo. He waz Mannuttmann insydde. And Min-nuttmann sed Hah Hah Hah menny timnes. His laffter shook the door and it filld up the roome.

1986
Not Long Leftt

The boy lived in this our world and in a diffrent one too. He was a boy who walked Up the staiurs twice and Down the staiurs only once. The seccondd time he went down he was not him. Mannuttmann you calld me long ago and Mannuttman I shall be. The boy saw the frendly old enymee hyding in the doorwais and in the shaddowes of the deep gutter. When he took a step, so did Mannuttman his enymee his frend. The Mumma grabbed his hand and she said too loud Sunny Boy You are still only seven years old sometimes I swear you act like a teenager.

Im sorry Mumma he saiud I will never be a teenager. Whats that I hear she said Dud you get that from your preshioys Minutman? You dont know hisz name. When they got to the cornoo at the end of the block the boy smild and told to his Mumma I have not long left. You will see. I have not long left? she said. Where do you get this stuf? He smyled and that was his anser.

What Happenz Wen You Look Upp

Lessay you stan at the bottum of the staires. Lessay you look upp. A Voice tellks you Look Upp Look Upp. Are you happy are you braav? You must look all the waye to the top. *All* the waye. Freddie is rite there—rite there at the topp. But you dontt see Freddie. You dont't you cant't see the top you dont't see how it goes on and on the staiures you dont't see you cant. Then the man geus out syde and agen heers the Voice. Look up look up Sullee it is the tyme you must look upp. Freddies Daddie you are,,,,, so look upp and see him. Are you goud are you nise are you stronng and braav are you standing on your fruhnt lahwn and leeniung bakk to look up hiuy in the skye? Can you see him? No. No you cant't. Beecuz Freddie is not there and Freddie is not there beecuz Mistr Nothing Nowehere Nobodie is there. He laft. Mistr Nothing Nowehere Nobodie laft out lowd. The man on his frunht lahwn is not happoy and he is not braav. No. And not Sytronng. Lessay that's truoe. Yes. Lessay it. And the Mistr Nothing Nowehere Nobody he is not there exseptt he is nevvr at the top of the stairs. And he nevvr leeves he nevr lefft. Hah!

The Boy and the Book

Once there was a boy named Frank Pinncushun. That was a comi-call naaym but Frank likked his naaym. He had a millyun frends at school and a thosand millyuun at home. At school his best frends were Charley Bruce Mike and Jonny. At home he was freends with Homer Momer Gomer Domer Jomer and Vomer. They never mayde fun of his naaym because it was goode like Barttelmee. Their favrote book was called THE MOUNTAIN OVER THE WALL: DOWN THE BIG RIVVER TREEMER-TRIMMER-TROUWNCE TO THE UNDERGROUND. It was a very long long book: and it was a goid storie. In the book there was a boy named Freddie. Al Frank's millyon frends wanted to be Freddie! He was their heero. Braav and strong. One day Frank Piunncushun went out to wlkk alone by him-sellff. Farr he went: soo farr. Littel Frank walked out of his nayberhooid and wlked some more: he wllkd over streeits over britdches and throou canyhons. He was never affrayed. Then he cayme to the Great River Treemer-Trimmer-Trouynse and what dud he doo? Inn he jumped and divved strait down. At the bottom was a huug hall were he culd breeth and wassnt't eeven wett! The waalls were hygh redd curtuns and the seelingg ewas sooo farr awaye he culd not see it. Guldenn playtes and guldenn cupps and gulden chaines laie heept up on the flore. Heloh Heloh Freddie yeled. Helo helo helo. A doore opend. A tall man in a redd cloke and werring a crownne came in the bigg roome. He was the Kinge. The Kinge lookt anguree. Who are yoo and whi are yoo yallingg Helo Helo?? I am Frank Pinncushun he sed but I am Freddie to, and I was hear befor. And we will have a greit fyhht and I wil tryk you and ern all the guld. Lessay I tel you sumethyng sed the Kinge. Lessay you liussen. Ar we kleer?? Yes, kleer, sed Frank. The Kinge walked farwude and tutchd his chisst. The Kinge said I am not I and yoo ar not yoo. Do yuoo unnerrstan me? Yes said the boy I unnerstann. Then he tuuk his Nife and killt the Kinge and walkkt into the heeps of guld. I am not me he sed and luukt at his hanns. His hanns were bluudee and drippt over the guld. He lafft thatt boy he lafft so herd hius laffter wennt up to the seeling. Freddie he kuld see his laffter lyke smoke was hius laffter lyke a twyiste roop mayde of smuck but he kuld nott see the seelingg. He niver saw the seelingg. Not wunse.

Acknowledgments

I should not like to lose the dedications to the collections *Houses Without Doors* and *Magic Terror.* The first of these was dedicated to Scott Hamilton and Warren Vaché, the second to Lawrence Block.

Of the stories previously uncollected, "Mallon the Guru" was originally published in *Stories: All-New Tales*; "The Ballad of Ballard and Sandrine" in *Conjunctions 56,* and "The Collected Short Stories of Freddie Prothero" in *Conjunctions 62.* I am indebted to Al Sarrantonio and Neil Gaiman, the editors of *Stories,* and to Bradford Morrow, the tireless and inspired editor of *Conjunctions,* for their intelligence, tact, sensitivity, and savvy.

Over the thirty-odd years in which I was writing these stories, I drew upon the friendship, love, and support of, among a hundred others, Ann Lauterbach, Valli Shaio and Gregorio Kohon, David Plante, Charles Bernstein and Susan Bee, Laurie Olin, Bradford Morrow, Abby and the late Donald Westlake, Gary K. Wolfe, Rona Pondick and Robert Feintuch, John and Judith Clute, Elizabeth Hand, Hap Beasley, Scott Hamilton, Warren Vaché, Kit Reed, Stephen King, Owen King and Kelly Braffet, Neil Gaiman, Morris Holbrook, Lila Kalinich, Michael and Ginevra Easton, Robert and Loyita Woods, Thomas Tessier, Harry and Martha Yohalem, Anne Ricker, David J. Schow, Ben and Judy Sidran, Leo and Amanda Sidran, Pat Cummings and Chuku Lee, Brian Evenson, Duncan Hannah, Paul Moravec, Bill Sheehan, and Bernadette Bosky.

Michael Fusco-Straub is a special case, having proven his loyalty, talent, and valor time after time.

For their consistent supply of inspiration and what often feels like company, I wish to thank Paul Desmond, Eric Alexander, Chet Baker, Bill Evans, Mike LeDonne, Miles Davis, Freddie Hubbard, Lester Young, Lee Konitz, Warne Marsh, Scott and Warren all over again, Clifford Brown, Charles Earland, Tommy Flanagan, Hank Jones, John Webber, and Joe Farnsworth.

I owe much to many brilliant editors, especially Lee Boudreaux, Alison Callahan, Laurie Bernstein, Bill Thompson, and the late Joe Fox. The present volume has been edited by smart, sensitive Robert Bloom. It is a pleasure to thank David Gernert for his brilliant, thoughtful, good-humored and powerhouse support, which begins by being professional and always quickly widens out to take in and accommodate the personal, which anyhow can only barely be separated from what is professional. David runs a magnificent agency, and he has my back.

Kathy Kinsner, Deanna Pacelli, Tiffany Jones, Este Lewis, Lizzy Crawford, and Jenny Calivas, who in home and office have been so kind, helpful, dependable, and funny, are all very dear to me. I wish also to thank Kathy Kinsner for putting in hour after hour of essential, last-minute work during the preparation of this book's manuscript.

Joy and pride warm every portion of my relationships with Benjamin Straub and Emma Straub, my grown-up children, as much as when they were the little enchantments that so bravely bore their names out into the world. Their existence continues astonishingly to enrich and deepen my life. Susan Straub remains the truest source of depth and enrichment in my life and is the one person in the world with whom a profound, shared psychic conversation shaped by ancient knowledge, love, respect, and an intimacy in the lowest, most honest registers, is always fluttering mothlike back and forth.

ABOUT THE AUTHOR

Peter Straub is the *New York Times* bestselling author of more than a dozen novels, most recently *A Dark Matter*. *In the Night Room* and *lost boy lost girl*, among many others, are winners of the Bram Stoker Award. He lives in New York City.